Catherine Jones was in the Ausband for twenty-five. They are now happily adjusting to Civvie Street in Oxfordshire with their three children.

Under the name of Annie Jones, Catherine was co-author of *Gumboots and Pearls* a humorous non-fiction guide to being an Army Wife.

ARMY WIVES

CATHERINE JONES
ARMY WIVES

PIATKUS

Copyright © 1996 by Catherine Jones

First published in Great Britain in 1996 by
Judy Piatkus (Publishers) Ltd of
5 Windmill Street, London W1

First published in paperback
in 1996 by Judy Piatkus (Publishers) Ltd.

The moral right of the author has been asserted

A catalogue record for this book is available from the British Library

ISBN 0-7499-3008 X

Set by Action Typesetting Ltd, Gloucester
Printed and bound in Great Britain by
Mackays of Chatham PLC

Acknowledgements

I am indebted to the following people for their help, support and encouragement while I was writing this book.

Alison Howard, Alison Baverstock, Sheridan Stevens J.P., Ann de Gale, Jayne and Robert Owen and Susan Brealey.

This book is for Ian –
without whom it would never have been written.

Chapter One

Had the wives living on the officers' married patch known what an impact Jenny Walker was going to have on their lives, they would have paid more attention to her arrival. As it was, most of her new neighbours barely gave the removal van a second glance as it drew up outside 23 Slim Road; it was a common enough sight on the patch – there was always someone moving in or out. Certainly Jenny, turning into the driveway of her new home, was completely unaware of arousing any interest at all amongst her neighbours.

At number 16, Gabriella Devereaux lay contentedly on her changing mat, patiently waiting for her mother to apply the baby lotion and then stick down the tabs of the clean nappy. While she waited, blowing bubbles and cooing, she examined her feet and then casually stuck one in her mouth. Pandora, unaware of her daughter's charming antics, was staring out of the window of the nursery, idly wondering about the new arrivals further down the road, although she was just too far away to get a really good view of the goings-on. All she could see was the lorry parked outside the driveway. She hoped the new people would be her sort; she'd found it hard to settle down in this cul-de-sac, and didn't have much in common with many of the other wives. Fiona Bain at number 25 was an exception, and she knew a couple of the colonels' wives in the next road. Pandora also had plenty of friends up in London, but life would be much more tolerable if she wasn't so lonely here. She longed for Rupert to get posted away from the Ministry of Defence and back to his Regiment, but they had only been here for four months, and it would be nearly two years before they were due to move again. She sighed and turned her attention back to Gabriella.

Next door, at number 18, Marian Cunliffe had also seen the arrival of the removal van and was standing behind her swagged net curtains being unashamedly nosy, knowing that no one could see her blatant curiosity. She hoped that the new family would have some nice children for little Emily and Charlotte to play with, not loud and boisterous boys. There were enough of those already in the road. As she watched, she saw a Volvo estate drive up and pull in behind the Pickfords van. A striking, very slim woman got out of the driver's seat and opened the rear door of the car, allowing three young children, two girls and a boy, to erupt. The woman leant against the car, giving her new house a long, appraising look as her offspring raced into the garden, shrieking and yelling in excitement. Marian decided that perhaps she would not encourage Emily and Charlotte to become too friendly – the girls were obviously wild. She brushed an imaginary cobweb off the curtain, then turned back to her room and continued to fussily straighten the already tidy bedclothes.

Annette Hobday, who lived at number 21, was busy feeding muesli to her daughter Victoria in the dining room at the back of her house, and missed the arrival of the newcomers and their furniture van. Not that she would have been particularly curious anyway. She regarded other people's business as their own affair, and neither was she prone to listening to gossip or repeating it. Nevertheless, she was a popular person around the patch, and the mothers appreciated the no-nonsense way she ran the mother and toddler group. She was being lobbied to carry on running it when Victoria moved on to playgroup next term. Annette knew she would be letting people down if she didn't, but she was rather hoping to get a part-time job to fill her empty mornings. Besides which, why should she do a voluntary job if she could get paid employment instead? She knew this wasn't what the Army would consider to be the right attitude – but stuff it, they needed the money.

Outside number 23, Jenny Walker perched on the warm bonnet of her car and decided that her new quarter, a 1930s semi, looked spacious and very appealing from the outside. She already knew that they'd been allocated a Type IV quarter, but it was much better than she'd imagined. She liked the hanging tiles and the bow windows. Not that it would have mattered if she had loathed the place; it would still be her home until the Army moved her on again. She wondered if her new house would look quite so attractive viewed in pouring rain and not in the bright, clear sunshine of early April. Even so, she had an instinctive feeling that the family would be happy here; she hoped she was right. One thing she particularly liked was that it was almost the last house in the cul-de-sac, which meant that it was wonderful from a road-safety point of view. Her children had lived almost exclusively on little-used roads and were accustomed to being able to ride their bikes outside the garden. Jenny had worried that moving to a quarter so near London, they would have traffic racing past their front door day and night. She stretched, ran her fingers through her short dark hair and gazed down the road at the other identical houses, their upstairs windows peering over their identical privet hedges. She saw a net curtain twitch and smiled wryly to herself, wondering how long it would be before the first of her new neighbours, overcome by curiosity, tramped up her path with some spurious excuse or other to find out who she was.

She strolled up the path to press her nose against a downstairs window. She cupped her hand over her eyes to cut out the reflection, but the curtains were half drawn and the deep shadow cast in the room made it impossible to discern any detail. She followed her children round to the back of the house, where the two girls were improvising a game of hopscotch on the patio paving and her son, aged four, was trying to climb a tree. She looked at her watch. Eight fifty. Ten minutes before the Estate Warden would turn up to commence the 'march-in' procedure. She tried again to see into the house, this time through the big French window that opened into the garden. She thought she could make out a fireplace, and she noticed that the curtains were a dreary shade of oatmeal – but at least they were neutral. She shuddered as she remembered the quarter she had been allocated a few years previously, with its orange curtains and carpets clashing with the red chair covers. It was like living in a nuclear reactor, she had complained. But as nothing was due for exchange or replacement, she had been told she'd have to lump it.

The three removal men settled down in their cab to another bacon butty and flask of tea. They were regulars on the Germany-to-UK run and knew that it would be at least an hour before they would be able to make a start – the time it took for the house to be inspected for damage and faults and all the paperwork to be completed. They felt sorry for Mrs Walker, moving on her own with three kids. It didn't seem right to them that her husband was being kept behind for military manoeuvres, but then they didn't understand how any woman would let herself be pushed from one place to another as often as these army wives did. There was no way they'd put their wives through this, they decided – not that their wives would have let them. A distant church clock struck nine times, and simultaneously two men turned into the driveway and walked, in step, up the path.

Two hours later Jenny was standing in the kitchen, gazing despairingly at the growing mound of packing cases.

'Where do you want this one, missus?' said the bearded man in Pickfords coveralls. Jenny snapped out of her reverie and made a valiant attempt to be cheerful and look as though she knew what she was doing.

'Er, put it in the girls' room. No, on second thoughts, the spare room.'

'OK. Do you want the other boxes marked "linen cupboard" to go in there too?' said the man.

'Yes, and anything marked "hall cupboard".'

God, thought Jenny, this'll take days to unpack.

The three removal men carried on ferrying Jenny's possessions from the van into the house. As they did so, they wondered how she was going to sort the place out on her own. She didn't look big enough to be able to cope with hefting home a bag of shopping, let alone moving these boxes around; she ought to have had a 'Fragile, Handle With Care' label stuck to her. In fact, she was remarkably robust, very fit and highly efficient, but she did nothing to dispel the illusion that she was weak and feeble if it made life easier for her. It had worked like a charm for her in the eight or so years she had served in the Army as an officer. She knew how to make her big brown eyes look as if they were about to fill with tears, to get the soldiers racing to her aid. Equally, if help was unwanted, she could smile politely while her eyes sparked a warning that anyone stepping too close would regret it. Jenny was no fool; she could go for femininity or feminism, whichever was most to her advantage.

At that moment, Jenny's three young children hurled themselves through the front door, excitedly exclaiming about the play park they had discovered at the end of the road on the corner of a little alleyway.

'... and there are loads of swings and a roundabout too,' shouted Elizabeth, the eight-year-old, drowning the voices of her smaller brother and sister.

'Oh good,' said Jenny. 'Then you'd better run along and amuse yourselves there. I've got a million things to do and I don't want you lot getting under my feet.' As an afterthought she added, 'And don't go too far, and be careful crossing the road. I'll call you when it's lunchtime – how do you fancy fish and chips today?'

'Hooray,' yelled the children in unison and then, just like the tide going out in Morecambe Bay, they disappeared out of the door again, almost bowling over two of the men staggering into the house with a tremendously heavy sofa bed. Jenny apologised, and supervised its positioning before pulling off the acres of protective wrapping. She then gathered up all the paper and bundled the mass of rubbish outside the front door for the men to take away in their van. The more she got rid of while they were here, the better. She knew she could not rely on the dustbin men to take it away these days.

As the men continued to-ing and fro-ing, Jenny returned to the kitchen and gazed again at the crates, boxes and piles of articles wrapped in paper, dejectedly wondering where to begin. Her innate cheerfulness was being pushed to the limit. She realised that unless she moved the washing machine to its proper space under the worktop, she was not going to be able to manoeuvre the cartons away from the cupboards to allow her to put stuff away. She grabbed hold of the heavy Hotpoint and tried to shift it.

'Bugger the Army,' she shouted at it, the end of her tether almost reached, as with all her strength she had only budged it a couple of inches across the floor. 'It's not fair!'

'Too bloody right,' a very plummy woman's voice said from the front door. Jenny spun round and walked into the hall to see who the sympathiser was. Standing in the open doorway was a tall, attractive woman in her late thirties, holding a tray with a teapot, milk bottle and a couple of mugs; obviously a fellow army wife. Jenny instantly recognised the wives' 'uniform' – navy pleated skirt, Laura Ashley frilly blouse, navy Guernsey and string of pearls. In this instance the ensemble was topped off by a velvet headband controlling her visitor's immaculate shoulder-length auburn hair. There was something about her simple but smart appearance that made it unlikely that she was the frilly-curtain twitcher down the road. Jenny, in tatty, faded jeans and a sweatshirt that needed a wash, as did her hair, spiky with lack of care, felt extremely scruffy.

'Hi,' drawled the stranger, 'I'm Fiona Bain from next door.' She indicated with her head that she meant the other half of the semi. Jenny congratulated herself about the curtain-twitching. 'I thought that you'd be ready for this and I wondered if you needed a hand.' She proffered the tray.

'Gosh, thanks.' Jenny smiled. She'd been gasping for a cup of tea for ages but the kettle hadn't surfaced yet. 'It's exactly what I need.' She smiled rather bleakly. 'I'm Jenny Walker.' She led Fiona into the kitchen and motioned her to put the tray down on a pile of packing cases.

'I don't suppose you could help me shove the washing machine across to here, could you? I can't get to the cupboards till I move it out of the way.'

'Sure thing.'

'Watch your clothes on that corner.' Jenny pointed to a jagged edge which was the inevitable result of too many moves.

'Isn't your husband around? Don't tell me he's had to report for duty already?' They started to manhandle the awkward appliance into position.

'No,' grunted Jenny with the exertion. 'He's had to stay on with the Regiment to run an exercise in Germany and he won't be here for another two weeks.' With a last heave from both of them, the machine slid into position. Jenny straightened up.

'Phew, thanks. I don't suppose your husband could lend me

a spanner so I can get it plumbed in?' she added, resting against the sink.

'He's in the States for a fortnight, but if I can find one you're welcome to borrow it. I'm not entirely sure where he keeps that sort of thing. He does all that stuff himself.'

Jenny wasn't the least bit surprised. She started to pour out the tea.

'Clever you being so practical,' added Fiona.

'It's only a question of tightening the nuts up properly.' Jenny giggled. 'I wouldn't mind tightening the nuts of some people in the Postings Branch at the same time.' Fiona roared with laughter.

'So how did you get conned into doing the move on your own? I'd have thrown my teddy in the corner if they had suggested this sort of thing to me.' Fiona leaned her long, elegant body against a cupboard. Jenny looked at her new neighbour's cool grey eyes and smooth, unwrinkled skin – she didn't look the sort who was prone to tantrums. But she could probably freeze hell with one look if she wanted.

'You know what it's like – they take a dim view of bolshie wives. And the man taking over from Nigel was coming from Ireland and he could only move his family over if I moved out, and ... Well, it's rather complicated, but muggins here got the short straw.'

'I'd have still said "on your bike" if they'd asked me to move on my own with kids.'

Jenny thought that it would have taken a brave man to make Fiona do anything she didn't fancy.

'I should've done, but Nigel's Commanding Officer came up to me at a dinner night when I'd had three sherries and rather too much red wine and gave me the "I'm sure an old hand like you can manage it" routine. I got the hard sell about the Regiment needing him, and in a fit of weakness I agreed. I wish I hadn't,' said Jenny morosely. 'I wanted to go and see the CO the next day when I was stone-cold sober and say forget it, but Nigel said I couldn't because it'd make him look such a bloody fool.'

'Poor you,' said Fiona, knowing that she would never have agreed to that sort of altruism. 'Listen, I'll push off now and let you get on. Don't worry about lunch, I'll rustle something up for all of you; did I see three children?' Jenny nodded. 'Twelve thirty, then?'

'You can't possibly do that,' said Jenny, overwhelmed by the generosity of her neighbour, whom she barely knew.

'Don't be daft,' said Fiona firmly. 'See you later.' She left before Jenny could argue further.

Jenny poured herself a second cup of tea, and feeling now as though she could at least get through the day, ripped the tape off the first of the packing cases and made a start. Fiona returned home and decided that Jenny was probably going to be fun to have as a neighbour, and at least she had a sense of humour. Perhaps she ought to have a dinner party in a few weeks to get to know them better. She wondered what regiment Nigel Walker was in. Not that it really mattered, but if he was in something downmarket like the REME, her husband might take against him. She despaired of James's snobbery – he was only a gunner himself, when all was said and done. The way he carried on was more fitted to the cavalry or the Guards. Still, assuming Nigel met with James's approval, it might be fun to have some people round to supper. She could invite the Devereauxs and the Ross-McLeods and perhaps the Hobdays – Annette Hobday was always good value at a party. She would mention it to Jenny when the poor woman had had a chance to get straight.

Fiona did not dwell on the mechanics of Jenny's move. She knew from her own experience exactly what would have been involved: hours spent scrubbing window frames with a toothbrush and bleach to shift mould, days bruising knuckles against wood-chip wallpaper, trying to eradicate every grubby fingerprint, and worst of all, the chore of cleaning the oven so it gleamed like new – not a dot of burned-on fat to be seen anywhere. The horrors of moving house had to be entirely eradicated from memory between times, like childbirth, otherwise it would be impossible to complete the process more than once.

It was hard to believe, thought Jenny as she carried on unpacking, that it was only three days since she had been desperately scouring away any evidence of her family's existence at 32 Sennelager Strasse. Already life in Germany seemed a distant memory now that the worst of the move was over. Although unpacking was as bad as packing, at least there was no deadline. No one would come and check up on your standards, like they did when you moved out. Jenny shuddered as she thought about the 'march-out' inspection, as the Army called it. No matter how often she underwent the process, she was never going to get used to the humiliation of every corner of her house (but no longer her home) being inspected for cleanliness before she handed back the keys. That was what made moving from one place to another so stressful. That was what made her like a bear for two weeks beforehand, and so exhausted afterwards. For a solid fortnight she seemed to have done nothing but clean and scrub, scour and polish – and when she wasn't doing that, she was yelling at her family not to mess it up again. Was it any wonder that so many army marriages ended in divorce?

Her first one had – foundering on the rocks of too-frequent separation followed by rows when they were together. For a moment Jenny wondered about her ex-husband: what he was doing, how he was getting on – *who* he was getting on. She'd heard he'd married again, and part of her felt a twinge of envy. There were no two ways about it, he'd been a phenomenal lover. It was a shame he'd also been a prize-winning, pompous, sexist chauvinist. She hoped his new wife didn't want a career as well as a husband. He hadn't allowed Jenny that luxury, and she didn't think the years would have altered his attitude. That was what had finally made her leave; the realisation that she loved her job more than him.

Jenny curtly dismissed him from her mind. She hadn't thought about him for years. She vaguely wondered why she thought of him now.

As Jenny moved about the ground floor of her house, arranging her possessions, she noticed the phone, sitting in a corner under the stairs. She wondered when Nigel would be able to ring her so that she could tell him about the new place – and that the move had gone as well as could be expected. Strictly speaking, it wasn't his fault that he'd had to go off on manoeuvres, although Jenny had a sneaking feeling that he'd found the prospect of three weeks in the field infinitely preferable to cleaning and packing. At least he'd had the decency to look totally shamefaced when he'd driven away in his Land Rover the previous Monday, leaving her and the children to deal with the removals and the march-out on their own.

Susan, a civilian friend who lived near Oxford and who'd housed Jenny and her homeless family over the weekend, had remarked that Nigel had been very canny when he'd allowed himself to be co-opted on to the exercise like that.

'That's not fair,' Jenny protested loyally, refusing to air her own suspicions. 'He helped me tremendously.'

'Oh yes? So why were you so knackered when you got here on Saturday? I'm amazed you were in a fit state to drive from the port.'

'I slept on the ferry,' said Jenny, as if that fact expiated Nigel's abandonment of his family at such a critical moment. 'Besides which, he had his own problems at work. His Commanding Officer is a complete wanker, and Nigel's having to wet-nurse him, hand over his Squadron to his successor and get everything ready for this exercise.'

Susan wasn't convinced. She stopped chopping vegetables for the Sunday lunch and said, 'So that makes it all right then. Nigel's CO can't look after himself so you have to cope with all this and three children single-handed. Face it, Jenny, if it wasn't for absolute bricks like you, the Army would fall apart at the seams.' Before Jenny could interrupt, she went on, 'And don't tell me that it's your duty, or you owe it to the Army, or any other claptrap, because the Army couldn't give a stuff. As soon as they've no further use for Nigel, he'll get the chop, just like the other few thousand who also thought they'd signed on for life.'

'What on earth makes you think that? They've said there's going to be no more redundancy,' Jenny said, with a hint of frost in her voice. She didn't like the Army being knocked, especially by an outsider.

'And you believe them?' The sarcasm was heavy.

'Of course I do. They've always said that they won't change conditions of service for people already in.'

'Oh, rot! They're looking at every way to make cuts. Even if they don't get rid of yet more people they'll have to find ways of decreasing the budget. They'll bin the boarding-school allowance before you can say knife, and the next thing that'll happen is that the rent for quarters will be increased to approach reality. Let's face it, apart from the odd bit of peace-keeping, what role is there for the Army these days.'

'Don't be ridiculous.' Jenny felt irritated, but she knew that a lot of what Susan said was right. She wasn't going to admit it, though. They'd been friends for a long time, but that didn't give her the right to be so critical. As Jenny stared at Susan's pleasant, honest face, she wondered for an instant if perhaps she was too closely involved with the Army to see its problems now that it had neither a clear enemy nor a role. It had been the linchpin of her life for getting on for sixteen years, and she was deeply loyal to the organisation and the people.

Susan met Jenny's stare and was unperturbed. 'If you ask me, you've got to get Nigel to give up the Army. The quality of life was never brilliant, but at least there were some perks as compensation, but what is there now?' She paused to allow Jenny time to answer, but Jenny only shrugged. 'You can't go on shunting your family around like this. Look at the children: Lizzie's been to three schools now, and she's only eight – and that's not counting playgroups. It'll be the same for the other two, and it's not fair on them. And don't tell me you knew what you were doing when you got married, what it would involve. You chose the life but they didn't, and it's very selfish of you to keep on inflicting it on them.'

Jenny wasn't about to concede that Susan's point had struck home. It wasn't fair on the children, and it wasn't only they who had a rough deal. Her mother, who lived alone in Devon, hadn't seen her grandchildren for two years. Her house was too small to accommodate Jenny and the children, but she'd been too frail to make the journey to Germany. It had been much the same story with Nigel's parents in Edinburgh, although there the problem was a financial one. They simply didn't have the money for an expensive air fare, and their Scots pride refused to allow Nigel to pay for the tickets.

'But even if I agreed, which I don't, that this is no life for the family, I'm never going to get Nigel to leave. The Army means everything to him. And what would he do if he came out?'

'The same as John did,' said Susan briskly, 'look for a job.'

It was this no-nonsense approach which had made Jenny notice Susan when they had met on their first day as officer cadets. They'd been friends ever since, and had gone out with their future husbands as a foursome. Then Susan's husband, John, had decided suddenly, after several years in uniform, that the Army was not for him, and had left to work as a personnel administrator for a firm in Oxfordshire. They had lived in one place for twelve years, in a rambling old house with some rather peculiar Victorian extensions which had been added before planning permission had controlled that sort of thing. On the outside the house was not very attractive, not ugly but lopsided, although it was festooned in a wisteria that disguised its faults, but the inside was spacious, airy and light, with numerous high-ceilinged rooms. Susan and John were so well established in their village that in the summer John played cricket for the pub and Susan helped with the teas. Their two boys had only ever lived in one house and had known all their school friends since they had graduated from the mother and toddler group in the village hall. Every time Jenny went to stay with them, she came away longing to settle down in her own home. She especially coveted the huge pine table in the blue and yellow kitchen – she longed for one just like it. Family life revolved around it; homework, discussions, meals and all other events took place there. At the other end of the kitchen were an Aga and a sofa. It was a home, not just where Susan lived. It was all so very different from the uniform walls of magnolia emulsion in the succession of dreary quarters with tiny kitchens, ancient cupboards and chipped gloss paint that Jenny had had to tolerate.

Standing in yet another inadequate kitchen and unpacking the sixth packing case that morning, Jenny asked herself if she really wanted to go through this every two years or so until Nigel reached fifty-five and was put out to grass. Another nine moves at least, probably more. She was interrupted by one of the removal men.

'Where do you want your husband's woodworking stuff? The garage?'

Typical man, thought Jenny. Why do they always believe that saws and hammers are boys' toys?

'No thanks. You can put the workbench and the tools in the

dining room. The other stuff can go in the spare room.'

Jenny suddenly realised that she was going to miss having a cellar, which was a standard feature in German houses. Where the hell was she going to run her business from? It wasn't anything very elaborate; just hand-painted bookends decorated with highly detailed three-dimensional wooden soldiers. But it gave her something to do and earned her some pin money at the same time. She'd started by making a pair of Guardsmen bookends for her son which had been admired by a friend, who'd commissioned a pair for her own child, and it had grown from there. Now her fellow wives bought them as gifts for their husbands, and Jenny would happily ensure the wooden soldiers wore the recipient's uniform, correct to the last button. However, the problem of a home for her workbench wasn't urgent. She could think about it after lunch. Jenny glanced at her watch. Hell! Fiona would be wondering where they'd got to.

She went to the play park at the end of the cul-de-sac and called to the children, still happily playing, to come and tidy up.

'Thank God it isn't raining,' she muttered, knowing that it would have been bedlam with the children underfoot and no toys available for them to play with; not even the TV plugged in.

'Hurry up you lot,' she said as they got back in, 'we've been invited out to lunch and we're late. Wash your hands right now.'

'But you promised us fish and chips,' protested Elizabeth.

'I know, sweetheart, but this is much easier for me, and I've enough on my plate right now. Besides which, it's very kind of Mrs Bain. She may have some children for you to play with, you never know.'

'Well, I wanted chips,' grumbled Elizabeth ungratefully.

'So did I,' joined in Jane.

'And me too,' said Christopher, who always agreed with his older sisters.

'Tough,' said Jenny. 'You'll eat what you're offered, and if I hear another word on the subject, I shan't bother to sort out the TV for you today, or find your bikes.'

'Mummy's grumpy,' said Christopher to the other two.

Jenny smiled inwardly but tried to maintain her stern expression in order to keep some semblance of discipline.

'Right, that's enough. Go and do your hands.' They raced upstairs, and after a perfunctory dabble under the cold tap were back in the hall as ordered, wiping their hands on their jerseys. As they left, picking their way between the piles of packing cases, some empty, some full, Jenny told the men where she could be found if there were any problems. She then herded her children down the path to the other half of the semi. Elizabeth rang the bell as Jenny had her hands full with Fiona's tea tray.

Fiona opened the door and greeted the children with the words: 'I hope you all like chips.'

'Do ducks swim?' countered Jenny on behalf of her offspring. Fiona led the way into the kitchen, and without a word took the tray and handed Jenny a large gin and tonic. She then offered the children the choice between Coke and lemonade. When their needs had been catered for, she showed them into the elegant sitting room redolent with the smell of flowers and furniture polish, and suggested that they might like to watch a video while she got lunch ready. Jenny glared a warning to them all not to spill their fizzy drinks on the pale-apricot upholstery.

'I haven't got children myself, but Elaine over the way has, so I borrowed a couple of tapes off her. I thought it would give you a chance to relax a bit if you weren't worrying about what they were getting up to.'

'You're a genius,' said Jenny, in admiration that anyone without children of their own would have the first clue about entertaining them so successfully.

'Not really – just a primary-school teacher, so I know exactly what it's like. By the way, I hope you didn't mind me assuming that you drank gin, but it's the first thing I'd want if I was in your shoes.'

'The gin's just wonderful.'

'Do I gather from what you said that you've come here from darkest Germany?'

'Yes.'

'We haven't been there for ages. What's it like now?'

'So different since the Wall came down and the Army

14

started to pull out. I think the Germans have discovered that the soldiers weren't too bad after all, now that the empty barracks are getting filled up with East European refugees. The locals would rather have squaddies than them any day. At least the soldiers have money to spend.' Fiona nodded in understanding as she expertly cooked chips and fish fingers and simultaneously produced a mouthwatering pasta and tuna dish for the grown-ups.

'It must be weird. When I was there last, the Brits were tolerated only because our soldiers were a marginally better option than rampaging Communist hordes.'

Jenny and Fiona chatted as she cooked until, fifteen minutes later, they were all sitting at her table tucking into lunch.

When they had finished, Fiona insisted on the children staying to watch videos while Jenny returned to get on with the unpacking. The play park having palled, the children needed no encouragement.

Back at her own house, Jenny found that the van was almost empty. By the same token, her house seemed to be bulging at the seams. There was hardly a square inch of floor space to be seen, and the furniture, although in the right rooms, was stacked higgledy-piggledy. She had a quick look upstairs and found that the men had reassembled the bunks for the girls. What angels. They had obviously realised that a woman on her own would have found the task impossible. She ran downstairs.

'It was very kind of you to do the girls' bunks for me. I couldn't have managed on my own.'

'That's all right, darlin'. Do you think you can do the double bed, or do you want us to have a go at that for you too?'

'Well, I got it apart, but...' Jenny thought of the heavy wooden base; she'd never manage to lift it into position on her own. 'Could you? It'd be so kind.' In fifteen minutes they were back downstairs. Jenny rummaged in her purse and took out a twenty-pound note. 'Here, that's for being so helpful – buy yourselves a beer or something.' The men thanked her, gathered up the drugget on the hall floor and the last of their packing materials, and began slamming the big doors on the van. Jenny returned to the kitchen and started unpacking yet another crate.

By the end of the following day, she had got her house

looking remarkably normal. Admittedly, the study had become a repository for most of the pictures and books and all her woodworking kit, and the spare bedroom was full of discarded packing materials, but she had made the ground floor look as though it had been inhabited for weeks rather than little more than thirty-six hours.

With life now able to function, Jenny turned her attention to the question of schools. She'd only been able to leave it this long because it was the Easter holidays, but they would soon end. She remembered that Fiona had said she was a primary-school teacher, so she might be a good person to tackle for information, although Jenny wasn't sure if she was working at the moment or not. Still, she had obviously lived in Slim Road for more than a few months and might well have done some supply teaching in the local schools, if nothing else. Jenny asked her to supper that night, but with a warning that she was going to pick her brains. Fiona arrived after the children were tucked up, and almost immediately Jenny broached her list of questions.

'Well, the choice is between these two schools, really,' said Fiona, putting a pencil tick beside a couple of names on Jenny's list. 'I think they are both equally good, and as far as I can gather the children on the patch are divided roughly between the two. It boils down to whether you want to walk or drive the kids to school in the mornings. But you'll have to visit them yourself to see which you like best, and to find out if they've got places.'

Jenny wondered what would happen if they were full. Well, she'd cross that bridge when she came to it. As it was, her kids would each have three teachers this year: the ones they'd left behind in Germany, the ones they'd have till summer, and then new ones in the autumn. It was amazing they weren't complete dunces, having to cope with that.

As they ate lasagne Fiona came fully up to expectations as a useful source of information. In fact she was able to recommend a name for just about every service, from TV repair man to hairdresser. Eventually Jenny protested that she was getting writer's cramp from taking so many notes.

'Well, I think I have covered most of the salient points, but you can always come back for more if I've missed something vital.'

'That's the problem with moving around all the time; so often I seem to discover the best hairdresser and the cheapest supermarket just as I'm about to move again. Still, with all you've told me, I don't think that will happen this time.'

'So, how many moves does this one make?' queried Fiona as Jenny poured her another glass of wine.

'This is the eighth since I've been married to Nigel, but I did four when I was working, including two with my first husband.' Jenny noticed Fiona's questioning look. 'I was in the Army too, and so was my ex.'

'Good God, no wonder you're so efficient at getting a place shipshape. It puts my paltry three moves firmly in the shade.'

While Jenny went to get some coffee, Fiona took the opportunity to nip to the loo. She came back holding one of the framed photographs she had found there, propped against the wall waiting to be hung. It was of a formal group of army officers sitting and standing round a minor royal, with half a dozen dogs lying in the foreground.

'What a coincidence, we've got a copy of this picture in our loo too. Your old man must know mine. Which one's your husband?'

'None of them,' said Jenny, suddenly feeling very sober and rather sick. 'It's my picture. That's me,' she said, pointing to a young woman with her long hair in a bun and wearing a smartly tailored green uniform, 'and as your name's Bain, I think you must be married to my ex.'

Fiona sat down abruptly.

'Dear God, how embarrassing.'

Chapter Two

The two women gazed at each other and then at the photograph again.

'He was called Pollock-Bain when I was married to him, that's why it never even crossed my mind that he was connected to you when you introduced yourself as Fiona Bain.'

'I insisted that he drop the Pollock bit before I married him. I couldn't stand the thought of the children in my class calling me Bollock-Brain, or some equally ghastly nickname.'

'I don't blame you. I loathed the name too. And you're right about the nickname; the soldiers used to call him Bollock-Pain.'

Suddenly Fiona laughed, rather nervously. 'This is a ridiculous situation. What on earth are our husbands going to say when they find out?'

'Nigel isn't going to find it very funny,' said Jenny sombrely. 'He's never liked the idea that I belonged to someone else first. He gets very upset if I ever mention him. In fact, it's the only thing I've ever known him really lose his cool over. It caused such a row once that I never dared go into the matter again. He knew James at Sandhurst and they had a big bust-up – it was something really unpleasant but I don't know what. I think this is going to cause a lot of problems.' She paused for a moment and then said, 'I shall have to go and see the Housing Commandant in the morning and see if there is another quarter available.'

'Don't be daft. You can't do that. Think of the upheaval; apart from just moving your kit, what about changing your address and phone number yet again? Besides which, I don't think anyone is due a posting for weeks. By the time you can organise another move, your husband and mine will have been back ages. Anyway, we can't keep you two and James apart for ever; your paths are going to have to cross eventually.'

'Oh shit!' swore Jenny vehemently.

Fiona thought that Jenny was referring to the animosity between Nigel and James, but in fact she was recalling her unhappy marriage and her eventual decision to leave Jamie, when the final, extremely unpleasant breakdown had occurred. She had been too young when she had married, blinded by the prospects of happy-ever-after, a regimental wedding and the glamour of his uniform; and perhaps most importantly, by his prowess in bed. Too late she had begun to have dreadful misgivings about marriage, but by that point she had felt she was in too deeply to back out. It had seemed easier at the time to go ahead with the wedding rather than face the humiliation of calling it off and, worst of all, facing her mother. She'd known only too well what her mother would have said. It would have been a diatribe about trouble and expense and the disapproval of other relatives. Getting wed to Jamie seemed the lesser of two unpleasant options. In a matter of months, Jenny knew what a ghastly mistake she had made.

She looked at Fiona. 'This is going to be extraordinarily difficult. I suppose Jamie's told you all about us.'

'No, James has hardly ever mentioned his first marriage. He did once, when we first got engaged. Um ...' Fiona hesitated, 'to be honest, he wasn't very polite about you, but I've only heard his side. Besides which,' Fiona hurried on, trying hard to be tactful, 'I've got to know you myself without knowing about your past, and I just can't link what I know now with the little that James told me then.'

'I walked out on him after a huge row about postings and careers,' Jenny said, then, in a rush, finding the whole business deeply embarrassing, 'But the marriage wasn't working and he refused to accept that I had a career in the Army too. What with that and the way he treated our house like an extension of the officers' mess, I'd just about had enough. Then he got posted to a job in Germany he felt wasn't good enough but I got offered a really cracking posting at a divisional headquarters a few miles away. He refused his posting and insisted that I turn mine down too. I decided I wanted my job more than him, so I walked out.' Jenny did not mention how James had harried and threatened her for weeks afterwards, trying first to make her come back to him voluntarily and then attempting to frighten her into it. By the time she had finally got away to Germany she had been terrified of what his apparent obsession might lead to. She was only thankful that her adjutant had had enough clout to get Jamie's posting changed to a job in London, to keep him as far away from her as possible. But she didn't tell Fiona this. If James was a reformed character, it would be spiteful to let on to his new wife the details of his past, and Jenny was not a spiteful person. But she was curious. She itched to find out what James's version to Fiona had been.

She said slowly, not wishing to sound too inquisitive, 'Do you think it might help me if I knew what he told you; how he saw it?'

'Well, he did tell me that you had done the walking out, and that by doing so you nearly wrecked his career because he'd been due a posting to work for a general in London and it was almost cancelled because of his marital problems. He said that he'd had a hard time convincing people he was still the right man for the job. He didn't say anything about a second-rate posting in Germany.' Fiona saw the look of amazement on Jenny's face. With absolute certainty she knew that James hadn't told her the full story. He had got the job with the General as a result of Jenny leaving, not in spite of it. But then it wasn't the first time he had altered facts to put himself in a better light. In the main, Fiona was philosophical about his interpretation of facts; he was ambitious, which was one of the reasons she'd married him. She'd always wanted the perks which went with high rank.

'Well, that's his side anyway,' she finished, rather lamely.

Jenny went to the sideboard and returned carrying a bottle of brandy. She poured them each a tot and recorked the bottle.

'I'm not sure how I'm going to cope, Fiona,' she said.

'Well, we've got about ten days before our husbands get back and we have to face the whole thing head on. You know, when you first said that James was your ex, I thought for an instant that this was going to be an amusing situation – like a TV sitcom. I can see now that it isn't.'

*

Jenny hardly slept that night, her mind refusing to stop going over past events and the bitter memories of fourteen years previously. She mentally rehearsed what she was going to say to Nigel when he phoned her, as he no doubt would in the next few days. She battled with the dilemma that perhaps it would be better for her not to break the news to him on the telephone but to wait for him to get back from exercise. But by that time Jamie would have returned from America. Might it be better to have Nigel's advice and support before she ran into James again? Then again, what could Nigel do in Germany except worry and brood?

The problem went round and round in her head, and on each circuit it increased in magnitude until it had assumed such proportions that Jenny was almost in tears. In the silent darkness of her bedroom she felt a despair that she had never imagined possible. Even in the worst moments of the break-up of her first marriage, she had been supported by the friendship of her fellow officers. Now she felt alone and vulnerable, and worse than that, she was afraid. What would James's reaction be when he found out? And what about Nigel? They'd seemed to be enemies before Jenny had appeared on the scene. Oh, God! What if Nigel did something stupid? It could ruin his career. He was doing so well, and his promotion prospects seemed just as good as anyone else's but something like this could screw up everything. Jenny knew only too well that officers with personal problems were frequently shunted into a dreary backwater while they got themselves sorted out, and their careers rarely regained their former momentum afterwards.

Jamie had always been far more ruthless than Nigel and if either of them was going to come out on top, it was bound to be him. He was a political creature, he'd done the right jobs, knew the right people, and they obviously knew him. Even when he'd been a subaltern he'd had a reputation for being merciless to his troops and a backstabber to his contemporaries. Now Jenny was at a loss to know why she'd found him so attractive in the past – possibly it was the faint aura of danger that he'd exuded. Obviously his reputation hadn't held him back in any way. He'd commanded the glamorous King's Troop Royal Horse Artillery and, according to Fiona, had expectations of being promoted at his earliest chance. He was now marking time in a staff job at Ministry of Defence Main Building, waiting for the Pink List, the names of those selected to be promoted to the rank of lieutenant colonel. Nigel was waiting for the publication of the list too, although he'd relied on his brains and ability as a leader, not scheming and manoeuvring, to get himself in the running. But this could really bugger up his chances.

She was on the brink of falling into an exhausted sleep when she was roused by a wail from Christopher's room. He'd woken up and hadn't been able to find his teddy. Frightened by the unfamiliar shadows in his new bedroom, he was wide awake and bolt upright, rigid with fear. Jenny soothed him and stumbled back to bed, barking her shins on an empty packing case. Tired, bruised and still worried, she clambered into bed. At about five, she eventually fell asleep. It seemed to her as though she had hardly dropped off when the alarm roused her again. Her hand groped out to switch it off before it woke the children too. Silly cow, she thought, why on earth did you set it? It was not as if the children were back at school, and it didn't really matter what time they got up, as the main event for that day was yet more unpacking and sorting. As Jenny rolled over in bed, she became aware of a dull headache.

She hauled herself from under the covers to go and put the kettle on. She knew that half a pint of hot, sweet tea would make her feel much better than any amount of aspirin. As she padded downstairs she heard Christopher come out of his room and open the girls' door. Less than thirty seconds later, the three of them came hurtling downstairs, clamouring for drinks of milk and asking for the television to be put on.

'No!' yelled Jenny. 'You all know the rules: no TV until you've dressed and had breakfast.'

'Don't be such a grouch,' retorted Elizabeth. 'It isn't as if we've got to get to school.'

Jenny saw red, and with a combination of a slight hangover and the lack of sleep she flipped.

'Don't you dare cheek me,' she roared. 'Get back upstairs, the lot of you. I don't want to hear from any of you until I say you can come down again. I've had enough, do you hear?' As she said it, she knew that she was being unfair, that the children didn't deserve to be lambasted like this, but she was so tired and miserable, and fed up with coping on her own. As the children trailed sulkily upstairs, Jenny broke into heaving sobs and curled herself up on the sofa, as though trying to hug herself better. Elizabeth and Jane had never heard their mother cry before, and they stood at the top of the stairs, frightened by the sound. After a few minutes they crept down again, and both proffered, silently, their favourite teddy to help comfort her. Jenny grabbed at them and the girls, and clutching them to herself she sobbed even louder.

Then the telephone rang. Jane squirmed free and ran to answer it.

'It's Daddy!' she shrieked to be heard above her mother's crying. 'It's Daddy, Daddy, Daddy. Daddy, Mummy's crying,' she continued, before Jenny grabbed the phone from her.

'Hello, darling,' she said, gulping back her sobs. Nigel didn't need her worries too; he probably had enough of his own. 'How's the exercise going?'

'Never mind that, what's the matter with you?' His Scots accent was soothing.

'Oh, it's nothing, really. I'm just a bit tired, that's all. The move's been a bit trying.' Jenny blew her nose.

'Jenny, I'm so sorry I haven't been there to help. I've been completely underemployed here. I'm going to ask Colonel Bob if he'll let me come home early.'

'Oh, you mustn't do it on my account. Honestly, the worst is over, and I'm sure it will only cause hassle if you ask to go.'

'Well, we'll see. Look, I'm running out of change. I'll give you a call on Saturday when I've got more time and money. I want to hear all about the new house and how you've got on. I trust there were no problems with the march-out?'

'No, we only got billed for the mark on the carpet in the spare room.'

'Tell me the details on Saturday. The money has run...' Jenny was left listening to the dialling tone.

'You didn't let us talk to him,' wailed Elizabeth.

'I'm sorry,' said Jenny. 'Daddy hardly had any money. He was just ringing to check that we'd arrived safely. He's promised to phone again at the weekend. If you're around when he calls, I promise you can talk to him then.'

Placated, the children began to go upstairs again. Elizabeth turned round on the landing. 'Mummy, are you OK now?' she asked.

'Yes, darling. I'm sorry I flew off the handle earlier, but moving house is so difficult. I've so much to think about, and when you lot aren't good it makes me tired and angry.'

'We'll try to be good. Honestly.' Jenny felt herself near the brink of tears again.

'I know you will. Now run along and get dressed, and then you can go and see what's on the box.' Elizabeth skipped off to her room, happily putting the crisis of ten minutes ago behind her.

Jenny had forgotten how much the children had missed British television when they had been in Germany. There was a channel for the British families run by the British Forces Broadcasting Service, but it had to cater for every taste and age group. Needless to say, many of the children's favourites were not included in the limited schedule, and early-morning TV for kids at weekends and in the holidays was almost non-existent. The children had been almost overwhelmed with the choice when they had first arrived back in Britain. But as Jenny had wryly remarked to Fiona, they'd soon come to grips with the problem.

Nigel put the receiver back on its rest and came out of the booth. There was hardly any noise in the Gastestätte, which was not surprising considering it was only just eight o'clock in the morning. There were a couple of farm labourers at the bar, downing a swift *pils* with a sausage and *bröchen* before heading off to work, but they were engrossed in their own conversation. Nigel nodded goodbye to the barman and walked out to the Land Rover parked outside. He pushed his floppy blond fringe out of his eyes and settled his beret firmly back on his head, tugging it expertly into position so that the cap badge was exactly above his left eye. His normal half-smile which gave him a mild-mannered appearance was replaced by a crease of discontent on his forehead. If he hadn't been in uniform he'd have looked more like a doctor worried by a declining patient than an army officer with a sharpened-steel brain.

'OK, Corporal Weaver, let's go.'

'Back to base, sir?'

'Yup. Wake me up when we get there.' Nigel slumped down in the front of the Land Rover, zipped up his combat jacket and pulled on his gloves. It was bitterly cold, grey and overcast, and apart from the brief visit to the inn to make his phone call home, Nigel had been outside, or at best in draughty farm buildings, for ten days. He was fed up with feeling cold, fed up with feeling bored and fed up with being frigged about by a senior officer who obviously knew nothing about logistics. Hearing his wife in tears on the phone had done nothing to improve his mood. He didn't feel like talking, and if Corporal Weaver thought that his boss was trying to get some shuteye, he would have the sense not to speak to him.

Thirty minutes later, they pulled up outside a huge barn on the edge of a big farm complex. It had been borrowed by the Army for the duration of the exercise. The family who owned it didn't mind, as they would get handsome compensation for any damage to the building or the surrounding area. In fact, if they were canny they would make sure that the leaky water trough and one or two other bits of ancient equipment were carefully placed to ensure that they got 'accidentally' run over and would have to be replaced by the British. Nigel climbed wearily out of his vehicle and walked past the Military Police sentry, showing his pass as he entered the building.

The sentry saluted him. 'Carry on, sir.'

Nigel could hardly be bothered to return the salute. He walked in through the wicket door into the barn and pushed back the blanket that had been stapled to the frame in a ridiculous effort to keep out the draught. All it seemed to achieve was to stop the smell of paraffin heaters and stale body odour from escaping.

'... so I said to the farmer that I couldn't accept his claim for his spring wheat being ruined by the tanks, and he said that it was OK, he would put his claim in again next week when the exercise actually *had* started.' The audience around the fat Anglo-German liaison officer roared with laughter at his story and then began to move back to their trestle tables, and their maps, to carry on planning the next phase of the exercise. A group gathered round the main table, where a huge map of

Westphalia was tacked down under a protective sheet of clear plastic. On it was marked all the latest positions of the units taking part in the exercise. Little rectangular boxes with cryptic symbols inside told a military onlooker whether the box represented a company of Black Watch or the HQ of an armoured division. Nigel ignored it and walked over to the logisticians' corner. He chucked his gas mask on to an empty canvas chair.

'Did you find them then, Nigel?' asked his second in command, a pleasant-faced captain who was monitoring the Clansman radio set.

'No. Fifteen pallets of fucking simmo go missing and all hell breaks loose. Anyone would think that it was real ammo that we had lost. It isn't as if anyone is taking this charade seriously anyway. We're hardly facing the Bolshevik hordes any more, are we?' Nigel pulled a chair across with his boot and plumped down on it. His morale was at rock bottom.

'I've just heard a rumour that they're going to call Endex early. Charles has opened a book that it will all be over by the beginning of next week. He should know, being the General's aide-de-camp.'

'Thank fuck for that,' said Nigel, scratching his stubbly chin. 'The only bit of good news I've had for a week. Well, in that case I'd better get back to the boys and tell them that if they don't find those pallets they'll be stuck here looking for them when everyone else is heading back to barracks.' Nigel's broad shoulders drooped slightly with tiredness at the prospect of going out again in his Land Rover. His shower and shave would have to wait.

'Does it really matter, Nigel? I mean, it isn't as if that stuff can do any harm.'

'Sorry, Phil, but we counted it out and we must count it home. We have to treat it as real ammunition for the purposes of the exercise, and that includes not losing the sodding stuff.' Nigel was feeling bitter. He had spent a whole year training to be an ammunition specialist; he'd done a tour of duty in Northern Ireland on bomb disposal duties, and had had two years in charge of clearing the giant Hohne ranges of unexploded ammunition. Now he was stuck in charge of issuing 'play' ammunition called simmo: boxes filled with stones used to simulate the real thing on exercises that did not call for live firing. Nigel did not feel as though his talents were being used to their best. He had become completely pissed off when, halfway through Exercise Green Light, the hierarchy had decided to go 'notional' on ammo.

'What do you mean, "notional"?' he had asked the Chief of Staff at the briefing. The Colonel, who had known that this would annoy the logisticians, ignored Nigel's faintly belligerent attitude.

'Well, as the pallets of ammo aren't arriving at the front quickly enough, we're going to give the gunners and the cavalry the grid reference of where the dump should be, and when they reach it we log the unit as having been resupplied. We don't have to involve your boys at all.' Nigel, astounded at the stupidity of this plan, forbore to point out that if it was a real front in a real war, the battle would have to wait for the shells to arrive, and the tank crews would hardly frighten the enemy by yelling 'Bang, Bang' at them. He also wondered what would happen if fuel didn't get to the tanks fast enough. He would like to see them go 'notional' on that.

Once that decision had been taken, there was little else to do but organise his troops into rounding up the pallets that had already been dumped on the ground and wait for the end of the exercise. That was when they discovered that they couldn't find one consignment. If they had been able to account for the lot, Nigel could have left Captain Phil Brooking in charge of tying up loose ends and pushed off home to his wife. As it was, he would now have to wait until the ammo was found – unless he could convince his boss that Phil did not need to have his hand held. Nigel took the radio mike off Phil and put it to his mouth.

'Hello, Delta One, this is Delta Charlie Four. Fetch Sunray. Over.'

'Hello, Delta Charlie Four, this is Delta One. Wait out.'

Nigel put the microphone back on the table and began to wait for the watch-keeper at the other end to go to the Colonel's bunk and haul him to the radio. Nigel didn't give a stuff if he was ruining his boss's beauty sleep. It was about time the fat knacker was made to make a real decision, Nigel thought, instead of arse-licking to the General. Nigel had a real hatred of anything that was second rate – and this extended to his boss, who in his eyes was a waste of space.

'Delta One, this is Sunray. Over.'

'Delta Charlie Four. The missing pallet cannot be traced. I would like permission to write off the lost simmo. Over.'

'Delta One. Request denied. Over.'

'Delta Charlie Four. May I have your reason for that?'

'Delta One. General's orders.'

'Delta Charlie Four. Out.'

Nigel turned to Phil, his tiredness suddenly getting the better of him. 'Bloody typical. He can't even make that decision for himself. He had to go to the General. Right, Phil, organise a search in the next quadrant. I haven't had any sleep since yesterday. You can manage for a few hours, can't you?'

'Sure thing, Nigel.' Phil grinned. He liked his boss. He liked Jenny too. She had always invited Phil's girlfriend to stay at their house when she flew out to Germany, and naturally had invited Phil to stay too. Sharing bedrooms in the officers' mess was still disapproved of officially, and not every OC would help one of his officers out like that. Not only that, but Nigel was a fair man too. If he gave you a bollocking it was because you deserved it, but once you had had your punishment he always considered the matter closed. There were some officers who had their shit lists; if you were on one of those, you got every rotten job, every extra duty. Major Walker was a bloody good OC and all the lads knew it. The trouble was, he was too nice, Phil thought, and that sort didn't always get promoted. It was the bastards and the thrusters who seemed to get on. Colonel Bob was a case in point.

After Nigel's phone call, Jenny went into the kitchen and put the kettle on for the cup of tea she so longed for. She returned to the hall and stared moodily out of the window that looked out on to the cul-de-sac, watching as patch life began a new day. A couple of men in their late thirties went past the end of her drive, wearing almost identical dark suits under Barbour jackets, heading for the same train to take them up to Waterloo and thence the Ministry of Defence. She fancied she recognised one of them and decided she had better get hold of a social list to find out who else lived in the quarters. She didn't like the idea of any more unpleasant surprises. She made her tea, and noticing that the children, now dressed, were engrossed in front of the television, went back to bed for a few minutes. She needed to do some thinking – deep thinking.

All that morning, whenever a moment presented itself, she tried to work out how best to tell Nigel the news, and attempted to come up with some options as to their best course of action. Her main problem was that she did not know how Nigel was going to react. The divorce had been twelve years ago, enough time surely for grown men to get over the past. Even as she told herself this, she was not convinced in her heart. Deep down, Jenny knew that Nigel was going to throw a track when he found out. She felt equally certain, that Jamie – only she must remember to call him James now – would also be less than pleased.

At lunchtime she had to call a halt to her cogitation, as she had promised the children a trip to McDonald's before their interviews with the heads of the two schools recommended by Fiona. The spring term was going to start the following day and Jenny hoped to have everything settled and uniforms bought so that the children could start on the first day of a new term.

Ultimately the choice of school had proved to be quite simple; one had a nursery department that was prepared to take Christopher and the other had not. Jenny wasn't entirely sure that the school was the best one, but as she had no choice it wasn't something to worry about. The school secretary explained that Jenny could buy the school ties and sweatshirts when they arrived in the morning, and no one would mind if the children did not have the right colour shirt for the first few days. Luckily the girls' school skirts were the correct shade of grey, but even so, thirty pounds for the rest of the uniform would have to come out of what little was left of their disturbance allowance. What remained of that was not enough to make a significant difference to her private fund, the small savings account she had opened some years before in which she squirrelled away a few pounds each month in an effort to ensure that one day they would have the money for the deposit on a home of their own.

Chapter Three

Early next morning Nigel decided to confront Colonel Bob with a request to be allowed home. He was frustrated at the way the exercise was being played, and he felt there was no role of importance for him. At first light he left the barn and walked over to the vehicle park. He spotted his Land Rover and saw that it looked empty. However, he banged on the bonnet and was pleased to see the rear suspension rock.

'Corporal Weaver, get yourself out of your sleeping bag, shower and shave and be ready in half an hour,' Nigel yelled.

'Right away, sir,' a muffled voice replied from the back. There was a violent shaking, a few swear words and the lanky and fully clad figure of Corporal Weaver tumbled over the tailgate, straightening his beret as he approached his OC. He saluted his boss when he reached the front of the vehicle.

'Do you want me back here or should I pick you up somewhere?'

'Here'll do.'

Nigel went to get some breakfast. Corporal Weaver was waiting for him on his return.

'Where to now, sir? Back to 39 Squadron to help search for the simmo?'

'No. We're going to find the Emerald City and the Wizard of Oz.'

'Come again, sir?'

'Divisional Headquarters and the Commanding Officer. And driver ...'

'Yes, sir.'

'Put your foot down.'

*

While Nigel was leaving the farmyard complex, his children were waking early, both excited and nervous at the prospect of going to a new school. They had been delighted, on their visit the day before, to see that it had a huge playground with loads of exciting climbing frames and play equipment, but they had been somewhat daunted by its size. Their school in Germany had been relatively small, and all their friends from the patch had gone to it. They had known almost everyone there. As the moment to leave home approached, Elizabeth's anxiety began to show.

'I wish we didn't have to move, Mummy,' she complained yet again, standing in the kitchen and watching her mother make the packed lunches. 'I liked my old school. I liked going to school with Rosie. I won't have any friends here. And they'll all laugh at me because I've got the wrong uniform on.'

'They won't, darling, and anyway, it's only your shirt that isn't right. I'll get you a new one for tomorrow. Promise.'

'But they'll still laugh at me *today*.' Elizabeth was starting to whine. 'Why didn't we go into town yesterday to get them?' Jenny found herself losing her temper. Why did her daughter insist on being so deliberately irritating?

'Stop being ridiculous. It was far too late for us to go back into town after we had finished with the schools, and you know it.'

'You don't care about us,' shouted Elizabeth. 'All you care about is moving house.'

'Of course I don't. And I don't do it because I like it.' Jenny slammed down the lid on one of the lunchboxes.

'Then why *do* you do it? I thought that when you were a grown-up you could do what you liked.'

Jenny tried to be reasonable. She grappled with her growing feelings of annoyance.

'It's not like that. I do it because of Daddy's job. If you want a nice house and lots of toys, then it's important that Daddy works.'

'I don't want nice toys. I want to go to school with Rosie.' Elizabeth's voice reached a peak of shrillness. Jenny was itching to hit her daughter. It wouldn't do any good but it would make her feel better. Jenny picked up the two plastic boxes with their hideous pictures of pink ponies with purple manes and walked as calmly as she could into the hall. Elizabeth trailed after her, niggling at her mother with the same perverse pleasure she found in picking a scab until it bled.

'I don't like England. I'd rather live in Germany.'

'Well, bloody well move back there then. At least it'll give me some peace,' Jenny roared back. 'Go on, clear off.' With a yell, Elizabeth fled upstairs, shocked by the outcome of her actions.

'No one loves me. Even you hate me,' she screamed at her mother through her sobs as she ran for the sanctuary of her bedroom.

With exasperation and sadness that she had driven yet another nail into the coffin of her daughter's self-confidence, Jenny wearily returned to the kitchen and began to wash up the breakfast things, while she gathered strength to calm Elizabeth down before sending her into a new school like a Christian to the lions.

An hour later Jenny was back in the house, having deposited all three children with their new classmates. It had taken a certain amount of prising to get Christopher to release his grip on her hand, but the sight of a wooden train set had eventually convinced him that being at nursery school was a much better bet than being at home with, as yet, only a few toys unpacked. Elizabeth and Jane's teachers had both made a big fuss of the two new girls – even though new pupils at a school so near an army patch were hardly a novelty. Though Elizabeth had basked in the attention, Jane had been overcome by shyness, but sporting their pristine sweatshirts they had gone off happily enough

On her return Jenny shut the front door behind her and resisted the urge to go straight back to bed. Feeling exhausted was not a luxury she had time for at the moment. Instead she hunted out her car keys, then backed the Volvo up the drive to the front door and began to load it with the rubbish from the spare room.

'Do you want a hand?' Fiona came up the path.

'No thanks, I can manage. It's not heavy, just bulky. I'm only taking it to the tip. The removal company said they couldn't collect their boxes for four weeks, so I told them to forget it.'

'You know where the tip is then?'

'Yes, I found it on the A to Z.'

'OK. Well, if you're sure you're all right, I'll leave you to get on. Come round for a coffee when you get back.'

'Do you mind if I pass on that today? I've still got so much to do. I'd like everything straight when Nigel gets here. Besides, it's a bit of a novelty not having the kids underfoot.'

Fiona nodded in understanding. 'Another day then.' She watched Jenny get into her car and drive off, accepting the excuse at face value.

In reality, Jenny did not feel pressured to complete her unpacking, but she was unsure of how to handle her friendship with Fiona now that the situation had changed so dramatically. She felt she ought to keep her distance, but her curiosity was aroused. Part of her wanted to find out why Fiona had married such a shit. She knew why she'd done it herself: she'd been young, naïve and mesmerised by the glamour. But looking at Fiona she must have been quite a woman of the world by the time James had wooed her into marriage. Perhaps James had changed, or Fiona had changed him? If so, how come Fiona could do it if Jenny couldn't?

She was also, although she was having a hard job admitting it to herself, faintly envious of Fiona. Nigel was a darling, there was no doubt about that. As Jenny thought about him she drove through the traffic automatically, barely noticing the other cars. She did love him so very much. He was marvellous with the children, had never denied her anything, was good fun, had a sense of humour – a paragon really. But she wasn't sure he had the mettle to vie with his contemporaries and colleagues for promotion and the top jobs. It simply wasn't in his nature, and Jenny knew from her own observations that unless he was prepared to fight dirty he wasn't going to go much higher. He'd done the right jobs, been to Staff College, but so had over a hundred other officers of the same age and with similar qualifications. Unless he did something to stand out from the crowd his chances were only fifty-fifty. In fact, in this new slim, trim army, they had probably been reduced even further. James, however, had all the right traits to ensure success. On top of everything else, Fiona also had the advantage of James in bed. He might have had a dozen faults, been a complete bastard and an utterly conceited shit, but he was the most stupendous lover. Jenny felt a faint fluttering in her stomach as she thought about it, and then had to slam on her brakes as, not concentrating on driving, she nearly went up the rear end of the car in front.

'Stupid cow!' the man yelled at her out of the window. Not that Jenny could hear, but she could read his lips. She mouthed back 'Sorry' at him, and he made an obscene gesture at her before driving away.

I've just put the reputation of women drivers back ten years, she thought glumly, but it made her concentrate firmly on driving; she did not want to have to tell Nigel she had damaged the car as well as everything else.

Later that day she and Christopher stood in the school playground waiting for the reappearance of Elizabeth and Jane. Jenny was oblivious that she was being subconsciously assessed by the other mothers for her suitability to be included in their cliques. Had she not had so much on her mind she might have responded to the tentative smiles and nods offered to her, but her abstraction made her appear aloof. The other mothers turned away. Her thoughts were suddenly interrupted by the strident school bell. In a tumbling, shouting mass of small boys and girls, Jane and Elizabeth suddenly appeared out of the grey and navy sea, clutching new exercise books and homework folders and ominously quiet about their first day. Eventually Jenny managed to winkle out the problems. Elizabeth was annoyed that she was back on a reading scheme again, having been classed as a free reader in her last school. She was also worried because she was now expected to be able to do joined-up writing.

'The others have been doing it ages and are good at it, Mummy. I can't do it at all and I look so stupid.' Her eyes brimmed with tears. Oh God, why can't all schools teach the same things in the same way? thought Jenny.

'And I've got these reading books,' said little Jane, her eyes wide with worry, 'and they've got lots of words in I don't know.' Jenny sighed, and knew that her children's self-confidence had taken yet another knock. She must try to be more patient with them herself. Perhaps when she wasn't so tired she would be able to make a real effort. The sooner they went off to boarding school the happier they would be, even if the idea of sending them away so young seemed heartless.

When they got into the house Jenny put all her thoughts about the unfairness of life behind her as she was swept into the after-school routine of helping with homework, providing drinks and biscuits and then trying to get toys unpacked and put away faster than the children could get them out again. By the time the children had been put to bed, Jenny felt shattered. She poured herself a large gin, opened a packet of peanuts and settled herself down to watch some early-evening rubbish. She had had enough of her thoughts on the subject of James and Nigel.

A complete slob, she reflected happily as she channel-hopped for something trivial and mindless. The door bell rang.

'Bugger,' she swore as she uncurled herself from the sofa. It was Fiona. Jenny switched on a smile and tried to look welcoming.

'I'm sorry to disturb you, Jenny. I expect you had just got your feet up.'

'No, not at all,' she lied. 'Come in and join me in a gin. What can I do for you?'

'Well, if you don't mind the interruption, I'd love one,' said Fiona, catching sight of Jenny's glass. 'I really only popped round to let you know that James may be coming home early. He had a meeting in Washington this week and was going on to a conference in Alabama on Monday, but there's been a tornado there and it looks as though it's being cancelled. He won't know till tonight – our time – but if it is, he's going to catch the redeye home and be back first thing tomorrow. I thought you ought to know.'

Jenny handed her a glass and took a large swig of her own drink.

'Thanks for coming to tell me. I don't suppose when he comes home will make much difference in the long run. I'm going to have to meet him eventually, aren't I?'

'I haven't told him about you yet. If you want more breathing space I could suggest we go away for the weekend – leave as soon as he gets back.'

'Don't be daft. You can't pussyfoot around my problems. It's not fair on either of you. You'd better break it to him when he gets back. I'm only dodging the issue because I'm a coward. I may find that he and I can be quite grown up about the whole business. The sooner I face it the better,' Jenny added ruefully.

'God, I can't say I envy you. You must be wondering "Why me?" I know I would be.' Jenny did not say that the thing she was really wondering was why Fiona had married James. Fiona didn't seem to be in a hurry to return to her empty house, and Jenny, too, suddenly discovered that she was glad of some adult company. She offered Fiona the 'other half' and they were soon chatting about matters of mutual interest, like the low level of disturbance allowance and the stupidity of putting beige carpets in quarters destined to house small children and dogs, and discovering shared friends from other postings. Fiona mentioned that she had spent some years in Hong Kong.

'Is that when you were a teacher?' asked Jenny.

'Goodness, no. It was before I left home. Daddy was the GOC.'

Bingo! Now she knew why James had married Fiona, and why he treated Fiona so differently. A general for a father-in-law would certainly persuade him to change his name or do the odd bit of shopping just to keep her sweet. All worthwhile for the right sort of clout in high places. And the new, less chauvinist James has probably seemed quite a catch to Fiona.

Fiona left after the second gin and tonic, as she thought that James might phone her again to let her know one way or another about his return to London. After she'd gone, Jenny cooked herself an omelette and then took herself to bed with a good book. But instead of getting engrossed in the story, she found herself thinking back to her three years with Jamie and the first night they had spent together.

She had not been a virgin when they had met, but neither was she experienced. She had lost her virginity at eighteen on her boyfriend's sofa during the FA Cup Final. It had hardly been a moment of grand romantic passion, as it had mostly consisted of Clive removing her clothes as quickly as possible, followed by a quick fumble between her legs – presumably to check that her anatomy did not differ from that shown in the biology textbook. She recalled how he had been so eager that he only got his trousers down as far as his knees before he rammed his penis into her, and he didn't even notice her wince of pain. Two strokes later it was all over. Apparently he and West Ham had scored simultaneously. He twitched and grunted and then rolled off. A great thrill no doubt for him, but all Jenny had got out of it was a sore fanny and a wet leg. She had finished with Clive as soon as was decent after that event, just a matter of days, certain that there had to be more to sex than that, and determined not to go to bed with anyone else until she had found someone whose idea of foreplay involved more than the removal of his socks and her knickers.

Once she joined the Army there had been any number of eager young men anxious to bed her, even though as an officer cadet, being caught in anyone else's bed resulted in instant dismissal, 'Services No Longer Required'. Susan had joked that in that instance it should have been phrased 'Servicing No Longer Required'. Illicit nookie was therefore not something to be dabbled in lightly. Some girls went away for weekends with their boyfriends to the safety and anonymity of hotels in Guildford or Farnham, but Jenny was always so skint – and so were her dates – that a dirty weekend was out of the question. It was only after her eight months of training, a full year after her fumbled copulation with Clive, that any opportunity for further sexual experimentation arose.

She was posted to the Depot Regimental Royal Artillery in Woolwich – a large basic training unit. Jenny was one of just a handful of women amongst thirty or so living-in officers in a mess which was a cross between a four-star hotel in its luxury and a museum in its décor. She had positively revelled in her glamorous surroundings.

Young, pretty and lively, she found that she was often the centre of attention of the junior mess members. For the first week or so she rarely had to buy herself a drink at the bar and never had to worry about a lift or an escort if she went out in the evening. It was very flattering, but Jenny was not that impressed by the young subalterns who were so keen for her attention. Naïve she may have been, but even she could see that corridor-creeping in the mess was the quickest way to get herself the reputation of regimental bicycle. She wanted to be treated like a sister, not a bit of available crumpet. Besides which, one of her instructors when she was a cadet, a formidable woman with gargantuan breasts and thighs, had warned them all about the pitfalls of mess life.

'Apart from getting yourselves posted at the speed of light, you will find that once you have lost your reputation you will never get it back. Any of you who think that they may stand a chance of finding a husband in the Army can kiss your hopes goodbye if you have the morals of an alley cat and have shagged your way through an entire officers' mess.' Captain Lawrence looked at the cadets in front of her, and their barely suppressed grins.

'You may think that this is funny, but no one is going to marry you if he thinks that the rest of the British Army knows where your birthmark is.' She glowered at the laugh this caused. 'I know that you all think that you are going to be career women who are going to make the rank of major at the very least, but generally, those who are most determined to make a go of the Army are usually the first up the aisle. Have I made my point?'

'Yes, ma'am,' the cadets had dutifully chorused.

Jenny had been exchanging looks with Susan during this lecture and not surprised to see her slipping her a note. Surreptitiously Jenny read, 'As Capt. L. is still single, do you think it is because she lost her reputation?'

Jenny considered the awesome figure of Captain Lawrence and then wrote back, 'Her reputation didn't get lost, it committed suicide.'

Jenny recalled this lecture a couple of months after she arrived in the mess. She was standing in the anteroom, admiring the Cuneo painting on the wall and trying to find the little mouse, when raucous laughter burst from the bar next door. Intrigued, she began to listen to the conversation.

'I know she's only thin, but I bet she fucks like a bunny,' said a young male voice, obviously belonging to one of the subalterns.

'Goes like a train, I reckon, but why hasn't anyone scored yet? God knows, I've bought her enough drinks,' said another. Jenny knew with absolute clarity that the conversation was about her. She felt her face colouring.

'I still say she's frigid, possibly even a dyke.'

There was a chorus of 'No!' and 'Of course not.' Jenny was horrified. Was that all that mattered to her fellow officers – whether she was screwable or not?

'OK, well if you're so sure you can get her into bed,' continued the voice that had expressed such doubts about her sexuality, 'let's have a bet on it. A case of champagne to the first one to shag her.'

There was a chorus of assent. Suddenly one of the subalterns, who obviously thought he was in with a chance, said, 'What do we have to produce as proof?'

There were several smutty suggestions, including stained sheets, but the consensus was Jenny's knickers. With her face burning, Jenny fled upstairs. She felt she'd never be able to face the other officers again.

Then James had been posted to Woolwich. He'd just come back from completing the arduous 'P Company' course to earn his Para wings and the red beret. He was tall, good-looking and had an air of confidence and self-assurance that made the other subalterns look like fifth-formers. Jenny was smitten by him as soon as she saw him. She had the good sense not to make her feelings obvious, but inwardly, every time he approached her she could feel her heartbeat increasing and knew that her face was flushing. James, on the other hand, was remarkably indifferent to her. The other subalterns might gather round her chair in the anteroom after dinner in the evening, but James would retire to a corner of the bar to read the newspaper. He often had to come into the office she shared with the Adjutant, but he always made a point of ignoring her and only speaking to her boss. She didn't expect to be attractive to every man who clapped eyes on her, but his complete indifference made her more determined to do something to make him acknowledge her existence. Nothing seemed to work.

About five weeks later, when Jenny had decided that the matter was a lost cause, she discovered that she was to sit next to him at a Regimental dinner night. She took special care as she got into her own mess dress that night, a gold brocade creation with a dark-green plaid over one shoulder. It didn't suit everyone, but with her dark looks and boyish figure it looked as though Norman Hartnell had designed it with her specifically in mind. She applied her make-up with skill and put her hair into an elaborate knot. She was not sure whether she was looking forward to the evening or not. She knew that if he was icily indifferent to her for the whole night then she might as well abandon hope. Perhaps he had a girlfriend elsewhere, or he was queer – there were loads of reasons why he might not fancy her. But this did not prevent her from having one last try for him. At the pre-dinner drinks she was careful to chat to other officers, aware of the admiring glances she was attracting. For her own part, she was astounded at how utterly devastating most of the men looked in their skin-tight mess overalls and bum-freezer jackets. The trousers, cut rather in the style of ski pants, made all the men, except the very fattest, look tall and slim, an effect that was emphasised by the short dark-blue and red jackets that barely reached their waists. Jenny could not help casting the odd admiring glance at the other officers' bottoms – they did look so tempting. She was just wondering what the reaction would be if she pinched one when a voice at her elbow said, 'Hello. I think I have the pleasure of escorting you into dinner tonight.' Jenny felt a surge of anticipation in her stomach as she recognised James' voice.

'Yes,' she replied, a shade too brightly, in an effort to appear casual. 'It looks as though you've drawn the short straw.'

'Not at all. Who do you think was given the job of drawing up the seating plan? I always look after my own interests.' Just then a bugler sounded a fanfare and the mess manager announced that dinner was served. James took her hand, placed it firmly on his arm and led her into the imposing dining room, while the band played 'The Roast Beef of Old England'. The dining room was splendid at the best of times, but with the tables now groaning with regimental silver and lit by dozens of candles in giant candelabra, Jenny was overawed. The gunner officers were well aware of the effect such glorious surroundings had on their guests and ignored the scene with studied nonchalance.

Jenny, almost overwhelmed by her excitement at sitting next to James and knowing that he had arranged it, felt unusually gauche and tongue-tied. James smoothly rescued her.

'Have you see the silver in our regimental museum?'

'No, is this some of it?'

'Good Lord, no. If we took that stuff out from behind bars, Lloyd's of London would have a fit. This is just the second-class silver.'

Jenny gaped. There was so much, and all of it ornate and massive, she could not believe that it was second rate. As she looked along the table at the gleaming pieces, culminating in the giant silver replica of a Howitzer field gun placed opposite the Master Gunner, the mess staff discreetly poured the wine to go with the smoked salmon. In the corner of the great dining hall a small chamber orchestra from the Royal Artillery band played a selection of Gershwin. Jenny ate mechanically, overawed by her surroundings and the company, and emptied her glass. Without her noticing the action of the waiter, as James spoke to her again, her glass was refilled.

Jenny began to relax, although she was still not sure she was going to be able to eat very much of anything, she was so wound up. She was unaware, however, that partly as a result of the wine and partly because of her excitement, the glow that she emanated, the sparkle and vivacity in her eyes, gave her rather ordinary prettiness an animation that made her look quite beautiful. Helped by the softly flattering light from the dozens of candles, and the gleam reflected from huge, ornate pieces of mess silver, Jenny outshone even James. James, for his part, was quite conscious that they made a very attractive couple.

The five-course meal was followed by port, coffee and cigars. Jenny had found that the food was so delicious she had had no problem with clearing her plate – contrary to her expectations. James had admired her appetite. He had also noticed how much she had had to drink. Jenny was completely unaware of quite how often she had drained her glass – the mess waiters had been so efficient – but James had been paying attention. He knew without any doubt that she would be quite tipsy when she left the table. He made sure he was right beside her when the moment came to return to the anteroom, and he helpfully supported her as she tottered, just a fraction unsteadily, out of the dining room.

'I think you could do with some more coffee,' he said quietly. 'The others are only going to play mess rugby now, so let's go and get some while the high jinks are taking place.'

'Where from?' said Jenny naïvely.

'I've a kettle in my room.' He led the way along the corridor and up three flights of stairs to the attics where the subalterns were quartered.

'Sit there.' He directed her shoulders towards an armchair and smacked her on her bottom. He then busied himself with the kettle and instant coffee. Jenny watched his back view dreamily, not believing her luck, that James, the most eligible of bachelors, was waiting on her. He put a record on to play; it was the Moody Blues' 'Nights in White Satin'. Jenny curled her legs underneath her in the chair and shut her eyes. She slowly became aware of a hand caressing her hair and the back of her neck. She arched her head backwards in pleasure.

'You're just like a kitten,' murmured James, kneeling beside the chair. 'I've wanted to fuck you from the moment I first saw you.'

'But I thought you were ignoring me,' Jenny said softly, incredulously.

'I was, but not because I didn't fancy you. I just knew that if I was too obvious, the others would give you a hard time. Dating a fellow mess member doesn't go down too well. Why do you think I find a dozen excuses every day to visit the Adjutant's office? It has nothing to do with his charms, I can assure you.'

'I didn't realise.' Jenny swung her feet on to the floor again and nuzzled her face against James' shoulder. His arm circled her waist and he drew her close against his body and began to kiss her face. First her cheeks, then her ears, her forehead, her nose and finally her mouth. She relaxed her body so that she slid off the chair to be on the floor beside him. Slowly and deliberately they both altered position so that they were lying beside each other on the worn carpet, their bodies together hard so that Jenny could feel the growing urgency in James. Then he moved, smoothly caught her up in his arms and swept her across the room to his bed.

'We may as well be comfortable, Kitten,' he whispered as he nibbled her ear. Jenny gave a little whimper of pleasure in reply. Slowly, carefully, he unzipped her dress and eased it from her shoulders. Then he began to kiss her body. Jenny started to writhe as her whole being began to ache for him.

She wriggled out of her dress completely and lay on the bed, naked for him to view. He was taken aback both because she had been wearing nothing underneath and by the size and hardness of the nipples on her petite breasts. Excitedly he leant down and began sucking and tugging on one of them. As he did so Jenny fumbled with the buttons on his waistcoat and his trousers. Jamie stood up, and with remarkable speed divested himself of his mess kit. He stood before her so she could admire his muscled torso and his huge penis. She eagerly leant across the bed and grasped it, pulling him towards her.

'Go on,' she said. 'Fuck me now.'

Jamie grasped her shoulders and pushed her back on to the bed. With a swift movement he straddled her body and, certain that she would be ready for him, thrust his penis between her legs and up into her warm, wet depths. Jenny bit her lip to stifle a shriek.

'Christ! You're not a virgin, are you?' asked Jamie, mortified by the thought that he ought to have been more gentle.

'No, I just got overexcited,' gasped Jenny. 'Please, please carry on,' she begged. At her bidding, Jamie began his slow, rhythmical pumping while simultaneously teasing her nipples with his fingers and kissing her as deeply as he could. Carefully, he increased his speed, and just when Jenny thought that she was going to explode with pleasure, he pulled himself out of her and bent his mouth to her wet opening. Jenny bit her lip again, afraid of making a noise that would alert others to what was going on in Jamie's room. As she got more and more frustrated by her desire to climax, she began to push her pelvis at him, urging him to spear her again with his mammoth organ. Sensing her desperation, he stopping toying with her clitoris and plunged into her once again at a frantic pace. Within minutes they were both sobbing and heaving with the intensity of the orgasm that had mutually suffused them.

Jenny had never known such pleasure, such emotions. She lay in James' arms feeling a sense of love and security she had never imagined possible. As she rested there, completely overwhelmed by such exertions and emotions, she fell asleep. She was unaware, as her eyes closed, that Jamie was weighing up her suitability as a prospective bride.

*

Jenny's book fell from her hand, and the thud as it landed on the floor woke her up. She rolled over in bed, checked that the alarm clock was set and switched off the light. As she snuggled down in her bed she felt guilty, dishonest about the way her thoughts had kept straying back to James over the last few days. Nigel would be livid if he knew; he would consider it not just disloyal but verging on the adulterous. Jenny gave herself a mental shake. She had to remember, too, that James had been hell to live with. God, he'd been a cold-hearted bastard if she'd done anything which he'd considered unsuitable or which might have jeopardised his career in any way. He hadn't been after a wife but a cook, social secretary and representative at the wives' gatherings from which he was naturally excluded. He'd been livid when Jenny had refused to reject her posting or to resign her commission just so that she could attend the same coffee mornings as the Brigadier's wife. She reminded herself that she must not lose sight of what a sod he'd been to her. Having made that clear to herself, she settled down to sleep.

Chapter Four

Jenny was unaware that the man to whom she was being mentally unfaithful had been doing a re-enactment of Daniel in the lion's den earlier that day. It was not his normal style to go in search of a confrontation, particularly with a senior officer, but his patience had come to an end.

'Nigel! What brings you up to the sharp end?' said Colonel Bob, or rather, Lieutenant Colonel Robert Clarkson, Royal Logistic Corps, Commanding Officer of Nigel's Regiment, which was a new one formed from the disbanded remnants of a number of others.

Nigel had encountered Colonel Bob in the middle of the headquarters complex. He saluted him out of habit and training, but not respect.

'I was wondering if I could see you for a minute, Colonel?'

'No problem. Come across to my wagon and tell me what you think of the exercise so far. It's going well, isn't it?'

Nigel restrained himself from saying that as most of it was being run as a sort of make-believe game it could hardly be doing anything else. He confined himself to saying, 'Absolutely, Colonel.'

He followed Colonel Bob through the closely parked vehicles shrouded in camouflage netting, carefully picking his way over the knitting-wool tangle of cables that snaked and curled their way between the tracks of the armoured personnel carriers, connecting everyone with the Signals complex and thence to all the troops on the ground. The Commanding Officer reached his APC, a sort of armoured van on caterpillar tracks, and opened the door. In the cramped but brightly lit space in the back of the vehicle were the maps, radios, personal kit and equipment required for the four people to man this particular desk around the clock. The reek of stale sweat, warm electrics, oil and cigarettes spilled out through the opening.

'I think everyone has pulled together very well on this exercise,' said Colonel Bob. 'Considering that we've never operated quite so closely with the Truckies before.' Nigel was dumbfounded by such a crass statement. Obviously his boss was trying to turn the exercise into some sort of personal success. The Ordnance Corps had always worked hand in glove with the Royal Corps of Transport; to say anything else was ridiculous. Things had hardly changed just because both the Corps had been disbanded and amalgamated into one; in fact, if anything it was going to make things easier. It crossed Nigel's mind that it was typical of Colonel Bob to misrepresent things – to make it look as though he had solved a knotty problem.

He was one of the people that Nigel put into the category of the three Ws – wimps, wasters and wankers; the problem was that he also had charm, which was why, so far, he had found favour with those above him. But he had never had an original idea and relentlessly, shamelessly plagiarised the work of those around him and took an unfair proportion of the credit. He was saved from being exposed by the essential loyalty of the Army and its eleventh commandment: 'Thou shalt not slag off thy superior officer to anyone'. Now he was in command he was finding it harder to maintain the charade that he was a well-liked leader of men, a logistician of note and a first-class officer worthy of the rank. He was required to make on-the-spot decisions without consulting his Squadron Commanders, his RSM or the chief clerk. Some of these decisions were not of the highest quality, and it was being noticed.

Colonel Bob was under a lot of pressure, and he was going to make sure that whatever else, no one would have cause to criticise the stores accounting procedures. There were going to be no write-offs because some stupid squaddie couldn't map-read. Nigel was well aware of this, and was equally aware that, if things went wrong, Colonel Bob would dodge the blame and ensure that one of his Squadron Commanders took the flak.

Nigel had been trained in unquestioning loyalty to his

superiors, knowing that they, in their turn, would support and champion their subordinates. Now that the Army was shrinking, the name of the game had become survival, not service, and Nigel had noticed that for a few officers loyalty, particularly downwards, was becoming an outdated quality of indifferent value. His contemporaries were amused by his surprise and disappointment at this, and agreed that it proved just now naïve and apolitical he was. It was amazing that someone as clever as Nigel couldn't see that the colonels were so busy fighting for their own continued existence that they had precious little time or energy to battle on behalf of anyone else.

'I think it was a shame that the brass decided that we should go national on ammunition,' said Nigel cautiously. 'I feel that if we were going to iron out any problems on resupply it would have been better to really dump the stuff for the troops to pick up, rather than just pretending to do it on paper. We might as well be the starship *Enterprise* and beam the stuff from A to B. It's also making the lads very bored now they've nothing to do.'

'I take your point, Nigel, but the General was very keen to keep everything moving. He didn't want the front-line troops to lose interest.' Nigel thought of his troops, now hanging idly around the stores dumps. Didn't his boss care about his men? Or was it more important to keep the General happy, regardless?

'No, Colonel, it'd be dreadful to have the gunners and the cavalry getting bored.' Colonel Bob missed the sarcasm in his voice.

'How are you getting on finding the missing pallets, Nigel?'

'The troops are looking for them. The driver swears he dropped them in the right place, but it was dark and raining, and frankly one field looks much like any other at night. Look, Colonel, I'm aware that it wouldn't be correct to write this stuff off, but it is only stones. If it was the real thing we could call on the Military Police to lend a hand; we could probably even get the Air Corps to help us with a thermal imager: but no one is going to put themselves out for a pile of tins with stones in them. If the driver was miles out we could search for them forever and not find them. Especially as he said that he camouflaged them really carefully.'

'I'm sorry, Nigel but I want that stuff found. I hope I make myself clear.'

'Certainly, Colonel. And this is partly why I've come to see you. Phil is perfectly capable of carrying on the search, and there is nothing else for my boys to do until Endex is called. I've heard a rumour that it's being brought forward anyway. I'm requesting permission to be allowed to push off early and go home to my family.'

Colonel Bob was taken aback. He was relying on Nigel to write up the post-exercise report before leaving for England, although he hadn't broached the subject yet. It would be most inconvenient if he went now. The Colonel would have to do it himself. Besides which, he knew that if there were any really difficult logistic problems, Nigel's abilities as a staff officer would sort them out. Although he mistrusted having such a talented man as his subordinate, he was ninety-nine per cent certain that Nigel was too honourable to stab him in the back and leapfrog his way past.

'I don't think it would look too good if you went. It'd be bad for morale,' he blustered, thinking of the unwritten report. 'I'm sure some of the others would be only too glad to be at home with their wives. I can't possibly agree to letting you go early. I'm surprised at you even asking permission.'

Nigel took a deep breath and tried to keep his growing anger under control.

'If it's so important that there is someone in charge, why can't you get my successor out here. For fuck's sake, I've even handed the Squadron over to him. It should be him pissing about on this exercise, not me.'

'I think you ought to cool down and think about what you have just said, Nigel.'

'I'm sorry, Colonel. I apologise, but I had hoped that you would see sense and allow me to go.' Nigel could see that there was no chance. He considered the possibility of just pushing off anyway. He was certain his boss would not have the courage to take any action – like court martialling him. It was the sort of thing which would reflect worse on the Commanding Officer than on the officer on the charge. Very senior men would want to know why a commanding officer had allowed things to get so far out of hand. Nigel pushed the temptation from his mind; it would also reflect badly on the Regiment, and it didn't deserve that from him.

'I'm sorry to have wasted your time. Goodbye, Colonel.'

He ducked his head as he left the low door of the APC and walked back to his Rover.

'Nigel!' yelled the Commanding Officer after him, feeling that he hadn't had a proper apology, but Nigel strode off, ignoring him. He had nothing more to say to the man.

Jenny slept well that night, despite a couple of rather disturbing dreams. As she was woken by her clock radio, she remembered some vague, muddled details, something to do with Nigel and James fighting over her, and then her ability to recall them was lost as an item on the news caught her attention.

The newsreader said, 'The bomb was placed under the car of a research scientist. It failed to go off and later an animal rights group claimed responsibility. They issued a statement saying that they would continue to target those people who tortured, maimed or killed animals, either in the name of science or for sport. A police spokesman said that some scientists and those involved in field sports should consider themselves at risk.'

Jenny turned on the taps of the washbasin and missed the rest of the bulletin. She felt sorry for the poor boffin, but having considered her husband, and therefore the entire family, a possible target since she could remember, she knew it was perfectly possible to carry on a normal life regardless. Well, she thought, this is one terrorist threat that isn't going to affect us. No danger of animal rights activities in Surrey suburbia.

She roused the children and began the daily routine of getting everyone dressed, fed and ready for school. After breakfast she returned to her bedroom to dab on some lipstick and powder and make her bed. As she shook out the duvet she noticed Fiona, looking smart in a chestnut two-piece which exactly matched her hair, getting into her car. Jenny concluded that she must be off to Heathrow to collect her husband.

Damn, she thought, I'll just have to keep a low profile this weekend. God, how I wish Nigel was here. She flicked the duvet back on to the bed and went to ready the children for school. Ten minutes later she was herding them up the road.

'Do keep up, Christopher. Elizabeth, don't walk so close to

the edge. If you fall you may go under a car. Christopher, *please* hurry up. We are going to be late.' Jenny felt that she would do better if she employed a sheepdog to keep them all moving in the right direction. Why were her children so awful when they walked down the road? Other mothers seemed to have perfect control over their offspring. Not for the first time Jenny thought of her days in the Army, when she could make a hundred men jump to her every word of command; yet now she could hardly get three small children to acknowledge her existence, let alone do as she asked. By the time Jenny and her gaggle of children reached the school gates she felt quite tired. She kissed them all goodbye as they stood in lines waiting to file into their classes, and went home to get a large mug of coffee.

As she was standing in her kitchen, gazing into the back garden while waiting for the kettle to boil, James was getting out of a taxi at the end of the road. The taxi driver had balked at driving over the speed bumps, found throughout the patch. He had complained vociferously about the damage they did to his suspension, and James had been too tired and jet-lagged to argue. He was also cross that he had been unable to contact his wife. He had phoned her from Heathrow, while he was waiting for his baggage to arrive on the carousel, and got no reply. There had been no choice but to join the queue for a taxi. Now, as he walked down the cul-de-sac in the spring sunshine, lugging his heavy bag and thinking about a hot bath and a cup of coffee, he suddenly realised that he didn't have any keys with him. Automatically he fumbled in his pockets, just to double-check what he already knew to be true. And if Fiona was out, how the hell was he going to get in?

As he pulled his handkerchief out so that he could ferret right into the fluffy depths of his jacket pocket, a few coins, lodged in its folds, flew out into the periwinkles which crept along under the privet hedge. James sighed in exasperation, put down his bag and crouched down to retrieve the money. Behind the periwinkles with their pretty blue flowers he could see half a dozen coins and, shoved deep in the hedge, a white carrier bag.

Why couldn't people take their bloody rubbish home with them? It was probably the yobs from the council estate who used the patch as a short cut to the school, he thought angrily. If it had been his hedge, and if he hadn't been encumbered with his luggage, he might have hauled it out to dispose of properly – like many in the military he objected to mess and litter. But it couldn't really be seen unless you peered into the foliage, and besides which, he might muck up his good suit if he crawled around in the undergrowth. He decided to ignore it and walked the ten or so yards to the drive that led to his front door. He looked for a note. Nothing. Then he remembered that Fiona kept a key next door. Keeping his fingers crossed that someone was in, he retraced his steps down his drive and approached Jenny's house.

After drinking her coffee, Jenny gathered her strength and went upstairs to carry on the process of emptying the remaining boxes still stacked in the spare room. She was itching to set up her little workshop again and had decided to appropriate a corner of this room for herself. As she worked she found a crate full of pictures for the children's rooms, their mobiles, posters and other items that she used to brighten up the drab paintwork. She had just nipped downstairs for her hammer and picture hooks when she heard the door bell ring. Grabbing the hammer from the tool box, she opened the front door.

'Can I have my ... My God, what are you doing here?' said James, recognising her instantly.

'Bloody hell!' she exclaimed simultaneously, and dropped the hammer on the floor; the shock of seeing him so unexpectedly was like experiencing a blow.

'What a surprise,' James drawled lazily. The speed with which he'd regained his composure was unnatural. 'Of all the coincidences – perhaps not a pleasant one, I think.' He wasn't going to let Jenny see how disturbed he was by this meeting and had assumed an air of cold detachment.

Jenny squared her shoulders, refusing to allow herself to be intimidated by him any more. 'Don't be so bloody rude.'

'I'm sorry, my dear, how ungallant of me. Put it down to the shock. This is very embarrassing, isn't it? What will your husband think of it all?'

'He's away on exercise,' mumbled Jenny, reminded of her vulnerability.

'Well, I should tell him before he gets back. Most people

don't like nasty surprises. I know I don't.' He looked hard at Jenny. 'You don't look any older than when we lived in Aldershot. I congratulate you. Now that we have dispensed with the pleasantries, do you have a spare key for my house? Your predecessors here used to keep one for us. Fiona has gone out and left me on the doorstep. Can you oblige me with one, or did she decide to give it a new home to save any embarrassment between us?'

'But I saw her leave first thing this morning. I thought she must be going to collect you from Heathrow.'

'So you knew I was coming back today. You and Fiona must have got chummy. Been swapping notes, have you?' James was irritated. He wondered what else they might have discussed about him.

'No, yes... I mean, I have got your spare key. Wait a minute, I'll get it.' Jenny fled into the kitchen and pulled it out of the drawer. Fiona had given it to her two days ago. It always made sense if you lived in a quarter; you never knew quite when the workmen would turn up to repair faults. The estate handymen knew the form if the occupier was out, and would invariably check to see if a neighbour could let them in. It was standard procedure. Besides which, Fiona had admitted that she'd a tendency to lock herself out.

While she had a few seconds in the kitchen, Jenny tried to pull herself together. The shock of seeing him there had made her feel most dreadfully shaken. She could not have imagined that after so long the situation between them was still so explosive. She leaned against the work surface and breathed in and out deeply a few times. She looked at her hands – they were shaking badly. She breathed deeply a couple more times and returned to the hall with the key.

While Jenny was in the kitchen retrieving the key, James was thinking about his ex-wife. He had forgotten just how alluring she was, how much he'd adored her. Why hadn't he been able to win her back after she had walked out on him? He'd wanted her, needed her so badly. Hadn't she realised how much he'd loved her – possibly still did? If only she'd been more flexible about her precious career. He felt a surge of envy for her new husband – she'd given it up for him so why hadn't she done it for James?

'Here you are, James, your key.'

'Thanks. I'll see you around, no doubt. Goodbye.' He had problems restraining himself from reaching out for her, putting his arms around her, feeling her fragile body, kissing her. He knew that living this close to her was going to be a torment to him. And as much as his body ached for Jenny again, his mind was filled with jealousy for her husband. Whoever he was.

Jenny shut the door. Her knees felt wobbly as she sagged against it. Slowly she pushed herself away and sat down on the bottom stair. Her mind was spinning out of control. She seemed to be incapable of thinking a coherent thought. Until a week ago her life had been predictable, even mundane, but now she was completely unsure of herself and her future. What would happen now that she was living next door to James? How would Nigel react? Would he insist that they move yet again? Jenny felt a *frisson* of fear. She was certain that this situation was bound to cause trouble for everyone. The question was, how much trouble?

She went back to where she had dropped the hammer, retrieved it and returned upstairs. She relieved some of her anxiety and tension by angrily banging some picture hooks into the children's walls.

'Sod him, sod him, sod him,' she said as she put up the peg for Elizabeth's dressing gown. The outward display of aggression helped to calm her down. It also made her focus her thoughts. If nothing else, she was going to be certain that the bastard was not going to get to her, and neither was she going to give him the satisfaction of letting him see she was scared of him.

The phone rang. Annoyed by yet another interruption, she ran down the stairs and brusquely answered, 'Hello.'

'Jenny, it's me, Nigel. I tried to get away yesterday but Colonel Bob wouldn't let me go. There's a big rumour going about that the exercise is going to get called off early. If it's true I'll get a flight as soon as I can. Maybe Monday. Don't worry about collecting me – I'll get home under my own steam.'

'Nigel, that's wonderful.' She made a desperate effort to keep her voice normal, not to blurt out about James.

'Jen, I've hardly any money. Talk to you when I know some

more. 'Bye.' He was gone. Jenny, her emotions so mixed she didn't know what she was feeling, stood by the phone, the receiver in her hand, and burst into tears. It was mainly relief, knowing that Nigel would soon be there to share the hassles of family life and the move, and partly anger that he never seemed to be able to call her when he had more than a couple of marks to put in the phone. And on top of it all was James. Oh God, what would Nigel say when he knew?

Well, thought Jenny, searching for a hanky, he will soon enough. Now that his return was imminent, actually breaking the news to him did not seem so difficult. After all, the problem was not of her making, and there was nothing she could do about it. She pulled herself together, blew her nose noisily and went back upstairs to carry on putting up the children's pictures.

She worked on in Christopher's room, her spirits rising at the thought of Nigel's return. She had almost finished when it was time to collect her son from nursery school. She looked forward to breaking the news to the children, especially as they hadn't thought that Daddy would be with them until the end of the following week at the earliest.

As she turned out of the drive, on her way to collect Christopher, she ran into Elaine Ross-McLeod, who was loading cases and travelling rugs into the back of her husband's immaculate, shiny new Volvo. Elaine had two children the same age as Christopher and Jane. She and Jenny had met when Elaine had to come over to Jenny's garden a couple of days previously to find Ruaraidh and Isabella. As the four children had collected up their toys and bikes prior to bedtime, she and Jenny had got chatting, trivia about schools, postings – the universal starting point of conversations for army wives.

Now Jenny asked, 'You off somewhere exciting?' as she saw Elaine shove a suitcase and a dog bowl into the boot.

'Only to see Malcolm's aged mother in Winchester. It's nice to get away to the country now and again. Get a lungful of air that smells of something other than traffic fumes.' Jenny grinned and Elaine continued, 'I'm taking the kids down after school and Malcolm'll get the train from Waterloo tonight.'

'I was wrong then. When I saw his car parked here this morning I though he must be skiving off.' Jenny knew that

Malcolm usually drove up to Horse Guards each day.

'Malcolm? Skive?' Elaine snorted an ironic laugh, her rather horsy face showing disbelief. 'Fat chance of that. He's a workaholic. When we go on holiday, his idea of hell is lazing on the beach. No, I've got the car because it's just easier if I get the kids and dogs away before the traffic builds up on the M3. If we wait for him to come home, the journey takes for ever and we get there so late the kids are beyond everything. The only problem is driving this car. I just can't get used to the gear box and it's like a tank after my little Fiat – I hate it.' Elaine heaved a case into the boot, then turned to Jenny. 'Oh, by the way, don't leave your car unlocked. Pandora Devereaux saw a bloke hanging around it yesterday evening. She thought he might have been planning to break into it.' A year before, terrorism would have been their first thought, not car crime. It was wonderful to feel relaxed, and army families had got used to it very quickly.

'Really? It's a bit unlikely. The radio came out of the Ark, and a C-reg estate is hardly the thing to go joy-riding in, is it?'

'Well, I'm not being rude, but that's rather what I thought. I mean, if I was going to steal a Volvo, a brand-new one is a more likely target. Apparently when Pan challenged him he told her that he thought he'd seen an injured bird flapping about under it – not the sort of story your average car thief would come up with. She didn't really believe him, especially as he made off straight away. Anyway, I thought you ought to know. If he comes round here again I think we might let the local police know. We had a couple of burglaries last year so it's just as well if we all keep our eyes open.'

'Thanks for the warning.'

'Well, I shan't get packed if I stand here gossiping.'

'And I must hurry to get Christopher or I'll be late. 'Bye.' Jenny waved and went on her way as Elaine continued to load up her husband's car. Jenny wasn't unduly worried; she thought that this Pandora Devereaux woman (what a name!) was probably overreacting. Still, they weren't that far from London, and the crime figures last year had been appalling. Perhaps she ought to try and get the car in the garage when she'd got rid of all the boxes.

Christopher skipped alongside her on the walk back home,

plainly delighted with the news about his father. He took a small rubber ball from his trouser pocket and bounced it along on the pavement. It never ceased to amaze Jenny how much he could cram into his pockets. More often than not she'd have to empty them of a half-dozen crayons, a couple of sweet papers, an empty crisp packet, several cars and some toy soldiers before she could put them in the washing machine.

'Do you think Daddy will take us swimming when he gets back?'

'I don't know. You'll have to ask him. Do you think it would be a good idea if we looked out the water wings for you, just in case?'

'Yes!' he shouted excitedly, and threw the ball into the air. He missed the catch and scrabbled on the ground to retrieve it. It's no wonder, Jenny thought, that he gets through his trouser knees so quickly. Still, summer is nearly here and he can go into shorts.

The two of them turned into the little alley, the short cut that ran between the hedges of the back gardens and led to their road, which was part of a medium-sized estate amongst several other similar estates. Anyone giving the houses a cursory glance might not realise that they were Ministry of Defence property, although a more observant person might be struck by the number of estate cars, and notice that the curtains in the windows were all made of the same material and the front doors were painted a uniform colour. Until a year or two back, the police had patrolled regularly and knew most of the inhabitants by sight, but the necessity for that had now gone, although outsiders were still discouraged from hanging around the quarters. Families living there would question strangers, very politely, the 'Can I help you, are you lost?' sort of challenge, which was so very off-putting to those with no right to be there.

Old habits die hard, and the young man who'd come down this alleyway the previous night and had met Pandora walking her dogs had received exactly this treatment. She'd seen him peering at the radiator grille on Jenny's car and had asked him if anything was wrong.

'No, nothing. I was ...'

The dogs, two springer spaniels, began to bark at him and

run around each other, tangling their leads.

'Quiet, boys!' Pandora commanded them. 'I'm sorry, you were saying?'

'I saw an injured blackbird,' he said hesitatingly. 'I thought it went under the car.'

'Oh.' Pandora wasn't entirely convinced, but it didn't seem the sort of excuse someone engaged in criminal activity would think up.

'But I must have been mistaken,' he said, and moved out of the drive on to the pavement.

'Oh,' said Pandora again, wishing she could be more assertive but frightened that he might turn nasty, although he looked a pasty-faced weed. Perhaps he really was telling the truth. She wondered if she ought to return home and call the police. While she was dithering, he nodded at her and walked down the cul-de-sac towards the main road. Pandora called the dogs to heel, and was distracted for a few seconds while she sorted out their leads. When she turned round he was just leaving their road. It was only after he'd gone that she realised he didn't have the carrier bag she thought he'd been clutching when she'd first accosted him. Perhaps he'd stuffed it in his pocket, she thought. The dogs tugged impatiently at their leads, eager to get on with their walk. Pandora, still wondering if she ought to ring the police, had decided to think about it on the walk and ask Rupert's opinion when she got home. But she forgot.

Jenny walked on down the road, listening to the chatter of her son, who was, as usual, trailing behind her. He kept dropping his ball and having to pick it out of the hedge or the gutter. Twenty yards away, over the shoulder-high privet, she saw Elaine slam the tailgate of the car and jump into the driver's seat. She must be going to fetch Ruaraidh from his nursery school, Jenny thought. Christopher ran past her and then jumped over the low wall by the swings. He played hopscotch on the paving stones as he crossed the play park. Jenny wondered if she ought to go out and get a bottle of champagne to celebrate Nigel's return. She called over her shoulder for Christopher to keep up and turned into the cul-de-sac that led to her house.

She heard and saw Elaine start her car and reverse it off the pavement. The rear wheels thumped down off the kerb and she backed straight across the road and ended up with the rear bumper hard against the hedge by Jenny's house. Jenny suppressed a smile as Elaine crashed the gears and got the Volvo out of reverse and into first. Jenny turned into her drive as Elaine, obviously not happy with the clutch, kangarooed down the road.

Christopher ran to catch up with his mother, and accidentally kicked his ball into the privet on the far side of their gate. He ran to the hedge and peered into the leafy gloom. Instantly his attention was caught by a white carrier bag which, dislodged by the impact of Elaine's car, had tipped sideways, revealing something inside it. He crouched down and reached into the twigs. The bag was heavy and he had to tug it to free it. He dragged it out and then sat on the pavement to examine his booty. What a prize! A splendid wooden box which would be perfect for putting his railway trains in. Carefully he drew it out of the bag and wondered how to get into it. All boxes had lids you could open. He heard his mother calling him to hurry up.

'I'm not holding this door open for you all day,' she said, her voice muffled by the hedge.

Christopher still couldn't see how to open the box, but Mummy would know. He could also ask her to get rid of the lump of metal taped to it. He clasped the box in both hands and began to walk up the drive. Suddenly he spotted a little dowelling pin sticking out of one side.

That must be it, he thought. That's how you open it. He began to wiggle the pin out as he walked. He wiggled it harder and was about three steps from his mother when it came loose.

'Look what I've got!' he said. Jenny, her attention on the free local paper which had been on the door mat, didn't look up as she replied.

'What, darling?'

'Look, Mummy. Look, a little light's come on now.'

It took all Jenny's self-control not to scream when she saw exactly what her son had clasped under his left arm. She knew in an instant that it was a car bomb – two years in Northern Ireland meant she was well trained in that field – and that Christopher, by pulling the dowelling pin out had just armed it. She felt so sick with shock she sat down on the doorstep. Trying not to frighten her son, she held her arms out towards him.

'Can I see it?' she asked. She didn't know if the detonator was worked by a timer or a mercury tilt switch, but if it was the latter and Christopher turned the box over... 'Please, darling. Let Mummy see.'

Christopher was standing right in front of her now, but still the box, with its evil red light, was tucked firmly under his arm. It didn't matter if it contained only a couple of ounces of explosive; at that range the flesh of his torso would be ripped from the bones, and the rest of him would be mangled beyond recognition. Real bombs didn't cause their victims to lazily somersault away from the blast before emerging from the smoke dazed but intact. Real bombs tore limbs off, burned flesh, and sprayed the minced remains over dozens of yards. Jenny knew that if the bomb went off now, neither of them would stand a chance, but she wasn't scared for herself; her only thoughts were of saving Christopher. Her heart was thundering and she could hardly catch her breath, yet she forced her mouth to smile, to try to look calm and normal.

Even so, Christopher could tell by his mother's voice that something was wrong. Perhaps she thought he'd stolen the box. 'I found it in the hedge, Mummy. It was thrown away – really. I can keep it, can't I?' He did so desperately want it.

Jenny had to swallow before she could answer. 'Let me have a look and we'll see.' She reached forward and touched it. She stared up at Christopher and smiled at him, trying to reassure him and willing him to let her take it. Very slowly she drew it out from under his arm, making sure to keep it absolutely level. She was shaking badly and terrified that Christopher would try and grab it back. Silently she was praying to God not to let it go off. Then she had it, safely grasped in both hands. Her mouth was dry and her breathing was shallow, but worst of all her hands were wet with sweat. Oh God, please don't let me drop it. Very carefully, very gently she put the box, heavy with explosive and the magnet to fix it to the car, on the step next to her. Then, trembling uncontrollably, she stood up again, took Christopher's hand, and before he could make a grab for the box, pulled him through the door and slammed it.

'What is it, Mummy? Tell me.' But Jenny did not answer. She had picked up the phone and took it as far away from the door as the flex would allow. She shielded Christopher with her body as she dialled 999.

'Emergency, which service?' enquired the nasal voice of the operator at the exchange.

'I don't know. I've got a bomb.'

Chapter Five

Jenny was transferred direct to the police switchboard while the operator routed the call simultaneously to the fire brigade and ambulance service. The civilian operator with the calm voice at the County Police Headquarters began to take the details, being careful not to fluster Jenny.

'Can you tell me exactly where the bomb is?'

The line was already being traced, held open in case anything happened before they got all the details. The trace showed the subscriber's address. As this information flashed up on the computer screen in front of the operator, she pressed the priority 'P' button to alert the dispatchers. There had already been one car bomb that morning, so the call was being taken especially seriously.

'On my front doorstep, at 23 Slim Road.'

'Can you describe it to me?' The ten dispatchers all had computer monitors in front of them and the 'P' message flashed on all screens. The most senior of them was an expert at listening with one ear to the emergency telephone conversations whilst keeping track of the whereabouts of all the response cars and simultaneously giving instructions over the radio to the drivers. He had once jokingly described his job to a friend as doing simultaneous translation for the United Nations while controlling air traffic for Heathrow. He'd heard the word 'bomb' a second before the 'P' message flashed on his monitor, and had pressed the button to get the details brought on screen before the operator had fed in the address. As the house number and road appeared he was already working out which of the response cars was nearest.

'It's a small wooden box with a magnet on top, and ... it's got a little light on the side which is on. I think that's important.'

'OK. I've got that. Have you any idea how heavy it is?' The dispatcher was on the radio to Kilo Golf One, the fast-response car that was patrolling two miles away. Constables Bennett and Davies were discussing the chances of the challenger for the heavyweight boxing championship when the call came through.

'Kilo Golf One proceeding,' answered Constable Bennett. Then to his passenger, 'OK, lights and music, please, maestro.' Davies switched on the siren and lights as they accelerated into the high street. 'ETA three minutes.'

'A couple of pounds, perhaps more.' Jenny felt calmer now she was in the hands of police procedure. Someone else was in control. She was asked some more details – how long it had been since it was found, and where exactly it had been discovered – all of which went on to the computer with the rest. Then the operator told Jenny that she should leave the house if possible.

'If I go out of the back door I'll still have to walk past the front porch. There's no other way out of the garden.'

'Just try to keep as far away as you can. A police car will be with you very shortly.'

By this time Jenny could hear the ululating wheec-wheec sound of a police car, although it was still in the distance. After she had put the phone down she grabbed Christopher's hand and led him, half running, to the back door and into the garden. She considered staying there but knew that the police would want to talk to her. She held Christopher firmly as she walked to the hedge at the side of the garden, and with the leaves brushing against her, she and her son edged their way towards the gate, giving the front door as wide a berth as possible. Every thirty seconds or so Christopher asked, 'What is it, Mummy?' but Jenny was so preoccupied with getting away from the device, so scared by the awful tragedy that might have happened, that she could only reply, 'Nothing, it's all right,' which even four-year-old Christopher knew was a lie. But he also knew that his mummy was very frightened, and that he would have to make do with this answer for the moment. He didn't think it was a good moment to make a fuss about the wooden box either.

The police car swept round the corner, brakes squealing as it halted. The two policemen were out of the car almost before the engine had fully cut out.

'Mrs Walker?' Constable Bennett enquired.

'Yes.'

'Can you show me where the device is?' Jenny pointed to her door. The wooden box stood out clearly against the dark-green paint.

'OK. I can see it. Paul,' he turned to Constable Davies, 'I'm just going to have a quick look to confirm details.' He sounded quite calm and in control, but inwardly he was very nervous about walking towards a suspect bomb. He'd been to the briefing on such devices; he knew that in theory if it had been moved, dropped, handled or whatever – and it still had not gone off – then just looking at it was not going to detonate it. But even so... He stopped thinking about it and walked quickly up the path. It was exactly as the radio message had said, a little wooden box with a big magnet taped to it and a red light glowing on the side. He ran back to his colleague.

'OK. I think the lady's right.' Then, to Jenny, 'Can you just make a couple of things clear for me? Where was it found?'

'I think my son found it in the hedge.'

'Right. It looks like they planned to plant it but got cold feet and dumped it. Can you think why anyone round here would be a target? I mean, assuming this is animal rights.'

'No. the Army doesn't do anything to animals.' Then Jenny, dazed and frightened as she was, remembered what Elaine had said about the man hanging round her car. She told them what she knew and said that they could get more information from Mrs Devereaux, and no, she didn't know where she lived, she'd only just moved in.

Jim Bennett relayed the details back to the control room, then said to Paul Davies, 'Get some back-up here, we're going to have to clear this road at least, plus we don't want anyone driving their cars until we have checked that there are no more of these things about. Oh, and find this Mrs Devereaux – we'll need a statement from her.' He looked at Jenny and could see that she looked very shaken, her face pinched and white and her brown eyes enormous.

'Would you like to sit down? Here.' He opened the back door of the police car and Jenny sank gratefully on to the rear seat. Christopher, unbidden, climbed in too. He wasn't going to miss the chance to have a close look at a real police car. This was the best excitement ever.

Davies radioed back to the control room that they had arrived and that he was starting evacuation procedure for a hundred-yard area while Constable Bennett looked after Jenny. As their call was received in the control room, confirming that the device looked real, definitely not a false alarm, a call was put through to the Joint Services Explosive Ordnance Disposal Centre in Oxfordshire, which was controlled by 11 Ordnance Regiment and covered the whole country, excluding Greater London, the province of the Metropolitan Police Bomb Squad. Twenty or thirty calls were received each day by the watch-keeper's desk. The vast proportion involved finds of old wartime ammunition, with a few well-intentioned but misguided false alarms – the most common being briefcases left behind in bus shelters or on trains. It was the job of the watchkeeper to get the facts from the relevant police force and then task the nearest bomb disposal team to the incident. Sometimes there was no urgency, but occasionally it was vital that someone was there in a matter of minutes. In this case the details sounded accurate; it had all the characteristics of what was technically called an under-vehicle improvised explosive device – a UVIED.

Immediately a call was made to the bomb disposal detachment based in the west London barracks where a team was always on instant stand-by. As the call was received, the team abandoned their game of cards and dashed for the white transit van with its distinctive yellow flash along its side. They were hardly in it with the doors shut before the driver put his foot hard on the accelerator and began racing down the road, siren blaring, blue lights flashing. Sergeant Parker picked up the cell phone and called the Joint Services Centre to ask for a police car to meet the van as they turned off the A3 and escort them to the address. By this time they were bucketing towards the M25, clearing a path through the traffic like an ice-breaker.

'Right, now the bomb disposal boys are probably going to have to talk to you when they get here, so if you can wait here for them it would be a big help,' said Constable Bennett to Jenny.

'Yes, I understand.' Jenny didn't mind where she sat; she still felt numb with shock. Her realisation of how dangerous the situation might have been, how seriously it was being treated was growing increasingly apparent as more and more cars arrived on the scene. By this time there were three fast-response cars and eight patrol cars. There also appeared to be a helicopter overhead, but Jenny was not sure if that was anything to do with the police.

Over the road, the first of the wives and families were being evacuated. The uniformed policemen and women were knocking at the doors of all the houses in the vicinity. It was hardly coming as a shock to most of the occupants, as they had been peering out of the windows since the arrival of the stream of police cars. Jenny watched in a dream as one after the other of wives left their homes.

A constable walked swiftly up to the door of number 21, next door to Jenny, the other side from the Bains. He rapped loudly and simultaneously rang the bell. Annette Hobday had been washing her hair upstairs and leant out of an upstairs window to see what the fuss was about. Her hair dryer had prevented her from hearing the racket of the police cars arriving.

'Good God,' she exclaimed when she saw the road crammed with vehicles, blue lights flashing. 'Hey you,' she shouted down to the police constable who was still hammering on the door. 'Up here.'

'I'm sorry, madam. There's a suspect package in the vicinity. I'm afraid I'm going to have to ask you to evacuate. Would you please alert the rest of your family and proceed as quickly as possible to the community centre.'

'OK,' she said briskly; she was not prone to histrionics. 'Give me two ticks and I'll be down.' She wondered for an instant whether to take her hair dryer with her, and decided against it. She wrapped a towel round her hair, raced downstairs, swept up Victoria, who was happily watching a video, and left the house. Annette was brisk, efficient and no-nonsense. There was no point in flapping about the whys and wherefores of the incident. The quicker she pushed off and did as she was told, the quicker the police could get themselves behind the cordon and out of danger. Her attitude probably stemmed from being brought up on a farm, where common sense and calmness even in emergencies had always been the norm.

Conversely, across the road at number 18, Marian Cunliffe was behaving as though she was going to have an attack of the vapours. Annette would have had no sympathy with her if she had known. She was not particularly friendly with Marian; they were such opposites. In fact, on occasions she was irritated beyond belief by Marian, who was fluffy, scatterbrained and coy, and who was now staring open-mouthed from a bedroom window, as she had been from the moment the first police car had screeched to a halt. She was deeply frightened and had had to force herself to open the door when the policeman had come and banged on it. Under normal circumstances, she would have simpered at him; she simpered at all men. But on this occasion, she had opened the door and just stood there, her baby-blue eyes wide and frightened. All she had been able to whisper was the word 'yes' in answer to his instructions. Mechanically she had returned to the kitchen, picked up her bag and followed the policeman down to the cordon. She was so busy worrying about her own safety, and terrified that anything might happen to her 'little nest', as she called her house, that it never crossed her mind to wonder about who had actually found the bomb, or who had been the target. Marian was self-centred, to say the least. Had she been on the *Titanic*, she would have made sure of a place in a lifeboat.

If she had known that Jenny was at the centre of all this, she would have been a little resentful. Deep down, Marian knew that she was rather feeble, and it galled her to hear other wives on the patch speaking highly of those who coped, who didn't have to be propped up by their husbands. The wives' grapevine had already designated Jenny as some sort of marvel, even though few had met her. Marian was well aware that never in a month of Sundays would she have been able to move from Germany on her own with three children. But then Marian had *never* moved by herself. When she had to move, she packed

Emily and Charlotte off to their grandparents for a fortnight, and her husband was made to take leave to help her clean the house. Ian Cunliffe put up with it because he knew that his wife would end up in a nursing home if she had to manage alone.

Next door to Marian, Pandora Devereaux, whose husband Rupert was in the Guards, was not impressed at the idea of having to take little Gabriella to the community centre. Pandora disliked the place. She thought it was a squalid little shack. Besides which, she didn't really like the wives who tended to frequent the coffee mornings there; Marian Cunliffe being a case in point. Pandora had asked the policeman if she could leave the area completely, by car, and had been most annoyed when she had been informed that no one was to touch their cars until the bomb squad had cleared them. She flounced down the road, Gabriella in her arms, with bad grace, and then remembered the dogs in the kennel in her back garden.

'Bugger,' she swore, and turned to retrace her steps through the cordon. She was used to getting her own way so was not impressed when the policeman politely but firmly told her she could not return. She informed him in clipped tones that if £800-worth of highly-trained gun dog got trashed by a bloody bomb she would hold him personally responsible. The policeman sighed and agreed to rescue the animals. She'd just got the dogs when Paul Davies caught up with her and asked about her encounter the previous night.

'And you think he was looking at the radiator grille?'

'Well, I think so. It could have been the number plate. I just don't know. I wasn't really paying attention. I'm sorry, I'm a rotten witness.'

'Do you think you would recognise him from a photograph?'

'I might.'

'Well, we'll probably ask you to come along to the station afterwards. Once we've sorted out the immediate problem.'

Pandora wasn't thrilled at the idea, but she could hardly refuse to help.

Surely not more police? thought Jenny as she heard the sound of yet more sirens. Christopher hung out of the window to see more clearly what was happening.

'It's a big van, Mummy,' he yelled at the top of his voice,

the excitement of the events taking place proving almost too much for him. The bomb disposal wagon drew up and a very young sergeant jumped out of the passenger door. He went over to the cordon and exchanged a few words with the police.

'Excuse me,' said Constable Bennett to Jenny a few minutes later. 'Could you come with me a moment?'

'Yes, but Christopher...' Jenny felt her son might cause havoc if left unattended in the car. Goodness knows what buttons he would start pressing, she thought.

'I'll keep him amused. The Army would like a word with you, that's all.'

Jenny was escorted to where the baby-faced sergeant was standing, just outside the cordon.

'Hello, ma'am,' he said. 'I gather your little boy has given you a bit of a fright. Could you just run through what happened for my benefit?' He sounded very relaxed, and Jenny felt more at ease as she explained how her son had brought the little box home.

As they were talking, the other members of the team had fixed a portable ramp to the rear of the van, down which they were manoeuvring a tank-like machine, about three feet high and four feet long, with half a dozen gadgets fixed to its superstructure. The sergeant asked the same questions as the woman in the police control room had done, and again Jenny described the box with its magnet and red light. He took an interest in the light.

'Was it on as your son was carrying it, or did it come on afterwards?'

'It must have come on when he was carrying it. I've had a word with him about it all, and he said that it lit when he pulled the little piece of wood out,' Jenny replied. She added, 'He armed it, didn't he?'

The sergeant nodded. 'You're well informed.'

'We lived in Ireland for a time. I went to the briefing for wives about security. They showed us then what a car booby-trap looked like. It was just the same,' she finished, almost in a whisper.

'Ok. Thanks for that. Have you somewhere to go where you can get a coffee and a sit-down? We'll be a while here. I'd prefer it if you didn't go too far. Just in case I need to talk to you again.' Jenny nodded.

A policewoman came up to her and suggested it might be an idea for Jenny to join the other wives at the community centre. The WPC took Christopher by the hand and together they walked down the road to the single-storey building that housed the thrift shop, mother and toddler group, and wives' club. As they walked through the patch, Jenny could see the police checking all the cars. They were peering in the wheel arches and under the sills. There were several dogs around too. Jenny suspected they might be sniffer dogs.

Being new to the patch, Jenny recognised only a few of the faces as she walked into the community centre. She nodded at them, acutely aware that she was the centre of their attention and the unwitting cause of all the fuss. Irrationally she felt guilty about it all. She was immediately approached by a smart blonde, with a size eight figure and fingernails that would have been the envy of a Chinese mandarin, who offered her a cup of tea. She looked as if she would have been more at home in a model agency than in the married patch coffee shop, but her smile was warm and friendly and she was obviously genuinely concerned about Jenny's wellbeing.

'My poor dear,' she said, 'what a perfectly dreadful thing to have happened to you. Come and sit down. You've had the most terrible experience.' Jenny found that she did rather want to sit down. Christopher had found a box of toys in the corner and was happily rootling around in it for cars and trucks, having elbowed little Victoria Hobday out of the way. He was plainly over the shock and was now busy ignoring Victoria, who was yelling in protest. Jenny was thankful that he was too young to realise just how close he had come to death.

The concerned woman standing beside Jenny patted her on the arm. 'I think we all dread this sort of thing happening, but it's such a shock when it does. Thank goodness your little body is unhurt.' She stopped, and then said, 'I'm sorry, with all this going on I have completely forgotten my manners. I'm Diana Marlow.'

'How do you do?' responded Jenny automatically. 'I'm Jenny Walker. I've only just arrived, so I don't know many people yet.'

'Yes, I know. I shan't introduce you to everyone here. There are far too many of them for you to remember, and besides, I don't suppose you will be able to take anything in. I imagine it won't be very long now before it's all over.'

Jenny nodded. She was still too shocked to be capable of conversation. The other wives resumed their chatter. Jenny listened with half an ear to what was being said. There was a pink fluffy woman, who appeared to be called Marian, who was gushing about her recent series of evening classes and was trying to persuade the others to take up watercolour painting too.

'It's just so relaxing, and my tutor is marvellous. He makes me feel like I'm a budding Turner. Oh, I know it's ridiculous but he just has that way with you. You really ought to come along and try...' she twittered on endlessly. The other wives had given up trying to get a word in and were nodding mechanically. Jenny switched off too, and shut her eyes. Suddenly she felt absolutely exhausted.

Pandora stood aloof from the group, with Gabriella perched on her hip, and wished that Elaine or Fiona was there. At least they talked sense – not this mindless chitchat. That Cunliffe woman never seemed to draw breath; she just droned on and on about her bloody painting. Pandora sighed deeply and wondered how much longer she was going to be stuck here with these frightful women.

Annette, having convinced Christopher and Victoria that they could share the toys, came up to Pandora. She didn't really know her; Pandora always seemed so unapproachable, even snobby. Annette couldn't be doing with that sort of thing, but suddenly she thought Pandora looked lonely. Perhaps she should talk to her. She summoned up her courage.

'Hello, I'm Annette Hobday. We haven't met yet. You haven't been here long, have you?' Pandora turned and gazed at her inquisitor. She recognised her as someone who lived on the patch, although she didn't know her name. There was something about Annette which Pandora liked instantly. It might have been her wide, smiling mouth, or her faint Yorkshire accent, or even the steady grey eyes that were looking at Pandora with interest and concern. Whatever it was, Pan felt inclined to be agreeable in return.

'No, only a couple of months. I'm Pandora Devereaux, and this is Gabriella.' As if on cue, Gabriella gurgled and smiled a wide, gummy grin. 'And have you been here long?'

Annette was faintly taken aback by Pandora's ultra-clipped diction but decided to ignore it. Just because she spoke posh didn't mean she was unfriendly.

'I've been here over a year, so I'm already beginning to wonder where we're due to go next.'

'I suppose you know everyone here?'

Annette scanned the room.

'Yes, except Jenny Walker, although I know who she is.'

'We all will after today,' said Pandora with sympathy. 'Poor woman – just moved house, hardly got settled, and the kid brings home a bomb.' She jiggled little Gabriella on her hip to make the child smile.

'Someone said he found it in a bag stuffed in the hedge,' said Annette.

'The carrier bag! Shit.'

'I'm sorry?'

'I saw a bloke hanging around Jenny Walker's car last night. I asked him what he was doing; I thought he was planning to nick it. He must have been trying to work out where to put the bomb.'

'Oh, come off it, he can't have been. And anyway, it's animal rights, not the IRA. What axe could they possibly have to grind with a family who has just got here from Germany?'

'Perhaps he got the wrong car,' said Pandora.

'In which case, who was his intended victim?'

'Let's grab a cup of tea and then go and see the police again – I think I ought to tell them about that bag.'

Deftly transferring her daughter to her other hip, she handed Annette a cup. She wondered why she hadn't noticed Annette before, and suddenly found herself suggesting that Annette might like to come round to her place for a stiff drink when it was all over.

'And call me Pan – all my friends do.'

They finished their tea and went to find a policeman.

Jenny was aware of another conversation as her stunned mind drifted aimlessly. Behind her, a couple of women were talking in low voices, the sort people assume at funerals and accidents when, vulture-like, they want to pick over the grisly details but wish to appear concerned rather than curious.

'Terrible business this, isn't it?'

'It's a good job it didn't happen to Julia.'

'I didn't know her. Who was she?'

'The woman who lived at number twenty-three before Mrs Walker moved in.'

'Why? Wouldn't she have been able to cope?'

'Nothing of the sort. She'd have probably taken it up to the MOD and shoved it up one of the generals.'

'Why on earth?'

'She was livid that her husband got made redundant. He'd been in the Army for twenty-odd years, they'd just got their two sons into public school and Richard, that was her husband, had been promised that he'd be all right. He'd definitely have a career till fifty-five. A year later he was told to go. Christ, was Julia mad.'

'I don't blame her. What are they doing now?'

'She's in Dorset, but he's having to live in a bedsit in London – it's the only place he can get a job. They can't sell the Dorset house because it's worth less than they paid for it, and the whole thing's a complete mess. The worst of it is, they'd never have bought the house if the Army hadn't assured Richard he was OK.'

Jenny thought back to her conversation with Susan: her fierce defence of the Army, her belief that the Army would always have its soldiers' best interests at heart. Poor bloody Julia, whoever she was, had believed the same. Jenny felt a wave of anger and resentment break over her, almost overpowering in its intensity. All those men, all those families who'd put up with separation, moves, exercises, shabby quarters, disrupted schooling, wars and terrorists, only to be treated so offhandedly. Discarded. Sacked. Goodbye. Christ, it was unfair. And suppose it happened to them? What would Nigel do; where would they live?

Jenny was in no state to think rationally, but the anger in her grew and totally eclipsed her loyalty to the Army; snuffed it out. No longer was she going to kowtow to the system. Nor was she going to be the dutiful wife, trundled out for dinner nights and expected to sit on committees, run the thrift shop or help at the SSAFA fair; but also to silently put up with the disruptions, separations and hardships that were part of their lives. They could stuff it. She and her family were going to take priority from here on in. If she didn't like something or didn't want to do something, she'd bloody well say so.

Outwardly, there were no signs of Jenny's resolution to rebel. She sat on her chair, clutching her teacup, pallid and expressionless. She knew Nigel wouldn't approve. His attitude was that she'd known precisely what she was taking on when she'd married him. And so she had. She'd also been promised exotic postings, job security and decent housing. It seemed that these were not necessarily part of the deal. Just endless wandering around north-west Europe with the threat of further reductions to the defence budget undermining morale, and the axe of future cuts hanging over everyone's heads.

The teapot was circulated again, Jenny at last drank her first cup and had a refill, and a group of women gathered at the window, fascinated by the drama that was happening a few hundred yards away.

A policeman appeared at the door.

'Excuse me, ladies,' he said to get their attention. In the silence as they all turned towards him, he continued, 'The army bomb disposal team has arrived and they are going to disrupt the bomb. You may hear a small explosion. It'll be nothing to worry about. However, I shall have to ask you to keep away from the window, and it might be a good idea to draw the curtains, just in case.' Immediately, Diana pulled the curtains across and then flicked the light switch. The policeman, job done, went back to the cordon.

The wives' conversations did not resume – they were all listening for the bang. When it became obvious that nothing was going to happen instantly, a few comments were made in low voices, and slowly the hubbub built up to its previous level. Jenny sat silently on her chair, holding her cup and saucer carefully on her lap, bracing herself against the sudden crack of the detonation. She was aware of her muscles getting tenser and tenser; she tried to relax but her body would not obey her. Her breathing became shallow and she could feel her heart rate increasing. Suddenly she knew she was about to be sick. Sending her cup clattering off her lap, she raced for the door marked 'Ladies'. She heaved and heaved over the bowl, a dry, racking retch. She had nothing to be sick on, as breakfast, her last meal, had been some four hours ago. She sank down to her knees and rested her head on the seat, too weak with nausea to do anything else.

'You poor dear,' said a voice. Jenny did not turn her head; she thought she might retch again. 'It's the shock. I think we had better get you to a doctor.'

'I don't have one yet,' mumbled Jenny.

'Then you must go to mine,' said the firm voice of Diana. 'As soon as you feel well enough, I'll take you in my car.' Once again Jenny felt as though she was being rescued by the kindness of her neighbours.

Twice in one week, she thought weakly; at this rate I'll be paying back favours forever.

Aloud she said, 'Thank you, I'll be OK in a minute.' Diana waited by the loo door until Jenny felt well enough to stand up, and then hovered beside her as she washed her face and hands. She was worried by Jenny's pallor – the girl had obviously taken it quite badly. She tucked one hand firmly under her elbow to support her back to her chair. Annette had just finished picking up the smashed china, and Marian was taking away the bowl of soapy water with which she had mopped the carpet. The other women were still chatting in groups.

Suddenly they all fell silent together as they heard a voice magnified and distorted by a megaphone say, 'Controlled explosion, my location, in one minute.' After what seemed far longer than a minute the voice yelled, 'Stand by. Firing.' Simultaneously there was a sharp, staccato crack.

'There, I think that's it,' said Diana. One woman peeked through the curtains.

'I hope we can all go home soon,' said Pandora, whose dogs, tied up outside, were barking crazily. There was a murmur of agreement. A policeman approached the building. Everyone started gathering up handbags and rounding up infants, expecting to be told they could leave.

'Ladies,' he said self-consciously from the door, 'I'm sorry that you've been inconvenienced, but can I ask you to bear with us a little longer. We need to check that nothing else has been planted, so we would ask you to stay here until the Army and the sniffer dogs have finished. It'll probably be an hour or so.' There was a groan of dismay.

'I was going to offer you lunch,' Diana said to Jenny. Jenny did not feel hungry, but Christopher would need something. 'It'll be nearer teatime before we get away.' Diana raised her voice and addressed the policeman. 'Can we go to the shops to get some bread and butter? The children need feeding.'

'Yes, that's fine if you don't cut across the patch.' The wives nodded at this news. They began to arrange amongst themselves who was going to go shopping for supplies. All Jenny wanted to do was to go home with Christopher and lie down on her bed. The strain of the last three hours – good God, was that all it was? – was making her feel as though she was losing control over her life. Seeing James was bad enough, without this on top too.

Oh, why isn't Nigel back? she thought.

An hour later they were all allowed to return to their houses. As Jenny approached hers, accompanied by Diana, who was still worried about her, they both noticed that it was still at the centre of the activity. A senior police officer ducked under the blue and white tape and came towards Jenny.

'Mrs Walker?' he asked as he held out his hand. Jenny nodded. The cameras were all pointing at the young sergeant who had dealt with the device and who was now letting the reporters look at his protective bomb suit. 'I'm afraid the media circus has come to town,' he continued with a grimace. 'An incident like this, especially because it involves a small child, does these maniacs no favours, and although they'll shrug it off as an accident, they will be livid at the adverse publicity. I know you have had an awful shock, but would you mind if the press took pictures of Christopher? It might do some good.'

Jenny was dazed. Was it OK for Christopher's picture to be all over the papers? Would Nigel object? Jenny wasn't sure, and she didn't feel up to trusting her judgement or making a decision. She really wanted to consult her husband, but how the hell could she? She didn't even know where he was. What would he say if he saw Christopher's face all over the papers before she could tell him what had happened? Jenny was at a loss to know what to say. The policeman carried on smoothly, aware that this was probably a difficult decision.

'I imagine you will want to contact your husband and let him know what has happened before you get involved with the press.'

'That's just it,' said Jenny, close to tears. 'I can't. He's on an exercise in Germany, and there's no way I can get in touch with him.'

'I see.'

Diana intervened. 'I'm sure there must be someone at the Ministry of Defence who could help. They must be able to get hold of his unit, wherever it is. I'll ring my husband and see what he can do.'

Jenny looked at the phalanx of reporters. A man in a suit detached himself from the rear of the group and came towards her.

'Hello. I'm Captain Tim Barry from the PR branch at the Ministry. I'm here to make sure that the press don't pester you too much. Also that they don't mention any details about this place that we would rather they didn't. Look, I know it's difficult, but they would appreciate a session with your son.' He saw that Jenny still looked doubtful, and carried on: 'A story like this might help save someone else's life – get people who may be at risk to check their cars and their mail. The police think it might have been aimed at Colonel Ross-McLeod, as he's quite a big wheel in the British Field Sports Association. And apart from anything else, it's good PR for the Army.'

Jenny knew she was being put under pressure to agree; she also knew that she ought to. It was her duty. Her new sense of rebelliousness made her want to tell them to forget it. The incident had put her son in danger, and the Army wasn't going to get a whole load of free publicity out of it. She was on the point of telling them where to shove their entire PR branch when she stopped herself. This wasn't the moment for her to try and score cheap points. If an interview with Christopher might stop it happening again ... How could she refuse? She made her decision and nodded her agreement.

'We'll let the lad settle down for a few minutes, and then the press can have a session with him. We won't let it go on for long and we'll be careful that he doesn't get upset. I don't suppose they'll want to talk to him much, beyond a few basic questions.' Jenny nodded again. The reporters were still engrossed with the sergeant, who was now giving an interview and demonstrating the skills of his wheelbarrow – the robot resembling a miniature tank that had had to be so carefully manoeuvred out of their bomb wagon earlier. After the machine had been put through its paces for the admiring press, and Christopher had been interviewed and photographed, Jenny and her son were quietly and discreetly escorted to the back of the house and privacy.

She had barely got her coat off and the kettle on when the doorbell rang.

'I'll go,' said Diana, who had accompanied her inside to make sure she was all right. Jenny could not hear the conversation on the doorstep. Diana returned.

'That was the bomb disposal chap. He came to apologise about a little bit of damage that got done when they dealt with the bomb. He thinks he may have cut the phone line. I've tried the phone, and I hate to say it but I think he's right. It's dead. Would you like me to report it from my house?'

'This is all I need. I can't even talk to Nigel if he phones, or tell the rest of my family not to worry.' Christopher started to clamour that he was still hungry. Jenny found all the things she had to do beginning to whirl around in her mind: collect the girls, ring her mother, get hold of Nigel, get the phone fixed ... It was all too much. She felt swamped by the problems. So much needed doing, but what should she tackle first? She couldn't think straight; she wanted someone to take over.

Diana saw that Jenny was not responding to her son. Her eyes were glazed, like doll's eyes.

'Come on, Christopher,' she said. 'I want you to show me where Mummy keeps the bread. Let's make some sandwiches together, shall we?' She got busy in the kitchen, rummaging in cupboards and the fridge for the fillings. When she had finished, she told Christopher to eat up – she was just popping out for a minute. Outside the back door, she managed to attract the attention of one of the policemen who was checking that they had missed no fragments of the bomb. She told him of the problem with the phone and suggested that maybe someone could get hold of the phone company on Mrs Walker's behalf – perhaps as a matter of urgency.

As she was talking Fiona's car drove up, and Diana saw her

stunned expression as she took in the police cars, bomb wagon, photographers and TV crews. Slowly she got out of her car and came towards Diana.

'What the hell is going on? What's happened? Is everyone all right?'

'Little Christopher Walker found a bomb in the hedge which had been dumped by an animal rights nutter who got cold feet. He brought it in to show Jenny.'

'Is he OK? And what about her?'

'Christopher's fine – it didn't go off, and I don't think he has a clue about what might have happened.'

'Jesus! Why on earth was it dumped here?'

Diana told her about Colonel Ross-McLeod.

'It's all OK now, but Jenny is pretty shocked. The poor girl seems in a bad way. I want to get her to a doctor, and I need to collect her girls from school.'

'Right,' said Fiona. 'Give me two ticks to do a couple of things at home, and then I'll have Christopher while you get Jenny to the quack – though surely under the circumstances he'd make a house call? Anyway, whether he does or not, I'll have the lad and get the girls from school. Tell Jenny everything's under control. In fact, I'll pop into see her myself when I come to get Christopher. Back in a tick.'

Fiona let herself into the house and almost tripped over a large grip that had been left in the middle of the hall.

'James, I'm home,' she called. Silence. She wondered where he was. He had probably taken himself off to a pub for lunch, she decided. He would not have fancied a cup of coffee down at the community centre with all the wives. What a day to get a supply teaching job, she thought. No doubt James would be in a bait because she was not around to pick him up from Heathrow. Well, he should have phoned to say he was coming back. Shit, that was all Jenny needed, James and a bloody bomb. Fiona didn't know that Jenny had already had to handle an encounter with him. She scribbled a quick note to James to say she was sorry she had missed him, and went next door to help Diana hold the fort.

Chapter Six

Jenny was sitting on the sofa with her feet up when Fiona returned. Diana was in the kitchen with Christopher, making a pot of tea.

'Hi, how are you feeling now?' said Fiona, the genuine concern in her voice mirrored by the expression in her grey eyes.

'Oh, all right. Well, not too bad, anyway.' Jenny's voice was dull, expressionless. She sighed, then said, 'It isn't as if anything happened. I mean, it's just my imagination which has made such a drama out of it all. Christopher wasn't ...' Her voice petered out and Fiona could tell that she was on the brink of tears. She could see Jenny swallowing down the sobs.

'No. And he's got no idea about what might have happened, and everyone will make sure that it stays that way.'

Jenny looked up, unshed tears hovering on her lower lashes. She smiled in gratitude, a thin, sad little smile.

'Thanks.'

Diana came in with the tea.

'Come on, Jenny, sit up and drink this.' She put the cup down on the coffee table and picked up a couple of cushions from another chair. 'Here. Lean forward while I make you more comfortable.' She plumped up the cushions and then wedged them behind Jenny to make it easier for her to drink her tea.

'Where's Christopher?' asked Jenny as she was passed the cup.

'In the kitchen with squash and biscuits. All the excitement has made him hungry. He's going to tell me all about his new school in a minute, so I'll leave you. Sing out if you want more tea.'

'Um, thanks.'

Diana shut the door behind her. Jenny took a sip of her tea, then said, 'You know, when I moved in here I thought this was going to be a happy house. Now I'm not so sure.'

'Why's that?'

'Just all sorts of things. First there's James, then the bomb, and then today I heard that the last people here got kicked out of the Army.'

'But that doesn't make the house jinxed.'

'No, I know. But I just wonder if anything else will happen while we're here.' Jenny sounded depressed.

'I doubt it,' said Fiona, with a confidence she knew was false.

'Julia – the woman who lived here before – tell me about her.'

'Why? There's not much to tell.'

'I don't know; curiosity, I suppose. Someone said that things have gone badly since her husband got the boot.'

'Yes. They've been unlucky. They just managed to get things wrong. I suppose they never considered the possibility that Richard would ever do anything else.' Fiona shrugged her shoulders under her camel cashmere sweater. 'You can't blame them; we all thought the Army was a safe job. Anyway, Julia was a paragon. Did all the right things for an army wife, ran the wives' club, went to meetings of the Federation of Army Wives, helped raised money for SSAFA ... you know the sort.' Jenny nodded. Everyone knew the sort. 'She'd packed her kids off to boarding school to be able to follow the drum. She always said that an officer couldn't do his job properly if he didn't have a proper family life. She had no truck with these wives who settle down in the country and just see their husbands at weekends. But they knew that they needed to get into the housing market for when he eventually retired. So they bought a place in Dorset to rent out while she lived in quarters. They didn't choose it with schools or jobs in mind.'

'I can imagine the rest,' said Jenny. 'No jobs to be had for miles around, the kids can't cope with the local state school, and they're stuck there because the mortgage is larger than the value of the house.'

'You've got it. Julia is terribly bitter. She'd devoted her life to the Army and to making sure she did all the right things to get Richard promoted.'

'What about her husband?'

'He was quite pragmatic at the time, but I don't know now. He's got a job in London which doesn't pay much, and he only sees his family at the weekend – I should imagine he's pretty disillusioned too.'

Diana returned to the sitting room, this time with Christopher, who was asking to watch a video. After much deliberation he decided to have Thomas the Tank Engine. He sat on a footstool, engrossed by the antics of his favourite character. Fiona noticed the time and left to collect the girls.

'Did you know Julia?' said Jenny.

'Yes. She was a member of just about every committee going.' Diana grimaced, and added, 'I have to chair most of them.' Jenny didn't think to ask why this fell to Diana. 'She was very committed to the Army. It was a shame her husband got kicked out.'

'She sounds as though she was quite a paragon.'

'Oh, she certainly was. In fact, she reminded me a lot of my husband's first wife. She was the same sort – dedicated to the wives' club and the welfare of the soldiers' wives. Knew what was expected of her.'

'So why...?' Jenny didn't quite know how to ask why Diana's husband had got rid of her and married Diana, who looked nothing like an army wife in her *haute couture* dress, glamorous costume jewellery, platinum-blonde hair and heavy make-up.

'She died,' replied Diana, who knew exactly what Jenny was getting at. If she'd known Jenny better she'd have also told her that Honor, her predecessor, had also been lousy in bed and a crashing bore. 'Anyway, enough of that. The doctor's going to be here in a moment, so let's get you upstairs and into bed. As I've persuaded him to come out and see you I think we should make it look as though we're not crying wolf.'

Had Jenny been more herself and not suffering from shock, she might have taken more interest in her benefactress and asked herself why this woman, who was such a head-turner, also chaired committee meetings and seemed to know her way round the system so well. With a modicum of thought she would probably have hit on the right answer – that Diana's husband, Roderick, was a very senior officer. It would not have been totally unfair to say that Honor had been partly responsible for his promotion before she died. Not because of all her efforts, although they certainly hadn't done him any harm, but because she had been so busy with her good works, her meetings, and her two adored and indulged children that she had had little energy left for him and still less for any sort of sex life. Roderick had found himself spending longer and longer in the office – it was preferable to home. His ensuing rapid promotion was almost entirely due to this, although Honor had silently, smugly, thought of the cliché about the good woman behind every successful man. After her death, with the two boys away at boarding school, there had been even less reason to go home early so he had worked even longer hours, driven largely by force of habit tempered by boredom. It was not, as his doting parents and loving in-laws thought, that he was working all hours to prevent himself thinking of Honor. Truth be told, once she was dead he found himself thinking of her surprisingly little.

Just a year after she had died, he ran into an old friend who lived with his new wife, Emma, in Chelsea. He invited Roderick back to supper, as his chum was plainly destined for nothing more exciting than fish and chips again. Visiting their flat at the same time was a girl who worked with Emma in the City. From the instant Roderick clapped eyes on her, he was smitten. Here was a girl who was independent, clever, chic and simply exuded sex appeal. She was the antithesis of Honor. Roderick decided that evening that if he was ever going to marry again, Diana was the only woman who would do. She might not be the sort of gal the Establishment would approve of, but he was convinced she would be the most phenomenal fun – especially in bed!

Conversely, Diana was not about to throw herself at any man. She was successful in her own right in a high-grade secretarial job in the City. With her looks and prospects she knew that she could have her pick of any number of men.

It took Roderick two whole years to woo Diana. Unashamedly, she played hard to get. He had no wish that she should marry into an organisation she did not fully understand.

He warned her in no uncertain terms about the separations, the moves, the tours in dreary places. He also told her what her duties would be. Amazingly this held a certain charm for Diana. She felt it would be rather like being the squire's wife in a small village. After her years working in the anonymous atmosphere of the City, the idea of being a big fish in a small pond was enticing. Besides which, the Army did seem undeniably glamorous. To Roderick's delight and surprise, she accepted his proposal. To Diana's credit, she was brilliant as a senior officer's wife. She did everything she was supposed to, except dress like one, which was why she was so refreshing.

Jenny lay on her bed while the doctor gave her a huge dose of sedative, quite unaware that Diana, who was busy drawing the curtains, fetching a glass of water and acting as nurse, was the current mistress of Flagstaff House, the large mansion which went with her husband's current job. Under the influence of the drug, and knowing that her children were in safe hands, Jenny slipped off to sleep.

Outside, all trace of the earlier excitement had disappeared. The journalists had vanished back to London to file their story. The police cars and the bomb wagon had gone. The sniffer dogs had been led away. In Jenny's kitchen, Fiona was busy getting tea. Diana, having checked that Jenny was fast asleep, went back to her husband's residence to break the news to Jenny's family.

'Does she want me to come up?' Jenny's elderly mother enquired querulously.

'I think she'll be fine by the morning. We're trying to get Nigel back from Germany, but someone here will stay with her until he arrives.'

'And you're sure no one was hurt?'

'Absolutely. Christopher thought it was a great adventure, and Jenny just had a bit of a shock. I'm sure she'll ring you herself tomorrow – the doctor has given her something to make her sleep for a few hours, otherwise she'd be telling you all this herself.'

'And you say Nigel will be coming home?'

'Yes, it's being arranged now.' Diana told a little white lie and hoped it could be – she was certain her husband could fix it. She also hoped she had succeeded in reassuring the old lady. It was all very well being told there was nothing to worry about, quite another thing to believe it.

Then she phoned her husband.

Lieutenant-General Sir Roderick Marlow KCMG CB DSO (late GLOSTERS) sat in his large office overlooking Horse Guards. He put down the phone and pressed the intercom button.

'Sir?' said his secretary.

'Laura, get me the SO1 G1 at HQ BAOR.'

'Just a moment, sir.' Laura had worked at the Ministry of Defence for long enough to be able to translate the jargon without a second thought. She picked up the telephone directory for the British Army's main headquarters in Rheindahlen and ran her finger down the column of the Administration Branch until she found the Grade 1 staff officer, Lieutenant Colonel Michael Cobham. Keeping her left forefinger on the number, she dialled direct with her other hand. The phone at the other end rang only once.

'Cobham,' the brusque voice said.

'I have a call from General Marlow for you – please hold on.' Laura patched the call through to the General's office.

'Sir, I've Colonel Cobham at HQ BAOR for you on line one.'

'Thanks, Laura.' The General pressed button one.

'Colonel Cobham? It's General Marlow here. I need your expertise. There's been an incident on a patch near London involving a bomb – some bloody animal rights group. No one was hurt but one family bore the brunt of the whole business and the wife is rather distressed. Her husband is currently on Exercise Green Light. Firstly I'd like someone to inform him of what has happened before it gets on the news, and secondly I think it would be a good thing if he could be brought home as soon as possible. It's not a compassionate case, as there are no injuries, but I'm sure he can be found a seat on an RAF flight.'

Colonel Cobham knew by heart the rules for compassionate flights home – it was one of his jobs. He also knew that it was perfectly possible to bend them, providing there was a good enough reason. This seemed to fall into just that category; the more so because a general was taking a personal interest.

'I'll see what I can do, General. What's this chap's name and unit?'

'Major Nigel Walker, of the Royal Logistic Corps. He's with the Logistic Headquarters.'

'I'll get on to it right away. Do you want me to pass details on to anyone in UK when I've got some news?'

'Yes, you can phone my staff here. I'll pass you back to my secretary and she can give you their phone numbers and all the details of the bombing. Thanks for your assistance. Good luck.'

The General, having put his considerable clout into getting Nigel home, passed the problem back to his staff, knowing that everything possible would now be done to carry out his wishes. He mused that rank really did have some advantages.

Twelve minutes later the phone rang in the operations wagon at the centre of the headquarters for Exercise Green Light. The clerk who took the call realised the urgency of the information, so having carefully noted all the details, he found his boss, Major Hammond, and handed the paper to him.

'Sir, we've got a compassionate case involving Major Walker.'

Major Hammond read the transcript made by the clerk. He knew the Walker family quite well. What bloody bad luck for poor Jenny to have this happen to her.

'Do you want me to get hold of him, sir?'

'No, we'll get his Commanding Officer to go and break the news to him. While he's doing that I want you to get on to the Army Air Corps and see if they can't give him a lift to Gutersloh. According to this, if we can get him there by 1800 hours there's a seat on a Hercules up for grabs.' The Major looked at his watch. 'We've got just over two hours – we'll have to step on it.'

Leaving his clerk to organise a helicopter flight, Brian Hammond ran along to Colonel Bob's APC. He found him sitting in a folding chair outside his vehicle, reading a thriller. No wonder the rest of the poor buggers working for him were so busy, he thought as he approached and saluted.

'Sorry to disturb you, Colonel, but we've had a call through from HQ BAOR. It seems there's been a bomb incident involving Nigel Walker's family, and although no one was hurt, he's wanted back home. The RAF have agreed to give him a lift on a Herc going back to UK tonight.'

Colonel Bob looked taken aback. His first reaction was one of disbelief. Walker had been trying to wangle a way off this exercise for a day or so now. Was this some sort of cock-and-bull story he'd got his cronies to concoct just to be able to bug out early? Brian Hammond, who disliked Colonel Bob, although he wasn't sure why, saw the man's raised eyebrows of disbelief. It was not the disbelief of shock but of scepticism. Why, for God's sake?

Irritated by the man's reaction, Brian said, 'The call came from the SO1 G1, Colonel Michael Cobham. His number is here. If you want any further details, perhaps you should talk to him.'

There was silence, as though the Colonel was weighing up the veracity of the statement – which indeed he was. Brian Hammond was incredulous. Didn't the man care? Any normal commanding officer would have been clamouring for details, expressing concern, but he hadn't even asked if the family was all right. What a bastard!

Eventually the Colonel said, 'Get the G1 on the line, while I organise my driver to take me up to Nigel.' His suspicious mind was still convinced that this was a put-up job, and he wasn't going to fall for it. He wasn't going to move until he had heard it from the horse's mouth.

'How are you getting on?' Diana asked cheerfully when she returned to Jenny's house. She had found Fiona and the children busy making jam tarts for tea.

'Fine, thanks,' answered Fiona. 'As soon as we've got this lot into the oven, we're all going over to the play park while they cook.' The children, sitting round the table, were making models out of leftover scraps of pastry. They beamed at the two women from floury faces.

'Jenny's still asleep,' said Fiona. 'I peeped in to check on her a few minutes ago. She seemed fine. Did you get your phone calls made?'

'Yes. Jenny's mother sounded a bit upset – not surprisingly – but I promised her that Jenny would phone her as soon as possible. And I got hold of Rod, who's going through channels to get Nigel back. Have BT dealt with the phone here yet?'

'I don't think so.'

Diana went into the hall and lifted the telephone receiver. It was still dead. Jenny could phone her mother from Flagstaff House, but what if Nigel wanted to ring home? She wondered whether to go back home and ring BT again, but decided to give them another half-hour. As she stood in the hall beside the bookcase, she spotted a pair of Jenny's bookends sitting on top of it, supporting some children's books. They immediately caught her attention. Even her untrained eye could see that the two miniature wooden officers, dressed in their ceremonial 'blues' and holding swords, were accurate right down to the cap badges. She wondered where Jenny had found such delightful things. If she could get one with the Gloucestershire Regiment's cap badge, it would make a wonderful birthday present for Rod.

'Fiona,' she called, 'have you seen these?'

Fiona came out of the kitchen, wiping her floury hands on her apron. Jane, curious to know what was interesting the grown-ups, followed her.

'Aren't they splendid!' exclaimed Fiona. 'I wonder where Jenny found them. I'd love a pair in gunner uniforms for James.'

'That's exactly what was going through my mind.' Diana turned to Jane. 'Do you know where Mummy got these book-ends?'

'She didn't buy them,' said Jane, 'she made them – she does Guardsmen too. Do you want to see where she does it?' She grabbed Diana's hand with her own sticky one and pulled her upstairs to the spare room, to show off her mother's small stock.

Nigel was sitting at his trestle table in the barn, bored senseless. Apart from coordinating the search for the missing simmo, he had had virtually nothing to do since his abortive trip to see his boss the previous day. He had sent Phil Brooking back to his billet. There was no point in both of them sitting here in discomfort. He was just contemplating getting in his Land Rover to go out and visit his troops yet again when he saw Colonel Bob push through the grey blanket over the barn door. Wearily Nigel stood up – this was the last person he felt like talking to.

'Nigel, ah – there's nothing to worry about and everyone is OK, but we've had a call from HQ BAOR about your family.' Nigel felt a tremor of fear run through him. It was only ever bad news if it had to be broken in person. He instantly thought about traffic accidents – then he realised that Colonel Bob was carrying on.

'...was a bomb dumped by some loony animal terrorist group which your son picked up.' Nigel's hands clenched involuntarily by his side – he'd seen the mangled remains after a car bomb had exploded. Colonel Bob had been watching Nigel intently as he broke the news. Despite having phoned HQ BAOR he still was not completely convinced that the story was true but even he realised that no one could let the colour drain from his face like that if he wasn't genuinely shocked.

'But if failed to go off. The bomb disposal team dealt with it and your family is fine.'

'Fine. What does fine mean? Jenny must have been terrified. I must speak to her.'

Now that Bob Clarkson's scepticism had been proved groundless, he actually began to feel a twinge of sympathy for his subordinate, although it was heavily overlaid with annoyance that he was now going to have to write the post-exercise report himself.

'Hold your fire on making a phone call, Nigel. It's been fixed for you to go home. There's a flight leaving Gutersloh in about ninety minutes, and the Air Corps are going to give you a lift. Get your kit together and get yourself home.'

Nigel's tense white face suddenly broke into a smile. He almost felt gratitude as he shook his boss warmly by the hand before running full tilt out of the barn and over to his billet.

Five minutes later he had almost finished frantically throwing his kit into his grip. His webbing and pistol, together with his sleeping bag and tin hat, belonged to the Regiment – he would have to get Phil to hand them back in. As he frenziedly tried to sort out his kit from the Army's and cram everything into his case, he heard the clatter of a Gazelle helicopter as it landed in the large farmyard. Phil watched as Nigel stuffed his shaving gear and PE kit in the top of the bag.

'Hurry up, Nigel, your taxi's here.'

'Christ, I'm going as fast as I can. Look, Phil, the pile of stuff on my bed needs to be handed back. I think most of it is there. If something is missing could you tell the QM to get hold of me before he docks my pay. I'll get the stuff sent back or replaced somehow. And can you fix to get the rest of my personal kit sent on?'

'Don't worry about that. Just concentrate on getting that flight out tonight and going home to Jenny.' Phil was almost more upset than Nigel about the news Colonel Bob had brought. He adored his boss's wife and couldn't bear the thought that wonderful, vivacious Jenny had been in so much danger. Nigel was worried too, although he believed the news that she was only badly shaken, not hurt in any way. However, deep inside, his gratitude had been replaced by anger. He was furious that he had been wasting his time in Germany because of his Commanding Officer and hadn't been in England, where he was really needed. If he'd been at home he might have seen something and prevented the incident from ever happening in the first place.

With a final heave on the zip, he closed his bag and raced across the dusty yard to the waiting helicopter. He held on to his beret as he ducked under the still-turning rotors, and with a final wave to Phil climbed aboard. As soon as the helicopter was airborne, Nigel gave a rebellious V sign to the retreating back view of Colonel Bob.

It took forty-five minutes for the helicopter to reach RAF Gutersloh. Nigel was deposited on a concrete pan about a hundred yards from the terminal building. He had barely leapt out before the revs increased once more and the chopper racketed skywards again. Nigel stood on the concrete watching it disappear eastwards and wondered where he should go next. As the silence of the early evening returned, he was aware of footsteps approaching him from behind.

'Major Walker? I'm Squadron Leader Brown, the station duty officer. I am so very sorry to hear about your family's close shave.' He smiled at Nigel and motioned that they should move towards the terminal building and away from the runway area.

'Thanks,' said Nigel. He was suddenly aware of the fact that he had been on exercise in the field for ten days, during which time he hadn't had a bath. Walking next to this pressed and polished officer, Nigel wondered if he smelt. 'Obviously the news of the incident has got around,' he said, widening the gap between them slightly.

'It was on the national news – your son is being turned into quite a little hero by the press.'

Nigel grimaced. He didn't altogether approve. He wondered whose idea it had been. It didn't sound like Jenny to allow that sort of thing. Some PR chap must have suggested it. There was no point in getting wound up about it; the main thing was that no one was hurt. He changed the subject.

'I don't know if there is any time before the flight, but I would really appreciate it if I could phone my wife and also have a wash somewhere.'

'No problem at all, we've half an hour before you have to be on board,' said the Squadron Leader, who had been trying with some difficulty to ignore Nigel's body odour. 'Follow me.' They had reached the rear of the terminal building, and he led Nigel through a door and across the concourse filled with regimented rows of plastic seats. He stepped over the black conveyor belt by the check-in desk and started up a flight of stairs that led to the administrative hub of the passenger terminal, hidden away on the top floor, where he directed Nigel into the duty officer's bunk with its en-suite bathroom. Opening the window in the bedroom, he now understood why the Army were nicknamed pongos.

When Nigel emerged from the bathroom ten minutes later, having had a rapid shower and changed into some relatively clean clothes, the duty officer led him along to his office. Nigel knew why the offer of a wash had taken precedence over making the call home, and didn't resent it.

'I'll get you through the switchboard,' said Brown. 'They're dragons down there, and you'll have to have my authority to phone UK at the firm's expense.' A minute later the operator reported that she was unable to connect the call; the line at the other end was out of order.

'Right,' said Brown. 'I'll phone the duty desk at Joint HQ Rheindahlen to see if they can get the info from the Ministry of

Defence. They may know more details anyway.' He got out the duty officer's folder to look up the correct number, and dialled. Nigel could only hear one side of the conversation, which he found intensely frustrating.

'Yes ... That's right, Major Walker ... Yes, in my office at the moment ... OK, give me the number ... Yes, I've got that ... OK ... Well, that's something ...' Nigel longed to grab the phone and ask questions, talk to whoever it was with the information, but he restrained himself. 'OK ... yes, I'll tell him. Thank you. Goodbye.' Nigel looked at him enquiringly.

'It seems that when the bomb was disrupted your phone line got severed. That was the only damage. They have confirmed most strongly that no one was hurt – the bomb was dumped in a hedge and your son picked it up. I've been given a number at the Ministry of Defence that you can call for more information. If you'd like to use my phone to call London, I'll pop along the corridor and fix for some transport to take you home from Lyneham.'

Five hours later, and Nigel was dismissing the car that had been made available by RAF Lyneham's Station Commander to get him home as soon as possible. He hadn't known when he'd arrived there that the Air Commodore had already been briefed by the Ministry of Defence about the army officer travelling on the Hercules from Gutersloh. He had been expecting a rail warrant to London and was touched by the Air Commodore's thoughtfulness. The car had met him as he left the C130 and had whisked him away from the base. It seemed an amazingly short time till he was standing on the doorstep of his new home, trying to detect any signs of the car bomb. The plastic cover on the wall where the phone line entered the house was shattered, but the wires inside it looked OK. Perhaps it had been fixed. He rang the door bell. A petite, blonde bombshell opened the door. Nigel was confused; he was sure his address was number 23.

'I'm sorry,' he said. 'I must have made a mistake. I thought this was the Walker house.'

'It is, I'm a neighbour. And you are ...?'

'I'm sorry. I'm Jenny's husband.'

'Jenny!' yelled the woman over her shoulder. 'Nigel's here.'

There was a flurry, and then she was in his arms, sobbing

and laughing and kissing him all at the same time. Then there was a shriek from a bedroom and the two girls hurled themselves down the stairs, two at a time, yelling, 'Hello, Daddy,' at the tops of their voices. They were all trying to hug him at the same time, Jane hanging on to his hand for grim death, jumping up and down and shrieking, 'Daddy, Daddy, Daddy,' over and over again. Elizabeth had her arms round his waist, her face buried in his tummy being sandwiched by Jenny, who was on tiptoe, kissing him. It was a while before things calmed down, and no one noticed that Diana had slipped away. Jenny would be fine now her husband was there; someone to take over and lift the strain of the last week from her fragile shoulders.

After the bedlam had subsided, Nigel realised that Christopher had not made an appearance.

'He's exhausted,' explained Jenny. 'He was taken for a ride round the patch in a police car and was allowed to play with the wheelbarrow. And he did a whole load of press interviews. I wasn't sure you would be keen about that, but a chap from Ministry of Defence PR came to see me and said it was OK. I wanted to ask you about it but they didn't seem to be able to get hold of you for ages. What with one thing and another, Christopher has had a bit of a day. I'll show you where his room is so you can see for yourself that he's fine.'

Nigel tiptoed into his son's room and stroked the sleeping child's hair. He had realised when he heard the news of the bomb how much he adored the boy. The gut-wrenching shock he'd experienced when he heard how close Christopher had come to death had shown him the aching, desperate void that would never be filled. To get that close to the black pit of horror had shaken him more than he cared to admit. Silently, and close to tears, he thanked God that Christopher was safe, kissed his son's little fist and then tucked it back under the covers and returned downstairs. Jenny handed him a beer, and then just sat and gazed at him, wriggling inside with happiness that he was home.

Chapter Seven

The next morning, Saturday, Jenny awoke and remembered with a glow of delight that her husband was home. She rolled over on to her side and tucked her body against his, her knees fitting into the crook of his, her hips curving round his warm bottom, her breasts pressed against his back. She nuzzled his shoulder blades happily.

'What does a man have to do to get some sleep around here?' Nigel murmured through a yawn.

'It's your fault,' Jenny replied softly. 'You shouldn't be such a delectable husband.' Her hand strayed from his chest to his stomach, and was about to explore lower when Nigel grasped it.

'Don't make promises you can't keep,' he said, turning his head so he could whisper into her ear. 'The children will be awake in a minute.'

'But you've forgotten about the joys of early-morning TV. They won't come in and bother us. They'll thunder straight down those stairs and be in front of the box for hours.'

'Promise?'

'Promise,' said Jenny firmly. Even as she spoke, they heard the click of a bedroom door opening and the pattering of feet on the stairs.

'Well, in that case...' And without saying anything more, they began to make slow, fulfilling and eventually passionate love. They lay in each other's arms for some time afterwards, waiting for their heart rates to return to normal, their breathing to recover. Then Nigel shifted his position slightly and rolled back on to his side of the bed.

'So where's my tea?' said Jenny impishly.

'All you've done is move house on your own and you think you can demand tea in bed. I don't know what things are coming to,' Nigel retorted with a grin. 'I suppose I'd better go and put the kettle on before you force me to make love to you again.'

'You're safe there – no energy left for that sort of carry-on. Well, not till I've had some tea, anyway.'

Nigel got out of bed and grabbed his dressing gown. 'I'll go and say hello to my mate Christopher while I'm at it.'

'Well, just be careful you're not interrupting a cartoon. He gets very stroppy if you do that.' Nigel went downstairs. Jenny could hear his feet padding on the carpet, a pause and the faint creak of the sitting room door hinges. Then came Christopher's excited shrieks and giggles of joy, and yells from the girls. Jenny smiled happily to herself as she snuggled under the duvet. Nigel was home, everyone seemed to have got over the trauma of yesterday, and nothing was going to spoil things now. Not even bloody James.

Comfortable, warm and content, Jenny was drifting off to sleep again as Nigel entered the bedroom, clutching two mugs and with the newspaper tucked under his arm.

'Tea and the paper,' he announced. 'And don't say I don't spoil you.'

'Ooh, goody.' Jenny yawned as she sat up, resting her tousled hair against the headboard. Idly she opened out the paper and nearly dropped her tea in her lap when she saw her son grinning cheerfully at her from the front page. *Army Major's Son in Animal Terror Outrage*, blared the headline.

'Good God!'

'Good picture,' commented Nigel. 'Let's read what they say.'

'Do you suppose he's in all the papers?' said Jenny. 'I didn't expect anything like this. When all those reporters wanted to talk to him I just thought it would be a paragraph or two on an inside page. God, if the *Telegraph* has done this, what sort of coverage will the tabloids be giving it?'

'Looks like Christopher is going to be famous for at least fifteen minutes. Now let me read the story.' They bent over the front page together, studying the paper's interpretation of the events of the previous day.

'When I think of how close Christopher came to meeting his maker...' said Jenny as they finished the article.

'He was probably fairly safe,' said Nigel pragmatically. 'Once those things fail, it usually means they are completely dud.' He knew that what he was saying wasn't strictly true. If the mechanism had jammed, a knock could easily free it, and then ... But better that Jenny was left in ignorance.

'Well, it's all very well for you to say that, but it was a bloody sight too close for comfort.'

'Yes, I know, and it's different when it's happening to you. It gave me a nasty turn when I heard the news in Germany. Still, it's over now, and it's all OK. Come on, let's get up and get on. Is there a pool here? I'll take them all swimming if there is.'

'They'd adore that. There's one down behind the main car park, near the centre of town.' Jenny began to get out of bed. Then she suddenly realised that if she didn't take this opportunity to tell Nigel about James now, there might not be another chance before the kids went to bed. Nigel had to find out before he ran into him. Mentally she braced herself and squared her shoulders.

'Nigel ...' He turned round and saw her serious face, her eyes looking huge as they always did when something was troubling her.

'It's OK, Jenny, Christopher's fine.'

'No. It's not Christopher, it's me.'

'Christ, you're not pregnant again, are you?' he joked. Then he saw her set mouth, her grave expression. 'What is it?' he asked gently.

'Nigel ...' She paused. Oh, come on, you silly woman, just say it. 'Nigel, James is our next-door neighbour.'

'You're kidding.' He sat on the bed. Jenny didn't have to say which James it was. There was only one. 'That bastard. Next door?'

'Yes, and I don't think he's changed much.'

'You mean you've met him?'

'Yesterday. He came round to get the spare key his wife keeps here. It happened just before Christopher found the bomb.'

'Shit.'

'My feelings precisely. I found out on Tuesday. I thought about asking for another quarter, but the hassle of changing our address and phone number again ... And besides which, I wasn't sure it'd be worth it. I mean, they'd probably only move us down the road. We'd still be bound to run into him.'

'God, I hope this isn't someone's idea of a sick joke.'

'No, I'm sure of that. It wouldn't be on any records, would it? Besides which, the housing people wouldn't know.'

'You're right. But it's a bloody mess, isn't it?'

'Absolutely. Look, I know you hate him nearly as much as I do, but I don't want you doing anything silly. We'll just keep out of his way for a while and see if things don't settle down.'

Nigel was surprised at how much loathing he still felt for Jamie Pollock-Bloody-Bain. It had been years since their paths had crossed at Sandhurst. Nigel worked it out: good grief, eighteen years. It didn't seem possible. James had been an arrogant sod then, and Nigel didn't consider it likely that time would have lessened that particular character defect. Ages ago, when Nigel had discovered that Jenny, the girl he was desperately in love with, had been married to Jamie, he had nearly finished with her. It was only because he had indeed loved her so very deeply that he had been able to put aside his feelings and go ahead with the wedding. But knowing that Jamie had made love to her first had never ceased to rankle, however petty it seemed.

'He's married to a general's daughter now,' said Jenny, breaking into Nigel's dark thoughts.

'Well, that's only to be expected. He wouldn't do anything that wouldn't be of help to his career. What's she like?'

'Actually, I rather like her. Very unpretentious, very attractive, but tough. In fact, I reckon that Jamie doesn't wear the trousers there. She made him drop the Pollock bit. Said she wasn't going to be called Bollock-Brain for anyone. I got to know her before I realised who she was. When she said her name was Fiona Bain, it didn't cross my mind that she was connected to him. If the penny had dropped I wouldn't have got so friendly with her.'

'Was that her – the dishy bird who opened the door last night?'

'No. Fiona's about five foot ten, fabulous auburn hair and

looks like she's stepped straight out of the society pages. The woman you met was Diana Marlow. She lives around here and looked after me yesterday when I got in a bit of a state.'

'Marlow? Did she say what her husband does?'

'No. Well, not that I remember. There were a lot of things I didn't take in yesterday.'

'Well, let's just hope you didn't say anything naughty. I know what you're like.'

'Why?' Jenny was intrigued.

'I wouldn't mind betting that she's connected to General Sir Roderick Marlow. I'd heard a rumour that his wife's a bit of all right. If that was her, then the old boy must have hidden depths.'

'Blimey,' said Jenny irreverently. 'You could be right.' She paused, considering what she knew about Diana. 'But she doesn't look anything like a general's wife; she's much too young and glamorous. All the ones I've ever met have been the most awful old bags. Still, she did say that her old man had been married before, and that his first wife was the pukka sort. Obviously he fancied something a bit more spicy the second time around. Well, if you're called for an interview without coffee on Monday, you'll know who to blame.' A vague memory of something Diana had said yesterday came to Jenny. 'I've got a sneaky feeling that she got her old man to have you brought home yesterday. When I didn't have a clue where you were.'

'Christ, so that's how I got back so easily. I thought it all went smoothly. Come on. We aren't even dressed yet, and if I'm going to get the children to the pool this side of Christmas ...'

In the house next door, James stood at the washbasin in the bedroom and regarded his lathered face in the mirror with approval. He peered closer at his reflection and was pleased to see that his blue eyes were clear despite last night's excesses. As he examined his face he noticed with satisfaction that his blond hair was still thick, with no receding evident. For someone of thirty-six, he thought, he still looked pretty good, good enough to pull a bird if he wanted. Fiona would give him hell if she ever found out about his conquests when he was travelling overseas. He didn't think she would find out, as he was always careful, just one-night stands. He wasn't the Casanova he had been – between his two marriages. Then, with a combination of good looks and a smart red Triumph Spitfire, he'd been able to screw any girl who'd taken his fancy. At the thought of his recent infidelities and his past affairs, his eyes flicked past his image to look at the reflection of his wife.

Fiona, sitting up in their big mahogany bed, met his gaze in the looking-glass. Even unmade-up, with her hair ruffled, she was stunningly attractive. She was one of those people who was unconsciously, naturally elegant. Lounging against the pale-yellow pillows, she looked like a model put there to enhance the expensive bedding rather than someone who had just woken up.

Fiona studied her husband's naked back view. He really was devilishly handsome, she concluded. His bottom was just perfect. It was a shame he was standing so far away at the moment. She could just fancy digging her fingers into his firm buttocks. She considered inviting him back into bed for another session of lovemaking – the first having taken place when he had woken up, as he always did, at six o'clock. God, he was good in bed. She felt herself getting aroused, a tightening in her loins. Then she noticed his expression. She thought that he looked distinctly smug, and decided that he probably was. There was very little about him that she missed; she could invariably guess what he was thinking. At the moment, she decided, he was admiring himself.

'You looked pleased with yourself. I'm surprised you haven't got a hangover,' she said.

'You know I never get hangovers, and I've nothing to be displeased about,' he replied as he started to shave. 'Things might be getting a bit tricky, though.'

'Why, what things?'

'Our new neighbours.'

'Hmm,' said Fiona. 'I gather you've seen Jenny again?'

'How do you think I got in yesterday? I had to get the spare key. I didn't expect you to be out when I got home.'

Fiona yawned and stretched like a cat.

'Sorry about that, but St John's rang up desperate for a supply teacher and I just had to go in.'

'I'd forgotten Julia and Richard had gone. It came as a bit of a shock to find that my ex-wife had moved in. Have you met her husband yet?'

'No, he's been away on exercise. He was rushed home early because of the bomb. He's called Nigel. Do you know him?'

'Nigel what?'

'Walker.'

James considered the name. No, it didn't ring a bell. The encounter that he had had with Nigel at Sandhurst had completely slipped his memory. If pressed, he might have recalled the final exercise, and a rather unpleasant business involving a cadet firing a gun by accident, but it hadn't really affected him. Besides which, James only ever bothered with people who would be useful to him; the cavalry and the Guards and those with connections and clout.

'Do you know who he's with?'

'The Logistics Corps, I think Jenny said.'

'No, don't know him. Never met him. Anyway, if you knew Jenny was my ex-wife, why did you leave the key with her? Why not with the Evanses?'

'Because Margaret Evans works silly hours. If I lock myself out I want to be able to get in at any time, not just when she happens to be at home.'

'OK. But you might have warned me. It isn't as if I haven't phoned home.'

'No. Well, I really didn't get much chance to tell you about her. You always seemed in a hurry when you called, and I expected you to ring back on Thursday night to let me know whether you were going on to Alabama or coming home. And you didn't.'

'I tried but I couldn't get a reply.'

'But that's ridiculous, I was in all eve—' Fiona suddenly remembered how she had popped in to see Jenny to warn her about James' imminent return, and how she had stayed for a drink. 'Well, almost all evening. You could have tried later,' she finished, rather petulantly.

'I was in a meeting, and then it was too late. Anyway, let's not argue over her.'

'Why didn't you mention her when you got in last night?'

'It didn't seem important. Besides which, you were so

nearly asleep I thought you'd be livid if I woke you up for a chat. All you did was mumble something about a bomb scare and then go back to sleep. It was like talking to the dormouse.' He finished shaving and began to rinse the last traces of foam off. 'So was it Jenny who had the bomb?'

'Yes it was, poor girl. She's had some tough breaks recently. She had to move here on her own with three children, and then her youngest comes within an inch of getting blown to bits. I hope you're going to be civil to her; she doesn't need any more hassle, and you two are quite old enough to behave like adults.' James thought she sounded like a schoolmistress. Any minute now she would threaten him with detention for being late home.

As if she had read his thoughts she added, 'By the way, why were you home so late last night? When I got back after lunch your bag was here but there was no sign of you. I thought you'd popped out for a pub lunch. I didn't expect you to be gone half the night too.'

'I went into work. I got back here around half past nine. You weren't here and I didn't feel sleepy so I went to the office to start my report on my trip to the Pentagon.'

'Couldn't you have done it here?'

'It's highly classified, silly. I have to do it on the word processor in the department.'

'God, you and your secrets.' Fiona had a suspicion that he made out everything was secret so he didn't have to invite her on his trips overseas.

'Anyway, then the Brigadier wanted to discuss something with me and invited me for a drink at his club. I tried to phone to tell you but the line was out. I had no idea about all the excitement that had gone on here. I'm sorry I was so late getting back but the old boy didn't seem keen to go home himself.'

Besides which, thought Fiona rather cynically, James was never one to miss the chance of having the undivided attention of a senior officer. A fact she didn't object to – as long as it really was a senior officer and not some office tart. She was absolutely certain that he'd had other women since their marriage. The knowledge annoyed her but she tolerated it. After all, James provided her with a decent standard of living, and he wasn't interested in having kids, which suited her down to the ground. She really didn't fancy the responsibility, and it left her free to walk out if his infidelities got too much. Fiona regarded her marriage as a means to an end rather than one of the more important aspects of her life.

After their leisurely breakfast, Fiona went shopping for a new dress and hat. She had several social engagements coming up, including a wedding, and it was a good excuse for a new outfit. James, deciding that fresh air would clear the faint muzziness in his head, the only trace of last night's excesses, went into the back garden. He surveyed the lawn and noted that it needed cutting. It was pleasantly mild for April, and the thin cloud cover was breaking up. It was going to be a lovely spring day. James decided that mowing the lawn would combine fresh air with exercise – but nothing too strenuous. He went round to the front to get the mower from the garage. As he did so he heard the noise of children, and then Jenny's voice in the next garden, although the thick privet hedge obscured any glimpse of her.

'Come on, you lot,' he heard her call. 'If you don't get in the car Daddy will go without you.' The excited shrieks of children's voices were followed by the sound of car doors slamming. He heard her call goodbye and then the front door shut. For some strange reason, James felt like a voyeur, standing there listening to Jenny without her knowledge. He wondered if he ought to go and apologise for his attitude to her the previous day. He had been unnecessarily rude, and it was not even as if their divorce was recent history. Anyway, she had also had that dreadful business about the bomb. Having just read the article about it in the *Times*, he now realised the extent of the danger. He did not admit to himself that he was searching for an excuse to see her. He waited for the car to drive away and then skirted the hedge to approach Jenny's front door.

He hesitated before he knocked. He felt a flutter of excitement course momentarily through his body at the thought of seeing her again. It had been a long time since the prospect of seeing someone had made him feel this excited. His encounter with her yesterday had brought back all sorts of memories. He pushed away his uneasy feeling of desire and tapped the knocker sharply against the door. There was a pause. James, feeling faintly, irrationally disappointed, wondered if Jenny had gone out too. He was just turning away when he heard the latch click.

'Oh, hello again,' said Jenny warily, peering round the half-open door. James thought how like a kitten she still looked, with her triangular face and those huge dark eyes. He felt his stomach tighten involuntarily with a mixture of happiness and lust.

'Jenny, I'm sorry about yesterday. I was unforgivably rude to you and I apologise.' James gave her his most devastating smile. 'I had no right to behave like such a sod. It must have been the jet lag. After all, it's a long time since we split up.'

'Fourteen years,' said Jenny, still feeling very cautious.

'I was shocked to hear what happened to your son. It must have been ghastly. People who do that sort of thing are mindless bastards, aren't they?'

'Yes, it was very unpleasant.' Jenny felt apprehensive. Why was James being so conciliatory? she wondered. What did he want?

'Look, Jenny...' James could see the caution in her eyes. 'We're both a lot older... Could we be friends if we tried? You and Fiona obviously get on. I don't know how much your husband knows about our marriage, but if we're going to live next door to each other, then perhaps we ought to get together to clear the air. Dinner one night, maybe?'

'I don't know. I really can't say until I've spoken to Nigel. It isn't that simple. There was a lot of bitterness, wasn't there, and I've only just told him that you live next door. We'll have to see.'

'Yes, you're probably right. It would be better to take things slowly. Well, think about it. The offer is there.'

'Thank you, James, and thanks for the apology. It didn't matter.'

'Yes it did. Anyway, I'll leave you in peace now, and Jenny ...'

'Yes?'

'Look after yourself. I really mean it. Goodbye.'

Jenny was taken aback by James's concern for her. She was sure she had detected real warmth in his voice. Then she dismissed the idea as ridiculous. She must have imagined it. But even so, she felt buoyed up by his kindness. She shut the door slowly and returned to the kitchen to carry on with the washing. As she sorted out the laundry, mainly her husband's filthy, smelly combat kit, she found her thoughts straying yet again to James. He was still utterly gorgeous to look at. She wondered if he was still phenomenal in bed.

That evening, while Nigel was relaxing in his deep armchair, his feet on the coffee table, Jenny said casually, 'I ran into James again this morning. He thinks we ought to get together for dinner one day.'

Nigel was piqued that James and Jenny had seen each other again. Part of him wanted to order Jenny to keep away from the man. Certainly he didn't want to share a meal with him. But then he reconsidered. It wouldn't do to make his hatred for James, or his reasons for it, too public. It might be considered bad form to hold a grudge for so long. The people who didn't know about the past wouldn't understand or care, and those who did would think better of him if he appeared to be magnanimous. For the time being, he would be civil to the man, no matter how much it irked him.

'OK. I don't see why not, if you don't mind. After all, he was married to you, not me. Are you sure?'

'Yes, I think so. It can't do any harm, can it?'

Nigel wasn't so certain.

Chapter Eight

A couple of weeks later Jenny was sitting on her dressing table stool, trying to ignore the growing feeling of excitement inside her. She tried to tell herself that it was nerves at meeting James again, but she knew that this wasn't the whole truth. Ridiculous as it seemed, she was looking forward to seeing him, like a lovesick sixteen-year-old on a first date. As she applied her mascara with a less than steady hand, Jenny's thoughts were in chaos. It was absolutely ridiculous for her to feel this way, she told herself. Just remember what the divorce was like – and the marriage: the rows, the threats, the acrimony. She glanced past her reflection in the mirror to Nigel, who was choosing a tie from the wardrobe. Christ, he'd be livid if he knew what she was thinking. Jenny looked at herself again and promptly smudged her mascara wand across her top lid.

'Fuck,' she murmured.

'Steady on, Jen.'

'Oh, don't be so bourgeois,' she snapped, glaring at him in the mirror. Nigel looked hurt. Jenny, to cover up her guilt at her outburst, busied herself with make-up remover.

Nigel finished tying his tie. 'I'll wait for you downstairs,' he said tersely, not understanding what the matter was. Perhaps her period was due.

Once he'd left the room, Jenny stopped all pretence at trying to get ready and looked herself in the eyes again. She thought back through the events of the last couple of weeks, and her encounters with James when he'd called at their house with such spurious excuses. Did she mind if he used the hedge-trimmer? Fiona had rearranged their sitting room and did the TV now disturb them? He was going to the newsagent, was there anything she wanted? She tried to analyse them; had he contrived the meetings at times when he'd have known Nigel was out? Was he just being neighbourly, or was there something more than that – more than just friendship? And how did she feel?

Jenny's brow creased with effort as she tried to convince herself that she was imagining it. He couldn't possibly still find her attractive – could he? But after twelve years of monogamy and motherhood, she found the idea of another man looking at her, as an object of desire, immensely flattering. Part of her wanted to believe it, even if it was just to bolster her own self-worth. That part of her could ignore the latent danger of encouragement. Nigel loved her, made love to her, but it was all so secure, safe and predictable. It had lost the passion, adoration and exploration of early love. It would be different with James ...

Abruptly she pulled herself up short. What the hell was she thinking of? She went across to the washbasin and doused her face with cold water, dried it and returned to re-apply her make-up. She was *not* going to get involved with James again.

'Jenny, Nigel, hello. Come on in.' Fiona flung open the door to allow them to enter, and greeted the couple with a kiss each. She turned to Jenny with a welcoming smile. 'Here, let me take your jacket.' She thought how vivacious and excited Jenny looked.

Nigel and Jenny could hear the hubbub of the other guests emanating from the sitting room as they waited for Fiona to hang Jenny's coat carefully in the hall cupboard. Nigel wondered, for the umpteenth time that evening, what on earth had possessed him to agree to this invitation. He just knew it was going to be a mistake.

Fiona ushered them through her hall and into her Liberty print and antique sitting room. Nigel, stiffly apprehensive, nodded at the couple already perched on the chesterfield, and acknowledged with a self-conscious smile the small group standing chatting by the French windows. Fiona guided them over to the pair sitting down. Jenny smiled a greeting at Elaine.

'Jenny, have you met Elaine's husband yet?' Fiona didn't wait for an answer but carried on smoothly with the introduction. 'This is Malcolm. Malcolm – Jenny Walker.'

Malcolm Ross-McLeod stood up as she approached, took her outstretched hand and kissed it.

'I'm delighted to meet you at last. Both of us almost unwitting victims of the same ghastly incident. I trust you and your son have fully recovered from it all?'

'Yes,' said Jenny, charmed by his easy good manners. 'We're all quite back to normal, except that to hear Christopher's side of the story anyone would think he'd single-handedly defused it himself. All that publicity has completely turned his head.'

Fiona slipped away to answer the door again, having said that James would be along with some drinks in a tick. Nigel looked around the room and wondered who the other guests were. When he'd had second thoughts about accepting the invitation Jenny had worked hard at persuading him.

'Fiona says it's going to be a big do, half the patch will be going. She wants us to meet some people called Devereaux, and the Hobdays – they live the other side of us.'

'Yes, but James will be around. That's the thing that worries me.'

'Oh, come on. I'm sure it'll be all right. And much better that we all meet up at a big supper party, where we have to be on best behaviour.'

Nigel had to admit that there would be safety in numbers. At a large party he could fairly easily avoid his host without appearing to do so.

Even as Jenny said hello to the Ross-McLeods she could sense that Nigel seemed tense. She hoped that it had nothing to do with James, although it was certainly the most likely cause. She was concerned that he was holding his enmity within himself, like the air in a balloon. Was it going to be expelled slowly, allowed to deflate, or was the encounter going to needle him into exploding? She still didn't know what it was that had made Nigel hate James since Sandhurst, but she knew her failed marriage to him had only made things worse.

Jenny swivelled towards Nigel, still standing beside her, and took his hand. She drew him closer to her.

'Nigel, I don't think you know either Elaine or Malcolm ...'

As the introductions were made, Malcolm noticed Nigel's tie. Nigel always wore his Northern Ireland bomb disposal tie to this sort of do. It was like a totem for him – he was not a natural socialiser and it gave him courage. It reminded him that there were worse things to face than a group of virtual strangers. Besides which, it usually proved to be a good conversation piece. Now Malcolm said, instantly recognising the significance of the logo, a jaunty yellow cat in a protective helmet, 'Where were you based when you got that?'

'Girdwood, west Belfast. But it was some years ago. I was out there in 1979.'

'Really? I was doing a tour in Londonderry about then. Did you know Bob Jones? He was our bomb man.'

Nigel's face lightened as he realised that here was someone who was not averse to talking shop; he loathed small talk. Elaine and Jenny could both see that it would be useless to try and engage their husbands in a more general topic which might include themselves. They were just about to indulge in some patch gossip when James brought round a tray of drinks. He insinuated himself into the centre of their group, and as he did so he bent forward and kissed Jenny on the cheek. It was only a brush of his lips against her skin, but Jenny felt a thrill of desire race through her body. It was so electrifying she was certain everyone must have noticed. She glanced guiltily at Nigel, but he was engrossed in conversation.

'Jenny! How lovely to see you. You must introduce me to your husband in a mo. Now then, Pimms, anyone?' James proffered tall glasses of inviting pale-amber liquid, which clinked with ice cubes.

'Gorgeous,' said Elaine. 'It really must be almost summer if people are beginning to think about Pimms again.' She took a glass and had a sip. As James turned slightly to allow Jenny to pick a glass, Elaine said with mock severity, 'You do know you're supposed to dilute this stuff with lemonade, don't you James?'

'Hell, I knew I'd forgotten something.' Then, more seriously, 'It isn't too strong, is it? I just thought it would get things off to a good start. Anyway, if it's too weak all you *can* taste is the lemonade – waste of bloody Pimms, if you ask me.'

He offered drinks to Nigel and Malcolm.

'Ah, you must be Nigel.' Then he looked harder. 'Have we met?'

'We were at Sandhurst at the same time.' Nigel was surprised at how little James had changed. He still had a slightly supercilious smile which permanently seemed to touch the corners of his mouth, and his thickly-lidded eyes had the same disdainful gaze.

'Your face is familiar, although your name didn't ring any bells when I first heard it.'

'No. Well, it's a common enough one.' There was a faintly belligerent tone in Nigel's voice as he said the word 'common'.

James didn't respond to the last remark, although he stared unwaveringly at Nigel as though he was inwardly debating whether or not to rise to the bait. Then, abruptly, 'Seriously, is the Pimms too strong? What do you think?' Nigel and Malcolm both took tentative sips and signalled that it was just fine. The tension eased. At that moment the Marlows and the Devereauxs entered the room, which was beginning to get quite crowded.

Diana paused for a moment in the doorway. Just as she'd expected, every head turned to admire her in her figure-hugging black and gold sheath dress that was cut so simply it looked as if it must have cost a fortune, which it had. It showed her slender figure off to perfection. Once she was sure everyone had noticed her, she moved forward again. The conversation, after a barely perceptible but gratifying lull, restarted. Behind her, unnoticed, stood General Marlow, who was escorting Pan and Rupert, having met them on the doorstep. Diana, who hadn't seen Jenny since the day of the bomb and Nigel's return, swept elegantly across the room to them.

'Jenny, my dear. How very well you look tonight. Where did you get that stunning dress?'

Jenny was startled. She'd been thinking that Diana ought to have been an actress, she had staged her entrance to such perfection. Her dress had been bought in Littlewood's sale, and she was so taken aback by the compliment that she blurted out the truth.

Rod Marlow, wanting to meet the woman at the centre of the bombing, had followed his wife, and now said gruffly, 'There, Diana, told you that you spend far too much on clothes. You must ask this clever woman to take you shopping next time you need a new outfit. I might be able to afford to retire if you shopped in the sales too.'

Diana smiled indulgently at her husband.

'Take no notice of him, Jenny. You'd hate shopping with me. I take hours to find anything I like, and then I can never get it in my size. Now then, before we go any further, let me meet your husband. I didn't get the chance to talk to him when we met on the doorstep. Has he got over the shock of finding his family were headline news?'

Pan and Rupert found acquaintances to join, James poured more Pimms, and, with alcohol inducing relaxation, the level of conversation racked itself up another notch. One thing the Bains' friends were all agreed about was the copious flow of alcohol at their parties. Judging by the Pimms, this one was going to be no exception.

James was acutely aware of Jenny's presence in the room, and although he circulated dutifully with the drinks, he spent more time than was necessary in her vicinity. Fiona noticed that he was drinking heavily – at this rate he'd end up smashed before the evening was half over. She cornered him in the kitchen to remonstrate.

'Lay off the booze, James,' she said without preliminaries.

'Oh, come on. This is a party, lighten up.'

'I've been watching you and you've been swigging it by the tumblerful. You'll be pissed before we get to the food if you keep going. What's got into you?'

'You're exaggerating.'

'I'm bloody not. Just remember that the General is here, and if you make a prat of yourself in front of him it won't do your career any good.' To avoid further argument, Fiona picked up a plate of canapés and swept back into the drawing room. James refilled his jug of Pimms, poured himself a glass, which he downed defiantly, and followed his wife.

*

'Of course there were advantages to missing out on the Falklands campaign. I might not have got a gong, but just think of all that available totty.' James had intended to confide in Rupert, but no longer sober, his voice carried across the room. 'Talk about troops' comforts!' Jenny stole a glance at the General to see his reaction to James' tale of mass adultery. Tactfully, perhaps aware that his host had drunk more than he ought to have done, the General was deep in conversation with Pandora. James bulldozed on. 'You know what I called the wives left behind? Whores de combat, ha, ha.' He laughed overloudly at his own joke, not noticing that no one else joined in.

Fiona grabbed him. 'Come and give me a hand with some things in the kitchen, will you, darling,' she said, as she led him firmly from the room. After a short pause, conversation resumed as though nothing had happened.

'That last comment from James won't do him any good,' remarked Nigel smugly to Jenny. 'You know how the Army feels about officers indulging in adultery.'

Jenny bit back an acid reply about *schadenfreude*. 'You could be right,' was all she said.

Nigel was about to ask her why she wasn't more pleased about James's gaffe when Fiona reappeared and announced supper.

Diana made her way purposefully across the room to sit next to Jenny. Jenny shifted up on the chesterfield to accommodate her.

'Hello again. Isn't this coronation chicken delicious? Fiona really is an excellent cook, isn't she?'

'Wonderful,' replied Jenny.

'And doing all this as well as working ...'

Jenny didn't say that she hadn't noticed Fiona doing much supply teaching lately. It would have sounded catty.

'So, tell me, Jenny, is everything back to normal with you?'

'Yes, fine thanks. Even Christopher has stopped mentioning it more than about six times a day.'

'And you've settled in OK?'

'Yes, thanks. It doesn't take long really, if you keep at it.'

'Good, I'm delighted to hear it. I was wondering ...' Diana paused.

Here it comes, thought Jenny. She's going to ask me to join some frightful committee.

'... would you be able to help me with the Federation of Army Wives?'

Shit, thought Jenny. I just knew it. Now, how do I get out of it?

'I'm very flattered you've asked me, but I was hoping to get my little business up and running again. In fact, I put an ad in the community centre only this week.'

'Oh, yes. Your bookends. But the Federation wouldn't take up much of your time. Only an hour or so each week.'

Jenny took another mouthful of chicken to give herself time to think. She'd sworn that she wouldn't do anything for the Army ever again. She was going to be utterly selfish and devote all her time to her family and her bookends. Besides which, she knew that once co-opted on to such a committee, the hour or so each week would soon expand into a couple of hours each day. All very well for the wives of more senior officers who rated a cleaner, paid for by the system, and whose children were at boarding school. They were the sort of women who had to stave off boredom by doing good works, and they felt that any other women at home all day should join their ranks and be glad of the opportunity.

'I really appreciate your offer, Diana, but may I pass for the time being? With Christopher only at school in the mornings, the few hours I do get to myself are really precious.' Then, to her disgust, she found herself adding, 'Perhaps when he goes all day ...' What a cop-out. She should have just told Diana to shove it – politely.

'Yes, all right. I do understand.' But her voice was a degree or so chillier than it had been at the start of the conversation. Jenny's refusal to join in was a definite black mark.

James's arrival with the offer of more wine defrosted the atmosphere.

'Come on, Jenny, drink up. It isn't as if you've got far to go to get home.'

Jenny thought that James sounded as though he'd done his share of drinking already. He used not to get drunk. He always used to be very careful. She remembered that he'd once told her that you could learn a lot by being sober when everyone else was one over the eight.

'OK, James, but just half a glass.' Jenny held out her glass, and he in turn held her hand as he poured the wine, a little unsteadily, into it. He stopped pouring when Jenny said, 'Hey, steady,' but didn't let go of her hand. Gently Jenny disengaged herself, and then covered her confusion by muttering something about seconds and getting up from the sofa. Fiona, watching from the doorway, didn't read anything into the incident. She was just thankful that Jenny and James seemed to be friends again.

After Jenny had helped herself to more food, she was reluctant to return to sit near Diana, and anyway, James was still there, chatting to her. She spotted a seat by the window next to the woman she now knew was Pandora Devereaux. Jenny, who'd already logged the Gucci loafers and silk shirtwaister, wondered if she was going to have anything in common with her. Well, it didn't really matter if she didn't. At least Pandora was unlikely to try to get her to volunteer for something.

'May I join you?'

'Be my guest.'

Jenny felt she should say something more, start a conversation.

'I gather it was you who saw the bloke who left the bomb in the hedge?'

'Yes, but I wasn't any help to the police.'

'Is your husband a Whitehall warrior too?'

Pan was quite happy to eat in silence. However, it was obvious that Jenny wanted to be friendly. Oh, well.

'Yes, he's got some tedious desk job.'

Jenny waited for a bit of expansion, or possibly even a question directed at herself. Nothing. Slowly she chewed a forkful of salad, wondering if she should try again or let the silence roll on. She tried again.

'Do you work?'

'Used to – then I had Gabriella.' Jenny suppressed a giggle at the name; how very predictable. Naughtily, she wondered what the reaction would be if she said her children were called Chelsea, Sharon and Darren. She restrained herself.

'What did you do?' If she didn't get the ball of conversation bounced back to her this time, she was going to give up.

Pandora finished her last mouthful of food. Now that she'd finished eating, she didn't mind chatting.

'I worked on the knickers counter in Harrods. That's where I met my husband. He came in to choose some for his girlfriend and ended up taking me out to dinner.' Pan knew that this tale amused people. She paused, waiting for the reaction. Jenny yelped with laughter.

'Did he buy the knickers after all?'

'Oh yes. I made him choose some perfectly disgusting scarlet ones that were wildly expensive, in the hope that his bird would hate him for it.'

'Did she?'

'I don't know – never bothered to find out.'

Jenny, almost in spite of herself, couldn't help admiring this woman's self-assurance and laconic style. She was surprised when Pandora said:

'Is it you that makes the Guardsmen bookends? Lady Marlow was telling me about them. She said they were wonderful.'

Jenny wondered if Diana would be quite so generous with her praise now.

'That was very kind of her, and yes, it's me,' she said.

'They sound stupendous. Do you do any regiment?'

'Yes, and you can have him wearing blues or service dress.'

'Guardsmen in bearskins too?'

'No, I usually paint them in uniform,' replied Jenny, deadpan. Pandora looked uncomprehending for a second, then she laughed.

'Have you got any in stock – Guardsmen, that is?'

'Yes, I've got Coldstreams, Scots and Irish. Come over any time. I'm always happy to do business.'

'Well, I was wondering – we're going to lunch tomorrow with a girl who's marrying one of Rupe's chums. I was going to take her some flowers or chocs, but a pair of your bookends sounds a lot more fun.'

Jenny wondered how to mention that a bunch of flowers might only cost Pan five quid, but bookends were going to set her back twenty. The direct approach was the only way.

'Look, I'd love to sell you a pair, but they come a bit more expensive than flowers.'

'Oh, don't worry about that.'

Jenny suddenly felt a fool. Of course, people like that didn't worry about the cost. She should have realised that Pan rarely, if ever, looked at price tags.

'I'll tell Rupe to take a bottle of claret rather than champagne.' Pan looked at Jenny expectantly. Jenny was at a loss to know why. Pan waited.

'Well, could I see one?'

'Now?' Jenny blurted the word out. 'I'm sorry, I didn't mean to sound rude, I just assumed you'd be coming round in the morning.'

'It's my fault, I should have made it clearer. We're going to the Isle of Wight – she has a weekend cottage there – and we'll be leaving at the crack, so – I mean, would you mind getting them now? I'll come round to your place if that's more convenient.'

Jenny thought of the chaos of children's toys in the hall, the disorder in her workroom. She'd left the place in a mess.

'No, I'll pop home now. I won't be a tick. Which Guards regiment are you after?'

'Coldstreams, please.'

'Right, back in a mo.'

Jenny slipped out of the sitting room and down the hall to the front door. For a fleeting instant she thought about making an excuse to Fiona, but she would only be gone a second. No one would even notice.

James, standing just inside the kitchen door, saw the movement in the hall and looked round to the front door just in time to see Jenny disappear through it. She had occupied his thoughts all evening. As he'd circulated with bottles of wine he'd found his eyes straying to her. At times, ostensibly talking to one group of people, he had been able to stand within touching distance of her. He had been close to her, inhaled her fragrance, and now, before he had had a chance to spend any time in her company, and be the subject of her undivided attention, she had gone. He followed her, wanting to know the reason for her sudden departure. Perhaps there had been a message from the babysitter – but the phone hadn't rung, no one had come to the door. Surely she was coming back? He would wait for her in the porch. He had to talk to her, he couldn't wait any longer.

Through the hedge he could hear her soft words to the babysitter as her own door was opened. Then, less than a minute later, the door closed again and Jenny returned to where James was waiting for her in the shadow of his porch.

'Hello,' he said quietly. Jenny, thinking about Pandora and the bookends, jumped as if she had been stung.

'Don't *do* that,' she hissed, not knowing why she wasn't talking normally.

'I'm sorry, Kitten. I didn't mean to frighten you, honestly. I saw you going and I was worried there was a problem, that's all. I was just waiting to see if you were coming back to us or not.' James, too, kept his voice low, and Jenny had the uneasy feeling that she was entering into a conspiracy; she wished he didn't keep calling her Kitten.

'I just went home to fetch something,' she explained.

James saw the glossy shapes in her hand.

'Let me see ...' He held up the bookends to see the little wooden statues better in the moonlight. 'These are brilliant. Where did you get them?'

'I made them.' Jenny was inexplicably overcome by a feeling of pride, that something she had created was being admired by James.

'You made them? But they're really good.' James realised as he said it what a back-handed compliment he had just delivered. 'No, I didn't mean it like that, but I just can't imagine anyone being able to turn out something that looks this professional without access to lots of machines and stuff. The finish is superb. I'm impressed, truly.'

Jenny began to shiver. It wasn't the chill night air which caused it, but excitement. She hoped James didn't realise. She didn't think he would; he'd drunk too much.

'You're cold, let's go in.'

As he handed back her miniature works of art, James let his hand touch hers again. Deliberately he stroked it. Without being able to resist the urge, he drew her to him and kissed her hard on the lips, probing with his tongue deep into her mouth. For a brief moment she responded, letting herself press against him, feeling his muscular, taut body. She had forgotten his smell, the masculine odour of raw sex. God, it was exciting. Then suddenly she woke up, came out of her trance. Shocked, she pushed herself away.

'No, James. Stop. What on earth are you doing? It's over between us – it was ages ago.'

James ignored her protestations. 'You know you're still adorable, don't you?'

Jenny shut her eyes, blotting out his fervour. She thought about how she looked in the early morning; about the stretch marks on her tummy and the other signs left from bearing three children. Was he saying these words just to flatter and cajole her? In a burst of understanding, and a feeling approaching smugness, she realised that he still wanted her. She still held a fascination for him. Stop it, she thought furiously. What on earth do you want James to be interested for anyway?

'Come on, I'm cold,' she said, pulling away. 'Let's go back in.'

Standing in the downstairs loo, having zipped up his trousers a couple of minutes earlier, Nigel listened, tense with rage, to the quiet exchange beside the open window. His hand gripped the towel rail, his knuckles absolutely white. During the silence after the brief conversation he'd known they'd kissed – and he'd gone cold with shock. What the hell did Jenny think she was playing at? Why the fuck had she let that creep kiss her? And as for James... He thought about going and confronting the pair of them. But then he thought, what good would it do? Confused and hurt, he decided that it would achieve nothing but an ugly scene. He swallowed his pride and rejoined the party. He didn't have a clue what he ought to do. He wasn't even sure he should mention it to Jenny. He couldn't prove what had gone on. If he accused her ...? Accused her of what? A kiss hardly constituted rampant adultery. Shit! What a mess.

When they got home, Nigel made love to Jenny. She was his, not James's, and there was no way that bastard was going to get his grasping hands on his wife.

Jenny was surprised by his passion, verging on aggression. She found his rough handling, his lunging and his silence exciting. There was something about his masculine domination of her which reminded her of James. At the thought of him, she knew she was going to come. Christ, she hoped Nigel didn't realise why she'd been so quick.

Nigel came almost at the same instant. He too had been thinking of James.

Chapter Nine

Nigel lay in bed, his mind restless, uninvited thoughts milling about, refusing to let sleep come although it was past one o'clock. He turned his head and looked across the pillow at Jenny, who was peacefully asleep, lying, as she always did, on her back with one hand above her head. Her thick lashes were curled against her unblemished cheeks, and her mouth was slightly open. She looked like a child, innocent, fragile and vulnerable. Nigel felt a lurch of love. He thought about kissing her but was afraid he might wake her. He tried to make his mind a blank, to bore himself to sleep, but memories of Sandhurst and his first confrontation with Jamie Pollock-Bain wheedled their way into his subconscious. As they did, like a weevil in a biscuit, they drilled into his thoughts and made his anger flare again.

Bugger it, he thought in frustration as sleep refused to come, I might just as well make myself a cup of tea. With utmost care he slithered out of bed, groped in the dark for his dressing gown and slippers, then crept downstairs. The neon strip in the kitchen flickered several times before its light became steady. He padded over to the kettle and switched it on. Almost instantly it began to hiss and grumble as the filament heated the water. It sounded loud in the silent house. He hoped it wouldn't disturb any of the family. While he waited, he leant on the sink and gazed out of the window at the dark garden. The kettle boiled, and he dunked a tea bag in his mug, warming his cold hands around it as he did so.

He took his drink into the sitting room and switched on the stereo, careful to keep the volume down low. He tuned it to an all-night music station. As he sipped his tea he looked at the pictures stacked against the wall, waiting to be hung. He would do it in the morning, he thought. It was the least he could do, and about the only job that remained. He had to admire his wife, he admitted to himself. The house was virtually straight and they had only been there three weeks. Jenny was a tireless worker when there were things to do. Even when they went on holiday she found it difficult to relax completely; she was always finding little jobs, like rinsing out the swimming things or sweeping the floor of the gîte. Nigel would get annoyed with her, as it made him feel guilty, sitting there reading a thriller. Jenny always protested that she didn't mind. She said she was happy pottering about like that, and if she wasn't worried, why should he care?

The music on the radio changed, and Nigel remembered that it was a tune that had been played at his commissioning ball in the Café Royale. It had been on 14 April 1975. 'Brown Sugar' was hardly easy to dance to in skin-tight mess kit, but all the newly-commissioned officers had managed it somehow, until a couple of the men had got their spurs tangled and had collapsed on to the floor, to the amusement of everyone else. He remembered the glamour of the ball, with the men dressed like peacocks in their mess dress. Some wore scarlet jackets, while others sported dark blue or black, faced with brilliant colours. Still others were embellished with yards of gold lace, outshining by far their girlfriends in their gowns. There had been the Light Division and the Gurkhas in deepest rifle green, the cavalry in a tumult of high-necked jackets and rich elegant waistcoats, and all of them sporting close-fitting mess overalls tapering down to highly-polished boots, some with spurs. The girls, however beautifully dressed, were eclipsed. It had been a perfect evening. Sandhurst had been good fun, he recalled. Or it would have been if that bastard Bain hadn't marred the last few weeks.

For Nigel, the Army had been a means to an end. Throughout his childhood he'd wanted to escape from his parents' dreary terraced house in an area of Edinburgh that was slowly degenerating into a slum. Across the road the houses were bigger and well maintained, with garages for cars. Nigel's father's bike lived in the yard behind their house; he used it once a week to cycle down to the unemployment exchange. When Nigel passed the eleven plus he thought he was going to get the chance to escape the guaranteed hopelessness of his future, but the dole wouldn't stretch to the cost of the grammar school uniform, and so, to save his parents' remaining vestige of pride, the place was refused.

The promise of paid employment and travel offered by army recruiting posters had tempted Nigel to enlist, but the recruiting sergeant had spotted his potential and insisted that he should try for a commission. Certain that his parents' financial status had no bearing on this offer, Nigel's ambition and self-esteem soared. All his life he had had to make do with second best – a second-hand bike, a second-rate school, a second-class ticket – and suffer the taunts of his less poor contemporaries about his lack of possessions and prospects. Christ, how he had been envious of those kids from over the road who had houses with gardens and fathers with jobs. This offer from the Army gave him the chance he had been denied at eleven. It was like a hot tip for the races. All he had to do was pass the Regular Commissions Board and he would be a winner.

When the card announcing his success dropped through the door the day after his return from four days of physical, mental and leadership tests, his parents had been inordinately proud. His father had done National Service in the Army but had never imagined that his son would ever be an officer. He, at least, had some realisation of the importance of Nigel's achievement. His mother was more interested in whether or not she would need a hat for Sovereign's Parade. They bought a bottle of sweet fizzy wine to celebrate and invited their more genteel neighbours to share the 'champagne'. Nigel was gratified by his parents' delight but mentally decided that in future he would only celebrate with real champagne. No more second best – ever.

Sandhurst had been a revelation. Like Sidney Carton's Paris, it had been a place of contrasts; the best of times and the worst of times. The outward elegance of the grand façades of the three colleges hid the harsh training regime. On one hand camaraderie and friendship, on the other rivalry and backstabbing; glamour and ceremonial contrasting with pain, mud and exhaustion. Nigel remembered his first sight of the Royal Military Academy and his feeling of awe at its grandeur, at the acres of playing fields, the lakes, and the three magnificent colleges: the modern grey concrete starkness of Victory College; the imposing bulk of Edwardian New College, built from red brick and cream stone, with its two huge wings that almost seemed to embrace the vast sports field in front of it; and finally, the beautiful white façade and neoclassical portico of Old College, with its famous steps that the cadets would march up after Sovereign's Parade.

He had arrived in spring, when the driveway leading to the colleges was flanked by magnificent deep-red rhododendrons. The ancient chestnut trees surrounding the sports pitches had all been acid green with their new leaves, and the grass and flower borders were immaculate and regimented; more reminiscent of a stately home than a military establishment. He had been one of thirty cadets who had been collected from the train at Camberley station by a matt-green army bus. They had eyed each other up on the train journey down from London, trying to assess if they were indeed all destined for Sandhurst. Naturally, there were a couple of the group who came from old army families and for whom the Royal Military Academy held few surprises or fears. These stood out from the others, lounging across the seats of the bus with an air of confidence, flaunting their knowledge of the jargon and their conviction of their right to be there. They wore blazers and slacks; not for them the coloured shirts and kipper ties of the others.

Nigel, who had not yet lived away from home and had not experienced the rigours of public or boarding school, was not sure he had made the right decision. Glenbank School, Edinburgh, had been more used to turning out boys for the docks or the dole queues than preparing them for the professions. Nigel felt at a distinct disadvantage listening to some of the cut-glass accents, but he hoped his Scottish accent would appear classless. He had enough wit to know the importance of background. If his voice didn't let him down, his background would be ignored. He was certain that if his lowly roots were discovered, the sneers he'd endured at junior school would be nothing compared with the more sophisticated derision that he could expect from those who'd honed their skills at public school.

The journey to New College, where all the cadets were to start their military careers, took no more than ten minutes. The banter on the bus trailed into silence as they approached the magnificent scene that unfurled as they were swept past the lake, and the rhododendrons gave way to the massive acreage of grass in front of the colleges. The bus pulled up on the wide gravel area at the front of the red brick of New College. One of the group of assembled platoon sergeants boarded the bus and roared from the front that they were to get off and line up. The order galvanised the overawed youths into action. There was a rush to grab suitcases and descend as quickly as possible. They called out their names and were divided into smaller groups, each one under the control of a colour sergeant. Nigel found himself in the middle of his group, his case at his feet, flanked by two boys who looked even more terrified than he felt.

'Stand up straight,' yelled the Colour Sergeant. They all braced up, pulled their shoulders back and tried to look as military as possible.

'What a long-haired shower!' screamed the Colour Sergeant in disbelief, his own hair cut so short at the back you could have filed your nails on it.

'Right!' he continued, in undiminished decibels. 'When I give the order, you lot pick up your bags, turn to the left and march to that door over there. And when you step off, you put your left foot forward first. What do you do, sir?' He pointed at the boy on Nigel's left with his pace stick.

'Left foot first, we march over there,' the lad said.

'We march over there, *Colour*!' bawled the Colour Sergeant 'You call me "Colour" because that is my rank. I call you "sir" because I have to. If you are addressed by the Sergeant Major he will call you "sir" and you will call him "sir". The difference is – you mean it, he doesn't. Understand!' The last word was not a question but an order. He continued with an increase in decibels.

'Right then. Left turn.' The group shuffled to face left. 'Pick up your cases.' They did. 'By the left, quick march.' Hesitantly they stepped out towards the open door and then into the cool, echoing interior.

Nigel's initial reaction was, how could a building that looked so magnificent on the outside be so completely hideous on the inside? It reminded him of a public lavatory. The walls were half tiled with dark-green glazed tiles, the remainder of the wall painted with light-green gloss. The floors were bare and echoing, but it smelt of polish and Brasso rather than of urine.

The boys were each allocated a room, told to check the contents against an inventory, sign for them and unpack. They were to wait in their rooms until told where to go next. Nigel's room was on the second floor, in one of the wings, so that from his window he could see the front entrance to New College and, across from the cricket pavilion, a corner of Old College. If he leaned out of the window he could see across the rugby pitch to the lake. Below him some more newcomers were being formed up and marched into the college, the manic yell of another colour sergeant sounding identical to the one who had just verbally abused Nigel's group.

He stared at the view, trying to memorise it. It was so different from the backs of terraced houses overtopped by the bus station, which was all he could see from his room at home. Now he was a part of all this. He felt an overwhelming surge of pride and self-satisfaction. He was a cadet at the world's most prestigious military academy – he was as good as anyone and he was going to succeed.

If only they could see this back home, he thought. He knew that they would be impressed. He could just imagine his mother's pride when she showed her friends in Edinburgh photographs of the place.

He turned back to look at his room. It was comfortable enough, with its own washbasin and an armchair, but with only a mat on the floor, no carpet. The floor had a shine on it that was truly magnificent. Nigel wondered who cleaned it. He found out the next day.

For the next six weeks, Nigel and his intake endured the worst the instructors could do. First they were shorn of their fashionable seventies sideboards and long hair, and then, disregarding the cadets' shaven-headed self-consciousness, the Colour Sergeant marched them across the Academy grounds to be issued with mounds of khaki clothing, none of which seemed to fit properly. During these weeks everything was done at the double. They learnt how to run for five miles without collapsing, who to salute and when, the difference between 'stand at ease' and 'stand easy' and how to wear all the pieces of issued uniform, from puttees to berets.

After drill periods and rifle practice they had to prepare their kit and their rooms for daily inspection, bull their boots, polish buttons and blanco belts. Not a speck of dust was to be found in their rooms, nor a single hair on their uniforms, or they would suffer with a re-inspection at a time calculated to cause inconvenience. Their floors had to shine like glass – just like their boots.

On top of this they had military theory to learn, like knowing correct radio procedure and call signs. By midnight most of the cadets had finished for the day and would head straight for bed. An unfortunate few, still struggling to get a shine on their boots, or to learn the proper way to encode a grid reference, would have to stagger on until the small hours or risk failure the next day. Nigel was lucky; he had mastered most of the early training with relative ease, but he was aware that the cadet in the next room was having a much rougher time.

Officer Cadet Kevin Day was finding army training a struggle. Although indisputably brainy, he was hampered by his lack of co-ordination, a fear of heights and a nasal West Midlands accent. From day one he had been the butt of the drill instructor's jokes. Nigel should have felt sorry for him, but really he was grateful. Like the other cadets, he kept away from Kevin, not wishing to be associated with him. For some, those with the breeding that removed them on to another social planet, Kevin represented a joke, an aberration of the selection board; but for others, with less confidence in their lineage, he might well prove to be a liability, make them guilty by association of the crime of 'not fitting in'. Nigel fell into the latter category; he was going to do nothing to jeopardise his chances now that he had got this far, and being linked with Kevin might do just that. While Kevin was around to take the flak, everyone else was safe from the attention and jibes of staff and senior cadets alike.

Nigel, however, could see straight away that as an officer cadet he himself was still only second class. He had more in common with Kevin than with those destined for the Guards, cavalry and infantry – although, unlike Kevin, he had had the nous to desist from referring to the loos as toilets. He was never going to be promoted to Under Officer – the equivalent of being a prefect – because he was not a natural officer, it wasn't in his blood. His proposed future career as a bomb disposal expert counted for nothing at Sandhurst. It didn't have the macho appeal of the Parachute Regiment or the exclusiveness of the Green Jackets. He was going to join a corps and was thus an 'oik'.

Nigel resented the prospects of those with the right military and social connections to ensure their progress through the ranks. Their advancement would be virtually automatic. With a modicum of luck he was fairly certain he could make it to the rank of lieutenant colonel, but to progress beyond that he'd have to work twice as hard to achieve the same outcome. Frankly, as a member of a corps, and with his background, it would take a miracle for him to get beyond brigadier. He also resented the fact that in order to make the grade and receive a commission he would have to become indistinguishable from his fellow cadets in dress, accent and attitude. He would have to be identical to those with all the advantages whilst still being denied them. It seemed to Nigel that it was like the brainwashing process which the creatures in *Animal Farm* had undergone, but that for him the slogan on the wall read 'individuality bad, uniformity good'. He wasn't sure he agreed with the principles underlying the training, but it wasn't his place to say so.

After six weeks Nigel's intake, divided into three companies, could move as one on the parade square. One hundred rifles were slapped to 'present arms', one hundred boots slammed to the ground in unison. They had learnt to be soldiers. Now they would learn to be officers.

To encourage *esprit de corps* each cadet was expected to push himself beyond his own capabilities in the inter-company assault course competition. For Nigel, naturally athletic, completing the assault course was tiring but not an unbearable feat of endurance. For Kevin it was hell on earth.

'Come on, Mr Day, sir! Don't be such a tart. It's only a bloody nose,' the physical training instructor bawled at him, as yet again Kevin misjudged his take-off for the twelve-foot wall and crashed impotently and painfully against it.

'Move yourself, sir. Mind over matter,' the instructor yelled mockingly as Kevin, winded and hurt, stood shivering beside the obstacle. To admit he couldn't do it would have earned him twenty press-ups in the mud, or, worse, the derision of his entire company. Nigel, who had been one of the last to set out on the course, could see Kevin's problem. Part of him wanted to write Day off as a wimp, but he knew how desperately hard the poor sod tried; a bloody sight harder than some of the upper-class slobs whose places in 'Daddy's Regiment' were guaranteed. It wasn't his fault he was such a waste of rations when it came to anything physical.

Nigel could see the pain and misery on the lad's face, and against his better judgement he yelled, 'Day, buck up and I'll give you a leg-up.' Kevin had straightened his aching body and with a huge effort had jogged towards Nigel and managed to get his boot into Nigel's cupped hands. With a mammoth heave, Nigel propelled him upwards and over the wall, where Kevin had sprawled momentarily in the mud before staggering on.

After they had finished and had stopped quivering with exhaustion, Kevin approached Nigel.

'Thanks, Walker. The PTI was about to have a real go at me.'

'It's OK,' replied Nigel, somewhat embarrassed at the pathetic gratitude. 'You're going to have to get it right for the competition, though. You'll have to go down to the wall and practise until you can do it.' Nigel was determined that his Company was not going to lose the competition due to a lightweight like Kevin. Kevin looked crestfallen. He knew that he just couldn't get over that bloody wall on his own. God knows, he'd tried hard enough.

'Supposing I came along to help you?' said Nigel reluctantly. Kevin looked doubtful. He didn't think anyone would be able to teach him how to do it. He certainly didn't want to exasperate another cadet, as well as the instructors, with his ineptness. Nigel could see the hesitation, but the man had to learn, otherwise the Company would lose the competition.

'It's only a knack,' he said encouragingly. 'I'm sure you could crack it if you really try.'

'OK then – thanks.'

On the next beasting round the assault course, the PTI had waited resignedly for Kevin to fail at the wall. To his amazement the cadet had scrambled unaided to the top and had vaulted down the other side. Frustrated that his carefully prepared sarcastic comments were not required, he had turned his wrath on an overweight but titled cadet who was relying on his family connections rather than effort to get him through the course.

Kevin was pathetically grateful and regarded Nigel as a real hero, his saviour. Nigel had never been the object of hero-worship before – he got a real buzz out of the fact that for the first time in his life, someone was looking up to him, respecting him. They had both been equally overjoyed when their Company had won the cup. Their broad grins were still apparent in the group photograph that now hung in the hall at 23 Slim Road, although the cup looked pathetically small, considering the effort, blood and pain that had gone into winning it.

Eventually their company, including Kevin, and the rest of the course was permitted to slow-march up the steps of Old College, the Academy band playing 'Auld Lang Syne', to be followed by the Academy Adjutant on his white horse. They had done it – they were officers, albeit only short-service commission, but now the Colour Sergeants, the Company Sergeant Majors, even the Academy Sergeant Major, the most senior warrant officer in the entire British Army, had to call them 'sir' and mean it – even to Kevin.

For those who wanted a regular commission, there were another two terms of academic study to complete, interspersed with more exercises. Now Kevin, destined for the Intelligence Corps, was able to repay Nigel, advising him about his essays, helping him with his military history studies – a subject Nigel found tedious in the extreme – and making sure he did not do badly at any of the academic work. In spite of Nigel's initial impression of Kevin – that he was waste of space and to be avoided at all costs – they had developed a friendship, so Nigel was not going to forget in a hurry the name of the man who caused Kevin to be dismissed from HM Forces. After everything that Kevin had been through, to be thrown out of Sandhurst – 'Services No Longer Required' – because a cocky, arrogant shit called James Pollock-Bain had spilled the beans about a negligent discharge was one of the worst injustices that Nigel had come across.

James had never suffered setbacks like Nigel. He'd attended a public school, albeit a minor one; his father had held a naval commission, and his mother was the cousin of a Guards officer. It had seemed likely that James would seek a commission in the Guards, like his relative, but he'd surprised everyone by applying for the gunners. He'd said that he wanted a career which would stretch him, and that he thought the gunnery course would provide the mental exercise he was after. The reality had been that he knew that the calibre of officers in the Guards could be very high indeed. James did not want the odds stacked against him more than necessary. He was pretty certain that by joining the Royal Artillery he would be in the top few per cent of his intake – a position he might not attain in the Guards.

However, by dropping the name of his mother's cousin James was easily able to cultivate friendships with cadets destined for the cavalry and Foot Guards. By virtue of his connections he was readily accepted into their social circle. With them he raised his eyebrows in extravagant mock horror when seeing some of the cadets, including the luckless Kevin, take frantic notes during the lesson on social etiquette. On leaving the lecture he had loudly commented, to the laughter of the other wags, that it was strange that officers now had to be taught to behave like gentlemen. Nigel, overhearing the remark and realising at whom it was directed, had taken an instant dislike to the man.

On the final exercise, James had been in the same section as Nigel and Kevin. His impression of Kevin as a yob who should never have been considered for a commission in the first place had not changed since the lecture on proper, officer-like behaviour. He found him utterly contemptible and ignored him as much as was humanly possible. Nigel he tolerated, but he resented the Scotsman's role on the exercise that made Nigel his superior. Then James, on watch in a trench one evening, had spotted Kevin's fawning attitude to Nigel – bloody sickening little sycophant, he had commented to a chum in the Royal Scots Dragoon Guards. All in all, he reckoned the Army would be better off without that type. The other officer agreed laconically, but he wasn't really interested. He was feeling far too uncomfortable to worry about such trivial matters.

They were dug in on a bleak exercise area in Yorkshire. They had been on exercise for nearly a week, during which time they'd had very little sleep. Now they were all cold, wet and exhausted. Kevin, on sentry duty late that night, had almost fallen asleep, and as he jerked himself awake, his finger slipped on the trigger and he fired off a single shot – a negligent discharge, a heinous crime in the Army. A negligent discharge for a soldier would result in a massive fine at the least; for a trainee officer, who had been drilled and schooled never to let it happen, it was possibly one of the worst offences he could commit. Kevin was dumbfounded at what he had done. With great presence of mind, Nigel, realising what had happened, let off a burst of automatic fire and yelled a challenge, in the hope that the single shot would go unnoticed in the confusion of a suspected attack by the enemy. The Colour Sergeant rushed up and asked Nigel what was happening, but Nigel was interrupted in his graphic tale of movement in the bushes by James, who told the truth.

'That man there, I don't know his name, had an ND.'

Nigel had tried to protest Kevin's innocence, but James was adamant. Kevin and Nigel were both charged by the College Commandant; Nigel received a severe reprimand because his actions had been honourable although misguided, but Kevin was asked to resign. With just three weeks to go to the end of the course, he was kicked out.

As Nigel sat now in the armchair, sipping his tea, he felt enormous anger twist inside him once again. What that man had done had been unnecessary. It had been a malicious, vicious action against someone who had struggled against disadvantage all his life. Had James subsequently felt remorse, Nigel might have forgiven him, but he had bragged to his cronies about cleansing the officer classes, and Nigel had no doubt that he was serious. He hated the man for his arrogant conceit in his own superiority, and he was not convinced that James had changed. Their proximity could only result in further animosity.

Chapter Ten

Nigel had been at his new job in the MOD for several weeks now, and the journey to and from London had long since palled. Even though it was still only spring, the trains were invariably hot, smelly and overcrowded. The first few trips had also been eased by the novelty of the view from the window; that was, if he got close enough to one to see out of it. In the morning, as a rule, he was lucky; his station was sufficiently far down the line for there still to be seats available when he got on. By Clapham the train was so crowded that standing passengers could hardly breathe, let alone admire the view. His chance of a seat in the evening depended on how recently the train had disgorged one lot of passengers as it sat silently waiting for the return trip. If it was about to pull out, he was likely to find himself standing until well past Wimbledon.

On some journeys he amused himself by scrutinising the backs of the Victorian terraces whose gardens ran down to the track, and wondering about the lives of the inhabitants. They bore little resemblance to the back-to-back housing he had known as a child. These bore all the outward signs of owner occupation: replacement windows, stick-on stone façades and extensions. It was easy to spot where the young families lived by the sandpits and the bikes and trikes in the gardens. The pensioners' homes, he reckoned, were distinguishable by the neat gardens, greenhouses and manicured lawns. Then there were the couch potatoes' houses: satellite dish in evidence, half-drawn curtains, untended gardens – all indicators of someone in residence who cared nothing for their surroundings, being happier to immerse themselves in the fantasy world of Australian soaps and the banalities of daytime TV.

Occasionally he spotted wild animals on the trackside. In particular there was a fox that sat, like an overlarge marmalade cat, on the embankment just outside Wimbledon station. Nigel wondered if it was train-spotting or observing the railway equivalent of the Green Cross Code. He also noticed how the banks beside the line were a sanctuary for any number of wild flowers and plants. As April had given way to May the grass had become filled with dozens of different flowers, and the lupins, buddleias and fuchsias, escapees from gardens along the line, provided a haven for butterflies.

But the pleasure of watching the changing scene to pass the time had ceased. A couple of mornings when his train had been cancelled, leaving him disgruntled and frustrated on the platform, shivering a little in the early-morning chill, had done nothing to improve his view of commuting. Especially as after one cancellation the next train was always so full as to be positively claustrophobic, even before it crossed the Thames at Putney. It was less enervating to try to shut out the trials of the journey. Nigel, like the other commuters, took to reading his paper.

A colleague in the office had told Nigel that in the summer the journey got more bearable, as the ladies on the train were wont to wear flimsy dresses in hot weather. He had tried to describe to Nigel the delights of being pressed hard against the body of a twenty-year-old blonde who was wearing nothing much more than a cotton shift and a dab of Eau de Gucci. Nigel, his anti-sexist principles roused, had given a rather dusty answer, but found later to his discomfiture that he rather relished the proximity of a pretty girl. He wasn't being lecherous, just appreciating something lovely. But he soon discovered the down side to the presence of pretty girls on the train. For every one of those leggy lovelies, there were an equal number of overweight frumps who oozed stale chip fat, cigarette smoke and body odour. Having one of those crushed against you, jowls shuddering in sympathy with the movement of the train, could get the working day off to a bad start.

On this day in early May, though, Nigel was completely unaware of either his fellow passengers or the scene outside the train. He was going over the events of the previous Saturday and wondering whether he should warn James off his wife. But the very fact of talking to James about it might be interpreted as an admission of inadequacy or jealousy. And the last thing he wanted was to give James a lever which he could use against him. Conversely, if he said nothing, might he not look like a cuckold? Nigel turned both sides of the argument over and over in his mind. He had been trained to work out the best way to defuse a bomb, how to plan a counterattack against the mythical 'orange' army and how to court martial a soldier. Nothing, though, which was the least use in assessing if his marriage was in danger, and if so, how to save it.

The obvious solution was to somehow get rid of James, but Nigel dismissed that. There were ways of getting someone posted, especially in a job which required as much security clearance as theirs did. A word in the ear of the vetting officer, some hints that James had had a string of conquests outside his marriage, coupled with a rumour that he used soft drugs, would probably be enough to see him off. But Nigel knew his conscience wouldn't allow him to do that. The conclusion he came to, the same one he'd come to on the numerous other occasions he'd wrestled with this, was that he'd do better to leave well alone. He couldn't see Fiona giving James up without a fight, and equally, after twelve years of marriage and three children, he didn't think that Jenny still had sufficient interest in sex – or energy, for that matter – to embark on an affair. Always supposing that that was what James had in mind. He was certain that Jenny would be faithful; Saturday had just been an aberration on her part. God, he hoped he was right.

The train jolted and Nigel looked up. Good grief, Waterloo already. He picked up his briefcase and joined the mêlée leaving the carriage and jostling down the platform.

Like the rest of the crowd about him, Nigel was completely unremarkable in his suit and tie, the uniform of the Whitehall Warriors, although, like the other army officers working in town, he probably had a higher standard of gloss on his polished black shoes than did mere civilians. There were a few deviants from this norm of business suit and tie, and those that did not conform stood out from the grey men around: a lad in a tracksuit and trainers, a Rastafarian sporting a rainbow-coloured hat, and a youth with a half-shaved head, black leather jacket and a ring through his nose. Nigel tried not to stare at him but could not help wondering how on earth he blew his nose. He decided he must be getting old if he found the latest fashions so odd. Had he not had a row with his father back in the seventies about growing his hair and wearing flares?

Nigel shuffled through the ticket barrier with the rest of the crowd. He was aware of the paradox that while the station was very noisy, all the people about him were silent. The racket came from train engines purring and whining, thousands of shoes scuffing on the polished stone floor, and the occasional announcement. Once out on to the main concourse, the press of people eased and Nigel was able to step out past the Festival Hall, over Hungerford railway bridge, and to work.

As he walked along the back of the old War Office he could see the massive bulk of the Ministry of Defence looming ahead of him, a monolithic 1930s structure. He briefly thought of George Orwell's Ministry of Love in *1984*. That had not been described as a very inviting building either. Nigel wondered if this place was what Orwell had had in mind.

He approached the North Entrance and cast his eyes briefly up at the huge stone statues of muscular Amazons that surmounted it, wondering whose fantasy these buxom women represented: the architect's, the stone mason's or some past field marshal's. Nigel decided, disrespectfully, that it must be the latter; they were certainly ferocious enough, and sufficiently large, to belong to a senior officer. Nigel thought they'd look more the part if they were dressed in baggy tweeds and pearls rather than lounging around, indecorously, in the nude. He walked between the two statues and up the steps, extricating his pass, like a credit card, from his wallet. Gone were the days of flashing one's army identity card at a security officer. High tech had reached into this bastion too. He approached the seven-foot-high security doors made of bulletproof glass, 'swiped' his card and tapped his personal code number into the panel, and the curved door in front of him slid open with a small hiss. The personnel entering the building progressed smoothly, as there were more than enough of these doors to cope with the early-morning rush.

As Nigel left the entrance hall he felt slightly uneasy. He

was not the sort of man to enjoy being this close to the centre of power and politics. There was something vaguely unsettling about the magnitude of the decisions that were made daily in this building, the sums of money spent, the power that was all too evident. Nigel was certain that for some officers here, probably the majority of those who had been to Staff College, this was the pinnacle of their career in the Army, the stuff they had dreamt about at Sandhurst. He had joined the Army to be a soldier. That was what he enjoyed doing. He wanted to be with a regiment in Germany, working with soldiers, or out in Bosnia. Those were the things that the recruiting posters had offered, that was what he had been trained to do. Nothing had been said, when he had joined up, about wearing a pinstriped suit and getting a train every morning. To him the battle of Waterloo was all about fighting the French – not scrambling for a seat on the 18.55 from platform five.

Nigel sighed as he waited for the lift to arrive; perhaps he would do better if he could view his posting here with more enthusiasm. Well, it was too late to worry about that. The pink list, was due out next month, and Nigel's fate had probably been decided already. Nothing he did now was going to have any bearing on his chances of making an appearance on this year's list.

Across the hall, he could see James deep in conversation with his boss. They appeared very chummy, obviously sharing some sort of joke. Nigel knew he ought to be more politically aware, be nice to the right people, but it had never been his style. It had probably got a lot to do with his Scottish upbringing, but he had always been of the opinion that his promotion should depend solely on his own merits – not on his connections. He knew that James took the opposite view, and he despised him for it. He wondered why it was that James's superiors couldn't see through it.

Nigel, like James, worked on the fifth floor of the Ministry, along with dozens of other officers and civil servants. It was a huge building, constructed around six central courtyards. Some people were lucky enough to get offices looking out either over the river or on to Whitehall. Mostly the allocation of these rooms was done according to rank, the Chiefs of Staff having quite sumptuous accommodation, and rightly so. There had to be some privileges that went with their status. Nigel, though, was only a major. That was pretty senior in the hierarchy of a regiment, which only consisted of around 350 men, but in the wider environment of the Ministry of Defence it ranked just above tea boy and below most civilian clerks; after all, they had unions to fight their corner for them and make sure they got their full entitlement of carpeting, office furniture and space. The civil servants who were employed in one department for years at a time were especially good at increasing their allotted office equipment to improve their perceived status amongst their peers. The military personnel were only ever *in situ* for two years and would just have got to grips with wangling an extra chair or so when they were moved on – and the hard-won chair snaffled by the nearest civvy as soon as their office was empty. Nigel could see from his first day that this was a bureaucratic world where importance was measured by the size of one's desk and the thickness of the carpet on the floor.

Nigel's office was a dreary affair that boasted a window that would have commanded a view of one of the inner courtyards had it not been shielded by a thick, grubby net curtain to prevent him being showered with flying glass in the event of a terrorist bomb.

He had his own computer terminal and monitor on his desk. The Ministry of Defence had managed to haul itself into the twentieth century during the last five years or so, and had concluded that since most officers possessed their own word processors at home, it might be to the Army's advantage to harness their computing skills. Thus they were no longer expected to draft letters for typing in longhand. How much simpler to draft them electronically and have them produced by laser printers; printers that could even head the paper with the appropriate crest and letterhead.

Nigel flicked on the light as he went through the door. He walked across to his desk, put his briefcase down and slipped his jacket off. The air in the building, as always on a Monday, was stale and musty. The office seemed oppressively hot and stuffy. Nigel had assumed that the May Day bank holiday would signal the end of central heating until October. Perhaps Whitehall, unlike the Army, was exempt from this arbitrary control. He turned off the radiator and opened the window a couple of inches to let some air into the place. You couldn't call it fresh air, not in London, but at least it was cool. Having done that, he wandered along to the clerks' office to see if there was anything in his pigeonhole, before returning to open his safe.

Compared with the little cubbyhole where he worked, the clerks had a spacious great room. It had to be big; generally ten of them worked there. But now, at just a few minutes after eight o'clock on the first day back after a weekend, there were only two people present: a young registry clerk and the warrant officer who was in overall charge.

'Good morning,' they said as Nigel came in.

'Hello there. Good weekend?' he enquired amiably.

'Not bad, thank you, sir,' replied Mr Murray, the chief clerk. 'You know, the normal sort of thing, took the kids swimming, cut the grass, washed the car. And you, sir?'

'Same as you really. I'm getting to the age when a quiet weekend seems very appealing. It's what family life is all about, in my view. I expect you had a much more exciting time, didn't you, Caroline?' said Nigel, who had spotted her look of disbelief that anyone could enjoy that sort of weekend. Caroline was a civil service clerical assistant and, at only twenty, her idea of a good weekend was to be out clubbing until the small hours of Friday night, followed by a party on Saturday and most of Sunday in bed recovering. Being a civilian, and young, she didn't call anyone 'sir'.

'Depends what you call exciting, really. I went out with my boyfriend mostly.' She tossed her head and made her short blonde curls dance, as though to prove to her employer her more than obvious charms. Her big, glitzy earrings jangled noisily. 'I haven't quite finished sorting out the mail from the weekend yet. If you give me a couple more minutes I'll bring it through to you.'

'I'm in no hurry,' said Nigel. 'I'll wait and take it through with me.'

He stared out of the window at the mass of people now pouring towards this building and the other ministries along Whitehall. He wondered if anyone else felt as he did about their place of work. Probably not. Most of them were civil servants and Whitehall was their Mecca. Nigel shrugged his shoulders, unable to understand the mentality, and turned away.

He wandered over to the array of pigeonholes on the far wall, one for each officer working in the department, about forty in all. He peered into his and hauled out the two files and a couple of inter-office memos that were lurking within. He really couldn't rouse any enthusiasm for another week shuffling papers across his desk and attending planning conferences. His mouth turned down at the corners in distaste as he read the title of the first file: 'Trucks – Fork-lift.' God, he thought, this has got to be the most boring file in the building, and I've got to deal with it. He wasn't even amused to see that it had a grading of 'secret', although he was at a complete loss to guess why such dreary machines could possibly rate such a classification. Perhaps we lob them at the enemy if all else fails, he thought humourlessly.

Caroline teetered across the office on her high heels and handed him a sheaf of flimsy faxes, for which she expected to be rewarded with a smile. She was miffed that her physical attributes were not having their normal effect on an officer, and flounced off. Not quite understanding the reason behind her sudden annoyance, Nigel returned, bemused, to his office.

Nigel and James both worked for the same department within the Ministry of Defence, although their paths had no cause to cross regularly. They both worked for the Deputy Chief of Defence Staff (Systems), which was the august title of a three-star general, a lieutenant general, with considerably less charm, humour and popularity than Roderick Marlow. Although Nigel knew the name of this man, only James had met him, and then only for an initial interview and at a couple of meetings. Nigel would meet him in due course, when the General's aide got round to fixing up the appointment. He was far too illustrious a person to deal regularly with the lesser minions beavering in the back rooms; besides which, the sub-departments had their own heads – brigadiers – to run things.

The General was in overall charge of an area within the Ministry entitled Operational Requirements, known to everyone as OR. There were a plethora of OR branches, each of which was responsible for deciding what their regiments or corps would need in the future in order to fight the next generation of wars and battles. The sappers had a branch, as did the cavalry, and so on. James's group looked at the future needs of the Royal Artillery. He studied the performance of new guns being developed, and the various permutations and combinations of ammunition for them. He was required to go to live-firing tests at gunnery ranges round the world to see how the various artillery pieces under consideration performed, and then report back.

Nigel, however, was in the vehicles department, and as he read through the file on his desk he learned that responsibility for forward planning for a new, heavy-duty fork-lift truck was his. His predecessor had already appraised him of other problems and projects, but judging from the memo from his boss at the front of the file, these would all have to wait while he got to grips with urgent requirements in this field. He flicked to the front of the file. It had been opened six years ago. Six years, and the MOD still hadn't managed to finalise the specifications. Nigel was staggered by the inefficiency of it all. He laid the file on his desk and began to read it through from the beginning. The only way he was going to be able to make a proper judgement about what was needed was to know all the facts and figures.

After a couple of hours, he closed the file. He might be bored by the subject, but at least he was now *au fait* with it. He had the lucky facility of being able to read copious quantities of documents and glean the salient points from them without getting bogged down by unimportant details. He'd made a few jottings in a notebook as he read, but most of the information he needed was now in his head; Nigel had a brain like a computerised database. One thing was obvious: before this project progressed any further, it was imperative that he should visit the manufacturer in Derby and discuss the whole issue with them. Nigel reread his boss's memo. If he wanted a full briefing on the progress of the matter, plus an assessment of the abilities of this piece of equipment to handle the Artillery's requirements for moving ammunition, and all by the following week, he was going to have to pull his finger out.

He pushed the button on the intercom.

'Yes,' said a female voice.

'Caroline?' Nigel couldn't recognise her voice, distorted as it was by the machine.

'Yes.'

'I've got to arrange a visit to Derby. Could you come in here so I can give you the details?'

'In a moment.' Her voice sounded sulky, even down the wire. Why, he wondered, couldn't this woman ever do anything with good grace? If he was honest with himself, he would admit to being faintly intimidated by her. He was of the old-fashioned school and had been led to expect that young women would be respectful to him by virtue of his age and seniority. He wasn't sure how to handle someone who had such a blatant disregard for life's courtesies and authority. He knew that if he took her to task she'd tell him to get stuffed, safe in the knowledge that there was bugger-all he could do about it. What with Jenny, and now Caroline, Nigel wondered if he had lost the ability to be able to relate to women at all.

Ten minutes later, Caroline stamped huffily into his office.

'Yeah?'

Nigel looked up as she strolled insolently across the square of carpet towards him.

'Ah, Caroline.' He kept his feelings of annoyance in check. 'I need to go to Derby to visit Hymax Vehicles. I'd like you to get on to them, fix a date, and then make my travel and hotel arrangements, please. If possible, I'd like to go up in the next couple of days.'

'OK, anything else?'

'No, that's all.'

Caroline shrugged, turned and left. Nigel returned to his work, busying himself with the contents of his in-tray. He deliberately put out of his mind the nagging doubt that this might not be a good time to be going away. The last thing he wanted to do was to leave Jenny on her own with James prowling around her.

While Nigel was beavering away in his office, Jenny was getting ready to go to the community centre to have a cup of coffee with the other wives. She had received the patch newsletter that detailed such information as the opening times of the thrift shop and who ran the babysitting circle. Blaring across the front page was a plea from Lady Marlow for a new representative for the Federation of Army Wives. Jenny grimaced when she saw it, and hoped that yet more pressure wouldn't be applied to get her to take up the post. Ignoring the advertisement, she turned to the next page and read with interest the details of the regular coffee mornings held in the community centre. She decided that braving one of these would be a good way of advertising her business personally. The notice on the board there hadn't produced much interest yet, and if she was going to avoid getting co-opted on to this, that or the other committee she'd better give the appearance of being far too busy. Obviously running a home and looking after three small children was considered to be no excuse at all.

She finished dabbing on some powder, tugged a comb through her short hair and smoothed down her skirt. She then ran down the stairs, grabbed her bag and went out of the house into the warm May sunshine. She felt very carefree as she swung down the road. She turned left at the end and headed for the single-storey pre-fab that was the hub of this little community. It was rather incongruous amongst the solid 1930s semis, but they were lucky the Army had given the wives anything at all. She remembered the last time she'd been there, during the bomb scare. Goodness, that was nearly four weeks ago; she must have been living here over a month already. Where had the time gone?

'Hello, Jenny. Lovely to see you,' gushed Marian, looking fluffy and vacuous as always. She really didn't have a bitchy bone in her body, and was invariably pleasant, but why, Jenny wondered, did she find her so annoying? Marian twittered on at her.

'Come along and we'll get you a cup of coffee. How do you take it? White with sugar?' Jenny declined the sugar. 'No wonder you're so slim,' rabbited Marian. 'I'm one of those poor unfortunates who has to watch what they eat all the time. I only have to think about nibbling a biscuit and the pounds just pile on.' She smoothed down her pink angora sweater. She reminded Jenny of a young Barbara Cartland. 'I imagine you can eat what you like, can't you? Still, with all those children to race after, and a boy, too ... I expect he's a handful, isn't he?' She smiled archly at Jenny. 'He must be his daddy's pride and joy. Is he at nursery school yet? How silly of me – he must be, a great big chap like that. Does he go to the one at the back here?'

The questions were not meant to be answered, and Jenny switched off. Comment and reply were really unnecessary – this woman was on auto-burble. As long as Jenny stood there, nodding now and again like a dog in the back of a car, Marian would keep her transmit button pressed down. Jenny tried to stop her eyes from glazing over.

'Jenny, can I be dreadfully rude and drag you away?' It was Elaine. Jenny didn't know if she was deliberately acting as saviour or if it was just coincidence. Not that it mattered; escape was possible. Marian was already prattling away at someone else.

'Come and have a word with Margaret Evans. She runs the babysitting circle here and I expect you'd like to join.' Jenny was carried away to the safety of a sensible conversation with down-to-earth Margaret Evans.

'Hi there,' she said to Margaret.

'Oh, hi, Jenny. It was a great party on Saturday, wasn't it? I bet there were a few headaches the next day.'

'That Pimms was lethal. Did you drink much of it?'

'Not after the first glass. I stuck to wine.' She added, conspiratorially, 'James was a bit tipsy when we left, didn't you think?'

'He did drink a bit, didn't he?'

'Did I gather you'd met before?'

'Yes, we were posted together years ago.' It was the truth, but not the whole truth. Jenny didn't think she wanted the patch to know about her previous marriage just yet – possibly not ever. Any patch was rife with gossip, and a juicy titbit like this would be fallen on with delight.

'Oh, you were in the Army too?'

'Yes, the WRAC. I was admin fodder mostly. I was with a gunner regiment that James was in.'

'Was he a complete bastard then too?'

Jenny didn't know how to answer that. It was one of those 'have you stopped beating your wife?' questions. And besides which, although he *had* been a bastard, Jenny suddenly felt loyal to him. Who was this woman to pass judgement on him?

What had he done to her to deserve such an aspersion?

She said, 'He was certainly ambitious,' and hoped that provided the right answer.

Margaret grimaced. 'Robert doesn't like him. They're both gunners, you see, and he says James is a sod to work for – very unscrupulous. To be honest, I think they're at daggers drawn for some reason. It's a good job Robert doesn't work anywhere near James at the moment. If he did, I think he'd have resigned by now.'

Jenny was glad she hadn't told Margaret that James was her ex-husband. Swiftly, she changed the subject. 'You like army life, then?' She knew that there were several wives who would be very happy indeed to see their husbands leave.

'Well, Will, my eldest boy, has settled so well at prep school, and Ben longs to go too, and if we don't get the boarding school allowance we couldn't possibly afford to keep them there.'

'How much is it these days?'

'What, the fees or the allowance?'

'Both, I suppose.'

'The fees are about three thousand pounds a term, and the allowance covers about half of it. It's a lot of money we still have to find, but it'll be easier when Ben goes to school this autumn, because then I can go back to working full time. I work part time now but the money isn't good.'

'What do you do?' asked Jenny.

'I'm a nurse. There's always agency nursing, or I might even try to get a job in a casualty unit. It's the night duties that really pay well, but I can't take those on when I've got to get Ben to school. What I like best is casualty work. It's proper nursing if you ask me. I used to do that before I got married. I really enjoyed it.'

'Don't tell me, you were a QA.'

'Yes, just like half the wives.'

'Well, those that weren't in the WRAC like me, or teachers in Germany.' They both grinned ruefully at the predictability of their pasts. Jenny liked Margaret; she was obviously a kindred spirit, sensible, forthright and cheerful. Jenny reckoned she would be a good shoulder to cry on if one needed to.

'At least you can look forward to going back to your career.

There'll always be a need for nurses. Not much call for ex-army officers, especially as there are so many sloshing around these days. I could quite fancy the idea of going back to work, but the instant you tell an employer your old man is in the Army, they look at the next candidate. There's no point in taking on someone who is going to be off in a year or so. I fiddle around making craft stuff to sell, but it's only a hobby. The kids'll have to go away to school, but heaven only knows how we're going to afford the top-up needed for a halfway decent school – unless I can get a good job.' Jenny sighed. 'It's all so bloody difficult.'

'I agree. If it wasn't for the boarding school allowance I think I would like Robert to leave. There's no chance of going anywhere nice these days, and Robert is bored to snores with all this peace. Silly, isn't it? Ninety-nine per cent of the world longs for peace, and my husband is itching for trouble to flare up somewhere so he can volunteer to help sort it out. Still, if he left, God knows what he'd do, but at least we wouldn't have to move again.'

Jenny thought again about Julia, and how she'd been shattered to find her husband out of a job. Her safe, secure, khaki world had fallen about her ears. Jenny didn't think that Margaret was the sort to want her husband to become a civilian. She struck her as someone who, deep down, loved patch life.

At that moment Pan burst into the room.

'Is Jenny here?' she said excitedly to Marian. Then, spotting her quarry in the corner, she almost ran over to her.

'Jenny, hold on to your hat. I think I've got some news for you. How do you think you could cope with an order for fifty bookends from one of London's best-known shops?'

Jenny stared at her, completely uncomprehending.

'I'm sorry, Pan,' she said, after a second or two. 'I'm really not with you.'

'The girl, Belinda, the one I went to have lunch with on Sunday – you know, the one marrying Rupe's friend – she's a buyer for the General Trading Company.' She looked at Jenny in exasperation; Jenny still looked stunned. 'She wants to sell your bookends in the Sloane Square branch of GTC.'

Jenny's face cleared as realisation dawned.

'Fifty,' she said. Then, with a shriek of joy, 'Fifty! How much are they going to pay?'

'I don't know, but quite a lot. We'll have to deal with the details later – when you get to meet their head buyer. I've got a bottle of champagne at home. I put it there last night when I got back from meeting Belinda. She said she would have to get her boss to confirm her judgement this morning – I waited for her to call before I told you anything.' Pan's face was alight with smiles. 'Isn't it wonderful? Jenny, it looks like you've hit pay dirt!'

Chapter Eleven

James walked into the big, airy clerks' office and dumped a couple of letters on Mr Murray's desk.

'Get these photocopied, Chief,' he said peremptorily, and then strode across to the table with the kettle to make himself a coffee. He passed Caroline's desk on the way.

'Hi, gorgeous. How are you?'

Caroline smirked, smugly. She liked being noticed, especially by such a hunk as Major Bain. Sally, the clerk in Plans, had told her that there was a rumour that he'd screwed one of the female officers in the map store. Caroline reckoned it was true; he looked the sort who collected scalps.

'Busy,' she said. 'I might have to work late tonight.'

Mr Murray, walking over to the photocopier, looked across at her in surprise. That didn't sound like Caroline. She was normally out of the door on the dot of five thirty.

James said, 'Tough luck,' and went to make his coffee. Caroline stared after him. Had he got the hint? Perhaps not, but then it wouldn't do to be too obvious. He had a nice body, she thought. He was probably quite muscular with his clothes off. She wondered if he had a hairy chest. She hoped not; she liked smooth men. While she was gazing at James the phone on her desk rang.

'Extension 5239,' she said, tearing her eyes off her idol and picking up a pencil.

'You're sure you can't see him till Thursday? ... OK, no I'll tell him. I'll get back to you if he wants anything else. 'Bye.' She replaced the receiver and buzzed the intercom.

'Major Walker,' said a tinny voice which carried clearly

145

across the office to where James was standing.

'Hymax can't fit you in till Thursday morning. They've got a delegation from Japan over for the next couple of days.'

Nigel, at the other end of the machine, paused for a second as he weighed up the implications of this.

'OK. I'll go and have a word with the boss. Fix up the train and book a hotel for Wednesday night, please.'

'All right.' Caroline released the button.

James finished making his coffee and walked back to his office. He sat down behind his desk and absently scratched his crotch. Little Jenny left on her own on Wednesday night – now that was an interesting bit of information.

Caroline came into the office with his photocopying.

'Where do you want it?' She licked her lips. James looked up at her and smiled slowly.

'On the desk. Where else?'

Caroline giggled.

James knew she fancied him. He could have her if he wanted. But he'd better not. He didn't think she'd be very discreet, and anyway, it was dangerous to screw the office staff. Word got around. He'd got her hint about staying on late after work but decided to ignore it. It was different when he went away on visits, especially the overseas ones. He could shag anyone then with impunity – Fiona never got to hear.

'Will there be anything else, Major Bain?'

'Not for the moment, Caroline. I'll give you a buzz if I need you.' Besides, he didn't want her; it was Jenny he was after.

'It's wonderful news, darling, but ...' Nigel, hardly through the front door, and still carrying his briefcase, wasn't sure how to carry on. He didn't want to dampen his wife's enthusiasm or take the gilt off her gingerbread, but he felt she was getting carried away by this taste of success. He could see all sorts of problems looming: where was she going to run the business from, how was she going to fill the order if GTC wanted them in the next few days – and who was going to look after Christopher and the girls after school? Moreover he'd got used to having a wife who was always around to look after his needs. He'd heard enough from various colleagues to know that working wives expected husbands to do their bit around the house. He couldn't admit it to Jenny, but he would almost prefer money to be a bit tight than have to start ironing his shirts and doing the shopping on a Thursday night.

'...but won't it mean an awful lot of hassle for you? Besides which, you don't know anything about running a business.' Nigel went into the dining room and poured himself a drink.

'Oh, don't spoil it for me,' said Jenny, infuriated by his practicality. 'I'm not going to worry about any of the details until I've been up to London to discuss terms and delivery dates with the shop. And don't worry,' she added, seeing the sceptical look in her husband's eyes, 'I shan't get myself into anything until I am certain I can handle it. Besides which, it gives me a perfect excuse not to get involved in any of Diana Marlow's committees.'

Nigel looked at her questioningly. 'I didn't know she'd approached you about that sort of thing.'

Jenny could have kicked herself. Silly bitch for mentioning it. She ought to have known Nigel would take issue about it. He was so predictably proper. He did his duty, so everyone else should too.

'Oh, it was nothing really. They're looking for a rep for the Federation of Army Wives. She asked me if I'd do it. I said no.'

'Why on earth? You'd be very good at it.'

'That's not the point. I was approached because I don't have a proper daytime job. Looking after three small children doesn't count.'

'What did Diana say?'

'Nothing much. I don't think she was all that pleased, but it's tough.'

'And what about me?'

'What do you mean, *what about me*?'

'It won't reflect well on me, that's all.'

'Oh, come on.' Jenny was beginning to feel annoyed. 'Your career is your affair. I gave up mine to have children, your children. Becoming a parent didn't mean you had to give up your job. Well, now it's my turn to do something that I want to do for a change. I've followed you about for ages, I haven't complained about the moving, but there's more to life than sitting on committees to make *you* look good.'

'Other wives do it. They don't complain.' Nigel's voice was getting louder. He took a large gulp of his gin and tonic.

'Well, I'm not going to. I think I can make a success of this and I'm bloody well going to have a go.' Jenny was incensed. She was a person, with a life to live, too. Couldn't he see that she didn't owe allegiance to the Army? It was his career, not hers. Now she had a chance to make something of herself, and he was worried in case what she did detracted from him. It wasn't fair, and with or without his support she was going to do it. Sod him! She flounced off to the kitchen to cook his supper, and expressed her frustration and rage by banging the saucepans and plates around noisily.

Nigel went to work the next day in a bad mood. Jenny was still sulking about their row and he felt let down by her attitude. Couldn't she see that it was important that she did her bit as a supportive army wife? What with that and the business with James, Nigel felt as though he was married to a stranger. Quiet, compliant Jenny had suddenly decided to rebel. Nigel could only think that it was something to do with James. But what? Perhaps Jenny regretted divorcing him. Surely not – James had been a complete chauvinist. Even Nigel knew that despite Jenny's accusations about him undermining her business opportunity, he was nowhere near James's league when it came to wanting women to stay in the kitchen. Perhaps, when all was considered, it would be better if Jenny was busy with her own business. At least she wouldn't have time to make sheep's eyes at James. Nigel felt his anger grow as he thought about James kissing Jenny. Bastard. It was a good thing they worked at opposite ends of the branch so their paths rarely crossed. Nigel wasn't sure he would be able to keep his temper entirely under control if they encountered each other too often.

His mood wasn't improved when his boss would only extend his deadline for his report on the fork-lift trucks by a couple of days. It probably meant that he'd have to work over the weekend to put the report together, after he got back from Derby. He didn't think he'd be able to get it all done on Friday. He'd write it at home but it was classified, so he'd have no option but to come into the office. Jenny was going to be even crosser with him. She wanted him home to look after the kids while she got on with turning out bookends. He didn't think she'd believe that it was all his boss's fault. More likely she'd have a go at him for not pushing for more time. Nigel wondered miserably if his marriage was heading for the rocks.

When he returned home he found Jenny and the children busy clearing out the garage. The bicycles and the mower were being moved down to the garden shed, and Jenny was putting all the other odds and ends – old plant pots, buckets and spades, and the other assorted junk that lurked in the corners – into some large cardboard boxes.

'Make yourself useful,' she said to Nigel, kissing him perfunctorily and somewhat coolly on the cheek and then thrusting a full box into his arms. 'Stick this lot at the top of the stairs, I'll find a home for it all later.'

'What's going on? The garage only gets sorted out when we move.'

'I'm going to set up my workbench in here. I'll have to start up some sort of production line. I've got four weeks till D-Day – Delivery Day. I'll need to have half a dozen pairs on the go at the same time if I'm going to be finished in time.'

'What happens if they don't sell?'

Jenny looked annoyed. 'You don't have much faith in my wonderful work, do you? Of course they'll sell.'

'Yes, but what if?' Nigel insisted gently.

'They get returned to me and, providing they're not damaged, I refund the money.' Jenny sounded faintly worried. 'But it won't come to that. GTC wouldn't be buying them if they weren't sure they can sell them.'

'OK, if you say so.' Nigel was in no mood to argue. What he wanted was to change out of his suit, read the paper and have a glass of cold beer. He didn't think Jenny would be best pleased if he sloped off to do that rather than helping her. He carried the box to the top of the stairs, then changed into jeans and a polo shirt. He looked longingly at the fridge on the way past and thought of the can of beer in it, then shrugged his shoulders and went out to the garage.

'I hope this venture of yours isn't going to cost me anything?'

'Not much,' replied Jenny. 'And I shall make sure I do a

proper costing before I give GTC a price. The only thing I shall have to buy, apart from materials, is an air brush.'

'And how much is that going to set me back?'

'They don't cost much, and I'll get a far better finish when I varnish them, and—'

'Hold on.' Nigel knew when he was getting a sales pitch. 'How much is not much?'

'I can get a really good one, that'll do the detail, too, for under a hundred pounds.'

'And how much profit will you make on fifty bookends?'

'I've told GTC that I'll probably be letting them have them for about fifteen pounds a pair; the wood and paint will cost around a hundred and fifty, so I stand to get around...' She rapidly did the sum in her head, '... six hundred pounds. Not bad for four weeks' work.'

'Less child-minding, less the air brush.'

'Oh, stop it. I'll enjoy doing it, and anyway, this may be my big break.'

Nigel was worried that this was exactly what it might be. Still, he'd cross that bridge when he came to it. He had too much on his plate at work to worry about her business. He changed the subject.

'I'll be away tomorrow night. I've got to go and visit a firm in Derby. I'll be back Thursday, late-ish.'

'Oh. All right. Will you want supper on Thursday?'

'I'll probably grab something on the train.'

Jenny nodded. Well, if Nigel was away it would give her more time to get everything ready to go. He'd probably get grumpy if she spent her evenings doing paperwork.

The next day, Wednesday, Jenny began to get herself well and truly sorted out. After she'd been to the timber merchant and selected her wood, she then went to a specialist model shop to get her air brush. It cost rather more than she'd told Nigel, but she paid the difference out of her slush fund. The home she'd promised herself could wait. She needed the money for something else now, and anyway, you had to speculate to accumulate, she told herself as she drew out several hundred pounds. She hadn't told Nigel that she'd need a proper workbench and shelves as well.

Having got the material problems fixed, Jenny went to call

on Annette Hobday. She needed a child-minder for Christopher in the afternoons and the girls once they had finished school. She hoped Annette could be persuaded to bail her out.

'Of course I'll do it. The going rate is two pounds per child per hour, and I'll give them all tea for you at five if you like.'

'It's a deal. It's great that I'll have the whole day without having to rush off to pick them up from school. Even a short break like that can be really distracting. Right, I must push off. I want to find someone to put up a load of shelves in my garage.'

'Look no further,' said Annette.

'Great, do you know someone reliable?'

'No, I mean yes. I'll do it for you.'

Jenny was taken aback. She wasn't sure. She wanted a proper job done.

'Look,' said Annette, seeing her hesitate, 'I was brought up on a farm in the Dales. I had to be able to turn my hand to most things, we all did. Don't worry, I'll do it properly. I know exactly what I'm doing.'

'I'm sorry,' said Jenny. 'There's no reason on earth why you shouldn't be able to. I've obviously been married to a chauvinist for too long. I've been brainwashed into believing that girls are only good for cooking, moving and breeding.'

'Bloody hell, if you really believe that, you're almost a lost cause. Anyway, when do you want me to do it?'

'Now? I mean, if it's convenient.'

'No problem. If you could just keep an eye on Victoria for me ... Have you got all the kit, rawl plugs and such?'

'Yes, I think so.'

'Ok, then you'd better show me exactly what you want doing.'

By the afternoon, Jenny was sitting at her workbench turning out her third figurine. Christopher was at Annette's, the girls would be picked up by her later, Jenny didn't have to worry about supper for anyone but herself, and her deadline seemed to present no problems at all. After her children had been returned, bathed and put to bed, Jenny cracked on. She had to admit that mass production was already proving a trifle tedious, but she'd decided that the easiest way to cope would be to make all the bookends, all fifty pairs, and then paint them. The painting would be much more interesting, as each model would be at a different stage. In the mean time there was nothing for it but to trudge on, turning out the wooden soldiers. Because of the noise from her electric saw, Jenny didn't hear the sound of the side door of the garage opening.

'Working late?' said James beside her.

Jenny leapt, and looked angrily at the nick in the side of the bookend where the saw had slipped in her hand.

'Don't do that,' she said fiercely.

'Do what?' said James, a picture of innocence.

'Surprise me like that.'

'I'm sorry, Kitten. I really didn't mean to. I just came to see if you'd like to have a drink with me this evening – for old times' sake and to show there are no hard feelings. Perhaps we could drink to the success of your business. What do you say?' His voice was smooth and deep; it unruffled her and calmed away her feelings of annoyance. As he spoke he could see her nostrils flare and her eyelids droop momentarily with lust.

Then, 'What about Fiona?' said Jenny.

'She's out. Won't be back till later.' Jenny didn't notice that he didn't ask about Nigel. Her mind was on other things. She was frantically trying to justify to herself her acceptance of his invitation. He *had* been her husband for nearly three years. And at least he was interested in her business, which seemed more than could be said for Nigel.

'OK, but you'll have to come over here. I can't possibly leave the children.' Having a drink didn't mean she was going to be unfaithful.

'No problem. I'll just pop home and get a bottle of wine. You still like Beaune?' Jenny nodded.

After James had gone she switched off her equipment and the lights and locked up the garage. She felt very confident that she was in control of herself, that she could harness her feelings. She and James were just going to have a drink and a chat.

On his return James looked approvingly at what Jenny had managed to do with the uninspiring colour scheme of beige carpet and magnolia walls. He felt instantly at home in her sitting room. It was not a designer showpiece like Fiona's, with picture bows and artfully draped fabrics that were not to be moved an inch out of position or the whole effect would be ruined. This was a cheerful family room that was lived in, not just looked at and admired. Jenny had not replaced the dull oatmeal curtains because, although they were uninspiring, they didn't clash with the yellow and blue covers on her chairs. In fact, their neutral tones emphasised the jolly pattern of the soft furnishings. She had a good eye for colour. On the large mahogany table opposite the window she had a dozen or so pictures of her family surrounding a big vase filled with an armful of irises, cleverly complementing the upholstery and reflected in a huge over-mantel mirror. On the walls were her collection of prints and watercolours. The effect was reminiscent of summer days and sunshine, as bright and cheerful as a cottage garden.

'I see your taste is as good as ever,' James remarked approvingly.

'Thank you. But it's Nigel's, too.' Jenny felt suddenly guilty, knowing that Nigel would disapprove of her entertaining James. James was just about to uncork the bottle when the telephone shrilled at them from the hall. Jenny went to answer it. Instantly she recognised Nigel's voice.

'Hi, darling,' she said. 'Good trip?'

'Fine. How are the kids?'

'All in bed asleep, I'm pleased to say.'

'You sound breathless. What have you been doing?'

'I was working in the garage. I had to run to reach the phone.' God, was her voice giving her away?

'How's it going?'

'Fine. I don't think I'm going to have any problems.'

'Great. Well, I was just phoning to see how you all were. I'm on my way out to get some supper. I'll see you tomorrow. 'Bye.'

Jenny replaced the receiver and returned to the sitting room.

'I'm sorry, James. I shouldn't have accepted your invitation. It was silly of me. I think you'd better go.'

'Oh, come on, Kitten. I only want to have a drink with you. Don't be such a spoilsport.'

'No, I'm sorry. Nigel wouldn't see it like that if he found out. Please go.'

James felt a surge of rage driven by frustration.

'All right. I'll go. You've become very boring in your old age, you know, Jenny. You used to be a lot of fun. Don't worry, I'll see myself out.'

Jenny sat very still on the sofa. She had no one to blame but herself. She'd been a fool to have anything to do with him.

James stamped down the hall to the front door. On the wall by the coat rack, a picture caught his eye. It was the one of Nigel and Kevin, flanked by the rest of their company at Sandhurst, holding the Inter-Company Assault Course trophy. With a shock, James suddenly recognised Nigel, remembered the incident on the exercise area nearly twenty years before.

Good God, he said to himself. Kevin and the negligent discharge. Now I know who you are.

Jenny, listening for the door to slam, was surprised when she heard it click quietly shut. She leapt off the sofa and looked into the hall, just to make sure that he'd really gone. Suddenly she felt overwhelmingly tired. She shelved any ideas about supper and went to bed.

Nigel, who'd only unpacked a sweater from his overnight bag, swept it out of the drawer and threw it back into his case on top of his washing kit, pyjamas and yesterday's underwear. He was pleased to be going home. The hotel room had been none too clean – dust on the mirror and some scraps of rubbish in the chest of drawers. If he'd been there longer he'd probably have complained, but it simply hadn't seemed worth it for such a short stay.

He was in such a hurry to be gone that he didn't notice that a crumpled-up piece of paper had got caught up with his jersey as he packed. He was in a hurry. His meeting had finished slightly earlier than he'd expected, and if he got a move on he could catch the earlier train. He'd been thinking about what Jenny had said to him. She was right. She ought to have the chance to do her own thing and stop playing the supporting role to his lead. It would do her good to run this business. He wanted to get home to tell her.

Jenny, bathing the children, didn't hear the key turn in the lock and didn't know he was back until he was at the top of the stairs.

'Hi, kids, hi, Jenny,' he said happily, pleased to be home.

The children shrieked with excitement. Anyone would think he'd been away a week, not just twenty-four hours, thought Jenny, a touch jealously. She was around all the time, so they never greeted her like this. She left Nigel to get the children out of the bath and play with them, and took his bag to their bedroom to unpack. As she pulled out dirty clothes, she almost missed the little piece of screwed-up paper lodged in the folds of his jersey. She picked it out and then folded the sweater up to put it back in his drawer. She was just about to chuck the scrap into the bin when she suddenly caught sight of the writing on it. Durex Featherlite.

Jenny reeled and sat down abruptly on the bed. She went cold with shock. Then she thought, it must have got in there by accident. But how? Had someone else put it there? Don't be ridiculous. How dare he! What the hell had he been up to in Derby? Couldn't he go away for one night without bedding some cheap trollop in a one-night stand? So things had been a bit tense between them these last few days. It didn't mean he had a licence to stray. Jenny conveniently forgot how close she'd come to going down the same path. She thought about confronting him with it, but this wasn't the time, not with the children up and about.

She sat there, dumbfounded, wondering what to do, then put the scrap in her pocket and went downstairs. She wanted to do something, anything to stop herself thinking about it right now. She found that her hands were trembling so much she couldn't peel the potatoes for supper. She bunged them back into the veg rack and got out pasta instead. Then she poured herself a very stiff gin and stared numbly out of the kitchen window, taking great swigs. She felt nearly as sick as when she'd seen Christopher with that bomb. She thought about confronting Nigel but she didn't want to know the details. It had, most likely, been a one-night stand, not a red-hot affair. She decided that it would be better to live with the uncertainty of doubt than to face the stark, cold reality of fact. Jenny took the condom wrapper from her pocket and threw it in the bin.

Later, at dinner, Nigel was hurt to find that Jenny's black

mood was no better than when he'd gone away. If running her own business was going to make her such a bitch, he was sorry that the opportunity had ever arisen.

He didn't seem to be able to do anything right these days, he thought miserably. Roll on tomorrow, when he could escape back to the office.

The atmosphere wasn't any better next door. For nearly a week, in fact since their party, James had seemed totally preoccupied. Had the General had a word in his ear about his behaviour that night? Fiona didn't like to ask, but something was certainly on his mind and she was getting increasingly fed up with his monosyllabic answers to her questions and his lack of interest in home life generally.

'Really, James, I don't know what the matter is with you. I try to make an effort and all I get is Neanderthal grunts. Do you or don't you want to come to Bath with me for a few days?'

'What, and get kept awake by your nympho sister bonking all night?'

'She's not a nymphomaniac.'

'She bloody is. If she didn't do it for free, she'd make a killing on the streets.'

'You're a fine one to talk. Everyone knows that you shagged your way through every British teacher in Germany before you married me.'

'Well, if I'm so shop-soiled, why *did* you marry me?'

'It wasn't because of your personality, that's for sure.'

'Really Fiona, you are childish sometimes.'

'OK then, I'll act like a child.' She picked up a glass of wine and tipped it over him, then walked from the room. James stared after her. Bitch. He went upstairs to his dressing room, took a clean shirt from the cupboard and went down to the pub. Fiona listened to his movements from her bedroom, filing her nails angrily. On impulse she picked up the phone and dialled her sister's number.

After more than a dozen rings, just when Fiona was about to give up, Victoria answered. She sounded as though she had just got out of bed.

'Hello, Bath 660875,' she yawned.

'Hi, Tors. It's me.'

'Oh, hello Fi.' Tors stifled another yawn.

'I'm not keeping you up, am I?' Fiona asked sarcastically. It had only just turned nine o'clock.

'Not at all,' said Tors. 'It's just that I've been burning the candle at both ends recently and when I got home from work I fell asleep watching the box. Your call woke me up. Hang on a tick ...'

Fiona patiently hung on to the phone. She listened intently to the silence but could not discern what her younger sister was up to. It certainly didn't sound as if she were talking to a man, there was only silence down the line. When was Tors going to find herself a bloke and settle down? She was getting a bit long in the tooth still to be leaping in and out of bed on one-night stands. She was thirty-three now, and not getting younger.

'Sorry about that, but I just had to get myself a gin and a fag before I settle down to a gossip. How have you been? I haven't spoken to you for ages.'

In reality Fiona and her sister hadn't spoken to each other for about a week, but they were very close, probably because neither of them had enjoyed boarding school and they had weathered the horrors of it together.

During school holidays, when Tors had still been too young to go herself, she had sat on her sister's bed and listened to her tearful report of how hateful it all was. Fiona knew that it would have been a waste of time to mention her feelings in her letters to her father and mother. The General would not have tolerated any namby-pamby ideas such as feeling homesick, and her mother was far too busy enjoying herself to want her life interrupted by a daughter begging to come home. Fiona would have been told to pull herself together and brace up. Tors understood, though. She was unhappy at home, as both parents were preoccupied with their own lives and had no time for her. If she was at school with Fi, at least they could be miserable together.

Fiona settled herself comfortably against her pillows and prepared for a long chat.

'James is in this dreadful mood,' she confided to her sister. 'Something to do with work, I think. The list for promotion is out soon and I think he's getting twitchy about it. I'm fed up with him. I suggested coming to see you for a day or two but he wasn't interested.'

'Well, come on your own. We'll probably have more fun anyway. Tell you what, Fi,' said Tors, 'are you busy the week after next? I mean, no teaching job or anything?'

'Busy? Me? You know how bored I am most of the time. I only do supply, and it's half-term then anyway. Why?'

'Well, I was thinking. I've got an old friend of ours from Hong Kong coming – you remember Jeremy Fulton, don't you? Well, he'll be staying at my place for about a week, the first week in June. How about you come down here too? It'll be such fun – we can all pretend we're teenagers again and be completely irresponsible. It'll be a bit of a squash, but if you don't mind sleeping on the sofa bed, or even on Jeremy, you'd be ever so welcome.'

There was a pause while Fiona considered this. She'd forgotten about Jeremy, though he'd been the object of her first real crush at fourteen. They'd met on an RAF flight taking children out to join their parents in Hong Kong for the school holidays. She'd sat next to him for the whole trip and he'd seemed so grown up, so assured, so handsome. They'd seen a lot of each other that holiday and the subsequent ones, climaxing with the summer holiday when Fiona had had her sixteenth birthday party at the Officers' Club, and he'd kissed her. She'd fancied herself in love and had written long outpourings in her diary. Then his parents had been posted, and that was the end of their entirely innocent affair. She knew that he was now a successful and wealthy banker, but other than that she'd lost touch with him years ago. She suddenly realised that Tors was still talking.

'... know you were thinking of getting away before then, but if it's me you want to see then that's the best offer I can make. If you're really desperate to get away from James, you could always go home.'

'Home? I'm not that desperate.'

'Well, come here then. It's bound to be a hoot. Oh, do say yes.'

'Look, it sounds great. And it doesn't matter that I can't rush off straight away. I'm sure I can put up with James for another week or so. He'll probably be quite glad to hear that he can rediscover the joys of bachelorhood. I'll get back to you as soon as I can to confirm that it's OK, but I don't think I'll mention that Jeremy will be there, so don't you either. Now, guess what? Hot news!' She told her sister about the reappearance of James's ex-wife. Tors was agog.

'What's she like? You always told me she must be a real cow.'

'No, I was wrong. Honestly, she's a poppet. Five foot six, and I don't think she could weigh more than about eight stone soaking wet. I don't know why, but when James said she was in the Army, I imagined this huge great lesbian with hairy legs, a moustache and sensible shoes. Not that it seemed possible that James would go for that sort of bird.' The sisters giggled at the incongruity of the picture.

Fiona was still on the phone when James returned from the pub.

'Well, go to your blasted sister's then,' he shouted at her once she'd put the receiver down. 'Go on, why don't you leave now? At least I'd get some bloody peace and quiet, instead of having you whining and nagging at me.'

'I don't whine and nag, or pester for that matter,' Fiona roared back at him. Unlike most women, her voice did not go shrill when she yelled. 'All I want to know is why you're in such a fucking awful mood. I don't know why you're so foul. What the hell have I done? What's so unreasonable about wanting to know that?' She paused for breath, glaring at James. 'Then when I suggest that I visit Tors, you make it sound as though I'm leaving you for ever. For Christ's sake, James, what's the matter?'

'I've had a lousy week in the office,' James lied. She was the last person he could tell about how frustrated he was feeling living next door to Jenny and not being able to have her again. 'Can't a man have a bad patch without the Spanish Inquisition?'

'I'm not bloody interrogating you!'

'Well, it sounds like it to me. And I suppose you told your sister what I said about her earlier. You've obviously been on the phone to her for half the fucking evening, so it must have cropped up in the conversation at some stage. Tell me, has

Victoria finished screwing the population of Bath and started on the rest of the West Country yet?'

'Christ, you're low. At least she's free to do what she wants, and she doesn't have anyone complaining about what she spends her money on.' Fiona was white with rage. How dare he talk about her sister like that? James was a shit, he really was. It would serve him bloody well right if she left him this instant.

James watched her with narrowed eyes. He wondered how long she would stick around if he didn't get on next month's promotion list. She liked a comfortable life and wasn't one for economising. She ought to get herself a job and stop idling round the house, expecting him to bring home the bacon. Christ, even Jenny, with three children, still found the time to run a business. He looked hard at his wife with her cool eyes and her spoilt, pouting mouth.

'As it's so bloody obvious that you like the good life, I suggest you stop spending your days and my money in dress shops and get yourself a proper job. Why don't you earn some money for a change, instead of just spending it?' He headed for the spare room. 'I shan't disturb you tonight, and if you want to go to Bath, the sooner the better.'

Chapter Twelve

The following Monday James sat in his office staring at his diary. He was looking at the week that Fiona was going to be in Bath, and was annoyed to discover that he was supposed to be in Germany at the same time. It was bloody annoying. Idly he tapped his teeth with a pencil. This wasn't what he'd had in mind at all. He'd hoped that while Fiona was away he might be able to lay siege to Jenny. He wanted her, more so now that he had remembered who her husband was – the officer who liked to associate himself with the yob element. Really, he'd have thought Jenny would have had better taste than to take up with the likes of Nigel. He sighed and went along the corridor to get the file on his visit to Germany. Surely there was a way to change the dates, or better still, get someone else to go in his stead.

'What can I do for you?' asked Caroline, running her tongue across her neat white teeth and putting her shoulders back to make her breasts stick out even more than usual.

James swallowed the obvious, lascivious reply – Mr Murray wouldn't approve – and said, 'I'll have the file on the ammunition trials on Hohne ranges next month.'

'I'll bring it through, Major Bain.'

'It's OK. I'll wait.' He sauntered over to the window to look down on Whitehall. He stared at the back view of Clive of India's statue as he waited for Caroline to extract the file from the right cabinet. He didn't see the Brigadier, head of Operational Requirements (Vehicles), come in, deep in conversation with Nigel's immediate boss, Colonel Figures.

'It's a quite remarkable piece of work. He's got right to the nub of the problem,' said Colonel Figures, the admiration clear in his voice.

'And you say he produced it in a day?'

'Yes. I gave the man a tight deadline because I wanted it before the end of this week. I thought he'd probably not risk it being more than a day or so late. I didn't bank on him getting it done so quickly.'

'I don't think I know this fellow Walker. Who is he?'

'He's new, came from Germany. He's the man whose kid found that bomb.'

'Right. I'd like to meet him. Fix an interview will you, Figures. In the mean time, I think you ought to get that report on fork-lifts to the General. I expect he'd like to see what Walker has to say.'

James continued to stand at the window, intent on the conversation taking place behind him. Nigel? Surely not? James had had him down as a no-hoper. After all he was in the Logistic Corps. The really bright chaps got into decent regiments. James didn't understand it. He went over to Mr Murray's desk.

'I couldn't help hearing what the Colonel had to say, Chief. What's Major Walker done that's so brilliant?'

'We've had a problem with the specifications for a new multi-role fork-lift for use on rough terrain. The file's been kicking around for a good few years now and no one seems to have solved the problem. It seems that Major Walker, after one visit to the factory in Derby, has got it all sewn up. This,' Murray indicated a thick plastic wallet containing thirty-odd sheets of paper, 'is his report.'

'Very impressive,' said James flatly. Nigel was obviously brighter than he'd given him credit for at Sandhurst. This knowledge certainly didn't improve James' temper as he took the file from Caroline and returned to his office to try to work out how he could wriggle out of the trip to Hohne.

'Where are my army shirts?' Nigel called to Jenny from the bedroom.

'They're in the second drawer down, in the big chest of drawers,' she yelled back from the kitchen. She finished ironing his green army-issue lightweight trousers and draped them over her arm to carry them upstairs. Laying them carefully on the bed, she said, 'Is there anything else which needs ironing before I put the board away?'

'No, that's the lot.' Nigel stowed the shirts and trousers tidily into his suitcase. 'I wouldn't mind taking the little holdall for my boots and shoes. Have you any idea where it is?' Jenny thought for a second or two and then dived under the bed. Triumphantly she produced it.

'This the one you're after?'

'Yup. Right – uniform, suit, ties, pants and socks, washing and shaving kit...' Nigel methodically checked off the contents of his luggage against a mental list. 'Yes, that seems to be the lot.'

'Tickets and Deutschmarks?' asked Jenny helpfully.

'In my wallet.'

'Well, if you're ready, we might as well make tracks. Children,' she yelled, switch off the television, it's time to go.' There was a shriek of glee from downstairs.

'Are you sure you don't mind taking me? I could have perfectly well got the train to Luton,' Nigel offered again.

'We've been through all that. It's no trouble to drive you there. Christopher can't wait to see the aeroplanes and we can all have a picnic on the way back home. Now come on, or we'll be late.'

'You know, I've no idea at all why they need me on this trial. As far as I can see it's all to do with firing ammunition, not moving it. I really don't see that anything I know about fork-lift trucks will have any bearing on how this new ammo performs.'

'Look, the Colonel, who seems to think very highly of you, wants you to go, so why are you arguing?'

'I'd just like to know the thought processes behind it, that's all.'

Jenny shrugged. It seemed immaterial to her. Someone had decided that he ought to attend this ammunition trial in Germany, and that was that. What was the point in worrying about it? All she knew was that she was stuck at home with three kids, it was half-term, and she was getting behind with her schedule. If she fell much further behind she wouldn't meet the deadline from GTC. And although she wasn't admitting it to herself, at the back of her mind was the nagging doubt that once Nigel was away from home, he might be tempted to screw around again.

Christopher was asleep on the back seat of the car, tired out by the excitement of seeing his father off at the airport, and the girls were seeing how many green cars they could spot. The traffic on the M25 was at a virtual standstill. Jenny turned up the car radio to listen to an old favourite being played. She hoped there might be a travel flash soon to tell her what the problem was. How she hated this motorway! The car in front inched forward and Jenny slipped the car into gear and budged up too. She was tempted to switch the engine off, but each time she considered it they seemed to move, even if it was only a few feet.

The disc jockey introduced the next record: 'Nights in White Satin'. Jenny was transported away from the monoxide fumes of the M25 to the glamour and luxury of the mess at Woolwich and the aftermath of her first regimental dinner night there. Guiltily, she remembered her liaison with James, and felt a warmth spread in her stomach as she recalled their passion, his caresses, their lovemaking ...

Angry hooting brought her back to reality. She had failed to move up to fill the gap in front, and the moronic driver of a K reg GTi was impatiently assuming that another ten feet nearer to his destination was going to make all the difference. Jenny shook her head in disbelief at the stupidity of the man and edged along a couple more yards of the tarmac. It's true, she thought, GTi is an anagram of git.

She returned to her thoughts of James. She knew it was dangerous that he still found her attractive. She wondered if he thought about her, remembered their lovemaking. She hoped he did. She wanted to be desired by a man other than Nigel, if only to prove to herself that she was still attractive. That was all it was, just a silly sort of reassurance that she could still catch a man if she wanted, that just because she was married to one man, and had been for nearly twelve years, she hadn't become repulsive. It had nothing to do with James's charms and attractions, she told herself; it was just a confidence boost. But deep down she knew she was deceiving herself.

*

Nigel stood by the luggage carousel in Hanover airport, waiting for his two battered cases to appear. The journey had been uneventful and pleasant enough, although the meal offered on the Forces' charter had been particularly unappetising. At last he spotted his luggage and swung the two cases off the rubber conveyor belt and on to his trolley. Swiftly he wheeled his way through the blue channel and out to the main concourse. Instantly he spotted a uniformed lance corporal who had obviously been detailed to meet someone.

As Nigel approached him he said, 'Major Walker?' Nigel nodded. 'Follow me, sir, there's a Land Rover outside.' They threw the cases over the tailgate and in no time at all were barrelling along the autobahn heading towards Walsrode, Fallingbostel and, ultimately, Bergen-Hohne. The Land Rover was draughty and the distinctive high-pitched whine of its engine, now that it was travelling at over a hundred kilometres an hour, prevented further speech.

Nigel sat in the front and gazed at the featureless German Heide, a sandy heathland where the scrub was interspersed with birch trees and pine forest. He wondered if Hohne ranges had changed at all since he had last been there. He was certain that the old Hitler-barracks would not have altered; they had been built to last for the thousand-year Reich, which made them as soldier-proof as anything could be. He wondered which of the several messes surrounding the range area he was going to be housed in, not that it made much difference to him; they were all the same.

He was looking forward to rediscovering the delights of mess life: early-morning tea in bed, three good meals and the camaraderie of the bar in the evening. That was one thing in Hohne's favour: you could guarantee a good crowd in the bar. The barracks were stuck in the middle of nowhere, which meant that the single officers tended to be around during the week, since there were no night spots to tempt them away. There was a brothel called Mic-Mac's, lightly disguised as a disco, down the road, but that catered mainly for the soldiers – the officers having access to the teachers' and nurses' messes for female company – though most of the squaddies preferred the company of a four-pack and a video in their barrack blocks to the dubious delights of Mic-Mac's amenities.

The next day, shortly after dawn, Nigel found himself being driven around the perimeter road of the Hohne ranges, the giant training area that covered thousands of acres of German countryside. The tyres of the Land Rover beat a rhythmic tattoo against the concrete sections of the roadway as they skirted the firing points and impact areas. To one side of the road there were farms and fields full of crops and animals. Picture-postcard buildings, window boxes gay with red geraniums, and farm machinery in regimented rows gave an all-round air of solid Germanic affluence.

The view on the other side of the road was chilling in comparison. There the ground had been churned up in places into the worst desolation described in a Wilfred Owen poem. The dusty sand of the area meant that in the summer a fine white dust covered the vegetation near the deep scores cut across the land by armoured vehicles racing into mock battles; in the winter this turned into a quagmire of mud and filth. The hulks of vehicles used as targets for live firing rusted and rotted like monstrous carcasses amongst the bleak scenery. But Nigel was unmoved by the contrast. This was just what he had expected. Hohne ranges had always been like this and probably always would be.

The driver suddenly swung off the range road and on to a large pan of concrete that had a view across a deep valley to a distant hillside covered in heather and stunted bushes. This was the firing point from which the guns could fire live rounds at the remote impact area. On the pan were two massive self-propelled guns and a large group of men gathered to watch the impending trial of ammunition involving the artillery pieces. Nigel jumped out of the Land Rover and went to introduce himself. Despite his doubts at to his value at the trial, he was looking forward to it. There was something magnificent about this type of firepower.

They felt the noise as much as they heard it, a massive shock that hammered through their bodies. As they watched, the huge barrel recoiled, the gun rocked back on its tracks and they saw the shell turn into a tiny black dot as it disappeared down the range. There was a small flash and a puff of grey smoke four miles away. Nearly twenty seconds later they heard the crump of the explosion. By that time their ears had almost stopped reverberating with the strange high-pitched, metallic ringing that had accompanied the huge roar of the blast from the barrel; even their earphones had not been able to protect them against that. Slowly the crowd of onlookers regrouped and began to deliberate on the performance of the gun. Measurements were taken, calibrations read, discussions held and notes made. The lengthy process of the trial ground on.

Occasionally Nigel was called upon in his capacity as an expert on mechanical handling equipment, abbreviated to MHE, to make a contribution to a discussion or argument on some salient point to do with the gun and the transportation of its ammunition. At other times he contributed to the proceedings by pointing out the requirements from the resupply point of view. At about thirty-minute intervals the guns would let rip again, each time with a slight variation on the previous firing.

After four hours of this, Nigel was bored senseless. His doubts about his value at this trial were right. He was completely wasting his time here. Christ, and he had the rest of the week to go. The more he thought about it, the less reason he could think of for his presence here. They'd have been far better off with someone from the artillery desk. The generals had obviously got it completely wrong – a logistician wasn't what was needed at all. And if he was honest, the boffins and the gunners only seemed to ask him questions as a courtesy, to show that they still realised he was there. He didn't think that anything he had to say would have any bearing at all on whether this particular artillery piece and its ammunition were brought into service or not. His only consolation was the beautiful weather: warm sunshine and no breeze.

God, he thought, what would it have been like, stuck here in a downpour? He was beginning to wonder if anyone would notice if he slipped away, or didn't come back tomorrow. His flight home was not until Friday, there was nothing he could do about that, but standing here was certainly a waste of his time. He strolled over to the green tent, where a supply of coffee and snacks was to be found. He passed the time of day with the corporal sent from the cookhouse in Hohne to cater for the personnel on the ranges. The poor chap was obviously as bored as Nigel. Then he helped himself to a couple of appetising tuna and mayonnaise sandwiches and turned to go out. As he did so his foot twisted into a small but deep pothole in the concrete, and he collapsed heavily and awkwardly on to his ankle.

'Fucking hell,' he roared as the pain lanced up his leg.

'Christ, sir,' the concerned corporal said as he ran round from behind his trestle table, knocking a stack of paper cups flying. 'Are you OK?'

'No, I'm bloody not,' said Nigel through clenched teeth. The pain was excruciating. The corporal flapped ineffectually for a moment in front of Nigel, and then made as if to move him.

'Don't touch me,' Nigel yelled, stopping the poor man in his tracks. 'I'll be all right when I get my foot out from under me.' He thanked his lucky stars he had been wearing boots and puttees, not barrack-dress trousers and shoes. He felt that his high army boots might be acting as a sort of splint if he had in fact broken his ankle. He tried to lever his body up to edge his foot round from under him. The pain was appalling and became even worse as his arms, failing to take the strain for any longer, allowed his full weight to sink back on to his damaged foot again.

The corporal dashed out of the tent, approached the nearest officer and explained what had happened. At the back of the pan was an ambulance, always a requirement when live firing was taking place, and the corporal and the officer ran over to it to alert the crew. Two minutes later Nigel was in the safe hands of experts.

'Hmm,' said the young-looking captain wearing the insignia of the Royal Army Medical Corps, 'nasty, this one.' He sucked on his teeth a little longer and then announced that he would have to cut Nigel's boot off. 'Once we've done that,' he said cheerfully, 'I can see how bad the damage is. I may have to send you down to hospital at Hanover to get it X-rayed. Sometimes it's hard to tell the difference between a sprain and a break.'

Nigel lay on the examination table in the medical centre at Hohne and looked despondently at the ceiling. He felt a complete fool. Fancy tripping over a hole in the ground like that. What a prat!

The doctor got busy with a scalpel and began to cut through

the leather of the issue boot. Nigel tried to keep his mind on other matters, anything but think about the throbbing ache in his ankle.

'Right, I'll be as gentle as I can, but this may hurt a bit.' Nigel knew from Jenny's ante-natal classes that tensing against pain was the worst way to combat it, but he couldn't help himself.

'Shit!' he said through his teeth, as the doctor inched his boot away from his grotesquely swollen ankle. He could feel sweat breaking out on his forehead as his foot twisted slightly when the boot came free.

'There, that wasn't too bad, was it? It's all over now.' Nigel wondered if the doctor wasn't some manic reincarnation of Dr Mengele – not too bad? It had been agonising. Slowly his muscles untensed again. At least taking his sock off wasn't going to hurt, and there was another bonus too – he'd get sent home now.

Jenny was in despair. She had just two weeks left to go, and she had only finished twelve models. Rows and rows of unpainted blanks stared at her from the shelves around the garage. The air brush was harder to use than she had first thought, and she had ruined a couple of nearly finished bookends with dribbles of varnish.

'I know it'll be quicker in the long run,' she said to Pan, who had popped in to see how she was getting on, 'but I haven't got used to it yet. And the light in here doesn't help matters. I could do with some better fluorescent strips in the ceiling, but the expense isn't justified.'

'Why don't you work with the door open?' said Pan, who was feeling distinctly chilly in her cotton sundress now that she was inside the cool gloom of Jenny's garage.

'Greenfly,' said Jenny shortly. 'The little buggers get stuck in the paint and wreck the finish.'

'What'll you do when you've finished this lot?'

'If I ever do, I shall go and lie down for a whole day, then I'll get to know my family again.'

'Is it as bad as that?'

'Oh no, Pan. Well, I'm a bit behind my timetable, that's all.' Jenny realised that she sounded as though she was regretting the order. 'It's just that the children have had to fend for themselves rather. It hasn't helped matters that Nigel is away in Germany this week.'

'So you don't want me to see if I can rustle up some more business for you? It's just that I thought, well, if you wanted me to, I could be your agent. Frankly, I'm bored with just Gabriella to keep me busy. As Annette only has Christopher in the afternoons I thought she might like to mind Gabriella for me in the mornings.'

'Yes, but if you're going to spend money on child-minding – I mean, you can't work for nothing, and I can't afford...' Jenny stopped. The question of paying Pandora was going to be tricky.

'Look,' said Pan, 'if it'll make you feel better, you can pay me a percentage for the orders I get you. That's normal practice.'

'Can I think about it?' Jenny had had to make a bigger initial outlay than she'd intended and now realised how slim her profit margin was. On the other hand, if she got some more orders, perhaps not quite so big and not in such a short time, she might be able to afford a band saw and turn them out quicker.

'No problem,' said Pan casually, hiding her disappointment that Jenny's reaction was only lukewarm. She'd fancied the chance to wheel and deal in some of her favourite London stores. What she was aware of and what Jenny wasn't, was Belinda's reaction when she had seen the bookends.

'These are absolutely brill. It's exactly the sort of thing we're always looking for at GTC. And it'll appeal to the tourists who just come in to gawp, as well as our regular customers. We'll certainly be able to shift dozens of them.'

Pan was certain they were going to fly off the shelves at GTC, and if they sold well there, then Harrods, and Selfridges and the other Oxford Street stores could probably be persuaded to stock them too. But there was no point in rushing Jenny. She would have to get used to the idea of running a proper business at her own pace. Having sown the idea, she left Jenny to think about it.

Jenny didn't think about what Pan had said; she was staring at the rows of unfinished bookends: forty-four pairs to complete, and only a week and a half in which to do it if they were to be at GTC's warehouse on time. They were all assembled, and some had their base coats on; it was only the painting to be done, but it was a job that couldn't be hurried. Jenny knew that if she rushed it, then they would end up substandard. She couldn't risk sending anything but the best to her first customer, not if she was going to make a go of this, as Pan had suggested. She wasn't sure if she was going to carry on; the hassle looked as if it was going to hugely outweigh any remuneration. One thing was certain: looking at the little statues wasn't achieving anything, but her growing feeling of panic and despondency was preventing her from thinking straight. She couldn't make a muck of this order; if she did they might send them back and all this effort would be wasted.

'Coo-ee, can I come in?'

Oh God, that was all she needed – mindless Marian and her motormouth. Jenny decided she would just have to be blunt with the woman.

'Yes, but I've not got time for a chat. I'm up to my eyes.'

'I know. I've just passed Pandora dropping off Gabriella for Annette to child-mind. She's off to play tennis with some friends – and she was saying that you were worried about getting finished on time. I wondered ... If there's a problem, can I do something? My art tutor says I'm very good at detail – oh! you'd like my tutor so much, he's so charming and he does such wonderful watercolours himself—' Jenny could see that Marian was about to go on to automatic pilot with her mouth. She really didn't have time for that; not now, at any rate.

'Sorry, Marian, but what exactly *do* you want to do?'

Marian looked slightly nettled by Jenny's brusqueness.

'Well,' her lips rather compressed, 'well, I was only going to say that if you would like me to help paint some of the detail, I would be happy to, but I don't want to impose myself on you.'

Jenny stared hard at Marian for a moment. She was torn between knowing that if she didn't get some help she was going to blow this order, and wondering whether being cooped up with this witless woman for the next week or so was worth it.

Marian was feeling irritated; after all she'd offered to help out of kindness, and it wasn't as if she'd offer her skills to just anyone. She hoped Jenny appreciated what she was doing.

'Can I give you a trial?' Jenny said eventually, having done some sums in her head. If this order arrived late GTC might not even accept it. And then what would she do with all these bloody bookends? 'Copy the detail from a finished one on to one of these with just its base coat on. I can't pay you much. Not more than three pounds fifty an hour. How long can you work?'

Not even a thank-you – really! Marian sniffed, and was tempted to tell Jenny that the offer was off, but the truth was, she was bored at home. She'd finished making the curtains and stencilling the kitchen cupboards. There was nothing more she could do to decorate her house. A little pin-money job would be rather pleasant. Charitably, she wondered if Jenny was just being so short because she was overstressed. That was probably it. Once she had some help, she'd probably enjoy having someone to chat to while she was working.

'I can work while Charlotte and Emily are at their friend's house. I'll have to go at three to collect them.'

'What about tomorrow? It's half-term, remember. Child-minding costs two quid per child per hour.'

'I know, but if I only come in the mornings Annette has said she'll look after them this week as a favour.'

Jenny wondered how many other women on the patch were privy to her problem with meeting her deadline. Obviously it had been discussed by quite a group of wives already. Not that she could gripe – everyone was being so helpful.

'OK, you're hired. But only if you don't make mistakes. I haven't time to sort them out, I'm on too tight a schedule.'

Jenny sorted out the brushes and paints for Marian, and gave her an example to copy. She resisted the temptation to look over her shoulder – that would be unfair on the poor woman – but, from her occasional quick glances at Marian's handiwork, she seemed to be doing OK. Jenny got on with painting gold buttons on half a dozen models in front of her. When she had finished she went across to Marian.

'Gosh! That's really good.' She couldn't help the surprise in her voice. Marian preened herself inwardly. She liked being appreciated.

'Keep up that standard, Marian, and I think I'm going to make it.' Suddenly the dreadful deadline that had been looming inexorably seemed attainable. Jenny felt the huge pressure begin to lift from her shoulders.

They worked on steadily until lunchtime, when Jenny suggested they both took a break and had some sandwiches in the house. For the first time in a week and a half Jenny allowed herself a lunch hour. So far she and Marian had finished two pairs between them and, with Marian picking up speed now that she was getting used to her task, they would probably manage another two or three pairs each before Marian had to collect her children. As she cut the crusts off the bread, Jenny wondered if she was going to be able to spare the time to take the children to the play park this afternoon. They had been shockingly ignored for too long now. Christopher was getting very truculent, and she hardly had time to see anything of them these days. Annette was great with them, gave them lots of fun, but when all was said and done, she wasn't their mother, and Jenny was paying someone to take her place, something she had sworn she would never do.

'Come on Marian, back to the grindstone,' she said when they had both finished their snack. She was beginning to feel more tolerant of Marian's prattle. At least when she worked she didn't jabber on, but concentrated on her painting.

'Ready when you are,' replied Marian. They walked into the garage that was laid out in such an organised way, thanks to Annette's talent with the power drill, with its new wall of shelves above their work tables and paints.

Marian said, 'What are you going to do with all this when you've finished this order?'

Jenny looked at her workshop. It was much too sophisticated just to go back to making ones and twos. Any special orders she might get from people on the patch would soon dry up.

'You know, Annette will miss your custom if you stop. She really likes having your children to mind. It means she's always around for Victoria, and she feels she's making a contribution to the family income. And I wouldn't mind a job for more than just a few days.' Marion surprised herself by being so forthright.

Jenny knew that Marian was right. She wouldn't be able just

to kick it into touch when she'd finished this lot. Pan's words about finding her more orders echoed in her brain. She resolved to work out the financial implications of employing Pan on commission. If the figures made sense, she would go and see her and take her up on her offer of acting as agent. Jenny felt as though she were taking control of her life again, in a way she hadn't done since she had first married. It felt good.

Chapter Thirteen

Fiona dropped in on Jenny just as Marian was wiping her hands with white spirit before packing up her brushes for the day.

'Hello, Jenny. Hi, Marian,' she said. She eyed the row of glistening soldiers. 'Production looks as though it's going well.'

'Yes. I've just put Marian on the payroll, and I think I've got a chance of finishing on time.'

'That's great. I just popped over to say I'm off down to my sister's in Bath for a few days.'

'Oh, right. Well, have a nice time. When are you due back?'

'Friday afternoon, I thought.'

'Have a safe journey.'

'I will, 'bye.' Fiona left without further ado.

'It was nice of Fiona to tell you she's going to be away,' said Marian.

'Hmm ... Oh, yes, it was.' But Jenny was more concerned that James was going to be on his own for a few days. Well, forewarned was forearmed, as they said, but was the sudden rush of adrenalin due to fear or anticipation?

'It's a very nasty break, Major Walker. We're going to have to set it under anaesthetic.' The QA captain, looking very attractive in her smart red and grey uniform, was sympathetic. The poor bloke was going to be in a great deal of discomfort for a few days yet.

'Great, that's all I need. How long will I have to stay here once it's done?' Nigel's face was an unattractive putty colour, which accentuated the sweat standing out on his top lip and forehead. If he had been feeling better he would have greatly appreciated the ministrations of the bubbly blonde by his bed, but right now all he wanted was to get rid of the pain.

'Oh, just a day or two, I should imagine. It won't need traction, but it'll be a bit sore for a while.' No point in telling the man it would be bloody agony for twelve hours and downright misery for a further forty-eight. 'Once we're sure that we've set it correctly, you'll be able to get about a bit, and then we'll see about getting you a flight.'

Nigel was lying in a bed in the near-empty men's surgical ward of the British Military Hospital, Hanover. He'd visited it often enough in the past, to commiserate with his soldiers who'd been taken ill or who'd been the victims of car crashes. Soldiers were, by nature, a fit bunch, so to see so many unfilled beds wasn't novel. No NHS-style waiting lists for British Forces overseas.

'We'll take you down to theatre in about an hour. We can't operate before then because of the coffee you drank earlier. Sorry about that, but there it is.'

'Can I have something to stop it aching?'

'I'll be giving you your pre-med shortly; that'll ease it a bit and make you feel woozy. It'll probably help quite a lot.' And by the time you realise that the pain hasn't got any better, you'll be on your way to theatre, she added silently to herself.

Jenny, sitting at the dining room table that evening, poring over a calculator and a notebook, was unaware of her husband's plight. The normally efficient system for notifying next of kin about accidents had failed. The BMH in Hanover assumed that the medical centre in Hohne had rung Nigel's wife while he waited for the ambulance; and the medical centre had thought that as he'd have to be admitted to the hospital, the staff there would carry out the procedure. As Jenny came to the end of her calculations with increasing excitement, Nigel was slipping into unconsciousness in the operating theatre.

Twice she checked her figures and twice she came to the same answer.

Surely I've made a mistake, she said to herself. This just can't be right. She'd allowed for the tax man's cut, she'd lopped off a chunk for VAT, she'd put in a generous estimate for the cost of materials, wages and child-care, but whichever way she looked at it, if she could get production up to fifty pairs of bookends a week, which she could with two other people like Marian, she could make nearly £15,000 a year profit. It seemed an awful lot of money. She checked her figures again. There was no mistake.

Excitedly she ran next door to Annette's house. 'Annette, is Peter home yet?'

'Yes, why? Is something wrong?'

'No, nothing. It's just that Nigel's away and I must go and have a chat to Pan. I was hoping you could keep an eye on the kids for me.'

'Of course.' Annette grabbed her keys, yelled a goodbye to Peter and shut the front door. The two women walked back up the path towards Jenny's house.

As they reached Jenny's front door she said, 'I'll only be about fifteen minutes, thirty at the most. Put it on the bill!'

'Don't worry about that. Go and see Pan – do I get to hear what the excitement is all about?'

'I'll tell you when I get back.' In her enthusiasm she almost ran down her path and on to the pavement. As she came round the corner, she barrelled into James, who was just turning into his gateway.

'Hey, steady on,' he said as he caught her by the shoulders and held on to her just a little longer than necessary to prevent her from losing her balance.

'James, I'm sorry. I didn't mean to bowl you over.'

'What's the hurry?'

'Oh, it just seems as though I can make a proper go of selling bookends.'

'Hey, congratulations.'

'Thanks, I can't stop,' said Jenny. Before he had time to reply, she swung past him and half ran, half walked down the road. James watched her back view for a few moments, then went to put a bottle of champagne on ice.

Tors was on the telephone, calming down a girlfriend who had just been jilted, while Fiona and Jeremy were poring over an old photograph album from Hong Kong. They were both feeling comfortably full after a large dinner which Tors had prepared in honour of their reunion after seventeen years. Mellowed by a couple of bottles of extremely good hock, a present from Jeremy, they were reminiscing about the good times spent in the Crown Colony. They sat together on the dilapidated sofa in the drawing room of Tors's first-floor, high-ceilinged Bohemian flat. Shawls, fans and cobwebs hung in equal quantities from the picture rail running around the room, and the floor was a jumble of different-coloured mats and rugs, collected by Tors when she had trekked across Africa. They had formed the inspiration for the designs and patterns that she now used in her jewellery business. The bold, bright colours on her bangles and necklaces could be found in shops all over the West Country. The mess which surrounded her at home, and her chaotic love life did not reflect her skills as an entrepreneur, which were more than adequate to support her very comfortably.

Despite the French window leading to the Regency balcony, the light in the room wasn't good, but it was still no excuse for Jeremy and Fiona to be leaning quite so close together as they squinted at the snaps taken nearly twenty years previously with an old Kodak Instamatic. The colour in the prints had faded to bluish tones, and the focus was not always sharp, but Jeremy and Fiona were still able to identify forgotten friends and scenes. The pictures jerked barely remembered incidents back into the forefront of their minds. In their memories, the weather was always perfect and the parties the best ever. Any boredom and discomfort, heat rash and unhappiness had been banished by time. They could only remember the idyll.

'What was the name of that awful girl whose father was some sort of civil servant? You know the one. She was dreadfully fat and used to prance around in tennis whites. No one would play with her because she was so boring.'

The light suddenly dawned for Fiona. 'Oh, I remember now. Norma, no, Norah.'

'That's it – nauseous Norah. I thought she had a crush on me at one stage. It was terrifying. She kept asking me if I was going to the summer ball.'

'Was that why you invited me? To make sure you didn't end up with her?'

'Not at all. I invited you because you were by far the prettiest girl in the Colony. I was surprised when you agreed. I thought you would be escorted by one of the Gurkha officers.'

The two old friends were oblivious to the ping of the telephone as the call finished, and to the click of the door opening. Tors surveyed their back view from the doorway before she drifted back into the room, swathed in an orange and green kaftan, cigarette in one hand, glass in the other. She noticed how close together her two guests were. You couldn't get a cigarette paper between them, she thought.

She heard Jeremy's comment and said, 'The officers out there were always frightened away by Mummy. She was so fierce to anyone who called to take us out that they never came back a second time.'

Jeremy swivelled round on the sofa to look at Tors, standing behind them.

'So why didn't I get the treatment?'

'I suppose she thought you were too young to have dishonourable intentions. Besides which, your parents were friends with ours.' Tors changed the subject. 'I'm going to have to go round to Molly's house for a while. The poor girl is in a rotten state and she wants a shoulder to cry on. If you could just leave the light on in the hall when you go to bed, I'll see you tomorrow.' She grabbed a huge length of cloth, which she flung dramatically over her shoulders, and slammed the front door behind her.

Fiona suddenly realised that Jeremy had not changed his position from when he had half turned to look over his shoulder. His leg was still pressing hard against her. Slowly she closed the photograph album and quite deliberately kissed him.

When Jenny left her some thirty minutes later, Pan got out an old indexed notebook that was tucked into the back of her bureau. She went through it, copying some of the names and numbers she came across on to a sheet of foolscap. She had been entirely honest when she had said that she had sold knickers in Harrods before her marriage. What she hadn't mentioned was that she had risen to be a junior buyer for the store before Rupe's postings, and pregnancy, had put paid to it all. She still had contacts in the retail trade, and although these acquaintances might not be able to help her directly, they would probably be able to steer her towards the people who could. As with all things, the bottom line wasn't what you knew, but who. If she was going to act as agent for Jenny, she was going to make damn certain that Jenny got as many orders as she could cope with.

It wasn't the commission which Pan stood to earn which made her so keen to help, but the prospect of finding a way to escape the boring routine of motherhood. As she'd said to a close friend a few months back, she would be the ideal mother if only she had a nanny. She was sure that Gabriella would have a much better deal if she spent her mornings with Annette, who adored doing all those boring, repetitive things like stacking beakers and playing peek-a-boo. Pan couldn't wait to get back into a smart suit and return to work.

Annette was as delighted as Pan when Jenny told her about her decision to try to expand her business. She'd enjoyed looking after Jenny's kids over the past couple of weeks, and had not been looking forward to the gap what would be left if Jenny didn't carry on producing her bookends wholesale. Even her husband Peter, who'd complained somewhat to begin with about the state of the house each evening, had admitted that the extra money was handy – now he'd got used to cutting a path through the mass of toys which blocked his way from the front door to his slippers. Jenny invited her to join her in a celebratory drink, but Annette declined. She had a mountain of ironing to tackle, and Peter really would throw a track if he didn't have a clean shirt for the morning.

Jenny poured herself a gin and went into the dining room to gloat over her figures again. She was just sketching out a plan for a better layout in the garage to accommodate a third workbench when she was interrupted by the doorbell. She expected it to be Pan with a list of possible stores to tackle, so she was particularly surprised to see James standing on her doorstep, brandishing champagne.

'How about you and Nigel joining me in a glass to celebrate your good news?' he said, walking uninvited into the hall.

'No, honestly, James. It's a very kind offer, but no.'

'Don't be ridiculous. Where do you keep the glasses?' He

strode purposefully through the hall and into the kitchen, where he began to open cupboards.

'Ah, here we are,' he said, finding a couple of tumblers.

'No, really, James. And Nigel isn't here.'

'Isn't he?' said James, feigning surprise with consummate skill. 'Where is he this time? Somewhere more glamorous than Derby, I hope?'

'He's in Hohne.'

'Then the answer is no. Poor man.' He put the glasses on the table and began to undo the wire and twist off the cork. 'It's tough that he isn't here to share the bubbly, but we mustn't let it spoil the fun.' The cork popped off and James got the first tumbler under the bottle just as the foaming wine began to cascade out.

'Please go away,' mumbled Jenny. 'This really isn't a good idea.'

'Rubbish, it's always a good idea to drink champagne when there's something to celebrate.'

'That's not what I meant.'

'Come on. I've poured you a glass now. One drink with me isn't going to hurt, is it?'

Jenny took the glass, knowing that by doing so she was entering into a conspiracy. She wouldn't be able to tell Nigel about this – he'd never understand. Then she remembered the condom wrapper in his suitcase.

'You're right,' she said defiantly, with a sudden change of heart. She took the glass and had a large swig. 'One drink never did any harm.'

She led him into the sitting room. Outside the hazy dusk of early summer was deepening. Midges were dancing under the trees in the garden, and a blackbird was prodding around on the lawn, hoping for a last meal before night fell. Jenny switched on a couple of table lamps and drew the curtains. Instantly the room was transformed by the warm golden glow from the lights. James sat in an armchair while Jenny sank into the sofa. She took another gulp and giggled; the champagne and her decision to expand had made her light-headed.

'It's like old times,' she said.

James shrugged. 'I suppose it is,' he conceded. There was a pause. Then he said, 'Tell me about your plans.'

Jenny needed no second bidding. She was bursting with excitement at the prospects of her business, and had been denied the chance of getting Nigel's approval and support. As she talked, she drained her glass. James moved over to refill it and then settled himself beside her. He remembered the look of lust in her eyes the last time he'd been in her company, and searched for it again, but she was too excited about her news to be thinking of sex. All the same, her dark-brown eyes, alive with passion about her prospects, were as arousing to James as ever. He put his own glass down and took hers from her hand, placing it carefully on the table by the sofa. He could have her now. She belonged to him, not Nigel, and he was going to prove it.

'I still want you, Jenny. Just as much as I did back in Woolwich.'

Jenny nearly collapsed with the surge of raw desire which flooded through her. James saw it in her eyes and moved closer to her on the sofa. He put his hand on her leg and slid it up her jeans, until it was burrowing towards her crotch.

'Oh, James,' breathed Jenny, her voice hoarse with craving. Expertly, James slid down her zip and pushed his fingers under the flimsy material of her panties. He discovered that they were soaked. He slid off the sofa so that he was on his knees, facing her. Carefully he undid her shirt buttons, and then the one at the waist of her trousers. Jenny arched her back as he began to stroke her body.

She opened her eyes and looked at James, and it was then that she saw an ill-concealed flicker of triumph. She realised that he saw her as a conquest, the recapture of a prize. She was just a military objective to be seized. Her desire evaporated in an instant.

'No, no. Stop it,' she said, clamping her legs together and starting to rebutton her blouse.

'Don't be ridiculous, Jenny.' He was now driven by primeval instincts more than his initial, planned seduction. She couldn't stop him, not now. He grabbed her wrist to allow her shirt to fall open again, and then bent his head towards her breasts. Jenny began to panic. She couldn't do it, not now, not here, not with her children upstairs. This was adultery and she wasn't going to commit it. It didn't matter what Nigel had done. Going down the same road was only going to make things worse.

'James, stop,' she pleaded. He gripped her arm tighter. Jenny struggled, which seemed only to excite him more. She didn't dare scream. It would wake the children, and they must be protected from witnessing this. James's chin was above her knee. With an almighty effort she jerked it upwards and heard a sickening crack as her patella connected with his face. James's expression turned from lust to hatred.

'You stupid bitch,' he snarled. 'What the fuck do you think you're playing at?' Blood dribbled from his mouth; he pulled a handkerchief from his pocket and dabbed at it.

'I said stop and I meant it,' panted Jenny, frantically buttoning her clothes now that he'd freed her arms.

'God, what a little cock-tease you are. I ought to teach you a lesson.' James rose to his feet and stood menacingly over Jenny. She looked at him, full in the face. She knew he mustn't see her fear, but she was convinced he was about to hit her.

'Get out,' she whispered. 'You barged in here, it was your idea. Not mine. You were the one who made all the moves. Now bugger off or I'll tell Fiona all about it when she gets home.'

'Bitch,' he spat at her. 'You wouldn't dare.' Jenny didn't reply; he was probably right. 'You're going to regret this.' She stared at him until he dropped his gaze and stormed from the house, dabbing at his still-bleeding mouth. He slammed the front door so hard it made the windows rattle, then Jenny collapsed sobbing in a heap on to the floor.

It was not until the next morning that someone at the British Military Hospital at Hanover rang Jenny to inform her that Nigel had been admitted. She'd been tense since breakfast, worrying about any moves James might make. He'd been so angry when he left she was terrified about what he might do next. When the phone rang she jumped as if she'd been jabbed with a pin. Marian, busy with her painting, didn't notice.

Jenny's hand hesitated for a moment over the phone before she grabbed it.

'Hello,' she said rather tightly, frightened that it might be James.

'Mrs Walker?' said an unknown voice. Oh, hell. It was going to be someone trying to sell her double-glazing or a new kitchen. She relaxed and was just about to launch into her 'this is a rented house, you're wasting your time and mine' routine when the voice continued.

'This is the admissions officer at BMH Hanover. I'm afraid we've had to admit your husband with a minor injury. I can assure you,' the unknown official hurried on, to prevent more than an instant of distress, 'that it's nothing to be worried about, and he'll be discharged tomorrow. However, as next of kin, it's our duty to inform you.'

'I see,' said Jenny, taken aback. 'What sort of minor injury is it?'

'He's hurt his ankle. In fact, it was a pretty nasty break, but it's been set and he's feeling much more comfortable. We should be able to discharge him in a day or two.' There was a pause while Jenny took the news on board. 'He'll be able to phone you himself soon. In the mean time, can I give him a message from you?'

'Oh, just wish him well and tell him how sorry I am.' Jenny racked her brains to think of something witty that would cheer him up, but failed. Rather tritely she said, 'Give him our love.'

'I'll make sure he's told, Mrs Walker. Goodbye.'

Fiona stretched luxuriously and opened her eyes to see Jeremy standing beside the bed, stark naked and proffering a cup of tea. She noticed he had a tan all over.

'Get up, sleepyhead,' he said with his attractive grin. Fiona yawned and stretched again, letting the covers slip from her curvaceous body and revealing that her auburn hair was natural.

'What time is it?'

'Nearly ten. Your sister has gone to work, having given me a lecture on my morals.'

Fiona made a moue of disapproval.

'She's a fine one to talk. She behaves like a cat on heat half the time. I hardly ever stray.'

Jeremy sat on the edge of the bed.

'Do I gather, then, that this isn't the first time?' He raised one eyebrow in query. Fiona shrugged and leaned forward in the bed, resting on one elbow. She gazed at Jeremy, a misleading picture of innocence.

'Look, I know that James sometimes plays away from home. I'd have to be a halfwit not to know. He's a very attractive man and he's no saint. I never ask him about what he does when he's away, and he doesn't tell me. I think he imagines I'd get frightfully upset if I knew. I know he justifies what he does by regarding sex and love as two separate issues, but he expects me to live by a different set of standards. Well, I just don't happen to agree with him; goose and gander get the same sauce.' She licked her lips. 'Anyway, let's not talk about sex, let's do it some more.'

She put her cup of tea down on the bedside table and pulled Jeremy into bed with her again. He was doubly attractive: not just an exciting lover, but wealthy, too. She wondered if he would object if she proposed a visit to him during the summer holidays. No doubt James would be too busy to go out to the Far East. That would be a shame.

Nigel, lying in his hospital bed, was flicking through some magazines thoughtfully supplied by the ward sister. He'd almost exhausted the pile; it wasn't a great selection: a couple of issues of *Country Life*, some car magazines and a few glossy women's fashion journals. The sort of stuff that he would never, normally, have looked at, but boredom had driven him to it. The WRVS trolley selling newspapers had not come round, and the bookshop was on the ground floor; Nigel had been told to stay in bed and rest his ankle completely. He had soon read all the articles and was reduced to looking at the advertisements. It seemed to him that any ad that was trying to sell something to do with the country always had people in it dressed in waxed jackets. It's like it's a bloody uniform, he thought. Slowly an idea for Jenny's bookends began to form in his head. He still wasn't keen on the idea of her turning them out full time, but there was no reason why she shouldn't have other sorts of figures decorating them, even if she reverted to just doing private commissions. Before he could forget it again, he rang his bell for the ward sister and asked for paper and a pen.

*

After the children had had their tea, Jenny took them all to the play park. Christopher was swinging happily while Jenny sat on a bench and reflected. Marian was a marvel, it looked as though they would easily make the deadline, she had decided to try to go into mass production, the sun was shining and her children were healthy and carefree. She had everything going for her, and yet last night she'd nearly wrecked the lot. If it hadn't been for that invidious piece of paper in Nigel's suitcase, and her stupid, stupid behaviour with James, none of her problems would have happened. With a feeling of cold horror, she wondered what Nigel's reaction would be if he found out about what had been going on while he was in hospital. Supposing James told him? Jenny shut her eyes in despair. It would be too stupid if this made them split up. It wasn't as if she'd actually *done* anything. But she'd thought about it. She suspected that in Nigel's head it would amount to the same thing. She'd been able to dismiss his infidelity; men had had flings since they'd come down from the trees. But for a woman to do the same ...

Christopher was totally engrossed in seeing how high he could swing. She let her thoughts wander back to the last time she and Nigel had almost split up, before they had even got married. God, that had been a mother and father of rows, and all because she hadn't told him who her ex-husband was. It had never crossed her mind that he didn't know she had reverted to her maiden name. She thought everyone knew. Neither had it occurred to her that he might know Jamie.

She remembered how they had met. She'd gone over to a cocktail party at Soltau with Susan. It hadn't promised to be a particularly scintillating occasion, since the local German population had been invited too. Formal do's with a language barrier thrown in for good measure were invariably tedious, but there was going to be a party for the Brits afterwards and Jenny was looking forward to that. When they had arrived, Susan had introduced her to a young Scottish officer called Nigel. He had seemed very proper and rather standoffish, but he was polite enough, and attentive to Jenny. His manners were impeccable, but Jenny could recognise Sandhurst training. He showed Jenny into the anteroom after she had hung up her coat, and suggested they stand near the fireplace.

'The food will all appear through this door,' he explained to Jenny. 'If you don't want to starve for the next couple of hours, I suggest you stick with me.' He had been proved right once the party got under way, and the waitress had bustled to and fro, passing right in front of them with trays loaded with meatballs, dips and chicken vol-au-vents. After a while Jenny had protested that she would not be able to manage the dinner promised later if she had any more to eat. Nigel, who had appeared so proper at the start of the evening, was soon making her fall about laughing, at the expense of their unsuspecting German guests, by speculating about their personal habits.

'My vife, Brunhilda, she has ze most vunderbar hairy armpits,' said Nigel, indicating a particularly large German woman busily shovelling a crumbling vol-au-vent into her wide mouth. 'Ve cut off ze hairs each month and ve use them to scour ze pans in ze kitchen. A gut idea, ja?' Jenny, who was just a touch tipsy, had giggled and begged Nigel not to continue. She was sure that if one of the formidable Germans had approached her she would not be able to open her mouth without roaring with laughter.

'I could cause a breakdown in diplomatic relations if I did that. Then what would my boss say?'

'I don't suppose he'd mind so very much. It would give everyone a chance to find out if our battle plans really do work.' Nigel grinned at her. 'I think it's quite a good idea. Shall we see if we can be really irresponsible and start World War Three?'

'You are a dreadful man, Nigel, and a bad influence. I shall have to pull rank in a minute and discipline you.'

'Oh, goody, are you going to spank me?' he said longingly. Jenny giggled again.

'Only if you beg me to.'

At that moment, Susan had turned up. 'I see you two are getting on. The booze is going to stop flowing any minute now, to give the Germans the hint that it's time they pushed off. We don't have to be on our best behaviour for much longer.'

'Jenny hasn't been behaving at all so far,' said Nigel. 'She has been making the most dreadful comments about our illustrious guests.' Jenny protested so loudly she caused several people to turn and look. She dodged behind Nigel, mortified.

As she sat in the sunshine now, watching her son swinging as high as he could, she recalled the fun they had had, all those years back. How Nigel had driven her over to the Mohne See and sung the Dambusters' March at the top of his voice as they walked across the dam; doing his bit for Anglo-German relations, he had said. How they had gone skiing together in the Hertz Mountains, and the night they had spent together in a guest house with the biggest bed Jenny had ever seen. They had bounced around in it for ages before going downstairs for supper. It was only when they were halfway through their meal that they realised that the house was so creaky that every movement upstairs reverberated down. Goodness only knows what the owners of the establishment had thought about the carryings-on in the bedroom earlier, Jenny thought.

Those had been wonderful days, when they both had good jobs, worked hard during the week and had the time, the money and the youth to make the most of their weekends. She recalled how Nigel had introduced Susan to a friend from his Battalion. As a foursome they had had even more fun. They had skied and tobogganed together in the winter, picnicked and walked in the summer and dined and gone to the cinema in the evenings. They never seemed to stop laughing or having fun. It had all been quite idyllic. Until the day when Susan had mentioned Jamie – and Jenny's past had been revealed.

She went cold, even now, just thinking about the row. Nigel had revealed a temper that she had no idea existed. He'd accused her of deliberately trying to conceal the details from him by not using her married name. Her protestations – that she had had no such intentions, that she had reverted to her own name because she hated her married one so much – had cut no ice with him. She had not been able to believe how angry he had been, how childish. The horror of it all was still vivid. No, thought Jenny, she was just going to have to hope and pray that everything that had happened in the past few days was going to be forgotten by everyone. If Nigel got that angry again, there was no telling how it might end.

Chapter Fourteen

'My cab will be here in a moment,' said Jeremy, as he zipped up his overnight bag with a typical flourish.

'So soon?' replied Fiona petulantly. 'You don't have to be in London till this evening. It's only one thirty now.'

'I've got a mass of papers to read when I get there. I've got a meeting first thing on Friday. The bank isn't paying me to enjoy myself, you know.' The bank, the Bank of Shanghai, was paying him and paying him very highly to clinch a deal with Barclays. His ability as a negotiator was why he was paid an extraordinarily large salary for such a relatively young executive. At barely thirty-five, he was one of the highest paid members of the bank's staff.

Fiona put her arms around him and kissed him again, letting her tongue linger succulently between his lips.

'So you have enjoyed yourself?' she murmured as she nuzzled against him.

'I'm glad I came.'

'Mmm, it was simultaneous,' said Fiona wickedly, sliding a hand down to his crotch. He gently untangled himself from her embrace and reflected again what a stroke of luck it had been that his mother, still friends with Tors's parents, had mentioned to them her son's brief visit to England, and that Tors had responded to the news with an invitation to stay. What he didn't know was that Tors's offer of hospitality had largely been engineered by Mrs Fulton, Jeremy's mother, and Tors's parents, who had told Tors how much Jeremy wanted to visit Bath. The three of them were conspiring in some matchmaking, since they had almost given up hope that their children would find suitable partners and settle down. When Mrs Fulton had suggested to Jeremy what fun it would be to look up his old school friend, she had not envisaged that it would be Tors's sister he had literally 'looked up'.

Jeremy had fallen on Tors's invitation when it had arrived; with the prospect of a week with nothing much to do – 'Go early to the old country, have a few days' break,' his boss had offered – the chance of a few days in Bath had sounded very pleasant. Having lived for nearly twenty years in Hong Kong, he had few friends left in England, and the idea of yet another sojourn in an anonymous Hilton hotel had not appealed. Worse was the possibility of being swamped by his geriatric mother's cloying and effusive fussing. Meeting up with an old friend and enjoying some company of his own age had been a far more attractive prospect. Fiona's presence had been an unexpected bonus. It was a shame she had got herself hitched to James, who sounded a bit of a bastard.

He gave Fiona a kiss on the cheek and said, 'It's been a great few days for me. I wasn't expecting to see you. No one told me you were going to be here.'

'Tors thought I'd like to see you again. She very sweetly invited me down. Besides which, I wanted to get away for a few days.'

'Didn't James object?'

'I didn't tell him you would be here, silly. And anyway, even if he knew, I could say you were mad about Tors.'

'I got the impression that our parents wouldn't mind some sort of liaison between Tors and me.'

'I'm certain mine would be thrilled. They're having a real panic about grandchildren. I'm blowed if I'm going to have any kids, and Tors doesn't want to settle down. I suppose it's our way of getting our own back on them. They didn't seem to want us as children. We both hated boarding school but we had to put up with it just the same. Now Mother only seems interested in us as breeding stock.'

Jeremy felt sorry for Fiona. Poor kid. In Hong Kong she had been the envy of all the army brats: pretty, clever, and with a high-ranking father. Perhaps she hadn't been so enviable after all. With sudden realisation, Jeremy discovered that he had more than just sympathy for Fiona; his feelings went deeper than that, despite his knowledge that she had a husband, although it was obvious that it wasn't a marriage made in heaven. But he was of the old school, where only complete shits went out deliberately to break marriages up. He wouldn't let on to her how he felt. They had both agreed that their affair was just some fun; neither of them was going to get involved.

'Poor Fi,' he said. 'You never did get on with your mother did you? I'm sorry we haven't had longer together. Perhaps you and James can come and see me out east later this year.' He heard the hooting of a car down in the street. He looked out of the window.

'That's my cab. You've got my address and phone number. I'll have to go now. Let's make sure it's not nearly twenty years before we get together again.' He kissed her tenderly, then grabbed his grip and left. Fiona, aware that she was going to miss him deeply, began to plan how she could go out to Hong Kong. On her own.

Nigel flew home from Germany on Friday and was greeted by Jenny and the children at Luton airport. From the moment he hobbled through the arrivals hall to the time they drew up outside their house, the kids bombarded him with questions and news, leaving Jenny no opportunity to get a word in edgeways. It was only when they finally got in that Nigel was able to ask how things had been going. He was genuinely pleased that she was so enthusiastic about her plans, despite his doubts about the viability of the project and its implications. He'd listened to her proposal, and although he was still uneasy about the commitment she was about to embark on, he could find no really good reasons to try and dissuade her.

Jenny, in her excitement, mistook his lack of objections for wholehearted support. She decided to put behind her any fears about his fidelity – or lack of it. They'd had some problems recently, but they were over them now. All she had to worry about was making a go of her business and – although she certainly couldn't discuss this with Nigel – whether James would retaliate in some way for Tuesday's débâcle. On the whole she thought it unlikely. After all, he'd made the moves, and if the sordid little incident was revealed, Fiona would be deeply unimpressed. Jenny couldn't see James risking Fiona, and therefore his connection to Fiona's father, over the matter. But even with such sound logic, there was still a niggle of doubt in her mind.

Family life returned to normal over the weekend, and Jenny was delighted to discover that Nigel had a week's sick leave. He'd checked her figures and hadn't been able to fault her costings, and he'd been glad that it was obviously going so well. Pan came to visit them to update them on the shops which had shown sufficient interest to demand to see samples. Fiona had returned, and James was staying out of the way. Breathing more easily, Jenny told herself that things were definitely looking up.

The following Monday, Nigel was ensconced in an armchair with his bad foot resting on the coffee table. To hand was a plentiful supply of magazines from sympathetic neighbours. He also had the TV remote control, a large cup of coffee and the radio. Jenny was spoiling him, he thought comfortably.

Outside, Jenny and Marian were beavering away in the garage. The order was almost completed. The shelves above the workbench were jammed with a battalion of gleaming miniature Guardsmen.

'We're going to do it with time to spare,' said Jenny.

'I knew we could. It's certainly been easier since we decided to do all the base coats first, then the detailed stuff.'

'I know. The trouble is, I get bored doing repetitive things. That's why I chopped and changed before, one minute varnishing, the next doing their faces. But I can see now that it was hopelessly inefficient.'

'When we get a production line set up, when you get more orders, it'll be faster still. Oh, hello. It looks like you've got a visitor.' Marian, from where she worked, could see a man approaching Jenny's front door.

'Hello,' called Jenny loudly. 'I'm in here.'

The man, an elderly gentleman in cavalry twill trousers, a cloth cap and a Barbour, put his head through the open door. He had a florid, puffy face which was suggestive of too many hours spent propping up bars, coupled with an inactive lifestyle. His mouth was set at a disagreeable angle, and he instantly reminded Jenny of a bad-tempered Persian cat.

'Mrs Walker?'

'Yes, how can I help you?'

'I'm Ted Roberts, the Housing Commandant. I believe your husband's on sick leave.'

'Yes, that's right. He's got a broken ankle.'

'I'd like a few words with him, if that's OK.'

'Yes, sure. The front door's on the latch. Just push it open and you'll find him in the sitting room. I expect you know your way around all these houses, don't you?' Mr Roberts – or perhaps it was Colonel Roberts, Jenny didn't know – ignored the pleasantries, nodded curtly and left.

'I wonder what that's all about,' said Marian.

Jenny shrugged. 'Probably some message from work he's been asked to relay.' The two women carried on working. A short while later, the front door banged shut as Jenny was carefully manoeuvring a still-tacky bookend on to a shelf so that she didn't damage the finish.

''Bye,' she called after the retreating back view. He didn't reply. Jenny thought she'd better go and see what it was all about.

'Nigel?' she said, entering the house.

'We've got to talk,' said Nigel grimly from the sitting room.

'OK. What's the problem?'

'Well, you can sack your plans for expansion, for a start.' Jenny stared at him, unbelieving.

'I'm not joking, Jenny. You can't carry on. I'm sorry, but that's that.'

'I don't understand. Why not?'

'You're not allowed to operate a business from a quarter without permission. And you have to have that permission before you start. If you don't stop, we'll get evicted.'

'Oh, they can't do that. It's just a threat.'

'They can, and they will. And what's more, if you don't toe the line, that dickhead Roberts will go to a higher authority to put pressure on me to make you stop. We're talking disciplinary action here.'

Jenny's shoulders sagged as she felt disappointment bear down on her. Why was it, she thought despairingly, that every time things seemed to be getting better, it all went wrong again? If Nigel did an ordinary job, if they lived in their own home, she could do pretty much what she damn well pleased. It was the fucking Army putting a spanner in the works yet again. She'd had a basinful of the Army one way and another. 'Can I at least finish this order?'

'He said he'd come back tomorrow to make sure you'd stopped, so I suppose if you can get it done today you'll be all right.'

'Well, that's something.'

Nigel could see Jenny's disappointment. It was a tough break for her, although he felt relieved that this would force her into abandoning the idea. He'd never been convinced that it wasn't going to cause huge problems.

'Can you get it done?'

'I don't know. We've got about twelve pairs to finish. If Marian and I work for the rest of the day, and this evening, we might just manage it. If all else fails, I could finish off the last ones on the kitchen table in the evenings. They'd never know.'

'OK. Well, go and tell Marian. I'll manage the kids this evening, and we'll get a takeaway so you don't have to worry about supper. Now get back out to the garage and stop wasting what little time you have.'

'Finished' said Marian.

'I've just got the epaulettes to do on this one and I will have too. There.' Jenny put the last brush strokes on the last bookend with a flourish. 'Well, that's something, at least.' She felt completely despondent. 'I couldn't have done it without you.'

'I enjoyed it. It was nice to feel useful. It's a shame it's all got to stop. If we had somewhere of our own ...'

Jenny nearly snapped at Marian, but it would have been unfair. Instead she shrugged and said, 'I know. But – oh, what the hell! It was a good idea, but that's that.'

'You couldn't rent somewhere, I suppose?'

'Oh, come on. It'd cost a fortune. If I'm going to go to all this trouble I want to make a decent amount of money from it. If I have to plough everything into overheads it just won't be worth it.'

'You don't think it's worth asking an estate agent? I mean, we'd only need a room, possibly two. Surely it wouldn't be more than a couple of hundred pounds a month?'

Jenny was so disheartened, she couldn't face the effort of making enquiries.

'No, I'm going to sack the idea. It's not worth the hassle. I might just as well give up and start being a proper army wife, and use my energies to run the thrift shop or something else equally worthy.'

Marian said nothing. It wasn't up to her. It seemed a shame, though, to give in without a fight.

After Marian had been paid and had gone, Jenny carefully wrapped her precious bookends in bubblewrap and put them into two large cardboard packing cases left over from the move. She'd drive them up to GTC's warehouse the next morning. When she'd finished wrapping them, she wandered disconsolately into the kitchen, pulled out her notebook with its meticulous calculations, and sat down at the kitchen table to go through everything again.

After half an hour she decided that it was hopeless trying to work out if she could afford to rent a place if she didn't know how much it was going to cost. She threw her workings back into the drawer and went into the sitting room, where Nigel was watching the late-evening news. Jenny was so fed up with the Army that she didn't feel like talking to him. She slumped angrily in a chair, feeling close to the bitter tears of self-pity.

'Cheer up,' said Nigel. Jenny glowered at him. It was all right for him; he still had a purpose to his life. He had a job, he earned money, he had a sense of self-esteem from being good at what he did. The daily routine of cooking, shopping, cleaning provided none of that. Frankly, Jenny told herself, half the time no one noticed if the house was clean or tidy. She only did it to fill the day and to make herself feel as though she was earning her unpaid keep. But her bookends had changed all that. She'd had the chance to make a real contribution, financially tangible, to do something lasting, of which she could feel proud. But the hope and ambition had been snuffed out by the petty rules and regulations of an organisation which was too big, too anonymous to fight against. She didn't even have a being on whom she could focus her rage, just a huge institution. Her anger simmered impotently and she watched the news stonily.

Nigel was aware of Jenny's mood and resented it. It wasn't

his fault. What was he supposed to have done, resigned over it? And then what – what would they have done for a house and money? Really, Jenny was unreasonable. He sighed heavily, and Jenny shot him a filthy look.

'I'm going to bed,' he said sulkily. There was no point in hanging around with her in a mood like that.

As Nigel stamped up the stairs, making more noise than was necessary with his plaster cast, Jenny felt the hot tears which had been brimming in her eyes tip off her eyelashes and roll steadily down her face. It had all been going so well, and now, nothing. She switched off the television and followed him.

'Did you get the stuff to GTC OK?' enquired Marian. She'd seen Jenny dropping her children off at school and had hurried to catch up with her before she got home.

'Yes, no problem.'

'What did they say?' She was dying to hear how they had been received the day before. She was a little put out that Jenny hadn't already told her.

'Nothing, really. I just handed the boxes to a warehouseman, and that was that.'

'Oh.' Marian had hoped to hear something more positive. It was clear that Jenny was still feeling low. Marian had some information for her but she wasn't sure how it was going to be received. She felt slightly intimidated by this capable woman, certain that Jenny could be brusque or even rude. She didn't like unpleasantness, and she found the idea of being upset by a neighbour quite alarming. But she owed it to Jenny to tell her this piece of news. She put her hand on Jenny's arm to stop her from turning into her drive.

'I hope you don't mind,' she said, looking into Jenny's lacklustre eyes, 'but I rang Carrington and Dean yesterday while you were up in London.' She paused, waiting for a response. 'They're estate agents. They do commercial properties too.'

'And?'

'They've got a small workshop on their books, in Egham, short lease. They want ninety pounds a week for it. I said I'd let them know.' Marian hovered nervously, waiting for Jenny's reaction.

'Ninety pounds a week?' Jenny's eyebrows rose in disbelief

at the price. 'That's ... three hundred and sixty quid a month. I don't know. I'll have to do some sums.' But really she'd already dismissed it as a non-starter; there was no way that she could increase the profit margin to cover that sort of rent. Besides which, it made the risks involved that much greater. But as Marian had gone to the trouble, it would be appalling manners not to go through the motions of looking at the possibilities. 'Are you in later this morning?' Marian nodded. 'Well, I'll come round at about eleven.'

'See you then.' Marian breathed a sigh of relief. It hadn't been so terrifying after all.

While Jenny was reworking her costings, Pan called in.

'Rotten luck, Jen. Just when I was beginning to make some useful contacts.'

'And when things were beginning to get going. I didn't realise how much it meant to me until Nigel told me I had no choice but to stop.'

'His jobs or yours, I suppose.'

'Something like that.'

'So what are you going to do now?'

'Marian thinks I ought to keep going. She's found a place I could work from, but I don't think I can afford it. Besides which, what's the point of getting it all organised when it'll have to stop anyway when we get posted?'

'That won't be for two years.'

'I know, but ... I mean, it's going to take a lot of organising. To cover the sort of rent I'd need for a half-decent workshop, I'd have to make sure we produced a hundred pairs a week. That means I've got to find some more helpers, get the equipment, sort out all the rules and regulations about employing people, VAT, tax, orders and invoices. The list of what it'll entail is endless, and I have to ask myself, can I be bothered for just a couple of years?'

'On the other hand,' said Pan, 'if you made a real go of it you could always get a manager to look after things if you got posted away, and just take your cut.'

'Yes, I suppose so,' said Jenny, unconvinced.

'Well, if you do make your mind up to keep going, you've got something else you simply must think about.'

'Oh, what's that?'

'Almost every store I've done so far has wanted to see your other range of products, and a catalogue.'

'What have you said?'

'I told them you specialise in military uniforms, but they weren't interested in other regiments.'

'I see. Well, I knew that I'd have to come up with something if I wanted more orders, but I've been so busy with this last job for GTC I haven't had a chance to think about it. You haven't got any ideas, have you?'

'Me? Good God, no. I've no artistic imagination at all.'

After Pan had left, Jenny carried on with her maths. The picture still didn't look too good, so she tried adding a pound to the basic price and started again. When she'd finished, she went across the road to see Marian. As she sat in the pink sitting room, crammed with furniture and ornaments, she wondered how on earth Marian had found time to dust and polish all her nick-nacks and help her out too. She must spend all her spare time cleaning.

Marian appeared with a tray, delicately covered with a lace cloth, with a cafetiere, two bone-china cups and a plate of home-made biscuits.

'What's the verdict?' she said.

'I don't think it can be done, not without making one hell of a lot and possibly putting up the price.'

'So what's wrong with that?'

'I don't think the market will stand it.'

'How do you know?'

'Just a feeling.'

Marian pushed down the brass plunger and poured the coffee into the bone-china cups. Jenny thought guiltily of the imperfectly washed mugs containing instant which was all she'd offered Marian when they'd been working.

'Well, why don't you ask Pandora what she thinks? She's been going round the shops, she must have some idea of the retail price of similar things. I imagine most shops make about the same profit margin – Pan will know.'

'OK, I'll ask her.' Jenny felt she was being pushed into keeping going, and she wasn't sure it was what she wanted. The problem was that three other people had become involved and had put a lot of effort into her original venture: Pan getting orders, Marian painting, and Annette having her house turned upside down by children. They'd put themselves out for her benefit, so didn't she have a responsibility to them? Which was more cowardly, to give up the idea and disappoint people, or to carry on against her better judgement?

When she returned home, Nigel was glued to the golf. Jenny thought of telling him about the workshop in Egham but decided against it. He'd find objections and they'd probably end up having a row. She decided to carry on without involving him – at least until she knew exactly what she was going to do. She wanted to take control, and if she told Nigel he'd influence her, even if he didn't mean to. This was, or wasn't, going to be her business, and she wanted the Army to have nothing to do with it. Whatever decision she eventually made, it was going to be hers.

Nigel returned to work on Friday. The joys of sick leave had palled, the golf had finished, he was bored and the prospect of the social intercourse of the office outweighed the envisaged difficulties of commuting with a leg in plaster. Besides which, Jenny was still barely talking to him, the atmosphere at home was leaden with suppressed feelings and Nigel felt that, as the object of her resentment, if he removed himself she might stop sulking quicker.

Caroline was sufficiently moved by sympathy to offer to make his coffee for him, and Mr Murray came through to his office to give him an update on events during his absence.

'... the General's secretary has rung me up twice to find out when the General can see you. Could you get hold of her this morning to fix it up? Colonel Figures wants you to look at the file on mobile cranes, and I thought you'd want to know that the Pink List is out on Monday.'

Nigel had forgotten all about the Pink List. He wasn't sure what his chances were. This was his first year in the bracket of those eligible to be selected for promotion to the next rank. It would be quite an achievement to be on the list at his age. If he got it, it might make Jenny feel better about things. If nothing else, there'd be a lot more money coming in; lieutenant colonels earned significantly more than majors.

'Do you know what the General wants?'

'Initial interview I should think, sir.'

'Right. Anything else?'

'No, sir.'

'If you could just ask Caroline to bring me the file on the ammo trial I was at the week before last, I suppose I'd better get on with this lot.' Nigel looked glumly at the pile of work in his in-tray.

'Well?' Marian looked at Jenny with a big grin. 'What do you think?' She hardly needed to ask; Jenny's enthusiasm was obvious. Her eyes were sparkling and dancing as she gazed around the bare workshop.

'Look, the light from that window is really perfect for the painters. I could set up a workbench underneath for them and put strip lighting over here for where I'll pack them up to send away, and some shelves along here to store the stock; it has real possibilities.'

The estate agent's representative could see that the deal was very nearly closed.

'How much did you say it was?' said Jenny, who was slightly irritated by the overattentive and deferential man from the commercial lettings department. He reminded her of Uriah Heep. Any minute now, she thought, he is going to say how 'umble he is.

'It's ninety pounds a week, which is a very reasonable price, I might add. This is a sought-after area for small businesses. It's close to major road networks and London. There are other people interested. We generally find that small units of this nature move very quickly.' Not strictly true, of course, but these two obviously wouldn't know that.

Marian studied the layer of dust on the window ledge, the grimy windows, and drew her finger across the dirt pointedly.

She said, 'So exactly how long has this been on the market?' The youth was taken aback. He had been expecting this to be straightforward; two women who were novices in the business property world should have been a pushover.

'Four months,' he replied sulkily. Perhaps this deal was going to go down the tubes too. If he didn't get someone to sign a contract soon he was going to be out of a job; business had been appalling recently. Maybe he could get his boss to agree to lower the rent. After all, some rent was better than none. He excused himself and went to his car phone to call back to the office.

Jenny was happily poking around the two stark rooms, envisaging them with a coat of whitewash, cleaned and swept, with some decent lighting. Half guiltily she realised she was feeling more enthusiastic about doing up these grubby premises than she had ever felt about sorting out a new quarter. But she had chosen this, it was hers. No one was going to lay down stupid rules about how many picture hooks were in a wall, or what colour paint she could use. It was her piece of space, and an escape from the Army.

'Mr Amps, back at the office, has suggested that our client may agree to come down to eighty pounds a week.' In fact Mr Amps had authorised him to come down as far as £70. Get rid of it, he had said. It's not earning anyone a bean empty.

'Call it seventy-five and it's a deal.'

'OK, seventy-five it is. If you'd like to come back to the office and give me names of references, we can complete the contracts. I'll have to ask for three months' rent in advance as a deposit, returnable when you vacate – assuming everything is in order.'

The lad showed them out and locked the shabby door with its peeling paint, and they followed his car back to the office to complete the paperwork.

Back home, Jenny sat down with a cup of coffee and her notebook to work out what she had to do before they could move into the new premises. She reckoned it would be a couple of weeks before it was all set up and ready to go. In the mean time she had to get on to the local job centre to get hold of at least one, but better still, two people who could paint. She thought about ringing Nigel at work to tell him about it, but decided against it. She wasn't sure how genuine his support had been when he'd got back from Germany; it'd evaporated quickly enough when the Housing Commandant had made trouble. She made up her mind to tell him when everything was ready to start production.

Nigel sat in the armchair in the Military Assistant's office, waiting for his summons to the inner sanctum to meet the

General. He wasn't particularly nervous; an initial interview was barely more than a formality: a few questions about settling down in his job, a polite but uninterested query about his new quarter, and possibly some comment or other about keeping fit or teamwork. These meetings invariably followed the same format. The buzzer on the MA's desk discreetly indicated that the General was ready to see Nigel. The MA got up to usher Nigel through the door.

'Don't sit down till he tells you to,' he advised Nigel quietly as he reached the door. Then louder, as he opened it, 'Nigel Walker, General.'

'Walker, come and take a seat by the desk,' said the General. The MA hid his amazement. Usually interviewees were kept standing for several minutes before being invited to sit – perhaps this was a perk because of his broken ankle. 'Welcome to OR Branch. I'm sorry to see that you've been in the wars.'

'Thank you, sir. It's much better, though.'

'Settling in your new post, I hope?'

'Yes, no problems.'

'You've obviously been getting to grips with some of the problems here. I saw your report on the new fork-lift from Hymax. Jolly good piece of work. I congratulate you.'

Nigel couldn't help smiling. The praise was genuine and unexpected.

'Thank you. It's very kind of you to say so.'

'Credit where credit's due,' the General said curtly. 'You'll hear just as quickly from me if you drop a brick.'

Nigel nodded.

'I gather your wife had a nasty shock shortly after she got here.' The General had been well briefed by his staff.

'Yes, although she seems to be over the incident now. Not that we were the target.'

'Wouldn't have made much difference if it had gone off.'

'No, sir.'

'Right then, Walker. Keep up your standard of work. First class.' Nigel stood and prepared to leave. The General had obviously pressed his buzzer again, as the MA had already opened the door.

'Good afternoon, sir.' Nigel walked towards the door.

'Oh, Walker.'

'Yes, sir?'

'One last thing – why were you at the ammo trials at Hohne and not someone from the gunners?'

'I've no idea. Colonel Figures told me I was required, but when I was there I didn't feel as though I had much to contribute. I assumed they wanted some input from me about loading the shells on to pallets, but that didn't seem to be the issue at all.'

'OK. I'll have a word with Figures.' The General indicated with a nod that Nigel was dismissed. The MA shut the door.

'The General was really pleased with that report you did,' he told Nigel.

Nigel shrugged. 'I know, but it's only that I actually got on with the job and produced it. I reckon everyone else had put off dealing with this bloody fork-lift because it was so boring.'

'Never mind that, it was a first class report. How do you rate your chances for the Pink List?'

'No idea. Fair to average, I suppose.'

'Me too. Well, we'll all know our futures on Monday.'

By the time Nigel left his office that evening, work had already got around OR Branch that he was the General's new golden boy. Some wag had opened a book on who was going to be on the Pink List, and had Nigel as the favourite, with the General's MA and James both at rather longer odds. Nigel found this very flattering but had the good sense to realise that his chances had been determined before he'd taken up this new job. While he was hopeful, he was also realistic, and he certainly wasn't going to tell Jenny until he knew for certain. He hoped that Jenny's mood over the weekend would be better than it had been recently. He was gratified when he discovered that it was – or at least she was sufficiently preoccupied with something that she wasn't sulking. He didn't risk an outburst from her by prying. He reckoned she would tell him when she was ready.

Chapter Fifteen

Nigel had been trying to dial home for over forty minutes before he finally got through.

'Jenny, guess what?' he said, his delight clear in his voice.

'I can't, tell me.'

'I'm on the Pink List. I'm going to be promoted.'

'Oh, Nigel. That's wonderful. Clever old you. When do you get it?'

'Not for a bit. But it's bloody good news. I tried to phone earlier but the line was engaged.'

'I'm sorry. I had some calls to make.'

'I gathered. I'll need the extra cash to pay the phone bill.' But Nigel was in such a good mood, he wasn't serious. 'I'll buy a bottle of fizz on the way home so we can celebrate properly.'

'And I'll get something nice for supper. Was there anyone else we know on the list?'

'I'll bring a copy of it home with me. You can see for yourself. Oh, by the way, don't say too much to Fiona; James wasn't on it.'

'Christ, he won't be pleased.'

'I haven't seen him yet to find out, but I imagine that's an understatement.' Nigel put the phone down, feeling immensely self-satisfied.

Down the corridor, James sat in his office, staring at the list. He simply couldn't believe that his name was missing. He'd been so confident of selection. The disappointment was almost overwhelming. He kept going over the twenty or so names of his rival Artillery officers who had been selected, most of whom he knew reasonably well, and tried to work out what attributes they had that he didn't. It made no difference that some of the officers to be promoted had been in the bracket for promotion for a number of years, and that this was his first shot at it; he still felt cheated by the system. He looked at the other pages to see who else was leaving him behind in the race for the red tabs of high office. His despondency grew when he saw men he disliked or didn't rate who had been picked. His finger moved slowly down the pages.

'He's a waster... God, not him... Oh, surely not,' he muttered with growing annoyance. Then the colour drained from his face as he read: Major N.F.J. Walker RLC. With a burst of rage and hatred, James crushed the sheets of paper and clenched them into a ball, his knuckles white, the sinews in the back of his hands raised with the huge effort he was putting into trying to destroy it. As if by so doing the published promotion would be stopped. Then, with fearful violence, he flung the ball across his office, where it smacked against the wall. The envy James felt about Nigel's possession of Jenny was now eclipsed by this savage jealousy of his success. He was glad he'd phoned the Housing Commandant's office, he thought vindictively, to blow the whistle on Jenny's business. That would teach the bitch to spurn him. If he could queer her pitch, he could probably do the same to that oaf Nigel.

Jenny was so delighted about Nigel's news that she longed to share it with someone. Locking the front door, she went down the road to see Pan. The June sunshine had real warmth in it; the leaves were fully out now, but still had the fresh green of spring, not the tired, dusty look of summer; and gardens were bright with geraniums and busy Lizzies. Jenny felt in better spirits than she had for a week.

Pandora was in the garden with Gabriella, who was crawling around on the grass, chasing the two springer spaniels, who tolerated her attentions with remarkable patience.

'Hello, Jenny. I'm just going to make some coffee. Would you like some?'

'Lovely. I'll keep an eye on Gabriella if you like.' Jenny settled herself on the rug on the grass, basking happily in the early heatwave.

'So, why are you slacking?' joked Pandora when she returned with two mugs of coffee and a beaker of orange for the baby.

'I've given myself a holiday to celebrate some good news.'

'What's that?'

'Nigel's getting promoted!'

'Bloody good. That's great news.' Pandora was genuinely delighted. She liked Nigel and Jenny, and was pleased to see that someone with obvious integrity and honesty had been selected. So often it seemed to be the scheming backstabbers who got to the top. Rupe had even gone so far as to say that it was an absolute prerequisite. Then a thought struck her. 'You'd better cancel the rent on your new workshop, though.'

'Why? Can't colonels' wives run businesses?' said Jenny with a smile.

'No. You'll be getting posted.'

Jenny sat rock still, her face suddenly pale.

'Bugger.' It had never crossed her mind.

'You can always set up something when you get to your new place.'

'I doubt it.' Jenny felt suddenly tired. The prospect of yet another move when she'd only just got over the last one filled her with horror. And every time she thought she'd overcome one obstacle, another one popped up. First it was Nigel's objections, then it was having to find a workshop, now it was a posting. Life was so bloody unfair.

'There's one good thing, though,' said Pan.

'I can't imagine what that can be.'

'Think of the disturbance allowance.'

'Yes, great.' But there was no enthusiasm in her voice. It seemed to her that there was no way she was going to succeed with this enterprise as long as Nigel was in the Army.

Nigel decided to knock off early. A couple of people had suggested he should go to a nearby pub for a few celebratory pints after work, but he'd shared a drink at lunchtime with some friends, and preferred to go straight home.

It was an hour after Nigel had left, and the building was beginning to empty, when James walked past his office. The door was wide open, and James could see that it was deserted and the cabinets locked. In the middle of the otherwise clear desk was Nigel's diary. James, on a sudden impulse born from inspiration, strode across the few feet between the door and the desk and took it. He returned to his own office, where he could peruse it at leisure. He was looking for one tiny scrap of information, and there was just a chance Nigel had stored it amongst the diary's pages.

Once back in his office, James opened the book and checked each page with care. The first few were clear of Nigel's writing, filled only with the obligatory printed information about bank holidays, and how to convert metres into feet and inches. Then there were two pages of phone numbers. This was what James was after. He recognised some of them: most were colleagues' extensions, a couple were obviously London numbers, and there were those which he was fairly certain belonged to units in Germany. Then his heart raced, as he found a six-digit number next to the word 'office'. Nigel was just like everyone else, thought James with malicious glee, as he copied down what he was certain was Nigel's safe combination disguised as a phone number. Swiftly he committed the number to memory, then wrote a memo to Nigel that he could 'deliver' to his office – if anyone found him there he wanted a good excuse.

He walked quickly back down the corridor to Nigel's office, leaving the door open so he could hear anyone approaching. He replaced the diary, rubbed his hands together and then spun the dial of the combination lock on Nigel's security cabinet. He made no mistakes, and it took him just twenty seconds to open it.

'Sir,' said WO1 Murray to Nigel when he came into work the next day, 'Colonel Figures wants you in his office first thing.'

'OK.'

'I'd put your flak jacket on, sir. He's in a bad mood.'

Nigel picked up the files in his pigeonhole in the clerks' office, collected his faxes and went to knock on his boss's door. He was still on a high about the previous day's events. Even Jenny had posed no problem, seeming to accept with relatively good grace that they'd probably be posted in the next six months or so, and certainly before their two years in London were up. Nigel mused that the Housing Commandant's visit had proved to be a blessing in disguise; if Jenny had really got things up and running she'd have been completely mad at the prospect of moving again. As it was, she'd seemed remarkably pragmatic about the whole thing. He'd been quite surprised that she hadn't made an issue of it. Obviously all that silliness about wanting to run her own business had just been a phase. He was glad she'd got over it; life could return to normal now.

'Shut the door, Walker,' said Colonel Figures. 'Did you celebrate yesterday?'

'Yes, I did, thanks, sir.'

'I thought you had. Lunchtime drinks?'

'Yes, but only a pint. There was a move to go on a bit of a binge after work, but I was keen to get home to Jenny.'

'Only a pint – are you sure?'

'Yes, sir.' Nigel felt a growing sense of unease. What had started off as a general conversation was now going in a specific direction, but he didn't know where.

'So, if you were sober when you left work last night, how do you account for leaving your office wide open and the hard disk still in your computer?'

Nigel was dumbfounded. He was certain he'd locked up. He had, hadn't he? He racked his brains – what had he done before he left for home? He'd been working on a letter to a transport regiment in Germany, then he'd phoned the Logistic Executive at Andover to fix up a visit. Then what? He was sure he'd switched off his terminal, put his files in the safe, taken out the computer's removable hard disk so as to disable it overnight, and locked up. He did it every night. He must have done it.

'But I did lock up. I must have done.' Nigel's forehead was creased with worry. The accusation being levelled at him was serious.

'Well, the duty officer saw that your cabinet was open when he did his rounds at six thirty. He said that he knew you'd been promoted and was going to shut and lock it for you without saying anything. He assumed you had other things on your mind and was going to cover up for you.' Nigel knew that this wasn't proper procedure, but it was accepted that everyone made the occasional oversight. He'd have done the same thing for a friend. 'But when he got into your office, he found the hard disk in your computer too. He had no option but to report it to security. God knows what information might have been compromised if he hadn't found it.'

'I'm sure I locked up, though, sir.'

'Well, you obviously didn't.' Colonel Figures's voice was icy.

'No, sir.'

'You'd better tell Mr Murray that you'll be duty officer for the next week. You obviously need the practice in security procedures.'

'Thank you, sir.'

Nigel felt bemused as he left the Colonel's office. He knew he'd locked up. The trouble was, it was an action he did every day – like cleaning his teeth. Supposing he'd been about to do it and been distracted at the last moment, might he have forgotten? He sighed. He supposed he was lucky to get away with five extras. He went back to his office and plonked the files he was still carrying on the corner of his desk. As he did so, he knocked his diary on to the floor. Strange, he thought. He always left it in the middle of his desk, not at the edge. Perhaps the cleaner had moved it.

'I've decided I'm going to go for it. I'm going to keep the workshop and I'd like you to start getting me some orders,' said Jenny. Pan looked at her in amazement. They were walking the dogs along the river while Gabriella was pointing excitedly to the ducks. Pan paused in her leisurely stroll and turned to face Jenny, her eyes screwed up against the bright glint of the sun reflected off the sluggish water.

'But you'll be going?'

'Not for a bit. I asked Nigel about when we could expect to move. He said it could be anything up to eighteen months, although it'll probably be in under a year. You were the one who said I could always find a manager.'

'Well, yes, but ... I thought you'd have longer to get it started. Surely it'd be a bit dodgy to leave someone else in charge if you've only just got it going?'

'It's a risk I'm prepared to take. I thought about it all yesterday. I've got a chance to make a real go of this. There's always been a risk that it might not do as well as I hoped and I'll have to sack the idea anyway. But supposing it does do well? I'm sure that I could keep it going if I could find a good manager. Anyway, if I don't give it a shot, I'll regret not trying. And I may never get a second chance.' Jenny stooped down and picked up a stone, which she threw into the water. Instantly both dogs charged down the bank and dived in.

'I'm sorry, Pan. I didn't mean the dogs to chase it.' They stared at the two liver and brown heads circling at the spot where the stone had splashed in.

'Oi, Wellington, Blenheim, come here,' bawled Pan. The two heads obediently turned and chugged towards the shore. As they emerged, Pandora ordered them to stay.

'Don't want them shaking themselves all over us.' For a second the dogs stood motionless on the muddy shore, then the instinct to shake themselves dry took over. The air around was filled with a spiralling mass of shining droplets.

'OK, boys. Heel.' They trotted up the bank to take up position.

'You couldn't train my children for me, could you?' said Jenny, envious of such command. Pandora grinned.

'I don't suppose you've thought about extending the range of your designs?'

'No, I haven't. But when Nigel and I were talking last night about his career and everything, he said he'd had an idea about the bookends when he was stuck in hospital.'

'And?'

'He suggested that I could try and do some country types in Barbour jackets. He wasn't meaning me to mass-produce them, but he thought they might make nice presents for friends who aren't connected with the Army. I didn't put him straight that I haven't given up yet.' Pan smiled at Jenny's duplicity.

'Hmm. Not very colourful.'

'Yes, but he's got a point. Think of all those hunting, shooting, fishing types.'

Pandora continued to look sceptical. Then she said, 'You know you said *shooting*, well, supposing you got more specific. What if you put a gun dog on the bookend too?' They both looked at the two springers.

'Awfully complicated to produce. I don't think it'd work too well.'

'Never mind. It was just an idea.'

'Anyway, I'm sure you can get shops to buy a whole load more Guardsmen before we flood the market and have to go on to something else.'

'Oh yes. I had some definite interest from Harvey Nicks, Harrods and Selfridges. I wouldn't mind trying John Lewis next, but I don't know if that'll be over the top. Being a chain, they may insist on a very large discount from the retail price. I don't know, but I can find out.'

'Great. Once I get it all set up, with some orders, hopefully, then I can tell Nigel.' The two women continued to walk along the towpath, enjoying the warm sun. Jenny was thinking about the rush with the GTC order, and the near-scramble to finish it on time.

'I think I'd like you to suggest to the shops that we are looking at stock for Christmas. That way I can pace production a bit. And by the time we hit Christmas, I'll know if I'm about to move house or not. I think that would be a better plan all round. Besides which, shops seem to gear themselves up for Christmas back in October, so that only leaves me three months anyway.'

'I should think that's fine. What are you going to do about finance?'

'I've got some funds tucked away which I hope will last until the money starts to come in. I've got an appointment to see the bank manager tomorrow to find out how to run this. It's all rather exciting.'

'Oh, Jenny, I do hope you make a go of it. You deserve to. I'll start going round the buyers again as soon as you tell me to.'

'I will. I just hope nothing else happens. And keep it under your hat. I think it'd be better if I present Nigel with a *fait accompli*. If it's up and running – or nearly – there's fewer objections he can raise.'

James was gratified to see that Nigel's name appeared on Part 1 Orders as duty officer for the following week. Even so, five extra duties wasn't a massive punishment. Metaphorically speaking it was the equivalent of a smacked wrist, not a kick up the backside. Still, thought James, if he got another black mark it wouldn't look too good. He'd have to look out for another opportunity.

He noticed that he was down for a weekend duty himself towards the end of the month. He supposed it was about his turn again, although they always seemed to come round faster than every four months. He initialled the Orders to signify he'd read them, then tossed them into his out-tray. He tried to ring Fiona to warn her about his impending duty, which would keep him at the MOD on a Saturday night, but the line was engaged. It didn't matter; he could tell her when he got home. He pulled the next file from his in-tray towards him and began to work on it.

At Slim Road Fiona was taking a call from Jeremy. He had meant not to phone her but he couldn't bear the thought of going back to the Far East without seeing her one last time; besides which, she had a talent he wanted to make use of.

'Jeremy. I thought you must have gone back to Hong Kong. I was about to write to you to complain that I didn't get the chance to say goodbye.'

'No, I'm still here; I'm not going back till the end of the month now. I was wondering if you could come up to town before I go and meet me for lunch? I'd like to say goodbye properly, and I haven't had an opportunity to thank you for the other week.'

'Lunch sounds heaven. Where do you want me to meet you?'

'Well, there's no such thing as a free meal. I want some advice from you before we eat. Can you meet me at Tower Hill tube station, at midday on the twenty-ninth?'

'God, you do plan ahead.'

'I'm booking you early to avoid disappointment.'

'What sort of advice do you want?' said Fiona intrigued.

'It's a surprise. You'll find out when we meet.'

'OK, I'll be there. No chance of seeing you before then, is there?'

'No, 'fraid not. I must visit my mother, and I've got a whole load of meetings and conferences before then.'

'OK. I'll wait for the twenty-ninth.'

'I must dash. I'm on a break between meetings and the next

one is about to start. See you soon. 'Bye.'

Slowly Fiona replaced the receiver on its rests. She was curious to know what Jeremy was up to, what he wanted her advice for. Well, she'd find out in due course, so there was no point in wondering about it now. She went up to her bedroom to go through her wardrobe and find something suitable. She might just have to buy a new outfit.

Belinda Cooper sat in the modern office chair, trying to look unconcerned, while the editor and feature writer of the 'Shop Front' page of the *Daily Telegraph* magazine discussed Jenny's bookends. Around her was the bustle of the daily paper: phones ringing, discussions being held, dispatch riders coming and going. Belinda was fascinated. She had taken the initiative to phone the magazine as soon as she had received the stock in the shop – the bookends had shouted excellence at a reasonable cost. The young girl she had spoken to had sounded quite enthusiastic and had asked Belinda to bring them along, after Belinda had stressed that the price, quality and originality of these articles seemed just the sort of thing they looked for to fill their pages.

'Who did you say the manufacturer is?' enquired the editor, who appeared to be in charge of the discussion. Belinda realised she was being addressed.

'Someone called Jenny Walker. She's married to a man in the Army. That's how she started, doing the military figures for friends.'

'How long has she been going?'

'On any sort of scale, not long. I think she'd been doing private commissions only until we found out about her at GTC.'

'Is she widely stocked around the country?'

'No, GTC has her bookends exclusively, although I gather she's hoping to expand, and I imagine she'd be quite happy to do mail order. Of course, if she got into your magazine it would be the most tremendous break for her. It would probably do her more good than anything.' Belinda knew that most people couldn't resist the idea of being a true benefactor to someone. She kept silent while the idea sank in.

'How did you find out about her? Did she come to you?'

'No. It was just luck. I'm engaged to a major in the Guards who's a chum of some neighbours of hers. I invited them to a lunch party and the wife brought me a pair of Guardsmen bookends as a present. I fell in love with them, and the rest, as they say, is history.' Belinda saw the exchange of looks between the writer and her editor. There were definite signs of interest. Belinda held her breath.

'OK,' said the editor, 'if I can keep these samples I'll send them up to our photographer. We can't give you a decision right away; it depends on what else comes in. And anyway, we're probably looking at six to eight weeks before we'd use them. I'll let you know in a week or two if it's on. If it is, you'd better tell Jenny Walker to hang on to her hat.'

What had not been said, but was going through the minds of both the journalists, was that this was the sort of story that was ideal for the women's page too. There could be quite a lot of mileage to be had out of Jenny Walker, one way and another.

Belinda almost skipped out of the Canary Wharf offices. That type of free publicity would do GTC no harm either. She longed to be able to pass on the news but decided she would have to keep it to herself until it was definite. It would be devastating for Jenny if it didn't work out. Although she had never met Jenny, Belinda felt that she would like her if she did.

Chapter Sixteen

Jenny was lying in bed, aware even through closed eyelids that it was getting light. Outside the open window, she could hear the level of birdsong increase from one distant but enthusiastically warbling blackbird to a cacophony of indistinguishable twitterings and cawings as the dawn chorus reached a peak. Downstairs the clock struck half past three. Light so early, she thought. But then it must be nearly the longest day.

She lay still, not wanting to disturb Nigel, and ran over what she still had to do at her new workshop before getting production going again. It had been swept and painted, and the carpenter and electrician were due to finish off putting up the shelves and the extra lights today. The job centre had found her a painter, and the bank manager had given her a mass of advice about the financial aspects: taxes, outlay, investment, capital goods and a host of other things she'd never heard of before. She was worried about the amount of money she was going to have to find to start with. She'd hoped she'd be able to cut corners on stationery and proper packaging, but had been assured by Pan, and indirectly by Belinda, that these things mattered, especially if she wanted new clients.

Over and above that, Jenny knew that she had to come up with a range of goods – one sort of bookend was not going to be enough. Lying in bed, feeling the cool breeze blowing softly through the window, her mind drifted back over Pan's idea for gun dogs. She really didn't think it would be possible to make them three-dimensional. Perhaps it would work if they were in just two dimensions – she'd have to try it out.

Beside her, Nigel began to snore softly. She gave him a dig

in the ribs; he was interrupting her deliberations. She'd have to tell him all about her plans soon, she thought. She hadn't liked keeping him in the dark for this long. In fact she hated secrets. As a child, if a friend had said, 'Shall I tell you a secret,' she'd always stuck her fingers in her ears and sung at the top of her voice to prevent herself from hearing the proffered confidence. She had always been terrified of the consequences of letting someone's greatest secret slip out.

She had only kept her plans so quiet now because she was afraid of Nigel's reaction. She knew that he saw her business as a threat to his own career. He'd resented that what with the bomb and then her bookends, he was known around the patch as Jenny's husband. He wasn't used to this, he was used to having the lead role, and Jenny was aware that it irked him that their neighbours were more concerned with her success than with his. She had been particularly careful to make sure that he had a chance to bask in the glory of his impending promotion, without her detracting from it in any way. But wasn't that typical of men? They felt it their duty to be the successful one in a partnership. It would be demeaning to most of them to earn less than their wives. Oh, they might joke about it with their friends, but it would rankle. No one ever speculated about a wife coping with a successful or famous husband, but how many jokes had there been about Denis Thatcher?

Her thoughts, floating from Nigel to her workshop and back, slowly became less clear as she drifted off to sleep again, where she dreamed of dogs retrieving paintbrushes.

'It really can't be worth it,' said Nigel in irritation.

'But it will be. I'm only renting the place, and I've worked out my profit margin so it covers the rent. Pan is only getting me orders up to Christmas, so if it isn't going to be a long-term success, I won't have lost anything.'

'And what if it is a success? We're going to be posted again, and I don't want you telling me we can't go overseas because you've got this millstone that you've just hung round our necks.' Nigel was livid. He thought she'd got over her ludicrous idea of trying to run a business. It was all that bloody Pan's fault. Jenny would never have gone this far if she hadn't stuck her oar in. What was wrong with being a housewife and supporting him, anyway? Couldn't Jenny see how important it was for him to have some proper back-up at home? Especially now he was getting promoted.

'But you've always said that there's precious little chance of us going back to Germany again. And if we do get sent there, then I shall either shut it all down or find a manager.'

Nigel shook his head. 'It'd be useless having a manager. You couldn't possibly run it from that sort of distance. Think of the phone bills. Supposing things went wrong? If I was commanding a regiment you couldn't expect me to drop everything to look after the kids so you could nip back to sort things out. I'm going to be under enough pressure as it is without having to look after things at home too.'

'But I promise it won't come to that.'

'How can you possibly make that sort of promise?' said Nigel in exasperation. 'If you only do this half-heartedly, it won't work. I know you. This means a lot to you and you'll put all your energies into it to make it a success. And where does that leave the rest of us? The kids farmed out to a child-minder, and me having to help run the house after I've put in a full day at work.'

Jenny felt close to tears. She'd never complained about having to do the ironing at ten o'clock at night after she'd put in a full day shopping, cleaning, cooking, and feeding and bathing the kids. Now here he was, happily implying that the twelve years of her married life had been one long swan, that being a housewife was a licence to sit around gossiping at coffee mornings. Did he have any idea how demeaning he'd just been? He'd devalued her worth as a wife into something slightly lower than a charlady. Why shouldn't she want to escape from the drudgery of it, and why did he see it as such a threat to himself if she did?

'Anyway,' said Nigel, 'I haven't time to argue the toss now. I'll be late for work.' He grabbed his briefcase and walking stick and limped out of the door, less concerned about being late for work than having to continue arguing when he knew that it was he who was being unreasonable.

'Bugger,' swore Jenny loudly after he'd gone. She wondered if he'd come round. She would far rather do this with his support than without it, but despite his attitude she was determined to carry on.

*

James and the General's MA, Major Brian Hanlon, stood together in the lift. The doors closed slowly and it began its smooth ascent to the fifth floor.

'Congratulations, Brian, on your promotion.'

'Thanks. I was sorry not to see your name on the list.' The tall, dark-haired Green Jacket looked suitably sympathetic. He'd worked for the General for a year and had honed his diplomacy to a fine art. He could look concerned and sincere under almost any circumstances now.

James shrugged. 'There's always next year,' he said, trying to sound casual.

'I thought it was a funny list this time,' said Brian Hanlon thoughtfully.

'Why's that?'

'Oh, I don't know, nothing really specific. There were some people I thought were sure-fire favourites – yourself, for example – and then there were some complete surprises.'

'Like Nigel Walker, you mean?'

Brian raised his eyebrows in surprise. 'Why Walker?'

'Oh. Nothing. Perhaps I'd be talking out of turn.'

'I had him down as a very able officer. He certainly impressed the General with one of his reports.' The lift came to a gentle halt and the doors slid smoothly apart. There was no one in the corridor as they made their way towards Brian's office.

'I must have got it wrong then. I'd heard a rumour that he had problems with the booze. Of course, I didn't believe it ...' James let the sentence hang there.

'I'm sure you must have got it wrong. He'd never have got his security clearance if there was a serious problem.'

'Yes, that's what I thought too. Anyway, I was jolly pleased to see your name on the list. I must buy you a drink to celebrate sometime. 'Bye.' James carried on to his own office, satisfied with his successful bit of rumour-mongering.

With a sense of defiance, Jenny drove with Pan to Egham to carry on organising her workshop. Under the now sparkling windows was a long table for the painters to work at, with three Anglepoise lamps spaced evenly along it. Overhead was a fluorescent strip light, and on the wall opposite were rows of shelves. In one corner stood a desk with a tatty, but serviceable, office chair. In the next room was Jenny's band saw and a lathe. The connecting door was wedged open with a piece of folded-up newspaper. Pan had been asked along because Jenny wanted advice as to what to put on the floor. Their feet echoed coldly on the bare concrete as they walked in.

'I considered leaving it bare, but it would look dreary, and I think we'll need something in winter to stop our feet getting frozen. I think it might feel damp if we've nothing down.'

'How much do you want to spend?'

'Bugger all, if I'm honest,' replied Jenny.

'What about rush matting?'

'It wouldn't be very hard-wearing.'

'Does it matter? You don't know yourself how long this is going to last.'

'True. I'm going to have to get a proper doorstop too. I can't stand that dreadful bit of newspaper.'

'Why don't you make one?'

'I could put a Guardsman on it.'

The same thought struck them simultaneously. 'Doorstops!' they both yelled.

'Well, there's one idea,' laughed Jenny. 'I had a thought about the gun dogs too.' She told Pan about her idea to make them in two dimensions. 'It would simplify things, and if they were painted well enough it might work very nicely.'

'I think that sounds superb. It would appeal to a completely different range of people too. Just think of all those lovely shops in places like York and Cheltenham. You must get Marian to help you make up some samples so I can get going. And once you've got a range of half a dozen items, you must get a little catalogue made. It needn't be anything spectacular, just a page folded in half, but it would make life much easier for me. We could send them out as fliers to some of the better-quality gift shops.'

'Sounds great, but where will we get the addresses from?'

'Don't worry about that. I'll nip down to the library and copy out some from the Yellow Pages. We'll start off in the obvious areas – the Cotswolds and the Lake District, perhaps.'

'I can't believe it's all going so well,' said Jenny. 'It's so exciting.' Then she pulled herself up short. There'd been a couple of other occasions recently when she'd thought everything had been going swimmingly, only for problems to arise instantly. She wasn't going to tempt providence again.

A couple of days later, Pan was standing in the General Trading Company by Sloane Square, admiring the display that Belinda had made from Jenny's bookends.

'What did I tell you, Pan? The punters love them,' Belinda drawled. 'When is your pal Jenny coming up with a new line? We'd love to have something new to offer for Christmas, although it's too late for consideration for our catalogue.'

'We're hoping that I'll be able to show you something quite soon.' Pan explained about the hunting, shooting, fishing theme for the new range.

'They sound absolutely terrific,' Belinda enthused. 'We'd be interested in those for our Bath and Cirencester shops too. We don't feel the Guardsmen are right for there. Look, I positively insist that I get first shot at them. If they are half as good as these Guardsmen we'll probably be thinking of quite a significant order. I've also got an idea to get us all some free publicity.'

'Oh, terrific,' said Pan. 'I was going to ask you about that sort of thing. What have you got in mind?'

'I shan't tell you just yet, in case it doesn't come off. Just make sure Jenny gets her stock levels up, OK?'

'I will,' said Pan. 'I'll see you in a week or so, Belinda. I must dash now. I want to see the shop manager at the National Army Museum, and then I'm off to Harvey Nicks.'

'Is it going well?'

'It's difficult to say. Apart from the Army Museum, everyone else wants to see a bigger range. Still, it's early days yet.'

Jenny's production line started bang on schedule on Monday of the following week. She and a youth called Eric, who had carpentry experience but had not had a job since leaving school a year earlier, cut out and assembled the bookends. In the larger room, Marian worked at the table under the window with Dulcie, who could only be described as 'ample' and who was an ex-painter from a bone-china manufacturer in Stafford. Her podgy fingers were unbelievably dextrous, completing figures at about three times the rate that Marian managed, whilst she never stopped talking. She even silenced Marian, which, as Jenny told Nigel, was quite a feat.

Marian was busy with the details for the human figure on the new range of bookends. The dogs had all proved to be trouble-free. She had ironed out most of the problems. Now she was refining the detail so that she and Dulcie would have a pattern to copy.

By the end of the first day, the shelves at the back of the room had begun to fill up at a satisfying rate with Guardsmen bookends in various stages of completion. Twenty a day was the target, and if they kept up with their first day's productivity they would reach it without difficulty. Jenny gained huge gratification from transferring the finished articles to the stout boxes printed in green with her logo, a wren sitting on a bookend, and slapping on the address of a customer.

'Right, that's the National Army Museum order done. I'll run it down to the post office before it shuts. While I'm out in the car, is there anything we need?'

'Some more tea bags,' said Dulcie. 'And the red paint is getting low.'

'I'll get them.' She put her head round the door of the other room and yelled above the din of the band saw.

'Eric, I'm going out.'

Eric could barely hear her and obligingly switched the machine off. The silence that followed the high-pitched whine was almost tangible.

'I'm going out. Do we need anything?'

Eric scratched his head.

'We could do wiv an 'oover down 'ere to pick up some of this dust. It'll get into the ovver room if we're not careful.'

Jenny looked at the growing pile of sawdust under the machinery and agreed with him. This saw might be more efficient, but it was also noisier, and the amount of sawdust it generated was phenomenal. The last thing she wanted was so much dust in the air that it began to affect the paint finish.

'I'll call in at the timber yard and see what they recommend. They must have this problem too. I think we'll need something more robust than an ordinary carpet-sweeper. Thanks, Eric.

Good idea, that.' The lad looked pleased. He wasn't used to praise.

Nigel was on the telephone when Colonel Figures looked round his door. He half stood behind his desk as he caught sight of his superior officer. He saw Figures mouth at him: 'My office – now.'

Nigel nodded and hurriedly finished the call. He wasn't unduly concerned as he limped down the corridor, the plaster cast on his foot making his steps uneven. He knocked on the open door.

'Come in, Walker, and shut the door.' Nigel did so and hobbled forward. 'How are things at home?'

'Fine, Colonel.' Nigel wondered what this was leading up to. His work was OK, Jenny's business had no implications at all as far as the Army was concerned – at least he didn't think so. What on earth was this leading to? Nigel wished that Figures didn't always start his conversations from this oblique angle.

'I just wondered. I was afraid that the pressure of this job, and a young family, might have been getting to you.'

'No, Colonel.' Nigel's perplexity showed in his voice as well as his face.

'You get to relax in the evening, when you get home?'

'Yes, everything's fine,' said Nigel, with mounting exasperation.

Colonel Figures realised that it was time to come to the point. 'There's a rumour going around the building that you're more fond of your beer than you should be. Normally, unless it affected your work or your health, this sort of thing would be overlooked, but your post is very highly vetted and I am wondering if we need to reassess your clearance. I'm telling you this now so you have a chance to sort it out before I have to get the security boys on to it.'

Nigel was almost incoherent with rage and righteous indignation. 'What... who... this is ridiculous, Colonel.'

'Do I take it, then, that you don't drink?'

'No, yes... Look, Colonel, I sometimes have a beer when I get home, and Jenny and I usually have a couple of bottles of wine over the course of a weekend. If that's excessive, then half the bloody Army are alcoholics.' Nigel was feeling belligerent. 'And since when did that amount cause problems? You say yourself that my work is up to speed.'

'There was that incident with your safe, the day you got Pink Listed.'

'Look, Colonel, I don't know what happened that day, but it had nothing to do with booze. I went to the pub with four other officers, we had one pint each, and we came back to work. Check with them if you don't believe me. I wasn't pissed and I swear I locked up properly.'

Colonel Figures sighed. He wanted to believe Nigel – he liked the man, and his work was undeniably good – but he'd heard the rumour from more than one source. He was certain that for a story to have that amount of speculation there would have to be some truth in it.

'I'd like to believe you, Nigel...' He didn't finish. The implication, of course, was that he didn't.

'Check it up with my neighbours. They'll tell you that I don't roll around the patch, pissed out of my skull. Surely, Colonel, if there's a rumour doing the rounds that I'm on the sauce, it must be because someone's seen me one over the eight once too often. And I can assure you it's just not true.'

Nigel wasn't pleading to be believed; he was too cross for that. He was sure that someone had either got the wrong man or was being deliberately malicious. But what really hurt was his boss's reaction. The man chose to believe the rumour and not the evidence in front of him. Nigel's work had always been good, submitted by the required deadlines. He'd never rolled in late for work or come in reeking of booze. And yet Figures seemed to believe an uncorroborated rumour rather than his own subordinate.

'OK, Nigel. But I don't want to hear that you've been drinking in your lunch hour again.'

'No, Colonel,' said Nigel flatly, wondering if Figures had ever transgressed. Silently he bet that the Colonel had attended a good few 'fat-boy lunches' in his time and partaken of the copious quantities of alcohol that invariably flowed at such corporate entertainments – but this was not the time to mention it. 'Is that all?'

'Yes thank you, Walker.'

Nigel strode out of the office with as much dignity as he

could muster, hampered by his plaster cast. 'He probably thinks I broke my fucking ankle because I'd been on the piss in Germany,' he muttered to himself, still tense with anger, as he returned to his office.

Underneath his rage was another feeling – one of immense disappointment. He'd tolerated the lack of loyalty and support from Colonel Bob out in Germany; he'd put it down to the fact that the man was an idle, ineffectual officer. He'd thought that it was a one-off, that other officers would be OK. And now Colonel Figures had distrusted him, disbelieved him, had preferred to put his faith in a rumour. Nigel was deeply hurt that the unswerving loyalty he'd always had for his superiors wasn't reciprocated. Despite the faith that had been shown in him by his promotion, Nigel felt a growing sense of disillusionment and disappointment with the Army. Increasingly he felt that this wasn't what he wanted any more. The camaraderie, the team spirit, the sense of common purpose against a common enemy was going. Individuals were now only concerned with their own welfare and advancement. This wasn't the Army that he'd joined, and he wasn't sure he wanted to be a part of it any more.

That evening, when Marian and Jenny returned to the patch to collect their children, Annette was keen to hear how the first day at the 'factory', as they called it, had gone.

'Really well, thank you. It was a lot of fun.'

Marian chipped in.

'Dulcie is amazing. She's a dreadful gossip, though. No one can get a word in edgeways.' She missed Annette's slight smile. She would not have understood the irony of pots and kettles. 'But even though she never draws breath, she is the most wonderfully neat painter. She told me that she used to work for the Wedgwood factory and did some of their more complicated patterns. Annette, you wouldn't believe how fast she can work.'

'No problems with the children, then?' asked Jenny, tired and keen to get home. She still wasn't used to the fact that someone else was now doing the lion's share of looking after her offspring.

'No, they've done their homework. I'm a real ogre and won't let them switch on the TV until it's finished. Charlotte asked me to remind you, Marian, that it's sports day next week and her plimsolls are too tight.'

Marian and Jenny collected up homework folders, lunchboxes that Annette had obligingly washed out, coats and other paraphernalia, then herded their children back to their own homes. Jenny closed her front door and leant against it. All she really wanted to do was have a stiff gin and lie down for an hour. What was on offer, though, was cooking her children's tea, preparing supper for herself and Nigel, bathtime, and the rest of her chores. Only when everything had been done for her family could she get on with preparing invoices and delivery notes to go with tomorrow's orders, and she would also have to read up on the regulations for paying National Insurance contributions for her staff. She doubted if she would be in bed before midnight. Perhaps when Eric and Dulcie had got to grips with everything, she would be able to do some of this at the workshop. She hoped so. She knew she couldn't carry on at this pace indefinitely. And she didn't dare ask for any help from Nigel. He'd have no sympathy at all. It was different when he got a high-pressure job and expected her to take on a bigger burden with the family to make life easier for him. Jenny thought ruefully that the old recruiting poster was absolutely right. It certainly was a man's life in the Army; women, even camp followers, seemed to have no place in it at all.

Chapter Seventeen

Fiona reached Tower Hill tube station at five to twelve. She emerged from the clean, tiled tunnel into bright sunlight. In front of her was a raised walkway to the sundial and a view of the Tower itself. Fiona leaned against the railing to wait for Jeremy, completely aware of how attractive she looked in the simple yellow dress she had chosen for the occasion.

'Hi, gorgeous.'

She spun round eagerly at the sound of Jeremy's voice.

'Hello. All finished for the day, or do you have to dash away after lunch to another boring meeting?'

'No, all I've got to do is pack my suitcase, finish off some personal business and give you the lunch I promised. I'm afraid I've got to catch this evening's flight back to Hong Kong.'

Fiona pouted. She'd hoped to share more than lunch with Jeremy. Hiding her disappointment, she said brightly, 'I'm intrigued about how I'm going to earn my lunch. I can't think how I can be of any help to you.'

'Well, Tors said something to me which made me think that you can. Come with me and I'll show you what it's all about.'

Jeremy linked his arm companionably through Fiona's and led her down towards the Tower Hotel. They passed behind it and turned down a side street, where he pushed open the door of an unobtrusive block of flats.

'Good afternoon, sir,' said the man behind the desk in the entrance hall. 'Can I help you?'

'My name is Mr Fulton. I'm meeting someone from Peabody and West here at midday.'

'Oh, yes. Follow me, sir. The gentleman is waiting for you.' He led them to the lift. When the door closed he pressed the button to take them to the top floor.

'You get a nice view from up here, sir,' said the doorman.

'I know. I was here last week.' The lift stopped with the barest of jolts and the door slid smoothly open. The hallway was deeply carpeted in pale grey and the walls were attractively painted in marbled pink tones. The doorman rang the bell by the door in front of the lift. A young man in a dark business suit opened it.

'Here you are, sir,' said the doorman, retreating into the lift.

'Mr Fulton. Nice to see you again. Come in,' said the stranger. Jeremy ushered Fiona in ahead of him.

The room was spectacular, light, high and airy, with a massive window running the whole width of the wall overlooking the river. Outside was a long balcony. Fiona crossed the unfurnished room, slid back the window and stepped out. The view was superb, dominated by the grandeur of Tower Bridge itself. Below, the river buses and ferries to Greenwich bustled importantly up and down. The panorama was stunning. Fiona turned to Jeremy.

'What a fabulous place!'

'I'm glad you like it. I've just bought it.' Jeremy turned to the young man. 'You've got the keys, then?'

'Yes. Do you want me to explain any of the features of the flat – the alarm system and the like? Or would you rather explore it on your own?'

'I think we'd rather find out all about it by ourselves. No doubt the service manuals are somewhere?'

'In the top drawer in the kitchen.'

'Right, well, if I can have the keys...?'

'Certainly. And may I just say what a pleasure it's been doing business with you.'

'Thanks.' Jeremy took the proffered keys and the young man left, shutting the door quietly behind him.

Jeremy joined Fiona by the window. They both looked down at the sunlight glinting off the river, at HMS *Belfast*, grey and stately, and at the solid walls of the Tower, with its imposing battlements and sense of dignity, despite being swarmed over by tourists and foreigners as if it was some sort of gigantic ant hill.

'I just want to know if you think this is a good buy. I've got to look to the future. In a few years I shall have to leave Hong Kong, and I thought that while I was over this time I should find a place to call home. Do you approve?'

'Jeremy, I dream about living in a place like this. It's fabulous. Have you thought about how to do it up, furnish it?'

'Not really, I'm hopeless at that sort of thing. I thought I'd pay someone to do it for me.'

Fiona looked at him incredulously.

'Pay someone to do it? Christ, I'd do it for free.' She could have bitten her tongue off, but the words had just slipped out before she had thought. How could she make such an offer? The only places she had decorated had been army quarters. What skills had she got compared with the sort of professional interior designer he would no doubt be able to afford.

Jeremy looked amazed. 'But that's why I'm taking you out to lunch. I was hoping to persuade you to do exactly that. Oh, not for free, of course,' he added hastily. 'I'll pay you the proper rate. Your sister told me all about your talents, and showed me some pictures of what you've done to the ghastly places the Army has given you to live in. I want the personal touch, and I know you'll produce something I'll be happy with. Would you agree to do it for one hundred pounds a day plus expenses? The only thing I ask is that you consult me on all major decisions. Now, if you think my terms are fair, I suggest we have a quick look round now so you can get the general feel of the place, and I can tell you what ideas I've already had. And then we can go to lunch and discuss it.'

Fiona was stunned. She couldn't believe her luck. A fabulous opportunity, an excuse to keep in close contact with Jeremy, and the key to this flat that was not going to be lived in by the owner for several years. She tried not to look too triumphant.

'Well?' said Jeremy.

'I'm sorry, it's a marvellous offer. I'd love to do it. It was just a bit of a shock. Come on, I want to see every nook and cranny.' She walked across the room, already envisaging it in blues and greens to complement the reflections from the river.

'Why don't you and I christen it first?' said Jeremy, taking her in his arms and giving her a lingering kiss.

'I didn't want lunch anyway,' murmured Fiona, as she kicked off her shoes.

'What the hell do you know about interior design?' said James incredulously. He put his knife and fork down and stared at his wife across their polished mahogany dining table.

'Enough. Anyway, I'm doing it for a friend of Tors's who wants the personal touch.'

'One of her discarded men?'

'Why do you automatically assume it's a man? Tors has women friends as well.'

'God, she's not bi now, is she? You know as well as I do that she shags everyone who enters her flat.'

'You bastard. You can never resist having a go at her.' Fiona looked angry, and James decided to move off dangerous ground.

'Anyway, who is this friend?'

Fiona carefully chewed a morsel of lamb cutlet. She didn't want to mention Jeremy, nor did she want to ruin James's illusion that the flat belonged to a woman. She hadn't lied yet – just been miserly with the truth. She picked her words carefully.

'It's a bolthole for a chum from Hong Kong, for when the colony gets handed back to the Chinese.'

'And how much is this "chum" paying you?'

'A hundred a day,' said Fiona, trying to sound casual.

James nearly choked. 'Bloody hell, that's more than I'm getting. She must be fucking nuts.'

'Perhaps you don't realise how much I'm worth,' said Fiona coldly. 'Anyway, I've got to have it done in three months, and I expect this is a one-off commission. It'll be back to supply teaching again after that.'

'We'd better hope this friend of yours is happy with what you do. She may get you more work, and if you carry on earning like that, I'll be able to retire early.'

Fiona said nothing. There was no way her money was going to allow James to start slacking. She wanted it to buy herself a decent wardrobe and have a holiday in the Far East. She earned it, why shouldn't she spend it? He wasn't going to get his sticky fingers on it.

Although James had been somewhat deprecating about Fiona's new occupation, he was rather pleased. It might keep the bitch from griping about him not being on the Pink List. Since it had been published she'd banged on and bloody on about the time when he'd had too much to drink at their party. How if he hadn't made such a fool of himself in front of General Marlow, he'd have been selected. He'd tried to explain that it had had nothing to do with that, but she hadn't listened. She'd hinted that if he didn't make it next year she might not hang around to see if he failed a third time. Fiona certainly liked the good things in life, and his salary was sorely stretched to provide them.

He changed the subject. 'I'm duty officer this weekend. I'll be away Saturday night.'

'Oh.' Fiona didn't care especially, not now she had something to keep herself occupied.

'Will you go away at all?' She usually took any excuse to escape off the patch.

'No, I think I'll stay here. I'll probably go up to London. I want to get some swatches from Liberty, and I wouldn't mind going to Heal's too.'

James shrugged. It didn't matter to him one way or the other. They finished their meal in silence, both wrapped up in thought. James was wondering if he could make use of Nigel's safe combination a second time, while he was alone in the MOD for twenty-four hours; and Fiona was thinking about the bed she was going to put in Jeremy's flat, and the use they would make of it – together.

The next day Nigel sat in his office trying, but failing, to concentrate on his work. He kept going over recent events in his mind: first there was that wild-goose chase to Germany which had resulted in him getting a broken ankle, but the injury had been his own fault and really the whole fiasco of the visit could have been put down to bureaucratic inefficiency. Then there'd been the business with his safe, and although he had no way of proving it, he was sure he'd locked it – but then no one else knew the combination. And finally there was this rumour going round about him being a drunk, although he had no proof that it had been started deliberately. So why did he feel as though someone was trying to have a go at him? He wondered for a while if it was sour grapes about the Pink List, but the Germany trip had happened before it was published.

Nigel racked his brains in case there was someone he'd upset who was now looking for revenge. The more he thought about it the more he decided that he was just being paranoid. Even so, he would like to know why he'd been sent to Germany when it was obvious that he would have been utterly unable to make any sort of contribution to assessing the ammunition being tested. The file on the ammo trials that he'd asked to look at several weeks ago had finally surfaced in his in-tray. It might well tell him who had made the crass decision to send him instead of a gunner. He was just about to pull it towards him to do some investigating when the buzzer on his desk sounded and Mr Murray reminded him of a conference that he was to attend in ten minutes. By the time Nigel returned, the file was once again buried under a pile of more pressing documents.

Pan stood in the doorway to the workshop, looking at the activity. Eric's band saw was, for once, silent. He was busy gluing. Dulcie, as ever, was nattering to Marian. Today she was conducting a one-sided discussion about the state of British television, but even as she held forth, her neat fingers never stopped deftly decorating the simple carving of a labrador. Every now and again, Marian, like a goldfish, opened her mouth to make a contribution to the conversation, but had to shut it again as Dulcie carried on without pause.

'... and I want to know why we always have to see animals, actually ...' She looked sideways at Marian while she wielded her paintbrush with amazing speed. '... you know...' she sniffed, 'doing it. I mean, we all know they do, but do people want to see it, that's what I want to know. And it's always on while me and my Ted are having our supper. It puts you off your egg and chips watching that sort of carrying-on. You mark my words, that David Attenborough will film humans at it one of these fine days, and it won't be called porn because it's him behind the camera, not some dirty old man ...' Pan tore herself away from the fascination of Dulcie's critique and wandered over to the desk. She stood in front of it and knocked on it with her knuckles. Jenny, startled, looked up.

'Oh, Pan. I didn't hear you come in. I was trying to read these blasted leaflets about National Insurance contributions.' She sighed. 'I don't know if it's because I'm dense or if it's because of the way they're written, but I just don't seem to be able to make head or tail of them.'

'You shouldn't worry about it so much. I'm sure you aren't breaking any regulations. Can't someone come round and give you advice, rather than you trying to work out everything for yourself? Or what about the bank manager – that's what he's there for.'

'You're probably right. Anyway, enough of boring regulations, you must have come over for a reason. How can I help you?'

'I came to pick up the new samples. I've got some buyers interested in seeing them. If you've more than one set I could use them both.'

'We've got two complete sets finished, one with a man and one with a woman, and five different dogs. Will that do you? They're in those two boxes by the door. I'm sorry they're so bulky – will you be able to manage them?'

Pan looked at them dubiously. She wasn't sure they would fit in her little runabout.

'I'll be able to get one in. I can always come back for the other tomorrow.' It would be a pain. She wanted to go up to Oxford Street tomorrow and had planned to set out early to get a parking space. Never mind. It couldn't be helped.

'Now we've got these, you ought to consider getting them photographed or drawn to go into a catalogue,' said Pan. 'We could reach a lot more shops with one. Think of all those places like Scotland and Yorkshire that I can't possibly get to.' She could see the expression of approval on Jenny's face. 'I'll get going on it when I've done my appointments today. I'll go and see that printer in Egham. I'm sure he'll be able to advise us.'

'It's a great idea, Pan. I'm sure he'll be able to give us chapter and verse on cost and minimum print runs. But don't worry about trying to take it on as well as tramping round the stores. I'll give him a ring this morning.'

'Great.' Pan caught sight of the clock on Jenny's desk. 'I must fly. I've got to be in London in an hour or I'll miss my first appointment. 'Bye.'

Pan grabbed one of the large cartons and sped out of the door. Jenny stared after her. She always found herself amazed by Pan's dynamism and resourcefulness. If only she could have such energy, she thought. But then that was what teamwork was all about. Everyone contributed their own skills. What would be really useful would be to have Nigel as part of the team, to take on the accounts and regulations. But realistically it would be stupid to expect him to give up a £30,000-a-year job. Especially as it was not yet certain that this business was going to become a going concern. They had the orders now, but there was precious little of her original £4,000 left. The first invoices were not due for payment for another eight weeks, and to get stock levels up to a reasonable level, more timber and paint were needed. On top of that, the wages and the rent had to be paid each week.

Jenny knew that she was between a rock and a hard place. She would either have to get a bank loan or slow down production. The first option would make her commitment to the business total; the second could be damaging. What if they got a big order and couldn't fill it? Jenny knew that she would have to discuss this with Nigel. Never far from the back of her mind was the knowledge that there was a posting looming up. There was very little possibility of him going somewhere really far away, like America, but there was still Scotland or Northern Ireland. She wouldn't be able to pack all this into a box and take it with her. The obvious solution was for her to settle here, but where did that leave Nigel? Like Scarlett O'Hara, Jenny pushed the problem to the back of her mind. I'll think about it tomorrow.

'Hi, Jenny, I'm home,' Nigel called from the front door.

'I'm upstairs,' she yelled back. She heard him and his plaster cast clumping swiftly up the stairs, his energy undiminished after a day in the office and the journey home. Jenny, feeling like a limp rag after a day at the workshop and an hour dealing with tea and tired children, felt a rush of jealousy.

'Well, don't just stand there,' she snapped. 'Grab a towel and make yourself useful. Dry Christopher for me while I wash Jane's hair.' She knew she was being unnecessarily short-tempered, but she was running out of hours in the day. If only Nigel helped more about the house. It was all very well him saying that he didn't mind if the place was a tip. She did. It wouldn't hurt him to push the hoover round occasionally, or to wash the supper things. His argument was that this business was her idea, and he didn't see why he should be expected to do a full day's work and then come home to even more work. It was the sort of chauvinist claptrap she had had from James, she thought bitterly.

Nigel could sense that there was a row brewing. He was just about to make a wisecrack about issuing flak jackets when he realised that this was not the moment. Sympathy was obviously required.

'What's the matter, Jen?'

She looked at him incredulously. What was the matter? She felt the pressure of her frustration and exhaustion building up inside her like a head of steam. What was the matter? Even a halfwit could see what the matter was.

'What the hell do you think the matter is? I haven't sat down for five minutes in the last six weeks. I'm trying to get a business going, run a home, cook, clean, shop. I do bedtime, bathtime, breakfast time and every other bloody time. I cook your supper and wash up, and then you ask me what the matter is? For God's sake, Nigel, use your brain. I'm exhausted, that's what.'

Jenny was unaware of the children staring at her, open-mouthed. They hadn't heard their mother have an outburst like this – even during the move she had been largely under control – and no one could talk to Daddy like that. In the stunned silence that followed, Jenny ran to her bedroom and slammed the door behind her. She flung herself on her bed, too exhausted to cry. In no more than a couple of minutes she was asleep.

Nigel finished putting the children to bed. They were consciously angelic in the wake of the storm, aware that this was not the moment to play up. He considered looking in on Jenny but decided that it would be better to let her calm down

He didn't want to risk her anger again. He didn't realise that she was out for the count.

Dejectedly, Nigel wondered if this business of hers was going to prove worth the hassle. He'd hardly seen her since she'd started it; she could only talk about bookends and orders. Sometimes it didn't seem worth even coming home. In fact, he had found himself staying progressively later at the office. Supper never materialised until eight thirty at the earliest these days, and if he got home early, like he had tonight, all that happened was he got nagged. He felt that he and Jenny were drifting apart, and he didn't know how to stop it.

He went into the kitchen and made himself toasted cheese. As he fiddled around with the cheese grater and the bread, he thought about the direction their lives were suddenly taking. It was obvious that if Jenny was going to be working full time they would have to have some sort of help around the house. Perhaps an au pair. He wondered wryly what Jenny's reaction would be to this suggestion.

Carrying his supper through to the dining room, he started to look at the papers spread out on the table. He leafed through the invoice book. His curiosity grew. Using the calculator, he totted up the orders she had had so far. Two hundred and seventy, including the GTC one. Four thousand pounds' worth of trade in six weeks. Not bad for starters, he thought. If they could improve on this, then they could have a real little gold mine. It was a shame there appeared to be a bit of cash-flow problem. He wondered if it was worth her getting a bank loan, but then dismissed the idea. It would be useless to commit themselves to too much if they were posted shortly after Christmas.

Pan was feeding Gabriella a disgusting-looking breakfast of sliced banana and soggy cereal. Gabriella, totally unconcerned by the appearance of her meal, smacked her lips appreciatively and banged her spoon down hard on the plate. It made a satisfying 'splot', so she repeated it. Without a word, Pan removed the implement and wiped the splashes of cereal from the front of her sweater. She sighed. She'd have to change before she went up to Kingston to keep her appointment with the buyer from Bentalls. Her daughter's antics might be all very charming, but Pan knew that unless she presented herself as a totally professional representative of Jenny's business, she would achieve nothing.

What they really needed was some publicity. Pan knew there was no money for expensive advertising, so they'd have to rustle up some free PR. The problem was how. She had no idea how to get the ball rolling on this sort of thing, and she was pretty certain that Jenny wouldn't either. She remembered that Belinda had said something about some publicity – but that had been a week or so ago and nothing had come of it. Perhaps she ought to quiz Belinda and see if they couldn't get something going. In the mean time she hoped that she would be able to persuade the shops she was visiting today to take half a dozen bookends. At least enough to make her journey and expenses worthwhile.

'I'm worried about whether or not Jenny is going to make a go of this,' she confided to Annette as she dropped Gabriella off half an hour later. Gabriella was placidly sitting on the carpet, playing with Victoria's toys, completely unperturbed by the recent change in her routine. In fact, she had a lot more fun at Annette's with Victoria for company, so she wasn't likely to complain about her mother going away so often.

'I know. It seemed such a surefire thing when it all started. I suppose we were swept away with enthusiasm and didn't know how little we knew about being in business. Do you think you will get many orders today?'

'It's hard to tell, but even if I only get a dozen or so, just three or four from each store, it'll keep things ticking over. The only trouble is, I've got to get a really worthwhile one soon if Jenny is going to expand; but that means more money. At the moment we're not doing much more than breaking even. She's invested so much in equipment she's going to have to carry on to recoup her outlay, but the big chains of shops may not be interested unless she can meet a bulk order quickly, which means more investment. It's like the chicken and the egg.'

'I offered to child-mind for her for free, because I know things are a bit tight, but she was adamant that if this is going to work, everything has to be done properly. She said she wasn't going to hang on through the kindness of her neighbours; if it's going down the tubes she doesn't want a raft of favours owing that she can't repay.'

'I can see her point of view, although talking about it isn't going to help.' Pan gave Gabriella a big hug and exhorted her to be good. 'I'll be back for her around one o'clock and I'll let you know how I got on then,' she said to Annette as she left.

Annette shut the front door carefully and returned to her charges. She would miss the money that the child-minding brought in if Jenny's business failed. She wondered if there was anything she could do to help.

For the umpteenth time that morning, the phone on Jenny's desk rang. While she didn't resent the fact, she found it mildly irritating that it kept breaking into her concentration. What she really needed was a secretary, but there certainly wasn't the cash around for that at the moment. The caller was Paul Cox, the printer, to tell that the proofs of her brochure were ready. She'd told him it was a rush job and he'd been incredibly helpful. Now the quicker she approved them, the quicker he could run off the two thousand copies she had ordered.

'Do you sell stationery as well?' she queried.

'What do you have in mind?' asked Paul.

'Envelopes to fit the leaflets.'

'Oh, yes, we can do those. Two thousand, is it?'

'I'll be down to collect the proofs this afternoon. I'll let you have them back on Monday.'

'OK. 'Bye.'

Jenny had barely replaced the receiver when the phone went again.

'Shit,' she swore softly as she picked it up. Then she changed her voice to her businesslike one,

'Hello, Wren Crafts. Can I help you?'

'Yes, I'd like to speak to Jenny.'

'Speaking.'

'This is Belinda Cooper from GTC.'

'Hi, nice to talk to you. Thank you for the orders. How are they going?'

'Very well. And I was thrilled with the new stuff. Pan showed me the samples yesterday morning. They're fabulous. Listen, I've got some really good news for you. Are you sitting down?'

Jenny expected a decent order and instantly pulled her order book towards her. As she did so, she wondered if she should give Pan the commission on this one; after all, the order had come direct to her. She didn't know what the rules were in that situation. She got no further in this line of thought as Belinda said:

'The *Daily Telegraph* magazine is going to feature your bookends in their 'Shop Front' section in the first issue in August. What do you think?'

'But that's marvellous, wonderful. How ...?'

'I got hold of them. Our three shops will be mentioned as principal stockists, but your address will be given too. You must ring the *Telegraph* today to pass on the details. Someone may come and visit your workshop too. Isn't it exciting?'

Jenny was almost too overwhelmed to talk. Her staff, aware that something monumental was happening, had all fallen silent, and were listening to Jenny's half of the conversation, trying to guess what it was. In a daze, Jenny took down the number of the *Daily Telegraph*.

'Belinda, that's brilliant. I don't know how to thank you. This'll mean so much to us. Goodness knows how many orders this will generate. What can I say?'

'You can buy me a drink when we meet, which I hope will be soon. I'll let Pan have an order for the new line just as soon as I've consulted with our out-of-town branches. In the mean time, keep the ideas coming. 'Bye.'

''Bye,' said Jenny. Then she turned to her staff and shrieked, 'We're going to be featured in a national newspaper! The *Daily Telegraph* ...'

But she didn't get to finish, as Marian, Dulcie and Eric were all jumping up and down, clapping and shouting and clamouring for details.

'We must get hold of Pan and tell her,' said Marian. 'She should share in the good news too.' She went to the phone and tried to ring Pan's home number. No reply. 'She's probably still up in town.'

'Calm down, everyone. I must ring the *Telegraph* and find out what they want and exactly when it's going to be in. I think I'm going to have to tell Mr Cox to add something about this on the leaflets.' Jenny tried to compose herself, but happiness welled up inside her and she found herself laughing aloud. This is no good, she thought, I can't make the call in this state.

'Come on, everybody. I'll make that call later. Let's go and celebrate!'

Chapter Eighteen

'Caroline,' Nigel said into his intercom, 'can you bring JSP101 through for me, please?'

'OK,' came her laconic reply.

Nigel sat back in his chair to await the arrival of the manual on service writing. He'd been tasked by Colonel Figures to produce a brief for the General on the requirement for an updated version of the long-wheel-based Land Rover. As this document would be looked at by some very high-ranking army officers and civil servants, Nigel wanted to be absolutely certain that it would be perfect. The manual, which contained the format for every conceivable sort of letter and document, from thank-you letters to written battle orders, would give him chapter and verse on exactly how to produce this complicated piece of work to the standard army format.

When it arrived, he began typing the information on to his computer as per the layout detailed in the large brown book on his desk. He knew that it would take him a couple of days at the least to finish it, and he worked slowly and meticulously, certain that he was producing something of the highest quality. Having put up a couple of blacks recently, he was keen to redeem his good name with a really cracking piece of work. He was just getting stuck in when the phone rang.

'Walker.'

'Nigel, it's me. I couldn't wait for you to come home to tell you the news, but my bookends are going to be featured in the *Daily Telegraph*. It'll make all the difference; even the big shops will take us really seriously now.'

'Jenny, that's really good news.' Nigel was stunned. He'd

always thought that his wife's craftsmanship was good, but not outstanding. Obviously he'd seriously underestimated her.

'The thing is, though, I'm going to have to plough some more money into this, because we'll have to be ready to meet a lot more orders than I envisaged.'

'OK, we'll discuss it when I get home tonight. I'm really pleased for you. Well done.'

'Thanks, darling. Love you.'

'Love you too, 'bye.' Nigel put the phone down, pleased at Jenny's good news and glad that she was over her temper tantrum of last night. He'd hardly dared talk to her this morning in case he set off another row. He'd wanted to point out that he earned quite enough for her not to have to work and he really couldn't understand why she felt she had to. She made her contribution by looking after the family. He simply couldn't grasp why this wasn't enough. Anyway, she'd certainly hit pay dirt now. Good old Jenny.

Now that the business was really taking off, they'd have to get some help at home, or Jenny would be rushed off her feet. If she wanted to work full time then she'd have to make sacrifices elsewhere. One of them would be having to give up the reins of the house to an outsider. Nigel didn't appreciate that to Jenny this would be no sacrifice at all.

Humming happily to himself, he returned to his computer screen.

The cork popped and the frothy liquid spilled into the glass held out to catch it.

'What fun, champagne,' said Jenny. 'I do love it.'

'I agree. And we've had quite a lot to celebrate, haven't we? What with my promotion and now your success.'

'Aren't we clever?' laughed Jenny. 'I'm sorry I was such a bear last night. I just had a bad day and everything got on top of me.'

'Never mind. With all these orders you're likely to get, I think we can run to a cleaner to come in a couple of times a week.'

'If she did the house and the ironing, I think I could manage the rest,' said Jenny.

'Right, well you'd better get an ad up in the newsagent's

window. The sooner you find someone the easier it'll be all round.' Nigel topped up Jenny's glass. 'Anyway, here's to us and success.'

'Success,' echoed Jenny. She took a sip and giggled as the bubbles went up her nose. 'I could drink this stuff all the time,' she said happily.

'Well, if you want to do that, you'll have to earn one helluva lot. Do you know what this costs a bottle?'

'Not really, and don't tell me. I'd rather not know.'

'What did Pan have to say about your news?'

'She was thrilled. It's also going to make her job an awful lot easier. She can go to the big boys now and tell them that the stuff's going to get a major plug in a quality daily. She's pretty certain Lewis's, Boots and House of Fraser will all be interested. Of course, we'll have to work flat out for the next six weeks or so, till the article comes out, otherwise we'll not be able to cope with demand.'

'You're certain that this will generate demand?'

'Oh, yes. I've no doubt about it.'

'Have you thought about the financial side?'

'Yes. I'm going to have to get a bank loan. I'll have to take on another painter, and I may have to buy another saw. I think that to keep three painters busy I'll have to help Eric. God knows when I shall find time to do the paperwork.' Jenny shrugged and sipped at her drink.

'It's a lot to take on if we get posted soon.'

'I know. I've been thinking about that too.' Jenny studied her glass as she said, 'Supposing we bought a house in this area and I stayed put with the kids?'

'No. Absolutely not.' Nigel was horrified at the suggestion.

'I thought you'd say that,' said Jenny morosely. 'I'll just have to hope that you get posted somewhere near London.' Inwardly she was fuming. Yet again, it looked as though the bloody Army was going to wreck her plans. Still, she had around six months before any move was likely to happen. She'd just have to hope she could make Nigel change his mind.

'Are you going to the reception at Lancaster House on Monday?' Brian Hanlon, the General's MA, asked Nigel as they waited for the lift on Friday morning.

'Yes, I gather it's a good bash.'

'As cocktail parties go, I should think it rates fairly high up the scale.' Brian looked at Nigel. It was hard to believe that this bloke was an alcoholic: clear eyes, steady hands, he looked the picture of health and sobriety. Still, Nigel's next-door neighbour had obviously had good reason to suspect something, and when Brian had made some discreet inquiries he'd heard the same from a couple of other sources – though he hadn't noticed that these had all been friends of James Bain. It had led him to wonder if perhaps that first piece of work Nigel had done for the General had just been a flash in the pan.

'How are you getting on with that brief?'

'Fine. I think it'll be finished today.'

'Good, because the old man wants it for Tuesday, but if he can have it earlier it means he's got time to bone up on all the facts. Makes life a lot easier for him if the Treasury field him some fast balls about costings.'

Nigel beavered away at his computer terminal all day. When he'd finished drafting the brief, he ran it through the Spellcheck programme, then got copies of various documents which he would attach to his masterpiece as appendices. By the time he'd finished it was after six o'clock. He was not prepared to put the whole thing together that night – he'd never get home. Instead he ran off a draft which he read through carefully for errors. It was perfect, even by his own meticulous standards. He took it to the shredder and destroyed it – it was classified 'secret', and it was easier to do that than account for it, file it and lock it away. Then he locked up, making absolutely sure that everything was put away and all his cupboards were secure. There was no way he was going to get hauled up in front of Colonel Figures again for leaving his safe unlocked.

By Saturday afternoon the Ministry of Defence was silent. A few overworked or overkeen officers had come in to their offices in the morning, but they'd all gone home at lunchtime, back to their families and an afternoon watching the third test match. James picked up the telephone in the duty officer's bunk and rang the switchboard.

'I'm going to be working in my office,' he told the operator. 'Can you transfer all calls to my extension?'

'Yes, sir. No problem at all. What extension will you be on?'

Glibly, James gave the young girl Nigel's number. Then he ran up the stairs to the fifth floor, went into Nigel's office and set to work. In five minutes he had Nigel's computer running and was scrolling through the documents to see what he could sabotage. At one point he was interrupted by an incoming call – a minor problem concerning the repatriation of a soldier in Germany. He'd jumped when it rang, his conscience being less than clear, but he quickly recovered his composure and gave thanks that videophones were still a concept for the future. Having dealt with the call, it took James thirty minutes to alter half a dozen documents on Nigel's computer so that they contained some fairly basic but sloppy errors. He also altered facts and figures, statistics which would ruin any conclusions Nigel had come to. James had no idea when Nigel would make use of these, but he rather hoped it would be soon. He'd carefully avoided anything which was dated too far in advance or which had already been printed and used.

When he'd finished he pressed the right keys to get the computer to save the documents with their new alterations, then he locked up, removed all evidence of his presence and returned to his bunk. With any luck, Nigel's reputation as the officer most likely to do well would be completely ruined. He might notice some of the alterations but it was pretty certain he'd miss those involving numbers.

Feeling satisfied with his work, James switched on the little TV and tuned into the cricket. That'll stitch the smug bastard up, he thought as he lay on his bed.

'This is crap, Walker,' said Colonel Figures as he threw Nigel's carefully prepared brief on to his desk.

Nigel looked at him in astonishment. 'It can't be, Colonel. I don't understand.' Oh God. Not again. What the hell was happening to him?

'Look,' the Colonel pointed to the second page, 'and here, and here. I can't pass this to the General with sloppy bloody mistakes like this all through it.' He stared hard at Nigel. 'You hadn't been drinking when you did this?'

'No, I hadn't, Colonel.' Nigel was appalled at the mistakes and even more outraged by the unfair slur. 'I don't know what is going on, but that document was perfect on Friday. I printed out a copy and it had none of those errors in it.'

'All right, show me the copy.'

'I can't. It was late and I couldn't be bothered to book it in so I shredded it.'

'Convenient.' The sarcasm was obvious. 'Frankly, I think you're lying. You thought you could get away with a second-rate piece of work and you're not prepared to accept you've been caught out. I'm deeply disappointed in you.'

'Please, Colonel. I'll sort out this brief and have it in your office by the end of the morning, but you've got to believe that I'm not responsible for those errors.'

'It's not good enough. And it isn't as if it's the first time I've had to talk to you about being sloppy.'

'I'm sorry, but I promise you it was perfect on Friday.'

The Colonel said nothing, just turned and left. Nigel sank back into his chair and tried to work out what was happening. He knew he was telling the truth. Why didn't his boss believe him? This was the second time he'd been unjustly accused of lying. He felt increasingly bitter.

The Army that Nigel had joined nearly twenty years ago had been an altogether different organisation, with different values. Their training had taught them to be loyal to subordinates and superiors alike, a loyalty which would in turn be reciprocated. But since the fall of the Communist empire and the Iron Curtain, the peace dividend had seen the end of the Army as a bastion for such old-fashioned sentiments. It had been turned into a business, with productivity replacing traditions and officer qualities being substituted by narrow-minded ambition interleaved with selfishness. Despite his future prospects, and the protection these now gave him against redundancy, Nigel wasn't sure he wanted to be a part of the Army any more. He might just as well move to civvy street for all the soldiering he was likely to do in the future – and he wouldn't have to bugger his family about every couple of years.

He turned his thoughts back to the document on the desk

in front of him. Damn, damn, damn, he thought. Why hadn't he checked it all through again when he printed it out this morning? But he knew why. It had been perfect on Friday evening and mistakes didn't make their own way on to a disk. If the disk had been corrupted, everything on it would have been turned into gobbledygook. But this wasn't rubbish; the mistakes had been put there on purpose. Someone must have hacked into his machine, and the security implications were horrendous. Nigel ignored the urgency of the corrections he was supposed to be making and rang the MOD security officer.

'Right, let's switch your machine on,' he said without preamble when he got to Nigel's office less than three minutes later. The accusation that Nigel had made over the telephone had caused him to cancel an important meeting and come up the stairs from the third floor, two at a time. It was unusual to see the lanky Intelligence Corps officer in a hurry, and a number of his colleagues began to speculate what could be causing Simon Coles to run.

'OK, the system logs the date and time when a document is accessed, in a hidden file. That means I can find out if anyone has been playing about with your machine when you've not been here.'

'I didn't know that,' said Nigel in admiration.

'We don't advertise it. But it means that when there has been a suspected security breach, we can find out pretty easily when it happened.' He tapped a password into the machine and was asked to verify his authority with another code word. Suddenly a list of files began to scroll across the monitor.

'What was it called?'

'Brief.LR,' answered Nigel.

'You're right. Someone was here on Saturday. Not you, I suppose?'

'No, I was at home all day. I imagine half a dozen people could verify that.'

'I believe you. The question is, how did they get hold of your disk? You did lock it away, didn't you?'

'Yes, I did. Since that time when it was found in my computer after I'd left the office, I've been double-checking that I've locked everything away.'

'I can imagine.' The tall major stared at Nigel. 'So this means that someone's got your combination.'

'But they can't have. I'm the only one who knows it – apart from your lot.'

'Point taken. Hang on.' Simon phoned his clerk. 'Check the envelopes with the duplicate safe combinations, please, and let me know if there have been any signs of tampering.'

'Will that take long?' asked Nigel.

'About fifteen minutes, I guess. He's got about five hundred to go through.'

Nigel raised his eyebrows. A lot of safes – so why had he been targeted? It had to be personal.

'OK, back to your security. You haven't told anyone your combination?'

'No.'

'And it's not a really obvious number, like your wife's date of birth, or your phone number?'

Nigel hesitated a fraction of a second, then said, 'No.'

Simon Coles looked at him quizzically; he knew that Nigel was lying or hiding something.

'Look, the more you help me the quicker we'll have this sorted out.'

'I wrote it down,' Nigel admitted quietly. 'I have to when I get a new combination. I always have a total blank about the number because I make sure it's random.'

Simon wasn't surprised. Half the MOD did this, against all regulations. When would these people learn?

'So where is it? In your diary, trying to masquerade as a phone number?'

Nigel nodded sheepishly.

'For Christ's sake,' said Simon. 'I suppose the only consolation is that you'll never do it again.'

'No, but that's cold comfort now, isn't it?'

'Too bloody right.'

Simon tapped away at the keyboard again and got the computer to make a printout of the information on the screen.

'Don't want to lose the evidence,' he said cheerfully. 'I'm going to find out who was logged into the building on Saturday, then I think we'll have our man – or woman.'

'Whoever did this didn't know about your tracking system, did they?'

'No, and I'd rather you kept quiet about it.'

'What are you wearing tonight?' said Marian to Jenny, who was driving her home.

'Tonight?'

'You haven't forgotten the Ministry cocktail party?' But Marian could see from the open-mouthed expression on Jenny's face that she had.

'Hell. And I haven't even got a babysitter. I suppose I'll have to ask Annette is she can do it for me. It isn't as if I didn't know about it. Nigel reminded me only yesterday.'

'You've had a lot to think about lately. What with trying to sort things out, and the excitement with that article.'

'If we get those orders that Pan is so sure of, we'll have to expand about threefold. Then we must keep coming up with new ideas to keep our customers happy. It's wonderful news, but I've got to make sure that I make the most of it.'

'You're lucky you've got six weeks.'

'Tell me about it. The editor of the magazine said it could go in earlier if I wanted. Can you imagine? We're going to have to work flat out as it is to be ready by the beginning of August. But I'm not going to think about it tonight. Tonight I am going to go out with Nigel and celebrate.'

Jenny, having squared things with Annette, who was more than happy to have the children camping in sleeping bags in her house, raced back home to find a suitable dress. She began to get more and more frustrated as everything she pulled out seemed either too big, too plain or not quite clean. The pile of discarded clothes on her bed grew. She began to wonder if she had a plain black top that would go with her black skirt. Rummaging in the back of her drawer, she found a black lycra leotard. It might do at a push, she decided.

Standing in her bedroom, wearing nothing but a skimpy pair of bikini briefs, she was not pleased when she heard the door bell ring. She grabbed her dressing gown and raced downstairs. Flinging open the door, she was delighted to see Pan.

'Pan! What can I do for you?'

'I just thought that you and Nigel might like to join Rupe and me after the reception. We're going on to the Ritz. Belinda's going to be there.'

'That sounds great. Only I shan't be going anywhere if I can't find the right thing to wear.'

'Problems?'

'Everything is either grubby or out of fashion. It's ages since I've been to a cocktail party. I just haven't got the right kit. I was going to wear a black leotard under a black skirt and tart it up with some glitzy jewellery.'

'Would a really ornate belt help?'

'Probably, but I don't have one.'

'I do. I'll bring it across in a minute.'

Jenny returned to her bedroom and slithered into her outfit. Looking in the mirror, she could see why three size ten dresses had fallen off her shoulders and gaped at the front – no wonder she'd lost so much weight, with all this rushing around.

When Pan returned a few minutes later with the belt, she felt a twinge of envy as Jenny reappeared at the door, the black outfit making her look even more waif-like. Never in her wildest dreams was Pan going to be that thin. It was a figure to kill for, she thought. The belt, a marvellous affair of black silk and gold lace, made Jenny's outfit look like something from *Vogue*.

'Perfect,' was Pan's vote. 'I'm going to change. I'll see you there.'

Jenny returned to her bedroom to brush her hair and fix her make-up. She really hardly needed any, but she dabbed on some powder and eyeshadow before stuffing the invitation and car park pass in her little patent-leather bag. Ten minutes later she was heading towards London, singing along to the hits from the seventies being played on Capital Gold.

As she rounded the fountain outside Buckingham Palace she could see the line of cars waiting to be admitted to the Lancaster House car park, in reality a cordoned-off part of the wide, tree-lined gravel verge of the Mall. She ferreted in her handbag and pulled out the yellow rectangle of card that would permit her entrance too. Slowly she edged nearer to the policeman who was checking credentials. Her turn came. She wound down the window.

'Good evening, Officer.'

'Evening, ma'am, can I see your identification?' Jenny complied. 'Thank you. Park next to the red Daimler.' He waved her on.

Jenny followed instructions and a few minutes later was locking her car, although looking about her there were any number of more desirable cars to pinch, she felt. Her battered old Volvo would be the last one a potential car thief would pick. She saw Pan pulling up at the checkpoint in her little Peugeot with its distinctive number plate. Only a Guards officer's wife could drive HUP 23. It made Jenny grin every time she saw it.

Nigel was waiting for her at the entrance.

'Hello, darling,' said Jenny, rushing up to him. 'You look awful. Bad day?'

'Bloody dreadful. I can't tell you about it now – too many people.'

They were standing just inside the grand entrance to Lancaster House, surrounded by dozens of other people milling about, waiting for their spouses to appear from cloakrooms and powder rooms. Jenny was deeply concerned. She couldn't imagine what on earth it was that could be so bad, but her imagination ran riot.

'You can't leave it like that, Nigel. You've got to tell me.' Jenny pulled him across the floor, away from the main crowd, most of whom were drifting towards the massive double marble staircase which led up to the huge salon.

'It's about James.' Nigel paused, but he didn't have a chance to continue as Pan, high heels clacking on the marble, walked quickly towards them.

'Hi, you two.' She offered her cheek for Nigel to kiss. 'Has Jenny told you about our plans for afterwards?'

'No, she hasn't had the chance.' He felt relief that he couldn't tell Jenny just yet about the day's events.

Pan filled him in. 'And don't tell me you can't afford it. With all the money Jen's going to be making soon, you'll be able to eat there all the time.'

Nigel grinned and pushed back his fringe.

'Come on, you two,' he said. 'Let's join the receiving line so we can have a drink – or are you waiting for Rupert?' He hoped not; he was badly in need of a drink.

'No – I said I'd meet him in there.'

They joined the queue waiting to be presented to a couple of VIPs. It took several minutes to reach the top of the stairs. Jenny and Pan handed over their invitations to the uniformed flunky.

'Major and Mrs Nigel Walker and Mrs Rupert Devereaux,' he announced in resonant tones. Jenny and Nigel were pleasantly surprised to see someone they knew heading the receiving line.

'Jenny, Nigel, how wonderful to see you,' Diana Marlow greeted them warmly. Jenny hoped she'd forgiven her at last for not joining any committees. As usual Diana was wearing a stunning outfit. This time it was sheer cream silk that clung so flatteringly it looked as though it had been poured over her like molten metal. Jenny instantly felt like a country cousin, despite Pan's belt.

'I long to chat, but I can't or we'll hold up the queue. See you later.'

Deftly they were passed down the line to her husband, General Sir Roderick Marlow, and a junior minister representing the Armed Forces, standing next to his mousy wife. Then they were into the grandest room Jenny had ever been in, excluding those she had gawped at from behind a cordon of thick red rope, guidebook in hand. It was like a wedding cake – white and gold and very Baroque.

Well-drilled waiters offered them drinks and canapés, the buzz of conversation grew and the room, despite its size, began to get crowded.

'Nigel, Jenny, hello.' It was Fiona. 'Come and join us.' She was surrounded by a group of people Jenny had never met, but who were obviously office cronies of James and Nigel's.

'I didn't expect to see you here tonight,' said Nigel.

Fiona looked at him uncomprehendingly. 'Why on earth not?'

Nigel realised he'd made a mistake. 'Forget it, I wasn't thinking.'

Fiona shrugged. The social chitchat got underway, oiled by the presence of alcohol. With steady regularity, uniformed waitresses passed among them proffering trays laden with delicious morsels: tiger prawn tails with a satay sauce dip, tiny slices of smoked salmon roulade, pastry barquettes filled with pâté. Jenny, high on excitement and not having eaten since breakfast, wolfed them down.

'I wonder what's kept James?' said Fiona. It was getting quite late. 'I was working at a friend's flat in Tower Hill, so if there was a problem he wouldn't have been able to phone me.'

Christ, thought Nigel. She doesn't know. No wonder she's here. He felt dreadful, but he knew that he couldn't tell her what had been going on. Shit, what a bloody awful mess.

Just then there was the most tremendous commotion by the door. From where Nigel and Jenny were standing, their view of what was going on was completely blocked. There was a crash of breaking glass and suddenly, surging through the guests, came James, drunk, dishevelled and angry.

'Where are you, you bastard? Where's Walker?' he yelled. He spun round to look at the sea of shocked faces and almost overbalanced. Then he saw his quarry. He lurched half a dozen paces to where Nigel was standing, ashen and silent. Two waiters and Rupert Devereaux hovered behind James, ready to restrain him if he lashed out – which looked imminent.

'I hope you're bloody satisfied, you bastard.' James' voice, slurred by drink, was almost incomprehensible. 'I hope you're happy with what you've done.' He stumbled again.

'Shut up,' said Fiona icily. 'You're making a disgusting exhibition of yourself.'

James turned on her. 'Piss off. It doesn't matter what I do. I've resigned. So all of you lot,' he swung round wildly, 'can take a flying fuck. And talking of fucks – your wife's still lousy in bed, Nigel.' Jenny shut her eyes; she felt ill.

'That's enough, Bain. Get out now, before I hit you.' Nigel took a pace towards James. Everyone else moved back. If there was going to be a brawl, they didn't want to be involved.

James swung his clenched fist drunkenly towards Nigel, who was easily able to dodge it. James lurched, lost his balance and sprawled on the floor. Fiona was white with shame and anger. James manage to get himself on to all fours, like a dog, and then suddenly, with a noise like ripping silk, he vomited over his hands and the carpet, a noisy, splattering geyser. A sweet-sour stench rose from the glistening pool. A wave of disgust swept across the horrified room. A few men said, 'My God,' and the women looked away.

'Fiona,' said General Marlow, 'take him home.' His tone was unequivocal. Tight-lipped, ashamed and full of loathing for her husband, Fiona grabbed a napkin from the arm of one of the waiters and threw it down beside James.

'Clean yourself up,' she hissed at him. James grabbed the napkin, levered himself to his feet and wiped his hands. He glowered at Nigel.

'I hope you enjoyed that,' he said, sounding suddenly more sober. 'You've ruined my job, my reputation, everything. I'll pay you back for this.'

'Don't be such a bloody fool,' intervened the General. 'It's all down to you. Now get out.'

Fiona stormed off towards the door, James lurching and stumbling in her wake. As he left, the relief that swept the room was almost tangible. The silence continued for a second or two, and then first whispers, then mumbles, and finally a dull roar of conversation broke out. But no laughter. Waiters scurried to clear up the mess, but the party was over. No one wanted to remain in the room and enjoy themselves. They all wanted to put as much space as possible between them and the sordid scene they'd witnessed.

'I think,' said Jenny, 'you'd better tell me what the hell has been going on.'

'And I think you've got some explaining to do too,' answered Nigel. 'We'd better go home.'

Pan didn't need to be told that neither Jenny or Nigel would be in the mood for the Ritz.

'I didn't go to bed with him,' said Jenny. They'd driven home in silence, both deep in their own thoughts, and were now seated on opposite sides of the sitting room.

'Didn't you? So why did he say so?'

'Jealousy, rage... I don't know.'

'But you kissed him. I know you did. I heard you at that party.'

'Oh God.' Jenny stared at Nigel, her face reddening. He'd known, but he hadn't let on. Why? She felt even more guilty, but it had only been a kiss. She didn't think he would believe that now, though. She felt hopeless. 'You must believe me, I hated myself afterwards. I knew it was stupid. I don't know why I let it happen, but nothing else did. Honest,' she pleaded. 'I haven't gone to bed with him. I wouldn't.

'I don't know whether to believe you or not. You know it was James that got me sent to Germany for that ammo trial? He was supposed to be going but he told his boss that they really needed an expert on moving the stuff. Because I know all about battlefield fork-lifts, they sent me. I reckon he engineered it so he could have a clear run at you.' Nigel stared hard at Jenny. 'I'm right, aren't I? That's when you and he ...' He couldn't go on. He couldn't bear the thought of Jenny and James together.

'No, nothing happened. Yes, he did come round, he wanted to have a drink with me – Fiona was away – but I sent him packing.' What a mess, thought Jenny.

'I suppose I'll have to believe you,' said Nigel coldly. But he wasn't sure he did.

'Are you going to tell me what happened today? Between you and James?'

He told her about James ruining his documents by hacking into his computer. 'I'd had to involve the security guys, so once they discovered who was at the bottom of it all, it was out of my hands. Simon Coles had to go to the General. Then it turned out that James had started a rumour that I'm an alcoholic. After that we began to look under a few more stones. That's when I found out about the Germany trip.'

'And the General asked James for his resignation?'

'It was that or a court martial.'

'Poor Fiona.'

'I know. She's the loser in all this.'

'Did you screw her?' Fiona didn't pause from flinging clothes into a suitcase.

'Would you care if I had?' James had removed his splattered, stinking suit and was lying on the bed in his underpants and socks. He was feeling lousy. His head ached and his nose and throat were sore. He didn't dare ask Fiona to get him an aspirin; he knew he'd gone too far, and she wouldn't have any sympathy with his plight now. Part of him admitted that he didn't blame her.

'Not in the least. You talk about Tors's morals, but I know about your sordid little flings when you go abroad. You're just as bad. What's another notch on the headboard?'

'Well, I didn't. I just wanted to make that smug sod Nigel squirm for a while.'

'You're low.' She snapped the locks on the bulging case. 'Right, well, I'm leaving you, James. I'm not going to Bath, so don't bother looking for me there. I'll see you in the divorce courts.' Picking up her handbag and the car keys, Fiona coolly walked out.

James stared dejectedly after her. He'd known this would happen as soon as he'd finished getting bawled out. When the call had come from Brian Hanlon he'd had no idea he'd been caught. He hadn't even suspected anything when he'd seen Simon Coles waiting in the MA's office too. It was only when Simon was told to go in with him that he began to feel uneasy.

He had never seen a senior officer so furious before. It had been terrifying. He'd been shaking when he left the office, his resignation already on the General's desk. He'd collected his kit from his own office and then gone to the pub to have a drink while he planned how to tell Fiona. When he tried to phone her she wasn't there, and he realised that she was working on the flat up in town and would go straight to the reception. That was when he had begun to get drunk.

Now he wondered what she would do. She obviously had something lined up, but James was feeling too ill and too battered to care.

Fiona certainly had her plans made. She would move into Jeremy's flat for the time being, and once she was divorced, she planned to move into his life too. Hong Kong, money, servants – a far better prospect than James. She had one last thing to do before she drove away. She knocked on the Walkers' door. Jenny answered it.

'Oh, God. Fiona. I'm so sorry.' She looked very pale.

'It's all right. I don't blame you – or Nigel. The stupid pillock did it entirely by himself.' Fiona shrugged. 'But I'm not hanging around here. I just wanted to tell Nigel something.'

'You'd better come in then,' said Jenny, still wary. Fiona walked into the sitting room. Nigel looked up, startled to see her.

'Don't worry. I'm not here for your blood. I just thought you ought to know that James was lying about Jenny. He's just told me the truth. My marriage may have gone down the tubes but there's no reason why he should bugger yours up too. So good luck. I'm pushing off for good. 'Bye.' And she left as abruptly as she'd entered.

'Thanks, Fiona. You didn't have to do that,' Jenny called after her.

'Bollocks,' she said over her shoulder as she went out. Jenny watched her car drive down the road and then shut the front door.

'So what are we going to do, Nigel?'

'I don't know. I've been thoroughly hacked off with the Army recently. When things began to go wrong my boss refused to believe that none of it was my fault. I thought Colonel Bob was a one-off – only worried about himself and not caring a toss for anyone else. But it seems rife these days. There's no loyalty, no sense of security. No one knows where the next axe is going to fall, so the brass are only concerned with being little empire-builders in order to make their job look more important than the next chap's.' Nigel sighed. 'This last business makes me wonder if I wouldn't be better off out of the whole thing. Civvy street's just as precarious, but at least we could stay put.'

'Oh, Nigel.' Jenny could hardly believe what she was hearing.

'You'd like it too, wouldn't you? You could keep going.'

'Let's not make too many plans just yet. I think we ought to let the dust settle.' But Jenny was hugging herself inside. Yes! This was what she wanted. With a shock, she realised that although the Army had been the centre of her life for over fifteen years, she didn't care that she might be taken away from it. A year ago she'd have been devastated by the idea, but not now. Now she felt as though she was going home – to her own home.

HER FATHER'S HOUSE
Emma Sinclair

Trevellan ... Her father's ancient Cornish home is the only constant in Jennie Veryan's young life, and Mark Curnow is her only love – though it seems she must lose them both. A proud and old family, the Veryans break up her romance with the land agent's son, for Jennie is the heiress to the estate.

Or so it seems. In 1950 an incredible rumour draws Jennie to Singapore, scene of her father's disappearance in the maelstrom of the Japanese occupation. And in her quest to discover the truth of her father's fate she uncovers a secret so shameful it threatens exile from Trevellan for ever ...

With its richly evoked backgrounds, sweeping narrative and enduring romance *Her Father's House* is the long awaited successor to *The Seventh Wave*.

THE BUTTERFLY
Anna Barrie

When Leo Chantry is released from a German POW camp he has only one priority: to secure the future of Molliston, his family home. Crumbling away from years of failing fortunes and the blithe neglect of his mother, Peggy, the Elizabethan manor will not survive another decade unless Leo marries someone with enough money to restore it.

Twenty-two-year-old Lydia Westley strikes him as aloof, combative and not particularly attractive – but when he learns she is also very rich Leo takes a second look. Lydia sends out some confusing signals. By turns disdainful and provocative, reticent then assertive, she shocks and unsettles him by mounting a seduction campaign. Unknown to Leo, Lydia too has a private reason for marrying that she is not revealing.

A wry, eloquent look at the hidden agendas two people can bring into a marriage, *The Butterfly* is evocative, witty and elegantly written.

0 7499 3010 1 £6.99

COME THE DAY
Una Horne

Theirs was a romance that should never have been – pitman's daughter Hannah Armstrong and Timothy Durkin, only child of Lord Akers' land agent, with a bright future at Oxford ahead of him. Heedless of his friends' advice Tim marries Hannah, only to break her heart by expecting her to live apart from him while he completes his studies. Stricken by the fear that he is ashamed of her, Hannah returns to her Durham village.

But things at home have changed since she last lived there. The miners are no longer prepared to put with the high-handed treatment of the likes of Daniel Durkin, Tim's father. The General Strike brings suffering to the miners, but it also brings opportunity and when Tim comes to reclaim his wife he finds Hannah an independent woman. This second courtship will not be as easy as the first – for Hannah knows her own worth as a woman who deserves to be loved ...

A stunning novel of pride and passion, *Come the Day* establishes Una Horne as the natural successor to Catherine Cookson as a chronicler of North-East life.

0 7499 3006 3   £5.99

DEVIL ON MY SHOULDER

Janet Mary Tomson

1642. Young Sorcha O'Neill is saved from the massacre which claims her family at the siege of Carrickmain Castle by Lieutenant Robert Hammond. He names her Dublin, the only word the wild, terrified Irish girl will speak in English, and takes her to his family on the Isle of Wight for refuge.

There she meets the shepherd Caleb Gosden, handsome in his way as Robert, but embittered by his past. Yet he is drawn to the still half-savage Irish girl, an outsider like himself. The tide of the Civil War is to take Sorcha on a long journey from her simple peasant roots but her destiny is bound up with those of Hammond and her sullen, unforgettable shepherd. And finally, with the fate of the prisoner of Carisbrooke Castle, King Charles I himself.

From the turmoil of the English Civil War to the court of King Charles I, *Devil On My Shoulder* is a compelling story of love and intrigue.

0 7499 3011 X £5.99

EVE OF DESTRUCTION

Martin Edwards

When Liverpool solicitor and amateur detective Harry Devlin takes on a client with matrimonial troubles, he becomes entangled in an intrigue which will have deadly consequences. His new client has been recording his wife's telephone conversations with her lover; the first mystery for Harry to solve is the identity of the woman's boyfriend.

Harry's own personal life is currently complicated by the enigmatic behaviour of both his partner in law and the woman he longs for. And soon he finds himself trapped in a maze where nothing is quite what it seems. Even when he discovers a conspiracy to commit murder, he cannot be sure who is the culprit and who the true victim ...

'(Martin Edwards) ... writes terrific crime novels'
– *Guardian*

0 7499 3003 9 £5.99

The very best of Piatkus fiction is now available in paperback as well as hardcover. Piatkus paperbacks, where *every* book is special.

☐ 0 7499 3005 5	Her Father's House	Emma Sinclair £5.99
☐ 0 7499 3008 X	Army Wives	Catherine Jones £5.99
☐ 0 7499 3006 3	Come The Day	Una Horne £5.99
☐ 0 7499 3000 4	Dying Fall	Judith Cutler £4.99
☐ 0 7499 3007 1	Second Marriage	Georgina Mackie £6.99
☐ 0 7499 3004 7	Dying To Write	Judith Cutler £5.99
☐ 0 7499 3010 1	The Butterfly	Anna Barrie £6.99
☐ 0 7499 3011 X	Devil On My Shoulder	Janet Mary Tomson £5.99
☐ 0 7499 3003 9	Eve Of Destruction	Martin Edwards £5.99

The prices shown above were correct at the time of going to press. However Piatkus Books reserve the right to show new retail prices on covers which may differ from those previously advertised in the text or elsewhere.

Piatkus Books will be available from your bookshop or newsagent, or can be ordered from the following address:
Piatkus Paperbacks, P.O. Box 11, Falmouth, TR10 9EN.
Alternatively you can fax your order to this address on 01326 374888 or E-mail us at books@barni.avel.co.uk.

Payments can be made as follows: Sterling cheque, Eurocheque, postal order, (payable to Piatkus Books) or by credit cards, Visa/Mastercard. Do not send cash or currency. UK and B.F.P.O. customers allow £1.00 postage and packing for the first book, 50p for the second and 30p for each additional book ordered to a maximum charge of £3.00 (7 books plus).

Overseas customers, including Eire, allow £2.00 for postage and packing for the first book, plus £1.00 for the second and 50p for each subsequent title ordered.

NAME (Block Letters) _____
ADDRESS_____

I enclose my remittance for £_____
I wish to pay by Visa/Mastercard Card.

Number ☐☐☐☐☐☐☐☐☐☐☐☐☐☐☐☐
Card Expiry Date_____

THE SCHOOLING OF STELLA

'Come now, Stella,' Miss Noble said sternly, 'you are a big girl and can take a big girl's punishment. At least a couple of dozen, I think.'

'No! No!' Stella answered, gasping. 'Please, Miss! Two dozen, and on the bare! That would hurt my poor bottom most cruelly!'

'Stella, you are wicked, and deserve to be hurt for your insolent pleading. Now I think it shall be three full dozen, yes, quite bare, till your bottom is quite red.'

By the same author:

MEMOIRS OF A CORNISH GOVERNESS
THE GOVERNESS AT ST AGATHA'S
THE GOVERNESS ABROAD
THE HOUSE OF MALDONA
THE ISLAND OF MALDONA
THE CASTLE OF MALDONA

To be published in February 1998:

PRIVATE MEMOIRS OF A KENTISH
  HEADMISTRESS

THE SCHOOLING OF STELLA

Yolanda Celbridge

This book is a work of fiction.
In real life, make sure you practise safe sex.

First published in 1997 by
Nexus
332 Ladbroke Grove
London W10 5AH

Copyright © Yolanda Celbridge 1997

The right of Yolanda Celbridge to be identified as the
Author of this Work has been asserted by her in
accordance with the Copyright Designs and Patents Act
1988.

Typeset by TW Typesetting, Plymouth, Devon

Printed and bound by
Caledonian Books Ltd, Glasgow

ISBN 0 352 33219 0

*All characters in this publication are fictitious and any
resemblance to real persons, living or dead, is purely
coincidental.*

This book is sold subject to the condition that it shall not,
by way of trade or otherwise, be lent, resold, hired out or
otherwise circulated without the publisher's prior written
consent in any form of binding or cover other than that in
which it is published and without a similar condition
including this condition being imposed on the subsequent
purchaser.

Contents

1	Taking it Bare	1
2	Beneath the Kilt	20
3	Rob Roy	40
4	Cane-kiss	63
5	A Spanking Quiz	77
6	Tea and Punishment	97
7	Sub	112
8	Taming the Bull	129
9	Kernece Football	143
10	Alberta's Secret	162
11	Ladies in Knots	176
12	Drudge	198
13	Tawser Bright	222
14	Ice and Honey	238
15	The Deep End	254

1

Taking it Bare

Stella Shawn felt her heart flutter as she inspected her nude body yet again in her bedroom mirror, putting off the fateful moment of donning her grey St Hilda's uniform for the very last time. She ran her hands lovingly around the mirror's polished oak frame, as though she were caressing herself. It seemed awfully daring – naughty, even – to look at herself thus, and in all her eighteen years she had rarely done so. Her guardians, though kindly, were nevertheless stern Black Country folk who did not believe in unnecessary extravagance. There were no mirrors in the bathroom or sitting-room, only a cracked Victorian glass in the hallway which was usually obscured by hats, sticks and umbrellas. Her oaken bedroom mirror was one of her few treasured possessions – indeed one of her few possessions – and she loved it since it was bequeathed to her by her late mamma. She regretted that it was too large, or rather too costly, to transport to her new home, Kernece College in Scotland.

She looked out over the familiar dull rooftops and chimneys of Stourbridge, which she was soon to leave forever. She knew it was forever, for although she had promised to return faithfully on the holidays from teacher training college, she felt in her heart that once she was in the wide world beyond the Midlands, she would not wish to return. An occasional visit to London, accompanied by her guardians, to visit the National Gallery or the British Museum, had been her sole introduction to the outside world. Although she enjoyed a ladylike proficiency at French and Italian, a visit to those countries was never suggested, partly because of the cost, but really, she suspected, because her guardian Mr Phipps distrusted foreigners. He often snorted about 'loose morals' encountered by unsuspecting English ladies. Even in the National Gallery, she had been hurried past the luscious canvasses of Botticelli, Poussin and Rubens, with their expanses of bare flesh, on to the homely paintings of the Dutch masters.

The thought of bareness excited her: she did not know why, but the people in those paintings seemed so at ease, a robe casually draped over breast or thigh with such artful grace that the cloth seemed part of its wearer's nudity. How different from her lumpish school uniform! Although she already felt nostalgic for St Hilda's, she looked forward to wearing clothes of her own choice; far from the dour respectability of Stourbridge, where a frill or ruff was taken as evidence of ungodliness. And her nostalgia for her girlhood days was tempered with eagerness: she wanted to get to Kernece College as soon as possible, to begin the adventure of being a woman.

Forgetting her nudity, she reached under the bed and withdrew a copy of *La Mode* magazine, which her friend Natalie Huggins had brought back from Paris. Natalie's mother was French, so she could respectably go there to visit. Natalie enjoyed tantalising her friends with stories of the impossibly handsome young captains and counts who had fallen madly in love with her. Stella was sure these stories were all made up, but even so, her heart fluttered at them. The other girls talked of dances, and parties and boyfriends, and how lovely it was to kiss; Stella's knowledge came all from books. Throughout her sheltered girlhood she had lived on a diet of King Arthur and his Knights – how she adored Sir Galahad! – the Welsh Mabinogion, the stories of Viking and Greek heroes, and the intrepid voyagers like Drake, Captain Cook, Sir Walter Raleigh, Vespucci, Columbus and Cabot. How she had longed to be aboard the Argo with Jason and his Golden Fleece, or breaking the Arctic icebergs with Frobisher.

How she had wept for noble Captain Scott, yet rejoiced for daring Amundsen who reached the South Pole before him.

In her dreams, she was St George slaying the dragon, or brave William Tell saving his son by shooting an apple from his head, or Joan of Arc fighting the English and being burned alive by her vicious conquerors. Always, she wept at such stories of goodness and heroism. Sometimes she was a crewman with Columbus or Drake, even though she was only a girl. But she somehow got on board by disguising herself as a man, although she knew, looking at herself, that her very full breasts and derrière would make this unlikely. In her dreams, sometimes, she was tied to the mainmast and her naked back was lashed with a whip, just like the other seamen. In one incredibly silly dream she was one of Amundsen's husky dogs, racing over the Antarctic ice with her back whipped by the tall blond Norwegian!

She had dreamt of being Fletcher Christian, defying cruel Captain Bligh aboard the Bounty and sailing off to a gorgeous island in the South Seas, to be surrounded by dusky, beautiful maidens whose breasts were bare and whose thighs were naked under the lightest rustling grass skirt. And sometimes she imagined herself one of those very maidens, obeying her Master's every whim. She saw herself lifting her skirt to be punished for some disobedience by a beating on her bared fesses, from the flat of his sword, with her Master splendid in tight breeches and golden seaman's earrings. In her dreamworld she was both Fletcher Christian, punishing his maiden, and the maiden herself. Her viewpoint shifted between the man, looking at the bared fesses of his woman, and the woman herself, feeling the searing sword-pain as the blade stroked her on the bare buttocks. Stella always shivered as she recalled that dream in all its vivid intensity. Whenever she thought of it, she felt awfully strange and tingly in her lady's place, and her curious little pink nubbin seemed to throb and grow, with an intensity that was half-pleasure, half-pain.

Stella had never taken the cane herself, although she knew that it was used at St Hilda's very occasionally: the Headmistress Miss Cox administered it herself to errant girls, and forbade them to speak of it afterwards. But the other girls guessed by the victim's flushed face and curiously haughty demeanour. Naturally shy and bookish, Stella had joined in none of the escapades of her more boyish comrades, and as a result had few friends and few enemies. Her bookishness, and her tall, imposing, stature, gave her a certain authority, which earned her the solitude of respect. She found the idea of a beating perfectly horrid, but wondered why she felt all shivery at the thought of being caned, and indeed why she returned to that terrifying thought so often. To be helpless and suffering at the hands of another seemed the worst of fates! And yet ... to be a husky dog, lashed bounding across the pure white snow, or strapped to the mast and showing her strength by taking her punishment without flinching: there was heroism in that. Sir Galahad, or Sir Lancelot – they would take a whipping without a murmur, if their King ordained. And she daydreamed that she, as Arthur's Queen, would take the same with a fortitude similar to the males' ... Stella longed to be a hero.

She knew that when a girl was caught smoking, or stealing, or telling a lie, Miss Cox would cane her. She supposed it was on the hand, or perhaps the calf, and did not understand why in her dreams the whippings always took place on the back or the fesses. Sighing, she riffled the pages of *Mode* magazine for the thousandth time. She looked with hunger at the gorgeous fashions, the short dresses and bobbed hair and high-heeled shoes worn by the models. They were smoking, coolly blowing blue plumes into the faces of dapper, handsome suitors whose eyes ached with yearning. Sometimes the photographs showed underthings: unthinkable in an English publication! The models had brassières, flattening their chests into lovely boyish shapes; they were corseted tightly, and had bright stockings of the sheerest silk, with lovely garter lace belts of varied shades to hold them up, and, incredibly, the very briefest of knickers, which scarcely covered their minks and their ladies' places!

One creation looked particularly lovely: a skimpy

pleated dress which the caption on the black and white photo said was red, and which left the knees uncovered. The shoulders too were bare, with no straps or anything to hold the dress up, and Stella wondered why the model's breasts did not pop out; perhaps there was some fearsome arrangement of whalebone straps hidden inside the dress. At any rate she wanted that dress, even if the stays did hurt! Her eyes lingered on the strapless dress. How she wanted it: and more, she found that she *wanted* to feel the tight whalebone biting her skin as her dress was held over her proud breasts, tantalising her adoring suitors with a glimpse of creamy flesh, yet firmly concealing her nipples. Was there a brassière under it? She could not tell, but she supposed she would be bare-breasted under the cloth, and – a luscious, naughty thought – perhaps would have no knickers either! In her heart, Stella already possessed that dress.

She looked glumly at the sensible grey flannel she would shortly don for her leaving ceremony, at the grey woollen stockings and coarse hemp garter belt with thick rubber straps. Then she looked again at the Parisian models. She knew that in London, too, the 'flappers' dressed thus. Women were able to vote now, and smoke in public, and get into taxis on their own – surely they had the right to wear lovely underthings and to look desirable? There were so many things a lady could use to attain the mysterious state of desirability: potions, creams, tweezers and scents. Judging by the small advertisements at the back of the magazine, the French readers seemed particularly fond of 'depilatories', which would leave a lady's arms and legs creamy smooth, without the painful aid of the razor.

Some of the creams seemed to be actually designed for a lady's mink, and the delights of having one's lady's place totally bare were described in winsome if rather roundabout language. Stella thought this extraordinary but was nonetheless intrigued by it. She wondered how a lady could be more desirable by being bare in a place no one was allowed to see. And once she had a husband, who was allowed to see it (Stella was sure), then being desirable surely wouldn't matter any more, because she would already have a husband. She thought suddenly that she did not want a husband at all, and was astonished at this boldness. Stella wanted above all to be desired, although she could not imagine being desired by any of the red-faced, tweedy young men of the Midlands that she had met and danced with at carefully-chaperoned church socials. Perhaps she would meet a dashing young man in Scotland, a clan chief with a sabre and a swirling kilt, like Robert the Bruce or Rob Roy or Bonnie Prince Charlie: a noble male burning with desire for Stella, full of bold deeds to prove himself worthy.

She had never told anyone about her dreams, not even Natalie Huggins or Miss Cox. She was afraid of being mocked, either because her dreams were so odd, or else because they were so simple that every girl had them. Perhaps every girl did, but they never talked about them. Did all girls dream of being Fletcher Christian, or St George, or one of Amundsen's huskies? Then again, perhaps such ideas would seem outlandish. Perhaps proper girls did not dream of being whipped at the mast, or beaten on the bare in the South Seas, but of a nice husband in Halesowen or Moseley, a Ford motor car, and a clutch of shiny, well-behaved children in a comfortable tree-lined avenue of red bricks and grey roofs.

Though she had never dared, she did sense she could confide in Miss Cox, whom she worshipped. It was Miss Cox whose inspiration made her want to be a teacher herself, and impart her gift of learning to other girls. She admired Miss Cox for her effortless and supreme exercise of power. Stella wanted, as a schoolmistress, to enjoy such power herself: to teach was to exercise power for the good. It was as a favour to Miss Cox that she was going back to School for the first day of September Term, although she had left classes the previous June. It was to receive her gold medal: a prize for her academic prowess and being the School Captain of Netball, Chief Monitor, and winning a glittering scholarship to Kernece College. She was to be presented to the new juniors as a glowing example of what a St Hilda's girl could achieve. Mr Phipps had wanted her to apply for Cambridge, but Stella was insistent that she wanted to be a teacher, and it was Miss Cox who had recommended her to Kernece, the finest and most exclusive College in Britain.

'You will be teaching *them* at Cambridge, Stella,' she said with a sweet lopsided smile and a twinkle in her lovely doe eyes.

Miss Cox looked just like one of the Parisian models. How Stella envied and adored her! But she had never dared tell her of the dreams. Sometimes her dreams had Miss Cox in them, too, and when the dream was over Stella found herself all sweaty and strange in her lady's place. It was as though she had wet the bed, although she had never done such a thing, even as a child. She would see Miss Cox's elfin body in her underthings, or sometimes bare, but always hazily, as though through gossamer. Once, she had dreamt she was St George, and Miss Cox, naked, was the dragon!

Stella was slaying her with a shining lance, which she stuck into Miss Cox between her thighs, again and again. Stella thought even in her dream that it must be very painful and could not understand why Miss Cox was urging her to strike harder and more rapidly. When she awoke, Stella was lathered in sweat, her lady's place all burning and tingly and nice at the same time, like being washed in a bath of hot milk. And in another dream, it was not Stella herself as Joan of Arc, but Miss Cox. Before the fire was lit beneath the brave heroine, Stella ripped her shining armour to reveal her naked body, then whipped her very severely on her back and her bottom until she was red with the pain, but Stella could not make Miss Cox cry out. That dream too made her awake all wet between her thighs.

She thought of these dreams as she recommenced her inspection of her body, the very act now seeming naughty. She longed for the compliments that men were supposed to shower on ladies they admired, but Stella could not remember ever receiving any. Was it her full, perhaps too imposing, body? Her tallness? Men wrote of women with perfect figures, but, infuriatingly, never gave details. Certainly, the models in her magazine all seemed elfin and boyish, almost waif-like. Was that a perfect figure? In which case, Stella could scarcely qualify as desirable: she had long hair, ash blonde and very silky, which she thought felt nice when she ran her fingers through it.

Her breasts were very large, although they stood up quite firm and pert on their own, without the aid of any corselage or brassière, and Stella was not sure whether she should be proud of that. Her fesses swelled quite handsomely, but were probably too big and smooth – and fruity! – for men who liked these gamine models. Yet in her fleeting glimpses of Rubens and Poussin, she had seen goddesses who were every bit as rounded and full-figured as herself, and they seemed to be the centre of the males' admiring attentions. Perhaps what was desirable changed with some unfathomable male logic every couple of decades, and that was why so many nice women never found a husband. Being a girl was so confusing!

She shivered as the desire suddenly washed over her that she longed to feel a man run his fingers through her hair, kiss her on the lips, touch her shoulder ... Touch her breasts! Touch her there, on her big plum nipples, and even ... No, surely not down there, where her full soft mink led to the pink lips of her lady's place. Did married people do such things? She could not imagine Mr and Mrs Phipps doing it! But something in her made her yearn for a man's hand to touch her there, even kiss her. She gulped at the wickedness of the thought. She knew from biology class how children were produced, that men had a 'sex organ' between their legs, like the stamen (or was it pistil?) of a flower, which they would put inside their wives in order to fertilise her.

There was no question of enjoying this operation: it was something a dutiful wife had to endure for the sake of her marriage. Males were apparently strange impulsive creatures, given to sulking if their wishes were not met. They apparently got pleasure from 'sowing their seed', as Miss

Foster the science mistress quaintly put it, and wives were supposed to gain pleasure from giving pleasure to their men. Stella thought this laudable and sensible enough, but surely Nature had allowed the female to take just the tiniest bit of pleasure at this act of creation? The immediacy of her final day made all these thoughts crowd into Stella's brain, flustering her.

She sighed as she reached for her uniform, left lovingly folded and starched while she had spent an impatient summer walking in the Brecon Beacons with Natalie and her family. School seemed already far away, and she was eager to leave for Scotland. But first she must listen to the speeches and collect her prizes and medal which would be her only mementoes of the long years at St Hilda's, apart from the dinner plate with the gold school crest which she had been unable to resist taking from the Prefects' common room on the last day of the Summer Term. Still, precious memories were not to be found in things, but in knowledge acquired and friendships made, and she was grateful for the first, if not the second.

But still she hesitated. She looked down at her full, lush mink, and wondered again why a lady would want to be bare down there. Then she reflected that it was perhaps no different from shaving her armpits. She played with her silky hairs, braiding them round her fingers, and then, suddenly, she thought once more of Miss Foster and her biology lessons. She was electrified with yearning for a male's pistil (stamen?) to swell up hard and enter her there, in her lady's place. A yearning to feel him lying heavy on her naked body and pumping hard at her loins until he sowed his seed in her. She gasped at the intensity of her vision and did something she had never ever done before: she put a finger inside herself.

She felt the inside of her lady's place all moist and oily, and as she moved her finger the moisture flowed more copiously still. Her fingers came to a barrier, a membrane that she guessed from class was her virginity. It needed a male to break it – a male's sex organ – and she longed for a male to enter her and break her, so that she could explore herself further! Her little nubbin was quite tingly now and she touched herself there, too, each caress sending shocks of pleasure through her belly and spine. She had never done that before: so much was happening to her at once that she felt giddy. And then her warm excitement turned to horror and remorse. It was her *thought*: she had wanted a *male* inside her or, more correctly, a male's sex organ. She had not thought of marriage or a wedding ring or a husband, or even a particular person, just a male organ, all stiff and full of sperm – as though she were no more than an animal.

Her heart was stabbed with agony and sorrow. She had been sinful in thought, which was as bad as sinning in deed! She was sure everybody would look at her and know that she was sinful. Why, being naked and looking at herself for so long was sinful enough, but to think of a sex organ in its awful, brutal nudity, without the marriage sacrament . . . Her eyes brimmed with tears, and she hated herself!

'Oh,' she moaned in anguish, 'Oh, Stella . . .'

Then she saw her silver hairbrush and knew she must be punished. Mr Phipps had never so much as spanked her, and she thought that to be caned or spanked, especially with a heavy brush, must hurt horribly. But she knew that she *deserved* to be hurt horribly. She grasped the handle of the hairbrush and bent over until her hair flowed over the carpet like a shining river. This was the position that boys had to take in *Tom Brown's Schooldays* and other stories, for 'six of the best'. Boys were wicked, and she had been wicked in thought – so she must take punishment like a boy.

As Chief Monitor, she had sometimes been obliged to send a seriously errant girl to a Mistress for 'a talking-to', and she had vaguely and guiltily accepted this might mean corporal punishment. But she did not like such thoughts, and for her own peace of mind suppressed them. Miss Cox had no need of *that*, surely? Now, Stella was about to discover for herself what 'that' felt like.

Trembling, and biting her lip, she lifted the hairbrush

and dealt her naked buttocks a stinging slap which brought tears to her eyes. She gritted her teeth and lashed her bare fesses again, and again, feeling them smart and glow with the awful pain. But when she had got to six, she knew that it was not enough, that she had to spank herself to her limit. Mingled with her determination was a pride that she could take as much as any male.

'Come now, Stella,' she said, gasping, 'you are a big girl and can take a big girl's punishment. At least a couple of dozen, I think.'

'No! No!' she answered herself in mock-falsetto. 'Please, Miss! Two dozen, and bare! That would hurt my poor bottom most cruelly!'

'Stella, you are wicked, and deserve to be hurt for your wicked thoughts, and for your insolent pleading. Now I think it shall be three full dozen, yes, quite bare, till your bottom is quite red and you are squirming and smarting like a fourth-former.'

'Pah!' she cried. 'You can make it four dozen, and I shan't flinch, any more than Tom Brown or Sir Walter Raleigh or brave Sir Galahad! Tan my bare bum and see if I care!'

Stella was impatient to continue her punishment. When the dialogue was completed to her satisfaction, a reckless glee seized her, and she made her blows as hard as she could, as though her poor bare bottom were a rebellious servant who must be tamed and corrected. She did not stop spanking herself until her naked buttocks had taken full sixty strokes of the hairbrush. She was gasping and flushed, and far from being displeased, she felt a glorious warmth and an intense, surprising tingle in her throbbing nubbin.

She rose and turned to inspect her bottom in the mirror, and the sight of her skin flaming red made her think she had the most beautiful bottom on Earth. Her lady's place simply flowed with hot liquid. Her mind was in turmoil; she felt her nubbin stiff and tingly, and her fingers could not help but creep there and caress herself. As a shock of pure joy at her woman's beauty coursed through Stella, she knew she was discovering herself as never before. Her body felt like the petals of a flower unfolding in the sun's warmth. Fleetingly, she wished it had been Miss Cox spanking her, and at that her whole body shook in a golden spasm of pure ecstasy. Though she did not know it then, Stella Shawn had masturbated for the very first time.

The feeling of warmth and joy with which Stella's masturbation had filled her lasted through her breakfast – with Mr and Mrs Phipps commenting on how ruddy-cheeked and healthy she looked – right until the moment she knocked on Miss Cox's door and was bade enter. Miss Cox too said that she looked well, and must have enjoyed her summer vacation. In fact, Stella's heart was so light with happiness that, in donning her dreary grey uniform, she had mischievously omitted to put on her knickers, and relished the swish of cool air on her mink and between her thighs as she walked.

'Yes, Miss,' said Stella, blushing, for she was sure from the glint in Miss Cox's eye that she *knew*. About the knickers – she must have guessed! – and about the other thing, too.

Stella wished *she* knew more about the momentous thing which had happened to her young body, a wondrous pleasure that Miss Foster had not mentioned in her biology lessons. Stella was certain it had lots to do with pistils and stamens and 'sex organs' . . .

'Well, Stella, I am glad you look so smart,' said Miss Cox, smoothing the upper breast of Stella's blouse. 'We have a busy day ahead. Speeches, then your presentation, then luncheon with the Governors. It is so good of you to make time for St Hilda's.'

'You look very smart too, Miss Cox,' stammered Stella with a blush. In truth, Miss Cox looked 'desirable': she wore a crisp white pleated skirt that swirled beautifully around her shapely calves, and a silk white blouse to match, with a little gold choker at her neck and pearl earrings. Her hair was done in the very latest style, cut short with little bobs at her forehead and curling around her cheeks – like one of the American 'film stars', Stella thought.

'Why, thank you, Stella,' said Miss Cox. 'We have a little time before the ceremonies begin, and I would ask you to sit down, but I am afraid there is some other business to attend to: so please remain standing.'

'Of course, Miss,' said Stella, puzzled. 'But what –'

'It is a little matter of a gold-crested plate.'

'A plate?' Stella started guiltily, for with sudden, awful certainty she knew well what Miss Cox meant.

'Yes, Stella,' continued the Headmistress with a wry smile, 'it is the plate which you took away on the last day of the Summer Term. That you *stole* from the School, Stella.'

'Oh! But, Miss, I didn't mean any harm!'

'Stealing is stealing. As Chief Monitor, you should have been concerned to set an example.'

'But no one knew!' cried Stella, her heart pounding.

'*I* know,' said Miss Cox evenly. 'And *you* know. You also know that wickedness must be punished, even when – no, especially when – it is committed by a girl in trust.'

'I'll give it back, Miss, I promise,' sobbed Stella miserably. Miss Cox put a consoling arm around her shoulder.

'Don't cry, Stella, my dear,' she said. 'I don't want your last and finest day at School to be spoiled. Of course you may keep the plate, that is not the issue. It is the matter of your wickedness and the punishment for it. Now, as Chief Monitor, you would administer small punishments – detention, lines, and so forth. But for more serious offences, you would refer a girl to me.'

'Yes, Miss.'

'And you must have known what that meant.'

'I never liked to think about it, Miss.'

'About what, Stella?' asked Miss Cox sweetly, wiping Stella's tear-stained cheeks with a scented lace hankie.

'The . . . the cane, Miss.'

'Does it frighten you?'

'Yes, Miss, ever so much!'

'But you realise that in this matter, I have no choice. The cane it must be. Of course, you are no longer at School, and may go now unpunished, with neither ceremony nor prize.'

'No, Miss!' cried Stella. 'That would be too awful! No, please ... Of course I accept! Anything from *you*, Miss!'

'Good,' said Miss Cox briskly. 'Well, this is a new experience for you, I suppose, unless you are beaten by your guardian Mr Phipps, which I doubt. I propose to give you four strokes, Stella. Are you sure you can take them?'

Stella felt her throat clutch and an icy chill in her heart. A spanking with a hairbrush was one thing, but four with the *cane* ...! She stared aghast as Miss Cox opened the bottom drawer of her desk and withdrew a supple, shiny little cane about three feet in length. It had a curved handle and a tip splayed in two. Trembling, Stella swallowed hard and stretched out her hands, palms up. Miss Cox smiled.

'No, Stella,' she said ruefully. 'Oh dear. You are a goose, aren't you? At St Hilda's the cane is given on the bottom – on the knickers, to be precise. So having accepted your punishment, you will please bend over my chair and lift your skirt up to your shoulders. Let me know when you are quite comfortable, and I'll begin.'

'Oh, Miss! I can't!' cried Stella, blushing in agonised embarrassment.

'Why ever not?' said Miss Cox severely. 'Don't be silly, Stella. You are a big girl now, almost a woman, and we haven't time to waste. When you get to Kernece College, you will find that you are expected to behave in a mature fashion, not to blub and squeal. And there is much at Kernece which will require all your power of understanding.'

'I'm not blubbing, Miss!' retorted Stella indignantly. 'It is just that ... that I have no knickers on. So there!'

Miss Cox smiled a delicious smile, her cherry red lipstick gleaming over her pearl-white teeth.

'Well, well,' she murmured. 'You *are* a big girl. Going knickerless is a serious offence, but since you are no longer at School, I must overlook it. However, you'll have to take your earned punishment on the bare, won't you?'

'On the bare?' stammered Stella, fearing not so much her punishment – although that thought was horrid enough – as much as the tell-tale redness of her already spanked bottom, and the indescribable shame of having to expose her bare nates to another's gaze. But she suddenly thrilled at the idea of showing herself naked to Miss Cox.

'Bare bum, Stella,' said Miss Cox quietly, and the gleam in her eye, now, was not merciful. 'Four tight ones on your naked bottom. Boys can take it – why, at Eton, they kneel at the block, trousers and knickers off, to take a full dozen with the birch! And I have only my little willow.'

She swished the cane in the air, and Stella shuddered at the fearful whirring noise. She gulped again.

'Very well, Miss,' she said.

'Good. I knew you would see reason. Well, let us get on with things. You may bend over now, Stella, and lift your skirts and petticoats as I have said. Place your legs well apart – feet touching the chair corners, I think.'

Her heart racing and her throat dry, yet filled with a curious tingle of desire, Stella bent over the chair and lifted her skirt and petticoats over her shoulders until the cloth caressed her shoulders. The chair back was quite high, and she was obliged to strain her long legs and support herself on tiptoe with her legs splayed wide. Her rubber suspenders were stretched tight and cut into her naked bottom. She could feel the air cool on the lips of her lady's place, and was shocked to feel deliciously naughty, as if the wickedness of exposing herself fulfilled a secret desire – as if she had always longed to be thus helpless and exposed! To her horror, yet with pleasure too, she felt a little seeping of the oily wet stuff moistening the dangling silky hairs of her mink.

She waited in an agony of fluttering anticipation for the first cut to fall on her unprotected buttocks, but instead felt the gossamer touch of Miss Cox's soft, cool fingers, stroking her globes very gently. She shivered with pleasure.

'Why, Stella,' said Miss Cox in a faraway voice, 'whatever has happened to your . . . to your lovely bottom? She is all red, as though . . .'

'Oh!' cried Stella. 'Is she?'

It seemed curious, yet somehow natural, to refer to her bottom as 'she'.

'I suppose I have been sitting down for too long.'

'Stella,' said Miss Cox sternly, 'do not lie to me. That *was* a lie, wasn't it?'

'Yes, Miss,' replied Stella miserably.

'Well, you'll take an extra cut for the lie. Five on the bare, Stella: think about it. Sometimes, you know, thinking about it is the worst part of the punishment. Now, tell the truth. You have been beaten already, haven't you?'

'Yes, Miss.'

'By your guardian?'

'Why, no, Miss! I had a wicked thought, and I spanked myself, with my hairbrush!'

And Stella blurted the truth: her dreams and longings, and her shame and puzzlement at them. Her helpless, subdued state seemed to make the confession easier. And all the time, she felt Miss Cox's cool fingers stroking her bottom – her 'bare bum' as she rather excitingly called it.

'Was I wrong, Miss? To have these thoughts, or to punish myself? I suppose you'll give me an extra cut for them.'

'Not wrong, Stella. Your thoughts are sweet and normal. And to have a "pash" for your Headmistress – why, I am flattered and pleased. You must know that I have always admired *you* . . . your strength, and your beauty.'

Miss Cox's breath was quite rapid, and her stroking of Stella's bare bum grew stronger and more insistent.

'Such a shame to stroke these beautiful globes,' she murmured. 'They would look lovely in knickers, little silk panties pulled up very high and tight between your fesses, so that it would almost be like flogging you bare.' She sighed. 'The cane is not the same as your hairbrush.'

'I know, Miss, but five it must be. And as tight as you like. I can take it.'

'Oh, they'll be tight. There is no other way. Very well, then. No silly blubbing or flinching or crying out, mind, or you get the cut over again.'

Stella heard the cane lift, then there was an awful swishing noise, and she almost jumped out of her skin as a white-hot pain seared her naked skin. She thought she had never felt anything so dreadful, and she had to clench her teeth to stop herself from crying out as her gorge rose.

'One,' said Miss Cox. 'Only four to go. Tight, was it?'

'Gosh, yes, Miss!' cried Stella. 'Oh! How it stings! I don't know how I shall take another four!'

'Well, you've chosen to, so you'll find out. Two!'

Stella could not help emitting a muffled 'Ooh!' as the cane cut her in exactly the same place as before. She felt her legs tremble and her bum squirm, and hoped this would not earn her a further stroke.

Miss Cox said thoughtfully that she would find Kernece College very interesting. 'Kernece is remote, and there is a noble beauty in remoteness,' she said. 'To be a teacher of others is the noblest profession, Stella. And to teach others, one must first learn to be taught oneself. You have been powerful in a small way at St Hilda's. When you reach Kernece, you'll find that, though a woman now, in many ways you will have less power than the meanest fourth-former. It is by learning to obey that one learns to command. Three!'

The third cut took Stella slightly lower, across the soft place where her bottom met her upper thighs, and was more painful than the first two put together. Yet now, Stella did not feel the need to cry out. She could not help her bottom squirming a little, but she felt with a glorious surprise that she had mastered the agony of her beating, that her pain was a warm, glowing, part of her.

'How I wish that *I* could have gone to Kernece,' said Miss Cox, her voice panting now, as though it were she taking the cane. 'Miss Dancer, the Principal, liked you at your interview in Birmingham. No other St Hilda's girl has even been accepted for Kernece, let alone awarded a scholarship. She is a particular friend of mine, as we were at Cambridge together. We share certain educational ideas, although I envy her, since in her northern fastness she is better able to put them into practice than I am in the cosy Midlands of England. But I took my present position gladly, as it is quite an honour to be a headmistress at the age of thirty. My, how beautifully your bum is reddening!'

Once more, Stella thrilled to feel Miss Cox's touch on her bare nates.

'There is an art of discipline, Stella. At Kernece, you shall learn that art, and carry my dreams with you. Four!'

The fourth cut seared Stella's bare like a burning lance, but she rode the pain, and found herself exultant. She dreamt she was a tough, muscled salt, strapped to the mast and whipped by Drake himself; or Joan of Arc, lips sealed as she was flogged at the stake. She could take it! And with this knowledge, she felt the moisture of her excitement flow quite copiously in her lady's place: now, it was a feeling she adored and craved.

'We have not much time, so I must finish. Oh, Stella, I should like to keep you here all day, and skin you with a beautiful slow dozen. But the ceremony awaits.'

'I could take a dozen from you, Miss. A dozen of your tightest. Gladly!' cried Stella.

'Oh, Stella . . .'

'Make it *half* a dozen, Miss, if that will give you pleasure.'

'A full six?'

'Yes! Oh, please, Miss! Then my wickedness shall be washed quite away.'

Stella could not believe it was her own voice she heard, that she was actually begging to be flogged!

'Very well. If it is any consolation, you should know that not all my canings are on the knickers. Some girls must take the cane on the bare, but there is not one of them who doesn't blub and squeal and wriggle. Although, Stella, it is very nice to see a girl's naked fesses wriggle and squirm. There is something satisfying and pure about it.'

'Make me squirm, Miss,' Stella whispered. 'I want to give you pleasure.' And as she spoke, her fount was wet.

At the fifth, ferocious cut, there was a loud snap, and Stella knew that the cane had severed the rubber of her garter straps! She felt her stockings sag, and did not care.

'Oh . . . You shall borrow one of mine,' said Miss Cox. 'Six!'

Then the sixth cut came, and this time Stella really did

squirm. The pain lifted her to a plateau of sensation she could never have imagined: so great that it was almost joy. Miss Cox took her with the cane vertical, full in the cleft of her buttocks, and she felt a new and vertiginous agony as the splayed tip danced briefly against the tight wrinkled bud of her bumhole! But her heart sang: she had taken 'six of the best', and taken it like a man!

'There. It is over,' panted Miss Cox, her voice laboured. 'I must fetch you another garter belt, a silk one this time. Wait, do not turn round just yet . . . Oh, Oh, *Oh!*'

But it was too late. Stella turned in alarm to look at Miss Cox, and saw her skirt up around her waist. Between her garter belt and stockings, her fingers were fiercely rubbing her naked lady's place, which was shaven bare! Stella saw this only for an instant, before Miss Cox let her skirt fall again to cover herself. She was panting, and blushed furiously, with a shamefaced grin.

'Well, Stella, now you know my little secret,' she said breathlessly. '*I* don't wear knickers either . . .'

2

Beneath the Kilt

The day's ceremonies were tiring but joyful. Stella was duly lauded and paraded before the dignitaries and new girls as an example of St Hilda's excellence. She finally left School with a sore bottom, but clutching her medal, and a prize of twenty whole guineas! It was more money than she had ever held in her life, and Mr Phipps advised her to open a bank account forthwith, which at eighteen years old she could do without his consent. She said she would take the bus into Wolverhampton and open an account there, calling first at Duckham's department store to purchase socks and stationery and other things for her new life at Kernece.

She did indeed mean to buy these things, but on entering the vast classical portals of Duckham's she was overawed by the array of goods displayed so as to make any lady's mouth water, and especially one from the West Midlands. There was counter upon counter brimming with scents, lotions, paints and creams. Beyond stretched acres of every imaginable garment, bag, glove, shoe or jewel for woman's adornment, and all of the latest London mode. There were underthings of creamy silk and satin: stockings, garters, knickers and brassières; camisoles, suspenders, bodices and corsets, in a rainbow of luscious hues. Stella had often wanted to linger in the paradise of Duckham's but had never had the leisure, or the money, to do so. Now, with her twenty guineas, she could.

On returning home, she hurried to her room and hid one

of her two large shopping bags under her bed. The other she dutifully showed to Mr Phipps. It contained a sweater, toiletries, some writing things, and sensible socks and knickers. Mr Phipps nodded approvingly.

'And the bank book?' he said.

'Oh . . .' said Stella, flustered, and lied to Mr Phipps for the first time ever. 'They'll send it on to me at Kernece.'

She reassured herself that it was only a white lie. There was no bank book, but there *might* have been.

That night, her last in Stourbridge, Stella waited until her guardians had retired and then opened her purchases. She touched them, smelled them, and reverently pressed them to her body. She did not yet try them, though: they were to wait for Scotland. She slept fitfully, dreaming of the long day's travel ahead: the train to Birmingham, then an overnight sleeper to Inverness, where a car would await to take her to Kernece. It was a pity she would not see all of the glens and lochs and heather in the velvet Caledonian night. But she knew that once in that romantic land, her tall, impossibly handsome chief would find her, and she would be properly robed for him. He would be kind, and have a mischievous twinkle in his eye, but with a streak of ruthlessness, perhaps even cruelty. He would not hesitate to – Stella gulped at the unbidden but beautiful thought – put her over his rippling kilted thighs and spank her bottom if she were naughty.

The next afternoon in Birmingham, Stella's mind still whirled with these daydreams as she said her tearful farewells to Mr and Mrs Phipps, and boarded the night train to Inverness. She had a compartment to herself, in a Pullman car – an act less of generosity by Mr Phipps than of his concern for the morals of a young lady travelling alone, even though Scotland did not *quite* count as abroad. He had to admit that the Scots had distinguished themselves in the Great War, although they were rather fond of their whisky. She had a book to read, one of the popular novels of Miss Celia Rummidge, whose adventures of dashing gallants and swooning maidens she normally enjoyed. But she was unable to concentrate, and thought:

soon I shall find my own gallant, and do my own swooning.

As the pleasant English landscape rattled past her window, she could no longer resist opening her precious shopping bag: after all, she was as good as in Scotland, and she would have to dress for dinner. She spread her things on the bed and gazed in awe at her treasures. Her heart fluttering, she stripped and looked once more at her naked body in the looking-glass. She blushed as she saw that her bare bottom still bore the lovely marks of Miss Cox's caning: the crimson flush had turned to a delicious purple, like the petals of an orchid, as though Miss Cox had painted a picture on her skin. It still hurt a little, but it was a nice comfortable hurt that made her grin ruefully, and gave her the cosy feeling that she possessed her own secret badge of honour.

The dinner bell rang in the corridor, and at last it was time to dress. Trembling a little, she inspected her new underthings, and chose black. She rolled on the sheerest black silk stockings, pulling them tight over her thighs; over them, panties of the same silk, with a rather garish lace fringe. The panties were cut very high and the cloth that covered her swelling mons was so narrow that stray golden hairs peeped out from her mink. She pulled the panties up as high and tight as she could, making the silk bite into her fount-lips and in the cleft of her bottom, which gave her a deliciously naughty pleasure.

Then she donned the matching silk garter belt, and fumbled with the straps until she had the stockings fastened. Garter belts were such a bother! Even though a nice bother ... Why could men not invent the essential – a garter strap that was easy to fasten – instead of inventing cannons and aeroplanes and things? She wondered if female clothing, even in the Twentieth Century, was a subtle male plot to keep women in their place: jackets without pockets, stockings that laddered, frills and flounces that got caught in things, awkward high heels, and all the accessories to think about! And while men measured their clothing in sensible inches, women's sizes seemed to mean nothing at all! Then Stella had a vision of a world without frills or flounces, corsets or lip gloss or high heels, everything measured in sensible inches, and shuddered.

Her black outfit gave her a choice of a brassière with deep-scooped cups to thrust the breasts up, or, in deference to the current elfin mode, a bodice or camisole which would flatten them into a boyish slimness. She chose the camisole, which buttoned at the front, but she cheated a little by not fastening the top two buttons – it would have squeezed a little *too* much – so that her upper bosom was buoyantly like two juicy peaches. She looked at her new red corset, a proper one of tight satin, which would go with her black knickers and everything, but no, she must leave room for dinner! Her corset would be a pleasure for another day, and she promised herself she would lace it *really* tight . . .

Her belly tingled, and she felt again that curious moistness in her lady's place as she gasped at her own loveliness in the glass. She applied kohl to her eyes, lipstick and scent, then put on a lovely choker of white imitation pearls, with clustered pearl earrings. Finally she slipped on a cocktail dress – the very thought of even owning such a thing made her giddy – which had the thinnest of straps and was cut very low over her breasts, pinched her waist quite adorably, then broadened into a swirl of pleats that caressed her thighs, the hem well above her knees. Red high-heeled shoes matched her dress, and she relished the smooth sliding of her silken feet into the sweet fresh leather. Finally she swept her long blonde mane with casual daring across her forehead to one side, and fastened it with a tortoiseshell barrette. She was ready for dinner.

Her table in the dining-car matched her expectations, with crisp linen and shining crystal. Conversation hushed at her entrance, and male eyes turned to her. Secretly delighted, she made a moue of hauteur as the fawning steward seated her alone by the window. He proffered the gold-tasselled menu, and asked if she would care for a cocktail. Stella was momentarily flustered.

'Ah, lemonade, please,' she said.

'I am sorry, Madam, we do not serve lemonade,' said the hair-creamed steward, a hint of a smirk behind his urbanity. 'We have Glen Troon mineral water, if Madam likes.'

'Yes, yes, that is what I meant,' said Stella, unconsciously smoothing her hair and fidgeting with her shoulder strap. Did she detect grins amongst the male diners, who all seemed busy with wine or whisky? They were a disappointing lot, really: businessmen in grey suits whose air buzzed with talk of orders and payments. Stella felt herself a flower in a sea of dullness.

Her mineral water arrived; it was fizzy, and not unlike lemonade. Stella was wondering if it would be a *faux pas* to put a spoonful of sugar in it, when her thoughts were interrupted by the steward again, who asked if she was ready to order. She rapidly perused the menu, found it mostly in French, and opted for simple roast beef, boiled potatoes and salad.

Shortly, there was a hubbub at the car entrance, and the steward reappeared, flustered himself this time, and asked if Madam would mind being joined by another single lady. Stella assented graciously, in truth pleased to have company, and shortly afterwards the leather banquette opposite her emitted a whoosh as a large female bottom plumped firmly down on it. This bottom was attached to an apparition of loveliness that had Stella fidgeting with her hair and shoulder straps once more, and feeling absurdly overdressed, or underdressed, or ... she wasn't sure at all!

The woman opposite was her own age, with short dark hair, dressed in the same up-to-the-minute style as Miss Cox's, that framed a strong, handsome, face with wide lips and high cheekbones. Her sparkling pearl choker and earrings looked real, and her cocktail dress of simple black artfully flattened what was obviously a bosom as ample as Stella's. Her waist was wasp-thin, and Stella supposed glumly that she wore the tightest, sweetest corset. Her dress was so short that Stella could see the tops of her stockings, with the skimpiest of suspender belts and lacy knickers, which the woman made no attempt to hide from the ogling male eyes! All at once, Stella felt terribly gauche and girly.

'Service on this bloody thing is bloody awful,' said the newcomer in a loud voice, not looking at Stella. 'Oi! Where's my whisky? Laphroaig, d'you hear? And a large one!' She focused on Stella for a moment, then on her glass.

'What's that stuff? *Water?*'

'They had no lemonade,' said Stella.

'Oi! Bring this lassie a whisky too! And bring her some lemonade! I don't care if you have to stop the train to get it, if a lady wants lemonade, she gets served lemonade, you bloody sassenach! Have a gasper, hen.'

She pulled out a packet of Player's Capstan and extracted a cigarette, which she threw on the table in front of Stella. Stella picked it up nervously, for she had never smoked, and was not sure of the correct etiquette. Her companion stuck the white tube in her mouth and pointed it upwards, cocking her head in haughty expectance, and at once the steward was there to light it for her. Stella did the same, marvelling at the assurance by which female beauty could extract service from a male. She took a nervous puff but did not imitate the other woman, who swallowed a ferocious lungful and exhaled with a grunt of satisfaction.

'I'm Morag. Who are you?' she said brusquely. Her accent was surprisingly plummy, a creamy aristocratic drawl which sat oddly with her coarse idiom, and Stella felt newly embarrassed at her slightly flat Midland vowels. She introduced herself and explained the purpose of her journey. Morag slapped a palm to her forehead, mock-dramatically.

'Just my luck!' she cried. 'A new squit. I'm at Kernece too, second year now. God, I shouldn't even be talking to you! I need that whisky!'

The whiskies duly arrived, along with a dusty bottle labelled 'American Cream Soda' (from Leeds). Morag sniffed her drink approvingly, then took an enormous swallow. Stella was at a loss, but told herself that she was a grown-up modern woman, and should smoke gaspers and drink whisky. She sipped the amber liquid and coughed at its fiery medicinal taste. Morag laughed, and told her to add 'some of that lemonade muck'. Stella filled the glass with cream soda, and sipped again, and this time found it palatably sweet. Already, Morag had drained her glass, and was calling for more. Sniffily, she pushed the menu aside.

'Have you ordered?' she demanded.

'Why, yes, I ordered –'

'Well, don't. The stuff on the menu is muck, for the sassenachs in suits. They keep the good stuff refrigerated, for the English nobs, may they rot in Hades.'

When further whiskies arrived, Morag told the steward to forget what Madam had said, and bring them both lobsters and a bottle of Heidsieck champagne. Stella felt the whisky warm her quite pleasantly, and thought that the Twentieth Century and women's emancipation were catching up with her all at once. She was even enjoying puffing on her cigarette, and found she could shape the smoke into pretty little rings.

'I'm sorry, Morag,' she said, 'but you don't sound like a Scot. I mean, your voice is very English.'

'Dear Stella, a lady never ever says she is sorry. Especially one as pretty as you.'

Stella blushed.

'This benighted country is the only one where polite society speaks in the accent of its class and not its birthplace. I'm a Highland lass, but brought up in the land of sassenachs. Kernece, for example, is about as far north in Scotland as you can get, but it isn't Scottish at all. A bit like Pembroke in Wales, which is awfully English. I should know – Daddy seems to own most of it.'

Two steaming lobsters were placed before them.

'Ah, tuck!' cried Morag. 'Eat up, it'll be hard tack when we get to Kernece. Worse for me, 'cos I'm a day late! Heinous offence! Probably get the steps, or the brank, or maybe a swishing at the block, if Dancy's in a foul mood. Well,' she said, seeing Stella's puzzled and alarmed expression, 'you'll learn all about that later, I'm afraid. I'm running out of excuses – this time I had to go to some dreary ball at Windsor, to find a noble sassenach husband. Hmph!'

Stella had never eaten lobster before, but wisely waited for the voracious Morag to show her how, and when she had mastered the art of shell-cracking, she found the succulent white meat delicious in its lemony butter sauce. Her whisky seemed to have emptied, and she started on the second, but Morag told her to keep it and take champagne. That too was new to Stella and she told Morag that she liked it much better than lemonade.

'Well, you'll get none at Kernece!'

Tremulously, Stella asked the meaning of the awful-sounding things Morag had mentioned: the steps, the brank, the swishing at the block. Morag laughed grimly.

'Punishments, hen! And you new squits have it the worst. You must learn to survive, or go under. A few girls can't take it and quit, which of course they may do any time, but they have to live with shame. You must be tough, Stella, for only by learning to take the discipline of teaching can you learn to impose it. And I don't just mean the cane and such, I mean using your power, your aura, for good. That is why I want to be a schoolmistress, not some doll of a Duchess, idling away my life at Biarritz and Monte Carlo and all those yawn-making holes. I suppose at whatever Dotheboys Hall you were at, you were a prefect and Captain of Netball and won a Kernece Scholarship and all that rot.'

'Why, yes,' said Stella, startled, 'how did you know?'

'You look the type. Well, being a Scholar isn't so bad, you get to wear a rather scrumptious long gown. But you still have to obey the Rules. Stella, Kernece is about unquestioning obedience: all excellence flows from that. You must be abased utterly in order to command. At first, you'll think you are back at school, only a thousand times worse. And it *is* a thousand times worse! You are back where school hasn't even been thought of! And half the battle of obeying the College Rules is *remembering* them! On top of them, there are the Game Rules, and the Army Rules . . .'

She paused, and her dark green eyes stared intently at Stella in a way that made her shiver.

'You are interesting,' said Morag. 'I see in you the strength to rule, but also the power to submit, which is perhaps the greatest strength.' She added cheerfully: 'You'll probably be bagged pretty quick for one of the Armies: I'm in the Reds, and I hope they bag you, but if you're bagged by the Blues, then we'll have to be deadly foes!'

Stella was glad of the drinks she had had, for they comforted her puzzlement and foreboding.

'I thought it was a College for grown-up girls,' she stammered. 'But all these punishments! I'm quite used to the cane,' she added proudly, telling her second white lie.

'Bare bum?'

'Why, yes. Of course.'

Morag nodded approvingly.

'I knew you were a lady,' she said. 'In Scotland, we favour a juicy tawse, because the punishment lasts longer.'

'But I had no idea. About the discipline, I mean.'

'Of course not! Kernece doesn't *advertise* itself. You'll be cold and get rotten food, and have to jump to it when a prefect calls for a drudge – that's the same as a fag at Eton. You'll have to work like a slave, and you'll always live in fear of chastisement.'

'Then, why do girls go there? Rather, why do they stay?'

Now it was Morag who looked puzzled.

'Because Kernece is the most wonderful bloody place on Earth,' she said.

Stella was careful not to drink at Morag's trooper's pace, but even so she felt herself pleasantly cosy and light-headed, and smoked her after-dinner cigarette quite luxuriously. Everything seemed nice, and even the prospect of cold showers and Scottish discipline – the mysterious tawses, branks and steps – seemed nothing for a strong English girl to cope with. It was dark outside, and the candle-lit dining-car did seem rather romantic, so it was quite natural that a tall young male should shimmer into view beside their table and ask in an soft accent as creamy as Morag's if he might offer the ladies a nightcap. Stella did not wait for Morag, but told him at once to sit down, and was thrilled with the authority in her voice; the more so when she inspected the young man.

He wore a kilt. Stella had only seen a kilt in pictures before, and this looked splendidly masculine, with a great bushy sporran and a lovely tartan of greens, pinks and golds that Stella would have loved to wear herself. His knees peeped from under the kilt, and were quite hairless and smooth, not at all bony as she had imagined. The young man was as blond as Stella, his hair cut very short, with a kiss-curl that Stella found adorable; his face was quite sunburnt, making it difficult to guess his age. He had piercing blue eyes under silky lashes, and a wide, strong mouth which curled in an engagingly modest smile. His tie was the same tartan as his kilt.

'I hope you don't think me forward,' he said, 'but the conversation of all these business types was beginning to bore me, and I thought . . . Well, I hope you don't mind. I'm not really very good with strangers.'

'You are more than welcome, Mr . . .?' Stella began.

'Isbister, Jamie Isbister.'

'You have an interesting name,' said Stella, when she and Morag had introduced themselves. 'Are you travelling far?'

'Oh,' he said, blushing, 'just to the jolly old family cottage. It's up in Sutherland, near Tongue. I've got a spot of leave – from the Army, you know. My name *is* curious. Actually, it's a place in Shetland, that my Viking ancestors sort of pillaged and whatnot, before they came down to Scotland and pillaged that too, before they were tamed by the womenfolk. I'm Lord Isbister, really, but I prefer Jamie, if you wouldn't mind calling me that. Or you can call me the Jarl of Yell! That's one of my monickers.'

'We're going to Sutherland – to Kernece,' said Stella.

'I've heard of that,' said Jamie. 'It's a sort of college for young ladies, isn't it? In fact I think my ancestors tried unsuccessfully to pillage it, but a tribe of ferocious women beat them off! Too mortifying for the Isbisters!'

'Yes,' said Morag, 'Castle Kernece has quite a history. Now, before we let you buy us a drink, sir, you must promise to tell us whether you are properly dressed as a Scotsman!'

'I don't quite follow, Miss Morag.'

'I mean, have you got any knickers on under that kilt?'

Stella's heart fluttered as the young man's face blushed crimson, with the sweetest of boyish smiles!

'Oh! I think I shall need a dram or two before I have the courage to answer that.' Flustered, he ordered them drinks.

'Your very good health,' he said. 'I am not used to such lovely modern ladies! I've been a soldier most of my time.'

'And for how long are you on leave?' asked Stella.

'As long as I like, really. I'm with Isbister's Guards. We're attached to the Highland Light Infantry, but I sort of run the show, d'you see. It is hereditary. Frightful bore, but one must do one's duty. We put up a good show at Ypres, then Gallipolli – in the War, you know. I was taken prisoner at Gallipolli, by the Turks, and when I got home, there ... there weren't all that many of us left.'

Stella felt that he had said more than he wished, for there was a moment of pain in his eyes, before he perked up and ordered more drinks. Stella was careful not to drink too much, but joined in the merry conversation, marvelling at Morag's wonderful bluntness, and feeling as gay as could be. The War! Isbister could not have been more than 23 or 24, if that, and her heart ached as she thought of this beautiful young man going to war at the tender age he must have been then. Scarcely older than her own father had been, who was now only a dim memory. Suddenly, she longed to comfort the young man, and soothe his pain with her woman's touch.

The night drew on, and Stella felt hypnotised by the soothing clatter of the rails, and the daring intimacy of Morag's conversation. Morag let fall a few hints about the regime of Kernece, and Jamie said it sounded just like Eton, and the conversation turned quite naturally to forms of chastisement. Jamie described the quaint ceremonies of Eton, where miscreants were paraded through College carrying the very birch which was to flog them kneeling at the block.

'A dozen on the bare!' he shivered. 'My, how it hurt! One got to keep the birch as a memento.'

'And did you receive many birchings?' asked Stella, her very words causing her fount to tingle.

'Oh! Yes!' he grinned. 'The War seemed tame after Eton.'

'Why, all properly brought up girls take it on the bare,' said Morag. 'There are no namby-pambies at Kernece. But now it seems these wretched sassenachs are shutting the bar, and we haven't had nearly enough, so I invite both of you to my room to share my own bottle of Drambuie.'

Stella found herself perched on Morag's bed in a compartment identical to her own. Golden liqueurs were poured, and she sipped sparingly and quietly, content to listen to the others.

'Now,' said Morag, 'it is time for us to learn the truth about your kilt, sir. Knickers or no knickers?'

'I hate to disappoint you, ladies, but I have knickers just like any other chap.'

'It is for us to decide whether we are disappointed,' said Morag with a mischievous gleam in her eyes. 'You will please show.'

'I say, that's not the sort of thing a young lady should ask a gentleman! I can't! I simply can't!'

'And no gentleman should refuse a lady's request,' replied Morag sweetly.

'I must agree, but, oh, you'll think ill of me!'

Stella said truthfully that she could not imagine thinking ill of him, and Morag added that she had seen plenty of men's knickers! Stella burned with curiosity to see Jamie's, and his mysterious bulge beneath. It seemed such naughty, splendid sport. Jamie shrugged ruefully, and began to slide his skirts up over his bare thighs.

'It's just that, well, men's knickers ... they aren't ... Oh, hang it, since you must, see for yourself!'

He pulled up the kilt, and Stella gasped in astonishment

and delight. Lord Isbister was wearing the loveliest, frilliest ladies' knickers she had ever seen! They were pink silk, with white ecru lace at the edges, and very tight indeed, so that the bulge of his stamen, or pistil, and the – gonads? – underneath, left nothing to her imagination.

'There!' he said miserably. 'Now you'll think I'm a bounder. The shame! Commander of the regiment, and dressing like a girly!'

Stella's eyes were fixed on his bulge, and she felt a sudden desire to remove the knickers and see what one of these strange, fascinating things looked like naked. She was going to say that he looked awfully sweet, and that men could wear pretty things just like girls, when Morag rapped: 'Indeed! I suppose you stole them from some poor girl. You *are* a bounder!'

'No!' he cried. 'I would never steal! They were ... given.'

'Rot!' retorted Morag, a gleam of real glee in her eyes. 'I say you're a bounder – my honour as a Kernece girl obliges me to report you to your regimental commander.'

'I am my regimental commander,' said Jamie glumly. 'You'd have to report me to Field Marshal Lord Stackenham. Oh, please don't, I beg you!'

'Well,' said Morag, 'We *could* be satisfied. If you will admit you are a beastly rotter, and agree to pay for it at once. You've been on the block at Eton, you know the form.'

'A flogging? Here?' gasped Jamie. 'Are you serious?'

'Of course. That curtain rail should serve nicely.'

'Oh! Heavens! I've never been beaten by a woman! But very well, Miss Morag, if it will please you. I swear I am innocent of any impropriety. It's just that, since the War, I – Oh, hang it, if you must beat me, get it over with!'

Without being asked, Stella fetched Morag the curtain rail, which was of springy steel a good four feet long. She shivered as she felt its smooth power, and the thought of the young man's bottom squirming under its kiss. Then her thought changed to her own bottom, naked and beaten, and her fount began to moisten in excitement!

'The knickers will have to come off,' said Morag quietly,

'for you're going to get it on the bare. A dozen stiff ones, Lord Isbister, my buck. Now, bend over and touch your toes.'

As Jamie Isbister lowered the frilly panties and obeyed, Morag gently touched the tip of his sex organ with the cane.

'Now, I know what happens when young men are flogged by a lady,' she said briskly. 'They get excited and their pea vine stands up most indecently! Well, there shall be none of that, otherwise the punishment is doubled. No, tripled!'

'There is no danger,' said the stooping male with sadness in his voice. 'You see ... Oh, dash it! I'll take your punishment because I know thrashing me will give you pleasure, and thrashing is all I deserve. I'm not a man! My pea vine *won't* stand! Ever since I was a prisoner of war ... The Turks dressed me in skirts and blouses and things, and made me a woman!'

'I see,' said Morag softly.

'And to my shame, I enjoyed it! I became their willing slave, and I survived thus, when so many of my comrades fell in the field. Ever since then, I have worn dresses, knickers and stockings and frilly things, to punish myself and remind myself of my guilt. So flog me, Miss Morag. As many strokes as you please, I shall take it thankfully.'

'Disciplining a male gives me pleasure, Isbister,' said Morag coolly. 'I think I'll take you completely naked.'

When Jamie had obediently stripped, she knotted his tie in a bow, as a ribbon for the balls beneath his sex organ.

'Wait!' cried Stella, giddy with yearning and tenderness for the sweet, broken-hearted male helpless before her. 'Here, you are almost the same size as me. Put on my dress. It shall be part of your punishment.'

She did not mean it: she longed to see his magnificent body robed as her, *become* her, under punishment. A strange feeling invaded Stella's breast: she had relished her own chastisement, and longed to see Jamie's bottom squirm under Morag's lash. But the thought of wielding the cane herself, and inflicting pain on another, seemed dreadful. Yet Jamie would look so lovely flogged as a woman: as her!

She stripped to her camisole and knickers, and handed Jamie the dress, helping him to put it on with trembling fingers. It was a tight fit, but robed him beautifully, and she had a glance of his poor limp pea vine. Even soft, it was wonderfully huge, and she wondered how such a monstrous, beautiful thing could ever fit into a lady's tender place. And as Jamie hugged the dress to himself, breathing Stella's perfume, she saw the sex organ tremble and thicken! He was *not* limp!

Suddenly he blushed, and said, 'Miss Stella, please don't think me rude, but it would be so much more shaming for me if I had your stockings on too, and your garter belt.'

Without a word, Stella divested herself of her shoes, garter belt and stockings and helped the young lord to roll the stockings up his muscled legs, and strap them to the garter belt. Her fount was sopping wet, and she did not care! Finally, she grasped his feet and with some effort squeezed them into her shoes.

'I'd give you my knickers, too,' she heard herself say, 'only you've been ordered to take it bare.'

He grinned sheepishly and nodded, then touched the tips of Stella's shoes, with the dress lifted over his back, and his legs spread well apart on Morag's orders. Then Morag began his beating. Her muscles quivered powerfully at her first stroke, and Jamie jumped, but did not cry. There was a long pause between lashes, but each stroke was awfully hard. Jamie's poor naked bottom quivered a little, which caused Stella to feel all wet and fluttery, especially as he did not make a sound in pain. Her heart melted at his bravery. *She* wanted to prove herself so brave!

'Gosh!' he gasped at the fourth stroke. 'You certainly lay it on hard, Miss Morag. These are the tightest cuts I can remember!' He reached out and pulled Stella's dress further up his quivering back, and then pulled his garter straps aside so as to bare his bum to her fullest.

'Wouldn't do to spoil Miss Stella's lovely dress with a stray cut,' he murmured, 'nor her stocking tops, if you want to give me a few on the thighs. How they loved that at Eton! And the birch on the back of the thighs is the Devil!'

'Quiet, sir!' rapped Morag. 'You are not here to give orders, my saucy Lord. You are here to feel the power of a lady's just chastisement.'

Stella watched in awed fascination as the young man's bum reddened; and the more she looked, the wetter she felt between her thighs. She could see his 'gonads', sweet little orbs, hanging between his buttocks, and tightening with a little jerk as each stroke laced his naked bum-flesh. She found it hard to breathe calmly, and looked down at her knickers to see a wet patch shining on the black cloth! Guiltily, she put her hand down to cover it and felt an astonishing surge of hot pleasure as her fingers touched herself there, on her little damsel, which felt all stiff and tingly. She hadn't meant to, but she could not draw her fingers away, and with Morag intently watching the man's bare red nates, she began to rub herself through her knickers, sending spasms of delight through her body at each touch on her damsel. The cane's rhythm seemed in strange, lovely harmony with the clicking of the rails beneath.

Morag looked up from her work above the trembling naked male, and smiled as she saw what Stella was doing. Then very deliberately, and looking Stella firmly in the eye, she hoisted her own skirt and put her fingers inside the waistband of her panties. She began to move her hand gently.

'I thought you'd be diddling,' she said softly. 'It is so lovely to see a male squirm, isn't it? I can never resist.'

She landed another fierce stroke on Jamie's bare, and he jerked at its impact.

'Oh, Miss,' he exclaimed, 'that was so tight! And it's lovely that you are diddling! I *am* giving you pleasure.'

Stella saw to her surprise that the pea vine which had dangled massively between the twin fleshy orbs had now disappeared! Or rather, it had risen from view and now stood trembling and stiff in front of the man's belly. Seeing this, Morag cried that his impudence knew no bounds, and she had a good mind to cane his balls, for a lesson.

'Let my rod flick down, right between your cheeks, and her tip catch your arsehole, sir. And then get further, right round the back, and land a cracker straight to those tight little jewels of yours! How would you like that?'

'You know I shouldn't like it at all, Miss Morag,' groaned Jamie, 'but you may tan my bum as much as you please. I am so joyful, Miss! You have made me stiff again!'

'It is wearing girlish things that has made you stiff,' growled Morag.

Stella thought that Jamie's excitement came from his beating, just like her own thrill at the swish of Miss Cox's cane on her bottom. And his pea vine stiffened just like her throbbing damsel! She knew if she continued to 'diddle' she would again reach that delicious spasm of warm pleasure. With Morag there, it all seemed so friendly and natural! Morag saw her gaping eyes, and said with a laugh that anyone would think she had never seen a naked male before. Stella blushed fiercely.

'I've never really . . .'

'You mean, never? So then you've never done *it* before?'

Stella thought she must mean the thing with pistils and stamens in the biology books, and admitted lamely that they were the full extent of her knowledge.

'Well,' said Morag thoughtfully, 'now isn't the time for *that* – Don't you dare move, *Miss*!'

She delivered a stinging crack to the man's crimson fesses, which made him jerk violently, and stifle a squeal.

'It must be a little more romantic, and Isbister here has probably forgotten how to do it properly. But we can extend your sainted biology lessons at least a bit. There! That is a good baker's dozen for you, *Miss*,' she sneered. 'And now we must put our girl's poor cock out of its stiff misery!'

After a final harsh cut, she threw the cane aside, and promptly knelt before Jamie's magnificently stiff sex organ, which trembled like a flower in the breeze. Still 'diddling',

Morag opened her mouth and began to lick the big shiny helmet at the top of the organ, nibbling it and kissing the peehole until Jamie's sex reared even stiffer than before, as though he was about to burst with seed. Then Morag plunged the organ deep inside her mouth, to the back of her throat, and began to suck very powerfully. The spectacle was unbearably exciting to Stella, and now she openly pulled down her knickers and began to diddle her naked fount. Morag watched her as she sucked, then suddenly disengaged, leaving the giant sex organ pink and trembling.

'You're the one with a pash for Isbister,' she smiled, 'don't deny it, I could see it in your eyes, you wee goose! So you can do the honours. Go on, just do like me, and when you hear gasps, and feel the cock start to shudder, you'll know the seed's coming. Then you'll taste it, all hot and creamy, and my advice is to swallow every drop of the sweet stuff while our friend jerks and yelps. They can't help that, you see, and it's awfully exciting.'

Trembling, as though mesmerised, Stella obeyed, and knelt in Morag's place. She felt the hard bulb of the sex organ – the lovely cock – between her lips, and it smelled and tasted nice: an acrid, oily sort of perfume. She slipped her mouth right over it; Jamie groaned with agonised pleasure, and she was surprised how big it felt, filling her mouth like a lovely big meringue. She pushed down, and felt it slip easily to her throat. Her fount was a veritable cascade of warm juices at her gorgeous feeling of being filled thus. She began to suck, pressing the shaft tightly with her lips, and was excited to hear Jamie respond with groans of pleasure. He clutched her hair, pressing her head to him as she sucked his manhood, and directed her hand to squeeze his orbs at the same time.

She diddled herself very fast, but suddenly felt a hand remove hers from her damsel, as Morag's cool fingers replaced her own. Without a word, Morag expertly masturbated her new friend – and delivered stinging, thrilling slaps to her bottom! – as Stella sucked and sucked at the lovely pea vine as though it were a new, wonderful toy. She felt a creamy hot wetness at the organ's tip, and then Jamie cried out loud, and the sex organ shuddered in her mouth, frightening her a little until she felt a hot jet burst from it and wash her throat with sweet oily seed. Jamie's cries became shrieks, rising in crescendo as he spurted into Stella's mouth. She could not hold back herself, and her cries mingled with Morag's as she came to a thrilling, shattering spasm of joy. Her pleasure increased by knowing from Morag's panting cries that she had spasmed too.

Stella was exhausted by her pleasure, and thought of bed; but outside it was growing light.

'Well!' said Morag brightly, 'we shall be in Inverness in half an hour. Better get your kit on again, Isbister, and return Stella's things.'

'No!' cried Stella, blushing furiously. 'His Lordship may keep my underthings, if he chooses. *And* my knickers.'

Jamie blushed too.

'That is too kind, Miss Stella,' he said, 'Oh, how can I thank you? Here, you take my panties. A fair exchange! Oh, and my kilt, for I have another with me.'

And when Stella had put on his gorgeous frilly pink knickers, and his kilt, smelling so musty and male, Jamie – Lord Isbister and the Jarl of Yell – kissed her full on her mouth, which still glistened with his own lovely seed. Stella almost swooned, and felt she must never wash her mouth again as long as she lived.

At Inverness station, Jamie said they must not bother with porters, as his servants would be there to meet him in his 'jalopy'. Morag assured them that Kernece provided its own transport, a sturdy Rolls-Royce which was necessary for the long drive north, where the roads were often nothing more than tracks. Outside, two gleaming Rolls-Royces stood waiting. One was flanked by three strapping blonde lasses in the fetching Isbister tartan, their kilts cut like ladies' skirts and sporranless. At a sign from Jamie, they picked up the luggage of Stella and Morag, and loaded it on the Kernece Rolls-Royce, at whose wheel sat a stern, muscular woman about Miss Cox's age but with cropped grey-flecked hair, and wearing a blue chauffeur's uniform.

'Ah, Clapton,' cried Morag, 'cheerful as always.'

'Miss Dancer'll have a warm welcome for you, Miss Morag,' said Clapton with a satisfied leer. 'A day late, again!'

'You are always welcome at my cottage,' said Jamie. 'Castle Isbister, you know. Come for tea, sometime.'

'Oh . . .' sighed Stella.

'Sometime,' said Morag firmly, holding Stella's hand.

'Just one thing,' said Jamie with a mischievous grin. 'That legend about what we wear under our kilts . . . Betty! Patsy! Ethel!' and he barked something in a strange Norwegiany sort of language. His three servants winked, and promptly raised their tartan skirts. Underneath, Stella saw that they wore no knickers at all, and, moreover, their ladies' places were shaved quite naked!

'See?' chuckled Jamie. 'In Scotland, it is the *ladies* who wear nothing under their kilts! One of the perquisites of being a Laird is that in my house, *I* wear the knickers!'

3

Rob Roy

Stella felt awfully funny and awfully grand to be wearing a lord's dress, and a lord's knickers, as the Rolls-Royce purred through the green highland glens. Although the kilt was not really a dress, and the knickers were after all ladies' knickers, still they were perfumed with the scent of his maleness, and *he* had worn them next to his skin ...

Her body still glowed from the pleasure and surprise of her love-play with Morag and Jamie, although she told herself coyly that it had really been a wholesome biology lesson. And her bottom still smarted a little from Morag's delicious slapping as she 'diddled' her from behind: *that* had been no biology lesson. How she wished she had taken the same cane that had flogged Jamie! As the Rolls softly carried her, these drowsy thoughts made her fount deliciously moisten once more.

The two women spent most of their journey half-sleeping after their wakeful night, with a brief stop for luncheon of delicious fresh salmon, oatcakes and 'bashed neeps', a lugubrious Scottish delicacy which turned out to be diluted turnips. They dined in a hotel overlooking the silvery ribbon of Loch Shin, where Morag assured Stella that there was a creature to rival the newly-popular Loch Ness Monster.

'Horns, and a big scaly tail, and fiery eyes and monstrous gnashers. In fact she looks just like Clapton!'

Clapton, toying with her bashed neeps, smiled grimly.

'Miss Morag likes her little joke,' she murmured, 'for she

knows that there will be few when we get home to Kernece. Aye, and smoke all you want, ladies –' Morag had just lit them each a nonchalant 'gasper' '– for there'll be none of that, either! Nor your slippery body-games. I know what you've been at on your train. I can smell it on you.' Clapton's voice was definitely Scottish, a fluting lady-like contralto which belied her tough, handsome features.

'As for monsters,' she laughed, 'there are strange things in Scotland, especially in our far north, and just pray you don't get sent out into the Parph!'

Stella was naturally puzzled by this word, and Morag explained that between the Castle of Kernece and Cape Wrath, lay forty or so square miles of bog and rock, an area so isolated that it had developed a unique flora and fauna.

'Of course the locals like Clapton here think it full of hobgoblins and fabulous beasties, isn't that so, Clapton? Och aye the noo!' Morag mocked.

'A body can see marvels and frights from the top of Kernece Tower,' said Clapton primly, 'which is why it is forbidden to ascend there. And I am not a local, as it happens, Miss Stella. I am from the City of Edinburgh.'

'Edinburgh! Where people are born with their clothes on!' hooted Morag as Clapton paid the bill. Stella noticed that their hosts did actually touch their forelocks as they left!

As the day wore on, and the shadows lengthened, the landscape became steadily bleaker, and they left the lush glens for a land of vast sky over barren moors and bare rocks. In the Highlands, the watchful, forbidding presence of the glens was almost palpable. Here, there was little to see: the landscape of Sutherland was a mysterious promise of things that might lie shimmering in the distance, and one felt that something unnameable always hovered just out of the corner of the eye. Stella thought it magical, precisely because of its sullen lack of magic.

Morag told Stella something of Kernece and her ways, but the closer they got, the more reserved her information became, and the more alert Clapton seemed to be. Morag's earlier flippancy was muted, and Stella sensed that there was much she held back. Stella studied their driver. She sensed a strength and power, a spirit which perhaps embodied the Spartan ideals of Kernece. She decided Clapton was more than a lowly chauffeur, and was now playing a role for her own, or Miss Dancer's, amusement.

Stella learnt that on arriving at Kernece, she would become a member of one of the five Houses, all of which seemed to be named after flowers. These were Poppy's, Marigold's, Bluebell's, Daisy's and Orchid's. Secretly, Stella wanted to be in Orchid's, as the name sounded so glamorous; the more so when Morag said off-handedly that she was in Orchid's, and Orchid's was simply the best House.

'I suppose Daisy's isn't too bad, and there are a few sound girls in Marigold's and Bluebell's, but Poppy's . . .!' She rolled her eyes. Stella wisely made no comment, but absorbed the information which Morag haphazardly imparted, noting that what Morag *didn't* say might be just as important as what she did.

She learnt that the three-year course at Kernece ('just like Cambridge!' said Morag in mixed pride and scorn) was divided into three forms: one for each year. Each form was divided into three classes, and in addition to the Form Mistress and various Class Mistresses, each girl had her own Tutor, who was responsible for her academic progress, while her Housemistress saw to her moral well-being and accomplishments outside the classroom. At the end of the first year, the first part of the 'Tripos' exam was taken, and a pass needed to progress to the second form. Those girls who did not pass were placed in the Remove, a sort of limbo where they remained until they did. Morag said that the Remove was 'not at all sound', although some of the girls actually seemed to like it, staying long and revelling in their unsoundness and 'getting up to mischief'.

It seemed Remove girls tended to be the spoiled daughters of powerful families, sent to Kernece to be tamed. Although a girl could be expelled ('for slacking, or blubbing, or not being sound!'), it was rare that any of the

Remove was disturbed in their 'mischief'. But now Morag made everything sound very jolly, not at all like the bloodcurdling warnings she had given before.

'What about the Armies, the Reds and the Blues?' said Stella innocently.

'Armies? Who told you about that?' said Morag nervously.

'Why, you did, of course.'

Morag nervously eyed the back of Clapton's shapely neck.

'Oh, it's some silly game the first years have, I think. It doesn't matter – Kernece has real games, and trophies to win! And there are the Girl Guides! That's super fun, if you can get in. You learn all about knots, and things.'

Stella daringly took one of Morag's cigarettes, lit it, and smoked.

'You told me the discipline is harsh.'

'Not exactly harsh, but stern. It has to be. We are on our own at Kernece – you don't go home to Mummy for tea.'

'Luckily, I can take it,' said Stella lazily, thrilling at the power of her words. She knew she told the truth.

'There's nothing much to it, Stella,' continued Morag. 'The tawse and cane, of course, but only if you break the Rules. And the Rules are so sensible, they're easy-peasy!'

'What about the the brank, Morag? Is that easy-peasy?'

'It's only a scold's bridle for chatterboxes! Why, I've had it, when I've been naughty.'

'You certainly have, Miss Morag,' said Clapton, 'and your bottom is no stranger to a bare tanning. I must explain, Miss Stella, that when – if – you are awarded the cane or the tawse which I prefer, it is always given on the bare.'

'Why, I am quite used to that,' said Stella airily.

'Used to lifting your skirt, dropping your knickers to your ankle, and being tawsed ninety-nine times on the bare bum before the whole College? For that can happen.'

'No, not exactly, but close,' said Stella defiantly. 'And what are these steps you spoke of, Morag?'

'That's a simple punishment,' said Morag. 'You have to

run up a given number of the Tower Steps, then run down again, a certain number of times. It is like writing lines, only it is good exercise instead of futile.'

'You have not mentioned Racing the Tawse, or Gauntlet, Miss Morag,' said Clapton. 'A very interesting punishment.'

'Oh, that,' said Morag, actually blushing. 'But it is rare, Clapton.'

'Not unheard of. I seem to remember you took it, and took it well, in your very first week. Caught smoking, wasn't it? This punishment is the ascent of the steps, Miss Stella, but it is done without knickers and barefoot, and the miscreant must hold her skirts up to show her bare nates. On every step stands a girl, who lashes her as she passes, the tawse being passed from hand to hand as she ascends. So to save her bum, she must try to outrace the tawse! It makes pretty theatre, and Miss Dancer is very fond of theatre.'

'Yes, and I did outrace the tawse,' said Morag proudly. 'I only took about fifty in the end. But stingers!'

The sun's rays were lengthening, and on the right Stella saw a low, brooding mountain, beyond it a grey ribbon of sea. Morag said it was Ben Hope, and that they would soon be at the village of Durness, then home in time for tea.

'Miss Dancer says that a lady must never be without her tea,' murmured Clapton. 'You'll have time to see Matron for your tea, then the Purser for your kit, Miss Stella. Then after tea, you can join the others for prep. You haven't been set any homework, of course, but I dare say Miss Dancer has seen to that. As for you, Miss Morag, I believe it's straight into number five kit and up to the Proctor's office.'

'I can *explain* why I am late coming up,' said Morag.

'Your excuses are wearing a bit thin, Miss Morag,' said Clapton dryly. 'Miss Dancer doesn't like lateness, nor girls who make excuses. I don't know what is in store for you, but I reckon a tanning will be the least of it.'

'Botheration!' cried Morag with forced gaiety. 'I say, Clapton, if it's you to give leather, you'll be a chum and go easy on me, won't you?'

Clapton turned round and grinned with pearl-white teeth. 'You know me better than that, Miss Morag,' she said slowly. 'I never go easy. But I have a Girl Guide meeting tonight. You might be taken by Miss Bulford instead . . .'

'Oh, no!' moaned Morag in real alarm. 'Not the Bull!'

'On the other hand,' mused Clapton with cruel amusement, 'my Guides are studying knottings and lashings just now, and it would be interesting to have a live model.'

They came to the windswept fishing village of Durness, whose greys and whites blended perfectly with the dark sea on whose edge it perched; then the road turned inland, past a long tapering firth, until they came to the hill which Morag called Farveall. Abruptly, Clapton turned off the paved road and on to a rough track which led through bog and rock. The jolting ride seemed to take an age: all around whispered stunted plants and bushes, the rocks etched into shapes that in the half-light seemed like grinning faces.

They came to a vast plain, and there before them stood a high fortress-like wall, with a mile or so between the wall and the glint of the sea. It was hard to estimate the size of the place, but Stella thought its grounds must cover at least a square mile! Over it loomed the only visible building, a monstrous dark structure indented with steps like one of the Great Pyramids, and topped by a curious bulb-like apartment – or dungeon? – which suddenly reminded her of sweet Jamie, of his sex organ and the purple swelling house on top . . . She knew it was the Kernece Tower.

'Welcome to Kernece, your new and happy home, Miss Stella,' said Clapton. 'Be aware that a student is expected to obey all the Rules right from her inception, and that ignorance of them is no excuse. Regrettably, this means that as a new squit you must expect your first unwitting weeks to be,' she paused. 'An interesting test. Miss Dancer says the best way to learn is by experience. And *I* say that sound flogging is the very best experience.'

'You mean, my bottom must expect the tawse?' said Stella, her heart suddenly chill.

'Yes,' said Clapton brightly, 'she certainly must.'

When the car drew up at the gateway of the massive granite walls, a prettily uniformed girl emerged from a little gatehouse built into the wall itself. Stella wondered where the granite came from, as there seemed to be none in the locality, and who had brought it hither. The uniformed girl carried a pen and notebook, and wrote something before nodding politely to their car. Clapton accelerated again, and Stella saw the girl lifting a telephone.

Outside the Castle walls, all was desolate bog and moorland, as though Nature had cast aside there what She had no precise use for. But inside ...! Stella was taken aback, for the walls did not abut the Castle, as she had expected. Instead she found herself on a long straight driveway lined with white classical statues of male and female nudes, as though at some opulent Roman villa. On either side stretched flower gardens, ponds and leafy arbours, with summerhouses and pavilions, and beyond were evidently playing fields for various healthy sports; Stella hoped netball was one. At the end of the drive was another wall, with slit or mullioned windows, crenellations and battlements, and this obviously was the Castle proper. Over all, in the centre, loomed the huge bulk of the Kernece Tower.

'It seems an oasis,' laughed Morag. 'Only an oasis must have irrigation: this one was achieved by drainage.'

'It's lovely,' breathed Stella. All her apprehensions were swept away: she knew that she wanted Kernece to be her home. The grounds were empty in the soft purple twilight of this northern land: she imagined them filled with laughing girls, skirts fluttering in the Caledonian breeze, and knew with happiness she would soon be one. They passed through a second large gateway, and were in a courtyard that seemed no less vast than the meadows outside. Stella realised that the Castle was not round, as she had expected from her storybooks, but nine-sided, with the Tower in the middle like the axis of a wheel. On five of the nine sides, large granite palaces clung to the outer wall, and Morag explained that those were the five Houses. Facing them across the other four sides, and flanking the gateway, were two much larger buildings, in whose shadows the car now stopped. These, it seemed, housed the body of Kernece.

'And much else,' Morag added ominously. Stella looked at these gigantic structures and thought they must be veritable labyrinths of secret passages and locked rooms, where the heroes of old conducted their arcane chivalrous ceremonies. She had visions of noble warriors surging forth to defend the desolate coast from the no less noble ancestors of Jamie Isbister, their weapons flashing under vast grey skies, while the prows of the longships loomed on the horizon, their dragon's heads like giant . . . pea vines! Stella gulped at the naughtiness of the thought, and wondered if the Norsemen went naked into battle, as she had read. She imagined Jamie that way, and felt all trembly inside. Perhaps his pea vine would be hard and standing stiff, like a fleshy sword to terrify the enemy. Nervously, she smoothed down her kilt, which now seemed soft and feminine, and smiled that her pink panties were a perfect match for the pink in the tartan, even though Jamie had said that a true Scottish lass wore no knickers.

Built into the base of the grim, gnarled Tower was a curiously pretty house, whitewashed and surrounded by a tiny garden of flowers and herbs, just like an English country cottage. This was Headmistress's House. Stella looked up at the massive steps cut into the side of the Tower, and shivered anew. They were wide and deep, so that 'racing the tawse' would be no skipping matter. Perhaps they had been built by a people longer in leg even than Stella.

The yard was filled with busy young women who clutched armfuls of books, and chattered quite merrily. All wore uniform, of surprising variety. Some had stern, almost military skirts of blue or brown, with jackets buttoned fully, partly, or not at all; some had fetching pleated skirts that swirled ankle- or knee-length. Many had very short skirts from which peeped enticing frilly knickers, and lovely garter belts holding shiny stockings in dark hues, and white or pastel blouses that seemed just a little too tight. Some girls had brassières plainly showing beneath their blouses, and some, with much tighter blouses, very evidently did not. Jewellery was apparent, with braided stripes, stars, badges and buttons, hair ribbons and flounced waistbands or garters, which Stella was certain all had some deep and as yet obscure significance.

They disembarked from the Rolls-Royce and stood by the doorway of the larger administration building. Incongruously in this northern twilight, all the College buildings were festooned with ivy and flowering creepers, as though their stern granite wished to imitate the homely beauty of an English school or church. Clapton helped them unload their bags, and said that Stella must wait for Matron, who would come with a drudge to carry her things. As for Morag, she must carry her own things and report at once to the Proctors' Office. Morag nodded glumly.

'Yes, number five kit, I bet,' she said. 'What a bore!'

She tried to yawn to show her disdain, but Stella sensed her bravado dampened. Then a young female of scarcely more than Stella's age came out of the Administration door and smiled warmly at Stella, bidding her a hearty welcome to Kernece. She was obviously Matron because she herself wore a uniform: the starched blue skirt and white petticoats of a nurse, with a pretty white linen hat, like a sailor's. But her surprising skirt was very short, with her frilly lace petticoats peeping beneath the hem, and it had a discreet slit at the right side. Both skirt and underthings left her softly shaped knees well exposed, as well as showing that she wore a garter belt and straps to hold up her dark blue stockings. And her shoes were not nurses' flat sensible pumps, but had high heels with pointed toes and looked fit for the gayest of parties. Her hair was in the latest bobbed 'flapper' style, and her lips were bright red in a rosebud shape just like the American 'film star' Stella had seen at the Wolverhampton Picture Palace – was it Theda Bara, or Clara Bow? Morag curtseyed to Matron; Clapton did not.

Matron was followed by two unsmiling drudges, and to Stella's surprise and dismay, they were branked. Each wore a metal harness on her head like a scold's bridle, with a tongue of steel that fitted in her mouth to prevent utterance. The drudges too wore extremely short skirts, but without frills, badges or ribbons, and their bodies were encased in stockings and blouse that seemed strangely all of one piece, and very tight on their skin. Their apparel was all in black, and to Stella's astonishment, it gleamed like rubber. It *was* rubber!

Morag saw Stella's surprise, and grinned ruefully.

'That,' she said, 'is number five kit.'

Matron directed the two drudges to shoulder Stella's bags and then took Stella by the arm and led her rapidly into the building, talking merrily all the while. Stella had just time to wave goodbye to Morag, who looked a little forlorn, and she hoped that Morag could bluff her way out of number five kit for her little misdemeanour.

'Such a pretty kilt!' fluttered Matron, in a pronounced Home Counties accent. 'The Isbister tartan, isn't it? Wherever did you get such a lovely thing? Are you entitled?'

'Well, yes,' replied Stella, blushing warmly, 'I suppose I am. It was a gift, from one of the Isbisters, actually.'

'Gosh!' cried Matron. 'I suppose I ought to curtsey to you, then! But you are only a new squit, Stella, so it shall be you who curtseys for a while. You are supposed to curtsey to me, you know, but it is only your first few minutes at Kernece, so we shall allow a little misdemeanour or two! Don't make it more than two ...'

She nodded playfully at the two branked girls, who were sweating profusely under their tight rubber suits.

'Sue and Avril were *very* naughty,' she said mysteriously.

Stella was reassured that her new surroundings bore the imprint of schools everywhere. There was the smell of carbolic soap and disinfectant, the dusty tiled corridors and drab green walls, and the high windows tilted open to emit the scratching of pens, the rustle of paper, the creaks and mumbles and bodily odours of girls grouped at their learning. Lessons were still in progress.

'Last period has just begun,' said Matron brightly, 'and then it's time for tea, which you'll take with me. I'll have time to give you a wash and a once-over before we have tea, then we can see the Purser for your kit, and to hand in your old things. Then after prep, it is buns and milk in Refectory – not sitting down – and after that to your dorm for a well-earned sleep! Nearly there!'

Stella frowned. She was to hand in her bags: did that mean that she would keep nothing of her own belongings, and be dressed and equipped every inch as a creature of Kernece? She was perturbed, but then felt a strange excitement at being a new girl in every sense. After the classrooms, which seemed endless, they came to a narrow, winding staircase and ascended at a sprightly pace which put the sweating drudges to some trouble, for they were obviously obliged to keep up on pain of further punishment. Stella felt sorry for them. Soon the sweaty schoolgirl smells were replaced by the odour of antiseptic, and the walls and floors were white. Matron stopped, and unlocked a gleaming door, marked 'Surgery'.

It was an ample room, with a deep window looking out over the gardens, distorted quaintly in its mullioned glass. Inside were racks of bottles and metal instruments, tubes and syringes, and everything Stella expected, though she was aware that there was probably no doctor nearer than Durness. A side door, ajar, led to a large gleaming bathroom.

'Right,' cried Matron briskly, when she had dismissed the drudges, 'no time like the present! Into the bathroom, Stella, and off with your kit. Your tea will taste all the finer when you've had a good scrubbing.'

Stella was nonplussed but sensed that she had to – wanted to – obey. Beneath Matron's cheerful exterior lay a soul of iron discipline. How cruelly and how casually she had treated the branked drudges! Stella entered the bathroom and stepped out of her kilt and blouse, folding them neatly, and stood in her underthings, then stood nervously as Matron bustled in her surgery. It was quite an elaborate bathroom, more like a beauty salon, Stella thought, with commodes and basins, and various appliances for hair or skin care, and others whose purpose she could not guess.

'Ready?' called Matron, entering the bathroom, and tut-tutted when she saw Stella in her underthings.

'No, you're not ready!' she cried. 'I told you to get your kit off, Stella. Isn't that plain English? I do hope you are not a disobedient girl.'

'Oh ...' stammered Stella, reddening. She was to be naked! Her surprise was equalled by her surprise at Matron's change of clothing, for now Matron wore a rubber suit very like those of the two drudges!

'It's a messy business,' explained Matron with a smile. Slowly and nervously, Stella stripped off her underthings, and when she wore nothing but her pink panties, she realised that she wanted to visit the commode, and said so.

'Yes, of course,' said Matron. 'Well, panties off, girl, and get on with it!' She pointed at one of the floor-bowls, and indicated that Stella should squat, but made no move to leave the room. Instead she busied herself with one of the machines, a large squat apparatus which gleamed with jars, bowls and tubes. There was a hissing of steam and a gurgle of water as the machine trembled.

'I'll just get Rob Roy here warmed up while you do your business,' chirped Matron. 'I hope he's in a good mood. We call him Rob Roy because he can be villainous if he wants!'

'I ...' Stella began, blushing, then understood that she was to be supervised at commode! She had never in her life imagined making her business in the presence of another. But Matron's sinister words rang in her ears; she would not be disobedient. It was bad enough to use one of these foreign squatting things, but to be watched ... and naked, too! Nevertheless Stella did as she was told, and her embarrassment was overwhelmed by her relief, and her pleasure at receiving an approving nod from Matron. She had obeyed without demur, and felt a glow of pleasure at her obedience. She thrilled when Matron said softly:

'My, you are a big girl, aren't you? In every way ...'

Stella decided to endure everything with unquestioning Kernecian obedience. She felt again that glow of strange pleasure in submitting to another's orders, particularly the orders of a woman whose striking beauty was emphasised rather than marred by the tight sheath of her sanitary rubber garment. Stella was gently strapped to Rob Roy by her wrists and ankles, with bare buttocks spread uncomfortably wide and legs stretched; then she flinched in shock as a greased tube touched the bud of her bumhole!

'Now, relax your sphincter,' said Matron, 'and you can take the tube all the way in. You have had irrigation before, I assume?'

'N-no,' Stella blurted. 'I don't think so.'

'You don't think so!' laughed Matron. 'Well, Rob Roy will break you in, and after a while you'll enjoy it, especially when you feel so clean and cosy afterwards. Loosen your bumhole as much as you can, and don't tighten when you feel the tube, you'll find he'll slide in quite smoothly all on his own. Irrigation is awfully good for a girl.'

Trembling, Stella obeyed, and felt the nozzle of the tube probe the tender inside of her anus, then gently thrust further and further, deep inside her most intimate place. She gasped, and Matron asked if it was hurting; Stella mumbled no, it did not hurt. But she did not say that her shock was from enjoyment! The tube, now deep at her very fundament, gave her a tickling, excruciating pleasure of which she had never before dreamt. When a hard spurt of hot water deliciously washed her anus shaft, she groaned in satisfaction that something so nice was actually good for you. So this was how she met her hero Rob Roy!

The irrigation took quite a long time; Stella was bathed with a mixture of hot and cold liquids and oils, which Matron explained were essences of various bog-plants.

'The Parph is such a rich treasure-trove,' she said, as the water from Stella's evacuating anus sprayed all over her rubber garment. 'If only the World knew ...'

Stella was embarrassed about the evacuation of her fluids, but Matron seemed to think it part of her job – she even seemed to enjoy it! She exhorted Stella to squirt harder.

'My, you've got a good strong bum!' she cried, stroking

Stella's squirming fesses with gentle fingers. Suddenly, in a flash of unexplained desire, Stella wished that Matron would lift her hand and spank her. She imagined Matron smacking her naked bottom quite pitilessly, and the thought made her become wet; not with the scented fluids that bathed her insides, but with her own warm fount-oil. She began to wriggle and squirm, as though the spanking were already taking place. The irrigation itself was such a sweet ticklish pleasure, but the dream of being spanked hard – no, *tawsed* – made her blush quite red with joyful desire. She wondered what the tawse was like: she had seen pictures of it, a fearful leather thong cut into four or five straps at the end. She knew she could take the cane, and wondered excitedly if she could take *that*. If Morag could, then so could she.

The session came to an end, as Matron took a long tube and hosed down Stella's whole body with a cold, fine spray, like a beast being washed down ready for auction in Stourbridge market. She adored being drenched, and began to twist and turn, stretching her arms and opening her legs. She bent over to let Matron see her naked fount-lips, and pirouetted as though in some aquatic ballet.

'Well, I think you're clean, now!' said Matron breathlessly, and Stella noticed that her face was flushed too. Her rubber suit glistened with the droplets of moisture that Stella had spurted over her. Matron gave Stella a towel and told her to dry herself while she got out of her wet things. To Stella's astonishment, Matron stripped in front of her, quite casually, and began to hose down her own body, which was shining with sweat. She gaped in awe and envy, for Matron's swelling smooth mons was shaved bare.

'Rubber is awfully sweaty, don't you think?' she said.

'I . . . I don't really know,' said Stella, wrapping the towel around her.

'Don't you use rubber gloves to wash the dishes? Or a rubber apron?'

'Why, no, a servant did that,' said Stella. 'I did have a rubber sheet when I was very little,' she volunteered, wishing to please Matron, 'because I used to . . . *you* know.'

'And do you still wet?' asked Matron, vigorously towelling herself.

'Heavens, no!' cried Stella with a fiery blush.

'Good. But you never know, so I'll make a note of it anyway. Now, in a moment I'm going to ring for tea, but first I want you to go to surgery and lie down on your back on the table. I just have to give you a little routine examination.'

Stella lay prone on the examination table, while Matron, clad once more in her fetching uniform, prodded and tapped her with various instruments. Stella was excited both by her own nudity and by being under the control of this beautiful, authoritative female. Finally Matron said all was in order but that she must do one last thing. She donned a thin latex glove and ordered Stella to open her thighs. Stella obeyed, and felt Matron's gloved index finger gently part her fount-lips and slide into her lady's place. The passage was easy, for Stella was well moistened with the juices of her excitement, and she felt awfully embarrassed, sure that Matron would notice. And Matron did notice. Her probing finger came to rest on the barrier of Stella's virginity, and she nodded sagely with a wry smile. But then she asked softly if Stella felt excited by being naked and accepting her attentions so passively.

'Answer honestly, Stella,' she said, and her finger accidentally flicked ever so briefly against Stella's damsel, making her start as a jolt of pleasure lanced her.

'Why, I hadn't thought . . .'

'Think now.'

'Yes, Matron, I suppose I do,' she blurted. The irrigation and being hosed and examined and everything, it made me feel like a beast at auction. Or a slave girl, naked, my body being felt by dark-skinned princes — one would buy me, a very handsome young lord, and make me his slave, and whip me on the bare if I was naughty, and oh . . .'

Stella felt Matron's finger withdraw from her lady's place and was suddenly horrified at her indiscretion.

'Oh, Matron, I'm sorry,' she cried, 'I didn't mean . . .'

'Yes you did, Stella,' said Matron with a broad smile, 'and remember a lady never says sorry.' There was a soft knock at the door. 'And now I think tea is served.'

Tea was indeed scrumptious. As she munched the hot crumpets, Stella felt butter and honey trickle on her chin and thought herself for a moment mischievously unladylike. Miss Dancer was right – tea was of supreme importance. She was careful not to spill anything on her new kilt, even though she knew she would have to hand it over to the Purser. She told Matron that she was excited about her new kit, and longed to dress herself as a proper Kernecian. She did not feel at all tired after her long journey; her irrigation and wash, and the lovely tea, made her feel as right as rain.

'Your kit will be for the morrow,' said Matron. 'A fresh start! Although you will wear your new nightie in bed. Don't worry, the other girls will think your kilt some special new uniform, and be frightfully jealous. There are many kinds of uniform, you see: it all depends on the Rules, and who you belong to, and everything. It can seem complicated at first. It is up to the Mistress of Perquisites to authorise change or adornment of uniform. Now, I cannot tell you what you will find in your kitbag. Miss Dancer supervises these things personally, and each girl's kit is slightly different, although in every kitbag is a Rulebook.'

She proceeded to explain some of the details of Kernece life, but Stella only half tried to keep up, knowing that she would be able to pore over her new Rulebook at her leisure. Matron added earnestly that there was a lot to know that was not to be found in the Rulebook.

'Imagine the Rulebook as a tree, that gives Kernece her life. Around the tree are garlands of flowers and tendrils, and within her branches are birds and butterflies, mice and squirrels,' she said. 'They are not part of the tree, yet the tree is unthinkable without them.'

She touched on the system of College ranks, uniforms, and badges, all of which were in the Rulebook, and the Societies and games which were integral to Kernece. These had their own Rules and badges, not to be found in any book. Stella was bold enough to ask about the Armies.

'Yes, the Reds and the Blues,' said Matron thoughtfully. 'Other Societies – like the Girl Guides and the Dramatic Society, the Knobkerry Club and the various game Societies – have written Rules and are, so to speak, official. The Armies exist, yet officially they do not'. She paused. 'In your dossier it says you are proficient at netball.' Stella nodded eagerly.

'A netball match has a finite timespan,' Matron continued, 'a score to be achieved, a fixed number of players and playing space, and a definite result. With the Armies, it is different. The Reds and the Blues wage a sort of war with each other, over territory, power, and ... affectionate loyalty. There are areas of College where a Blue girl will not walk, because they are Red territory, and vice versa. Rather like the razor gangs in Glasgow, but we women are more subtle. This war has no fixed space, no Rules, no objective, and no result. No one knows how it began or whether it will end. It is a war of the spirit, victories measured in smiles or tears, although it has its ... physical aspects, too.'

Puzzled, Stella changed tack and said that Miss Dancer was a personal friend of Miss Cox, her former Headmistress. Matron frowned and said she should not expect too much from that. If anything, she would receive harsher treatment, either from the Prefects, from the other girls, or from Miss Dancer herself. In a girl's first days as a new squit, those of slight seniority took delight in tormenting those who had none. There would shortly arrive one of her House Prefects to escort her to prep, and she advised Stella to behave well. House Prefects were very important creatures in the hierarchy of Kernece, with fairly wide powers of punishment, including the tawse.

'Study your Rulebook carefully, because you must know whom to salute, and how; where you may walk, where you may run; what days your skirt must be high or low, your buttons fastened or open. You must know when you may speak, and when to be silent. It tells you the correct way to deal with males: we have a few, as drudges, but since the Great War strong brave males are hard to come by. We women must become strong and brave ourselves. You must also be aware of the correct demeanour for the rituals of Hallowe'en, Knobkerry Night, Up-Helly-Ya, your House Day, and the rest.'

Stella suddenly remembered that she had not been told which House she was to join, and Matron blushed in sudden confusion. She bit her lip.

'Oh,' she said, 'that is remiss of me. I have it in your papers.' She rose, and fetched a surprisingly thick dossier then leafed through it. She eventually told Stella that all was in order, and she was admitted to Poppy's House. Still frowning, she said it was rare for her to commit remission.

'Why, that is all right, Matron, thank you,' said Stella.

'When you join your House, you must be prepared for initiation rites,' said Matron. 'Accept them without protest, and remember that at all times the wisest course is to submit. You see, females are divided into those who achieve by dominating, and those who achieve by submitting. I sense, Stella, that you are a submissive, and Kernece is a harsh Mistress who will give your nature ample freedom to blossom. Your friend Morag is dominant, which is why she is always getting into scrapes. Those of us in authority, like me –' she smiled ruefully '– sometimes find that we cannot be what we *really* wish. By the way,' she paused, as if guessing Stella's thoughts, 'pay no attention to what Morag says about Poppy's. It is a good house, if rather eclectic.'

Matron had not removed her hand from Stella's thigh, and it seemed to have crept upwards; Stella noted that this warm pressure did not displease her.

'Stella, I must ask you . . .' said Matron rather coyly. 'There is much in your dossier, and I feel I already know you well. But when I examined you, I saw that your bottom was faintly blushed, as though by chastisement. Tell me.'

Now Stella's face blushed. She thought of Morag's lovely smacking of her bare bottom as she sucked Jamie's pea vine on the night train. But it could not be that, it must be Miss Cox's cane, or her own sturdy hairbrush. So she still bore the crimson of her spankings. She felt awfully proud, and decided to tell Matron, whose uniform, and medical surroundings, were a soothing invitation to confidences. She blurted out the details of her caning by Miss Cox, ending: 'But I didn't think I was doing wrong in taking the plate, Matron! Although I know I deserved my punishment.'

She did not tell of her joy at the cane's cut, nor of Miss Cox's pleasuring herself by rubbing her shaven lady's place at the sight of her squirming reddened fesses.

'But there is more on your bottom than that, Stella,' said Matron with a knowing smile. 'In my profession, I see many crimsoned fesses when examining miscreant girls after chastisement. One learns to read their bottoms like a book.'

Stella blurted all at once that she had also been spanked with a hairbrush.

'By whom?' insisted Matron.

'Oh...! By myself, Matron. I don't know why. I wanted to feel what it was like. And to my amazement, I liked it!'

'Well!' exclaimed Matron, with a flush of surprise and genuine happiness. 'It seems you are fitted to be a Kernecian. I suppose you know already that a Kernecian's bottom is no stranger to cane or tawse.'

Her grip tightened on Stella's thigh, quite high up toward her lady's place, and Stella found herself placing her own hand on Matron's. Her skin was lovely and cool.

'I am familiar with the cane, Matron, but not the tawse. And the unknown is sometimes frightening.'

'Stella, would you like to go forth into Kernece knowing, rather than unknowing?' said Matron quietly. 'It can be arranged. I overlooked your new squit's failure in not curtseying to me, but I can remember it.'

'You mean...'

Matron nodded.

'A tawsing, here and now?'

'Just 21,' Matron said. 'To give you the taste. Your first

licking at Kernece. When I saw your lovely bottom, Stella, I . . . I knew I wanted to lick her some day.'

Stella's heart pounded, and she felt a sudden moisture between her thighs. She had longed for this!

'It is very sudden, Matron,' she said with pretend coyness. 'But I submit.'

Matron rewarded her with the loveliest of smiles, and curtly ordered her to take the position. Stella was thrilled to be treated in such a grown-up way, and that she knew what 'the position' meant. At once, she tidied her tea things and stood with her legs wide apart, then raised her kilt neatly above her waist and lowered her pink knickers to her ankles. She touched her toes and waited. The air was cool on her bared nates. With mounting anticipation she heard Matron unlock a drawer and swish a heavy object rather alarmingly in the air. Stella felt cold leather pressed to her lips, and Matron said it was customary to kiss the tawse before and after punishment.

As she did so, kissing each of three wicked thongs, Stella felt Matron's skirts and stockings brush against her face, wreathing her in a delicious bouquet of femaleness. It was just as delicious as Jamie's manly odour, but in a different way. Stella wondered why there were two sexes at all, then wondered why there were *only* two sexes, when there was such a wealth of joy that people could give each other. Her musings were interrupted by the first lash of the tawse, descending on her tight bare fesses after a warning swish. She jumped and forced herself not to squeal as her throat caught. Oh, it stung! And another twenty seemed a horrid prospect! But she gritted her teeth. She had asked for it: she would take it.

Matron was strong, and each lash made Stella tremble. After the fifth cut, her trembling became a squirming as she felt her naked bottom smart and redden. But now the strokes blended with each other in a cosy rhythm, and Stella's panting abated. The pain was warm and comforting now; a happy part of her, even an act of worship on Matron's part. Stella remembered the girlish jibes about her big bottom. They seemed silly now, for she became aware that her pears were beautiful and deserved to be adored and kissed, whether with lips or thongs. She also felt content in her abasement as she heard Matron's harsh breath. *She* was doing all this work. Stella, the submissive one, had simply to stand 'in position' and receive her bountiful flogging.

When it was over, her bottom stung beautifully and she longed to look at herself in the glass. She kissed the tawse once more, and then on a daring impulse knelt and kissed the tips of Matron's shoes. At this, Matron's panting became quite laboured, and her eyes were heavy-lidded in her flushed face. Stella did not wish to give the game away by saying she could have taken the punishment twice over, or even more. And Matron was in a different mood, now. Her nostrils flared as she spoke with harsh breath.

'Stella, I was remiss in not telling you your House,' she said hoarsely as Stella smoothed her knickers and kilt. 'Kernece makes no exceptions. It is necessary that I atone.'

She kissed the tawse and handed it to Stella.

'Control is part of submission,' she whispered, 'just as to obey is to rule. Tawse me, Miss Stella, please. As hard as you can with those sweet muscled arms of yours.'

Swallowing her astonishment, Stella took the tawse, feeling it strong and lithe against her fingers, like a playful kitten. She felt her lady's place quite wet with excitement and pleasure, but she tried not to let it show. Matron bent over in position, raised her skirt to show her suspenders and knickers, then lowered the panties around her ankles. Stella saw to her delight that Matron's panties too were sopping wet! She felt cool and in command as she daringly told Matron that she was a naughty girl and was to take 21 hard lashes on the bare.

'No,' whispered Matron. 'I am senior. It must be three times 21, Miss. I beg you.'

Stella trembled at the thrilling wetness which warmed the whole of her lady's place, and signified her agreement. She lifted the tawse, which was surprisingly heavy. She delivered her first lash to the bare buttocks prettily framed by stocking-tops, garter-straps and belt. Matron grunted in satisfaction, and after Stella became one with her instrument and was stroking the exposed bare orbs very hard, her grunts turned to a deep throaty moan. Matron's bottom began wriggling uncontrollably. Stella's flogging arm rose and fell in a hypnotic rhythm, which she imagined to be the rhythm of the railway train. As she flogged, her lady's place grew wetter and wetter until her head was giddy with desire and joy. She longed to bend and kiss those flaming red orbs that took their flogging with such sweet shivers. She was unable to stop her free hand from straying beneath the hem of her kilt and up her oily-moist thighs, to the lips of her fount and then to the throbbing little damsel that nestled all stiff and tingly between their swollen folds.

Stella almost cried out as she touched herself there, and began to rub at the rhythm of the flogging. Dimly, she was aware that she was at stroke 46 ... 47 ... She saw that Matron's thighs were glistening with her fount-juice, trickling from her fleshy lips and forming a shining damp patch across her stocking-tops. 51, 52 ... Stella rubbed herself furiously, longing for that sweet warm spasm to flood her again. At the sixtieth stroke she felt it come. Her hand trembled and she almost dropped the tawse, biting her lip to stop herself crying out as beauty flooded her quaking body. And then, to her amazement, Matron let out a harsh moan, and another, harsher still and higher. Her moans grew to a crescendo of shrieks as her naked bottom fully squirmed under the last few strokes of the tawse. Both women panted heavily as the punishment ceased. Stella realised that Matron, whose fingers were firmly on the floor, must have spasmed at her whip's kiss alone! She felt quite overwhelmed with joy at making a woman spasm thus.

'Oh,' gasped Matron as she rose, 'Oh ...'

As Matron was smoothing down her skirt over her pulled-up panties, and making sure her garter straps were properly fastened, there was a knock on the door. With no pause it burst insolently open to reveal a girl taller and stronger than Stella. Stella would have thought her a vision of beauty, had it not been for the haughty cruelty in her lips and eyes. Her breasts were free of brassière or corselage and thrust proudly against a dark blue blouse, with wide plum nipples clearly outlined. Her pleated blue skirt swirled around her full thighs, and she had long thoroughbred's legs and ankles which gleamed in white silk stockings, atop blue and very spiky shoes even more daring than Matron's own. Over her blouse she wore a lovely poppy-coloured cashmere jacket, laden with badges and carelessly unbuttoned, over which her shimmering mane of auburn hair cascaded free.

'Bulford! You know it is against the Rules to enter without permission,' Matron stammered. Bulford ignored her.

'Rules are made to be broken,' she said to Stella, 'except the Rules *I* make. You're the new squit, and I've come to get you your kit at Purser's, then take you to Poppy's for prep and whatnot. Sorry to interrupt your girly fun, Matron,' she added with a sneer.

'Stella, this is Miss Amanda Bulford, the Senior Prefect of Poppy's House,' said Matron with frosty dignity.

Amanda Bulford chucked Stella under the chin, staring into her eyes with her own of cold, piercing blue.

'I like the cut of your jib, new squit,' she said at last. 'Yes, I think I do ... You'll get on at Poppy's if you remember the Rule – there is only one, you see. That is: when I call, you come! Now shoulder your wretched civilian bags and follow me at the double!'

Matron nodded helplessly that Stella must obey, and Stella followed the firm, swaying bottom of the long-legged Amanda down the corridor. She struggled with her heavy load to keep up. She gulped. She was in the hands of The Bull!

4

Cane-kiss

Stella's bags suddenly seemed awfully heavy, and her discomfort was increased by the smirks of the girls who tripped past her in the corridor. Those who had been new squits for only a day found it pleasing to find one junior even to them. Stella sweated, despite the cold, which was bracing rather than damp. She noticed that in addition to the usual musty perfumes of school, there was another, sweeter, scent, and at last she identified it as the scent of sphagnum moss. No doubt it drifted from the Parph outside.

They turned into a dusty office, where a young lady in a dark blue smock sat finishing her tea-plate and wiping crumbs from her lips. She was quite handsome, with the frown of one in office-bound authority. She blatantly scrutinised Stella, and Stella averted her gaze from the piercing blue eyes which seemed to wordlessly undress and examine her.

' 'Lo, Purser!' cried Amanda Bulford. 'Got a new inmate at Poppy's, come to collect her kit.'

'Bit late, aren't ye?' muttered the Purser in a Scottish sort of way. 'Tea has been and gone.'

'It is all in order from Miss Dancer, for a lady must have her tea! Even you, Purser of my heart,' replied the Bull. 'Now – Shawn, Stella; Poppy's House; eighteen years of age. Me: Bulford, Amanda; Senior Prefect. Get the drift?'

The purser muttered that she got the drift, and went into a cavernous storeroom. She emerged with a bright blue canvas sack, rather like a sailor's, with Stella's name stencilled on it in poppy-coloured ink. Stella thought it rather fetching, and imagined herself walking up the gangplank as a crewman on Jamie Isbister's longship, setting off to far Shetland to plunder and ravish maidens and ... mmm!

'Sign here, here, and here,' said the Purser, brandishing a flurry of papers. As Stella did so – without having time to read the text – she felt the Purser's eyes on her, the probing more intense for its complete silence.

'Now bring your civilian kit into the storeroom,' said the Purser, scribbling Stella's name on adhesive tags which she slapped unceremoniously on her cases and boxes. Stella followed her into a large baggage room, lined with melancholy stacks of girls' personal things. As well as cases, there were lampshades, fluffy toys, sewing machines, china teasets, and even birdcages: all the homely things a lady might want to keep for herself. She felt a bit forlorn. Her whole life was to be stored here in the bowels of Kernece, and she would enter College quite naked! The Purser gave her a linen bag and said that when she went to bed, she was to put her daywear in it, and leave it for a laundry drudge to collect. With that, Stella shouldered her kitbag and followed the Bull once more, this time out of the building and across the crowded courtyard.

It was almost dark now, so Stella felt welcome at once in the brightly-lit hallway of Poppy's House. Still following the Bull's brisk, military pace, she had little time to admire the surprisingly sumptuous furnishings, or the stern portraits of Old Kernecians which stared down at her as she mounted the marble stairs. Once on the mezzanine, however, things were less than sumptuous. They went down a long corridor of bare boards while the Bull fired instructions that Stella tried to follow: there was the day-room, a sort of common-room with comfortable chairs and a fireplace; there the ablutions; these the Prefects' studies; and behind this, an oak-panelled door, the study of the Housemistress, Miss Rime.

At the end of the corridor was an enormous chamber

whose walls were lined with beds half-concealed by wooden, doorless cubicles: the dorm. Each bed had things stored underneath, and an ample locker beside, with a water-jug on a bedside table. Stella saw that the wooden partitions between beds afforded some privacy, but that a girl could never conceal herself completely from view. Nevertheless each cubicle was decorated with little flowers and knicknacks, all neat and tidy, and festooned with hanging clothes and underthings – heartening proof to Stella that a girl always knew how to make herself at home.

The dorm was oblong, and smelled of sweat, underclothes and disinfectant. At the narrow ends were ten beds, and along the side walls, twenty-five. The centre was empty, and Stella was surprised at this apparent waste of space, until she realised that every girl could thus be observed by every other girl. Four of the cubicles did have doors, however, placed in the middle of each wall, and the Bull said curtly that those were the Under-Prefects' quarters; the full Prefects slept in their studies. There was no one there, and the Bull added that girls needed Prefects' permission to visit the dorm during day hours. Stella was shown her bed, right in the corner, and evidently at the most junior end of the dorm. It seemed that bedding was graded by seniority, and certainly the seniors' cubicles at the far end were much more imaginatively and brazenly decorated than the humble quarters of the new squits. In addition, the seniors had bedside lamps, to supplement the few bulbs which hung from the white ceiling.

Stella was pleased by the Spartan contrast of white ceiling, polished brown floorboards and poppy-coloured bedcovers with nice pastel blue sheets. As Stella deposited her kitbag on her bed, a bell clanged in the distance. She longed to inspect her new things, but it was time for prep. She hurried once more after Amanda Bulford, out of Poppy's, and across the quadrangle back to the classroom building. Here, she was shown to a desk in a great hall presided over by a Prefect on a dais. She was wearing a sky-blue sash, which would have been awfully sporting were it not evidently a sign of authority, like the tawse which dangled beneath it at her waist. The Bull sat Stella at a desk which already bore her name card, and said briefly: 'Remember the Rule.'

And then Stella was alone, feeling quite bewildered amid the rustle of papers and groans as the girls commenced their homework assignments. The girls seemed to be arranged in years, judging by the charming simplicity of the first-year uniforms and the individualism of the senior girls. The juniors were ranged on the right-hand side of the great hall, where Stella was seated right at the back, almost beside the plain wall of polished granite. She noted that all the girls, including the seniors, wore at least one item of uniform which distinguished their House. While the colours were dispersed throughout the assembly, some mysterious process of osmosis meant that each section had a preponderance of one colour; poppy, marigold, purple orchid, light blue and daisy white.

The first year uniform, worn complete, was very pretty. Stella looked forward to wearing it, even though, or perhaps because, it was so frilly and young and ... The only word she could think of was the Bull's word, 'girly'. It was a very short pleated skirt, allowing the girl's suspenders – and sometimes knickers too – to be seen when she was seated, with sheer stockings and sensible silver-buckled shoes. It was completed by a loose blouse and hair frequently worn in pigtails or a 'pony-tail' (Stella had seen that in *Mode*), tied with lovely little ribbons, bows or flowers.

Numerous desks were vacant, and Stella supposed these were girls who were excused prep to attend some Society like Clapton's Girl Guides. Morag was nowhere to be seen, amidst at least, Stella thought, three hundred souls. She wondered if Clapton was busy using her body to illustrate the intriguing knottings and lashings. The thought suddenly and wickedly excited her, but she was confused at her excitement; an excitement at the picture of Morag's nude body, trussed in intricate knots and helpless, perhaps in order to receive the tawse on her exposed bare bum! However she was indeed alone, she thought ruefully, except for the warm smarting of her own tawsed nates. She thought about her bottom, having nothing else to think about at the moment: how she had always been jealously teased for having such full, ripe globes, as though there were something wrong in that. Now, their glowing made her feel that her fesses were beautiful and friendly, and that the teasing was just jealousy. She wondered if boys were teased for having big pea vines, and imagined Jamie mocked by his schoolfriends, jealous of his lovely big sex organ. Stella thought it would be so nice for her to possess one like that, and blushed.

Her reverie was interrupted by a friendly yet hurried voice, who welcomed her to Kernece. She looked up, then on instinct stood and curtseyed, guessing correctly it was the right thing to do. The Mistress looked pleased, and introduced herself as Miss Noble, her Tutor. She was tall, with a smart grey short-skirted suit and a pretty flounced pink blouse. She looked more like a businesswoman than a teacher. Her hair, blonde like Jamie's, was tied back in a stern bun with a flowered chignon. Her suit was quite close-fitting, and Stella could see that her figure was quite slim and mannish, although her breasts were large – larger, it seemed, than her bottom. Nevertheless Stella sensed kindness, and smiled.

'My, what a pretty kilt!' Miss Noble said. 'The Mistress of Perquisites might give you permission to wear it at Hallowe'en, if you are a good girl. But when you come to my study tomorrow before your first class, it'll be a first year Poppy's uniform, Stella! I am sure you'll like it. I must fly, but I have brought you a little book on the history of Kernece; see if you can learn as much as you can, and I'll quiz you in the morning.'

She laid a sumptuously-printed booklet on Stella's desk, and was gone. Stella opened it at once, and began to read eagerly. There was a preface, which was a sort of potted version of the Rulebook, and she was grateful to have that, though she thought even this summary complicated enough. Then there were stories of various doughty Headmistresses through the centuries, all pictured unsmiling and grand, frequently holding a tawse or even a cane and standing beside a vase of orchids or poppies. One Head, whose name was coupled with that of Eton's famous Dr

Keate, was shown actually *birching* the decorously bared nates of a Kernecian at the flogging block! Stella shivered. Kernece was very old; yet there seemed to be no mention of its actual foundation.

Eventually Stella's attention was distracted by the hubbub around her. She looked up and found herself in the midst of subdued conversations, glances and passed messages. The Prefect in charge frequently rapped on her desk in exasperation as Under-prefects patrolled the narrow aisles, calling for quiet. Stella realised that the young women of Kernece were like schoolgirls anywhere, and that her forebodings of girls fearsomely disciplined like 'robots' (a new word which sounded fascinating) were perhaps exaggerated. She was interested in the behaviour of the two girls in front of her, who seemed in dispute over some trifling and thus infuriatingly important matter. They exchanged rude glances and hisses, flicked balls of inky paper, and were only still when the warning cane of an Under-prefect tapped on their desks.

'D'you want the Steps, Perkins?' she rapped.

'It was Gilfillan, Miss!' snorted Perkins plaintively.

'Was not!' countered Gilfillan.

'Both of you, shut up, you . . . you girlies!'

'She's the girly! Not me! Just because Florence Tate gave me a kiss and her ribbon to wear . . .!'

'Do your prep, I am not interested in your girly nonsense,' hissed the Under-prefect. 'Last warning!'

Stella was amused and incredulous that these were young women of her own age. It seemed that the donning of 'girly' uniform had a corresponding effect on the behaviour of mature young ladies, and wondered if she would be the same. She even thought it might be nice to be a girly again.

Suddenly there was a loud squeal, and the Under-prefect whirled round, furious.

'Gilfillan pinched my bum!' howled Perkins.

'Did you, Gilfillan?' demanded the Under-prefect.

'What if I did?'

'Did you? Tell me!'

'Shan't say. I'm not going to descend to *her* level.'

'Gilfillan, you have broken the Rules by that remark,' said the tall Under-prefect very quietly, her eyes glinting.

'She pinched my bum very hard, and tried to rip my knickers. That's breaking the Rules twice!' shrieked Perkins.

There was an expectant hush in the hall, and the Under-prefect looked up at the Prefect in charge, who nodded. 'Right,' said the Under-prefect gleefully, 'you are both for it!'

'But *I* didn't do anything!' they wailed in unison.

'A summary chastisement,' continued the Under-prefect. 'One of you is guilty of bullying, and the other guilty of telling tales, it doesn't matter which is which, for you are both going to get a tanning. Stand up, both of you, and bend over your desks, position four!'

'On the bare! Oh, please, no!' wailed Perkins.

'You know the Rules. Hurry! I want those bums bare and stretched! Now, skirts up and knickers well down!'

As sluggishly as possible, they obeyed, Gilfillan with a little shrug, pretending not to care. But obey they did, and Stella was fascinated – and excited – to see two lovely bare croups stretched over the gnarled desktops. The women clutched the sides of the desks, as if they knew the drill. Their panties spanned their parted thighs like frilly tightropes. Stella wondered how many they would get, and chided herself for hoping it would be lots.

The Under-prefect detached a short, whippy little cane from her belt, and pressed it against both women's lips in the Kiss of Obedience, as Stella's booklet called it.

'A nice juicy seven,' she said briskly. 'I'll take you one cut each in turn. Shut your eyes – no peeking at each other's bums, or you'll get the cut over.'

She proceeded to lace the women's naked fesses with seven very tight cane-strokes, which they took without a murmur. Towards the end, both were wriggling and clenching their naked buttocks – quite yummily, Stella thought, guilty at the moisture which had begun to seep in her lady's place. She wished, suddenly, that *she* would have the courage to do something wicked, and have to bend over her own desk, lifting her kilt and lowering Jamie's pink panties, not for a tawsing, but for a real *caning*. And in front of the entire assembly! Her throat caught at the enormity of her secret desire. To be stripped – yes, bare and bound, too! – for a tawsing, or caning, while everyone watched and saw how bravely she bared herself and *took it*! Her booklet made it clear that the tawse had the advantage of longer, hence more humiliating, punishment, while the cane was convenient for short, quick pain when time was of the essence.

When the caning was over, both women kissed the rod again, and with undue slowness pulled their knickers up. There were smug grins on their flushed faces as they showed their beautifully crimsoned bottoms to their comrades. Stella thought it was as though the two had a secret pact, that their rivalry was only a theatre and they had *wanted* to take the cane bare, in order to tantalise the others. Stella was certainly tantalised, and in her confusion she felt her lady's place quite moist with excitement. She longed to put her hand right inside her panties and rub herself on her stiff, throbbing little damsel, but, sighing, did not dare. She was sure, though, that many of the other girls felt the same. The atmosphere at prep was, after that, subdued and quiet, as though every girl felt the same as Stella and was impatient to be alone for her private joy.

Prep was concluded without further incident, and Stella followed the rest to the Refectory, to line up for an informal distribution of currant buns and either hot milk or cocoa. The conversations around her were excited arguments as to whether Gilfillan or Perkins had taken it better, and whose bum would remain red the longer. Stella was ignored, and thought it wise to follow a group of Poppy's girls back to the dormitory, where she thankfully reached her new bed, and opened her kitbag. She withdrew the first packed item, which was an absolutely *gorgeous* frilly nightie, in poppy colour, and knee-length. Happily she stripped with as much modesty as her cubicle would allow, and put it on. She had a nice toilet bag too; amid the raucous crosstalk of her new dorm-mates, she asked her neighbour to remind her where the ablutions were.

'Come with me,' said the girl, a pleasant, wiry young lady with jet-black hair and very dark Mediterranean skin, but with a plummy lilting accent just like Morag's.

'I'm Alberta,' she said. 'New squit like you, only I'm a day senior!' She laughed at the absurdity of this. Stella introduced herself, and asked if she was from London.

'Why, no,' said Alberta, 'I'm Italian, actually. An Eyetie from Bolzano, don't you know!' She seemed to think this frightfully amusing. 'I wonder what star sign you are. I'm sure we'll be chums,' she said merrily.

They brushed their teeth amidst a chaos of giggling girls and the whoosh of flushing commodes. All around were the barks of Prefects telling everyone vainly to hurry up, and that anyone not in bed by lights-out was for a number seven at least. Stella felt too tired to ask what a star sign or a number seven was, and sank gratefully into her surprisingly soft bed only seconds before everyone hushed, and the dorm was plunged into darkness softened by moonlight. Her bed made a funny crinkly sound, and when she put her hand under her bottom, she found that between her mattress and her blue cotton sheets, there was another sheet of smooth rubber. There was the jug of water on her bedside table, and a glass, and she found a lovely chamberpot under the bed, with a flowery poppy pattern.

The Under-prefects did not, it appeared, have to go to bed till much later, and after a final, totally superfluous bark of 'No talking!' the inhabitants of Poppy's dorm were left to their night-time peace. Stella noticed that the dorm locked automatically from the outside, so that egress, but not ingress, was possible: hence the provision of chamberpot. At once a babble of conversation broke out. Alberta was full of eager questions, but Stella was now exhausted, and said she would answer in the morning.

'Never apologise!' whispered Alberta. 'But sleep while you can, Stella. If your first night is anything like mine, then you might not get much sleep at all. Kernece has already taught me that when you have strong discipline, you also have strong indiscipline.'

* * *

Sleep came soon, but Stella awoke well before dawn. She felt quite refreshed, though troubled by a sudden vivid dream, in which her bedclothes had been ripped from her, a light shone in her eyes, and steely fingers pinioned her body. She shook her head and groaned, trying to snuggle under her blankets, and then found that it had not been a dream. A torch shone on her eyes, and her wrists and ankles were held, while her nightie was pulled up to her neck, exposing her naked body. A hand gagged her mouth while unseen assailants conversed in excited whispers.

'Welcome to Kernece, new squit,' sneered one voice.

'Isn't she a mossy bitch!' added another.

It seemed her assailants were three in number, for a third melodious voice trilled sweetly:

'Let's tan the slut straight away!'

'Muffy, you are always in a hurry. And you always want to be the boss!'

'I say we follow the procedures, Tuffy. We have all night long, you know.'

'Buffy, you're holding the bitch's mouth. D'you think she'll stay on honour to keep quiet if you let go?'

'I think so,' said – evidently – Buffy. 'She seems too scared to move. Will you be quiet for your initiation, bitch?' Stella nodded a fervent yes, and was ungagged.

In truth, Stella was not really scared. Deep down, she had expected something like this, and in a way welcomed it. To be initiated meant that she would be one of the other girls, and it would be quite mortifying *not* to be initiated!

Stella felt tickling fingers run all over her body like little mice, and she felt quite excited, despite her apprehension. She could, of course, cry out but sensed that the rest of the dorm was observing her gleefully in the cold moonlight. And besides, she had given her word not to. The grip on her wrists and ankles was quite firm, and she could not move. Rather than try, she said quietly:

'If I must be initiated, then do whatever you like with me, ladies.'

Her voice sounded dangerous and thrilling. She shivered with a strange pleasure in giving herself completely and helplessly to whatever attentions Buffy, Muffy and Tuffy might bestow on her. A hand paused on her mink, and began to squeeze her hair roughly, like a sponge.

'She *is* a big mossy bitch!' cooed Muffy – or was it Tuffy? 'I've never seen so much flax on a slut's hillock.'

'Perhaps she uses cream or something,' said Buffy doubtfully. 'I bet she has a big cave! Have we enough moss?'

'And a monster bum!' The torch was extinguished, and Stella felt a cool hand kneading her naked buttocks, and then fingers touching the very lips of her fount! She trembled, not in fear but in anticipation. To her horror and delight, she *wanted* it to happen to her! The moonlight illuminated the dorm clearly, and she saw her three aggressors as shadowy figures dressed in Poppy's frilly nighties, but with funny leather belts, wristbands and necklaces which glinted with sharp studs. She glanced to her side, and saw Alberta sitting up on one elbow, watching intently and a little nervously. But Stella grinned and shrugged, and was happy to see Alberta smile back. She craned her neck: the whole dorm was sitting up watching her.

'We are the initiation committee, bitch,' said Muffy, who seemed vaguely in charge. 'And we have to decide what degree of initiation it'll take to make you a faithful Poppilian! Number one is out of the question, you are far too big for that. Look at those utterly enormous udders! And the muscles! I suppose you play a lot of soppy netball.'

'Well, yes,' stammered Stella. 'I was Captain of Netball at St Hilda's.' Muffy, Buffy and Tuffy guffawed in unison.

'Number two, I suppose, then,' said Buffy. 'Now, who is to be Spank Mistress, or shall we take it in turns?'

There was some argument about who was to hold Stella and who was to spank her, and Stella quietly loved being the centre of so much attention, until Tuffy said: 'I think she'll go to number three! I was at Clapton's Girl Guides tonight, and we learnt all about knots and lashings. There was that Morag – you know, the snotty bitch in the Reds – and she was a model. Lovely, it was, to see her all trussed like a turkey! Let's do it to this one.' Stella murmured that she knew Morag.

'Then that settles it! Number three, and you'll get the same as your bitch friend.'

'Who's got the tawse?'

'Oh ... I forgot.'

'Buffy, you are a mossy bitch! It'll have to be the belt, better still, three belts together. Let's get 'em off.'

'Wait a minute,' said Tuffy, peering at Stella's fesses, 'she's crimsoned! She's *already* been tawsed. And not just the tawse, there is cane-kiss there too!'

There were murmurs of admiration.

'So soon! And who did this to you, new bitch?'

Stella was about to explain, but suddenly shook her head and refused to tell, her refusal causing great glee in the Buffy, Tuffy, and Muffy camp.

'Super! *Now* she's for it! Number three with a vengeance!'

Stella was released, and helped to her feet, then very gently led to the open space at the centre of the dorm. So that was its purpose! A blanket was spread for her, and she was made to kneel, with her hands clasped on her buttocks and head bent down between her thighs. Her nightie was taken right off, and thus she was nude, feeling the pale moonlight shine on her bare body. The Under-prefects behind their closed doors gave no sign of interest, or even of their presence. Tawseless, Muffy was nevertheless equipped with rope, and amid gleeful exclamations of 'half hitch', 'round turn', and 'square lashing', Stella was efficiently secured into a tight bundle of knots and ties.

Her arms were stretched behind her and fastened to her ankles, while her head was squeezed right between her thighs. Ropes looped around her knees and calves to form a tight corset around the back of her neck. Her breasts were bound and squeezed ever so tightly, like the sternest of brassières, and Muffy fashioned a makeshift corset of ropes that harshly constricted her belly, leaving her buttocks bare for her whipping. Just as Tuffy was about to loop a final rope across the cleft of her buttocks and her fount, Muffy cried that she was a silly bitch for forgetting the moss, which was the most important thing. Now Stella felt a cool damp cluster of moss pressed firmly into her lady's place, filling her to bursting!

Another clump of moss was unceremoniously thrust into her mouth, gagging her anew. It tasted fragrant and bittersweet. The little flowers and stems tickled her pleasantly in both places. The moss in her lady's place was uncomfortable but felt pleasantly naughty, like wearing wet knickers. Stella suddenly jerked as she felt a fingertip brush her damsel, and a spasm of excitement filled her.

'I say, her winkle's stiff!' The finger tickled her damsel again, and Stella moaned through her moss-gag.

'And it's a big one! Hard and swollen up, and her squid-mouth's all wet and oily! The mossy *bitch*! We'll whip that out of her!'

'I say we make up a number *four* initiation, just for her! No limit to the drubbing, until the slut squeals!'

This was enthusiastically agreed, and Stella could feel the buzz of excitement in the dorm, as she realised she was now to be whipped until she begged for mercy. But she thought, I am a St Hilda's girl, and I want Miss Cox to be proud of me. And more, I am going to show myself a true Kernecian. I *shan't* squeal for mercy!

Her bum was high in the air, and she could not move in Muffy's quite expert bonds. To her strange new delight, she did not want to move. She relished her helplessness, the tingling in her damsel, and the now copious flowing of excited wetness in her fount. She longed for the whipping to start, and heard with trembling anticipation the sound of belts being loosened and then knotted together in a flail.

The flail whooshed in the air with a fearful whistle, heralding a cut that made Stella wince. She felt the studs bite her naked buttocks, much harder than any tawse, and jerked in her bonds as the stroke fell, but did not cry out. The flail was passed from hand to hand, and the strokes rained on her bare without mercy or anything but grim determination. Stella determination to take it was equally grim; she was glad of her mouthful of dampening moss.

The flogging was interspersed with cries and grunts.

'Squeal, bitch!'

'Lace her harder!'

'She's squirming nicely, and look at that red! We'll have her crimson – dance the black bottom! – and she'll have the makings of a true Poppilian!'

Stella's heart swelled with pride at this back-handed compliment. She felt herself already a true Poppilian, and a true Kernecian; St Hilda's in grimy Stourbridge seemed so far away. As each lash of the three-thonged whip caressed her bare nates, she imagined how her bum would look in the mirror, and longed to show herself to Morag – and to Jamie! And at that thought her damsel tingled quite unbearably, her fount a veritable torrent of her juices. She no longer kept count of the lashes on her bare, noting only that Buffy muttered it must be at least fifty by now.

'Submit, bitch!' she cried, 'then you may take the Oath!'

'Before one of those rotten Armies gets to her,' added Muffy under her breath.

Stella shook her head. She would never submit, or call stop, for she was already, truly submitting. She floated serene as an empress on a white-hot ocean. Time and place had no meaning; she was filled with the pain and beauty of her helplessness. Her bonds seemed to caress her like lovers' fingers as she squirmed and jerked at the force of her lashes: they were her lashes, her property, a sweet part of Stella. And her tormentors were *serving* her!

She glimpsed a stealthy figure cross the dorm and open the door to someone outside. Suddenly Stella's flogging ceased, for through the door burst a party of women with blue hoods masking their heads. They were all dressed in blue jackets and tight trousers, like men's! They made straight for the centre of the room. Muffy, Buffy, and Tuffy melted into the shadows as surprisingly as they had emerged, and Stella felt herself lifted and cradled between strong arms.

'Are you Stella Shawn?' said a voice. Stella nodded, yes.

'Excellent. Purser was right, you're a big tough one. And already wrapped for us! These girlies are *so* obliging!'

She pronounced it 'obleeging'. Then she cried:

'Stella Shawn, you are bagged for the Blues!'

5

A Spanking Quiz

Already a glimmer of dawn stirred outside the windows of Kernece. Stella was wide-awake, and her whipped bottom still smarted quite warmly, but she was joyous and excited. It felt strange to be carried naked and trussed, and with two orifices crammed with moss, through the deserted corridors of the slumbering Castle. She smiled blissfully as she imagined what her guardians, or even Miss Cox, would make of it. Already, she loved Kernece: it was such an adventure!

The women kept up a brisk pace, bearing Stella out of Poppy's, across the yard, and into the administrative building. There, they twisted through unlit passages and dusty porticoes. Stella gave up trying to get her bearings; unfamiliar as yet with the Castle, she suspected she was being taken by a route unknown even to its familiars.

'Tuffy is one of us, Stella,' said the group's leader in a kindly voice. 'A good Blue! Purser, too; she had already told us about you. And then Tuffy spotted you at prep, and knew you were ripe Blue meat!'

Stella had never been described as meat before, but took it as a rather nice compliment. She wondered if Jamie would like being described as ripe meat. Perhaps he would! She felt the brooding tension of the wakening day; even with the College deserted, Stella could sense the bustle and warmth that hovered ready to come into being. Whatever was to happen to her, it would surely be fast, before her empty bed was discovered and her absence noted at dorm roll-call. Well – she gulped – many ordeals were fast.

They came to an alcove, dust-shrouded, in a side-turning off a deserted passage that looked as if it were always deserted. It was very narrow, and the stone ceiling low and bumpy like the cobbled floor. despite her discomfort and apprehension, Stella's mind wandered again to the days of old Kernece: she saw troops of soldiers in chain mail sweating with vats of boiling oil to pour over the attacking Isbisters, all fierce and proud and naked ...

A door creaked open, and she was bundled inside a large vaulted room illuminated by a glowing fireplace, in which a cauldron simmered. A waning moon gleamed through a slit window. She was gently placed on the rough stone floor, unbound, and helped to her feet. She stood rather confused, rubbing her sore limbs and fiery bottom as she adjusted to the dim light. She saw a large round table – just like King Arthur's, high chairs and armchairs, and the huge fireplace decorated with gargoyles. Beside it in shadow stood a lovely tall wooden carving, a giant shaft – like a pea vine! – which on inspection she saw to be the prow of a Norsemen's longship, with a grinning dragon's head painted in shades of gold and blue. The women who had abducted her swept off their hoods, revealing lustrous long hair which tumbled over their mannish garb.

'Welcome to the Army of the Blues, known as the Sisterhood of the Dawn,' said the group leader. 'You will take a cup of tea to refresh yourself this dawn, your first!'

'Thank you,' said Stella. She was suddenly conscious of her nudity, though the room was lovely and cosy after the cold of the empty corridors. 'I am honoured. May I have my nightie back?'

'There will be no need of raiment, Stella. The Sisters greet the dawn naked and in submission. You are not yet a soldier; soon, after you have made your first obeisance, you shall be a true Kern of the Blues.'

A metal goblet of hot liquid was handed to her, and she drank gratefully, pausing over the curious sweetish taste. The leader smiled and, to Stella's surprise, began to strip off her raiment, the other women doing likewise. Stella saw that in the recesses of the chamber there were other women, all nude! They now came forward, smiling, to greet her, until Stella found herself surrounded by ten Kerns as naked as herself. But at the end of the room, recessed in shadow, was a wooden throne, upon which a woman sat who was not nude. To Stella's surprise, she wore the most delightful but unmilitary costume – an outfit of powder blue. A flounced blouse with billowing pagoda sleeves; gossamer chiffon skirts, layered like a ballerina's tutu; sheer shiny stockings and a clearly visible suspender belt and garters, with silk knickers; and lovely patent leather shoes with sparkling sequins. She looked divine, with blonde, almost snowy white hair, cascading over her lush breasts that were well displayed by the low cleavage of her blouse. In her hair she wore the most delightful spray of bluebells and orchids. She reminded Stella of Peter Pan's Tinkerbelle, rather than a warrior! Her dainty lady's hands were busy weaving bouquets of small flowers.

'Do you like your tea?' asked the leader, nude now. The moon and the firelight vividly glinted on her pert, high-nippled breasts which Stella noticed were pleasingly beaded with sweat. She supposed she must have been heavy to carry, and apologised for it.

'I do like this tea,' she added quickly. There were little savoury biscuits too, with a meaty taste, and she felt quite well breakfasted already.

'Never apologise, Stella. It was our privilege to carry a new comrade, and to serve her. Happily we took you before you had a chance to swear any silly Poppilian oath, so it shall be your oath to the Blues which binds you – forever! After that, you can make as many oaths as you like, for they don't matter. The tea is a secret of the Blues; there is moss, and flowers, and roots in it. Parph tea! Just as our forebears drank before battle, in ancient Karnak.'

The name was familiar, and Stella said so cheerfully, feeling oddly at home sipping moss tea with a lot of nude females in a dungeon at dawn. She forebore to ask what the nice biscuits were actually made of. In her throne, the girly female was impassive with her flowers, observing them.

'I have read of Carnac in Brittany,' she said, thinking of Tristan and fair Ysolde. 'And the sunken city of Ys.'

'Yes – and there is Karnak in Egypt, and a Karnak in India, and in Cornwall, too. The realm of Karnak spanned many lands,' said the leader solemnly. 'Kernece is a Scottish variant of the sacred name, and we, the Blues, hold to her old rites. Blue is the colour of life and the sky and sea; red is fire and destruction, anger and shame.'

'A plague on the Reds!' cried all the nude women in unison, which rather startled Stella.

'Yes, a plague on the Reds!' she said hurriedly, even though she knew Morag was one of them. She wondered what sort of initiation – another initiation! – she was to go through, and soon learnt. There was to be a blood-curdling oath, never to betray any of the Blues' secrets, even under torture by the hated Reds. Torture! Stella had not thought Kernecians would go *that* far. She asked what the secrets were that she must not betray, and was told that she must know as few as possible; only the Supreme Battle Jarl knew them all. She would learn the signs of recognition, and how to tell a Red. Sometimes Reds were captured and interrogated, and after fierce torture it turned out that they were Blues all the time, their secret names so secret they were not even known to members of another Cohort. The leader said that her secret name was Heather.

'We are divided into cells, or Cohorts,' said Heather. 'Each with a secret meeting place, and none known to the other. We are Cohort Anemone, in zone three. The whole of Kernece is divided into zones, some occupied and some unoccupied; like squares on a chessboard. Territory is gained by occupying sectors into which the zones are divided, and when one Army has occupied the majority of sectors in a zone, then the whole zone is theirs.'

Stella asked how sectors and zones were occupied.

'By being there,' said Heather earnestly. 'And by leaving tokens or indelible signs, that must stay for a day and a night without being destroyed. They must be blue, obviously, and you shall learn our coded signs. Some of them so encrypted that even other Blues are hard put to recognise them as Blue signs. Sometimes two Cohorts are busy occupying a sector or an entire zone at the same time! And then the matter of intimate possession is settled by trial before Jarls. That –' she gestured to the throned woman '– is one of the Jarls of Cohort Anemone. Her secret name is Charity, and we must obey her as slaves! The space you occupy, Stella, is now a Blue sector: that is, your bed, your desk, your changing-room locker, your seat in Refectory, and so on. You gain control of another girl's personal territory by making her an affective sector. That is, by gaining control of her affections, and taking tokens of love from her.'

So that was what Gilfillan and Perkins were squabbling about at prep! The ribbon and the kiss from Florence Tate...

'Situation maps of Kernece are revised every week; at the moment, we Blues are on an upsurge, with two zones and ten isolated sectors conquered last week alone! The maps are sacred, and kept by the Norns, who must destroy each map as a new one is prepared.'

'Do the Norns dress as prettily as the Jarls?' asked Stella innocently.

'Sometimes, Norns and Jarls are one and the same,' said Heather. 'It is not for us to know. We are shown the maps, and must memorise. And of course, Stella, the only sign of recognition we must give to other Cohort members is a secret one. If you meet me, or any of these Kerns – footsoldiers – outside, then it is as if we have never met.'

Stella said, puzzled, that if they were classmates they would have to meet anyway.

'Then you must meet in a distant way, Stella! Think of the excitement of mingling with secret comrades, and having to treat them with the excruciating politeness of a stranger! Don't all girls love to hold a secret? To spend every moment on alert, probing for weakness or betrayal in friend and foe alike! Other girls live lives of shelter and comfort, obeying the Rules like good Kernecians. We

Kerns obey the Rules too, but we are only pretending to obey them, and thus obey them more strictly than anyone else, to hide our dissimulation! If, for example, you are tawsed or caned by a Prefect you know to be a Blue, you must not let her show favour; rather, you must beg for sterner punishment!'

Stella's duties were to train hard, in preparation for Ragnarok: the ultimate battle between good and evil, when the Reds and the Blues would face each other for a fight to the death. In the meantime, she must perform any task her Cohort gave her, take territory and prisoners, and be ruthless in torturing and interrogating any captured Red for her secrets. She must be prepared to lie, and cheat, and – again, in order to allay suspicion – this meant she must strive to tell the truth and be honest in all things!

'That way, they won't suspect,' said Heather gravely.

'What if I am asked point blank – say by the Bull, or Miss Rime, or even Miss Dancer – if I belong to an Army, or belong to the Blues themselves?'

'Why, then you tell the biggest whopper of a lie,' exclaimed Heather triumphantly. 'You tell the truth. You say yes, and they will *think* you are lying. The stupid Reds always tell *real* lies! Now, we must proceed with the ritual. You have much to learn, and after your oath you shall be given your first task.'

Stella took the oath, and thought it an exceedingly strange kind of oath. The nude females were arranged in a circle and she had to stand in its centre, bent over and touching her toes, with her buttocks spread wide, as though for a caning. That was what she expected, a sort of ordeal of endurance. But after she had sworn to be eternally loyal to the Blues, never to betray their secrets even under threat of extreme discomfort, and to obey orders unquestioningly or else expect the most horrid things imaginable, she felt soft lips kissing her toes, and then her anus bud! Her ordeal was tickling! Each of the nude females prostrated herself to kiss Stella on anus and foot. Then Heather said she was ready for the ritual.

Charity now rose from her throne and minced on

beautifully high heels towards the circle of nude women. She carried a scroll of parchment, which she unrolled to reveal a hand-drawn map in pencil. She curtseyed to Stella, and handed her the map, which she examined with little comprehension. It was evidently of the nonahedral Castle of Kernece, with plans of each floor in great detail, and various sections coloured red or blue, or red-and-blue stripes. Stella said she might need a long time to study it in depth, and Heather replied there was no need, as maps were obsolete as soon as they were produced, so fast did the battle lines change. She jabbed a finger at Orchid's House.

'This is your objective,' she said. 'It is to be an affective attack; that is, you must win the heart and loyalty of one of the toughest Reds. So, quite a challenge for you. Our intelligence reports reveal that her battle name is Morag!' Perplexed, Stella nodded humbly.

'For your next summons to Cohort, you will be given a secret sign, using your secret name. Do not ask what the sign is, you will know when you are told it. And now for your initiation ritual.' Stella's pulse quickened.

'Oh, yes,' she murmured.

Charity brought a large basket of daisy chains and placed it in the centre of the circle. At Heather's signal, the nude Kerns closed on Stella and placed garlands of daisies around her neck and waist, each woman kissing her lips and touching her fount.

'Charity will now give you your initiation task, which shall be a harsh punishment, Stella. Are you ready? I can see from your bottom – she's a corker, by the way, quite delicious! – that you've already taken the tawse, *and* the cane, and in addition that rather clumsy but effective belt-lashing from Tuffy and her chums.'

'I am ready!' cried Stella, thinking, *now* comes my caning, and my bottom, when I have the chance to show Morag, will be such a beautiful artwork! Charity approached her bearing a cane four feet in length and a full inch wide, which made Stella gulp. The beautiful 'girly' then knelt and kissed Stella's bare toes, before handing her the cane.

'As your Jarl, Stella,' she trilled in a soft voice, 'I command you to cane my naked fesses three times thirteen.'

Stella could hardly believe her ears.

'I thought . . . I was the one to be caned,' she stammered.

'No,' said Charity, 'you are the one to be *punished*. It is I who shall be caned. You must strike me as hard as you can. I shall kneel for you, with my head on the floor, and you must lift my skirt high and then lower my panties to my stocking tops. Prove yourself a worthy Blue, Stella, and obey without question.'

'But . . .'

Stella was in anguish. She had never caned anyone before, not even at St Hilda's! Although her young body had awoken to the joy of submitting, or seeing other girls submit to a caning on the bare, the idea that she should administer chastisement herself shocked her somehow. And Charity, the Jarl – as one in authority, surely *she* was supposed to administer chastisement to her Kerns!

'Why do you hesitate, Stella?' said Heather in a worried voice. 'We know you are strong, that you are one of us.'

And then Stella remembered that if she became a Prefect, as she wished and intended, she *would* have to chastise girls on the bare. She had hoped to cross that bridge when she came to it, but it seemed that she had come to it already.

'Surely you can take the pain of flogging me, Stella,' murmured Charity. 'Or are you nothing but a mossy bitch?'

'Right!' cried Stella, stung into action. 'Thrice thirteen it shall be, my girly Jarl!'

She lifted Charity's skirt and pulled down her frilly panties, to reveal a quivering bare croup of lovely shining alabaster. She raised the heavy cane and, with a gasp, cracked it hard across the twin orbs. Charity moaned, and her taut bum quivered gorgeously as a red glow appeared at once. Stella was nervous – she had hurt Charity! But when Charity whispered that she could do better than that, and must cane like a Blue and not a mossy bitch, Stella's passion was unleashed. She raised the cane again and laced Charity's naked, quivering buttocks unmercifully, drawing the sweetest squeals and moans from her subdued Jarl as she counted the strokes in a loud, grim voice.

The glowing buttocks danced before her in their sweet red fire of pain, topped by the pure blue of the flogged woman's skirts. It was as though the crimson of her whipped bare nates were an invasion of Reds into the sacred cleanliness of the Blues! Sweat dripped into Stella's eyes: she saw only those lovely squirming buttocks, and wished that it could be *her* so prettily robed and so harshly abased in chastisement! And at that thought, the moisture in her fount became a flow, a cascade of hot oil which moistened her naked thighs. Her belly trembled with desire as she counted the strokes, and far away she heard her hoarse cry of 'thirty-nine'!

Panting, she lowered the cane, and wiped her eyes of sweat. Charity was moaning still; not softly, but louder and louder, though the caning had stopped. Her buttocks glowed like firelight in the warm dawn rays which now flooded the chamber. To her surprise, Stella saw that Charity's hand was between her glistening wet thighs. She was – had been – diddling herself as she took her flogging! In astonishment, Stella turned and saw that each of her naked Blue comrades had her hand on the lady's place of her neighbour, and was diddling her softly. She watched the naked human daisy chain gleaming in the soft dawn. Stella felt giddy and helpless with desire; she did not know what to do, and stood still as Charity turned, still diddling herself. She knelt with her face against Stella's bare mink.

'Now, Stella,' she whispered, 'the final part of your ordeal, and you are full Blue!'

So saying, she put her wet tongue to Stella's throbbing damsel and began to kiss and lick her until, in no more than a few moments, Stella felt beauty well up in her. She cried out along with Charity and all of her naked comrades as they spasmed in a beautiful dawn of pleasure and joy.

'Now you are truly one of the Blues, Stella, you have greeted the dawn with your sisters!' cried Charity.

It was time to don her nightie, and creep back to dorm, where Tuffy would let her in.

'You must call her "Tuffy",' said Heather. 'That is her secret name, you know.'

Stella was quite thrilled to be part of a secret army playing an imaginary game on an imaginary board, with imaginary rules and imaginary names.

'And what is my secret name to be?' asked Stella.

'Your secret name is henceforth ... *Stella!*'

'So I suppose my summons to Cohort will be something like, "Stella, your next Anemone Cohort meeting is in room 3b at dawn on Friday, signed Heather of the Blues", chalked on a blackboard?' asked Stella with unusual irony.

Heather beamed. 'Now *there* is a cracking idea,' she exclaimed.

Tuffy was at the dorm door to let her in, with a sly wink, and Stella was back in bed just in time for the strident whistle and the glare of lights that were to rouse her from it. She saw the Bull standing in the doorway, hands on hips and whistle in her mouth like a cigar. She scrambled out of bed like the others, grabbed her washbag, and joined in the rush for the ablutions. Alberta smiled knowingly at her and told her to hurry, if she wanted commode. Stella realised she did – the moss tea was strident in its demands for evacuation. The rush was mostly unlearnt new squits, for the older girls haughtily bided their time. Alberta said that she would not join Stella at ablutions, as she always went alone, not wishing to be nude in front of others.

'It is just a thing of mine,' she said rather shyly.

The ablutions were cavernous, with showers, baths, washbasins, and a line of squatting French commodes at the rear, with no concealment. Stella hung her nightie on a free peg, and found a vacant commode. It was really just a hole in the floor with footrests and constantly sluicing water, and Stella realised she would have to get over her distaste at such foreign ways, which seemed *de rigueur* at Kernece. She wondered if commodes were part of the 'auld alliance' between Scotland and France.

It was curious, but somehow liberating, to be attending to her business with a throng of other naked girls. They laughed and splashed each other amidst curtains of hanging knickers, petticoats and camisoles, which certain Poppilians evidently preferred to launder themselves. Underprefects barked 'Come on!' and 'Hurry!' with little effect. As Stella anxiously queued for Buffy to finish her shower, the Bull appeared and barked even more loudly, telling them all that they were a lot of mossy slugs and needed hurrying. She unhooked an enormous coiled hosepipe from the wall, turned a tap, and began to spray the entire ablutions with a jet of icy water. Even girls who had already finished were wet anew, which Stella thought not very practical, until she realised the squirting was for the Bull's own pleasure.

'She does that just when you least expect,' groaned Buffy. 'And when you don't bother to shower, then she doesn't! Ow!' The jet of water caught her full on her pert young breasts. Stella found herself dancing in the spray, and quite enjoyed submitting to this indignity, like a helpless slave. She would have enjoyed Alberta's naked company, but assumed her new friend had made her own mysterious arrangements.

Back in dorm, the Under-prefect gruffly said that Stella and Alberta were to sit next to the Housemistress, Miss Rime, at breakfast. There was half an hour or so for bedmaking and dressing beforehand. Alberta explained that very mossy girls neglected to make their beds until after breakfast, hoping that the Under-prefects who inspected would be too hurried to notice imperfections and award punishments for a creased corner or slovenly pillow.

This was the moment Stella had been waiting for: she opened her kitbag and withdrew all of her new things, laying them out neatly on her bed. She had oodles of lovely clothes: pullovers, underthings, corselets and bodices and a greatcoat. There were rough work overalls, boots and socks and gorgeous stockings and frilly knickers, and brassières! She marvelled at how much could be crammed into a kitbag, and longed to try them all on, but Alberta warned her not to take all day. She hung them neatly in her little wardrobe and put the soft undies in her drawer, after hungrily sniffing the gentle silks and satins. She was left with her day uniform, and her leather back-satchel of school equipment. Her day uniform was sumptuous enough! She had always thought of school uniform as dour and unprepossessing, and had to remind herself proudly that she was a young Kernece lady!

Everything was a shade of poppy: the skirt, garter belt and shoes were the darkest, almost a wine colour, while in sumptuous contrast were the stockings, panties, blouse and camisole, in a creamy pastel shade like strawberry ice cream. There were oodles of underthings: all in lush silks, mousselines, satins and lace, and in a rainbow of poppy shades, dark and light. There was even a proper grown-up corset – a gorgeous creation of whalebone and satin and with eyelets that, when knotted, looked ready to squeeze her as thin as a pencil! Alberta said that was called a *guêpière* which translated into English as the rather inelegant 'waspie'. Stella just longed to try them, but Alberta said they should be kept for special occasions, not for the hurly-burly of the classroom. She regretfully stored her fichu scarves, her camiknickers, bloomers, bustiers, and petticoats. She kept just one pastel petticoat for day wear, however, whose ecru lace trim peeped naughtily below the hem of her ultra-short pleated skirt.

She felt such a thrill as she pulled her lacy panties very tight around her lady's place, then slowly rolled her new stockings over her bare legs and with trembling fingers fastened her garter straps. She felt so clumsy that Alberta laughed and said she would help; Stella smelt her musky perfume as her hair dangled over her breasts and she expertly snapped the wayward straps into place. Suddenly she noticed that she had an extra single garter strap, and felt a thrill that someone from the Blues – Tuffy, perhaps – had given it to her in secret. She strapped it round her upper thigh, next to her panties, and felt awfully proud and bold.

'Oh, nothing at all,' she answered with daring nonchalance when Alberta demanded to know what it was. She put on her lovely snug bumfreezer jacket and fastened the three shiny silver buttons, feeling its soft fabric and realising with a pleased start that it was cashmere wool. Then she slipped on her shoes and buckled them tight, and at last she was ready. Stella felt so grand to be one of the throng of identical new squits on her way to her first – no, second – Kernece breakfast.

All the girls lined up by their Houses in the long corridor outside Refectory, while Prefects took another roll-call. The Kernece uniform was the same for all Houses except for the colour, and Stella thought the array of House colours awfully pretty. They were like a bouquet of bright flowers, arrayed in the austere granite vase of Kernece. Inside the refectory, girls were seated by House: six tables to each, with a Prefect at the head of each of five tables. The Housemistress at the sixth, her place apparently rotating every day. The Under-prefects sat one or two to a table, amidst the girls, and at the end of Refectory on a stage, stood High Table, where the Mistresses ate.

Stella thus found herself beside Miss Rime, an engaging, cuddly woman a little older perhaps than Miss Cox, but extremely well-preserved. She had an ample figure neatly encased in a smart grey suit, white silk stockings, and a poppy blouse. She made small talk as breakfast was served. She quizzed Stella about the Midlands as though it were some marvellously exotic foreign land, and said that she was glad they could meet now, informally, as she was so busy.

'After your first few days, I'll have you for tea, Stella, if you like,' she said. Stella replied it would be super. 'Today, first thing after Assembly, you will go to Miss Noble, your Tutor. She will have your Scholar's gown for you and tell you about your timetable. As you perhaps know, classes are of 55 minutes, with a five minute break between each. So that makes three classes in the morning from nine until midday, two hours for luncheon, and then two in the afternoon from two until four. That's when most girls go to the tuck shop! Tea at six, then prep or activities. Then buns and a little time for reading before bed! If you finish your prep early, to the Prefect's satisfaction, you may ask to be excused. Saturday and Sunday are half-days.'

Stella was taken aback.

'I would have thought . . . church . . .' she said awkwardly. Then she remembered that the breakfast had not commenced with saying grace as she had expected.

'Church? Oh, yes, church. Here at Kernece, we think such matters are best left to the individual. You are not little girls, you know, you are grown-ups now. There is plenty of leisure time for . . . church.'

She said the word with a vague irritation, and proceeded to ask how Stella was settling in, telling her that the Prefects would teach her the House routine. Miss Rime added that she hoped she liked her breakfast. Stella was glad she had had the 'Parph' breakfast already, for in front of her was the most unappetising breakfast she had ever seen. There was a plate of porridge, thin as soup; and a plate of a rock-hard yellow substance like rubber, which she learnt was scrambled eggs or, as Alberta whispered, 'vommo'. Limp toast with sour marmalade and pats of greenish-grey butter were washed down with tea which, while stewed beyond taste, was thankfully strong. Miss Dancer's enthusiasm for a lady's tea evidently did not encompass other meals.

Stella lied politely that it was delicious, and Miss Rime beamed, apparently believing it was. She added that Miss Dancer would interview her in the next few days, but that because of her desire to interview each new entrant individually, there was sometimes a considerable wait. This did not displease Stella; she felt there were already quite enough bearings for her to get.

After breakfast, there was bed inspection in the dorm, and Stella's meticulous bedmaking passed muster. She saw one or two beds unceremoniously ripped apart by an Under-prefect, earning a later, unspecified punishment – and a further punishment if remaking the bed meant a late arrival at Assembly. Alberta said that faulty bedmaking did not merit the tawse or cane, but sometimes the Steps, and more usually a spanking.

'On the bare?' said Stella casually.

'Why, of course. What other sort of spanking is there? You wouldn't want your panties to get spoiled, would you?'

As instructed, Stella said a regretful goodbye to her kilt and other civilian things, leaving them in a laundry bag. On a mischievous impulse, she kept the frilly knickers Jamie had given her, hiding them in her locker. She followed Alberta down to Assembly, yet another roll-call, and a rather dull ten minutes of routine announcements about various Societies or meetings. There was no cheery College song or anything: as Miss Rime had said, they were grown-ups. There was, however, a moment when girls were invited to bring up 'Matters Arising' or 'Grievances'. There were none.

As Assembly broke up, Miss Noble descended on Stella and warmly greeted her, instructing her to follow her to her study. She was excused first lesson, and Miss Noble explained that as each Tutor had a restricted number of students, she was able, unlike Miss Dancer, to see each of them soon after the beginning of Term. They passed through milling throngs of girls who were clutching and dropping stacks of books and papers, jostling and laughing. None seemed to be wearing a Scholar's gown, and Stella wondered how many Scholars there actually were. She caught sight of Heather, and a couple of the other Blues, but gave and received no greeting, and felt awfully proud of her secrecy. Of Morag there was no sign, and she remembered that, by chance, Morag was her first task as a Kern of Anemone Cohort. Or, she wondered, *was* it chance?

Miss Noble's study was amidst a warren of oaken doors, a convenient distance from the hubbub of classrooms. She invited Stella to take a seat, giving her a neatly scripted copy of her timetable. She told her that everything Stella needed to know about her studies was there, together with directions to each classroom and to her own form room, together with the schedule for prep in her various subjects, and so on. Stella glanced at her timetable, and it was indeed thorough. There were periods for every subject in which she had excelled at St Hilda's and, in addition, lectures on educational psychology, methods of discipline, and something called sociology.

'You'll learn the layout of Kernece quickly,' Miss Noble said with a smile of her delicately painted red lips. 'But don't be afraid to ask – it's a bit of a maze sometimes. There are all sorts of places which are out of bounds, to staff and students alike! Now I shall give you a little quiz, to see if you've spent your prep wisely.'

Miss Noble crossed her legs, and Stella noticed that she too had quite a short skirt for a Mistress, almost from the pages of *Mode*. It was black and pleated, and Stella could see her stocking-tops, garters, and even had a glimpse of frilly black knickers! She looked very 'schoolmistressy' with her plain white satin blouse and black jacket, and a bumfreezer like Stella's. But her lips and eyes *were* painted, and Stella felt a little jealous. Miss Noble had intriguingly lithe haunches and a very narrow waist with generous but very firm breasts that stood out quite pertly against her tight blouse, her thimble-like nipples being surprisingly plain to see. Stella idly wondered if she were corsed, and decided she must be. Her face was porcelain white, like a doll's, and her blonde hair was combed – or ironed! – straight and shiny around her strong shoulders.

'Then we'll give you your Scholar's gown, I expect you are eager to have that,' she grinned.

'Oh, yes, Miss!' cried Stella.

'Or would you rather have it on for your quiz?'

'Please!'

'All right,' said Miss Noble, getting up and opening a drawer. 'Take off all your clothes, except your panties.'

'I beg your pardon . . . take off . . .?' Stella stammered.

'Yes!' said Miss Noble brightly, holding up a small, sheer black garment. 'This is your Scholar's gown, Stella. Worn next to the skin, and an especial privilege here in the north, where it can be *very* cold.'

Stella obeyed, wide-eyed, for she smelled and saw that her Scholar's gown was made of shiny black rubber! When she was nude, she took the gown and stepped into it; it was soft and silky to touch, and was an unusual one-piece garment with a gusset that buttoned at the lady's place, under her buttocks, and straps over the shoulders. The belly and croup were covered, but the breasts left delectably bare, although upthrust by the strong rubber! It was *almost* a corset. She slipped it over her bare skin and found it a perfect fit. Its touch was so slippery-smooth and the gown was so snug around her fesses and lady's place that she thrilled as though she had a second skin. She longed for her mirror.

'My, Stella, what a lovely bottom you have!' said Miss Noble suddenly. 'And I can see others have thought so too. You have already taken bare chastisement, haven't you?'

Stella blushed, and answered yes.

'Brave girl. Now, you may wear panties with your gown, or not, as you please,' said Miss Noble. 'Most girls don't. Anyway, put your kit on and we'll get down to our quiz.'

When Stella was dressed, she could not help thinking that she would wear the gown with no panties. Its touch was so sly and smooth, like a caressing hand, that she could scarcely concentrate on Miss Dancer's questions. These were fired at her quite rapidly, and Stella soon became confused. Miss Noble did not tell her whether she had got the question right, which was even more confusing.

'How many players in a side at Kernece Football?'

'Six under a crescent Moon, seven if the Moon is full.'

'Who was "Tawser" Bright?'

'A famous Headmistress of the 1860s.'

'How many jacket buttons may a new squit have undone when going through Hadrian's Passage?'

'A new squit is not allowed in Hadrian's Passage.'

'How high is the Kernece Tower?'

'349 feet. No, 347.'

'And how many Steps are there?' Stella hesitated.

'Mmm . . . 304?'

'What is the Labyrinth?'

'A group of cellars for the chastisement of seniors.'

'How do you address a Prefect who is in the Remove?'

'A member of the Remove may not be a Prefect.'

'When may a Kernecian in uniform lawfully wear no knickers?'

'At Hallowe'en, or Knobkerry Day. No, wait, on Knobkerry Day it is *forbidden* to wear knickers. Or is it Hallowe'en?'

The questions became harder and more obscure, and eventually Miss Noble pursed her lips and tut-tutted with a rueful shake of her head.

'Dear me, Stella. We aren't doing very well, are we?'

'I . . . I'm sorry, Miss,' stammered Stella, blushing desperately. 'I did study the book, and I thought I knew most things.'

In truth, the distraction of her lovely tight rubber gown – as well as the sight of Miss Noble's beautiful thighs, and the frilly black bulge of her fount as she crossed and uncrossed her legs – had made Stella tingle with a strange, uneasy desire. Her bottom constantly reminded her of the thrashings she had taken. To her embarrassment, she kept thinking of the blows of tawse or flail, and of Charity's gorgeous buttocks squirming under her own cane – though she still felt awkward about giving, instead of taking, punishment. As a result of all these thoughts her fount was determinedly seeping with moisture.

'We'll try a few more,' said Miss Noble rather sternly. Try and buck up, Stella.'

Some more questions followed: what was the minimum petticoat length for a second-year girl?, on what days were girls to dress in trousers and a House necktie?, what prize entitled the winner to roam freely in the Parph?, and so on. But Stella was all at sea. At last, Miss Noble sighed and shook her head.

'It's no good, Stella, I'm afraid I must fail you. And your very first prep! Dear me. Miss Dancer will not be pleased. At Kernece, you are thrown in the deep end, and must learn to swim with the others – right away! It'll be a blot on your College record, you know.'

She sighed again. Stella felt so wretched to have disappointed her pretty Tutor that she was afraid tears might well.

'I wish there were some way out of this,' said Miss Noble. 'I do hate paperwork, you know.'

'Miss, I know I've been remiss,' said Stella, 'and deserve punishment. But to have my name marked, and on my first day! Oh, I'd rather ...'

'Rather what, Stella?' said Miss Noble, her eyes shining.

'Oh! Rather have my *bottom* marked!'

Stella blushed furiously, and hung her head. There was an electric pause, and then Miss Noble said slowly:

'Well, you have only been slightly remiss, Stella. I suppose ... A little spank might settle your fault.'

Stella's head remained hanging, and her heart beat as she tried to sound penitent and disguise the sudden excitement she felt. Had she *deliberately* got her answers wrong, hoping for this very punishment?

'Yes, Miss, if you say so,' she whispered. Oh please yes, Oh please! her heart sang.

'It'll have to be bare bum, you know.'

'I know, Miss.'

'Very well! That settles things. It's a bit of a bother, but you must lift up your skirt and undo the gusset of your gown. Raise the rubber crotch-flap and lower your knickers so that I can have a good view of your fesses.'

Stella did so, hoping that Miss Noble would not notice how wet her upper thighs were with the juices that now flowed from her quivering fount – or perhaps hoping that she *would* notice. At Miss Noble's direction, she placed herself over her Tutor's skirted knee, with her head almost on the floor and her long legs spread as wide behind her as the barrier of her stretched knickers would permit. She breathed rapturously of Miss Noble's wonderful perfume; her Tutor smelled as cool and sweet as moss!

'Right, Stella!' said Miss Noble, and Stella felt a hard hand slap her naked bum. Another spank followed, and another, and as Miss Noble spanked her now squirming charge, she emphasised each smarting blow with a single word of her lengthy chastisement.

'You have been remiss Miss Stella Shawn and I have no place for remiss students you must promise to behave properly at all times in future if you wish to become a good Kernecian otherwise you will be no stranger to the brank or the Steps or any other punishments to which I sentence you and they shall go in the punishment book is that clearly understood and the next time I have occasion to tan you it shall be the tawse or cane and on your bare not just a mere girly's spanking a caning till you wriggle and squirm and beg me to stop but I shall not stop tanning your bum until you are truly a good girl and a good Kernecian there now!'

Stella's fount was cascading wet as the spanking stopped, and her fesses glowed as red as her flushed face felt.

'Oh, yes, Miss!' she cried as she got up, 'I promise to be good, and thank you for my punishment! Gosh, how you can spank! I'm smarting so beau – I mean, so hard.'

'I cane much harder,' said Miss Noble quietly. 'And I hope I shan't have occasion for *that*!'

On impulse, Stella knelt and kissed the tips of Miss Noble's shoes! She heard Miss Noble pant hoarsely.

'Or perhaps I hope I shall,' Miss Noble whispered. In the distance, a strident bell rang.

'Goodness, time for second lesson!' said Miss Noble. 'You are in Miss Rose's class – biology, at which it seems you distinguished yourself at St Hilda's. Miss Rose shall, of course, be in attendance.'

'I don't understand, Miss,' said Stella, smoothing her uniform.

'Why, you are to teach the class,' said Miss Noble. 'The best way to learn to teach is by teaching! At Kernece, you *are* thrown in at the deep end!'

As Stella said goodbye, she saw Miss Noble's hand touch, or caress, the front of her skirt, on her lap , where Stella's gushing fount had left an enormous wet patch! Moreover, she could see that Miss Noble's stocking-tops were glistening with liquid that was not Stella's ...

6

Tea and Punishment

There were a dozen girls already seated in Miss Rose's classroom when Stella entered, as well as Miss Rose herself. She was a thin woman with handsome but severe features and, like the others, she wore a white smock: the biology room was partly a laboratory. To Stella's surprise, Heather and Morag were there, and all stood to greet her as she entered, with a sullen' 'Good morning, Miss.'

Miss Rose took her aside and said that this was class A of the second year. Stella's task would be to oversee a test on their prescribed holiday study, for which last night's prep had been a final revision. Miss Rose would remain in attendance, but not interfere: Stella's job was really to maintain discipline rather than to teach anything. There were questions already chalked on the blackboard, and Stella felt awfully grand as she mounted the podium and ordered the girls to begin. Her nervousness disappeared, and she began to scan the questions on the board, then skimmed the biology textbook and was pleased to find that she already knew most of it. Here she was, a Mistress at her podium: she *could* teach if she wanted to! It seemed their prep had contained much about pistils and stamens, and also what were called 'male and female human reproductive organs'.

For the first few minutes there was silence except for the dutiful scratching of old-fashioned ink pens, and Stella looked idly round the austere laboratory, thinking that teaching was going to be such fun! Then she began to scrutinise the second years' uniforms under their open smocks, comparing them to her own.

The new squit's uniform she had donned with such pride such a short time ago now seemed rather girly and frivolous. She was acutely aware that the stern, knee-length skirts, dark shoes and stockings of the second years were much more dignified. However, as the girls emitted groans of frustration and scratched their heads over their test, Stella felt at home in the familiar odour of a classroom. Suddenly a red-headed girl from Marigold's House put her hand up and said, 'Please, Miss?' in an innocent voice.

'Yes?' said Stella, trying to sound stern.

'How do you spell "penis"? Has it got two "e"s?'

Stella blushed hotly. She had heard of that word, but never countenanced using it! She looked at Miss Rose, who shrugged to indicate that Stella must deal with the matter.

'That is not in your test,' stammered Stella. 'Nor, I believe, is it in your textbook.'

'Yes, Miss, but it is so much shorter than "male reproductive organ", isn't it? To save time, I mean.'

'You will save time by not wasting it with foolish questions!' said Stella, recovering some of her aplomb.

'But, Miss –'

'Silence!' cried Stella, and after a flutter of muted giggling there *was* silence, to her relief: but not for long. Another girl, from Bluebell's, put up her hand.

'Please, Miss? If you *do* know how to spell "penis", are you allowed to use it?' There were more giggles, this time not so muted, and the giggles turned to subdued remarks. Stella reddened again.

'I ... Yes, all right,' she said in confusion, realising that she was not sure how to spell the word herself.

Now, another two hands were raised, one from Poppy's and one from Orchid's. Stella nodded to the girl from Orchid's.

'Does that mean we can say "vagina", Miss, instead of "female reproductive organ"?'

'Yes, you may,' said Stella, beginning to feel desperate.

'How do you spell "vagina", Miss?' said the Poppy's girl. 'Is it with a "j" or a "g"?'

The redhead promptly put her hand up again.

'Miss, it's not fair if some of us know the spellings and some don't, because then we get penalised for bad spelling!'

'Then write "reproductive organs" as it says in the book!' Stella exclaimed.

'Then we waste time and they don't,' cried another voice.

'May we write "breasts", then, Miss, instead of "secondary female reproductive organs?"' said a voice.

'Or "bosoms"?' said another.

'How about "titties"?' said a third, and the whole class burst into laughter.

'Be quiet, the lot of you, and get on with your work!' cried Stella, and abandoned her position at the podium to get closer to her obstreperous charges. This meant that she could no longer survey all the girls at once and, too late, she realised her mistake.

Behind her, she heard a sly whisper, so low that it was almost imperceptible, but meant for her to perceive.

'I can see her knickers!' The laughter that greeted this was not imperceptible, and Stella felt wild with frustrated embarrassment.

'Hasn't she a big bum!' came another, louder, whisper.

'And big secondary female sex organs.'

'I'll bet she needs a brassière like Tower Bridge to hold them up.'

'Two brassières, probably, one for each titty!'

'Silence!' cried Stella desperately: to no avail. Miss Rose sat impassive and frowning, her arms folded. Now the taunts were quite open and no longer whispered.

'What a girly!'

'Only a new squit, the mossy barnacle!'

'I bet she doesn't know what a penis *is*!'

'*Or* a vagina!'

Stella's normal placidity dissolved in a furious rage.

'I do know what a penis is! Of course I do!' she roared, and there was pandemonium as the girls simpered, 'Ooh!'

And then there was a remark, clearly and insultingly loud, from a voice Stella recognised.

'I bet she's telling the truth,' it said. 'I bet she knows all about a penis. I bet she's even sucked one like a lollipop and swallowed all the juice, too!'

Stella whirled round in outrage.

'Morag!' she cried furiously. 'How *dare* you! You will apologise before the class for your insolence!'

Morag remained silent as the others simpered 'Ooh!' again at Stella's acquaintance with Morag.

'This is outrageous! Answer me, Morag, damn you!'

Stella was shocked to hear herself utter a foul word, and this time Morag did answer.

'You look sweet in your poppy knickers, girly,' she said.

'Oh!' Stella cried as the classroom erupted with laughter, and in a blind rage struck out at the woman she thought had been her friend. Morag made no attempt to duck the blow, but Stella's aim was false. In her fury, all she did was clip Morag's breasts. It was enough. At once there was a deathly hush; Miss Rose stood and approached Stella.

'Carry on with your work, girls,' she rapped, and they obeyed. She turned to Stella and shook her said sadly.

'This is an appalling matter,' she said. 'Miss Shawn, you have broken a cardinal rule of Kernece: the prohibition of any blow struck in anger. The case shall have to go to Miss Dancer. And, even if there were no witnesses, I should not be inclined to excuse punishment for this outrage.'

Tears of shame and rage welled in Stella's eyes. She tried to stammer her excuses, but words would not come, for she knew in her heart she had no excuse.

'You will leave my classroom and go straight to Headmistress's house,' Miss Rose continued, 'and tell the truth to her secretary, Miss Fortis.'

Stella bowed her head and, full of bitterness and self-loathing, left the room fighting back her tears. Her only crumb of comfort was that she was being trusted as a grown-up to go to Headmistress herself and tell the truth. She had been so looking forward to meeting Miss Dancer. And now she would do so, under the worst possible circumstances!

She crossed the yard with a heavy heart, and full of foreboding: her whole future seemed now in doubt, all thanks to the stupid chance that had made her cuff Morag. Or was it fate? Stella was troubled as she could not decide between the two. Her romantic reading of heroes and destiny had made her believe in an all-powerful fate. But now she reflected that it was chance that had led Morag to delay her return to Kernece, chance that had led her to Jamie Isbister. Was it chance, though, that Morag had deliberately provoked her? Morag must have known the likely result.

Stella was scrutinised with ill-concealed disdain as she told Miss Fortis what had happened. The Headmistress's secretary was a female of middling years, well-preserved yet dressed strangely in a costume very similar to a new squit's uniform. She had brightly-painted lips and a chignon of flowers in her hair, which was flecked steely grey and knotted surprisingly in ribboned pigtails. She was trim, like most of the females Stella had seen – except for the cuddly Miss Rime, who evidently liked even the austere food served at mealtimes. Therefore her short little pleated skirt and frilly blouse did not sit oddly on her, but, had her expression not been so dour, would have seemed rather a pleasing conceit.

'Well, you'll be for it, Miss, I expect,' she murmured in a Scottish growl, picking up a telephone. She spoke briefly to Miss Dancer about the case, and there was a pause, while Miss Fortis listened with a grin of satisfaction. She put the telephone down and told Stella to attend Miss Dancer for tea at a quarter to five. This sounded good: she would be spared Refectory, and Miss Dancer would no doubt provide a yummy tea. Perhaps she would just get a nice motherly talking-to!

'You may expect more than tea, I think, Miss,' said Miss Fortis with a leer that chilled Stella's heart.

The rest of the day passed in an uncomfortable daze, with Stella scarcely able to take in anything of her lessons. The third class was French, at which she acquitted herself well even though she was not really paying attention. Luncheon was even more horrid than breakfast, with cardboard potatoes and a strip of meat that looked, and tasted, like wet string, and shone with an eerie luminescence that put her in mind of the mysterious Parph and its flora.

'Rainbow meat!' said Alberta gaily, and asked her why she was so glum. Stella did not explain, saying merely that she was very tired. She ate little: Alberta finished her plate.

Afternoon classes were a double period of sociology, of which Stella could make neither head nor tail. She was with her first form intake, the new squits, but noticed that there was a fair sprinkling of girls with senior uniforms. Most of them looked bored and superior, and had that indefinable air of casual elegance given by wealth taken for granted. The girl beside her, in the fetching white of Daisy's House, whispered that they were the 'slackers' of the Remove, who had to repeat their first year. She added that sociology was all rot, and that anyway Miss Marsham the teacher was a bolshie communist! Stella did not know if it was rot or not, since her nervous agitation of the morning had given way to a miserable somnolence. She knew she would be punished, and was sure it would be the humiliation of the Steps, with all her comrades jeering the new squit at her ordeal. She would no doubt be given some horrid nickname. She pinched herself awake, and tried to take notes.

'And so,' Miss Marsham droned, 'we see that all human society is based on power and ownership, expressed by the ever-renewed conflict between classes. The social or affective power struggle is most intense, however, between the male and female of our race, a parallel conflict which transcends even the class struggle. Even in feudal or, nowadays –' she smirked grimly '– in socialist societies like the USSR, the economic power of the male has always been balanced by the affective power of the female, and her ability to enslave the male and direct him to her own ends. One party must always dominate, and one submit. Or as Lenin succinctly puts it, "Who whom?". It is normal for submissive classes to rebel against their dominant oppressors; rare for those dominant to rebel against their own dominance! *But it is not unheard of*. There are sometimes other motivations than simple economics. As young ladies, you shall learn that by submitting to the class structure of

Kernece, you shall learn supremely to dominate the world outside. In particular, the male of the species.'

One of the Remove girls ostentatiously yawned.

'Unless,' added Miss Marsham maliciously, 'you are a *bourgeoise* of the Remove, in which case it is doubtful you shall learn anything at all.'

Stella soldiered dutifully on through the lesson, but the thought struck and stayed with her that she had not yet spied any males in Kernece, and realised that she rather missed their odd-smelling, incomprehensible, yet comforting presence. The bell rang for end of classes and, when they had received Miss Marsham's permission to depart, there was a headlong rush in the general direction of the reading room. Stella found herself swept along without really knowing where she was headed, until a girl breathlessly told her: 'Tuck Shop!'

They came to the end of a long queue of giggling, expectant girls. First, second and third years all mingling amicably in the strange democracy of hunger, and fussing with hair and dress as though preparing for a dance or party. Stella suddenly realised that she was starving! Dimly she told herself that she would get tea at Headmistress's, but she did not know *what* she would have there.

She looked at the money in her pocket-book and reminded herself that it had to last all term; she would deposit it with the House Bursar, as Miss Rime had advised, and whence she could withdraw as much as she wanted at any time. Meanwhile she decided to have a little treat: some chocolate, or sweets or cake, perhaps. Stella remembered that as a Scholar, she received an extra 24 pounds a term from the Kernece Scholarship Fund (one of the good works of Tawser Bright) and suddenly felt extremely rich! When she came to the doorway and saw the plain counter with the jars of toffees and fudge, gaudy boiled sweets and biscuits, with rows of bottles of lemonade like suitors at a ball, her mouth actually watered.

She now saw why the girls were so keen to get to the tuck shop: behind the counter she saw her first male at Kernece. He was superbly tall and had a cupid's face with full rosebud lips under a thicket of black curls, like some ancient Greek hero. His skin was tan, and his boyish – or really, Stella thought, girlish – good looks were in contrast to the whipcord of his muscled arms as he performed his unheroic tasks. He worked fast, pouring, measuring, and sifting sweaty coins, and smiled rarely; when he did, there was smirking sullen arrogance to the crease of his beautiful lips. Stella sensed herself competing for his smiles like the others. His name seemed to be Jakes, and when her turn came, she found herself ordering toffees, and chocolate, and cake, and lollipops, *and* lemonade!

'I'm new, you know, Jakes,' she blurted. 'It's all a bit strange to me. What a lovely . . . tuck shop you have!'

Jakes grinned slyly.

'They all say that, Miss,' he replied in a thick accent of the purest cockney.

'And do you work at Kernece full time?' said Stella, feeling awfully gauche and oopsy.

'Day and night,' he replied lazily. 'I'm sort of a general factotum, and Miss Dancer believes in keeping a male hard at it. Still, it's drier than sailing the Atlantic for Newfoundland cod.'

'Newfoundland!' blurted Stella. 'That is a long way from . . . from London.'

'It certainly is,' he said. 'But once a fisherman, always a fisherman. Caught my first whelk off Southend Pier when I was a nipper, and never looked back.'

He finished wrapping her purchases and told her it would be two shillings and sevenpence-halfpenny. As she fumbled with coins, Jakes stared very deep into her eyes, and said mildly, 'I'm still a fisherman, Miss.'

She left the tuck shop feeling on top of the world, and conscious of the envious glances of the other girls. She didn't care. Jakes had actually smiled at her!

Stella found a casual bench in the reading room and leafed through a week-old copy of *The Scotsman* as she munched her sweetmeats and washed them down with lemonade. She became quite enthralled with the stories in the newspaper, about things she had never heard of, so that its elegant English prose seemed like a new foreign language for her to master. What was an 'Arbroath smokie', a 'chib', or a 'Dunfermline pudding'? She was fascinated, and looked up at the clock just in time to see she had two minutes to get to Headmistress's! Dismayed, she saw she had eaten everything she had bought, and was sure she was too full to have tea! It could not be helped; she scurried across the yard and presented herself, breathless but suitably meek, to Miss Fortis. It cheered her up to think of Jakes's smile, and the other girls' jealousy. Then, promptly at a quarter to five, the Headmistress's door opened and she was admitted to Miss Dancer's study. A woman stood by a large sofa, and Stella gaped in surprise to see who else was in the room: Morag was seated in an armchair to one side of the room.

Stella would have known Miss Dancer was Headmistress, even without her soft-spoken introduction. She radiated an aura of steely authority, both in her overpowering physical presence and the stern understatement of her dress. She looked Stella straight in the eye, with her own eyes that were deep pools of jade. Stella blushed and looked away, as though Miss Dancer had seen into her very soul! Miss Dancer was petite, and dressed entirely in black silk, except for sheer white silk stockings. Her shoes were black and pointed, with high heels, and she wore a long-sleeved sheath dress that just covered her knees. The dress was surprisingly low-cut, revealing the globes and plum nipples of a very firm, upthrust bosom that clearly had no need of a brassière. Her waist was so narrow, above a ripe hour-glass croup, that Stella would have sworn she was corsed, had not the tightness of her dress made plain that she was uncorsed and pantiless. Only the outline of her suspender belt interrupted its smoothness. Her only jewellery was a thick gold necklace, over which her jet-black hair coiled thick and lustrous. Her skin was a perfect alabaster white, with crimson lips budding in the snowy face. She wore austere half-moon glasses in a gold frame. Stella thought that Miss Dancer was power itself.

Her study was sparsely furnished, but comfortable, with

an imposing oak desk and some abstract paintings on the wall that Stella imagined were 'futurist', or 'art deco'. In subtle harmony, there were also paintings of the previous century: sumptuously detailed nude females in the neoclassical style, which Stella thought daringly beautiful. On the low table in front of a cheerful fire sat a plentiful tea, with cakes and buttered scones and honey, and Stella groaned inwardly that she had already gorged on tuck. She was invited to sit on the sofa, where Miss Dancer joined her, as Morag poured tea for them all. Stella nervously sat, and now Miss Dancer smiled, showing perfect teeth and emitting a little purr like a cat, or a tiger.

'Well, Stella Shawn,' she said in a mild, quizzical voice, 'it seems we meet sooner than I had anticipated. Your behaviour in slapping Miss Morag Tallon was ... Well, I think you know how serious.'

So that is Morag's name, Stella thought.

'Against the Rules, of course,' said Miss Dancer, 'but Stella –' she laid a soothing hand on Stella's knee, which was trembling a little '– the Rules are based on common sense. And your dossier, as well as the glowing testimony of my friend Miss Cox, suggest you are a lady of common sense.'

Stella was pleased to be addressed as a lady, and sipped her tea, forcing herself to join the others in scones and a curiously delicious jam. Suddenly she found to her delight that her woman's appetite was not at all sated.

'How do you like your tea?' said Miss Dancer. 'It is Lapsang Souchong, my favourite, although there is Earl Grey or Darjeeling if you prefer. And this jam is made from Parph raspberries, as we call them. They are very plentiful in summer, and we make preserves.'

Stella waited to swallow her food, and said that it was very nice. Miss Dancer nodded approvingly. She lowered her half-moon spectacles and looked at Stella over the top, with a mildly reproachful expression.

'At Kernece, Stella, your training will be quite harsh, as I think you already know. In fact I understand you have already taken punishment on the bare; your charming initiation into Poppy's, for example.'

'Y-yes, Miss,' said Stella. Miss Dancer's smile was warm.

'And I know that Miss Noble has a firm hand.'

Stella gulped. How did Miss Dancer know these things?

'And you shall in time come to administer discipline yourself, I have no doubt.'

Stella did not mention her caning of Charity, although she was by now sure that Miss Dancer knew *everything*.

'But while corporal punishment is the cornerstone of proper training, it must be administered with love, not in anger. A lady must always know how to control herself, and in cuffing Morag Tallon you have not done so. Do you agree?'

Stella nodded, yes. What was the use in complaining about Morag's horrid provocation?

'Well, then?' There was a pause, and Stella realised she was supposed to speak.

'I . . . I suppose I must expect punishment, Miss.'

Miss Dancer placed her hand again on Stella's knee.

'But do you *wish* to be punished, Stella?' she said softly, looking into Stella's eyes. This time Stella did not flinch, but her heart leapt with the joy of her sudden understanding.

'Yes, Miss!' she cried. 'I desire to be punished!'

'Good,' said Miss Dancer briskly. 'Finish your tea, Stella, there is no hurry. And I have decided that, while I should have no hesitation in sentencing an older lady to the Steps, in full punishment kit, the nature of your offence makes a simple caning more appropriate.'

'Yes, Miss,' said Stella numbly.

'Bare bum, of course.'

'Of *course*, Miss,' replied Stella, and she heard her words spill with eagerness.

'Now,' continued Miss Dancer, 'how many strokes do you deserve? Think before answering, because what you say is what you'll get. Too few, and you will be left with a slacker's guilt. Too many, and I might think you were showing off, which is unladylike. But you'd get them, and you might have to sleep on your tummy, and take your breakfast standing up.'

Stella's head whirled. She had given Charity a full 39, evidently a significant number to the Blues. She still felt uncomfortable at her pleasure in giving, rather than taking, the cane. But then Charity's bottom was accustomed to it. Why, Stella Shawn was accustomed to it! If she said 39, Miss Dancer might guess the secret that she was in the Blues; anyway, she shivered as she looked at Miss Dancer's athletic body and her whipcord arm muscles. 39 from *her*! Stella promised herself she would not be cowardly.

'I'll take 27, Miss,' she said in a sharp breath.

'Perfect,' said Miss Dancer warmly. 'And as part of your punishment you will bare your bottom to Morag.'

Stella blushed crimson at this humiliation, but she would not change her mind. She would take it. Suddenly, the pressure in her belly – and her nervousness – made her wish to visit the bathroom, and she asked Miss Dancer's permission.

'Morag knows where it is,' the Headmistress said, 'she will take you.'

Stella lifted her skirt and petticoat, lowered her panties, and squatted on the commode, while Morag made no move to go. Stella was quite full of tuck, and concentrated on the private pleasure of her evacuation. When she had her relief, she asked Morag bitterly what had made her do this. Morag sneered that she knew Stella was a Blue, and so they were enemies! Stella could not hide her astonishment.

'How –' she began.

'We have our spies,' said Morag, putting her face uncomfortably close to Stella's. 'You see, Stella, we Reds are all of us doms – dominant females. As such, we are predators, we fight an aggressive war. We need victims! You Blues are confused, you are *defensive*. You're an Army of doms, but run by pathetic submissives like that girly Charity. So all your aggression is wasted on your own leaders, because that is what they want! I'm going to cane *you*, the enemy. And you won't get on as a Blue Kern, Stella, for I've marked you as a sub, not a dom!'

'I was Head Girl of St Hilda's!' she replied with a bravado she did not really feel. 'Of course I'm a dom!'

She stood and wiped herself, washed her lady's place and pulled up her panties. She had the glimmering of an idea.

'No need of that,' sneered Morag. 'Those panties are coming off right away. 27 on those lovely bare globes! Oh, you stupid, stupid sub!'

'Not so stupid,' said Stella coolly. 'If I am a sub, then I'll enjoy it, won't I? And as for being a sub in the Blues, then I am destined to *lead* the Blues! *You* will never lead the Reds! Too much dom competition.' Morag bristled in anger.

'There are limits to enjoyment, sub,' she hissed. 'I'll cane you tighter than you've ever imagined!'

'And I,' said Stella sweetly, 'shall take it.'

They returned to the study, where the tea-things had been cleared. Miss Dancer was sitting at her desk, all briskness.

'Let us to the business, ladies,' she said. 'Stella, you will please bend over the back of the armchair, with your feet spread to its legs, then raise your skirts and lower your panties to your knees. You must take your punishment like a lady: that is, without crying and with no flinching. Although I shan't mind squirming. Indeed I expect it.'

Stella obeyed, and in her flogging position, grasped the chair arms for support. She felt so bare and helpless with her naked bottom upthrust to the gaze of the other women: yet it excited her! The more so when she felt Miss Dancer's soft hand stroke her naked fesses, and touch her secret blue garter. She had forgotten it, and now Miss Dancer *knew*!

'Oh,' said Miss Dancer, 'such lovely globes, Stella! So soft and sweet! They deserve a very special blush. Let me see, shall it be the yew, the ash? The willow? There is even a hickory. The ash, I think. Here, Morag.'

She heard Miss Dancer hand Morag the cane, and tell her to make the strokes as hard as she could; words which sent a terrible thrill up Stella's spine. She was given the long cane to kiss, and her beating began. The pain of the first stroke was horrid. The second, in just the same place across her soft bum-flesh, was worse. It was all Stella could do not to cry out as her throat caught, or to flinch as she heard the whistle of the cane heralding each cut.

Morag panted harshly as she flogged Stella's naked bottom. She was fierce – a dom, all right. Stella could sense through the fierce cane-strokes the exultant pleasure that her friend was taking in punishing her, and to her joy realised that Morag was indeed her friend after all. The caning was a bond between them, a giving of love and pleasure. She was giving her friend, the dom Morag, what she wanted, and in doing so experienced the beautiful joy of submission to a loved other!

She reached a plateau where her severe discomfort crossed the threshold of pain and became a fierce glow of happiness, pride and desire. She gasped, not at the cane strokes, but at the feeling of wetness that was flowing in her lady's place! She felt the oil of her fount trickling down her naked, quivering thighs, and was sure – hoped – that Morag and Miss Dancer saw too! She imagined it was Jamie caning her, or Matron, or the surly Jakes. Her bottom was wriggling now in pure lustful pleasure.

Her bare bottom glowed, and she could imagine the lovely pink flush she would keep as Morag's sweet present. The flogging was expert, but she wondered why both Armies were doms? Were there so few subs? She thought of Charity and Matron and her own self . . . surely there were more like her? Were Morag's dominant comrades in the reds, and hers in the Blues, only pretending? Were they denying their true natures – were they *really subs in disguise*?

The caning continued remorselessly, and Stella glowed with joy at another's happiness: at the happiness of two others, because Miss Dancer was shifting nervously in her chair, and her face was flushed. As though mesmerised, Miss Dancer raised and lowered her glinting spectacles to the rhythm of the cane, and Stella thought there was something odd about the lenses. At last Morag panted, 'That's it!' with a final cut that took her with sweet cruelty across the soft backs of her upper thighs, and Stella genuinely jumped at the searing pain of *that* stroke. There were tears in her eyes as she stood and replaced her clothing, but they were tears of gratitude. She bowed and thanked Miss Dancer, and then, without warning, knelt to kiss Morag's shoes!

'Why, that is very sweet of you, Stella,' said Miss Dancer. 'You are ... a good girl. And you shall have a little reward for your fortitude. Morag, lift your skirts and lower your panties. I want Stella to see your croup!'

'Oh, Miss' said Morag, squirming in embarrassment.

'Will you obey, Miss, or do I give you the same again?' rapped Miss Dancer. Morag turned and lowered her knickers, and Stella saw with wonderful pleasure that her bottom too was criss-crossed and glowing crimson!

'Morag!' she cried. 'Oh, my best chum!'

'You see,' smiled Miss Dancer sweetly, 'there were two guilty parties in this affair. Morag received her punishment with the same cane before tea – but she only took 21!'

She dismissed the two women, bade them remember their lesson – Stella rubbed her bum and said that she would never forget! – and then put on her impressively bossy spectacles again. In the yard, Morag looked angry. Stella sensed that she was embarrassed at having to show her lovely reddened bum, and clasped her hand. Morag did not resist, but growled with, Stella was certain, a hint of envy, 'In a way, it is a pity you are nothing but a sub, Stella. How I despise stupid subs!'

'How can you despise the thing you, as a dom, need most?' replied Stella sweetly. The very word dom gave her a naughty, melting thrill.

'Hah!' snorted Morag. 'Jakes needs women, but he despises them ... If you eat a fish, don't you despise it for being so stupid as to get caught?'

'No,' said Stella. 'I love it.' And then smiled at Morag, for now she knew how she was to complete her task for the Blues, and gain Morag's 'affective sector'.

They parted to go to their Houses, and Stella suddenly realised what was unusual about Miss Dancer's spectacles: the lenses were nothing but plain glass.

7

Sub

In the days that followed, Stella found she adapted easily and quickly to the routine of Kernece. Classes presented little problem to her, and she found the varied studies quite exciting. Even sociology began to assume some murky significance, and on the occasion when she was required to teach a class, she found that she could keep discipline by actually teaching the girls something interesting. She sensed they had more experience of life than she, but she knew more about books, and had more stories. She enthralled them with tales of her heroes, and particularly Joan of Arc.

Mealtimes were dismal, but the presence of the enigmatic Jakes and his tuck-shop made up for that. Stella surmised that the College must make a handsome profit out of tuck, which was why the meals were so insipid. Tea was the exception, but by teatime most girls were so full of tuck that the tea-things were taken away half-full, no doubt to be served again the next day. She wondered if the girls would spend so much money on sweetmeats if they were served by another girl, and not by Jakes.

At ablutions, her well-adorned bottom earned her the admiration of the other Poppilian new squits, who had not yet been graced with lashes. She assumed a slight air of superiority, as one who could 'take it'. Her new chums waited eagerly for her to lift her nightie in the morning and casually show her well-blossomed nates, even though the blooms of her chastisement were gradually fading. This attention did not go unnoticed by the Bull, who took special delight in squirting Stella's naked bum with the ice-cold hose. Sometimes the jet of water played around her front, to soak her mink and lady's place, and whenever her damsel was tickled, Stella found this humiliation unbearably thrilling!

The other Prefects were quite nice, and seemed to live in as much awe of the Bull as everyone else. The Underprefects were not taken very seriously, having little power; they were rather embarrassed at not being full Prefects.

She behaved herself, had a friendly tea with Miss Rime – whose mountains of rock cakes really were rock cakes (no matter, since she happily scoffed them all), and played netball with some success, being promoted to the 'A' team of the first years. Miss Harker, the Games Mistress, seemed to take an especial interest in her, chatting to her amicably at after-game ablutions. She eyed Stella's breasts quite a lot, and her bum too. She told her that she had a good figure, so should expect a trial at Kernece Football. When Stella asked her to explain this mysterious game, Miss Harker smiled and said that she must read her Rule Book.

Her meetings with Miss Noble were, of necessity, brief but she knew there was a strange electricity in the air whenever they met. She longed for the moment when Miss Noble would have occasion to punish her again. She thought the same about Matron, and half-wished to sustain a bruise at netball, to have an excuse to visit her. But she was comforted by the Rule that each Kernecian was required to take an irrigation once every calendar month.

She worked hard at her varied subjects, and Miss Noble explained to her that most Universities or Training Colleges were cursed by specialisation: some girls were qualified to teach only maths, or French, or history. At Kernece, girls were trained not to be Mistresses but *Headmistresses*, commanding the whole range of their pupils' studies. In this, Miss Dancer was a fervent believer in the doctrines of Kytetroos of Naxos, the legendary sage of the Fifth Century BC, whose Academy amongst the olive groves of the Greek island drew female students from the highest classes of Athens, Macedonia, and even Sparta.

Miss Noble explained that even when the city states of Greece were at war – which was usually the case – their daughters mingled happily at the Academy of Kytetroos, who taught that the noble discipline of olive branches on the naked female body transcended the male foolishness of warriors.

Stella thought often of Jamie Isbister, but found herself thinking of Jakes too, since he was the only personable male on view. There were others: lugubrious gnarled fellows of sturdy physique and indeterminate age, who performed menial tasks such as cleaning, fetching supplies from Durness, or repairing stonework. All seemed to answer to the name 'Jimmy'. Jakes was to be seen quite a lot, looking infuriatingly precious as he ambled about his tasks, or disappeared mysteriously into doorways accompanied by Clapton, although he was never seen actually *doing* anything.

She frequented the Library, assiduously studying her Rule Book, or improving her mind with the History of Scotland and the northern isles, with their wonderful heritage of kilted warriors, longships and Norse plunderers. She had a curious daydream about Jamie, in which he seemed to have black curly hair. She had no secret messages from the Blues, and wondered when she would be summoned to her next meeting of Cohort Anemone. This put her in mind of her task, to occupy Morag's sector by means of gaining control of her affective space; she had a shrewd idea how to do it, but the trouble was getting alone with Morag. The second years tended to remain aloof from the new squits.

The bracing northern air, and the hard work and games, gave her young body a keen appetite, and Stella was aware it was not only for food, or Jakes's comforting tuck. She had night dreams about Jamie, and of Jakes too, and they were naked, with hard pea vines somehow intertwined like branches or crossed swords. Lying waiting for Rousing Bell in the half-light, in the strange state between sleep and wakefulness, Stella found that her hand would stray under her nightie to her naked fount, and rest on her damsel.

This she would flick and rub to send shivers of tingling, naughty pleasure through her body.

She was aware of what she was doing, but pretended it was only a dream, until one morning she awoke earlier than usual, and found that her drowsy fumbling had time enough to flood her with pleasure and longing. She imagined herself in Jamie's arms, his lips covering her naked body with kisses, then seeing his pea vine, all stiff and rearing like the dragon's head of a ship. It would approach her open fount lips for the thing of which she had read, but had never dared think of doing! The 'reproductive act', as Miss Rose's textbook primly put it. She knew it was only for married women, and a painful duty at that. Why, then, did she dream of it so much? The idea that she wanted it was unthinkable.

And Jakes was there in her dream, his lips creased in a sullen moue. His pea vine was behind her, and it was a huge writhing whip, with a forked end where his pee-hole nestled between two gigantic split halves of his bulb. Jakes was rhythmically undulating his hips as he whipped her bare buttocks with strong cuts that stung her body like hot wire. And as Jamie's stiff manly stem touched her damsel (though it was really her own thumb), and she knew he was going to enter her secret body with that massive penis, he drew closer and closer. She wanted to be filled with his lovely hard male's thing! And Stella masturbated herself to a glorious, melting orgasm that made her mewl with such loud joy that she woke Alberta.

'Oh, there's nothing wrong, dear Alberta,' she said, hiding her flushed face beneath the covers. 'Just a dream, a terrifying dream'

And thereafter, Stella masturbated in her bed every time she permitted herself to daydream of Jamie. She permitted herself frequently, and masturbated a lot, telling herself she was a prisoner of her dreams. That reassured her: she was being a sub to her own body and her own desire. Except that the more she masturbated, the more she wanted to: the more she longed for Jamie to carry her off in his arms, and grace her with the reality of his stiff pea vine with its fountain of spurting creamy love.

She longed too for Jamie to whip her! She thought a lot about the beatings she had already received, and about Morag's words, and marvelled at her new bravery, timidly daring to admit that she had come to crave beating. She only dimly understood *why*. But, yes, she was submissive, and she was proud of it! It was as though a new and wondrously simple world had opened its gates to her.

She still felt uneasy at painfully caning another, but Charity's pleasure had given Stella her own pleasure. She relished the effects of her caning, and could pretend that the squirming of the naked fesses, the shuddering of Charity's body, and the delicious reddening of the flesh under the cane's lash, were somehow the work of someone else. Her desire had come from imagining herself in Charity's place, Charity's flogged bottom her own. And part of her wonderful lightness of heart was the feeling that suddenly – and for the first time – she knew that whatever troubles assailed her spirit, they would all be washed away by kissing a dom's feet. By doing her bidding, and kissing the cane that was to lash her bared nates. Or, she added, kissing *his* feet . . .

Sometimes she wished to be Joan of Arc, dressed as a lovely handsome boy (her features fused with Jamie's), or in bright armour at the head of her troops, sword in hand. Then captured, robed as a girl and submitting to the whips and shackles of the cruel English. And finally, her naked body red with lashes, giving herself to the merciless embrace of the flames. She saw herself as the wondrous boy-girl, with the body and strength of a dom, but the heart of a girlish sub: shining with the holiness of total submission. And once, when she tossed and turned in her dream of Joan, she awoke to find the bed-things damp; the rubber sheet beneath was wet! Flustered, and scared of being punished for it, she asked Alberta for advice. She laughed and said Stella was no different from other girls, except that she was lucky to have the rubber sheet, and should simply put up with it until laundry day on the morrow. Alberta was so wise!

She often longed to take her hairbrush, and administer

a very good spanking to her own bottom, to calm her itch – but that would be impossible in the dorm's lack of privacy. There must be somewhere private in Kernece! She looked at the sweetly drowsing Alberta, and wondered if she would consent to whip Stella on the bare. Or would she be horrified and withdraw her friendship? Then she thrilled at her answer: Alberta knew of the incident with the wet rubber sheet, and that Stella was guilty of not reporting it, although she was not yet sure from the Rule Book if her act was actually an offence. To assuage her guilt, then, Alberta would surely agree to whip her, between chums. The thought was lovely and cosy; she resolved to find a private place.

She knew that despite her lovely new craving, the thought of being punished was, paradoxically, still terrifying to her: the stern face of her Mistress sentencing her to flogging, the ritual of lowering her panties and raising her bared bum, the humiliating bending over. Then she realised that this ritual humiliation and frightened expectancy was actually part of her submissive pleasure; the waiting, the uncertainty, the *imagining*, made the chastisement subtler and sweeter still. And the pain, when it came, was horrid and eye-watering. But it was like a cold plunge: once the first shock was over, the icy water became a delicious hot bath, making the pulse race, just as the shock of the cane became gasping, invigorating joy.

At the beginning of her second week, it was announced that Florence Tate was to be publicly chastised, for cheeking Clapton before her Girl Guides. Florence was to receive the Steps and, more than that, the terrifying punishment of Racing the Tawse. The Central Notice Board announced that members of College had been chosen by lot to form the gauntlet, the others being required to watch. Stella's name was on the list; Morag's was not. The day before the ordeal, Stella sent little notes via the mail drudge to Heather and Charity in their respective Houses. She did not sign the note, but wrote 'Top Secret' on the envelopes, thinking this would please Heather.

Florence's punishment was to take place before tea,

when the dusk would make the spectacle more sinister, and this gave the girls time to visit the tuck shop to stock up with a picnic for the entertainment. A late tea would be provided; it seemed the punishment was expected to last until dark. Stella was pleased that the last lesson was chemistry. The lesson was quite chaotic; everyone was so excited by the coming distraction. Jakes's smile was broader than usual as tuck money flowed.

'A flogging always gives you an appetite, eh, ladies?' he said. Stella treated herself to toffees and eclairs, and a bottle of sweet dark lemonade from Glasgow, called, inexplicably, 'Heavy Duty'.

The excitement was palpable as the women rushed to secure a good vantage point, and there was a breathless hush as Florence was led by Clapton to the base of the Steps. The crowd was mixed by years and Houses; like the tuck shop, the spectacle of punishment created its own democracy. Before joining the gauntlet, Stella wormed her way to Morag.

'So,' sneered Morag, 'luck of the new squit, eh? My little sub in the gauntlet!'

'I say, Morag, old chum,' replied Stella in a rather girly voice, 'no hard feelings. My bum's still sore from your cane, but it was all good sport, wasn't it?'

'No, Stella,' said Morag, 'it was not.'

'Well, be a brick and hold my tuck for me, will you? You can have some if you like – this lemonade's super, but leave some for me. I bet the gauntlet is thirsty work.'

Morag agreed, and Stella ran to join the gauntlet. Florence was gagged with cords, bound by the wrists, and her legs tethered in a sheepshank knot, forming a rough hempen shackle. Her humiliation was evident as she awkwardly walked in front of her comrades and waited at the base of the Steps while Stella ascended with the other chastisers. Florence had to climb 140 steps, so 140 girls made the ascent to their appointed places. Stella found herself at number 60; even that climb was exhausting due to the ungainly sizing of the Steps, and she quailed at the thought of actually having to run up them! She gazed up at the remaining steps, with the bulbous, curiously oval, swelling of the out-of-bounds chamber on top, like a cap or helmet. The Steps seemed to stretch to heaven! She wondered who had built them, and for what purpose. Climbing 60 steps was hard enough; poor Florence had to climb 140, bound and filled, *and* take a tawsing! To climb right to the very top was almost unthinkable, tawsed or not.

A Prefect told them that the drill was simple: the tawse would be passed from hand to hand as Florence climbed, and their job was to give her a lash, or many lashes if she paused, before she went to the next step. If she stumbled, she was of course to be helped, but the flogging might not abate. All the women stood on the left side, so that on her ascent, Florence's buttocks would take their strokes from the left; on her descent, from the right, thus ensuring that no part of her croup was left unadorned by the lash.

Giving cheek to Clapton was not a wise move, Stella thought, as she watched Florence being stripped for punishment. Her humiliating gag and leg shackles were removed, but so were her skirt, shoes and panties. Her blouse was knotted around her waist, and she wore only suspender belt and stockings, with neither knickers nor shoes. Not only would she run the gauntlet bare bum, but almost barefoot, with her hands still tied behind her back! And there was a gasp of horror as Clapton produced a handful of small objects like sweets, some of which she thrust into Florence's mouth.

'She's taking the Parph apples!' exclaimed the girl on the step below Stella. 'She must have really given cheek!'

Stella learnt that Parph apples were a small, extremely bitter fruit which grew on stunted bushes amidst the moss. The chastised female was obliged to hold her mouthful intact as she ran her gauntlet. No matter how severe her flogging, she must return each fruit unbitten and unspilled.

'If she makes a mistake,' said Stella's companion with relish, 'then it's the Labyrinth for her!'

Florence took the fruits in her mouth, then stooped slightly and parted her thighs. Clapton gave her the other fruits, and Florence placed them inside her lady's place!

Clapton dealt the first blow with the heavy tawse, and Florence started her clumsy scamper up the Steps. The tawse flew from hand to hand, waiting for her as she stumbled to the next step. Frequently she missed her footing, and received two, or even three, lashes from the same female. The atmosphere was electric as the tawse neared Stella's step. She was unhappy at having to inflict pain, but moist with excitement at the same time. She wondered if Joan of Arc had been obliged to run a similar gauntlet by her English captors, and shivered at the thought of one day having to Run the Tawse herself. She saw Florence approaching now, gasping for breath, her face streaming with tears and sweat, and her heart melted in sympathy for her.

'The poor girl,' she found herself murmuring.

'Don't waste your sympathy!' rapped her neighbour. 'She asked for it. She didn't *have* to take the punishment.'

'Asked for it?' gasped Stella, as the half-naked captive shuddered at a particularly vicious lick from the tawse. It seemed to slap its way across her entire croup in a sensuous embrace. 'Something so hard and cruel? How . . .?'

'I mean she *formally asked* for it. Don't you know the ways of Kernece yet?'

Stella was confused, but heartened. So it seemed Florence was a sub too! Or perhaps she was doing the honourable thing in requesting such a harsh punishment. She was sure the Parph apples, though, were an added nuance from Clapton. At any rate she felt better as she was handed the heavy tawse and watched Florence painfully climb to her step. With a fluid motion, she lifted the tawse, and cracked Florence a smarting blow right across her flaming red buttocks. In the same motion, she handed the tawse to the next female, like a smooth pass at netball.

Florence was not permitted to pause at the 140th step, but had to immediately commence her descent, and when she lumbered past Stella for the second time, it scarcely seemed to matter how hard Stella laced her. Florence seemed to have gained her second wind, and was no longer trying to outrun the tawse, but moved slowly and deliberately with the strange dignity of an automaton. Her bare bottom was a mass of red now, and her face was flushed and glistened with sweat; but there were no tears, rather a radiant glow in her eyes. Stella felt no qualms as she delivered her strong cut to the quivering naked fesses that passed before her; Florence Tate was truly a *sub*!

When it was over, Florence knelt and kissed the tawse that had flogged her, then was presented with her tawse as a memento. As she accepted it, and bowed to Clapton, there were thunderous cheers, and she was carried away shoulder high. Stella ran down the Steps, to test herself, and found Morag waiting for her.

'You took your time!' drawled Morag. 'Still, you didn't do too bad for a new squit. Take your tuck back, it was pretty good, and I'm dying to go to ablutions.'

Stella took her half-eaten tuck; her lemonade bottle was two-thirds empty. She followed Morag to the nearest College ablutions, open to all years and Houses, and looked round to see if they were being followed. They were.

The central ablutions was a cavernous chamber behind the gymnasium and steam baths, which Stella looked forward to trying. It was arranged much as the Poppilian model, only much larger: a row of squatting commodes flanked by open shower units and washbasins. Stella followed Morag's rapid steps into the ablutions, grinning mischievously at her friend's urgency; Stella was herself followed by Heather, Charity, and a throng of eager Blues.

Morag swore: every commode was occupied. Stella watched her hopping from one foot to the other, and after an age, two girls vacated their commodes at once; Morag rushed, and had her skirts up and panties lowered before she had made herself quite comfortable, while Stella took a more leisurely pace. When she was comfortably asquat, she commenced her own evacuation to the accompaniment of Morag's moans of 'Ahhh!' as she relieved herself. These sighs grew in joyful intensity and Stella reflected on the power of Heavy Duty lemonade to fill as well as refresh. But suddenly the excited chatter of the ablutions was hushed, and Morag looked up, puzzled. Stella tried to keep a straight face as Morag blushed fiery red, realising that all eyes were on her, or rather her lady's place, and a few fingers pointing. Laughter burst out, rising to a crescendo of cheers. Morag looked down between her thighs.

'What . . .?' she cried. 'No! Oh! Cripes! Oh, *fuck!*'

Stella had never heard such an unladylike word used before. She had heard of it, and thought it was only for the use of matelots and uncouth males. Nevertheless she placed a hand on Morag's shoulder, and Morag's head whirled round.

'You . . .!' she hissed as Stella joined in the helpless laughter. 'Your beastly lemonade! You bitch! You mossy fucking sub bitch!'

Stella cupped her hand under Morag's fount, which still gushed with hot liquid, and held up her hand to the company.

'I claim Morag Tallon as my prisoner. A prisoner of the Blues! Her sector is now Blue territory!' she cried, and was cheered wildly. Morag was livid, but there was nothing she could do, either to stem the flow of her water or to hide the fact that it was bright blue! As soon as was decently possible, she reaccoutred herself and stormed from the building, swearing revenge, while Stella was heartily congratulated by Heather and the others.

'A little potassium permanganate works wonders,' she said. 'We do know a thing or two in the West Midlands.'

As she hurried towards Refectory to line up for the late tea, Morag emerged from the shadows and fell into step with her. It was what Stella had hoped and expected, for she knew that her triumph over Morag was not yet complete. A victory for the Blues, certainly, but not yet the affective victory she intended to have. So when Morag hissed that she would waylay her after prep and drag her to the secret room in the Labyrinth, in order to thrash her bottom to jelly, Stella interrupted her and said sweetly: 'Why, Morag, there is no need to drag me to this secret room, wherever it is. I shall come willingly. I know I have offended you as my friend, and must make it up to you.

But you understand: it was Army orders. Even so, I am quite willing to make amends.' Secretly, she was delighted to discover a secret room which she had no doubt she could use for her own purposes, involving the delicious Alberta.

'I am not your friend,' cried Morag as they reached the line for tea. 'You subs – you think it is all a game! Make amends, indeed! You'll be crying and howling, Stella Shawn, when I've finished with you!'

Stella bowed her head and said meekly:

'If that will give you pleasure, Miss.'

Stella ate her tea mechanically, too excited to relish the quality of the day's one fine meal, and concentrated only perfunctorily on her prep. After prep, in the period of free time, she went out into the yard, shivering as the cold Scottish night bit into her, and wondering if she had time to go to dorm and fetch her poppy-coloured cardigan, which in the first half of Term was permitted only after dark. She did not; Morag was waiting for her in the darkness, her Orchid's jacket buttoned up. She took Stella firmly by the arm. They crossed to the other administration building, and went in through a side door Stella had not noticed before. In fact, she thought it strange that at Kernece there seemed so many neglected or forgotten nooks and crannies, like the Anemone meeting place – when there was such a complement of Jimmys to tidy everything. It was as though the mystery of Castle Kernece was somehow maintained deliberately, so that girls could get up to just such mischief as Morag planned.

They went down a spiral staircase which smelled of must and cobwebs, and was bitterly cold. Morag told Stella that she would soon warm up. They emerged into an empty cellar, where there was a barred oaken door, and Morag said that was the true Labyrinth, where new squits were not normally allowed. Stella wondered about the word 'normally': what could abnormal circumstances possibly be? She could have sworn she heard a low, anguished moan coming from behind the locked door, but had no time to investigate.

The cellar was humid and hushed, dimly lit from the staircase, and the wind whistled faintly on the surface. Morag led her past the barred door to another, which creaked open and led to a winding corridor, which was completely dark. She knew her way; Stella followed nervously, and almost cried out as she felt her face brush a cobweb. At last a door opened, and they entered a small chamber, where Morag produced a petrol cigarette lighter and lit a candle which stood on the room's floor. There were of course no windows, and no furniture, other than a squat device of wood, with curious straps and hinges. Morag said smugly that she had discovered this cell, and that she did not think anyone else knew of it, though she was not sure.

'It is part of the Labyrinth, really,' she said, 'but this sector is unused. Formerly, there were many more dwellers in Kernece than there are now.'

There was a bolt on the door's inside, and Morag fastened it. Then she put her hands on her hips and looked Stella up and down. A sly, cruel grin spread over her face.

'All alone, girly,' she drawled. 'Are you sorry you came?'

'N – no,' stammered Stella, suddenly unsure of herself.

'That is the block,' said Morag, gesturing at the squat wooden device. 'The arms and legs fold out, and . . . well, You'll see! Pretty, ain't she? I keep her polished, in case some pathetic sub new squit needs a proper tanning. Pity I've no drudge to do it. Or maybe I have . . .'

She suddenly unbuttoned her jacket to reveal that she wore a belt, which was no ordinary belt, but a leather many-thonged whip! She swished it in the air, and it made a frightful whistling sound. Stella looked aghast. It was no tawse, but a cat o' nine tails. Its wicked short thongs were tipped with dully gleaming steel.

'On your knees, sub,' she ordered, and Stella obeyed. Morag sauntered around her prone body, flicking the whip but not quite touching her with the tips. Morag laughed.

'I'm going to strap you to the block, Stella, in the most uncomfortable position, and punish you for your filthy trick with a whipping the like of which you have never dreamt of. Potassium permanganate, indeed! The oldest, stupidest trick in the book.'

'It worked, though, didn't it, Morag?' said Stella.

'You call me *Miss*!' cried Morag.

'Well, Miss, aren't you punishing yourself for being so stupid as to fall for my trick?' said Stella.

'*I*...! You slut! You'll clean your flogging-block before I thrash you! Get to work, with your tongue!'

'Yes, Miss,' said Stella meekly, and felt a sudden thrill – of *power* – at being given, and obeying, such a humiliating order. There was a thin layer of dust on the flogging-block, and Stella crawled to it on hands and knees, and began to lick. It tasted bitter and she had to pause frequently to spit the dust out, but she finished proudly and had the flogging-block gleaming. She was drenched in sweat, and aching, but now it was *her* flogging-block! She inspected the hinges and armrests, and saw how she was to be positioned; her belly thrilled at the thought of her constraint, and her fount began to moisten.

'Now, sub, knickers off!' cried Morag. Stella wriggled out of her knickers without getting up from the floor, and handed the slightly damp panties to Morag, who sniffed them.

'Wet already, sub?' she sneered. 'You won't be, for I'll whip you dry! Now for the block. Take your jacket off.'

Soon, Stella was fastened by wrists and ankles to the splayed limbs of the block which had her almost in a cross shape. It stretched her arms and legs to the limits of endurance. Her head hung free almost to the floor, but she could scarcely move it, as tight leather bands over her blouse constricted her waist and shoulders. There were similar straps on her thighs and calves. Morag contemptuously flicked up Stella's skirt and petticoat, high over her back, revealing her bare nates which a high ridge on the block forced upwards into a most exposed and humiliating position. Her buttocks were higher than her shoulders, and deliciously spread so that she felt the cold air caressing her open fount and anus bud.

'Ooh...' moaned Stella, and her moan was a sigh of

sheer pleasure to be thus helpless and trussed as a sacrifice to the loving whip of her friend. It *was* a loving whip, although Morag herself was not yet aware of it. Morag misinterpreted her sigh, and told her that she was right to be scared.

'I'm not going to blindfold you,' she said, 'because I want you to watch your tears drip on the floor as I whip your bum. But to stop your silly squealing, you can have your panties back.'

Stella felt her very own knickers, balled and thrust tightly into her open mouth, gagging her.

'Mmm,' she sighed, and felt her fount flow quite copiously! She felt her wetness seep on to the naked skin of her thighs, and was sure Morag would see it glisten in the flickering candle-light. She wanted her to see it, and whip her the harder for feeling such pleasure!

'There's more,' said Morag. 'You'll want feeding, I expect, so I brought you some Parph apples. Not for your big mouth, though.'

Stella gasped as she felt a tickling at the very entrance to her belly, her anus bud itself, and then a tickling sensation as Morag pressed the hard little fruits one after the other right into her fundament, filling her completely until her anus must have taken a good half-dozen of the apples. She was astounded: after the first shock, and the resistance of her bum-muscle, she had relaxed and let the insertion proceed smoothly. She was thrilled at how beautifully the little hard orbs filled her. It was so lovely and naughty that for a moment she imagined it was Jamie with his stiff pea vine who was filling her thus! At that, her lady's place became a sea of wetness, and she knew Morag must be aware of her soaking fount and the sparkling of her juices flowing down the backs of her thighs.

Without warning, the flogging began. The first whipcrack took her by surprise so that she jumped and cried out in her startled pain. It hurt awfully! Morag was right; she had never dreamt of anything like it. It was far more than the searing lash of the cane, or even the heavy pounding of the tawse: nine white-hot needles burning her naked flesh all at once in a stern caress of agony. Her throat caught, and she panicked for an instant, wondering if she could take it. Her panic increased as the second lash took her in the same place, or places. It seemed that every inch of her exposed nakedness was wreathed in pain.

'I'm not going to give you a specific number of strokes,' Stella,' said Morag pleasantly. 'I'm going to flog you till you beg me to stop. Just moan loud and shake your head firmly, and I'll know. We'll see how true a sub you really are. Anyway, I dare say you won't want to miss buns.'

The lashing continued, and soon Stella felt her bottom squirming quite uncontrollably. She could not stop her buttocks from flinching as she heard the whistle of the whip. As she flinched, the fruits wedged in her anus were squeezed tight, giving her a strange thrill amidst her agony. Her bottom was on fire. Then, at the fifth stroke, she experienced a wonderful lifting sensation. It was as if the pain had taken her over completely like some wild winged stallion, and she was now riding on its back, naked and free above the clouds. She exulted in her flogging, and wanted it never to stop! She could hear Morag panting harshly, and knew she was having to work hard. She was so glad she could not speak, for her enforced silence must be quite infuriating to her whipper.

The lashes fell, but the steady rhythm gradually became uneven, and now Stella's moans of ecstasy were accompanied by Morag's, of frustration or exhaustion, or . . .?

Morag's moans became sighs, and the whipstrokes quite erratic, and Stella suddenly knew that Morag was masturbating as she flogged her. The knowledge that her reddened, squirming bum could inspire the lovely Morag to masturbate made Stella's juices flow quite uncontrollably, and she felt that now familiar warm tickling in her own belly. The strokes continued to caress her with their livid pain, and at each stroke she flinched, deliberately now, relishing the squeezing of the hard fruits inside her anus. There was no mistaking the warmth in her belly, the throbbing of her stiff damsel and the shivers that traversed her spine. She was at her plateau ... Now, beyond!

Morag's panting made her wetter and wetter. She must have taken thirty or more strokes, and still longed for more!

'Say stop, damn you, say stop!' gasped Morag. 'Oh ... Oh ... how I need this! Say stop, you bitch sub! I won't stop. I need your bum, Stella. I need you! Oh, *Oh!*'

Morag was at orgasm, and Stella knew she had made her affective conquest! At the sweet words 'I need you', her belly writhed in sweet ecstasy as her spasm of joy flooded through her, making her quiver in a glorious submission to her pleasure. She could not control herself, and felt the most gorgeous caress of her anus membrane as one after the other the Parph apples exploded from her bumhole, spattering Morag whose groans of pleasure heralded each impact.

When Stella's beating was over, Morag unstrapped her with trembling fingers. Stella rose, removed her panties from her mouth and stepped decorously into them. Morag's face was flushed and her whole body was trembling. Stella was overjoyed to see the large wet patch which darkened her purple orchid skirt at the joining of her thighs, mingling with the stains of the splattered fruit which Stella's anus had shot squarely to her whipper's fount!

'Well, sub,' Morag stammered, trying and failing to sneer, 'I hope you've learnt your lesson.

'Yes, Miss,' said Stella.

'And whatever I may have said ... I didn't mean it.'

'No, Miss. I am yours to command.'

'Just forget I said it.'

'I obey, Miss,' said Stella, kneeling to kiss Morag's shoes. 'I shan't.'

8

Taming the Bull

Stella found that something Morag had said preyed on her. It was at ablution, before her caning in Miss Dancer's study. She had spoken of Jakes, that he 'needed' women, yet despised them. How did he need them, and what did he do to assuage his need? Was it something to do with biology; with the power of the pea vine, as Stella saw in her dreams and which made her *masturbate* so much? She used that word to herself now, for she had seen it in textbooks and now understood what it meant. But it still made her shiver. The other thing made her shiver even more: a hard penis, actually put inside a lady's place! The very thought made her wet, yet shocked and terrified. She had tasted Jamie's cream, and that was one thing, it was sweet and lovely. The thought of the cream spurting inside her naked place was frightening, yet wickedly tempting. Was that what Jakes did with the women of Kernece? And with how many? All? Morag, even? Stella's head spun, and she resolved to educate herself in this mystery. Above all, she wanted to know why the beautiful Jakes despised women. Was it because they took his seed from him? She thought it would be a useful task to teach him not to despise women.

Her drowsy thoughts of Jakes were dispelled early in the morning after her submission to Morag, by a shattering whistle that made her jump, and a shriek of 'drudge!' from the distance. She was surprised at the speed with which the dorm awoke as one. The girls slipperless and clad only in nighties, rushed to the door. Buffy, Muffy and Tuffy scampered gaily in the lead. She was confused: Rousing Bell had not yet sounded, and it was only half-light outside.

'Come on, Stella!' urged Alberta. 'You don't want to miss breakfast! It's the Bull! Last one to get to her study has to be her drudge, for as long as she wants!'

But Stella was still drowsy, the lovely glowing smart of her flogged backside making her lapse again into her daydream. When she finally shook herself out of bed and padded to the doorway, the rest of the dorm was already stumbling back to bed. She followed the corridor against the stream, glumly aware that she would be last to arrive, and hence the Bull's drudge. She was right. The Bull stood at her door, waiting with a grim smile as Stella walked evenly

'Ah, Shawn, the new squit, Matron's girly! I thought it might be you. You lazy slut! Into my study, drudge!'

Stella obeyed. The Bull's study was a spacious bedsitting chamber, with, surprisingly, its own ablutions, and a rather dramatic view over the Parph. Its white walls were decorated with photographs of young men in military uniform, and one of a strikingly handsome young woman: the Bull herself. In the photograph, she was brandishing one or other implements of sporting prowess or, Stella noticed with a shiver, instruments of correction. The furniture was almost mannish in its relaxed, leathery comfort, and a good fire burned in the grate, with a pungent sweetish aroma that Stella surmised was peat moss.

'Heard about your little trick with the good old pot perm! Very smart. I remember cousin Stackenham doing that to me a while back, but I whacked his bum for it, the rotter! With his own sword! So you're in the Blue Army – rather gave the game away with that little stunt. I suppose you think you're special, whacking that idiot Charity on the bum I don't doubt. Well, we'll soon see about *that*.'

Stella wanted to disagree, but the Bull went on merrily, 'You are my drudge for as long as I want, Shawn. You can miss breakfast – you'll trough with me – and classes too, on my say-so. Now take off that nightie, and put these things on. I've plenty of cleaning and jobs for you, and I expect you'll be hopelessly slow. We'll see if you can make tea.' She pointed towards a little kitchen alcove, with a sink and gas ring.

Stella remembered that her first class was actually a free period, with which her timetable was plentifully studded, and which was meant to be spent studying in the Library: her free afternoons being intended for sports. She did not think anyone would notice her absence. The Bull handed her a bundle of clothing and told her to strip off her nightie. Nervously, Stella lifted her nightie until her mink was bare, but hesitated as the garment reached her breasts. To be naked in ablutions was one thing, but it seemed somehow improper to be naked in another person's private room. The Bull snorted at her to hurry up, and said she was a mossy little slut, though her tone was not unkind. She took Stella's nightie and sniffed it, making a face.

'Pooh! You stink, drudge! I suppose I should scrub you, but you'll work up a good lather at drudgery, and anyway your uniform's been worn by plenty of other drudges. Although you might find it a tight fit. Those bubbies are a bit grand for a new squit! And that bum ... Well, I'd say she needs a good tanning for being such a whopper, but I see that's been attended to.'

Stella did not understand what being a new squit had to do with possessing a large croup, but unfolded the unfamiliar garments. Uniform! It was certainly a strange one, and smelled odd. She held the things up, and saw that they would indeed be a tight fit.

'Pretty, ain't it?' said the Bull. 'Number eight kit, not many of them in College. I annexed this from the Purser, because I like to see a drudge dressed properly.'

Stella began to put on her uniform, and found it a squeeze. She had expected a drudge's kit to be some coarse smock of rough cotton, but this was more like a frilly maid's uniform at some exotic London banquet. The fabric was deliciously thin, and she had a black blouse, short frilly black skirt, white stockings, suspender belt and petticoat, high-heeled poppy shoes and – to her amazement – a poppy corset! The ensemble was topped by a frilly white maid's cap, and Stella was both surprised and tickled to find that all the garments were made of thin, silky rubber! She had rarely worn white stockings, and never ones made of rubber.

She first put on her corset, and the Bull insisted on knotting it for her. Stella gasped at the tight constraint which she felt pushing up her already swelling 'bubbies' and forcing the tops of her buttocks out. She wanted to look at herself in the glass, as it felt so tight and naughty! She slipped on the rest of her things; they squeezed her too, though not as tightly as her corset. Her blouse was open quite deep, showing her breasts pressed hard together like two ripe fleshy melons. There was no brassière, and she observed to the Bull that there were no knickers either. The Bull grinned and snorted that a drudge should not wear knickers, as it made her bum easier to lick, and gestured towards a rather frightening tawse which hung above her bed.

'A girl's like a horse: needs a lick on the crupper from time to time, to keep her at it,' said the Bull thoughtfully, as though to herself.

'We'll bathe before tea, drudge,' she said, not looking at Stella. It was as though Stella could have been anyone at all. The Bull used the royal 'we', meaning herself.

'Put the kettle on for tea, and we'll have toast with that. Meantime you can heat some water and scrub my back.'

As the dawn glimmered outside, Stella busied herself at her tasks, She felt oddly excited that the Bull treated her as a drudge, not even as a person. Stella felt nothing more than an animal – a horse with a big crupper! – and as the water boiled she imagined herself a captive of the proud Isbisters; paraded naked, and hearing her crupper and bubbies arrogantly discussed as though she were nothing more than a beast of burden. Jamie would be there, of course, idly flicking her body with the tip of his sword ...

When the water was ready for the Bull's ablutions, Stella filled the sink and fetched sponge and soap and towel. She was already proud of her efficiency as a drudge, and thought her new role far more exciting than lessons, or the dreadful breakfast of stewed tea and 'vommo'. The Bull was sucking on a mouthful of Parph apples from a big bucket that stood beside her gas ring. As she swallowed the bitter juice, she spat the stones and gobbets of juice and flesh on the floor. Stella guessed she would have to clean this up on her hands and knees: she hoped it would be on hands and knees, skirt high, with a lick to the bum from that juicy tawse to encourage her! She grinned at her wondrous naughtiness, and indicated to the Bull that her ablutions were ready.

Then, to Stella's surprise, the Bull slipped off her quilted nightgown and stood naked in front of her drudge. She wore a nonchalant expression, as though she were quite alone. First, she positioned herself in a squat on the commode, and noisily did her business. When she airily waved her hand, Stella was proud that she had anticipated the command, and was ready with white tissue paper. Then the Bull rose, and placed herself at the sink, handing the soap and sponge for Stella to scrub her back. Stella bent to her task, and did not stop at the Bull's back.

She was entranced by the beauty of the Bull's body; a lithe, ripely-muscled frame that had not an ounce of fat, but swelled as fully and as handsomely as Stella's own breasts and buttocks. Her creamy skin was beautifully enhanced by the mane of silky auburn hair that caressed her back and breasts. The Bull stood akimbo, allowing Stella to sponge her most intimate places, then suddenly turning so that she might do her front. Stella did so, taking her time at scrubbing the wondrous breasts, with their big plum-red nipples twice the size of the Parph apples which the Bull kept chewing and spitting. Stella was pleased that at her washing, the nipples became deliciously tense, and the Bull's face turned just a tiny bit red! She passed down the firm belly, soaping a rich lather, then scrubbed the strong horsewoman's legs, and the surprisingly dainty feet.

'Make sure you get all the jam from between my toes, said the Bull rather crudely. Stella had the occasion to kneel and her skirt rode up to reveal her bare nates as she paid particular attention to the feet.

'Now, drudge, you deserve a lick or two on the bum,' said the Bull, 'as you seem to have forgotten somewhere.'

She pointed at her lady's place, adorned by a mink of superb, silky lushness that seemed to extend halfway up her belly, almost to the sweet dimple of her belly-button! Gulping, Stella went to work with her sponge. The Bull casually parted her thighs and held the cheeks of her bum open, so that Stella could wash the lips of her fount, and her anus bud too. She saw that the Bull's fount was glistening slightly, as though her attentions made her excited. Stella found that her own fount was just a little bit moist at the thrill of her 'drudgery'. The Bull's damsel was very big and Stella found her fascinating, resisting the urge to put the sponge down and touch the nubbin with her naked finger. It was like a crimson thimble, standing sweetly between the fleshy folds of her fount lips, and Stella was sure it was just a little hard.

'You've a good pair of jugs, drudge,' said the Bull suddenly, with a bird's-eye view of Stella's upthrust bosom. 'I think you'll go for Kernece Football. I bet Miss Harker's noticed you too, starkers in the showers.'

Stella replied diplomatically that Miss Harker did like to chat with her when she was showering. The Bull snorted that she was not in the least surprised.

'She hasn't bagged you yet, for her team?' she said anxiously, and Stella said she was unaware of any bagging.

'Good. Then we'll bag you for ours. First game tomorrow afternoon! I don't care if you have free periods or not, just rearrange them and tell them we said so.'

Stella did have the afternoon free for games. As she was towelling the Bull dry, she asked what Kernece Football actually was. The Bull roared with laughter.

'You'll find out! It's in the appendix of your Rule Book, you mossy slut! I dare say you haven't got that far yet.' Stella said that was true.

'Well, Kernece Football is tough. Are you tough, drudge?'

Stella moved towards the tea-kettle, and said proudly that she had been Captain of Netball, which caused the Bull to guffaw even more.

'For one thing,' she said, 'in Kernece Football, there is no ball, not as such. And precious few rules, either, short of a prohibition on murder.'

Stella gulped, and served the breakfast, being permitted a cup of tea and piece of buttered toast herself, which she had to eat standing up while the Bull lolled in her armchair. Her quilted robe fell carelessly open to show her fine legs and the strands of her wet mink-hair curling on her soft thigh-skin. Stella thought her a picture of indolence.

After her breakfast, the Bull carelessly threw crumbs and crusts on the floor, which was of bare burnished boards adorned with thick hearthrugs, and told Stella to get on with cleaning the floor while she dressed. Stella looked for cleaning things, and had been right: there was a bucket, dustpan and cloth, but no mop. She smiled and got down on her knees with a bucket of cold water, and began to brush. When she had swept away the crumbs, she went to work with the bucket and cloth, throwing herself into the task with vigour. She paused when she saw the Bull standing over her, in uniform now, and holding her tawse.

She wore the same poppy jacket, but her skirt was not the long blue one Stella had seen at Matron's. She had a pleated and very short skirt, which showed her superb legs in bright silk stockings. These stockings, like her blouse, were a leaf green which formed a piquant contrast to her jacket. Stella was suddenly envious of a senior's privileges, and especially of a Prefect's. She had lovely shoes, too, in a darker shade of green. The Bull casually flicked her bare bum with the tawse, and told her to work harder, then sat down with her legs over her chair and lit a cigarette. She puffed contemptuously and flicked cigarette ash right in the places that Stella had washed, so that she was obliged to do it again. Stella knew she was being teased, or humiliated, and did not mind! Especially when the Bull delivered a proper stinging tawse-lash to her naked croup, which made her jump, and the frilly skirt slither across her bare skin, while the lace-ends of her corset bounced and tickled the tops of her fesses. She found that quite nice, and rubbed her bottom with exaggerated gestures to please the Bull.

'Ouch, Miss!' she cried each time the tawse struck her nates. 'My bum smarts so. You are awfully cruel!'

The Bull would smile when she said this, and usually rewarded her with another cut from her lash, so that Stella found herself cleaning over and over in the place near the Bull's chair, where she was in easy reach of the tawse.

'Yes, I am, am I not?' she said pleasantly, dropping the royal 'we' in her enthusiasm. 'Runs in the family. The Stackenhams have always loved discipline, my girl. Pater used to tell me about flogging the men in South Africa before Ladysmith; and Grandmama, who was Russian, wouldn't be outdone. She told us that when she was little, *her* Pater would have the serfs stripped naked and flogged with the knout while they were having supper. She said it was awfully thrilling to see a naked man, or woman, writhing under the lash while they were eating their borscht. Perhaps that is why she used to serve borscht so much.'

She rewarded Stella with another, seemingly effortless lash. It caught her right at the cleft of the buttocks and hurt abominably, so that Stella shuddered and overturned her bucket. Her bum really glowed now, and she was trembling with mingled fear and pleasure, because she knew what was to happen. It occurred to her that she might have overturned the bucket accidentally on purpose.

The Bull rose to her full height, and towered over her crouching drudge. The talk of flogging seemed to excite her, and her face glowed.

'Well!' she cried, stepping over the puddle of water, 'We should make you lick that up, but we're in a good mood, so we'll be lenient. Over the chair with you, drudge, and skirt well up for a proper tanning! A good dozen on that lovely crimson bare of yours will teach you manners!'

Stella meekly obeyed, her heart pounding, for she was not displeased. She buried her nose in the chair cushions, smelling the warmth from the Bull's own bottom, and stretched her fesses in the air as high as she could. The Bull noticed.

'My, anyone would think you were begging for it,' she said. 'Most drudges squeal and squall something rotten.'

'I am obedient, Miss,' said Stella softly. 'If I have earned a flogging, then flogged I must be. Would you like me to make you some borscht to eat as you lash my bum?'

She grinned to herself at her impudence, and was rewarded with a strangled 'Well!' from the Bull. 'That's insolence, and not so dumb!' she exclaimed angrily. 'For that, slut, you'll get *two* dozen. And one for luck! Keep count!' Stella said nothing, but waited.

The first lash was harsher than all the others, but not as hard as Morag's cat-o'-nine-tails. Though the stroke made her buttocks squirm quite tensely, Stella knew she could take it. Even this early in the morning! The second and third strokes came in quick succession, and then the Bull paused. Stella had to admire the woman; the strokes seemed to come with a fluid, graceful ease that did not make her gasp or pant.

'I'm enjoying this,' chuckled the Bull. 'Golly, I'll make you dance, you stupid drudge.'

'Do you flog many girls, Miss?' asked Stella in a voice whose calmness took the Bull somewhat aback.

'Why, yes,' she said. 'I've reddened oodles of bare bums, and I love every minute of it. Yours is special, though: she's already well poppy, and I shall make you into a true Poppilian!'

'I should like that very much, Miss,' murmured Stella. 'So I can be proud when the other girls see me at ablution.'

'Hmmph!' cried the Bull, and recommenced the beating, as Stella counted in a hushed voice. The strokes really were hard; the Bull had not lectured her about flinching or squirming, so flinch and squirm Stella did. She could not help herself, and wondered if two dozen were too much, but then at the tenth or eleventh she reached that wonderful serene plateau again. She became one with her flaming bottom, and seemed to float on air, her pain a distant warm event taking place outside her for her own pleasure. She exaggerated her squirming, hoping it would please and excite the Bull – a sign of her willing submission.

At the fifteenth, Stella could not stop herself from giving a long, low 'Mmmm' of pure joy as a particularly hard cut jolted her with a spasm of searing pain. The seeping moisture in her fount become a trickle that wetted the tops of her thighs. The Bull paused again.

'You are a tough one!' she said. 'I could have sworn that was a cry of pleasure! Are you enjoying it, drudge?'

'Oh, no, Miss,' cried Stella. 'It stings most horribly! My poor bare bottom! You hurt her so!' The Bull laughed.

'*I'm* enjoying it,' she said. 'I love seeing a girly squirm and cry. I am so happy with my lot. Wouldn't you just *love* to be me?'

Stella did not answer, and her silence seemed to upset the Bull, for her strokes became faster and faster. Stella was emboldened, her slit now slippery with her juices, and she began to moan, 'Oh, yes, *yes* . . .'

'You *are* taking pleasure!' the Bull exclaimed, as though thunderstruck.

'Have you never heard of subs and doms, Miss?' said Stella almost contemptuously. 'Well, you are a dom, you take pleasure in flogging –'

'Yes!' cried the Bull, a little too hastily. 'Always have, always will. Why, Pater entrusts me with beating the serving maids at Stackenham Hall . . .'

'So that is why I'm dressed thus!' said Stella. 'It stands to reason there must be those of . . . a different persuasion. Have you never been flogged yourself?'

'Of course, when I was a new squit. But chance treated me well. I hated it!'

'Are you sure?'

'I like doing it. I like seeing a girly's bare crupper well squirming. I like seeing yours squirm.'

'Gosh,' said Stella, 'hurry up and finish, Miss, so I can rub my bum! She's really smarting so beautifully. And if it gives you pleasure, why, I cannot *stop* myself squirming."

'You are a strange one,' said the Bull as she brought the flogging to a tumultuous end, with Stella allowing her fesses to dance in an exaggerated sensuous rhythm, a ballet of pain. When it was over, she stood and rubbed herself, not bothering to smooth down her skirt, so that the Bull had a clear view of her shining wet thighs and fount. There was a puzzled expression on the Bull's face. Stella now stared her out, directly in the eyes, until the Bull blushed and averted her gaze. Stella took the tawse from her limp hand.

'In answer to your question, Miss: no, I wouldn't like to be you. But you would like to be me, wouldn't you? A girly new squit again, just for a moment. Admit it.'

The Bull bit her lip, then smiled – shyly!

'I'd never thought ... Well, you took such pleasure. I don't know ... Oh, hang it, anything for a giggle!'

Her smile turned to a grin, and she lifted her skirt, revealing her deep poppy knickers. 'It will be just like old times, before chance elevated me ...'

'It is no giggle, Miss,' said Stella gravely, throwing the tawse aside. 'Take your blouse off.'

'Is that needed? I mean, my knickers, yes, but –'

'Of course I'll have your knickers, Miss,' said Stella severely. 'But you weren't afraid to be unrobed when I was just a drudge, washing you. The blouse, please.'

Slowly, the Bull unbuttoned her blouse, and her full ripe breasts spilled out so lovely and bare that Stella had to restrain herself from kissing the big dark nipples that stood so round and erect at their softly curving tips. She took the blouse and went to the kitchen where she found the bucket of Parph apples. She soaked the blouse at the sink, then emptied the entire contents of the bucket into the blouse, which she knotted tightly to make a cruelly-knobbed truncheon. She swung it experimentally, and felt unsure; it was so heavy and so hard. Yet she had to *teach* the Bull ...

'Now, crouch on the rug, Miss Bulford,' she ordered curtly, 'with your thighs spread and your bum in the air. Feel free to bite the carpet if you need to.'

'How ... how many?' gasped the Bull, paling as she saw Stella's weapon. Stella put her stiletto heel on the crouching woman's neck.

'As many as you like,' she said. 'For you like flogging, Miss, so you are going to flog yourself!'

She handed the weapon to the Bull. She ordered her to begin beating herself on the bare buttocks, with all her force, until she decided she could take no more.

'*I* decide?' wailed the Bull. 'That isn't fair!'

'We'll see how tough you are,' Stella sneered. 'Begin!'

The Bull groaned, and lifted the weapon, then smacked it with pleasing force on her bared high nates, making herself flinch. She repeated this three or four times, until her flinching became a delicious squirming of real discomfort.

'Oh, it *hurts*, Miss!' she wailed. Stella ground her heel into the Bull's neck and ordered her to beat herself *much* harder.

'You like it, don't you?' she whispered.

'No! No! Oh! It's harder than Jakes's whip! Oh cruel chance! Oh!'

'You can always stop if you wish,' said Stella, pretending to yawn, but pondering the mention of Jakes. Languidly, she reached for the Bull's Rulebook which lay on her desk, and opened it at the appendix.

'I'll just inform myself about Kernece Football while you get on with things,' she said, pretending to be bored. 'I might as well use the time constructively.'

In truth, her fount was flowing very copiously with hot oil as she saw the delicious blush that now suffused the Bull's magnificent bare buttocks. And to her delight, she saw a glistening on her victim's thigh-skin; the Bull too was flowing with fount-juice! As the flogging continued, the Bull's strokes became harsher and harsher, her wriggling and mewling more frantic. Stella found the section on Kernece Football, in very small print, and what she read almost made her drop the book.

'Oh!' the Bull cried. 'It's worse – I mean it's better than Knobkerry Night! You wicked mossy bitch! I must . . .'

And with that, Stella saw the Bull's hand feverishly clamp her fount and begin to rub her damsel. She watched, tremendously excited – almost beyond control, as the Bull masturbated in time with her flogging. Her bottom was now a beautifully deep crimson. Then Stella herself lost control, and sighed as her fingers found her own engorged, throbbing damsel, which she flicked and rubbed until her whole body glowed with spasming pleasure.

'So that's what you want,' she said faintly, and roughly took the truncheon from the Bull's flogging hand.

'Don't make me stop, I beg you!' gasped the Bull.

'I am just starting,' replied Stella. 'Turn over, and press your knees up against your bubbies so that I can see your bum and thighs.'

When the Bull was on her back, and in this position, Stella roughly squatted right on top of the Bull's face, with her thighs spread wide and her damsel positioned above the other woman's mouth.

'Now tongue me while you diddle yourself, bitch!' she blurted. 'I won't be left out.'

She gasped with joy as she felt a hot wet tongue flicker against her throbbing nubbin. She began to beat the bared buttocks and thighs that the Bull stretched before her, laying her whole weight on the woman's head and holding the weapon with both hands. Raising her arms above her head to their full length, she dealt blow after severe blow as the Bull continued to masturbate, her hips writhing in a sensuous dance and her fount gleaming with her copious fluid. Stella could feel her own flow anointing the Bull's tongue and lips, and knew that her liquid was so copious that the Bull's chin and shoulder must be quite soaked.

She could scarcely control her own writhing as she came to her plateau and knew that soon she would orgasm. She laid the truncheon suddenly aside, and bent over, drawing her knees in so that her thighs tightly cradled the Bull's wet cheeks, and placed her own mouth on the Bull's glistening swollen fount lips. She gently removed the flicking fingers and replaced them with her own tongue, licking the Bull's swollen hard nubbin until it seemed so big she could take it between her lips. She did, chewing and gently biting the stiff limb as though it were a Parph apple. The Bull's moans became a howl: her love juices drenched Stella's mouth as both women cried out and spasmed in their ecstasy.

'Well!' said the Bull, getting unsteadily to her feet, 'I suppose my bum's all crimson like some mossy new squit's.'

'Yes, she is, Miss,' said Stella, smoothing down her skirt. 'And she is lovely. Did you like being me?'

'Hmmph!' snorted the Bull. 'Like doesn't come into it. Chance brought you to me, and permitted you to bewitch me for a moment. The Whip of Chance is everything at Kernece.'

'Surely, fate . . .' Stella began.

'You haven't properly studied your Rulebook!' sneered the Bull. Her bare breasts bobbed sweetly in her agitation, as she forgot her lovely nudity. 'Everything here is decided by lot! To be a Prefect, to be sent to the Remove . . . Even the Headmistress herself is decided by drawing lots. Of course they can be influenced in many ways, especially if Clapton favours you. She is Mistress of the Lots just now, and even that rank is decided by lot.'

Stella blurted that she wanted to know about Jakes's whip, and the Bull reared up, telling her a slut of a new squit should not ask questions. Then, just as suddenly, her face softened and Stella saw sadness behind her hauteur.

'You'll find out,' she said gently. 'Oh, you'll find out.'

Stella asked if there were any more tasks for her, and the Bull said that she could go to her lessons. She added, though, that Stella was remiss in not properly polishing the floor, and the curtains needed to be washed, and . . .

'Oh, there are so many things to do!' she cried, blushing. For a moment, Stella saw a sweet, innocent girlish face beneath the handsome features of the Head Prefect. 'Just remember, Stella Shawn,' she added – shyly, 'when I whistle for a drudge, the last girl to present herself gets the task. Be sure that when I whistle, you walk slowly. Now, I'll see you tomorrow for Kernece Football.' Her tone was again brisk and haughty.

'It sounds awfully tough, Miss,' said Stella uncertainly.

'Oh, it is. And it'll be worse for you.' Her gloating sneer told Stella that she was now the Bull once more. '*You* are going to be the ball.'

9

Kernece Football

Stella lined up nervously outside the inner gate with a dozen other girls, ready for her first essay into Kernece Football. The Bull was there, and Miss Harker, and there seemed no love lost between them; neither paid Stella much attention. The two teams – seven a side – exchanged loud sneers, with little discouragement from their principals. Stella recognised Heather, and Charity, Tuffy, and Florence Tate, as well as her erstwhile suitor Gilfillan. Alberta was there too, the only one to nod at Stella. Each girl carried a little kitbag, but as she had received no instructions to do so she was now frightened that the Bull's taunt was nothing but the truth: she was not exactly to be a player in the game.

There was a gurgling roar, and a frightful smoky smell, as an ancient army lorry pulled up beside them. Jakes was at the wheel. With the teams, Stella climbed into the back of the lorry, and they chugged briskly off in the direction of the playing fields, which Stella already knew well. She wondered which one had been set aside for Kernece Football, as they seemed to be all occupied. To her surprise, the lorry passed the playing fields and headed out the main gate on to the stony track, then turned a sharp right and drove around the perimeter of Kernece. The giant wall shaded their heads from the warm afternoon sun. Then Jakes turned off even that poor track, and they were riding over spongy bog: they were heading for the Parph!

The lush grounds of Kernece, and her watchful but somehow comforting Tower and Walls, drew further and further away as the lorry lurched over the bleak expanse of moss, rock and shrub. The Parph was like nothing else Stella had seen, and she would have thought herself on another planet, had the air not been tingling and moist with the distant sea. There were outcrops of stunted trees and bushes, bright with bilious fruits, and curious darting winged insects, cawing birds and the scurrying of mice and lizards. Stella shivered: what a strange place it seemed to play football.

At last the lorry's path became smoother, as the undergrowth thinned and they found themselves on a vast mossy plain, levelled as though by some celestial steamroller. They stopped; Stella saw that little mounds of stones marked the outline of a circular playing field. At each end of the field was a hut made of the same stones, with a narrow entrance, like a prehistoric cairn. In the very centre of the circle was a circular grove of trees, about her own height, which bore Parph apples. It looked very lonely there, and Stella wondered why there were no other trees around it. The trees were surprisingly straight, as all the others she had seen had been very gnarled and knobby, and she supposed the moss fertile. In the centre of the circular grove was another, much thicker tree, and that one was indeed very gnarled and bulbous.

She peered at the tree as Jakes opened the back of the lorry. She saw that its indentations looked very like the breasts and bottom and thighs of a female, while the curious hanging branches with their dark evergreen leaves could have been a woman's hair. Jakes was curiously attired. He wore a rough leather jacket over a bare brown chest which was hairless, like a girl's, and with breast-muscles that in the glinting sunlight gave his strong, hard breasts the aspect of a girl's too. Under this he wore a long, flowing kilt that came down to mid-calf – almost a woman's skirt – except that it bore no tartan but rather pretty painted designs of birds and insects and trees. They looked like those of the Parph, and an image of a giant lizard, or dragon, flicked his scaly tongue out to catch them.

For a moment, she saw the grove as a circle of pea vines – of male sex organs, of standing penises – clustering round a trapped female, ready to deliver their fruits to her! Or was it they who were trapped by the female? There was a light breeze, and a watery sun, which Jakes pronounced first-rate weather for play. At once, the two teams began to strip off their uniforms, placing their clothes neatly in the lorry. Stella did not know what to do, and now the Bull took her by the arm.

'Normally, you'd be in the team,' she said. 'But for your first outing, you are going to be the ball, so as you can get the hang of it! You'll have a splendid time, and a special treat at the end. The thing is, your bubbies and bum are just right; I'm so glad *la* Harker didn't bag you first.'

Stella wondered what the special treat could be. She had in fact studied the small print of the Rule Book scrupulously, and learnt that upon the discretion of the referee, it was customary for the winning team at Kernece Football to administer ritual chastisement to the losers. Perhaps being the ball and not in play, was the treat.

She was surprised to see that the team players took off all their clothes, including panties and stockings, but were still not naked. Underneath, they wore sheer clinging catsuits of thin rubber, one team in green and the other in black. It seemed that Jakes was the referee, and he produced a whistle like the Bull's. Then the Bull and Miss Harker began to rub some foul-smelling lubricant into the rubber suiting of their teams, while the girls rubbed their bare hands with what smelled like honey.

'Well, take off your clothes, Shawn!' snapped the Bull.

'All of them?' said Stella, feeling rather foolish.

'Of course! I'll be with you in a moment. Prance around a bit, girly, and get the feel of the moss. I bet you have never played on moss before!'

Nervously, Stella obeyed, neatly folding her uniform and underthings and placing them beside Alberta's on the back of the lorry. She felt terribly self-conscious, and her skin was all goose-pimply; to hide her embarrassment, she took a few nervous steps on the lush moss. The effect was electric; it was as though her toes had sunk into a delicious foaming bath, and the moss seemed to caress her feet with its soft spongy flowers. There seemed to be no foundation at all, and it was like walking on rubber. Stella began to think it was probably better to be the ball. She allowed herself to stumble on the moss, and was delighted when she bounced up from her fall as though from a trampoline!

She was interrupted by a summons from the Bull, who ordered her to lie face down on the moss, with her hands behind her back. Stella obeyed, and saw the opposing teams clustered around her, while Jakes carried a coil of hempen ropes from his lorry. She first felt hair-clips fasten her hair in a bun, and then, to her shock, felt her hands bound very tightly behind her back. Her ankles were tied together too, although loosely. The bonds were of thin, coarse rope, about half-an-inch thick, but sturdy and supple. Several ropes were looped around her belly, starting under her breasts leaving them naked.

With each loop, a member of each team took a turn at fastening a knot, and she heard enthusiastic cries – 'Bowline! Sheepshank! Timberhitch!' – along with names of knots she did not know, like 'Turk's Cluster', 'Stragglebeard' and even 'Anemone' (this from Heather!). She remembered that many of the girls had worn Girl Guide badges on their uniform jackets. It seemed that the teams were vying to constrict her in the tightest and strangest of ties which the other team would not know how to unravel. The ropes were coiled around her belly, but left her buttocks and breasts entirely bare. There was a thin, and rather uncomfortable, strand of rope pressing tightly against her fount, inside the very lips of her lady's place, and its coarse fibres itchy against her damsel.

Her unsheathed breasts were pushed outwards, as were her fesses, until Stella felt like a cluster of ripe melons! The knotted ropes coiled round and round her body, their accumulation pushing her protuberances more and more tightly outwards, and fashioning her a corset of ropes which she found oddly becoming. Her thighs were strapped; shoulders, back and calves were criss-crossed in the most elaborate knottings, with loops and bows that Stella thought brutally pretty. Her neck, breasts and buttocks were free, but otherwise, she was trussed and helpless. Though her ankle ropes were quite loose, she would be able only to hobble. Jakes looked on with an approving seafarer's eye, occasionally murmuring encouragement that a particular knot should be even tighter. Although the bulky knots rubbed against her uncomfortably, the intricate pattern of ropes nevertheless acted as a sort of cushion.

The Bull began to rub her with the lubricant, generously applying it all over her bare flesh. She paid particular attention to her breasts and croup, which protruded quite tightly from their hempen prison. The game had seemed bizarre when she read its rules in the Book, but now that she saw the pitch, the strange grove and the two cairns, she understood. The ball was a human being, and she was oiled to make catching her difficult, just as the players were oiled to prevent being pinioned by their opponents. The honeyed hands were for a better grip on the protuberances of the ball which were permitted to be in play: her own breasts and buttocks! So that was why the Bull had been pleased to recruit a big-breasted girl.

Next, Stella was helped to her feet and made to waddle in her bonds towards the central grove, while the two teams took up position on either side of it. All except the goalkeeper bunched tightly around the grove into which Stella was led. When she was pressed against the central tree, Jakes blindfolded her with a rubber thong, and then twirled her round until she was slightly giddy. Stella understood the procedure. She was to walk from the grove, not knowing which team she would face. The lucky team would then grab her, while the other would attempt to get her away from her captors. The idea was to carry her into the team's cairn, where her captors would try and unloose her knots, keeping the ropes as trophies. While her captors were trying to unbind her, the other team would battle to get into the cairn and release her, then carry her to their own cairn. The winning team was apparently the one who loosed the last knot, or, in case of a dispute, the team which already held the most trophies.

Such were the principles; rules, as well as fixed positions, seemed quite in abeyance. The only rule which was adhered to was the method of pinning and transporting the ball: only the breasts and buttocks might be used as handles. This was called 'The Jarl's Rule', although the Book did not specify which ingenious Jarl had thought it up, or when. There was also a procedure for a 'Berserk' which was like a scrummage at Rugby Football, and would be ordered by the referee if the fighting became too wild. The Berserk did not make the fighting less wild, but enforced its more orderly conduct.

Stella emerged from the grove in her blindfold and was promptly set upon by a clutch of furious hands which grabbed her quite expertly by breasts and buttocks, and dragged her towards one of the opposing cairns. There was obviously a practised technique for transporting the ball: the breasts were used for locomotion, to drag Stella along the springy moss, while the buttocks were used for propulsion and steering. With swift and rather painful twists and squeezes, Stella found herself half dragged and half bounced along the moss. Despite her oiled breasts, they were gripped fiercely, twisted halfway round with the nipples against the sticky palm of a honeyed hand. After her first shock and discomfort, Stella found herself actually enjoying being the helpless ball; it reminded her of the fearsome rides at the funfair in Sutton Coldfield, although more brutal.

All around her were noises of fighting, and squeals of pain as the players thumped and twisted each other with heavy thuds, trying to get possession of Stella. There was a Berserk, in which the scrummage echoed to cries of pain and indignation as buttocks and fount lips were pinched and pummelled. At last she felt her captors tackle *en masse*, and she was dropped unceremoniously to bounce helpless on the springy turf, until other, stronger hands grabbed her breasts very fiercely, dragging her in the opposite direction. She recognised the smell a powerful musky scent that seemed strangely mannish and beautiful, like Jamie.

'It's me, Stella,' panted Alberta's voice. 'I've got you! We're going to win!'

Stella could not remember which team Alberta belonged to, but she was sure it must be the Bull's. At any rate she was quite happy to be so roughly dragged by her lovely dorm neighbour, and indeed found her status as bouncing ball very exciting. To be a plaything of others, bound and helpless! She only wished Jamie were playing, and that the hands clasping her breasts and croup were strong male hands . . .

Finally she was carried into the cairn and felt feverish hands undoing her knots, while outside a noisy battle raged. They did not get very far at untying her before the opposing team burst into the cairn with great whoops of savage glee, and dragged her off in the other direction. She began to wonder how the ball must feel at her strenuous games of netball! The procedure was repeated, but it took hours for the ropes to be gradually unbound from her body, and she was sure her breasts must be black and blue with all the tugging and slapping they had received. But she found also that she enjoyed being handled as a plaything. She wanted it, and wished the players would treat her more roughly.

Even Alberta did not speak to her any more, but treated her simply as a mute object, worse than a slave-girl. Stella shivered with tell-tale signs of excitement as the harsh ropes rubbed implacably against her fount lips and nubbin. In her humiliation, she felt wet pleasure between her thighs. Her breasts were mauled, but mauled with a certain expert tenderness, and she began to learn how to thrust herself and go limp so that they would form more malleable handles for the players. She learnt, too, how to tense or relax her buttocks so that they gave a firm grip. She favoured neither side over the other, and she sensed that her compliance was appreciated, even overhearing mutters that she was a 'topping ball'! What was the topping ball's treat to be?

At last she was nude, the last rope stripped from her while a great bottom sat firmly on her face to ward off attempts at recapture. She was glad it was Alberta's bottom, and she breathed in her friend's bum-scent through the tight rubber sheath. She was enjoying this when at last Alberta's team, which was indeed the Bull's, was proclaimed victorious. Miss Harker's team looked glum. Silently they all began to troop towards the grove, Jakes in the rear. Alberta and her comrades carried the now-nude Stella, who enjoyed the cooling wind on her bruised bare skin. Of the losing team, Heather looked very apprehensive, and only the submissive Charity looked cheerful, relishing no doubt the penalty that was to come.

Jakes produced from his holdall a warm robe for Stella, and a short springy whip made of knotted creepers; about two dozen, she reckoned, so that it looked like a green flail. These he handed gravely to Stella, but not without a twinkle in his eye. The losing team lined up to take their punishment for losing! It seemed that each girl must ascend the mighty tree-trunk and raise her legs so that her thighs and arms cupped the bark and held her to the tree, the effort of doing this presumably being part of the punishment. The chastisement was, however, more symbolic than hurtful, since each girl was to receive only one stroke on her rubber-sheathed fesses, and one on her bare back. It was the humiliation of crouching desperately against the giant motherly treetrunk which made Jakes's eyes shine, and Stella wondered if he had devised this penalty.

'Right!' barked the Bull gleefully. 'Let's be having you! Lash 'em proper, Stella!'

Stella was pleased that the Bull had called her by her first name. She nervously held the heavy flail, and saw that it still had little aphids crawling in its green depths. She thought of her beating of Charity, and of Matron, and of naughtily making the Bull chastise her own buttocks. But that was somehow different. She knew that she *could* do this – only two strokes, after all – but still she recoiled at giving pain to those who did not wish it.

'Is this my treat?' she asked the Bull. 'A flogging?'

'Why, yes, girl. It is in the Rules, as you know. Hurry up, it is getting cold, and Jakes has to get back to open the tuck shop."

'The Rules don't say who is to take it.'

'Well, it is the losing side, everyone knows that.'

'But the Rules aren't *specific*, Miss.'

Jakes gently butted in.

'I think Miss Stella is right,' he said. 'Perhaps the Rules are remiss. A flogging there must be, with the green whip, but then who is to take it?'

'*I* shall take it!' cried Stella, flinging aside her robe, and giddy with excitement. She was to be Joan of Arc, flogged at the stake! Nude, she clambered up the treetrunk, before anyone could object in their astonishment, and anchored herself with her fount resting on a swelling nubbin that seemed to be the tree-woman's navel: her head cradled between the massive breasts, and her feet stretched right round the trunk to rest on the tops of the croup. It was as though the tree were embracing her, taking her to itself, and she cried that each team member should give her the two strokes as ordained.

'This is most irregular,' snorted Miss Harker.

'Chance works in funny ways, Miss,' said Jakes, 'and as referee I deem this acceptably chanceful!'

Stella noticed that when his kilt swayed in the breeze, there was a pleasing swell to its skirts, as though the zephyr had filled them with soft, firm clouds.

'What is the girl to be punished for?' snapped the Bull. 'She didn't lose the game, she was the ball! And a jolly good one, very submissive and pliable. I chose her myself!'

'And that is what I must be punished for,' cried Stella. 'For being a plaything, submissive and pliable. For being a jolly good ball!'

The flogging took place; Stella noticed that Alberta's strokes were amongst the strongest, and sighed with fierce pleasure as her friend's lashes bit her naked skin. The flail was a hard and fearsome weapon. She hoped the little insects were not disturbed too much as their green home thudded remorselessly on to Stella's nates and shoulders.

To be flogged on the shoulders was a new and voluptuous experience for Stella, and she daydreamed that she was a sailor at the mast of Columbus's ship, or King Richard the Lionheart in the Saracen dungeon. She took it all without a murmur except for little gasps of joy and satisfaction at her abject pain. She was sure she was not overheard in the ever-growing hum of the Parph wind, to which the flail's whistle was sweetly married. But the flail was heavy, and each stroke made her jump at its force; she found that her lady's place rubbed sharply against the wooden outcrop where she nestled, and caused her a pleasure that made her moist. When she climbed down, her back and buttocks glowed intensely, and the falling rays of the sun illuminated the tree where her fount had pressed; the bark was shiny wet.

Back at the lorry, the girls put on their uniforms again, and Stella was cuddled and kissed, and the taunts of earlier were supplanted by fervent discussions of tuck. Stella, uniformed once more, was about to climb aboard, when Jakes beckoned her. She went to the front of the lorry, where he grinned down at her from the driver's seat.

'You have forgotten your treat, Miss,' he said softly.

'But I thought I had my treat,' she stammered.

'No. Your treat is to ride with me, in the front seat, like a grown-up lady!'

Stella looked at the Bull and Miss Harker for guidance, and sensed that both strong women were somehow in awe of whatever power Jakes possessed. They shrugged helplessly.

'Hop in, Miss,' said Jakes. Stella hopped in.

The cab of the lorry was smelly. There was a slight odour of petrol, and on top, perhaps to mask it, was an overpowering marine smell, which on its own was quite nice. Stella looked round the cab and saw bundles of wet seaweed, and strings of mussels, whelks and other unspeakable molluscs, hanging from the roof! And then, close to Jakes, she smelled an unusual man-scent of the expected sweat and grime, but mixed with the scents of chocolate, toffees and tuck. The smell was curiously attractive.

'I like to be reminded of the sea,' said Jakes simply. 'That's why it is so wonderful here in the north: Cape Wrath and the wild Atlantic. That's home for me! When the Great War was over, I couldn't stand London any more, so I went off on the boats. I was a boy sailor at Scapa Flow, you know, just up there.' He pointed vaguely north. 'There was the Battle of Jutland . . .' then he went suddenly still.

'I suppose all sailors have tattoos,' said Stella suddenly, not knowing why, then blushed. She saw no tattoos on his arms. Jakes nodded and grinned almost shyly.

'I have many keepsakes of the sea,' he said, concentrating on navigating the bumpy track. Stella was jolted uncomfortably, and at one particularly hard bounce she grabbed at the nearest support, which was Jakes's thigh, under his pretty kilt. Only what she touched was not his thigh. Her hand came to rest just above his knee, and there was something else there; something that common sense told her had no right to be down there, but which she felt tense and tremble slightly even at her fleeting touch. Jakes grinned and looked at her but said nothing, and Stella's blush became a fire. She thought of the deference shown to Jakes by the Bull and Miss Harker, both his superiors, and wondered if riding in the lorry's cab was such a treat after all. Her eyes strayed again to that strange form under his skirt, and she itched with curiosity. She gulped, and at the next jolt, touched him again, *there*. She noticed a hard protuberance, like metal.

'Do you like wearing a kilt?' she asked rather foolishly.

'It's airy,' said Jakes.

'It must feel funny – I mean, a man wearing a skirt.'

'It's not a skirt,' retorted Jakes scornfully, 'it is a kilt. A skirt indeed! Anyway, how are you feeling, Miss? That was a spiffing match. You took quite a pounding.'

'I'm all right,' said Stella gaily. 'I quite enjoyed it, really. A few aches and bruises, that's all.'

'You deserve a *real* treat for being such a stout lass. Some tuck at my shop! Real tuck, from my secret store. We've a good hour before I open, and it doesn't matter if

I'm late. What are they going to do, sack me?' He burst out laughing. Stella wondered why Jakes was unsackable.

After depositing the teams back at Kernece, Jakes led her through the lulled corridor to his tuck shop. The other women watched her go with strange looks, half-envious, half-sympathetic. Whatever it was, they *knew*. She told herself that she was not obliged to go with Jakes, but then dismissed her fears as stupid. It was only tuck, for heaven's sake! And this was Kernece! No one broke the Rules, not even Jakes! Unless Jakes made his own Rules ...

She found herself in the unlit tuck shop, surrounded by the piled delights at which she had previously stared hungrily, clutching her sixpences. But there was another locked door at the back of the shop, and Jakes opened this to admit her; then swiftly locked it again. They were in a small storeroom, and Jakes flicked on the electric light. Stella gasped, for it smelled so deliciously sweet that her mouth promptly watered. There were almonds, chocolates, Turkish delights, nougats, a thousand sweetmeats, and Jakes grinned smugly as he told her to help herself. He went to a small basin and made her a jug of sherbet as she quite forgot her ladylike reserve, and raided the jars and boxes, cramming the sticky good things into her. They were not ordinary sweetmeats! Each delicacy was in the form of winkles, cockles, oysters, or whelks; there were sugar candy dolls of males and females, with the sex organs in vivid detail, and the males' quite naughtily stiff! Giggling, she chewed marzipan pea vines and balls, or toffee buttocks.

'I make 'em myself,' said Jakes lazily. 'They are not for everybody. But I like to see a lass enjoying herself.'

'Make them? Where?' mumbled Stella, her mouth unforgivably full. Chocolate and crumbs and bits of melted sweets dribbled down her chin and uniform, but such was the lovely glow in her tummy that she did not care a jot!

'That's for me to know, and you to find out,' said Jakes, enjoying himself. 'I have access to the Labyrinth.'

'You seem to know a lot, Jakes,' she said. 'What about this Kernece Football: the tree, and the cairn and everything? Do you know about that?'

'It is very old,' he said, his face sombre. 'Goes back to the Viking days, maybe beyond that. The tree was sacred, and they sacrificed slaves and warriors there, which are the same thing. I won't say how, it would horrify you. They fought duels, then were whipped as they were sacrificed. Kernece Football is a watered-down girly version. Miss Dancer holds to it strongly, and she must be obeyed.'

Stella thought of the ancient warriors, doomed to sacrifice, fighting their vain, heroic duels with flashing swords under the cruel northern sky. Their only fate was to be the whipping, the sacred tree, and the sacrifice. She blurted her fantasy to Jakes.

'They did not fight with swords, as such,' he said, 'and fate had nothing to do with it. They were chosen by lot, by the Norns.'

Stella thought they must have wrestled, but Jakes said that was not the case. He murmured that she must have eaten her fill, and that he should be opening the tuck shop proper. But Stella was emboldened with food and curiosity, and said derisively that the gluttonous squits could wait. And she found her gaze fixed on that mysterious swelling beneath the folds of Jakes's embroidered kilt. She smiled at him in what she imagined a coy, kittenish way.

'You said you would show me your tattoos, Jakes,' she purred. Jakes answered that he had said nothing of the sort. But his eye gleamed as he spoke with feigned shyness.

'Oh, all right. But you must promise not to touch.'

Stella promised enthusiastically, with her fingers crossed, telling herself that made it all right. Slowly, Jakes lifted the front of his kilt, and Stella gasped, dropping a toffee-apple on the floor. Jakes grinned in a strange mixture of sheepishness and pride.

'That's why I like to wear the kilt,' he said. 'It is more comfortable for *this*.'

Jakes was blessed, or cursed, with a pea vine that must have been eighteen inches long, and whose tip came down almost to his knee! Stella could never have imagined such a monstrous thing. It was very thin, no more than an inch until the abrupt swelling of the bulb, which was adorned with a thick and obviously heavy gold ring, right through the shiny skin of his massive helmet. And the whole length of the penis – she still gulped at that word – was emblazoned with tattoos, of fish and sea creatures and harpoons. It was hideous, yet magical. At her enthralled gaze, the penis began to stiffen and tremble, like some uncoiling sea-serpent, and grew even longer! Jakes's stare was now deadly serious and he fixed her with a gaze that seemed to pierce the very heart of her womanhood.

'I was shipwrecked,' he said slowly, as if in a trance. 'It was far to the north of Labrador, an Eskimo island called Uklukluk, and I was the only one to survive the wreck. We hit an iceberg! Just like the Titanic, only our trawler went down even faster. I had to stay there until the pack-ice melted, and in that time, the women took charge of me. You see, they remembered the old days, when the Norsemen came in their long ships, and thought I was one of them. Even though I'm not fair, due to my Italian blood. But I was from the east, and I was ... well-endowed, as their men are not. They wanted it to be more, like Gunnar Gunnarsson, Erik the Red, and others whose names they babbled. First, they pierced me there, at my tip, and put in the ring which their tribe had kept all through the centuries, for *me*!'

Stella longed to touch the curious ring, and the pea vine too, but desisted, and busied herself with fudge instead.

'Then they suspended blocks of ice from my penis, to stretch it. It hurt abominably! The ice took a long time to melt, and when it was just a pebble, it was replaced, with another, heavier block. All the time my penis grew and grew, and when it was this length, I was tattooed. And then I had to do battle with the champion of the Inuit – "the People" as they called themselves – who had had the same treatment. I did battle, and won, and for a short time, before an icebreaker came from Montreal to rescue me, I was champion of that tribe. I had every woman ... That is how the ancient slaves of Kernece did battle before they were sacrificed. They duelled not with swords of metal, but with swords of flesh: with their stiff penises!'

Jakes's grin now became a leer.

'They have probably told you that I've had every woman in Kernece,' he added.

'Yes,' faltered Stella. Jakes nodded.

'And I'll probably have you as well,' he said matter-of-factly. Stella shuddered, not in fear, but at the terrible wash of desire that filled her and made her fount moisten with hot oil. She looked mesmerised at the mighty penis, wanting it inside her lady's place . . . now! Used to submitting to females, she wanted to submit to the champion of the tribe, the power of the male symbolised by the fearsome, ugly beauty of his giant penis. She reached out and touched the golden ring at its tip, then ran her fingers down the soft sinuous shaft, which reared like a dragon, making her start. The glow of food in her stomach was matched in sweet harmony by a fire of desire in her belly, and she knew it was hopeless to resist.

'You like my whip?' drawled Jakes.

The pea vine swelled and swelled, although it did not thicken much, rather lengthened, lifted, and stood in a great rigid arc that reached up to Jakes's breasts. Jamie's had stood straight and true, but this one curved obscenely, like a bow. As it trembled, the fishes tattooed on it seemed to dance and swim. The bulb swelled enormously, so that the ring, which was pierced deep inside the man's pee-hole, was flattened and stretched against the shiny crimson helmet. It seemed to give slightly, and suddenly there was a click, as the ring was fully stretched. From its thick waist sprang a flail of thin golden rods, about seven or eight inches long, like a little many-thonged whip!

Outside, there was a murmuring from the corridor as the queue wanted the tuck shop to open. Stella was oblivious. She had dreamt of Jamie's pea vine inside her, but this was here and now, this was the moment: it was her fate!

'I'll take you now, girly,' said Jakes, grinning quietly. 'My cock says so. What other treat can a girly have? Bend over and touch your toes, skirt up and knickers by your ankles. You know the drill. I'm going to give you a proper swiving with my big stiff whip, and after that no other man will satisfy you.'

Numb with frightened lust, Stella obeyed, feeling the trickle of moisture from her fount on her thigh-skin as she bent over, like a boy for his six of the best. Then Jakes had his fingers inside her very lady's place, roughly probing and kneading her throbbing damsel! He grunted.

'Already wet, eh? That's good. You *are* a submissive girly. Well, you took one good flogging today, and that bum looks as though she's been well attended to, so I'll swive you properly, with a real whip.'

Stella twisted her head to look, and saw Jakes doff his jacket and kilt, and he stood before her entirely nude. He began to undulate his hips in a sensuous, almost inhuman, rhythm. Only his belly and thighs moved, the rest of his body as rigid as his whip; but the whip began to whirl round and round as his belly-dance grew more and more frantic, the golden flail dancing from the ring at his whirling bulb. Suddenly Stella felt a sharp, smarting pain as her bared buttocks took a lash from his whole stiff penis and the sharp thongs of the flail at its tip. It was like the splayed cane of which Stella had read, with which the natives were flogged in the rubber plantations of Malaya. Her heart cried in sympathy for them, because her pain was horrid.

Jakes's rigid penis was as hard as an iron bar, and as heavy, and the splay of the whip at its bulb brought tears of smarting pain to Stella's eyes. She did not know how many he intended to give her; but gradually, as she accustomed herself to the rhythm of his flogging, it became *her* flogging, her property, and she did not want it to stop. She relished this new submission – to a male!

'Come on,' she whispered, as, outside, there was a faint clamour of 'Tuck! Tuck! We want our tuck!' Jakes was sweating freely now, and the more he exerted himself, the cooler Stella became, the more her belly danced in pleasure at her joyful submission.

'Harder, Jakes, harder!' she murmured.

'My, you are a cool girly!' he panted. 'But still, girlies are stupid, you know? Give them a bellyful of sweets, and ...' He broke off to cackle. 'I shall flog you with my whip until you beg me to stop!'

'Ooh' groaned Stella, as her hand crept to her tingling stiff damsel and she began to openly masturbate in front of her strange new paramour! 'That will be never! I love it so! Jakes, you may flog my bare bum forever and ever! Your penis is so big! You are champion of the tribe!'

She knew males liked to hear such things.

Jakes saw her masturbating, and that seemed to inflame his ardour still more. He put his fingers, now, right inside her lady's place and felt her brutally. Stella moaned, but thrilled at his touch.

'You've a nice tight cunt,' he gasped. 'What's this? A virgin! Well, it won't be my first . . . I'm going to fuck you now, my cock's so full of spunk for you, little girl, and I'm going to spurt it all into that sweet cunt of yours till you overflow!'

Stella was pleased. She had never thought of her lady's place, her – 'cunt!' – as sweet. Jakes delivered a final stinging cut with his penis whip and then she felt the metal of his penis-ring, the rods retracted, tickle the lips of her fount, sliding inside her oily wetness and followed by the massive bulb. She gasped as she relaxed to let him inside her, and loved the helpless sensation of being filled and taken. He paused when he came to her virginal barrier.

'Soon, girly, you'll know the sweetness of a male's seed,' he hissed. 'That is what your cunt is for. Just as I feed your bellies with sweetmeats, so I feed your cunts with the juiciest spunk. You females know no limit to your appetites, Miss: you are our *receptacles*.'

Stella had no time to ponder the import of these words, for, just as Jakes drew back for his thrust into her precious virginity – which, it seemed, fate had decreed was not so precious any more – there was a sudden piercing cry from outside the tuck shop.

'Jakes! Are you in there? Open up at once! This is a disgrace!' It was Miss Dancer's voice.

Jakes suddenly withdrew his penis from Stella's fount, and muttered 'Oh, hell!' Stella was bitterly disappointed; the pressure of Jakes's penis inside her, together with the insistent pressure of her own masturbating fingertips, made her on the point of orgasming. But Jakes speedily donned his clothing and rushed through the storeroom door to fling open the shutters of his tuck shop, where his flushed face was greeted by a clamour of hungry Kernecians. Miss Dancer remained to supervise, her face stern and her arms folded.

Gradually, Stella came to her senses, and the thrill of submission turned to irritation at being beached on her orgasmic plateau. She resolved that she should not be deprived of her pleasure; she had missed the tuck queue, but she would be fed! Surreptitiously, she crept on all fours to the counter where Jakes was busily serving, and put her head underneath his kilt. He started, but under Miss Dancer's steely eye could not interrupt his tasks, nor give the game away. And Stella knew this. Grinning wickedly to herself, she raised her head and put her lips on his balls. She covered them with her mouth and began to gently chew them, imagining they were candied toffee-apples. Jakes groaned.

Then her hand went to his still-throbbing shaft, and with a few flicks she had him stiff and trembling again. She reached her whole arm right up to the bulb, which was swelling just beneath the waistband of his kilt, even though he had hitched it up over his belly. Surely Miss Dancer and the girls must be aware, must see her hand, too, as she began to vigorously stroke and rub his swollen bulb, making the little golden flail jangle loudly.

'Oh ... Oh ...' moaned Jakes: 'Two shillings and threepence, please ... Oh ...!'

It did not take long before Stella felt the golden whip-thongs moisten with a droplet of spunk from his peehole. She rubbed his penis very hard and ruthlessly, so that a great creamy jet spurted from it, all over her hand, to Jakes's moans and gasps of pleasure.

'Whatever is the matter, Jakes?' rapped Miss Dancer, but there was a wry softness in her voice: she *knew*!

The sperm from Jakes's whip seemed inexhaustible; as she masturbated him with one hand, Stella rubbed herself feverishly with the other. As the stream of hot creamy seed cascaded over his shivering balls and into her avidly licking mouth, she exploded in a spasm of joy and ecstasy. She swallowed every drop of his creamy seed, like a delicious dessert to all the sweetmeats that filled her, and when his spasm had subsided and his whip softened a little, she gave his balls the tenderest of kisses, and whispered:

'Thank you for your sweetness.'

'Why,' stammered Jakes, 'no one ever said that before, Miss.'

'What?' rapped Miss Dancer.

'Nothing, Miss Dancer.'

'Good. I believe that Miss Shawn excelled herself at Football.'

'Yes, Miss Dancer.'

'And did she enjoy her treat?'

'I believe so, Miss.'

'Excellent. She is a good girl. I think she has spunk.'

Stella licked her lips. She knew she wanted the sweetness of the male, but now, her appetite satisfied, she knew that it was Jamie's seed she wanted inside her ... cunt.

Finally, the customers left, satisfied, and Jakes was able to shut the tuck shop. Stella noticed wryly that his penis was soft again; it seemed that a male milked of his spunk had no further desire to penetrate a receptacle.

'Well, Jakes,' she said, kissing him lightly on the lips, 'you may not have had me, but I have certainly had *you*. There is just one thing. With your lovely big penis, you may be champion for now, but I know someone who can whip you in naked combat, and who will ... Because I shall make him.'

She added silently to herself, that for someone who seemed to disparage girlies and receptacles, Jakes would look uncommonly nice dressed as one.

10

Alberta's Secret

Joyously and graciously, Stella accepted the routine of Kernece as her own. After only a few weeks, it seemed that she had been there since time immemorial, and she had to remind herself that in all the talk of Hallowe'en and Knobkerry Night and Up-Helly-A, it was in fact her first experience of these festivals. Of Hallowe'en she had heard, since it was some pagan rite they had in Scotland and Ireland, at roughly the same time as the civilised English Guy Fawkes Night. Knobkerry Night was a mystery, although she knew a knobkerry was some ferocious Scottish cudgel, no doubt used to resist the incursions of Jamie Isbister's blond ancestors – how she pined for sweet Jamie! She knew that Up-Helly-A involved burning longhips and drinking mead or something from skulls of vanquished warriors, the Isbisters no doubt figuring prominently in its annals. There was some grumbling when Miss Dancer announced that this year, due to some mysterious concatenation of dates and planets, the three festivals would be so close that to save time and money, – 'Especially money!' whispered Alberta loudly – they would be merged into one: Hallowe'en on October 31st. The grumblings were rewarded with one or two choice public beatings in Hall, which cheered everyone up, and preparations became feverish and secretive.

Stella's triumph in occupying Morag for the Blues stood her in such good stead that she was not called upon to perform further. Nor did she need to administer the cane to Charity or any of the map-making Norns, being content to hold the squirming women for their desired beating. She gathered that a starring role awaited her at Hallowe'en, shrouded of course in last-minute secrecy. At one Cohort meeting, she dared Heather to take the cane and prove herself a true Blue, but the suggestion was booed. To *take* a beating was for girly subs like Charity, who took cane just as they submitted joyfully – for strange sub reasons of their own – to the responsibility of command, leaving the Kerns free to 'conquer, loot and pillage' as Heather stirringly insisted.

'What if *I'm* really a girly sub?' asked Stella slyly.

'You? Never!' scoffed Heather. 'You are one of us. Of course you can take a beating, with gritted teeth, from Miss Dancer or Clapton, and that shows how tough and *dom* you are! But the idea of enjoying it . . .! Why, you'd have to be like Charity here!'

She emphasised her words by delivering a hearty kick right to Charity's bottom, as though her leader were a football. Charity breathed deeply, and rubbed her bottom as if hoping for more.

'Even if you wanted to take Charity's place as leader,' Heather continued, 'you'd have to take a lacing that she couldn't. And no one can take more than Charity!'

Charity nodded, and smiled as she was rewarded with a second kick, so hard it nearly toppled her. Stella mentally filed this information. She wondered what it would be like to be beaten by the redoubtable Clapton, and what excuse Clapton would find. She suspected that a lashing from her would be accompanied by many knots, and little love. For the meantime, she found the question of Alberta more and more intriguing, and wondered if she was conceiving a pash for her chum. Of course, she still dreamed of Jamie, and now of Jakes too, and masturbated quite frequently, but somehow Alberta crept more and more into her dreams. Her very proximity lent Stella's self-pleasuring a piquant, frustrating edge. She would turn her head to see Alberta's black hair spread like petals on her pillow. As her fingers brought her throbbing damsel nearer and nearer to the warm shudder of her orgasm, she would imagine Alberta and Jamie entwined, Stella embracing them, and Jakes there too, his dark curly hair somehow flowing into Alberta's . . .

Her desire to see the shy Alberta nude grew more and more powerful, as did the thought of persuading Alberta to whip her: it would somehow cement their friendship for Stella to bare her nates to Alberta's lashes. She had seen her in uniform, of course, and in her nightie, and in the rubber football suit, but Alberta was adamant that it was unseemly for her to be naked with others. Stella thought this must have to do with her Italian religious upbringing – although Alberta's plummy vowels in her deep, melodious contralto did not *sound* Italian – and the authorities seemed to tolerate her timidity. She was allowed both to commode and shower alone, and have her monthly irrigation from Matron in private.

'She allows me to keep my panties on, you see,' she confided to Stella, with a lovely blush. 'That is, I pull them down at the back, but hold them up at the front. And if I get a thrashing, I can keep my panties on too; it's still bare bum, for I pull them up really tight, so that my fesses are quite nude for the tawse. Not that panties would make much difference.' Stella seized this opening.

'I've never been chastised on the panties, or in skirt,' she said mischievously, but telling the strict truth. 'Always bare bum. I wonder what it's like?'

'Oh, just as painful, I'd imagine,' said Alberta. 'I don't like being beaten! And think of the damage to your panties! Why, the Bull would rip them to shreds.'

'I bet a loving whip-hand would be able to lace a bottom in panties without damaging them,' said Stella coyly.

'A loving whip-hand!' cried Alberta. 'Is there such a thing?' Stella put her palm on Alberta's wrist.

'There is yours, sweet Alberta,' she whispered.

'Mine? Whatever do you mean?'

'I said I'd bet – Of course, if you're not game, I suppose your skinny frame doesn't need to win a free feed from Jakes's tuck shop.' Alberta's eyes lit.

'You mean, I should lace you in panties? What would you get out of it, Stella my love, except a sore bum?'

'You remember when I – you know, all over my sheets?' said Stella with feigned timidity. 'Well, I still feel awfully guilty about it. I know I should be punished.' Alberta squeezed Stella's hand in sympathy.

'You must have had a religious upbringing,' she said. Stella was momentarily confused: it was modest Alberta who was supposed to have suffered a religious upbringing!

'Why no,' she stammered, 'I mean, yes, C of E, of course, but – damn it, Alberta, please help me! Take the bet, I beg you. I know a secret place, it's beside the Labyrinth.'

'Of course I shall help you,' said Alberta, 'you lovely, guilty girl! I wonder if I shan't rather enjoy flogging your big bum, panties or no panties ...'

The dusky afternoon air was heavy with a beautiful scent of moss and autumn flowers that excited Stella as they crossed the yard. It was as though Alberta already knew her way to Morag's secret room, and Stella guessed that 'secret' was simply a term of endearment. Alberta was equipped with a thick cane, which, she explained to her doubtful partner, would be quite kind to the precious fabric of her panties, if not to the skin beneath. But the mystery of the secret room heightened Stella's tense pleasure; her fount was wet as Alberta shut the door and flexed her cane. Stella gave a little shiver, half of fear and half of awaited joy. Her mouth was dry. She wanted to get started, get those first hard cuts over with, and feel herself swept by the blissful rhythm of her chastisement.

'I – I feel so much better,' faltered Stella with a gulp.

'You won't when I start whacking you,' said Alberta, taking off her jacket. Stella noticed how strong and sinewy Alberta's arms were. Her muscles rippled prettily as she swished the cane in the air.

'I'm used to taking, not giving, and I hate the pain. But I think I'm going to enjoy giving it to you.'

'I certainly hope so,' said Stella nervously, wondering if

she was being foolhardy. It was tuck time. She thought of the girls clamouring for Jakes's sweetmeats, and for a moment wished she was there. But that was silly! She had demanded punishment – she craved punishment – and would take it. She smiled, knowing that her jitters were as always part of her pleasure.

'I suppose you'll want to strap me to the block,' she said casually. Alberta frowned.

'Yes, it would be nice,' she replied, 'but it takes time, and we don't want to miss tea as well as tuck. You aren't going to run away, are you? Although you can stop me any time, and then you pay me double tuck! You see, Stella, I plan to give that bottom of yours a nice slow skinning.' She stroked Stella's fesses through her skirt.

'Raise that,' said Alberta softly, 'and bend over. Touch your toes, and spread your thighs wide.' Stella obeyed, and felt Alberta's fingers running lightly over the thin silk of her panties, like little tickly mice.

'How I'd love to cane you on the bare,' whispered Alberta, and at her words Stella felt the wetness grow sweet and hot between her swelling fount-lips.

'Oh,' she said, genuinely taken aback. 'How I should love that too, Alberta. It would be such a – jape.'

'More than that,' said Alberta. 'But there is one thing: if I lose, and tear your panties, what is my penalty?'

'Why, you must buy me tuck,' said Stella promptly.

'Only that?'

'It is open to – *ouch*! – discussion.'

Stella's sentence was interrupted by the harsh descent of Alberta's cane on the stretched silk of her panties. The cut smarted terribly, and Stella thought that she might just as well be taking it bare! Another followed quickly, then another, and after the fourth, Alberta's pace slowed into a steady, almost hypnotic rhythm. Now Stella's breath was easier, and she sighed with pleasure rather than anguish. She accommodated herself to the smooth, searing jolts of pain which she rode proudly as though a wild stallion bucked between her thighs.

'Gosh,' she sighed, 'those are tight! My bum stings so! Are you sure you're not experienced, Alberta?'

'Not with a girl,' Alberta panted hoarsely.

'You mean you've caned males?' cried Stella. Alberta's strokes suddenly faltered.

'Oh,' she burbled. 'Yes. Just in play, you know. Pretending. But a girl's bottom is much more beautiful.'

'And you caned them, *pretending*, on the bare?'

'I admit I've seen men's bums bare.'

'And what do they look like?' Stella persisted, impishly, as her bottom squirmed gently to the rhythm of the swishing.

'Bony,' said Alberta. 'I say, you are wriggling quite a lot, Stella. Am I really hurting? It makes such an awful thrash, it certainly sounds as if you're bum's getting a real Dancer treatment. Panties rumpled but intact!'

'Yes, you are hurting!' gasped Stella, clasping her buttocks tightly together so that she could feel the panty silk caught in the valley of her fesses.

'Alberta, when this is over, may I – may I see *your* bottom? Just for an instant? You could pull your panties up tight, as though for a beating. I'd like to see if she is as lovely bare as she looks under your nightie.'

'Yes, Stella. Yes,' whispered Alberta.

Stella felt her fount quite soaking now, and the jerks of her fesses very tight and shuddering as the cane kissed her panties. She imagined a whole row of men's bums, all bare and bony and squirming under Alberta's lash as Stella looked on, her fingers – no, Alberta's! – playing ever so delicately on her tingling damsel.

'Mmm,' she gasped, feeling herself writhing quite shamelessly as the cane-strokes brought her nearer and nearer to her plateau. Would Alberta continue the flogging, and bring her there? Or would she touch her . . . Oh, how Stella longed for that! Alberta's firm lips on hers, and her strong fingers diddling her, soppy wet girly that she was! Alberta said she saw a big wet patch on Stella's panties.

'Don't tell me you've . . .?' she murmured quizzically.

'No! *You* know,' replied Stella coyly. 'A beating always does that, makes me flow with – naughty stuff.'

Alberta was silent except for a puzzling sigh, and her stroke faltered.

'You *do* know, don't you, Alberta?'

'Yes, of course. Oh, Stella, I shouldn't feel this way about you, I want to take those panties off and hug and kiss you all over. There! I've said it! I've been improper, and I suppose *I* deserve beating.'

Stella told Alberta that she had at last won her bet.

'And,' she said, rising, 'before you get your tuck, you promised I could see your bare bum.'

'Oh,' wailed Alberta, 'it wasn't meant to be like this!'

She turned quickly and put her hands in front of her skirt, but not fast enough to stop Stella noticing her embarrassment. Blushing, Alberta bent over and lifted her skirt. She then pulled her knickers tightly in the cleft of her buttocks until her fesses were bared to Stella's view, prettily framed by her garter belt, straps and stockings. Stella touched the smooth creamy skin of Alberta's croup. She saw and felt two delicious bum-orbs, tight and shiny as apples. But Alberta's embarrassment was impossible!

'How do you find my bum, Stella?' said Alberta in a small voice. 'If you must flog me for my impudence, please be quick, because I hate to be beaten. *You* seem to like it. Are you then a sub?'

'Yes, Alberta, you are right,' said Stella, stroking the girl's lovely bottom. 'So I would have no pleasure in beating you. Your punishment shall be ... You must act according to your words. You must kiss and cuddle me!'

With that, she deftly slipped her fingers under Alberta's hand, between her thighs. Alberta yelped in surprised outrage, and jumped up, but it was too late. Stella had felt her, there. The two women faced each other.

'So that is why you will not be naked,' said Stella coolly. 'I had never dreamt of such a thing. This is impudence, not just to me, but to the whole of Kernece!'

Alberta took Stella's hands in hers.

'Do not give me away. I'll be your slave forever. Anything! I beg you,' she pleaded, 'as one girl to another ...'

'But, Alberta, it seems you are not a girl,' said Stella. 'That bulge you are vainly trying to hide is a rather magnificent *penis*. And standing so stiff and lovely for me!'

She put her arms around Alberta, who had begun to sob, and comforted her – him! Stella pressed the young man tightly to her. Her fount melted in warm oils as she felt the ramrod stiffness of the pea vine hard against her belly, the swollen helmet tickling her navel through the straining skirt-cloth.

'I never guessed!' she murmured, smelling the sweet manscent through Alberta's silken black tresses. 'How ...?'

Alberta's lips were on Stella's shoulder.

'I wanted to be a girl, that's all,' Alberta sobbed. 'To wear beautiful things, and perfume, and know what it is to be pure, and serve. I told Jakes, my cousin, from our English family. He thought it a tremendous jape, and gained me a place at Kernece. He has influence. So only he, Miss Dancer, and Matron know.'

Stella drew a deep breath, and slid her hand under Alberta's skirt and panties. Alberta did not resist as she curled her hand's around the tight balls, then began to stroke the throbbing smooth shaft of the erect penis. She reached the tip, the hard shiny skin of the bulb, and found Alberta's pee-hole, which she began to rub very gently. She told herself that she was not betraying Jamie, for Alberta was truly a girl, was she not? And as for betraying Jakes – Why, Jakes with his monstrous sex organ was a mere biology lesson! Alberta moaned and trembled with pleasure.

'Oh, no, stop ...'

'You don't mean stop, Alberta,' said Stella softly. 'When a girl says no, sometimes she means yes.'

She placed Alberta's hand between her own thighs, squarely on the moist swollen lips of her fount, then directed the male's fingers to her stiff damsel.

'Boys like being rubbed, I know,' she said, thrilled at her new authority, 'and so do girls. Don't you rub yourself? I mean until the spunk comes?' Alberta nodded, yes.

'And what do you dream of when you rub yourself?'

'Oh, Stella, I dream of *you*!'

'And how often do you pleasure yourself thus?'

'Every night, sometimes twice or more. It is agony! Your sweet body only feet away, and it might be an ocean. It is no pleasure! It is a moment of pure wisdom, which vanishes and leaves one forlorn. Pleasure, Stella, can last. Wisdom, when the spunk comes, is a flash of pure beauty, and it is gone in an instant.'

'Perhaps that is why we girls are not wise,' said Stella artfully, 'for we can have pleasure that lasts and lasts!'

Stella herself was trembling and her fount felt like a delicious river of love for this boy and his smooth gentle body. Gasping, she knelt at his feet and lifted his skirt to the full, lowering the panties so that the throbbing pea vine sprang up. Comfortably kneeling, she stroked the penis and balls and stared entranced at the magnificent apparatus of the male. There was no hair there; Alberta had a completely shaven mink. Or were some boys bare, she wondered? She diddled her own damsel, now, and a spasm of pure desire transfixed her. She wanted that penis inside her, wanted to *feel* the spunk that Alberta would give to her sacred lady's place as she gave him wisdom.

Suddenly she drew back from her thought. A cold thrill of warning and desire gripped her heart: *that* was for Jamie!

'I won't give you away, Alberta,' she panted, 'but in return you *shall* be my slave. You must obey me: make me worship this pea vine, and serve you, and beat me when I wish it. That is your servitude, and hard it shall be. Now, kneel by me, and we shall continue our sweet game . . . my boy!'

Alberta knelt, and clasped Stella's fount once more, hissing that she was not a boy, but Stella's girl-slave. Stella looked Alberta deep in the eyes, and her heart melted at the soft beauty of her new slave, which was the more haunting because of Stella's real confusion. Was Alberta boy or girl? The hard penis she clutched left her in no doubt. And yet . . . The glimmering of an idea took shape. She wanted Alberta so much, wanted to feel that hot strong flesh inside her, filling her.

As she slowly rubbed Alberta's penis, being careful now

to avoid the shiny glans, she asked Alberta about Italy and schooldays there; the games that she knew young men played with each other. Alberta blushed deeply, and said that there had been wrestling games, as well as mock-chastisements.

'Mock-loving, I suppose? With your pea vines? Inside each other, thrusting and rubbing till the cream spurted from you, in your boyish desire for "wisdom"?' Alberta nodded. The thought of males together made Stella feel quite funny!

'We ... We made girls of each other, sometimes,' blushed Alberta. 'And I thought that I wanted to be a girl, to feel like a girl, so I took things from my sisters' wardrobes – dresses and stockings and panties, *you* know. I just felt so beautiful and calm and *serene* when properly dressed! And one day I dressed up and went out into the streets of Bolzano, and everyone thought I was one of my sisters! I was so thrilled – my pea vine, as you call it, stood up all stiff! I had seen that my sisters shaved their whole bodies, so I did too. I so wanted to be like them because I love them so much. A pity I was past eighteen summers before I discovered my love of dressing – my truth!

'Two years later, I came into money from my father's estate. He owned the biggest chain of pastry-shops in the South Tirol, making strudel and apfeltorten for the Austrians, with shops from Merano to Trentino and even branches in Graz, Trieste and Vienna! So it was easy to contact my cousin Jakes in North Woolwich and gain entry to Kernece. I love it so! Although, I love my pea vine too, and know that I can never really be a girl, nor I suppose do I want to. She stands so much when I dress properly – it is as though girly things make me more of a man. I never really liked being beaten, though I can take it as a girl; but I do love to see other bums wriggling! I want to be a Prefect at Poppy's, where I can beat girls' bottoms, and let my pea vine stand without them seeing! Knobkerry Night shall be wonderful, the ceremony loved by Kytetroos of Naxos.'

Stella learnt that the festival came from Africa: it was

held once a year in honour of the goddess Minerva, whom the Africans called Neith, or Night. Minerva was personified as a nude black female arched over on her fingertips and toes, fount and breasts to the heavens, and spangled with jewels to represent the stars. The women of Kernece would be drawn up in two bodies to fight with clubs, and those who fell in the mock-battle were declared 'false maidens', and had to pay forfeits. The loveliest of the warriors wore shining armour, just like Joan of Arc! Stella too thrilled at the contest of Knobkerry Night, although she reflected ruefully that with the insatiable Jakes around, there could not be many true maidens left at Kernece.

'So my sweet Alberta is a dom,' whispered Stella. 'But *you* shall be *my* girl, and I shall be your boy. It would be no sin. You could put your girl's pea vine inside me, and thrust until you spurted, but I would still be virgin.'

Alberta sighed. Stella abruptly turned and kissed her, then presented her reddened fesses, knickers lowered and skirt up. She had heard that this was what naughty boys did, at their games, and gulped at her wickedness. Her damsel throbbed; she knew she must be filled by her new slave's stiff flesh. Her fingers could not stray from her damsel: she rubbed herself until her smarting fesses writhed in a sinuous dance of her desire, and she knew Alberta's resistance was melting. She drew her cheeks wide with her free hand, exposing her anus bud, and waited. She heard Alberta moan, and felt her stiff, smooth helmet tickle the soft skin of her anus.

'Oh,' she moaned suddenly, starting with pleasure as she felt the hard bulb probing inside her tight little hole. 'Will it hurt? Caning I can take, but not real hurt.'

'Only a little,' said Alberta. 'You must relax your bum-muscle, and let me slide all the way in, and then it will be glorious. You'll see. But you're a bit dry ...'

Stella felt the whole weight of Alberta's body straddle her, and a hand touch her swollen fount. Alberta took the oils that flowed from Stella's slit, and applied them to the pea vine so that the massive organ was smooth and glistening. It slipped deep into Stella's fundament, met resistance, and then, as Stella relaxed fully, thrust right to her core in a wonderful filling rush. Stella gasped, masturbating herself as Alberta's penis thrust gently up and down in her bumhole. It *was* glorious! She squeezed her bum-muscle on Alberta's sex organ, drawing sweet moans of pleasure from her slave. She thrilled at the thought that she could do this lovely thing as much as she wanted, and still be a virgin! She thought of Jakes's penis inside her bumhole, and shivered. Could her tender place take *that*?

Now she felt Alberta's hands on her breasts, touching the bare under her blouse, and grasping her nipples. She squeezed and rubbed them between lovely strong fingers so that they tingled and stood stiff like hard walnuts, throbbing in time with her tingling damsel! Spasms of warm joy transfused Stella's body; she breathed the male scent of Alberta's hair wreathing her own, and, helpless with desire, she knew it would not be long before she orgasmed.

'It is fabulous,' she gasped, then blurted: 'Oh, Alberta, you feel as big as Jakes!' Alberta laughed, not cruelly.

'I thought so!' she cried. Stella protested that no, Alberta's penis was the first inside her body, yet she had ... *seen* Jakes.

'No one *sees* Jakes, without more,' Alberta laughed. 'And no one is as big as Jakes. That is his hold over women, Stella, and his power at Kernece. It was chance that brought him here, and chance too that only Jakes can satisfy Miss Dancer and Clapton. *I know: their founts are so big!* Oh, this is so lovely, Mistress, I shall come – take my wisdom!'

'Please, Alberta,' whispered Stella. 'Spurt your hot cream inside me as soon as you like. Oh, Alberta, my love, *fuck* me!' Stella felt herself one with Morag. She could use that word, and knew she would use it again!

'I obey. You are my Mistress, now. But I was supposed to enslave you! I am one of the Reds, Stella. Morag set me up to this. I was supposed to gain possession of your affections, and now it is you who have gained me! It is my first time to fuck a woman, and you take my virginity from me, Mistress, as my joyful gift.'

Delirious with joy and power and desire, Stella ordered Alberta that *she*, Alberta, must become as big as Jakes. By wearing a rock and a chain, concealed under her uniform skirt and petticoats, Alberta was to achieve the same huge penis, on the order and pleasure of her Mistress. She would always be the most wonderful woman, and she was to make herself the most wonderful male. Alberta assented!

Stella felt Alberta's penis shudder and heard her moan, as a hot drop of liquid came from her peehole. Then the whole penis began to buck, and Alberta's seed came in fierce, loving spurts, washing Stella's insides with its hot flood. She cried out and knew she was about to orgasm, and as the spurts of hot cream seemed endless, her whole body spasmed as though every corner of her young body were bathed in Alberta's male essence.

At that moment the door opened, and Morag strode triumphantly into the chamber. Mistress and slave were tight in their embrace, but with Alberta's penis safely hidden under her panties and skirts. Morag crowed with delight.

'A victory for the Reds! Well done, Alberta, you have tamed the girly slut!'

'No, Morag,' said Alberta with quiet pride, 'it is she who has possessed me.'

Stella rose, and smiled at Morag, then ordered her to lift her skirts.

'What! You impudent girly!'

'You impudent *Mistress*, Morag. Or don't you wish to obey the rules of warfare? I conquered you, remember.'

She stared coolly, deep into the jewels of Morag's lovely hard eyes: Morag blushed, and obeyed. Then Stella knelt, and kissed Morag's feet. She ran her tongue and lips up her stockings and garters to her panties, where she kissed the swelling mound through the cloth until the panty silk was quite wet and Morag gasped.

'Oh, you sweet slut,' she moaned. 'Oh, how good it is, you gorgeous mossy bitch – *Mistress*!'

Stella raised her own skirts high, and told Morag that she was to spank her naked fesses. Stella knew that she had, and would always have, Morag under the spell of her self-abasement. Slowly, she removed her own blue garter and fastened it to Morag's thigh, nestling against her fount.

'Yes, Mistress,' Morag murmured, and began to spank Stella's bare. And as Stella's already crimson fesses blushed under their spanking, she looked up and smiled.

'You see, Morag?' she said sweetly. 'Another victory for the Blues!'

11

Ladies in Knots

A stiff breeze whipped clouds across the darkening October sky as Stella crossed the yard on her way to Matron's Surgery. She shivered, hoping it was not too late to arrange for her monthly irrigation, in time for Hallowe'en the next day. She was perplexed, and the gaunt Castle walls seemed to echo her perplexity, as she was still uncertain what was to happen at the forthcoming festival. She had received hints that hers was to be a major role, something to do with her apparent success as a Kernece Football! But Miss Noble said it was a matter for Miss Rime, and Miss Rime said it was a matter for Miss Noble. The Bull dropped hints, but said it was an Army Matter. Alberta seemed to suspect something, but smirked when asked, saying it was a House matter. Jakes just smirked, telling her only that she must be well cleansed in every orifice for Hallowe'en, 'for witches and warlocks detest clean passages'.

'Hallowe'en!' cried Matron, tousling her hair with pencil-black fingers. 'I'm always so busy at Hallowe'en! Everyone wants their irrigations all at the same time, so I have to do them in batches.' She looked up, and smiled, blushing so prettily that Stella blushed too.

'Oh, it's you, Stella. You sweet young lady – how are you faring at Kernece? You look radiant. I suppose you've been bagged by one of the Armies, and mustn't tell me about it. I'm so curious, and so envious! But I mustn't prattle. Of course I'll fit your irrigation for when we can be alone.'

Her eyes were anxious.

'Please say you'd like that, Stella.'

'I should like that so much, Matron,' Stella answered softly. 'But it might be wrong for me to seem favoured over others.' Matron bit her lip.

'I suppose so,' she sighed. 'But, you know, you are entitled to as many irrigations as you like, if you can find a place for me in your busy timetable.'

Stella put her hand on Matron's and stroked her.

'Always, Matron.' Stella sighed. 'I have, as you say, been bagged. And not just by an Army. I have befriended Alberta – made her my slave! – and I request that I be permitted to take my irrigation with her in attendance.'

'That is impossible!' cried Matron, then stared at Stella, understanding the truth.

'You know ...' she whispered.

'Yes, and the secret is safe with me.'

Matron stroked her chin, and frowned, which made Stella feel sad, so she gave the older woman a light kiss on the lips. Matron's frown turned to a rueful smile. She told Stella that her knowledge was very dangerous, as was Alberta's presence here, in defiance of the ancient Charter of Kernece, which admitted men to the Castle only as the lowest drudges. Stella insisted that she alone was to blame.

'No,' sighed Matron, 'it is Jakes who is to blame. A male with such irresistible power! I take it, Stella – we are both grown-ups – you know what I allude to?'

'I have ... *seen* Jakes, Matron,' said Stella carefully. Matron laughed gently, like a little bird, and stroked Stella's cheek.

'No one just *sees* Jakes,' she said, 'you sweet mossy thing. And I suppose Alberta has told you why he has power?'

'Yes ... I find it hard to believe. Oh, I could believe anything of Clapton, but Miss Dancer ... But, Matron, if Jakes does such things to girls ... Why, from my biology lessons, I do know the likely outcome of such – dalliances.'

'How prettily put! Jakes has power in other ways. His time at sea, and amongst the tribes of the far north, have taught him secrets of the herbs, and mosses and plants. Jakes knows the Parph and her bounty, Stella. There are herbs which Mrs Stopes's Society would love to know about, herbs which harmlessly divert the natural courses of a woman's body – But it's getting late! Miss Dancer herself will be here for her irrigation any moment, and then I have to shut the surgery. Miss Dancer likes to receive a complete irrigation.' She giggled shyly, then sighed again.

'Oh, Stella, I dread to have you strip for me, for I know how I shall feel. And I'll want to be naked with you, and be punished for my naughtiness. Wait – Alberta is due directly after Miss Dancer. You wanted to take irrigation with her. It is proper, if Miss Dancer is chaperone! I'm so excited!'

She telephoned for a drudge, who was sent to find Alberta and summon her promptly for her cleansing. Just as she replaced the receiver, there was a polite knock on the door, and Matron opened it to admit Miss Dancer. Matron, flustered, welcomed the Headmistress, and Stella curtseyed, to Miss Dancer's satisfaction. Once again Stella was aware of the power of Miss Dancer's piercing jade eyes, as she stared coolly at Stella over the rims of her half-moon spectacles. Now, she was dressed as though for the business at hand, still in black, with a simple satin blouse, low-cut to reveal the swelling tops of her pert breasts. She was wearing a short skirt of a lustrous fabric that Stella saw close up was sheer latex. The skirt was very tight, and the rich, firm orbs of Miss Dancer's buttocks were displayed in luscious prominence: Miss Dancer evidently was a stranger to panties. Stella thrilled that if Matron's plan was accepted, she would shortly be witness to their full, splendid nudity alongside her own bare fesses with which Miss Dancer was already intimately familiar. There was no sign of a suspender belt, so her stockings, also of thin black rubber, were tight enough to stay up by themselves. Stella felt envious: belts and straps were such a fuss!

Matron had a hurried, whispered conference with Miss Dancer, and Stella blushed with joy and relief as she saw

Miss Dancer nod her agreement. Miss Dancer looked at her watch and said that the girls must not miss their tea, and Matron said that she had therefore taken the liberty of sending for Alberta already. The Headmistress looked at Matron with a sly smile, and joked that such presumption in one of her girls would merit the sternest punishment.

'But you are not one of my girls, Matron,' she continued smoothly, 'and neither, as it seems Stella has discovered, is sweet Alberta. I do hope you can keep a secret, Stella.'

'My honour as a Kernecian, Miss!' cried Stella proudly.

Miss Dancer smiled, then led the way to the lavage chamber. With surprising nonchalance, she began to unfasten her dress and stockings, allowing Matron to unbutton the blouse as she did so. Stella was enthralled at the spectacle of the smooth rubber hose rolling neatly down the equally smooth naked legs, shining as though no blade of hair had ever disfigured them. And when the skirt dropped into Matron's waiting hand, Stella gasped at the ripeness of Miss Dancer's swelling bare mons. The alabaster skin was as smooth and shiny as the shaven legs: not a hint of hair marred the porcelain purity of that majestic fount, and so big was her swelling that the dimple at her pubic bone was a soft shady cavern. The fount-lips too were of regal splendour: pink folds of shining gentle skin which thrust proudly below the curve of the mons, and whose only coyness was in concealing the soft bulge of Miss Dancer's damsel. Stella suddenly longed to make those folds wet with oil, to slide her finger between them and prise them apart to reveal the delicious erect truth of Miss Dancer's nympha ...

With a start, she heard Miss Dancer chide her for not hurrying to undress herself. Blushing anew, she obeyed, feeling awfully clumsy as she fumbled with straps and hooks and stockings. Matron took her uniform and folded it neatly, and as the two women, nude, positioned themselves by the bank of irrigation devices, Miss Dancer said brightly that they must be well cleansed for Hallowe'en, and especially for Knobkerry Night.

'Then the purifying flames of Up-Helly-A,' she added, licking her lips. 'I have long wanted to unite our three festivals, and the stars have this year been propitious. Thus does celestial harmony lead to terrestrial economy.'

There was a knock on the door, and Stella heard Alberta admitted, with Matron's brief words of explanation. Alberta appeared to hesitate, but Matron responded firmly. When Miss Dancer's name was mentioned, Alberta, blushing, was led into the steamy chamber where the other two women awaited their irrigation with spread legs and raised bottoms.

'Well, Alberta,' said Miss Dancer, 'you have blabbed, and one can scarcely be pleased with you. I dare say a punishment is in order, but for the moment we shall attend to our business. Stella here must exert quite a power over you, to get you to betray your – our – little secret.'

'Not so little, Miss,' said Stella impishly.

'We shall see, Stella,' said Miss Dancer. 'Alberta – strip, Miss, if you please.'

Shyly, Alberta did so, revealing a penis already quivering before the ladies in a delicious state of half-tumescence. Miss Dancer scrutinised the smooth organ, and chuckled to herself, murmuring that Jakes had nothing to be alarmed about. Stella noted with satisfaction that her prescribed gravitational exercise had already begun to work, and Alberta's sex organ was already pleasingly long and distended even in its half-flaccid state. To Stella's surprise, tears welled in Alberta's eyes, and her friend said that it was cruel of Miss Dancer to mock her.

'Oh, Alberta,' said Miss Dancer, putting her hand on Alberta's helmet, which had the effect of stiffening the sex organ further, 'it is a lovely penis. I make no fun of you. Take your place beside your friend Stella.'

Alberta obeyed, and when the three bodies were strapped into place, Matron busied herself with tubes and nozzles.

'I take the complete lavage,' said Miss Dancer, 'that is, in fount and *in ano*; you, Alberta, for obvious reasons, cannot, but you, Stella –'

'No, Miss,' interrupted Matron. 'Stella is virgin.'

'Still?' said Miss Dancer, raising an eyebrow. 'After meeting Jakes, and Alberta too?'

'Y-yes, Miss,' stammered Stella, grimacing as Matron's deft fingers applied jelly to her anus bud and then inserted the first cleansing tube, pushing it quite deep on the first thrust. Matron, dressed in her hygienic rubber once more, exclaimed that Stella's shaft was pleasantly relaxed now, and Miss Dancer's smile became a broad grin. She whispered that she understood, that Stella was indeed a very modern young lady, and that this little party was awfully jolly. Matron turned levers and taps, and positioned jars which looked to Stella like witches' cauldrons, and with great hissings and jets of steam, the irrigations commenced. A huge hard flow of hot soapy liquid flooded Stella's anus, filling her until she felt her belly would burst, and just as she thought she could hold it no more, it was sucked rapidly out, to be instantly replaced by another, hotter stream. Tanks were filled and drained as the three women – for what, Stella thought, was Alberta but a woman, *her* woman? – writhed and squirmed and sighed, straining against their straps with faces flushed hot and blissful. Stella took Alberta's hand and squeezed it, seeing with a little tickle of desire that the penis had risen to its full glorious height. Alberta blushed, and said that it was to do with glands, that the pressure in the bumhole could make a man stand, and even reach orgasm, without his pea vine even being touched! Stella opined that she would be glad to see this in operation, and could no doubt insert the information in her next biology homework for Miss Rose. Alberta, sighing, began to caress Stella's naked breasts, making her nipples tingle and stiffen!

'I shall do my best, Mistress,' said Alberta, and as the gurgling rush of hot and cold fluids seemed to transport her like a frail petal bobbing on the ocean's tumult, Stella felt her fount grow wet. She watched Alberta's penis begin to tremble and stiffen, then a little white droplet appear at the peehole! Caressing Stella's stiff, throbbing nipples excited Alberta, and Stella thrilled that her slave was indeed going to sperm for her! Matron saw it too; face flushed and eyes agleam, she increased the heat and the pressure in Alberta's anus until Alberta's squirming became a veritable dance of discomfort and obvious ecstasy.

'Oh, Matron, you're scalding my bumhole!' she cried. Matron turned a tap, and now Alberta cried that she was freezing. Miss Dancer's hands reached out amid the clouds of steam, and Stella saw them caress Alberta's tight testicles, stroking them and squeezing them as though testing fruit. Liquid cascaded from both Miss Dancer's nether holes, and Stella saw to her amazement that the Headmistress's fingers had crept to her own shaven fount, where she was vigorously rubbing the engorged pink beauty of her huge damsel. Miss Dancer began to moan, no doubt thinking her hands were shrouded in steam, but surely aware that her voice was heard by all. Her regal authority seemed to have dissolved, and she was now no more and no less than a naked woman, writhing in pleasure amid other slippery bodies. It seemed to Stella that the helpless tickling discomfort of irrigation released Miss Dancer from her magisterial shell, and brought her to the beauty of naked freedom: rather like the naked helplessness of a flogging.

Her grip tightened on Alberta's balls, and Alberta moaned, the penis shuddering now with a daemonic energy like a seer about to gush forth in wisdom. Stella could not resist; one hand cupped Miss Dancer's over Alberta's balls, and stroked her as a friend, while her other busied itself on her own throbbing damsel. Her fount was quite wet with hot oil as her giddy fingers tenderly massaged her stiff nympha, sending a stream of slippery liquid over the soft, trembling skin of her inner thighs.

Then Alberta gasped, and her whole body shuddered. She cried out in helpless ecstasy as the penis bucked like a stallion, and a great jet of white creamy sperm cascaded from its peehole. Stella's belly tingled and she felt her body glow with desire and pleasure, as the maddening pressure of the spurting liquids in her anus drove her to masturbate more and more vigorously. The strokes of her fingers matched the jets of sperm which spurted from Alberta's sex organ, like white-capped waves on a whipped sea. Stella had not dreamt that the sperm could spurt so fast, so hard and so far: it was as though the testicles contained some godlike pumping muscle, a daemon or succubus whose strength existed independently of its host.

She looked round and saw that Matron too was masturbating at the spectacle. It was as if all three women, awed and reverent, were witnessing the birth of godlike wisdom in the white seed which flowed from Alberta's throbbing penis. Matron's fingers were locked between her thighs. She was vigorously, even desperately, rubbing at the place where her damsel was, as though trying to pierce her rubber sheath. And then, the three women's cries joined Alberta's, as Stella felt the warmth of her climax surge in her young body, and knew that the others felt the same.

Alberta's cries subsided to sobbing moans. Her sex organ was shiny with sperm, and Stella saw Miss Dancer's hand leave the softened testicles to clasp and rub the softening shaft. Her hand glistened; she placed her fingertips to her fount, and then to her lips, which she anointed with the creamy seed. She then applied her fingertips to Alberta's lips and tongue. Sighing with the hot afterglow of her orgasm, Stella did the same. She felt Alberta's penis sticky and hot, and then the tickling of her slave's tongue against her fingers as it licked her bounty of sperm. With trembling hand, Matron followed suit.

Stella saw twilight in the yard outside the Surgery window. Faintly, in the distance, she heard a seagull's cry. Miss Dancer spoke, her voice dreamlike, as if her nudity and Alberta's sperming had freed her dark female.

'This shall be the best Hallowe'en ever! I remember when Master Jakes first came to us. Ah! I suppose you both know ... About myself, about Clapton, about our secret bodies. It was happy chance that brought us all here. There *was* a man, once, a real man, but he lies in Flanders now. We women must look to ourselves for love. Miss Cox taught me that, years ago, when we played innocently with each other, giggling at commode and touching each other until our touching became more than play. And we whipped each other's bare for our naughtiness, thinking ourselves absolved by the pain – even that was the truest love. Dear Miss Cox!

'What do men bring but destruction and savagery, and ... power? If only all males were as sensible as Alberta, and robed themselves as women! How much serenity and love there would be in this world! Yet still we women must worship that power; of the life tree, the dragon, the long ship's prow, the tower ... The sacred phallus! We have forgotten so much dark wisdom of the old times, but here by the Parph it survives. Up-Helly-A, when the long ship is burnt in sacrifice ... Some say that in olden days a live maiden was bound inside her! Hallowe'en, when witches and warlocks roam, to take their pleasures with mortals. And our gentle modern version of Knobkerry night.'

In response to Stella's and Alberta's raised eyebrows, the Headmistress continued mischievously, 'For the week before Knobkerry Night, the men of the long ships were free to roam the Scotch villages at night, and lift the skirts of any woman they found abroad, then rip off and capture her breeks, or panties! Of course the women were free to remain indoors, where the men were forbidden to go, but few did! Mostly, when they had given up their breeks, they would rush home and reclothe themselves to venture forth again. On Knobkerry Night, the warriors could claim any woman whose panties they held and strap her to the prow of the long ship. She had to take a swiving, or a thrashing on the bare with her own knobkerry! A woman who had lost, or contrived to lose, her breeks to more than one warrior had to take each of them in turn – either a swiving or a naked thrashing. She then had the choice of marrying any one of them: a choice which her chosen warrior was obliged to obey. In this way many advantageous marriages were made, and people have forgotten that the custom was instituted by the women themselves.

'At Kernece, we must do without Norse warriors and the swiving, but we have our knobkerries ... Except the night Master Jakes arrived. That first Night, he won my panties.

He took me to the sacred grove, and bound me to the life tree. Then he flogged me bare, using his monstrous sex organ as a whip! I was inflamed and curious: I begged him to swive me too, and he said he might – such arrogance of the male! – if I took another, proper thrashing with my own knobkerry. I looked at his sex organ which had reddened my bare bum so beautifully, and I felt thrilled with her smarting so that I could not but agree. The beating with my knobkerry frightened me at first, but then I imagined the rod a bigger, more powerful sex organ. I came to a giddy pleasure I had never known before. After I had taken a good three dozen with the knotty cudgel, he parted my cheeks and thighs, and put his rod into my cavern. His huge whip filled me utterly! It was glorious, it was the first time a man was capable of properly swiving me! And for the first time I knew joy.'

Miss Dancer was interrupted by a crash as Surgery door opened, and a familiar voice called for Matron. It was Clapton, and Matron gulped and hurried to obey. The three were still strapped to the irrigation machine, and they heard an urgent conversation, with Matron vainly trying to fend off the newcomer.

'No, Matron,' said Clapton in her calm, menacing, voice, 'I am in a hurry. Tea's over, prep is about to start, and I must get to the Labyrinth to practise my special Hallowe'en knots for the Girl Guides' class. Three of them, you say? Why, I'll join them, we are all girls together!'

Matron was evidently trying to suggest that this was not so, but Clapton burst into the chamber and surveyed the three nude figures through the steam.

'Why, Miss D!' she cried cheerfully. 'With two new squits. Miss Stella, and our Italian lassie! I say, Alberta, what a lovely tight little bum you have! Eminently tawsable! Don't turn away, she'll feel my naked lash soon enough, girl.' She paused, as Alberta vainly squirmed to hide.

'Girl?' said Clapton. 'My, Oh, my . . . This is a disgrace! How can it have happened? Jakes's doing, I'm sure! But I'll have you for this, Dancer. You *knew*!'

Clapton's hand darted to Alberta's flaccid penis, and held it tightly, then moved to squeeze the balls. Matron bustled in, flustered, and pretended not to notice anything untoward as she unfastened the straps of the machine.

'A male at Kernece!' cried Clapton. 'And quite a male! Not quite Jakes, eh, Dancer, but then nobody is! *You* must have known too, Matron!'

Matron said nothing, but sheepishly looked at Miss Dancer for guidance. Stella watched as Alberta's penis, lengthened by the exercises with weights, swelled and began to stand under Clapton's noticeably expert handling. Miss Dancer stood and suddenly slapped Clapton's hand away.

'If you would like to undress for your irrigation, Miss Clapton,' began Matron, but Miss Dancer interrupted her.

'Keep your hands off the male, Clapton!' she cried. 'As for having me, as you put it, only chance and the lottery can "have" me! But you'll suffer for your impudence!'

Her mouth creased in a sneer, Clapton returned Miss Dancer's slap, this time with quite a fierce punch which caught Miss Dancer squarely on her naked breasts. She recoiled in pain and astonishment. In a reflex that was almost immediate, she balled her fist and struck Clapton in her belly. Clapton's sneer deepened.

'So you want to fight, Miss?' she said. 'You'll have to hit better than that.' And again, she dealt a stinging, contemptuous slap to Miss Dancer's breasts. They quivered, to Miss Dancer's evident embarrassment. Her face was red with anger as she lunged at Clapton, and to Stella's surprise, the petite woman managed to topple the larger Clapton by the force of her lunge. Miss Dancer sat on top of Clapton, the two women grappling furiously in the soapy puddles.

'She's mine, you bitch!' hissed Miss Dancer. 'Master Jakes too. I had him first!'

'But I have him whenever I want, slut!' cried Clapton, struggling and slipping in the suds as she tried to escape Miss Dancer's pummelling. Miss Dancer began to rip at Clapton's flimsy clothing: she had come for her irrigation in a simple skirt and blouse, with no underthings, and it was not long before Clapton's clothing was in tatters and her soapy body as naked as her assailant's. Stella was excited by Clapton's powerful nudity.

She was very strong, and her breasts jutted quite prominently, but without any swing, as though they were all muscle, rather like Jamie's. The nipples were quite wide, but flat like hard brown pennies. Her thighs, too, were honed to athletic tautness, and rippled as she squirmed under her drubbing. The belly was a flat slab, and under it her mink was unshaven and unadorned except by flecks of steely grey like those of her close-cropped head. But her mink had more hair than her head! Stella knew that she herself was blessed with a lush mink, and had become proud of it; now she wondered if hers compared to Clapton's. It seemed an acre of thick scrubby hair, that sprawled over half her belly, unlike Stella's forest of soft silky curls. It was as though the factotum wore the very Parph at her fount!

Both women flailed, their naked limbs entwined like some writhing sea-monster, and Miss Dancer's fury seemed to erupt from a deep resentment of her servant and colleague. Jakes, and his huge manhood, seemed to be the issue, and Stella wondered why they could not be happy sharing him, as Jakes evidently had enough lustful energy to share with all. Her fists mercilessly pummelled Clapton's face and breasts, and even dealt powerful blows on the lips of her fount, causing Clapton to jerk and squirm in very real discomfort.

It was as though Miss Dancer did not mind Jakes 'fooling' with drudges and new squits, or even with Matron, and, Stella had no doubt, Miss Noble, Miss Rose and the others. But for Clapton, who was almost an equal, to claim supremacy over Jakes hit her too near the bone. But her fury did her no good, for it was clear that Clapton's powerful muscles could with one spring of uncoiled force overturn her tormentor.

And so it happened: with a terrible scream of rage, Clapton hurled the smaller woman from her, and leapt up, slithering in the soapy puddles. She grasped Miss Dancer's hair, which she pulled fiercely back, causing Miss Dancer to shriek and lose her balance. Clapton's other arm darted between Miss Dancer's thighs, and pinioned her by a tight grip on her fount-lips. She squeezed them most brutally and held her opponent thus immobile, the hair and fount locked in an unbreakable grip. Stella, Matron and Alberta watched the contest with terrified fascination, and Stella found herself excited by the brute spectacle of the two naked women fighting. Her fount began to moisten, quite copiously! And she saw that Alberta's penis was rock-hard!

Clapton rose to her full height, her breath harsh, holding Miss Dancer off the floor by her hair and still squeezing her lady's place with white knuckles. Stella momentarily saw her as a Norse berserker of old. The three stood in awe of the imperturbable Clapton's new ferocity. From Miss Dancer's throat came a piteous mewling as her dark hair strained at its roots, and Stella felt awfully sorry for her. The tableau seemed frozen in time, full of awful possibility. Then, suddenly, Clapton gave a profound wail of sorrow, and placed Miss Dancer gently on the floor before hugging her fiercely in her bear-like arms.

'Oh, Miss Dancer, my love, how could I do such a thing?' she moaned. 'I am sorry, so sorry, for my horrid vicious temper! After all our friendship, how could we let a mere male come between us? Wretched Jakes, with his stupid big cock – he is yours! If only you'll forgive me!'

Stella was quite astounded at this turnabout, the more so as she saw Clapton did not remove her hand from Miss Dancer's fount; rather she softened her grasp, so that her hand was now caressing and stroking Miss Dancer's open fount-lips most fondly and tenderly! Stella saw Clapton's thumb reach for the damsel, and press hard, so that Miss Dancer moaned too and began to cover Clapton's lips with eager kisses, while burying her hand in Clapton's thick mink

'There is nothing to forgive, Clapton,' she murmured, 'for it is I who am at fault. I should have told you! But you know Jakes's power. He shall suffer, I promise. Meanwhile, I must be punished for leaving you in ignorance.'

The two combatants were oblivious to the others as their loving hands stroked and pinched buttocks, founts, and breasts. Their heads bobbed as lips found their way to stiffening nipples and trembling bellies. Miss Dancer gasped that although Hallowe'en was on the morrow, tonight would have been the postponed Knobkerry Night, and therefore she had authority to declare it unpostponed.

'The festivities may start now,' she moaned, as Clapton knelt to tongue her damsel, her deft fingers masturbating her own fount as she did so. 'Oh – don't stop!' She looked round with lust-sugared eyes at her enthralled spectators.

'We are five, the sacred number of the pentangle. It is a quorum, and we may begin. First, Clapton, you must whip me soundly. Yes! Don't argue, and don't take your tongue from my clit yet. Please, please make me come! And punish me more for taking such pleasure! You must tie me, bind me with the tightest knots. There is no need to go to the Labyrinth for your practice. And then, my whipping – on my bare, and hard, if you please. Oh, I'm coming! Oh, your sweet tongue, my angel – whip my clit with your tongue! Oh, yes! *Yes*!'

As Miss Dancer shuddered in her orgasm, with juices trickling shiny and sweet all down her thighs, Clapton on all fours with thighs spread wide, emitted a little squeal. Her fingers drummed the stiff, engorged 'clit' (Stella found the word exciting!) which peeped like a lovely soldier's helmet from the thick lips of her swollen fount. When both women's moans of delight had subsided into quiet purring, they embraced each other and kissed anew. Then Clapton ordered the willing, and now inflamed, spectators, to assist in Miss Dancer's binding. Stella's fount was unashamedly flowing with the juices of her excitement, and she surmised that Matron was the same, while Alberta's penis stood as hard as an oak.

Matron ventured that it was unfair to leave them out of the festivities. 'I am as guilty as Miss Dancer,' she insisted. 'I should be whipped, and harder!' Her eyes gleamed as she spoke, and her face was flushed. Stella too wanted to feel the muscled arms of Clapton expertly flogging her, which she was sure would be very hard indeed. She was attracted to the woman, now that she had seen both her hard male side, and her soft female submission to the joy of orgasm. She knew that Matron's bottom felt the same tingling lust for whipping as her own. Miss Dancer, once more the Headmistress, even in her willing submission to Clapton's rod, agreed that Matron too deserved whipping. But, she explained, it would be awkward for Clapton to whip them both satisfactorily at the same time.

'Lace me first, I beg you!' cried Matron. This too was agreed. Stella, though, was full with the wanton aroma of lust that scented the steam of the bathroom, and dared to demand some reward for her *own* naughtiness. Clapton murmured that Miss Stella was a spunky filly, for a new squit.

'Then my reward shall be my punishment, too!' cried Stella. 'For my insolence, you shall *all* flog me!'

Stella smiled so sweetly that no one dared refuse her, though Clapton murmured that she suspected Miss of being a sub. Then, all eyes turned to Alberta, who seemed nervous.

'Please do not whip me,' Alberta said in a small voice.

'No,' said Clapton thoughtfully. 'You are the cause of all our improprieties, young lady, so your punishment shall be something else. We shall make you into a man! It is Knobkerry Night, by Miss Dancer's decree, and while Matron has tawses and canes aplenty, I'm afraid we have no knobkerry. So you, Alberta, shall be our knobkerry!'

With that, Clapton ordered the others to seize Alberta and hold her down on her back while she fetched her twine and ropes. She returned with a bountiful armoury of hemp, and, ignoring Alberta's pleas for mercy, began to bind the balls and penis! Stella and the other women watched in ecstatic fascination as Clapton's fingers whirled in a kaleidoscope of sheepshanks, half-whips, bowlines and reefs. Alberta's penis was soon wrapped in twine and grew into a huge, bulging shaft that bristled with artful lumps, striations and curlicues – just like a real cudgel, but with the tiniest aperture at the tip. The whole engine was anchored firmly to the penis with a criss-cross of tight loops around Alberta's ball-sac.

Stella gasped: there seemed no end to Clapton's art as Alberta's penis became a veritable tree of hard knots, as big as – no, bigger than! – the mighty sex organ of Jakes. She wondered why the size of the penis exerted such a fascination over her woman's heart. Was it as a symbol of power, or because a mighty tree brought forth more fruit? Although, a sapling whipped more painfully . . .

Clapton pronounced herself satisfied with her work, then warned Alberta that if her sex organ softened at all beneath the fearsome knotted exterior, she would get the harshest bare whipping any Kernecian had ever received. Alberta put her hands on her hips, looked down at her massive new penis and said smugly there would be no need of that. Now it was the turn of Miss Dancer and Matron to be trussed for their chastisements. Matron thankfully peeled off her hygienic rubber garments – Stella saw her panties were soaking wet! – and, after fetching a veritable Harrod's emporium of tawses and canes, lay naked beside the Headmistress. Clapton took the thicker cords, and said she would bind each woman differently, for sport. There was no need for them to be restrained, as they spread their bare limbs eagerly for the ropes. Matron was to be tawsed, and Clapton said she would 'crab' her. Matron lay on her belly with her thighs well splayed, and was told to bend her arms behind her back.

She did this, her wrists pressed together at the small of her back, in a twisted mockery of prayer. Clapton bound the wrists together. From them, she looped another rope tightly around Matron's breasts, producing a pair of heavy clothes pegs which she pinned to Matron's nipples! Stella thought this pretty tough, for the rope from her wrists was fastened to the clothes pegs; so if Matron attempted to move her arms, she would feel considerable discomfort on her clamped nipples. Taking her by the ankles, Clapton slowly bent her legs back until her calves were pressing her thighs. She did not stop: the thighs were now lifted, and forced upwards and back to a degree Stella thought incredible, until her ankles touched her elbows. Two knots fastened her ankles to the elbows, and two further ropes stretched the short distance from ankles to bound wrists. The thighs remained well splayed like the wings of a butterfly so that Matron's fount gaped pink and open. Her straining calves and forearms were a pretty frame for the buttocks awaiting their tawse-strokes.

Clapton then said that she would 'clam' Miss Dancer. She instructed her to sit and cross her ankles, which Clapton tied, and bend forward until her head was cradled by her thighs and calves. In this humbled position, Miss Dancer was turned over and Clapton knelt on the backs of her knees so that her thighs were pressed on to her breasts. Her head actually peeped through the frame of thigh and calf, her bound ankles cradling the back of her neck! Her arms were then taken and wrapped across her breast, with her wrists fitted under her armpits, and fingers almost touching her toes. Her wrists were bound together by a series of knots across her upper back, and each wrist was then bound to each ankle, in a crisscross of ropes about six inches long.

Miss Dancer's bare-shorn fount was spread wide. Stella's own fount grew wet at the sight of the thick parted lips with the glistening pink flesh within, and the hard, swollen cherry of her damsel now exposed in sweet trembling nudity. Miss Dancer's thighs and buttocks were stretched bare and helpless for the cane, so tightly bound that she would be unable to gain even the small satisfaction of wriggling to soothe the pain of the lash on her bare skin. The bodies of both trussed women glistened with the soapy water in which they lay, crab and clam in their pools!

The floggings began. Clapton took Matron first, selecting the thickest tawse with a tip splayed into four tongues of hard leather. She positioned herself behind Matron's fesses, so that she could drive the tawse on her vertically, the leather snaking down on Matron's spread buttocks and thighs, and dangerously close to her vulnerable lady's place. One false move and Clapton's tawse would land right on Matron's exposed fount! Miss Dancer's eyes were bright as she saw Clapton complete the preparation: she gagged Matron by stuffing her captive's panties into her own mouth, upon which Matron sighed – not with protest, but in satisfaction. Miss Dancer went 'Mm! Mm!' as though *she* were gagged, or wanted to be, and soon she was. As she had no panties, she took Stella's in her mouth, which made Stella proud.

It was marvellous to watch the ripple of Clapton's naked muscles as she tawsed her tethered captive. Sweat poured in rivers down her body as she lifted the tawse to the very height of her arm. She then delivered a fierce lash both to Matron's buttocks and upon the exposed insides of her thighs, the tenderest and most painful place Stella could imagine. She shivered at the thought of being flogged there – it would be awful, like being breast-whipped! But her fount tingled with warm moisture at the dreadful thought, for her heart told her she craved such humiliation.

Clapton expertly flicked the tawse so that its wicked tips swished the air just a glance from Matron's fount-lips, before cracking on the stretched bare arse-skin. Balanced on her belly, Matron was unable to cry out, or wriggle, or even to flinch. She took a full hundred strokes of the tawse.

Panting heavily, Clapton threw the instrument aside. Stella could see that she too was excited by the beating; her eyes were thin slits of desire and her nostrils flared in her reddened face. She looked at her work, the crimson mass of skin that was Matron's beaten croup, and her belly twitched. Her hand moved as though involuntarily towards her mink, but then stopped and reached instead towards the assortment of canes. Miss Dancer looked up expectantly as Clapton tried a few, swishing them with a fearsome whistle. She finally selected a thin, whippy cane about four feet in length and with a crook handle, for Miss Dancer's punishment. She lifted it above Miss Dancer's proffered buttocks, and was about to deliver the first stroke, then paused, frowning.

'Wait!' she cried hoarsely. 'What about *my* punishment, Miss? I struck you, remember? Miss Stella has bagged a juicy flogging for herself – it's only fair that I should receive one too! I've made Miss Alberta a fine knobkerry, and ...'

Miss Dancer was unable to answer through her gag, but Alberta now spoke, with face and eyes inflamed by lust.

'I'll beat you well with my knobkerry, Clapton,' she said, 'and I promise you'll regret asking for it!'

There was something in Alberta's imperious, and utterly masculine, tone that hushed the women. Clapton bowed her head and whispered, 'Very well, Miss. Thank you', before setting to the caning of her Headmistress.

The first lash descended on Miss Dancer's helpless nates, laying a thin mark of vivid crimson. Like Matron, she was bound so that she could not flinch nor squirm, and Stella saw her eyes water at the force of the stroke. The first was followed rapidly by another – on the backs of the thighs this time, which made her sob behind her gag. Thereafter she was silent, but her body shuddered at each cut, which began to redden her nates and the tender soft thigh-skin in a pretty diamond pattern. Stella shuddered too, for she knew that cuts to the thigh-skin hurt more than anything. Suddenly she noticed that Matron was jerking and wobbling on her belly, and that no one had thought to release her.

She stooped to do so, but Matron shook her head and grunted through her gag. She did not want to be released, but to swivel, the better to watch the chastisement. Stella obliged, and saw Alberta position herself behind Clapton, hands on her hips and waist writhing as if her whole body was a whip. Alberta swung her hempen knobkerry with such force that it cracked quite loudly on Clapton's buttocks, making her pause in mid-stroke, and sigh with satisfaction. The knobs and striations of her penis-adornment were really quite sharp, and though the knobkerry could not have the force of a cane or even a tawse, it nevertheless left a pleasing crimson on Clapton's naked croup.

Alberta's waist gyrated rapidly, alternating fierce backward and forward strokes, so that for every lash Clapton bestowed on Miss Dancer's globes, she received two on her own. Stella marvelled at her slave's balletic grace as she penis-flogged Clapton, and soon Clapton's fesses were quite as red as Matron's or Miss Dancer's. Stella itched with the desire for her own chastisement, and wished they would hurry to get to her turn. Looking down at Matron, who was moaning in pleasure and excitement, she saw that there was a veritable torrent of shiny love-juice cascading from the parted lips of her fount! Stella could not resist. She knelt and put her lips to the swollen shiny fount-lips. Matron groaned loudly, and Stella began to lick her hard, then found the engorged stiff damsel and flicked the throbbing tip with her tongue. Matron jerked and squealed as Stella tongued her, at the same time rubbing her own stiff clit.

My damsel, she thought, Oh, my *clit*! She is so lovely, for these are such lovely words for her ...

She masturbated until she knew she was at her orgasmic plateau. From Matron's moans of joy and the flow of love-oil which drenched Stella's lips and tongue, she knew that she was going to bring Matron to a climax. Clapton looked round suddenly and smiled at her, as her own fesses squirmed and danced at Alberta's fiery assault.

'Yes!' cried Dancer, 'Oh, yes, Miss Stella! Who needs males, the ugly brutes?'

Suddenly Alberta responded by ceasing the flogging and grabbing Clapton's swinging breasts by the nipples, quite roughly, to pull her down into a bending over position.

'I'll show you, bitch!' cried Alberta with a fierce male dominance that quite thrilled Stella. 'I'll show you what you need! Keep flogging your girly friend, while I ...'

Alberta slapped Clapton's trembling fesses and prised them firmly apart, revealing her anus bud, then reached to Clapton's fount and rubbed her vigorously.

'You're wet for it, bitch!' he cried triumphantly, and rubbed his knobkerry with the oils from Clapton's fount until the hempen cords shone brightly. Then he put his knobkerry squarely on the bud. With two or three hard thrusts, he pushed his gnarled man-shaft deep into her fundament. Clapton groaned, but did not resist, and her caning of Miss Dancer took on a new vigour as Alberta administered a powerful fucking to the woman's anus.

Stella was dripping with excited juices as she watched, and she knew that masturbating herself was no longer enough to bring her to fruition. Rolling Matron's trussed body on to her side, she slithered her legs in a scissors to clasp Matron's torso, and with one foot on her neck, she ripped the gag from Matron's mouth with her toes. Then Stella put her toes right into her mouth, where Matron at once began to tickle her with a delicious sucking. At the same time, Stella positioned her own fount so that it pressed tightly against Matron's, and she felt their juices mingle like two rivers of beauty. Their clits met, and Stella shuddered with a spasm of pure electric joy as the two throbbing stiff damsels flicked against each other like swordsmen's rapiers.

Matron was the first to come to orgasm, and Stella's climax followed soon afterwards, both their bodies twisting and jerking in the flood of pleasure that accompanied this delicious clit-fucking. She heard Alberta cry out too, in orgasm, and Clapton's voice became a crescendo of rapid shrieks. Stella was dazed with her joy, drenched in sweat, and oblivious to everything except the pulse of her own young pleasure as she felt unseen hands grasp her. She was spread face down, her fesses parted.

Her arms were positioned behind her, and her wrists fastened. She felt stern ropes tightly coil her legs and torso, and heard the slapping of hard knots pinning and locking her into a wonderful contortion, so that she felt like the folded petals of a rose. She gasped with muffled joy and fear as she felt the massive knobbed engine of Alberta's penis tickle her open anus bud, then thrust forcefully inside her, filling her soft innards right to the core. Alberta began to fuck her in the anus as other fingers and tongues vied to tickle her swollen, throbbing clit. Stella was delirious with joy; the hempen cock filled her utterly, and her fount flowed with love oil, which she felt trickle hot and wet on her straining thighs. She cried out in delight at her submission: she was taking it, and being joyfully, wondrously *taken*!

A tawse descended on her taut bare buttocks, and then there was a cane-stroke, followed by a smarting slap from a bare hand, then a stinging lash from the stiff knobkerry. She was held down, and it was her pleasure to submit thus. The whipping grew more intense, and her cries of real pain and her piteous pleas for mercy went scorned or unheeded – as she intended them to be. The strokes of cane and tawse seared her naked bottom with white-hot pleasure, and she wriggled and squirmed, straining against her tight bonds to show her captors how much their tormented, willing plaything she was. Her anus was filled, her fountlips wide and licked, chewed and nuzzled, and her clit tickled unbearably with the caresses of tongue, breast, toe and finger. She was a slave, a plaything, and at this knowledge she felt herself shudder in the most intense orgasm she could ever remember. She seemed to float on a hot cloud of joy, outside time and space. She heard herself shriek long and loud.

'Oh! Oh! Ooh ...! My ladies, do not trouble yourself who owns Jakes or any man, for *I* am *everybody's* ...'

'Yes,' said Alberta, her voice soft and female one more, 'who needs men? Vicious beasts! We ladies can pleasure ourselves.'

'Who needs men?' echoed Miss Dancer. 'Well, Stella?'

'Speak up, Miss, you wet little sub!' added Clapton harshly. 'Men? Fuck the monsters! I wish we had one here, to show him what for!'

'Please whip me harder, ladies,' cried Stella faintly, feeling that the wash of her orgasm would never ever leave her. 'Please don't stop! Make my bum as red as lipstick!'

'Men! Who needs them?' cried the others in exultant unison, as together the women flogged their girly's writhing bare globes. There was a soft click as the door opened.

'I think you all do, ladies,' drawled a familiar, insolent voice. It was Jakes.

12

Drudge

'And what have you made of our friend Stella?' said Jakes. 'Clapton's trussing, and how the poor bitch squirms! A *mussel*, I think. And a mussel with quite a beard.' He grinned at Stella's sweat-soaked mink, all damp and straggly above the open pink lips of her glistening fount.

'Cousin Alberta, they've made you a knobkerry, how awfully sweet! But I believe *this* is what you want, ladies, in your girly pretence at sport!'

Jakes was wearing a knee-length 'kilt', of heavy work cotton, and he lifted it to reveal his naked genitals. He grasped his enormous penis and began to whirl it insolently round and round like a child's paper windmill. Miss Dancer and Clapton looked at each other, and then at Jakes, daggers in their eyes. Stella saw that her companions, including Alberta, were not minded to tolerate arrogance, and were sincere in their cries of triumphant womanhood. It was not the moment for Jakes to strut; yet strut he did.

'Just broke in a filly,' he chirped. ' Florence Tate – my, did she have a tight box! Not like you two old girls with your aircraft hangars for lairs!' Subtlety, Stella surmised, was not a strong point of Jakes's.

'I thought I was going to split her! But she couldn't get enough. Lovely girl, squealed like a piglet when I inserted! There's something about a virgin, one gives you an appetite for another, and I thought of little Stella here, the Kernece football. They told me where you'd gone, Miss, and here you are all trussed and ready for me.'

As he spoke, the whip of his penis had hardened until it stood hard and menacing so that he was no longer able to whirl it round. Stella sighed in resignation; Jakes had been on the point of taking her virginity, in the tuckshop, and Stella had thought it her fate to submit. But chance had sent Miss Dancer to interrupt! Afterwards, she thought that her flower was fated to be plucked by Jamie. Now it seemed that fate had sent Jakes again! It was awfully confusing.

Well, her fount *was* deliciously wet, yearning to be filled, and that was perhaps fate as well. But she had not foreseen the outraged femininity of Miss Dancer and Clapton.

'Stay away from Stella!' barked Miss Dancer, raising her cane as though in attack. 'She is virgin, and you shan't have her, Jakes! Clapton, untie the virgin. Jakes, your insolence shall not go unpunished this time.'

Jakes watched in his own confusion as Clapton speedily undid the knots that bound Stella. She stood up, rubbing herself where the knots had bitten; especially her bottom, which had been bitten by more than mere knots, and glowed a lovely flaming red. Stella grinned proudly! Jakes perked up, thinking the grin was for him.

'Come on, Stella, you know you are gasping for it,' he said crudely. 'Part those thighs for me, and feel a real cock in your cunt. First time is never forgotten, and I've already knocked on the door of your cherry, remember? I'll have plenty of spunk left for these other cunts afterwards, but cousin Alberta will just have to watch and diddle that tiny dick of hers.'

Although Stella thought 'cunt' a lovely word – how could it be otherwise, when it described such a lovely place? – the other ladies evidently did not. Diplomacy was not the strong point of the arrogant Jakes; complacency was, and it was his undoing. As if by a silent command, Miss Dancer, Alberta, and Clapton seized him by the arms and legs and forced him to the floor. He struggled helplessly, his penis (to Stella's eyes) sadly wilting. She felt sorry for him! She remembered his sudden gentleness when she had said a kind word after their embraces in the tuckshop:

that he was unused to receiving kindness from ladies. So, Stella thought, he has to put on this rough male façade, this false carapace of arrogance. If only I could have him to myself, to tame and dress him, and make him my slave!

'The male Jakes, with his obscene sex organ, is the cause of our women's misfortunes,' muttered Miss Dancer as though to herself.

'Let's teach him a lesson!' cried Alberta, family loyalty destroyed by genital insult. 'Flog his bum till he squeals!'

'Not enough,' hissed Clapton. 'Besides, he might enjoy it. I'll kick his balls for him, he won't like that. It hurts a male an awful lot, like a blow to the funny-bone.'

She drew back her foot, ready to kick the helpless male. Alberta blanched and quavered that it was too harsh a punishment, and Stella saw that the male in her recoiled at the enormity of such a blow: mysteriously, far more painful than an assault on the funny-bone.

'No,' said Miss Dancer. 'We'll punish him tomorrow, at the celebrations. Take him to the Labyrinth and bind him, let him stew as he dreams of all he's going to suffer. And you will suffer, Jakes,' she spat, 'for all your ... For everything you've ... Oh, take him down, I can't bear it!'

'I'll kick the bastard just once,' said Clapton, and as her leg was about to whip a ferocious blow to Jakes's precious soft balls, Stella suddenly interposed herself. She grabbed Clapton's leg and twisted it so that Clapton fell heavily. She cried out and punched Stella in the breasts, making them shiver, and Stella felt a severe pain, so without thinking she struck back. She hit Clapton in the belly and on her fount. She felt urgent hands pull her away, and she stood, panting, in front of Miss Dancer, who reached solemnly for her plain spectacles! She was the Headmistress again, all the sport of the last hours forgotten.

'Stella Shawn,' she said, 'you have struck a College servant, and interfered with the execution of her duties, which is unforgivable. You will be taken with the miscreant Jakes to the Labyrinth. There you will don the uniform of a drudge and await your punishment tomorrow. After your punishment, you shall witness the painful punishment of your *friend* Jakes, and shall wear drudge's uniform ever after. Stella Shawn, I sentence you to join the Remove!' After a brief pause, she added rather petulantly that Florence Tate was to be dressed as a drudge, and join the Remove as well. 'You mean, the drudges *are* the Remove?' stammered Stella.

'Rich bitches, and subs all of them,' sneered Clapton. 'You'll be quite at home there, Miss, if you survive your punishment.' She laughed deep in her throat.

'All I did was to protect Jakes and his lovely manhood,' Stella sobbed. 'It doesn't seem fair, but – yes, I'll gladly take my punishment, Miss. Please tell me what it is to be?' Miss Dancer smiled thinly: Stella sensed that she was taking revenge both on Jakes and herself for her own weakness in submitting to womanly lusts.

'The Steps, Stella,' she said quietly. 'Running the Tawse – *all* the Steps, right to the top of Kernece Tower.'

'That has never been done before,' said Matron, her face pale. 'Not even in the days of Tawser Bright!'

'No, it hasn't, has it?' smiled Miss Dancer.

Trembling, Stella followed the curious party across the dark yard, to the steps where, it seemed so long ago, Morag had led her to the secret punishment room. She shivered in her Poppilian uniform, which seemed skimpy and inadequate in the cold that heralded a northern winter, although her stockings were quite snug. But she reflected that a drudge's drab would probably be colder still, and she would not have silk stockings. Jakes, carried by Matron, Clapton and Alberta, had stopped struggling. He hung limply in their cradling arms, his clothing decorously shielding his nudity from the curious glances of the few passing Kernecians. Stella realised she had missed tea, and was hungry. She was also missing Prep, and would miss cocoa and buns – and, no doubt, bedtime in the cosy Poppy's dorm. Even the Bull's bark would seem friendly to her now. How could her friends turn so suddenly against her? Miss Dancer preceded them, lighting candles and switching on the sparse electric bulbs to illumine their gloomy passage through the Labyrinth.

Stella felt a tear: all she longed for was to be loved, and serve her friends. Then she felt better: if she excelled herself as a drudge, then she *would* serve them, and would be loved! The first thing, though, was to find out what Clapton had in mind for Jakes, and to help him. She had just now seen the fervour which could grip women, and suspected that when the celebrations began in earnest, the darkest and most destructive passions could be loosed.

They passed cells from which Stella heard, or imagined she could hear, the most fearful groans. Or was it the grim shadowy lights playing tricks on her imagination? The squeaks of bats above the cobwebbed rafters were no trick, as she jumped at a bat's sudden whirling inches past her face. They came to an empty cell, into which Jakes was carried by Clapton and Alberta, his protests and wriggling having begun once more. But it was all to no avail, as the heavy door slammed shut behind him. Stella shuddered; Miss Dancer said she and Matron would be back in a moment, once they had dealt with Stella. After many twisting corridors and stumbling on broken floors, Miss Dancer produced a large key and opened a door which was three times the size of any cell. Beyond, Stella could hear moans, but also cries of play, laughter, and argument. Miss Dancer grinned benignly.

'Your new home, Stella, perhaps for longer than you imagine. The Remove Dorm.'

Matron protested feebly, but bravely, that Stella had had no tea or tuck, and Miss Dancer replied that the drudges knew how to look after themselves.

'Welcome to the Remove, Miss Shawn,' she said, gently pushing Stella inside. The door boomed as it shut after her.

At first, there was cacophony. The Remove Dorm was much bigger than Poppy's Dorm, and much more crowded. Stella thought herself in a dungeon rather than a dorm, or even a London Underground station at rush hour (she had experienced Piccadilly on one of her visits to the National Gallery). It was not a bare cube of a room, like an ordinary dorm, but a twisting jumble of bulges, nooks and crannies, with uneven floors and haphazard lighting.

It was rather as though several dorms had been knocked together to make one. The throng of girls were laughing or wrestling, sleeping, eating, or begging to eat, weeping softly, or playing excited games of chance. Stella had expected a cowed, sullen mass of drudges, but these seemed well occupied. A few heads were lifted at the door's opening, but no one paid her much attention. Underprefects prowled the mêlée casually flicking tawses and barking largely unheeded orders. There were sloppy palliasses ranged around the walls, or piles of tattered clothing, and these seemed to be the beds. She found an empty palliasse in a corner, and sank down to rest.

She noticed that the door opened and closed a lot, with much coming and going, indeed like a railway station. The faces were unfamiliar: the Remove did not normally contain first-years. There were little cubicles and offices, with telephones in them, which would ring frequently, when an Under-prefect would should 'Drudge!' followed by a name, and a destination. The named girl would then scurry to put together the semblance of a drudge's uniform before embarking on her errand. These Under-prefects did not have the discontented look of the ones at Poppy's, for here they were evidently true Mistresses of this chaotic underworld. The electric lights overhead were quite bright, and Stella sensed that they were never turned off. In all the hubbub, the word 'Hallowe'en' cropped up frequently.

Even in the underworld, there was a hierarchy. Some girls were piteously naked, their clothing presumably stolen by older or stronger girls. If summoned as drudges, they had to beg for a uniform, promising favours which Stella sensed were quite ominous. However, since the dorm was quite hot and stuffy, being naked seemed to Stella a desirable state. She saw some haughty girls nude, who were not piteous, but whose fesses or backs were well crimsoned with lashes. She guessed from their boldness that whipped girls were permitted the comfort of nudity, and perhaps a certain freedom of unseemliness already paid for.

Some favours were paid at once, and to Stella's astonishment, the older or more powerful girl would often lift her skirt to reveal her fount naked for a quick 'diddling' with tongue or fingers! This was carried on quite shamelessly, and she saw that many girls lying on their palliasses were openly diddling themselves. Or else they were couched with two or three others, engaging in what Stella thought the most pleasant practices, had their surroundings been less squalid and less public. It was as though the very shamelessness of intimate acts performed in full view of all lent an excitement to the acts themselves,

There were fights and pleading over the humblest scraps of tuck, and as if the discipline of cane and tawse were not enough, the dorm was liberally furnished with stark, ugly punishment cages. Most of these contained girls bound in various positions of chastisement. Some of the young women squatted clammed or crabbed, but most were vertically suspended. They hung by chains from armpits, nipple clamps on painfully stretched breasts, or bent double at the waist; and sometimes, upside down, from the ankles. All were nude except for bonds of varying discomfort and intricacy, which Stella supposed reflected the gravity of their offence.

Arms and legs were strapped into positions of grotesque discomfort, mouths were clamped with heavy steel gags, and some were hooded in black rubber. As well as nipple clamps, she saw clamps for the fount-lips themselves: one miscreant was hung upside down, gagged and masked, suspended by chains from her waist, clamped nipples, ankles, and fount-lips! Her arms were forced behind her, tethered by the wrists to the roof of her cage; her naked back and fesses were purple with tawsing. All her bonds were tight, and the victim shifted constantly as she tried to ease her discomfort. She was not helped by the haughty girls who amused themselves by throwing rotten fruit and cake at her helpless body, scraps of which were promptly fought over by the squalling naked drudges, who were themselves frequently punished for their rowdiness, to be bound and pelted in their turn!

Some of the punishments were impish rather than gruesome, although still evidently uncomfortable. One girl was 'secretary spider', as Stella learnt from the excited chatter around her. She craned her neck and saw an unfortunate girl trussed so that all her limbs were bound into an oval ball, like a black egg, or a spider contracting itself for protection. She was gagged and masked thus, and entirely sheathed in black shiny rubber, with only her naked fount-lips visible. In this position she was suspended from the roof of her cage by a single strand which looped around her breasts and armpits. She hung scarcely an inch from the floor, and was obliged to swing herself back and forth in order to moisten postage stamps with the lips of her fount!

The stamps were placed singly by the leering Underprefect in the most awkward recesses of her cage. The unfortunate girl knew when a stamp had been successfully moistened only by the cheers of the crowd, which redoubled when a dearth of excited juices at her fount – and Stella understood that to be bound thus *was* exciting – caused her to take recourse in a more effective, but less appealing method. She would make a trickle of commode, at which she earned gleeful yells of 'poo!' and usually a few strokes with the tawse on her wobbling bottom. The moistened stamps were promptly stuck to big buff envelopes, and Stella grinned as she wondered if the nation's loving parents knew how their Kernece prospectus brochures had been packed.

There were flogging pillars, too, with straps and masks for the unfortunate victims. From her corner, Stella witnessed a particularly harsh beating with six-foot canes. The recipient was bound upside down to a long pole, like a telephone pole, with rubber straps the whole length of her legs and very tightly around her breasts, with buttocks and shoulders left bare. Once hanging, her face was fastened into a gagging mask at the bottom of the pole and, like this, she was flogged by two Under-prefects at once, each on either side of her inert body. To the great cheers of the throng, one tormentor applied her cane to the girl's shoulders, while the other attended to the exposed fesses. As the strokes landed two at a time, the sheathed body jerked and writhed like a shiny black electric eel. Stella counted to forty-three strokes before she dozed off into an exhausted sleep.

She was woken by a rough shaking of her shoulders.

'What . . .?' she muttered, shielding herself from a dazzling torch beam. The overhead lights had been dimmed, though not extinguished, and though the Dorm still bustled, most of the occupants seemed intent on slumber.

'You're on my bed, you fucking new squit!' growled a familiar voice, then burst into peels of laughter.

It was Morag! Tenderly, she kissed Stella's lips, then lay down beside her and embraced her. This pleased and excited Stella, for Morag was quite naked. She saw on Morag's body the livid crimson of a recent flogging, both on her shoulders and bottom, and her fingers flew to her lips as she cried 'Oh!' in horrified sympathy. Morag laughed more.

'It was nothing! Didn't you see me going to bat for those two mossy Under-pre's? They can't flog for toffee. Going to bat,' she explained to the puzzled Stella. 'Hanging upside down, like a bat!'

As if in sympathy, the bats squeaked at each other, high in the rafters.

'Oh, Morag, it must have been awful,' murmured Stella, running her hands lightly over Morag's reddened buttocks. 'What are you doing here? How long . . .?'

'The bat's nothing!' answered Morag airily. 'And you can be nude, afterwards, and don't have to drudge. It's quite decent here, really, because the Under-pre's have all been drudges themselves. I've been here a week. A little dispute in class with *la* Marsham. I told her she was a rotten bolshevik.'

'The Remove, just for that! A beating, yes, but . . .'

'Then I told her all the bolshies ought to be shot.'

'Even so . . . The Steps, perhaps.'

'Then I said she was aptly named because her cunt was so narrow only a rose stem would fit up it, and she was the only woman in Kernece Jakes refused to fuck.'

'I see. Rather insulting.'

'Not just that. When I agreed to apologise, I said that last part was a lie! Never mind, what are *you* doing here?'

Stella explained everything, including Alberta, and at once Morag became very serious. After enquiring about Stella's rumbling stomach, and providing her with a welcome feast of stale sandwiches and scraps of cake, she said that they must do something about Jakes's plight.

'You'll run the Steps with ease, Stella, my Mistress, even though you'll have a very sore bum afterwards. But I *know* you can take it. You'll even like being a drudge, you beastly sub, you!'

She kissed Stella, who blushed. It was true!.

'But I suspect Clapton has it in for Jakes. She hates him for having her in the thrall of that giant cock. Who knows what she has in mind? Hallowe'en, and Up-Helly-A, and Knobkerry Night – They are wild enough on their own, but all at once! Anything can happen. I think Clapton wants to rid Kernece of the cause of her bewitching, and have revenge too. Alberta must watch out. We'll have to free Jakes – who knows what they've done to him already? Clapton's probably kicked his balls – Oh! I can't bear to think about it.'

Stella said that Miss Dancer would probably restrain Clapton for the moment, but she wondered how they were to gain egress from the Remove Dorm. Morag scoffed that it was easy, she had only to wait for the phone to ring for a drudge.

'At this time of night?' said Stella, not knowing what time of night it was.

'You'd be surprised ... Ah! there's a stroke of luck, it's Petunia's phone, she's a Red, and quite a brick. Quickly, now. I'll come with you. We'll have to be clamped, though.'

The two presented themselves to the Under-prefect Petunia, who seemed as sleepy as Stella, and quite happy to assign her the drudge's task. Morag said that as Stella was a new drudge, Morag volunteered to show her out of the Labyrinth to her task. Petunia yawned and agreed, then reached for her book. She told Stella and Morag to sign, then ordered Stella to lift her skirt and remove her panties, handing them to her for safe-keeping. She sniffed them appreciatively, leered and said 'Blue, eh?' before putting them in a drawer which was full of panties. Stella guessed she was not going to see them again. A trophy for the Reds, perhaps ...

Then she was clamped! Petunia parted the lips of her fount, and fastened two tight steel pegs to them, then did the same to the already nude Morag. The pegs were connected to balls of twine, Stella's twice as thick as Morag's, and the ends of the twine were clipped to Petunia's desk.

'All in order,' said Petunia, and handed Stella a slip of paper with her destination written on it. 'Morag, to door of Labyrinth; Stella, across yard to Staff Building. Report here when you return, with your chitty signed properly, otherwise you'll be caged – not that I care. And if you're not back by dawn, I'll reel you in on your twine – you won't want that, I dare say.' She handed Morag a key, returned to bed and began to snore.

'See?' said Morag. 'It is easy to get out of here. She's not supposed to entrust me with a key. Actually, I can pick locks quite easily, and so can most of us drudges, and no one really cares. No one wants to go anywhere, even when Clapton comes down to open the cages and use the naughty ones for Girl Guide practice. I think they like it, really.' She said that they had no time for Stella to kit herself as a drudge, so she would have to go to her task in her girly Poppy's uniform, even though knickerless. The twine was both to lead the drudge back to the Dorm, and a method of ensuring she did not spend suspiciously long away, in which case, the Under-pre would probably start reeling her in.

'Pretty painful, I imagine, being reeled in. But no one ever tries to escape. Perhaps we are really all subs ...'

Morag passed various dishevelled palliasses, and helped herself to bits of discarded clothing, to make a ragtag uniform, which she handed in a pile to Stella. Her last acquisition was a pair of the sweetest frilly blue knickers, whose owner, however, was moved to protest at their removal. She sat up in bed, crossly, hands over her naked breasts in girly modesty.

'Give me my knickers back, Morag, you bitch! Please?' she cried. It was Charity, of the Blues' Anemone Cohort! 'Oh!' the submissive continued, recognising Stella. 'I'm sorry! How can I ever atone for my insolence?'

And, answering her own remark, she turned round, threw off her blanket, and presented the sweet globes of her bare croup thrust upwards towards Stella's hand! Morag grinned, shrugged, and took the bundle of clothes, Charity's knickers on top. Stella, with a sigh, applied a few dozen firm slaps until Charity's bare nates glowed quite red. Charity smiled angelically and murmured thanks, then snuggled down to sleep again. Stella remarked, laughing, to Morag, that perhaps she was really a dom after all. Morag said that in the Remove, anything was possible. Stella responded by saying *this* was then possible, taking Charity's knickers and slipping them on, albeit awkwardly, over the twine.

'We subs never like to be without our knickers, you know,' she said solemnly, 'so we can always have the pleasure of taking something off.' Morag laughed.

'They will never think of looking for Jakes *here*.' Morag exclaimed as she opened the door. 'We'll make a girly of the brute. Isn't this fun?'

Stella thought of the magnificent Jakes robed in a Kernece uniform, and despite the uncomfortable fount-clamps and the daunting prospect of her punishment in the morning, had to admit that yes, it *was* fun. There was indeed something to be said for being a naughty girl in the Remove.

It was slightly awkward to walk with the heavy twine curling from the clamps at her fount-lips. But there was something rather exciting about it too, as though Stella were a helpless slave, which indeed she supposed she was. The twine was thickly greased, so that it would not snag or catch, and so that no matter how many turns she took, the Under-prefect would have no difficulty coiling it in. Morag said that it was quite possible to undo the clamps, for comfort or deceit, but that if the twine was reeled, it would disappear with a snap, and to have been found thus remiss and deceitful merited truly dreadful punishment. Also, it would cause no little inconvenience, since the ball of twine contained the key to permit the drudge's re-entry to the labyrinth. It was 'Drudges' Honour' to remain clamped: once a new drudge had gained trust, like Morag, clamps were not strictly necessary; in this case, Morag had the clamps because she was not the one on drudge.

They reached the door of Jakes's cell, and found it locked. It was a matter of moments for Morag to pick the lock, with a hairpin and a piece of wood, and they entered. Jakes was a dreadful sight. He was sleeping fitfully on a harsh stone floor, and naked except for shackles which bound his wrists and ankles behind his back, bending him back painfully in a crab position. The ring at the end of his bare penis was locked to a clasp on the end of a thick rope, and fastened to a post in the flagstones; and on a second rope, twin clamps were fastened to his balls themselves, tight on the soft skin under the precious orbs! Morag explained that this was an Edinburgh Harness, a device used in Victorian times to prevent 'spermatorrhea', since any erection of the penis or tightening of the balls would result in the most severe discomfort. Stella thought that Jakes was unlikely to feel like sperming just now. Worst of all, he was branked: his curly head restrained by the harsh steel of a scold's bridle.

Quickly, Morag knelt and began to gnaw at the ropes attached to his manhood; Stella joined her, and in five minutes they had the ropes severed. Jakes was now awakened by a rub on the shoulder, and awoke bleary-eyed; Stella's heart melted, for she saw he had been crying. She hated Clapton for doing this to the proud male, however arrogant he was. The beauty of the plan was explained to him; he would hide in the Dorm, a girly amongst girlies, and when Hallowe'en was over, he could reappear in his tuckshop as though nothing had happened.

Once the excitement of the celebrations had died down,

Miss Dancer and Clapton would be far too embarrassed at their foolish scheme to admit to their defeat. In fact Jakes's power would probably be increased! This appealed greatly to the now tear-free Jakes, who nodded enthusiastically through his brank. The brank was not locked, and Stella unfastened it. Morag tried without success to pick the lock on his shackles, while Stella worried about the time, and being reeled. But she decided that Jakes's safety was more important, and she would unclamp herself if need be. This thought safely in her mind, it was followed by others, more mischievous: she could not forget her anguish at seeing a male's cheek stained with tears.

Morag solved the problem by heaving up a flagstone and crashing it spectacularly down on Jakes's shackles, neatly smashing the locks. This done, she silenced Jakes's awkward thanks and gave him his new kit: a nice, gaudy uniform that was a mishmash of garments from all the Houses. Jakes looked uncertain. 'Must I?' he quavered. 'Dress as a girly?'

'Unless you want to go nude,' said Morag.

'In front of girlies?' he scoffed, his old bravado returning. 'That has never bothered *me*.'

Morag pointed out that a naked male, especially one so unmistakable, would rapidly be discovered by their enemies. Stella dared him to go on and dress, as he would look super, and she meant it; so Jakes ruefully assented. He donned a short pleated skirt, silk stockings and knickers – 'not forgetting the garter belt!' cried Morag mischievously – with a brassière and Orchid's blouse, and an untidy, rather moth-eaten wig of long brown hair.

Stella cried that he looked as pretty as a picture, and kissed the glowering male, with a little caress to his penis, which trembled under his Daisy's skirt. Jakes took to smoothing down his new clothes and pulling his stockings smooth, and Stella said that there would be plenty of time for admiring himself in the mirror later, which made him blush. They speedily left, Morag escorting Jakes back to the Dorm, while Stella made her way to the outer door of the Labyrinth, equipped with Morag's hairpin and piece of wood, and Jakes's brank.

She looked up at the forbidding Tower, glinting under the moonlight, the stars wreathing it like grinning Norns. Tomorrow, she thought – no, today! – I'll be running up there, my bum smarting like the devil. And I won't mind! *I'll take it*. She crossed the yard slowly, allowing her fount-twine to pay out, and instead of going into the designated building, she entered the other, where she knew Clapton lodged. She found the room. Other Kernecians spoke of it with awe, and there could be no mistaking it: right at the top of the building, down a corridor where it was the only room. The place seemed to smell of Clapton: clean, sharp and brutal, like the blade of a guillotine. The door was unlocked, so she had no need of her implements. There, on a simple frame bed, lay Clapton, swathed in a blanket. The furnishings were stark; all elaboration was reserved for Clapton's beloved equipment. There were racks of polished canes and tawses, chains, cuffs, shackles and whips, greased ropes and cords. Clapton was sound asleep, lying on her back with her head bent to one side. Stella made her selection, then paused, looking at Clapton's head so peaceful on her pillow, with her hair splayed so sweetly in the moonlight. She had to remind herself of the reason for her task, of Jakes's cruel abandonment, bound in his cold cell.

She threw back the cover from the sleeping woman, causing her to stir, and before Clapton fully awoke, she snapped cuffs around her wrists and ankles, fastening them securely to each end of the bed-frame. Clapton's head jerked up, and she tried to rub her eyes. Her mouth opened to yell, but, oddly, she did not. She looked on almost dispassionately as Stella quickly clamped the brank over her head, depressing her tongue with the heavy metal flap and clicking the device shut at the nape of her neck. Clapton's eyes burned through her face's prison like bright coals in a brazier. Stella stepped back and surveyed her prisoner.

She had prepared a few contemptuous words, but somehow speech would not come. Clapton was silent, and did not attempt to struggle: she lay still, bound and strangely beautiful in her humiliation, the rays of the moon playing their ghostly white light on the thick forest of her minkhair. Stella gasped, for she felt herself moistening at her fount, thrilled by the strange new power of her domination. She had forgotten the time: it did not seem to matter. Deliberately, she went to the washstand and filled a basin of cold water, then took soap and a cut-throat razor. She set these things on a little table and placed it next to Clapton's waist. Now, Clapton became visibly agitated. She began to shudder and moan and shake her branked head from side to side, guessing Stella's purpose. Stella smiled.

'Yes, Clapton,' she whispered. 'You are very proud of your lush mink. Just as Jakes is of his penis – the cock you long to possess for your own. You grow your mink so full and beautiful to hide behind, don't you? Hide the fact that you haven't a man's thing – Well, we'll see what you look like!'

She began to strop the razor back and forth, testing it on her tongue. It tingled, and she hummed appreciatively to signify it was sharp. Then she took the soap and water, and began to lather Clapton's mink, rubbing the soap thick and hard until the whole mink blossomed with scented foam. Stella felt the thick fount-lips swell ever so slightly to her touch, and felt Clapton jerk as her fingers brushed the nestling clit, which was stiff as a button! Clapton trembled and let out a long, low moan of despair.

Stella's fount was very wet, now, and her breath came sharply as she parted the soaking hairs and placed the razor blade just outside the fleshy fold of Clapton's fount. She saw the cunt-lip glisten: Clapton was wet, too, at the thought of her humiliation! Clapton's glowing, fearful eyes were fixed on the razor blade in Stella's raised hand.

Suddenly, Stella put aside the razor. She dropped her uniform skirt and took down Charity's blue panties to reveal her own bare mink. Then, with trembling fingers, she soaped herself there, feeling her clit stiff and throbbing and her cunt-lips swelling bounteous and hard as she touched herself. When she was fully lathered, she took a deep breath and stroked herself with the razor. The wet hairs came away easily; she rinsed the razor, and made another stroke, and another, careful of the lips of her slit, until her whole mons gleamed naked in the moonlight.

'There, Clapton,' she cried. 'I'm a bare girly. Wouldn't *you* like to be?'

Stella then put away the shaving things, rubbing the ripe swelling of her shaven mons and thrilling at the wonderful naked innocence she felt. She knew that thus shorn, she could never do wrong nor suffer any wrong.

With a thick rope, she bound Clapton's ankles together, looping the rope around the bed. Then, by a methodical series of piecemeal bindings which ensured Clapton was never free to escape, she had her captive bent forward, her hair knotted to the ankle rope. Her arms, legs and waist were linked by tight chains and shackles, with the arms held twisted securely behind her back. Now the brank came off to be replaced by a light rope gag. Finally, Stella unfastened her own clamps and fixed them to Clapton's cunt-lips.

Stella stood and surveyed her handiwork.

'I think you get the idea, Clapton,' she said. 'When you've gnawed through your gag, you are free to gnaw your way through your ankle rope. Then you can move and walk, but with your arms behind, you can't get at the metal shackles. You can either make your way down to the yard – it'll be dawn soon, and you'll see everybody going in to breakfast – or you can wait for Petunia's tug on my cunt-twine, and go to the Remove Dorm. The choice is yours.'

On impulse, Stella stripped herself completely, then helped herself to Clapton's clothes from her closet. She dressed herself in a stern grey suit with a short pleated skirt, grey stockings and garters, white blouse and a bumfreezer jacket with slightly padded shoulders. There was a ribbon at her neck which she tied in a flouncy bow, and she helped herself also to Clapton's brightest, shiniest black patent leather shoes, and stern black satin panties which were *very* tight and skimpy. It felt thrilling and lovely to be her own captive! She bundled her own soiled Poppy's uniform under her arm, and in response to the mute pleading in Clapton's eyes, she lifted her new skirt and rubbed her shining bare mons, and said softly:

'No, I'm not going to shave you, my girl. Clapton is already shaved.'

Stella skipped joyfully out into the yard once more. She made her way up the stairs of the other building, to the room indicated on her chitty. These were sleeping quarters, and she knocked timidly on the door.

'Drudge, Miss,' she said.

'Come in, Stella. What kept you? I've waited so long.'

Stella took a deep breath and entered. It was the voice of Miss Noble, her tutor! She was standing by her bed, wearing a short black nightie, and barefoot. Her blonde hair was combed flat and unpinned, sweeping down over her large breasts whose curving tops were quite generously displayed by the low 'v' of the nightie. Her long smooth legs, too, were pleasing to Stella's eye, and Miss Noble's body, with her mannish tight buttocks, seemed to possess a harmony that her name graced. Her arms were folded below her breasts.

'Well, Stella, I summoned you especially for drudge, just as soon as I learnt you had been sent to the Remove. It's a disgrace! One of my girls, a drudge! You have let me down, Stella, and made me very sorry.'

Miss Noble sniffed, and looked as though tears might come, but the gleam in her eye belied her sorrow. Stella looked round the spotlessly clean bedsitting room, unable to see any task for her. It was furnished simply, with casual elegance; there were numerous classical paintings depicting the male nude in heroic poses. Stella noted that all were shorn of body hair, including the mink, and all seemed to have small penises! Except for one, in pride of place, which showed a handsome muscled young man endowed generously, though not quite of Jakesian proportions, who wore a garland of flowers and held a scroll. Benignly he observed the flogging of one naked female by another, holding a quirt of olive branches. Stella found it a sunny, serene picture. Miss Noble noticed her attention.

'Kytetroos of Naxos,' she said, 'who laid the principles of female, and Kernecian, education. His colour was red, you know – I think of him as the first of the Reds.'

Miss Noble lifted her nightie a fraction over her creamy thigh, to reveal it adorned with a red garter!

'Our secret,' she said mischievously. 'Now, perhaps you would like to see the real Kytetroos.'

Stella assented. Gleefully Miss Noble opened a drawer and unwrapped a bronze statuette depicting the same features of Kytetroos, but in the form of a satyr, and with his naked penis now monstrously erect. Miss Noble smiled and rubbed the penis lovingly. The metal organ shone with wear.

'He brings me luck,' she said simply. 'Touch him.'

Stella accepted the statuette, and looked at the grinning face of Miss Noble's mentor, as she caressed his stiff cock. Down all the centuries, she felt she knew Kytetroos. Miss Noble said that Kytetroos was a hero, for he had saved the island of Naxos during one of the endless Greek wars.

'Naxos was always a peaceful and pleasure-loving island,' she said dreamily, taking the statuette and replacing it carefully in its drawer. 'In the time of Kytetroos, there was a war with the Spartans, who coveted the olives, wine and honey of Naxos. A Spartan force landed: Kytetroos knew that the Naxians would be no match for Spartans, toughened by their military upbringing of hardship and the lash. So he challenged the Spartan commander: he would be bound and flogged by the Spartans, to show Naxian bravery! The commander accepted, and ordered him stripped. The soldiers were awed by the hugeness of his penis standing stiff, like a god's! Kytetroos was devoted to the arts of peace; he taught that warlike and destructive impulses in males come from shame at having small penises. This seems self-evident today, Stella, but Kytetroos was the first to understand it.

'Nude, he took a hundred lashes with a quirt of olive branches, and boasted that there were thousands of Naxian penises to which his was just a sapling. After his whipping, he was still gloriously erect! The Spartan commander complained that he saw only women there. As one, the students of Kytetroos stripped and beseeched the Spartans to whip them, too, on the bare! This was done: each took a hundred, without protest, and at last the Spartans decided they were no match for the Naxians, and sailed away. And thus, Stella, does Kernece inherit the arts of peace.'

Stella saw that the front of Miss Noble's nightie was swirling in her agitation, and that there was a damp patch at her fount. The story had excited her too, but she asked what her drudgery was to be. Miss Noble smiled, and fetched a cane from the stand by her door. The canes were brightly polished, and she selected the longest and thickest one. Miss Noble stood holding the cane behind her back, across the tops of her slim fesses.

'No drudgery, Stella. I'm afraid you must take punishment for your insult to me. You have let me down, Stella.'

'I meant no harm, Miss,' said Stella numbly. 'And I'm to be punished anyway: I must Run the Tawse.'

'I know. And that means you may well wish to leave Kernece afterwards. I shall not see you again, or – or have occasion to chastise you.' She sighed, biting her lip, and now her eyes did mist. Suddenly she frowned.

'I am afraid you will have to strip,' said Miss Noble, her voice trembling, 'for it is to be bare bum. Well, you can keep your stockings on, if you like, but the panties must be off completely. And I want the blouse off, too, for you'll have to take it on the back as well.'

Stella unfastened Clapton's skirt and let it fall to the floor, explaining coolly how she came by it. Miss Noble laughed at the story, and said she had spunk. She saw Miss Noble's eyes bright on the bulge of her shaven mons under the tight black panties, and impishly decided to leave them till last. She removed her jacket, undid the bow at her neck and slowly opened the blouse buttons, finally shucking it off and letting it fall with her skirt. She shivered as her long hair tickled the nipples of her bared breasts, and made them stiffen slightly. Miss Noble swallowed hard.

'I think I'll keep my shoes and stockings on, Miss, if you don't mind,' said Stella.

'Very well, but the panties, Stella! Off with them!'

Now, Stella pretended to be shy, and fiddled with the elastic waist, hesitating before slipping the panties down just to her dimple at the top of her mons. She knew that Miss Noble was agitated; she could see that there were no mink-hairs peeping.

'Stella!' she murmured weakly. 'Don't tantalise me! Take them off. I beg you!'

With a flurry, Stella pulled off her knickers, right down to her knees, and stepped out of them. The effect on Miss Noble was stunning. She blushed fiery, and her hand flew to within an inch of Stella's bare mound.

'Oh, Stella . . .' she gasped. 'So beautiful! You are shorn. You are one of us!'

Her hand hovered, trembling, and Stella took hold of it and gently placed Miss Noble's fingers on her naked mons. Her touch was cool and lovely, and at its tingling pressure, Stella felt moisture flow within her fount. Sighing, Miss Noble said that her punishment must begin. She ordered Stella to bend over her leather sofa, with her head in the cushions, as she might want to bite. Stella obeyed, nervous eyes on the cane as Miss Noble swished the air.

'And I'll want you on tiptoe,' said Miss Noble, all businesslike. 'That way you can't squirm too much to lessen the smarting. And you will smart, Stella, I promise. I'm going to take you on the bare, shoulders as well as bum. Nice and slowly, to give you time to relish the pain of each stroke, and just when you think the sting is fading, there'll be another stroke to refresh it.'

The cane whistled to Stella's bare nates, and its impact made her jump. It *did* smart, quite horribly! Two more strokes followed with cruel speed, and Stella's legs and bottom danced in agony, toes and fesses feverishly clenching.

'Oh, Miss,' she gasped, 'that smarts so! How – Oh! *Ouch*! How many must I take?'

'Why,' panted Miss Noble, 'as many as you can stand, Miss. There!' And another stroke fell, this time on Stella's stretched bare shoulders. 'I must say, Stella, you take beating awfully well. You've learnt a lot about Kernece.

'I don't think I'd fail your test, now, Miss. Ooh! That was tight! You know, the one you spanked me for. There's only one thing that intrigues me –' she stopped to squeal as Miss Noble took her with a powerful stroke squarely on the backs of her stockinged thighs, making her eyes water.

'Mind Clapton's stockings, Miss, you'll rip them with those thigh-strokes! Oh, how they hurt!'

'Hang Clapton and her stockings,' was the reply.

Miss Noble assumed a rhythm, lacing buttocks and shoulders in turn, so that no part of Stella's body had time to recover from one bout before the pain of the next flooded her. But gradually, she stopped counting the strokes, and her bite on the leather cushion became less fierce, as the warm glowing agony suffused and transported her.

'What is it that intrigues you, Stella?'

'The Kernece Tower,' said Stella, her bottom squirming as though in time with her gasped words. 'I long to know what is at the top, in the locked chamber.' Miss Noble laughed.

'I don't think anyone knows,' she said. 'No one dares! Certainly not me! There is supposed to be some sort of curse, something to do with the Norsemen. A treasure captured from the Isbister warriors, that they had brought from the East. The Vikings pillaged all over the place, you know, as far as Egypt and Greece! They were real men ... But how we girls love such stories, romance and tattle!'

'Jakes might know,' said Stella, writhing tight-lipped under cane-strokes to her bare shoulders.

'He would,' agreed Miss Noble glumly. Then she whispered, 'Is that all that intrigues you Stella?'

'Miss, you said I was "one of us". Are you shorn, too?'

'Oh, lovely Stella ...'

Miss Noble moved from behind the prostrate girl to stand in front of her face, which Stella raised. She continued to cane, but now landed her strokes vertically, single strokes to each buttock, making Stella's bottom wriggle quite uncontrollably. Miss Noble lifted the hem of her nightie to reveal her fount, as shiny and naked as Stella's own! Beneath the mons glowed two red, swollen cunt-lips, glistening with rivulets of love-oil which Stella saw trickling openly down Miss Noble's inner thighs. She reached up and touched the cunt, feeling the smooth mons with her fingers while her palm rubbed the oily fount-lips, and found Miss Noble's damsel stiff and quivering in its fleshy nest. Stella's own cunt soaked. Delirious with pain and pleasure, she put her fingers in and out of Miss Noble's slit, rubbing the oily flesh and caressing the swollen nympha until, her cunt flowing, Miss Noble moaned and shuddered and said she could not continue the beating.

'But you must, Miss!' cried Stella. 'I'll be a clam.'

She shifted and placed her back on the floor, then lifted her legs and clasped the backs of her thighs to her belly, exposing the ripped stockings and fiery red buttock-flesh. She then, cheekily, ordered Miss Noble to be at ease – she should squat on Stella's face, fount against Stella's mouth, and cane her from that position. Trembling, Miss Noble obeyed her order, and Stella felt the hot slippery weight of Miss Noble's fleshy cunt sink heavily on to her open mouth.

Miss Noble resumed the flogging, the tip of the cane biting fiercely as she took Stella with vertical strokes on the bum and thigh-backs. All the time, Stella's tongue and lips were busy licking the engorged nympha and sucking the precious fluid which cascaded from her Tutor's swollen cunt-lips. Stella vigorously masturbated as she took the caning and pleasured her loving tormentor, caressing her fesses with the soles of her feet. She knew she would make Miss Noble orgasm, and when she did, her whole body writhed in ecstasy, so that Stella had to clamp her tightly to her face. She heard the cane clatter to the floor, and felt Miss Noble bend forward, pressing her own face to Stella's fount, and thirstily sucking her juices as her tongue maddened Stella's stiff nympha with spasms of pleasure.

In moments, Stella cried out in her own climax, and the two women fell sobbing and laughing and kissing, in each other's arms. Miss Noble pulled off Stella's stockings, then wiped Stella's wet cunt with them, and pressed them to her lips, before rubbing Stella's oil over her breasts. Stella ripped Miss Noble's red garter, and did the same, rubbing her nipples then pushing the garter right inside her wet slit; she whispered that it was a trophy for the Blues.

'My pure sweet Stella,' gasped Miss Noble. 'Shorn, like a soft lamb. Yes, you are one of us, so bare and so womanly ...'

The first rays of the dawn were peeping through the window, glinting on the two soaked bare bodies.

'It will soon be time for me to Run the Tawse,' said Stella, stroking her Tutor's hair. 'All the way to the top of the Steps.'

Miss Noble sat up. 'First, it is time for *my* punishment, Stella,' she said severely, then broke into an impish smile. 'I failed my test, remember? I was remiss: I couldn't answer what was at the top of the Kernece Steps, in the locked room.'

She shifted and knelt before her charge, her nightie around her neck and her bare buttocks thrust up in their taut, slender loveliness.

'A spanking, please, Miss,' she whispered, 'just like the one I gave you. And I'll test you while you spank me – each spank accompanied by a word, as you recite all you have learnt of the Kernece Rulebook.'

Obediently, Stella raised her hand for the spanking.

'But, Miss, that is chapters and chapters! I know the Rulebook almost by heart!'

'Yes,' smiled Miss Noble, as the first blow fell on her quivering naked bottom. 'Yes ...'

13

Tawser Bright

Stella wore a bright red nightie of Miss Noble's; the two women slept in each other's arms, and the sun was high when they awoke. It shone from a bright, blue winter sky that seemed to give its benison to the festival which was already noisily under way. The two women rubbed their eyes and looked down at the hubbub in the yard. It seemed that every Kernecian was there, whirling and carousing in a joyful mêlée, and wearing costumes of the most outlandish nature. Girls carried portions of uniform from every house, adorned with accoutrements of their own: bandannas, ribbons, even spiky helmets or sheepskin boots with spurs at the ankle! Some carried fearsome clubs, or knobkerries, as Stella surmised. Some had their faces painted to look like daemons or witches. All were festive.

And amid the throng, the drudges, just as gaily attired, toiled to erect a mighty long ship, whose prow was a dragon with a slender neck that broadened into a huge grinning bulb of a head. But the dragon's face had wide blue eyes, full lips and the long flaxen hair of a northern woman! Stella had never thought of a dragon as female before – especially as the bulbous head, long neck, and twin dimples of the ship's forward hull reminded her strangely of Kytetroos's, or Jakes's, male organ. Under the long ship were piled bundles of twigs and branches, to make a fire.

Stella watched as Miss Noble busied herself with breakfast things, saying that Stella would need it. There was a strange democracy at work below. Drudges circulated with punchbowls of, presumably, mead, or trays of cakes and cooked meats. Proctors and Prefects and Mistresses mingled with their charges, as merrily as the rest. Stella spied the Bull, clad in a sumptuous military greatcoat, which she pulled open from time to time as though to frighten, but revealed to great cheers that she had only a bright poppy bra and knickers on underneath!

Everyone had one conceit or other; there was Miss Rose, all in crimson, dressed *as* a rose, which gave her the appearance of a lovely red vulva; Miss Harker the Games Mistress was encased in brown leather, like a football bladder; even Miss Dancer was there, smiling, dressed in virginal white, like a bride. Once or twice, Stella thought she recognised Jakes's mousy brown wig, but he was well disguised. Only Clapton distinguished herself by her stern grey everyday uniform, as she gazed sullenly up at Miss Noble's window. Stella sighed; Clapton awaited her. But a lady must have time for breakfast . . .

She withdrew from the window, and looked through Miss Noble's bookshelf. Amongst tomes of philosophy and poetry, she was pleased to see her own favourite romances of chivalry and heroism. One curious leather volume caught her eye, and she took it down. The title and author's name were proudly embossed in gold: *Notes On The Correction And Discipline Of Young English and Scottish Ladies*, by Miss Patience Bright, D.Phil. (Akad. Kytetroos). Miss Noble served her a tray of tea, toast, and boiled eggs, and, tucking up her red nightie, Stella crossed her legs and settled down to read. She rapidly became enthralled, as in the crispest and most decorous Victorian prose, Tawser Bright described things that Stella had already experienced, and things she longed to try, that made her belly flutter: the Saddle, the Belt, the Rail, the Trapeze . . .

'There can be no education of Young Ladies without firm discipline,' Stella read in the introduction, 'and no discipline without a loving and strict hand. To bring tears to a miscreant's eyes with harsh words and bad temper is an insult to our fair sex, and produces only spite, resentment, and shiftlessness. A stern and reasonable punishment with tawse, whip or cane, charitably given, and proudly taken, effects repentance and good resolve for improvement, and does honour both to the chastiser and chastised, as well as to the womanhood of both.

'As there are gradations of offence, so must there be gradations in severity of punishment and subtlety of the corrective instruments. In some cases, a mere spanking suffices to bring the offender to her senses; in others, a sound tawsing, or the short shock of a caning, is appropriate. The punishment should meet the crime. For example, to an offence repeated over a long period, the tawse is indicated, as the long duration of a tawsing of a hundred lashes or more will give the miscreant ample time to reflect upon her misdeeds. For a sudden, thoughtless offence, the sharp pain of caning, perhaps only a couple of dozen strokes, will concentrate her mind wonderfully.

'The aim of punishment is first and foremost to reform the offender's outlook and morals, and to make her thankful that physical pain has absolved her character of moral stigma, that is, her slate is "wiped clean". In all but exceptional cases, punishment should be given on the bare; that is, the offender's nates should be exposed naked to the correctional instrument. Sometimes a whipping is indicated on shoulders as well as buttocks, and here complete nudity is required, with the offender securely tied to a whipping frame by wrists, waist, and ankles.

'However, most punishments are administered to the naked buttocks, whose soft fleshy expanse and extreme sensitivity are most conducive to moral reflection, both during the chastisement and afterward, when the recipient of correction is reminded of her fault by the discomfort of sitting down. The nudity of the fesses, her secret, private place exposed to the world, causes the penitent to reflect upon the nudity of her soul, alone before the instrument of her correction.

'To this end, a just ritual of humiliation is a necessary part of chastisement, especially where a serious offence merits chastisement before one or more witnesses. No silk, nor satin, may sheath the miscreant's buttocks from the awful shame of their exposed state. She may be obliged to divest herself of her clothing piece by piece, folding each garment neatly on risk of further punishment for untidiness.

'The order of removal is important, beginning with the outer garments, the skirt, jacket, shoes and stockings, and of course garter belt and straps if worn; then the unhooking of corset or stays, the graceful stepping from shift and petticoat, and finally the removal of the panties themselves, which should be accomplished in a firm and decisive motion, without hesitation or blushing. Even the simple lifting of a nightdress to the neck, for a bare-bottom spanking with the flat of the hand, should be carried out with due ceremony and gravity.

'It is the same where the gravity of the offence requires the binding or trussing of the offender, which may involve the wearing of a hood, gag, or brank. This has the effect of holding the body still and incapable of Unladylike squirmings to alleviate the rigours of punishment. Bound and helpless, a Young Lady is obliged to reflect on her own helplessness in the face of Nature, and the wrong of offending Nature by her Unladylike, hence immoral, act.

'A binding must be applied to a Young Lady in a state of complete nudity, and the intricacy of the knots applied to the offender's stripped body, as well as the contorted pose which usefully tight fabrics such as rubber or leather shall oblige her to adopt, shall reflect her own contortion of proper morality which has led her to offend. The careful thought which has been applied to her trussing shall remind her of the thoughtlessness of her own improper act.

'At Kernece, we are blessed with a Tower, whose ancient Steps provide a perfect theatre for the ritual chastisement of an errant Young Lady. As she ascends, the tawse-strokes her bared nates receive at each Step incite her to moral thoughts, for each Step carries nearer to Higher Things and Moral Excellence. A Young Lady who should manage to reach the very top of the Tower would achieve

Moral Excellence indeed, for there lies a chamber whose secrets legend denies to the eyes of Kernecians unless they have fully accomplished such a moral ascent. The Young Ladies of Kernece have devised various means of concentrating the mind in order to endure the painful ascent as far as the top, but these matters of local interest need not detain the reader of this general work.

'It must be remembered that a chastisement amongst Ladies is a social occasion like any other, and that all politenesses and proprieties must be observed. The Lady administering the chastisement should be careful to say "please" when ordering the removal of clothing or the adoption of a binding position, and "thank you" when each instruction is obeyed. The recipient of chastisement should likewise remember to ask politely for her instructions, to thank her chastiser as they are given, and to give sincere thanks when the chastisement is completed.

'It is fitting for unhurried Ladylike conversation to take place during the whipping itself, to emphasise that a Lady never departs from civilised politeness, even in the most demanding circumstances. It is seemly for the Young Lady, as her nates are being served by the cane or tawse, to make helpful suggestions for enhancing the efficacy of the punishment, or for her chastiser to request small adjustments of position, to the same end. Also, it is appropriate for refreshments to be served, usually after completion of the punishment, when both parties may make observations on the manner of its execution and acceptance.

'As in all social manners, sincerity is of the utmost importance: both giver and recipient must genuinely desire the chastisement, and be pleased and grateful when it has taken place. Civility and not passion must rule, and after her whipping, a Young Lady who rubs her inflamed bottom should do so in the happy knowledge that she has been treated fairly and with kindness.

'Like any Lady who is steadfast in her insistence on proper behaviour, I have a certain experience of chastising Young Gentlemen as well as Young Ladies, and have been kindly requested to entrust my observations to print.

However, I feel that the moral and physical aspects of male chastisement have been amply, and, I venture, more expertly dealt with, by my colleagues at our great Public Schools, and so the scope of the present volume precludes a detailed discussion of the correction of young males.

'Therefore, to the Lady whose duty it is to chastise some wilful Young Gentleman – and which of us are not thus obliged, from time to time? – I can only refer her to my advice on the chastisement of the female, with some significant asides. Female offences are generally offences of taste or manners, rather than morality; the male, having little taste and a natural propensity to immorality, usually offends in a coarser and more brutal manner than the female, and it is tempting for a Lady to think his punishment should therefore be brutal. This temptation should be resisted.

'Certainly, a Young Gentleman's whipping may be more vigorous, and the implements of his chastisement perhaps sterner: the efficacy of a sturdy bundle of birch rods on a male's naked posterior is well-known. Mere spanking may be discounted, as the male with his coarse humour will dismiss it as tickling, and may even enjoy the touch of a Lady's reluctant hand on his exposed parts! No, a male should always be whipped or caned, always soundly, and always on the bare. But he should be treated with the same politeness and good taste as any Lady, in the hope that being confronted with civility may teach him some of it!

'Which brings me to the question of delicacy. A Lady may understandably be repelled by the very thought of observing, let alone having contact with, a male's naked posterior, especially when the attentions of the rod are causing it to wriggle in a way that could strike a Lady as lewd. I have found it extremely beneficial, both in kindness to a Lady's sensibilities and as a means of taming the male's natural rowdiness, that a male who receives punishment from a Lady *should first be made to robe himself as a Lady*.

'The embarrassment of being robed by expert female hands, or invited to robe himself while a female watches, dangling the instrument of his correction in front of him, will soften the uncouthness of the most fractious Young Gentleman. Imagine his dismay, the weakening of all rebellion and pride, as he finds himself scented, corsed, and skirted, in petticoats and stockings, with a pair of pinching high shoes, if one can be found to accommodate his clumsy male feet. Imagine, too, as the clever females shower him with compliments, the dawning that his new raiment actually makes him look pretty, and that there is more to life than beer, mud, smells and cricket bats!

'The question of male punishment is thus easily answered: the male's will to resist is completely sapped by his new, tasteful attire, and the cane or whip may be applied with thorough propriety to a very thin satin petticoat or shift, revealed as he lifts his skirts to bend over, and covering his intimate limbs from a Lady's gaze, while affording little protection from her just chastisement.

'I thoroughly recommend this method of punishing males to Ladies obliged to do so, as I myself have used it with considerable success. My only caution is this: I have found that certain Young Gentlemen, far from being deterred from impropriety by being chastised in Lady's robes, will appear before me again and again to receive this very same punishment, sometimes for offences so trifling as to make one think they had committed them on purpose!'

Stella scarcely noticed that she had finished her breakfast, nor that Miss Noble had whisked away her tray, and was standing before her with a smile.

'Enthralling, isn't it?' said Miss Noble, then sighed. 'But I don't think we can put it off any longer: it is time to go down and face the punishment Miss Dancer has decreed.'

'Clapton has decreed, more like,' said Stella defiantly. 'But I don't care. I'll take it. And since I'll be stripped to Run The Tawse, I'll jolly well go down there nude in the first place, just to show them! But Tawser Bright's book *is* enthralling, and I wonder about those "devices" girls used to get to the top of the Steps . . .'

Miss Noble said that Stella was a brave girl to appear nude, and would be a splendid recruit for the Reds, if she desired. As for the devices, to her knowledge not one had ever worked, or at least anyone who had been to the secret chamber at the top of Kernece Tower had been too frightened by what she had seen to tell anyone else. She frowned, and put her hand to her lips. Stella stretched, doffing Miss Noble's red nightie, which she had grown quite attached to, and stood nude, her breasts pressed to the window.

She did not care if Clapton, or the Bull, or anyone, saw her; they would all see her soon enough, and cheer as the leather reddened her naked skin. How fondly she thought of Tawser Bright and the cosy proprieties of her Victorian world, with her politeness and civility and Moral Excellence. Her book seemed a far cry from this young and brutal century. Stella wondered if the Tawser would recognise her Kernece in the crowd of baying and whooping young women down in the yard, their bodies glowing with carefree lust and mischief below the tall prow of the long ship. Already, a hapless drudge had been caught, stripped and tethered to the ship's prow, her naked body greased and the knobkerries lifted for her flogging. The whole scene seemed to hark back to an older and darker age. Or perhaps Kernece had never left it.

'Well, Miss, I'm ready,' said Stella with iron in her voice.

Miss Noble spoke, looking thoughtful. 'There was something about ice cubes,' she said.

There was a roar of applause as Stella appeared at the doorway, blinking in the bright sun and her naked skin pimpling in the breeze. She saw Matron, dressed in a starched nurse's uniform, and was encouraged by the kiss of encouragement she blew. She expected a formal procession, led by Miss Dancer and a leering Clapton, to take her to the Steps and her punishment. But the democracy of Hallowe'en overruled any authority, and she was seized by a throng of merry Kernecians, whose faces were flushed with cold and mead, and enthusiasm for a new plaything. Stella was to be that plaything.

As she was held, she heard loud suggestions from

Prefects and drudges alike as to her warm-up for the Steps' ascent. Clearly, her Running the Tawse was to be the high point, not the whole, of the celebration. Miss Dancer and Clapton now stood to one side, surrounded by Mistresses, watching curiously, while Matron busied herself with a makeshift first aid station. All the Mistresses, like the Prefects, carried tawses, but these seemed ceremonial. Miss Noble squeezed her hand, and whispered that everything would be all right. Stella watched her then approach Florence Tate, and speak to her, before going to join the other Mistresses.

A dispute arose between the faction which wished Stella to make it to the top of the Steps and into the secret chamber, and those who opined that a 'mossy new squit' had no chance. The dispute became physical: certain foolhardy Prefects attempted to restore order, and were rewarded by gleeful buffeting and seizure of their tawses.

Some malefactors were apprehended and dragged by Prefects to the long ship, where they replaced the unfortunate drudge who had been crimsoned by knobkerries. Each was then replaced by another in turn, eagerly stripped and hooted by their comrades. Stella was almost forgotten as the mead passed. The beatings were carried out with girlish enthusiasm, and Matron fussed with her bandages and liniments. It seemed that on the day of Hallowe'en, all discipline was suspended, and that when the early darkness of the northern lands descended, pandemonium would surely break loose. Stella hoped for her punishment before darkness fell. She realised that the circle of Mistresses around Miss Dancer carried their tawses for self-protection as much as to vainly try and enforce discipline!

She was not altogether surprised to find that Heather and Tuffy were amongst those who held her by wrists and ankles. She did not try to struggle from their grasp, which seemed half-hearted. Fingers stroked her shaven fount, with little coos of admiration, and she knew she could break free if she wished. She winked at Heather and the grinning Tuffy, to no avail, then demanded if the Blues weren't going to help.

'Shush,' cried Heather. 'It's a secret! No one must know, it is part of the grand battle plan!'

'What is the grand battle plan?' asked Stella.

'That is a secret too!'

'To catch the Reds off guard, I suppose,' said Stella.

'Exactly! The Reds expect us to rescue you, so we won't! *That*'ll fool them. If you *take it*, and pretend to be a sub to the tawse, you might be promoted to Jarl!'

Stella wanted to ask what was the difference between submitting to the tawse and pretending to submit, but the Bull intervened, grinning fiercely, and fiddling with the buttons of her military coat. She held a fearsome whip, and a goblet of mead, which she invited Stella to taste, pressing the vessel to her lips. Stella found it sweet and warming. So, evidently, did the Bull, for she drained the cup and bellowed for more. Then she barked at the women to release Stella. This was done, and Stella stood facing the Bull, hands meekly behind her back.

'Well! Stella Shawn, Miss Hoity-toity, for the Tawse, eh?' she cried.

'An unlucky chance, Miss,' said Stella softly.

'Ha! No such thing! Clapton is Mistress of the Lots! She fixes everything! But Clapton is an old haybag, and you are my drudge, so *I'll* do the honours, and have the first lash. I haven't forgotten how beautifully you squirmed when I beat you. How do you like my coat? Cousin Stackenham gave it to me in a bet. I wore out a birch on his bare bum, the cad! And this horsewhip – a regimental one, don't you know – I'll wear *her* out on your bum before the top of the Tower!'

Stella smiled sweetly and said she was sure Cousin Stackenham's bum had blushed as beautifully as the Bull's own when she beat herself with the flail of Parph apples. The Bull flushed. Stella added in sudden mischief that she had glimpsed her bra and knickers, and that it was very cold, and she would not mind having such kit herself. The Bull laughed derisively and undid her buttons, sweeping her coat dramatically aside to show her body naked but for her tight underthings. Shivering as she was, Stella could not but feel a pang of desire at the sight of the Bull's superbly muscled belly and thighs. She admired the lushness of her mink and the firm swelling of the breasts whose wide saucer nipples were clearly outlined through the thin poppy satin bra. Her auburn mane dangled dreamily across her bra, stroking the nipples, and Stella found herself wishing she could be a lock of the Bull's silken hair. There were inquisitive glances from Heather and her comrades as they apparently pondered the mystery of Parph apples.

A fresh goblet of mead was served, and the Bull took a hearty swallow, then asked Stella if she wanted some. When Stella assented, she was ordered to get down on her knees. She obeyed, and The Bull told her that if she wanted mead, she would have to lick it! She poured the liquid down her front, so that her bra, belly and knickers were soaked! The onlookers roared, and a crowd began to gather, drifting away from the wailings of the thrashed girls at the long ship. Smiling with the serenity of her willing submission, Stella raised herself and applied her tongue to the creamy breast-flesh above the Bull's bra. Then she licked the satin itself, flicking her tongue again and again on the big plum nipples, and making them stand stiff. She went on to lick the woman's downy flat belly, then came to the panties, which were well soaked in mead.

Stella chewed the satin panties, sucking firmly and swallowing the heady drink. Coming to the curve of the fount, she licked and licked until what she tasted was not only mead, but the soft love-juices of Amanda Bulford's swelling cunt-lips. She felt the Bull breathe rather deeply, and there was the hint of a sigh, until the Bull pushed her head away, and said she would be tipsy if she drank more. Stella stood, her own fount moist in her excitement. Boldly, she told the Bull to strip herself of her bra and panties. The Bull stared, livid with rage.

'This is scandalous!' she cried. 'You'll get what for!'

'I'm getting what for anyway,' said Stella, 'and I might as well be hanged for a sheep as for a lamb, *Amanda*. The bra and panties, please. Why, it is Knobkerry Night – I should have panties on for you to rip, Amanda! Or do I have to tell everyone the full story of the Parph apples?' She stared her straight in the face, and the Bull lowered her eyes.

'How you whipped yourself, and loved it?' hissed Stella, so that only the Bull could hear.

'Hallowe'en ...' the Bull muttered sheepishly. 'Just for a giggle ... keep the troops happy.'

To great cheers, she stripped, and handed Stella her underthings, which Stella triumphantly donned. Perhaps it is the mead, she thought giddily, or perhaps the awesome power I have as a sacrifice-to-be – the power of having nothing to lose. There were hurrahs and shouts that she should thrash the Bull, and calls to fetch Parph apples, although there was uncertainty what was to be done with them.

'The whip, too, please,' said Stella, enjoying her bravado. Numbly, the Bull handed her the heavy whip.

'Now kneel, and lift your coat well over your bum, then kiss my feet and ask me to stroke you.'

As if mesmerised, the Bull obeyed, murmuring that Stella would pay for this. But the misty desire in her eyes belied her words, and she whispered that Miss Stella should please lace her on the bare. Stella thrilled as she felt the woman's lips and tongue softly licking her own feet. She looked at the gorgeous breadth of the Bull's creamy, firm buttocks spread before her, and could not resist cracking the whip smartly across them: once, twice, then a dozen times. All the while, the Bull's licking of her feet grew fiercer and more loving. Stella glowed with joy, for by her domination she would give the Bull the pleasure she craved, but did not dare admit to! Heather and the others urged her to give the Bull a proper thrashing, and the group gradually became the focus of general attention. Miss Dancer's circle approached; Clapton detached herself from it, her face dark.

'Do you like your treatment, Amanda?' said Stella, remembering Tawser Bright's advice on politeness. 'I do hope so, for it's what you've always wanted, isn't it? A good thrashing in front of your drudges. To be a sub, like *me*!

'Oh – Oh –' moaned the Bull, her naked bottom writhing. 'Oh, don't stop, Miss. I'm all wet, I – Oh! Ooh!'

The Bull's squirming naked ecstasy was interrupted as Clapton snatched the whip from Stella and cried that she would get further punishment for this disgrace.

'There's plenty of time before your ordeal, Miss Stella,' she crowed. 'I think we'll have you ride the crossbar for a while. We must spare your bum for the tawse, but your back deserves a seeing to, I think, *Miss*.'

The Bull protested that Stella was *her* slave, but the crowd's loyalty now switched to Clapton, and Stella was borne without protest to the centre of the yard. Here, a sort of Rugby football goal had been erected next to Miss Dancer's house, in the shadow of the Steps; except that the crossbar of this goal was only two feet from the ground, and the sideposts no more than six feet apart. Stella saw that Miss Dancer was smiling thanks at her: the combined festival was proceeding splendidly!

Under Clapton's direction, Stella was placed squatting on the crossbar, so that her fount took her full weight, pressing with extreme discomfort on the wooden rail about two inches wide. Stella felt herself frightened but excited, as though in a lustful dream, as her legs were bent under her, and crossed very tightly under the bar. Her bare feet poked awkwardly up. Her arms were crossed behind her back, and bound at the elbows, with her wrists positioned just above her ankles. Then her ankles were pushed higher and higher until her toes and fingertips touched. She thought she could scarcely be constricted more, but she was, allowing Clapton to strap wrists and ankles together with leather thongs.

Her tormentor stepped back, and looked approvingly as she flexed the Bull's whip. The Bull, red-faced, huddled in her greatcoat and said nothing. Stella, meanwhile, was forced to balance on the insidiously painful rail by squeezing her thighs and calves against it, in order not to topple over and strike the ground. Every effort to keep her balance made the pressure of the wood between her fount-lips more agonising. Clapton said that she could not see a girly so ill at ease, – '*Miss*,' – and fetched two more ropes, with heavy metal clamps fixed to the ends.

The clamps were fastened, so tightly as to make her eyes water, on to Stella's nipples, whose stiff swelling beneath the tight bra satin made removal of the bra unnecessary. The ropes were then stretched and secured to the top of the goalposts. Thus was Stella painfully and precariously held, the nipple clamps adding cruelly to her discomfort, since the support ropes jerked her breasts at her slightest sway. To complete her trussing, Clapton in her fury tore off one of her own shoes and thrust the leather tip deep into Stella's mouth.

Without ceremony, Clapton lifted the whip and began to lash her naked shoulders, rocking Stella's tethered body at each stroke. Tremors of pain shook through her clamped nipples and pressed cunt. The pain streaked across her soft shoulders, searing her like white-hot needles, and in her distress, she was glad of her leather gag to chew. The strokes came faster and faster, and she heard Clapton hiss that this would teach her to make a girly of another lady. The throng cheered ecstatically, none louder than Heather and Tuffy, and through her tears Stella thought ruefully that she was certainly helping the Blues' grand plan.

She lost count of the whipstrokes, and after a while her tears came less thickly; her bare back grew used to the burning pain of the lash, which seemed almost like a fiery, familiar caress. Suddenly there was a snap, and she fell violently forward, breaking her fall on the bar with the heel of Clapton's shoe. The whipping had torn the bra-strap, and the bra, together with the nipple clamps and tethering ropes, flew free of Stella's body. Such was Clapton's fury, however, that she did not stop her whipping. Stella was able to balance herself on the bar by using the shoe-heel in her mouth, and her new prone position meant that her buttocks were high and exposed.

Now Clapton began to aim the whip low, catching her full on the panties stretched tightly over her upthrust fesses. Stella gasped as the first arse-stroke flamed against her globes, and she realised that the panties were wet, and had been for her whole beating. The whip to her buttocks was truly her friend! But then Stella heard a cry from the newly enlivened Bull, and a scuffle as she sprang at Clapton.

'My bra, you bitch! You've ruined my bra, and you're not going to ruin my panties!'

The whipping ceased, and Stella twisted her head to look. The Bull had thrown off her greatcoat, and, nude, was sitting on top of Clapton. She punched the older woman ferociously on her breasts and between the thighs, with powerful blows right to the fount-lips. With her other hand she was ripping Clapton's clothing so that her skirt was torn, her stockings shredded, and her tight black knickers revealed. One naked breast hung awkwardly from Clapton's dislodged black bra. The Bull seemed intent on having these garments to replace her own poppy ones. The two women writhed on the ground, one nude and the other approaching nudity as her skin was exposed, pinched and beaten by the avenging Bull.

Miss Dancer's voice rang out angrily.

'Stop it at *once*, Kernecians! This is out of order! A Prefect and a College Servant, squabbling like drudges! Clapton, the lots you have drawn may stand – Miss Shawn's punishment will go ahead – but you are no longer Mistress of Lots! You, Miss Bulford, are consigned to the Remove.'

'But, Miss,' said the Bull, 'a Prefect cannot be a member of the Remove.'

'That,' replied Miss Dancer, 'is because you are no longer a Prefect. It is a House matter, of course, but I am sure Poppy's Housemistress will agree with me.'

Miss Rime paused in her gulping of cake to nod fervently that she did indeed agree. Miss Dancer then ordered Stella unbound, and said that in view of the Kernecians' excitement, it was fitting that Stella should Run The Tawse forthwith. The fun and games were over, and proper business must proceed. Stella bowed her head and was led the short distance to the Steps, and as she passed Miss Dancer she begged her not to be too harsh on the Bull and Clapton.

'I was loving it, Miss,' she said. 'As you were well aware.' Miss Dancer took a deep breath, sighed and smiled.

14

Ice and Honey

Stella stood at the bottom of the Steps, watching as the Prefects, drudges, even Mistresses mounted, to flog her. She saw Alberta, and her chums from Poppy's and the Blue Army, standing near the top. Even Miss Noble was there for her. There was no sign of Jakes. And Morag herself gave a little wave: she was standing on the very highest step but one, as though that were reserved for Stella herself. She felt emboldened that Morag had faith in her.

The yard was silent, now, and Stella shivered in the cold wind. Much of the day had slipped past, and shadows were already beginning to lengthen. Soon it would be twilight, and the time for bonfires and lanterns and the bewitchment of Hallowe'en's darkness. Stella's arms were still bound behind her back. She was barefoot, wearing only the poppy panties, and flanked by Clapton, Matron and Miss Dancer. The Bull appeared at her side, ready to ascend to her Step, and asked Miss Stella for the privilege of ripping her panties, in the tradition of Knobkerry Night. Stella smiled, thinking this awfully sweet and touching. She was about to agree, when Florence Tate intervened.

'I was the last to Run The Tawse,' she proclaimed, 'and as such, I have the right to attend the next, Miss Stella. It is in the Rulebook, page 219, footnote D.' Miss Dancer thought for a moment, then nodded her assent.

'So, Clapton,' said Florence Tate boldly, 'you may put

away your Parph apples, for Miss Stella's tawsing will be otherwise enhanced.'

Clapton glowered but said nothing. Florence lifted her arm, and ceremonially ripped off Stella's panties, stuffing them in the manner of a keepsake down the front of her own skirt. She knelt and kissed Stella's feet and bare bottom, rose and bowed to Miss Dancer, then took Stella to one side. First she unbound her wrists, announcing that it was her right to replace that constraint with a harsher one – Miss Dancer assented – and bound Stella's hair back with three hairpins, which she said mysteriously that Stella might need. Then she produced a gleaming container from under her skirt. The container was, on closer inspection, a rubber tube which bulged with its frosted, jagged contents.

'I had to telephone Mrs McWhirter's fish cannery in Durness,' said Florence breathlessly. 'She came in her van straight away, bless her, when I explained that a Lady's honour was at stake.'

'What is it?' asked Stella.

'It's dry ice, for your bum, Stella! It has to be in a bag, otherwise it'll burn your skin. It is much colder than water ice: you know, it is the stuff they use to make smoke in stage plays. I'm not sure what the rubber sheath is, and –' she blushed '– I didn't like to ask. But it's lubricated with special oil, so it will slide into your bum easily.'

Stella was mystified, and said so.

'Hurry, Miss! Part your bum-cheeks, so I can shove it right inside you. This will hurt horribly! It will be so cold, it'll feel like molten lead inside your bumhole! The point is, you won't even notice the tawsing, you will be so concerned to leap up those steps and melt the ice with the friction of your body. And the old books from Tawser Bright's time say that a girl who gets to the top, and has one ice cube left, can name any forfeit or favour she likes! It's never been tried before. Just imagine it's a penis, a lovely hard man's cock in your bumhole. Only it will feel more delicious and bigger than any penis you've ever had.' Florence blushed again.

Stella held her bum-cheeks wide, and felt the tip of the

rubber bag nestle against her anus bud, then thrust firmly inside her. She had to stifle a squeal. It was so big, so knobbly and hard, and cold, strangely as though a white hot lance had penetrated her. Florence thrust, until Stella's arse-globes closed, locking the tube of ice inside her. She shuddered at the searing pain, and said to Miss Dancer that she was ready – no, desperate! – to start her climb. Miss Dancer lifted her hand, and Stella began to race up the Steps, followed by the heaviest tawse she had ever seen.

Florence had been right; she leapt over the Steps two at a time, throwing her tawsers into confusion, so that the flogging tool had to be thrown over their heads to catch up with Stella. The strokes fell on her unprotected nates, and they were indeed harsher than she had ever known, but she registered the fearsome pain of the tawse somehow at a distance, as if she were observing a classroom experiment. She knew that it was her pain, that her bare bum was reddening as she took it, but it seemed at the same time to belong to a faraway place.

All she felt was the engulfing, burning chill of the ice-pack within her anus. It suffused her with a deadly glow of cold fire, and she pumped her freed arms desperately in time with her pulsing thighs as she raced to get to the top. The pain of the ice suffused her utterly, gradually numbing her lower body so that the tawse-strokes became more and more remote. Stella would have raced up a thousand Steps, to lessen the horrid freezing fire in her tender anus!

Her eyes blurred with stinging sweat, and as she ascended, she felt the swollen bag in her bottom begin to shrink. There was icy liquid mingling with the sweat on her thighs. The dry ice was melting! She looked behind her, noting that she was halfway up the Steps, and saw that plumes of steam were spurting from her anus as she ran, like a dragon's breath! She knew she could make the top, and now, she had to slow down and clench her buttocks tightly, in order to clasp her precious bum-cargo. The secret chamber loomed in her sweat-blurred eyes like a holy citadel, and she knew she must penetrate it. The rubber tube shrank more and more rapidly as she neared the top, her heart and lungs pumping. Below her she could see the great green expanse of the Parph, and beyond, the grey, white-capped ocean, patrolled by tiny fishing boats and wheeling ducks and seagulls. She exulted in her strength of body and the power of her resolve, and felt herself Mistress of Kernece!

Panting, she reached the last Step but one, where Morag awaited her. She stopped and drew breath, for Morag had to wait for the Tawse to catch up! Morag took it, and dealt a fierce stroke to Stella's quivering bum.

'My, how red you are, Stella!' she cried. 'So lovely!'

Stella took her whipping hand and pulled her after her, on to the top Step. She said that she must take the last stroke there, to complete her ascent, and perfect her claim to the chamber. She bent over to touch her toes for Morag's tawse! She took a hard lash perfectly placed across her naked fesses, to wild applause from below. Then, Stella opened her bum-cheeks and extruded the glistening ice-pack, now a shrivelled ribbon of rubber. There was only one of the precious cubes left intact, right at the end! She took the rubber tube and whirled it round her head like a lariat, then hurled it to the crowd, to land at Miss Dancer's feet.

It remained now to gain her rightful access to the secret chamber. She told Morag to lead her comrades down; she must be alone for her task. Now, she understood Florence's gift of hairpins. She unbound her hair, letting her long blonde tresses flow in the October breeze, cascading deliciously over her naked shoulders and breasts. She felt like the princess of her own Tower. She approached the heavy wooden door, but had no need to pick the lock; the door creaked open at her touch, on hinges long unoiled, releasing a musty yet intriguing reek of stale air. She took a deep breath and entered, shivering: the first Lady in years, perhaps in centuries, to behold the Norsemen's Treasure of Kernece.

The secret chamber was a bare stone cell, smaller than the menacing bulb of its exterior suggested. A slit window allowed a thin ray of sun to illumine the clouds of dust which Stella's feet stirred. Cobwebs hung thick, and the dust was speckled with the carcases of insects. All around were piled stacks of earthenware jars, about three feet high, which she thought she recognised from pictures: they looked like amphorae from ancient Greece. The jars were sealed with thick stoppers of a clear amber substance. She tapped one, gingerly, and saw a magnificent jewelled scarab inside the lid. It *was* amber! There was some writing chiselled on the side and she bent to look; in crabbed letters, it read 'Naxos'. She did not know whether to be frightened or intrigued but intrigue got the better of her. She began to chip at one of the amber stoppers.

It would, she saw, be a long task. How many centuries had these jars lain here, and what could they possibly contain? As she chipped away at the seals, her mind wandered to the bold Norsemen, roaming and pillaging far to the East. Had they, then, visited Naxos, and stolen these jars of treasure? Had they met Kytetroos himself? There must have been Norsemen in his era, just as in our own, she thought, feeling that somehow, there had *always* been Norsemen.

Her fingernails cracked, and she looked for a spike or peg to use as a tool. She knelt and poked in the dust, but found nothing, and suddenly she saw a shadow blocking the sun's ray above her. She jumped in fright, and looked up.

'Is *this* what you are looking for?' drawled Jakes, wigless now but still dressed in his girl's uniform, with his skirt and petticoat raised, showing his garter belt and straps, but no panties. He held his monstrous penis naked in his hand, and it was fully straining and erect. At its tip, the splayed thongs of his metal whip danced menacingly. He reached past her, glanced through the door, and closed it.

'They've all gone,' he said. 'There is a fire, and they are having their feast, before they burn the long ship for Up-Helly-A. We are all alone, Miss.'

'What are you doing here, Jakes?' she stammered. 'I thought nobody had ever –'

'No *woman*,' said Jakes. 'But as you can see, I am not a

woman. And I have been waiting for you, for I mean to complete my man's work. Still virgin? Not for long. *This* is the treasure you and all females seek!'

He slapped the shaft of his stiff bare penis, making his tattoos writhe: Stella found herself dry-mouthed but tantalised despite herself. Jakes advanced on her, lazily. Crouching, Stella looked for a weapon; there was none.

'Don't worry, girly,' he said, 'I'm not going to take you by force. I don't have to. You're going to beg for it. They all do! Aren't you wet in your cunt, already, just thinking of my cock fucking you?' Stella frowned in annoyance, realising that her fount *was* a tiny bit moist! Damn Jakes and his accursed maleness! Damn her own womanhood!

'No – I was just thinking – You look awfully nice, Jakes. Awfully sweet, as a girl. It makes you somehow more manly!'

There was a flicker of softness and pleasure in Jakes's eyes, the same softness she had glimpsed in the tuckshop. Then his male carapace closed over him again, and he sneered, 'Is that the best you can think of, girly? Nice? You won't find it nice when I give your bum her whipping. You'll beg for it, of course. How red she is from that tawse, and how beautifully my cock rose, watching you! But she's not nearly red enough.'

'Mmm! Yes!' murmured Stella coyly. 'I say, the uniform suits you. Especially the skirt, and the petticoat, and the blouse is a nice fit. It goes well with your stockings.'

She saw Jakes look down and give a little pat to his skirt-bum, and make sure his stockings were smooth.

'What is in these jars?' she asked, still on her knees.

'Who cares? Bones, probably. Burial urns. Who would put anything valuable in stupid jars? I come up here, you know, to be alone with my thoughts, and to get away from all you damn women. Alone with bones . . . That's funny!'

'Why do you wish to get away from women, Jakes, when you want us so much?'

'It is you who want me! And this!' He stroked his stiff cock again, making the whip-fronds whirl prettily. Stella was entranced. She *did* want him inside her. But she knew it would be wrong, for her *and* for Jakes. He must be taught . . .

'Oh, I do want you, Jakes!' she cried, not untruthfully. 'You're a real man! And like all real men, you'll have to *catch* your female!'

Suddenly, she sprang to her feet, and aimed a kick right to his exposed bare balls. She knew this was the way to hurt a male, but she did not want to hurt him, or any other. Aiming her kick straight at his core, she brought it like lightning to within an inch of his skin, then arrested her foot. Jakes's reactions were like lightning too, as she correctly guessed. He whirled round, his arms flailing, and toppled the topmost amphora, which in turn crashed into others. They all fell to the stone floor right beside Stella, bursting and splintering to drench her with their contents. She scarcely had time to note what had happened before she was out the door and scampering down the Steps she had so painfully ascended. She hurtled to the yard, passed the astonished crowd, girls occupied with their barbecued bones and meat juices dribbling down their chins, astonished at this naked apparition. Stella snatched a plump bone from a drudge.

'Sorry!' she cried to the wind. Gnawing as she ran, she sped out the gate, turning towards the scent of the sea and the sound of the swirling gulls and ducks. She wanted to get away from Jakes, but knew he would catch her. She heard him rushing after her, peppering the air with curses, and wondered what the festive crowd would make of him, with his penis a flagpole. Playfully she threw the gnawed bone at him, and headed for the Parph, and the field. There she would find the sacred grove, and the Tree. She knew that if it was to happen, it must happen there, on her own woman's ground. *She* must be in control.

The mossy ground was damp and silky under her bare feet, seeming to speed her on. Her hair streamed in the wind and she felt exultant as her strong legs, caressed by flowers, flew across the darkly scented terrain. The Norsemen's Treasure of Kernece was oddly sticky and sweet-smelling on her bare skin, but she had no time to think further what the it might be, save that it seemed a very odd treasure indeed. Ducks hooted overhead as though in greeting. She felt like Helen of Troy, or one of the Sabine Women, fleeing her prince while longing to be caught by him in the blissful submission of sheer helplessness. The virile male must conquer his willing victim!

She turned once or twice and saw Jakes gaining on her, and she slowed her pace. His penis shone before him like a wonderful lance, with the knight's pennant of the golden whip-fronds shimmering in the low sunlight. She reached the football field, and headed for the grove. Her heart leapt; it was perfect! She clung to the beautiful gnarled Tree, caressing the breasts and thighs, as Jakes came to her.

'You have me, Sir!' she cried. 'I am yours! Take me if you must! Whip my bare body for my wilful flight. Take my virgin hymen, but show gentleness and mercy!'

'I'll whip you Miss, said Jakes, with surprising gentleness, 'but not before you've had my cock inside you.'

Before he could touch her, Stella cried 'Oh . . .' and let herself slip down from the Tree. Her back pressed the cool moss, and she looked up at the sky, thinking how beautiful and perfect it all was. Her cunt flowed with her sweet oils, trickling down her shivering thighs to perfume the moss which was her bridal bed. Jakes came nearer and nearer, his cock trembling and stiff, as though caressed by the breeze.

The whip was sheathed back in its ring, now, and she flowed with moisture as she imagined that hard golden circle smoothly penetrating her folds, to be followed by the giant mystery of the manhood which bore it. He knelt before her, and Stella opened her thighs as wide as she could. She parted her wet cunt-lips with trembling fingers to show her stiff swollen damsel, and her glistening pink passage awaiting his touch, his entrance, his possession. The gleaming helmet of his cock was an inch from her swollen, waiting cunt-lips. She shut her eyes and murmured, 'Yes . . .'

Suddenly there was the bang of a gun, and a male voice.

'I say! Miss Stella! Well! I was just passing, with my girls – Betty, Patsy and Ethel, you remember – and – After the ducks, you know – And – well! You seem to be all smeared in *honey!* What *is* going on?'

Stella opened her eyes and saw, flanked by three smiling blonde lasses, the puzzled, beautiful features of Jamie, Lord Isbister and Jarl of Yell.

'I know what is going on, my Lord,' said one of the strapping blonde lasses, with a broad grin, and followed with a burst of the Norwegiany language. Jamie Isbister blushed crimson, and raised his shotgun.

'Jamie! No! Put it away!' cried Stella, raising herself on her elbows. 'You are man enough without it, Sir!'

Betty, Patsy and Ethel giggled their agreement, and Jamie obeyed, but instead took a riding crop from his belt. Stella stood, and demanded what he proposed to do.

'Why, I'm going to do what any Isbister would do, or Cousin Stackenham for that matter! I'm going to whip this scoundrel! Even that Stackenham filly Amanda would take off her frilly maid's uniform for a moment and do the same!'

He ordered the lasses to go and tend to their horses, which could be heard whinnying in the distance.

'Shan't,' said Betty, Patsy and Ethel in unison. 'We want to watch the fun.'

'You, sir,' roared Jamie – Stella thrilled at how *manful* he was!, 'bend over for your thrashing! You may be kitted as a Lady, but you'll touch your toes and take your thrashing like a Gentleman!'

Jakes got to his feet, and put his hands on his hips.

'Ha! You'll have to fight me for her. And I'll beat you. What have you got for a weapon? a tickler and a popgun! I've got *this!*' And he proudly tapped his cock, which Stella thought seemed stiffer than ever, at the expectation of combat. Her already wet fount flowed still more copiously, at the thought of two males doing battle for her! And she saw the three lasses hugging each other with excited giggles, their hands boldly creeping beneath their kilts.

'Jakes is right,' she said. 'First, you two Gentlemen have

not been properly introduced, and the civilities must be observed. Jamie, this is Jakes; Jakes, Lord Isbister.' Jamie frowned and bowed stiffly. Jakes nodded with a puzzled look.

'Jakes was going to take my virginity,' Stella continued, 'and I was going to let him. But you, Jamie, are a Lord, and you may choose to fight for my virginity, if you wish to be *my* Lord, and – and take it for yourself.'

There! She had said it. Her heart beat wildly as her fount gushed with desire for the young Lord, a desire which she knew had never left her.

'Jamie – remove your clothing,' she ordered, her voice trembling now. 'And you, Jakes, do the same. I want you both naked, and you shall be armed with the weapons Nature has given you. You shall fight for me with swords, Gentlemen: the swords of your manly flesh.'

Betty, Patsy and Ethel were now so excited that they were quite open in their mutual caresses, with fingers darting feverishly under ruffled kilts. Stella saw glimpses of creamy thigh and swelling shaven founts, and longed to stroke herself! The ducks hooted overhead, as though cheering the spectacle of their own hunter at bay.

Nervously, Jamie and Jakes stripped, both warily eyeing the other, and Stella thrilled when she saw the long sweet shaft of Jamie's beloved cock. He was not quite as big as Jakes – a fact Jakes noted with a triumphant smirk – but Stella knew that Jamie's centuries of nobility, and the ferocity of his ancient Jarl blood, would give him victory!

Stella ordered them to face each other, keeping hands on hips, and said that the rules were the same as fencing with épée or rapier. She watched as both penises, fired by the lust for combat, stood to their full height. Stella's heart was in her mouth; she thought her Lord's cock, erect and straining, was the most beautiful weapon she could ever dream of. Two heroes were to battle for her: now *this* was the stuff of romance and chivalry!

The three blonde lasses evidently thought so too, as they blatantly kissed, stroked and masturbated each other with kilts fully raised to reveal the sweetest shaven founts. Jamie did not seem to find this breach of aristocratic discipline unusual. Stella found herself smiling as she wondered what Cousin Stackenham would have to say – or the 'filly' Amanda – the Bull, with her frilly maid's uniform, indeed! She decided that the three lasses should interrupt their sport and act as scorekeepers: a point for a hit on the thigh; two for the belly; three, for a hit on the opponent's bulb; four, for a hit right to the balls! The prospect of this carnage cheered the lasses, and they fixed their eyes intently. Stella added boldly that any failure of erection would result in instant defeat, failure to be decided by her as referee.

On Stella's signal the contest started. It was lovely to see the two erect cocks flail as they parried, thrust and riposted. What Jakes gained by the size of his penis – which, Stella was thrilled to see, was not all that much! – was made up by Jamie's dexterity, and the cunning swiftness of his jabs and parries against Jakes's ungainly manhood. Gradually, it was clear that Jamie was the more skilful, and his jabs to the belly grew sharper and evidently more irritating. Jakes was reduced to making clumsy lunges, using his cock as a sort of broadsword. Neither cock showed any sign of wilting, and Jamie's points were mounting, with stroke after stroke to his rival's thighs and belly.

Suddenly Jakes, with an angry roar, made a fierce lunge and caught Jamie straight on the balls with his shining helmet! Jamie groaned, and Jakes followed his thrust with another, this time to Jamie's peehole. And then a third, to the balls again! Jamie staggered back, his eyes tight with pain, and to her horror, Stella saw his penis start to wilt! He looked at her, pleading, as Jakes, now points ahead, advanced for his *coup*. Unthinking, Stella parted her thighs and opened her cunt-lips to Jamie's gaze, then put her finger to her throbbing clit and began to rub her damsel.

Jamie smiled and took a deep breath, and his cock became as stiff as the Tree herself. He sidestepped Jakes's lunge, and stabbed him directly in the balls, then stabbed him again! Jakes groaned and tottered, and Jamie closed in, forcing his cock around the base of the other's shaft.

With an expert contortion of his belly muscles, he bent Jakes's giant organ sideways, using his own cock as a merciless lever! Jakes sagged, and Jamie drew back his hips. With a sharp, blurring thrust he struck Jakes full in the balls, with his own orbs! Stella's hand flew to her lips: it had not seemed very hard – how could it? – but she didn't know exactly how painful such a blow might be.

It did not seem to cause much discomfort to Jamie, who fell on the staggering Jakes and straddled him. His cock locked on his opponent's and he forced him bit by bit to his knees, then flat on the ground! Jamie looked up in triumph, and the three lasses gave their employer the thumbs up signal. Helpfully removing any hint of bias, Jakes groaned that he submitted. Jamie at once released him, and helped him to his feet, with a hearty handshake.

'Good show, old sport,' he panted. 'No hard feelings, eh? Hope you're not, you know – All fair in love and war, what.'

Patsy, Betty, and Ethel at once threw themselves on the still-proud Jakes, more specifically on his penis, which showed dangerous signs of wilting. Cooing and kissing, they nursed the organ back to a pleasing erection. After some good-humoured jostling, they took it in turns to lift their kilts and mount him, arms round his neck and thighs around his waist. Their wet shining founts spread firmly to take his massive bulb inside. Jamie said nothing; his eyes, and his stiff cock, said everything for him. Without a word, he scooped Stella in his arms and carried her back to the base of the tree. Here she lay with thighs wide and fount dripping, this time for her true Lord.

'Yes,' she moaned, her feet touching the back of his neck as his massively stiff penis thrust smoothly inside her.

'Do you mean it?' he gasped. 'Truly?'

'*Yes!*' cried Stella. She felt the briefest of discomfort, then ecstasy. Stella was no longer virgin.

Jamie's cock seemed inexhaustible as he fucked Stella with the tenderness of a lady tending a flower. He took her in the cunt; in the mouth, her tongue and lips worshipping her Lord's penis; and from the rear, where she crouched with her bottom upthrust as though for a beating. He took her once in the anus, spanking her bare fesses as he did so. She orgasmed three times before she lost count, and her orgasms melted into one hot ocean on which she floated as though drowning in pleasure. He proved capable of fucking for ages without sperming, and as soon as he had done so, he was stiff for her again! Not far away, Jakes was being thoroughly tested by the voracious blonde lasses. He lay on his back with his head on his hands, grinning with something gentler than his usual arrogance as the women writhed on his cock.

Stella's blissful reverie was interrupted by a sharp cry from Jamie, just as she sensed he was about to sperm once more. She looked up and there stood Morag, beaming, with her finger tickling Jamie's anus!

'You mossy bitch!' she cried. 'I came to see if you were all right, and look at the pie you've got to eat!'

Stella laughed, and gently showed her Lord Jamie that Morag should take her place. Were they not all friends?

'There is plenty of pie for everyone,' she said, and watched as her Lord came to his sperming in her friend's cunt. Then she strolled to where the wriggling Jakes was pleasuring Betty, or perhaps Ethel, yet again. Without a word, the lass yielded her place to Stella. Jakes's massive engine slid into her dripping cunt with the gentlest of thrusts, and she began to writhe, gasping, in her turn.

'See, Sir?' she said loudly, so that all could hear. 'You do not have to be arrogant to be a true man, just as my Lord needs no gun or whip. The penis is whip enough. He has had me in cunt, and now I have you . . . Remember that, to be a Gentleman, you must not treat Ladies with disdain, nor hide from them in a tower. And we Ladies must learn not to hide ourselves in towers! We need to be whipped, by Gentlemen, whose penises are not weapons, but flowers! And all a true Gentleman needs to please us is not heroism or glory or sneering disdain, but a big cock and good table manners!' And, crying to Jamie as he renewed his worshipful fucking of Morag, whose body shone with power and beauty:

'A live cock is better than a dead hero!'

At these words, Jakes's sperm spurted so strongly that it overflowed down the wet insides of Stella's thighs, mingling with her own juices. The three lasses rushed to lick it from her.

The party arrived back at Kernece on horseback, to find Hallowe'en in full swing. It was nearly dark; bonfires had been lit, and there were ghoulish masks and turnip lanterns. They were about to light a fire under the long ship, but Stella, welcomed heartily by Miss Dancer, and sullenly by Clapton, cried that she was due her forfeit. The long ship was not to be touched by flame, as her prow was a woman, like the Tree where Stella's own womanhood had so gorgeously flowered. Instead, the forfeit was that Stella herself be bound to the prow, and spanked on the bare, by every Kernecian, including Jakes, and including Jamie and his lasses, who Stella pronounced honorary Kernecians! One spank each, as Stella whispered a single instruction, which the recipient was honour bound to obey.

Florence Tate opined that this was within the Rules. Before the spanking, drudges were sent to retrieve the treasure from the secret chamber, and a spoonful was given to each Lady before she delivered her spank.

'Strange, that the top of the Tower should contain honey,' said Miss Dancer.

'What else would you expect a treasure to be, Miss?' replied Stella. 'And when it is gone, there is plenty of our very own treasure, to take its place. I am sure Kytetroos would have approved of Parph apples.'

Stella found her spanking most relaxing, and was pleased that the Kernecians took their instructions so willingly. Only Jakes seemed doubtful.

'Miss Dancer's slave? And dressed in frillies? If you say so, Miss Stella,' he said, 'but what will Clapton think of losing my services?'

'Clapton will be delighted to have as her own slave a young man, also dressed in frillies, with a penis which thanks to my gravitational enhancement, will shortly be the equal of yours, Sir,' replied Stella.

Towards dawn, in the Remove Dorm, Stella and Morag lay side by side. Sleep would come to neither.

'What jolly instructions!' said Morag. 'You are a clever little sub. If you really are a sub, that is. Isn't it time you made up your mind?'

Stella whispered that she already had.

'And just to prove I'm a sub, we'll go and see the Bull,' said Stella. 'I am sure she wants a drudge at this hour. And if she doesn't I'll jolly well order her to want one.'

Morag said that it was a master-stroke to abolish the Armies, with all their time-wasting games.

'I haven't abolished the Armies!' retorted Stella. 'I've just amalgamated the Blues and the Reds, so that there is only one democratic Army: the Purple! And you can only tell rank from the way a Lady shaves her mink.'

'But everyone now has to shave her mink completely.'

'Exactly,' said Stella. 'So the Army is *really* secret.'

Morag wondered what instruction Stella had given Jamie, and was told airily that it was nothing much. He was to install a direct telephone line from Isbister Castle, to summon Stella as his drudge, whenever she desired to be summoned. Which would be two or three times a week . . .

Stella opened the Bull's door, without knocking.

'You wanted a drudge, Miss?' she barked. 'Here I am.'

'I . . . Did I?' said Amanda Bulford, rubbing the sleep from her eyes. 'Yes, Miss, I suppose I did.'

Stella delivered a stinging slap to her bare left buttock, which peeped from her tousled nightie. The Bull squeaked.

'You call me "bitch" or "slut", not "Miss",' said Stella firmly. 'I am a drudge, remember? Now get your frilly maid's uniform on – I know you have it secreted – and then make us some tea. Then you can lick my feet clean, and when the tea is ready, get down on all fours with your bum bared for a thrashing, And your back can be our table while I cane you.'

'Yes – slut,' said the Bull, and went to obey. As Morag and Stella enjoyed their tea, their sips were punctuated by the swish of the Bull's own cane, and its owner's howls.

Stella grinned and said to Morag that it was quite easy to be a sub, if one knew how; but Morag looked broody.

'You and Isbister, Clapton and Alberta, Jakes and Miss Dancer – Sometimes a girl sort of pines for a steady male.'

'*Now* I remember,' said Stella. 'There is another thing for you to do, Miss Amanda, when you have finished making me thrash you. Your Cousin Stackenham: military man, eh?

'Yes, Miss,' said the Bull. 'Ouch! I mean, yes, you mossy bitch.'

'Heart in right place, but needs bum warmed occasionally?'

'Very much so.'

'Big cock?'

'Why, yes.'

'Get him here pronto,' drawled Stella. 'I want him to meet my best friend ...'

15

The Deep End

The new Mistress looked round her quarters, and breathed a sigh of pure joy.

'Oh, thank you, Miss Dancer! It is the summit of my dreams, these long years! My own post at Kernece! How pleased I am to renew our friendship – this time as colleagues, though I am your subordinate! But to be a Mistress at Kernece is better than to be Headmistress at the grandest establishment on Earth! I thank you, Miss.'

Miss Dancer ran a finger along the window sill, disturbing a layer of dust.

'You shall meet other old friends, too. Meanwhile, I think your apartment has not been well serviced; I'll have a drudge sent along at once, and leave you to unpack.'

She smiled and withdrew, and the newcomer began to take her clothes off for her bath, cooing with delight at the compact luxury of her new home. She put the kettle on for tea, and elected to take a shower-bath. While the tepid, but plentiful, water cascaded down her back, she took her razor and made sure that her body was properly shaved. A few naughty little mink-hairs had grown during her long journey north, and she couldn't have *that*!

There was a knock on the door.

'Drudge, Miss,' said a female voice.

'Come in, I shall be out of the shower in a moment. Meanwhile, you may set to your work. You will please make us some tea.' The door opened and the drudge entered.

'At your service, Miss,' she said obediently. 'May I welcome you to Kernece. My, this apartment does need cleaning! I'll set to it right away.'

Over the hiss of the shower, there were the sounds of brushing and wiping in the apartment.

'Miss,' said the drudge, 'there is a lot of dirt here, and I shall do my best, but as a drudge I must be prepared for your displeasure if I am remiss in my task. I trust Miss Dancer has explained that all drudges are subject to the sternest discipline. The naughtiest of drudges wear a special uniform, similar to a French maid's, with a very short frilly skirt and without knickers. I am wearing such a uniform now – I had the honour of designing it myself, actually. The skirt is easily drawn up to reveal the bare globes, should they require punishment.'

'Why, yes – but I am sure there shall be no need of that! On my very first day . . .'

'I am *not* so sure, Miss. And your very first day at Kernece is no different from every other day. We are all thrown in at the deep end.'

The new Mistress emerged from her shower, wrapped in a large towel, and saw the drudge at work on her hands and knees, with her bottom raised towards her. Her uniform *was* fetching: a black satin bustier with a white frilly apron, black shoes and stockings fastened to a very tight suspender belt, pinching the waist which was visible above the peaches of her croup. The uniform's deliciously short frilly skirt rode high over her bum. As the drudge had said, she wore no knickers, and the creamy globes of her bare bottom were a delight. Her long blonde hair cascaded over her back and breast.

'I fear, Miss, that I have already proved remiss at this work, and a lazy drudge deserves severe punishment. It seems I have let the kettle boil over, too. What must you think of my sloppiness! I shall fetch the rack of canes, so that you may select a suitable implement for my chastisement. Or there is the tawse, if you prefer, though I recommend the cane, as it is more painful.'

The drudge looked up with a serene, twinkling

expression, and the new Mistress was so astonished she let her towel fall to reveal her naked breasts.

'Why, Stella Shawn!' she cried. 'What a lovely surprise! The idea of my caning *you*, dear girl – it is impossible!'

'At Kernece, nothing is impossible,' said Stella, rising. 'I shall fetch the canes, and make the tea, then bend over to receive the chastisement a naughty drudge deserves.'

As she smoothed her frilly skirt and apron, there was a brief glimpse of her swelling fount. Stella Shawn was shaven too! Tea was prepared, and the rack of canes brought.

'I recommend this one,' said Stella gravely. 'It is the whippiest and the hardest. Now, I shall bend over while we let the tea brew. Or, I could straddle the sofa, on tiptoe.'

This course was agreed upon, and Stella drew her skirt well up over her back, revealing the fullest, silkiest fesses imaginable. She explained that there was a special seam in the back of the skirt to prevent it falling back over the bared nates during chastisement.

'I am quite proud of my design,' she said. 'A drudge must always be reminded of her place. Now, Miss, after my punishment, I suggest we take tea and discuss the finer points of your, and my, performance. And you will please not take it amiss if during my caning I give little pointers as to its greater efficacy. A chastisement between Ladies is after all a civilised occasion, and the niceties of Ladylike politeness and conversation must be observed at all times. You may, for example, care to tell me something of your journey here as you cane my bottom. Therefore, I think a slow two dozen and one strokes should be appropriate.'

Bemused, but excited – her fount felt moist with desire to redden those creamy buttocks – the new Mistress let her towel fall, and, naked for greater comfort, began the beating of her naughty drudge. She let fall a few pleasant remarks on her uneventful journey to Kernece, and the kind welcome from her sweet-tempered driver. But her emotion prevented her from sounding as casually Ladylike as Stella obviously expected. Meanwhile, the caning was punctuated by remarks from Stella, as her bare bottom twisted and wriggled juicily under the hard strokes.

'A little more to the left, perhaps, Miss. Ah! Yes! That really stung! And the back of my thighs, don't forget. Oh! *Ooh*! You certainly do know how to thrash a girl. Or should I say, you have not forgotten. This is most satisfactory. You are a worthy prize for Kernece ...'

Breathlessly, her fount soaking, the new Mistress put all her force into lashing the naked fesses of this impossibly serene drudge. She knew that the wetness of her desire could not be denied, and that more than a caning would – must! take place. She came to the end of the beating, and could not help but touch herself on her throbbing damsel as she contemplated the delicious crimson arse-globes her cane had so lovingly caressed. Stella politely thanked her for the punishment, and added that it had been most skilful.

'My, Stella, you have changed,' cried the new Mistress, as she bade the drudge rise, and come to her arms to be embraced. 'You have been here quite a time. I should expect you to be at least a Prefect, by now.'

Stella looked up and smiled.

'I am a naughty girl, a low drudge,' she said.

'Yet you talk so firmly, you are so – grown-up. One would think you were the Headmistress herself!'

Stella gazed at her with wide eyes as silky as moonbeams, then rose with arms outstretched.

'Why, Miss Cox,' she said to her former Headmistress, 'whatever makes you think I'm not?'

NEW BOOKS

Coming up from Nexus and Black Lace

There are three Nexus titles published in January

Emma's Secret Domination by Hilary James
January 1988   Price £4.99   ISBN: 0 352 33226 3

In this, the final instalment of the *Emma* series, Emma returns to London only to fall back into the clutches of her cruel former mistress Ursula. Realising that she has missed the bittersweet delights of lesbian domination, she begins finally to enjoy Ursula's attentions – but this only serves to anger and humiliate the prince, who is still her master. How will he administer the discipline she deserves?

'S' – A Story of Submission by Philippa Masters
January 1998   Price £4.99   ISBN: 0 352 33229 8

When S answers an advert which seems to promise an escape from her dull life, little does she realise that her fantasies of total submission are soon to be fulfilled. Entering into a secret world of domination, subservience and humiliation, she explores the bounds of her sexuality, finally realising the depravity of her darkest desires.

The Governess at St Agatha's by Yolanda Celbridge
January 1998   Price £4.99   ISBN: 0 352 32986 6

Miss Constance de Comynge's unusual education and correctional techniques are always in demand – by the residents of her village, the staff and pupils of the young ladies' acadamy she founds, and a number of other gentlemen of the locale. Nexus are reprinting some of their best-selling titles throughout 1998. This is the second book in the popular *Governess* series.

A Degree of Discipline by Zoe Templeton
February 1998   Price £4.99   ISBN: 0 352 33233 6

A new disciplinary law for young offenders has come into force and affects two naughty but naive young ladies, Juliette and Lucy, in quite different ways. They soon find themselves at a leading corrective establishment, Carstairs, and realise that their interest in discipline and humiliation is more than just academic, developing a taste for administering as well as receiving punishment.

Private Memoirs of a Kentish Headmistress
by Yolanda Celbridge
February 1998   Price £4.99   ISBN: 0 352 33232 8
Having learnt the delights of discipline, Miss Abigail Swift is keen to share that knowledge with others. She sets up an exclusive training academy for naughty young ladies at Orpingham Hall, with an intricate system of rules, ranks, and corporal punishment and restraints – all designed to teach her pupils the rudiments of correction.

Unhallowed Rites by Martine Marquand
January 1998   Price £5.99   ISBN: 0 352 332 220

Twenty-year-old Allegra di Vitale is bored with life in her guardian's Venetian palazzo – until temptation draws her to look at the bizarre pictures he keeps in his private chamber. Her lust awakened, she tries to deny her powerful cravings by submitting to life as a nun. But the strange order of the Convent of Santa Clerisa provides new temptations, forcing her to perform ritual acts with the depraved men and women of the convent.

Lake of Lost Love by Mercedes Kelly
December 1997   Price £5.99   ISBN: 0 352 33220 4

Princess Angeline lives on a paradise island in the South Seas. Married to Prince Hari and accepted into the native culture and customs, she has a life of ease and debauched sensual delights. When Prince Hari's young manservant is kidnapped and used as a sex slave by the cruel and depraved female ruler of nearby Monkey Island, Angeline sets about planning his rescue.

The Succubus by Zoe le Verdier
February 1998   Price £5.99   ISBN: 0 352 33230 1

When Adele, a young and innocent ballet dancer, learns that her dance company is in danger of losing its funding, she is only too happy to put on private performances for a wealthy patron of the arts. In order to save the company, she must dance the role of the sex-crazed Succubus, and learns to relish the role as it awakens a voracious appetite for new experiences in her which must be satisfied.

Ménage by Emma Holly
February 1998   Price £5.99   ISBN: 0 352 33231 X

When Kate finds her two flatmates in bed together, she is surprised by the strength of her arousal. When one of them asks her to join in, she leaps at the chance, little realising the extent of the experimental and perverse games they will soon come to play. The pleasure she experiences is beyond anything she had ever dreamt of, but will the implications of the kinky ménage à trois become too much?

NEXUS BACKLIST

All books are priced £4.99 unless another price is given. If a date is supplied, the book in question will not be available until that month in 1997.

CONTEMPORARY EROTICA

THE ACADEMY	Arabella Knight	
AGONY AUNT	G. C. Scott	
ALLISON'S AWAKENING	Lauren King	
BOUND TO SERVE	Amanda Ware	
BOUND TO SUBMIT	Amanda Ware	
CANDIDA'S SECRET MISSION	Virginia LaSalle	
CANDIDA IN PARIS	Virginia LaSalle	
CANDY IN CAPTIVITY	Arabella Knight	
CHALICE OF DELIGHTS	Katrina Young	
A CHAMBER OF DELIGHTS	Katrina Young	
THE CHASTE LEGACY	Susanna Hughes	
CHRISTINA WISHED	Gene Craven	
DARK DESIRES	Maria del Rey	
A DEGREE OF DISCIPLINE	Zoe Templeton	Feb
THE DOMINO TATTOO	Cyrian Amberlake	
THE DOMINO ENIGMA	Cyrian Amberlake	
THE DOMINO QUEEN	Cyrian Amberlake	
EDEN UNVEILED	Maria del Rey	
EDUCATING ELLA	Stephen Ferris	
ELAINE	Stephen Ferris	
EMMA'S SECRET WORLD	Hilary James	
EMMA'S SECRET DIARIES	Hilary James	
EMMA'S SUBMISSION	Hilary James	
EMMA'S HUMILIATION	Hilary James	
EMMA'S SECRET DOMINATION	Hilary James	Jan

FALLEN ANGELS	Kendal Grahame	
THE TRAINING OF FALLEN ANGELS	Kendal Grahame	
THE FANTASIES OF JOSEPHINE SCOTT	Josephine Scott	
THE FINISHING SCHOOL	Stephen Ferris	
HEART OF DESIRE	Maria del Rey	
HIS MISTRESS'S VOICE	G. C. Scott	
HOUSE OF INTRIGUE	Yvonne Strickland	
HOUSE OF TEMPTATIONS	Yvonne Strickland	
THE HOUSE OF MALDONA	Yolanda Celbridge	
THE ISLAND OF MALDONA	Yolanda Celbridge	
THE CASTLE OF MALDONA	Yolanda Celbridge	
THE ICE QUEEN	Stephen Ferris	
THE IMAGE AND OTHER STORIES	Jean de Berg	
THE INSTITUTE	Maria del Rey	
SISTERHOOD OF THE INSTITUTE	Maria del Rey	
JENNIFER'S INSTRUCTION	Cyrian Amberlake	
JOURNEY FROM INNOCENCE	Jean-Philippe Aubourg	
JULIE AT THE REFORMATORY	Angela Elgar	Feb
A MATTER OF POSSESSION	G. C. Scott	
MELINDA AND THE MASTER	Susanna Hughes	
MELINDA AND THE COUNTESS	Susanna Hughes	
MELINDA AND SOPHIA	Susanna Hughes	
MELINDA AND ESMERELDA	Susanna Hughes	
THE NEW STORY OF O	Anonymous	
ONE WEEK IN THE PRIVATE HOUSE	Esme Ombreux	
AMANDA IN THE PRIVATE HOUSE	Esme Ombreux	
PARADISE BAY	Maria del Rey	
THE PASSIVE VOICE	G. C. Scott	
PRIVATE MEMOIRS OF A KENTISH HEADMISTRESS	Yolanda Celbridge	Feb
RUE MARQUIS DE SADE	Morgana Baron	
'S' A STORY OF SUBMISSION	Philippa Masters	Jan
THE SCHOOLING OF STELLA	Yolanda Celbridge	
SECRETS OF THE WHIPCORD	Michaela Wallace	

SERVING TIME	Sarah Veitch
SHERRIE	Evelyn Culber
SHERRIE AND THE INITIATION OF PENNY	Evelyn Culber
THE SPANISH SENSUALIST	Josephine Arno
STEPHANIE'S CASTLE	Susanna Hughes
STEPHANIE'S REVENGE	Susanna Hughes
STEPHANIE'S DOMAIN	Susanna Hughes
STEPHANIE'S TRIAL	Susanna Hughes
STEPHANIE'S PLEASURE	Susanna Hughes
SUSIE IN SERVITUDE	Arabella Knight
THE TEACHING OF FAITH	Elizabeth Bruce
FAITH IN THE STABLES	Elizabeth Bruce
THE REWARD OF FAITH	Elizabeth Bruce
THE TRAINING GROUNDS	Sarah Veitch
VIRGINIA'S QUEST	Katrina Young
WEB OF DOMINATION	Yvonne Strickland

EROTIC SCIENCE FICTION

RETURN TO THE PLEASUREZONE	Delaney Silver

ANCIENT & FANTASY SETTINGS

CAPTIVES OF ARGAN	Stephen Ferris
CITADEL OF SERVITUDE	Aran Ashe
THE CLOAK OF APHRODITE	Kendal Grahame
DEMONIA	Kendal Grahame
NYMPHS OF DIONYSUS	Susan Tinoff
PLEASURE ISLAND	Aran Ashe
PYRAMID OF DELIGHTS	Kendal Grahame
THE SLAVE OF LIDIR	Aran Ashe
THE DUNGEONS OF LIDIR	Aran Ashe
THE FOREST OF BONDAGE	Aran Ashe
WARRIOR WOMEN	Stephen Ferris
WITCH QUEEN OF VIXANIA	Morgana Baron
SLAVE-MISTRESS OF VIXANIA	Morgana Baron

EDWARDIAN, VICTORIAN & OLDER EROTICA

ANNIE	Evelyn Culber
ANNIE AND THE SOCIETY	Evelyn Culber
ANNIE'S FURTHER EDUCATION	Evelyn Culber
BEATRICE	Anonymous
CHOOSING LOVERS FOR JUSTINE	Aran Ashe
DEAR FANNY	Michelle Clare
LYDIA IN THE BORDELLO	Philippa Masters
MADAM LYDIA	Philippa Masters
LURE OF THE MANOR	Barbra Baron
MAN WITH A MAID 3	Anonymous
MEMOIRS OF A CORNISH GOVERNESS	Yolanda Celbridge
THE GOVERNESS AT ST AGATHA'S	Yolanda Celbridge
THE GOVERNESS ABROAD	Yolanda Celbridge
PLEASING THEM	William Doughty

SAMPLERS & COLLECTIONS

EROTICON 1	
EROTICON 2	
EROTICON 3	
THE FIESTA LETTERS	ed. Chris Lloyd
MOLTEN SILVER	Delaney Silver
NEW EROTICA 2	ed. Esme Ombreaux

NON-FICTION

HOW TO DRIVE YOUR WOMAN WILD IN BED	Graham Masterton
HOW TO DRIVE YOUR MAN WILD IN BED	Graham Masterton
LETTERS TO LINZI	Linzi Drew

Please send me the books I have ticked above.

Name ....

Address ....

....

....

.... Post code ....

Send to: Cash Sales, Nexus Books, 332 Ladbroke Grove, London W10 5AH

Please enclose a cheque or postal order, made payable to Virgin Publishing, to the value of the books you have ordered plus postage and packing costs as follows:

UK and BFPO – £1.00 for the first book, 50p for each subsequent book.

Overseas (including Republic of Ireland) – £2.00 for the first book, £1.00 for each subsequent book.

If you would prefer to pay by VISA or ACCESS/MASTER-CARD, please write your card number and expiry date here:

....

Please allow up to 28 days for delivery.

Signature ....